THE TREE OF YOUNG DREAMERS

THE TREE OF YOUNG DREAMERS

Frank Sousa

Library of Congress Control Number:		2014903444
ISBN:	Hardcover	978-1-4931-7609-0
	Softcover	978-1-4931-7610-6
	eBook	978-1-4931-7608-3

Rev. date: 07/16/2014

To order additional copies of this book, contact:
Xlibris LLC
1-888-795-4274
www.Xlibris.com
Orders@Xlibris.com
542696

CONTENTS

PROLOGUE

This book, *The Tree of Young Dreamers*, is dedicated to all of us laborers-in-the-field readers everywhere who never thought in our wildest dreams that a book would be dedicated to us.

The follow-up novel, *The Tree of Lost Dreams*, will be dedicated to my family and our close friends whom I all love dearly, along with everyone who has given me a boost forward along what at one time appeared to be a lost cause.

Young Dreamers follows the teenagers who ride the limbs of the Big Tree. Each transposes himself into a pirate high in a swaying ship's mast, telescoping for plunder or into a silver-bullet Lone Ranger or sword-wielding crusaders, a bucking bronco rodeo rider.

The girls spied on the heroic boys from behind bushes, both giggling at their antics while feeling an inner thigh urge they did not understand.

Johnny DaSilva is the leader of the Big Tree terrors.

Housing the most fertile imagination, he gave nicknames to all.

The titles are badges of honor, although in today's politically correct society, they would be termed "bullying." The chubby member was called Skinny, the thin member Fats, the left-hander in the gang was Righty.

And Johnny, as payback, was not given a nickname.

It was a time of the Depression of the 1930s, and there were no big bucks, digital Buck Rogers-type ray guns. A triangular piece of wood leftover from a construction job was their pistola, and a branch shaped by nature just for the Tree Boys was a perfect Colt carbine rifle for their General Custer's Calvary boys.

During the Depression, no one was poor; they just didn't have any money.

Both the boys and girls were sexually immature in comparison to today's enlightened youths.

One Aunt called Johnny's devastating legacy of two complete opposite grandfathers, one of "an English conscience and Portuguese passion."

This set his hormones into a ping-pong mode.

His sexually pinball bumpering was accented by both planned and accidental incidents involving older women.

If things were not topsy-turvy enough, add the fact that their fathers, uncles, older brothers, and Danny the Doughnut Man, were off fighting World War II, one more war to end all wars.

Thus, a big hunk of the Big Tree boys' lives was spent using every ruse their young imaginations could dream of to get into the service and the fighting and, of course, of the heroic action they dreamed of, longed for. There you have a plateful.

Johnny lugged a stuffed full backpack, as these were the days that Catholics and Protestants did not marry each other, and the old English did not marry Johnny-come-lately foreigners.

And what could have been his coup de grace, there were two beautiful young women more than interested in him.

One was the most popular girl in the class, Yelena, wealthy and beautiful, and the other from a family as poor as Johnny's, Bernadette, who was sexually abused by her father. She handed herself around, feeling she was not worthy until Johnny momentarily wore the costume of a white knight for her.

So please enjoy this first novel; after all, it is dedicated to you.

CHAPTER 1

JOHN—AUGUST 13, 1932

"For I cherish the old rugged cross!"

The old man with the shock of wild milk-white hair that looked like the foaming rapids of an absolutely insane white water river was in his finest voice ever and thus would also be at the top of his painting talents on this day. Religious song, house painting, and family were his holy trinity.

He remained free of pride, he believed, despite the fact he realized he was the absolute best at his art form. He believed, to quote himself, "A proud man always falleth downward when sitting nose tilted upward on his high horse, for in his pride he had mistakenly sat on a straight-up corncob believing it a throne." The old man, John, liked to embellish others' quotes in such a complicated manner that others could not repeat his wisdom.

His house-painting prowess was a self-opinion kept to himself, that registered no self-congratulations other than a small smile of contentment. Certainly, a humble-enough approach to win God's approval. Those whose houses he painted also had smiles of contentment. The strokes were smooth, bringing out the very best in the wood grain and thus the home.

But his hourly charges for painting each house varied. If the wage earner of the house made seventy-five cents an hour, the cost to have his house painted was seventy-five cents an hour. Ahhh.

If the master of the house made an ungodly five dollars an hour, Mr. John Shiverick charged an ungodly five dollars an hour. Ohhh.

While his house painting drew "The old gent is good," from the house owners, his real fame or infamy was due to his shoe-painting prowess. Opinions varied among the mothers whose children returned home with a bright coat of house paint on their shoes, boots, or sneakers and occasionally even on bare feet. The latter were children who only had one pair of shoes—Sunday, go-to-church shoes, rarely worn as weekday shoes, except during the winter, of course. But in the winter, a heavy sock was worn over the shoes to protect them.

His most severe critics were the neighborhood mothers whose children were wearing nearly new shoes, their best shoes, or their only shoes. He not only painted them, but also daubed them with outlandish colors if the kids so desired.

The parents' opinions did not matter as much as that of the children. The old man's words to all were "The happiness of the wearer is God's wish."

Mothers of the children who went barefoot weren't quite as upset with the old man as the house paint he applied was easily scraped off smooth feet or feet with a layer of dirt or sweat. Not so those of porous leather.

As he pushed the paint cart, he led them in a singsong prayer to God almighty, their voices sounding not unlike a cricket chorus, shiny faces lifted heavenward. He had thought many times, *Someday a grandson . . . will be part of . . . the chorus . . .*

The praying and singing that took place as he pushed his giant wheeled cart of house paints was often accompanied by a combination of jigs, Maypole dancing, and vibrations similar to that of a hoochie-coochie belly dancer.

A smattering of the Catholic and Jewish mothers begrudged his Episcopalians-only-need-apply approach to adults entering the hallowed gates of heaven. He believed that children of all leanings could make it to heaven, that little ones that stood before God's eye were all loved.

The painting of the shoes and sneakers and even bare feet was a little much and, yes, to some, entirely too much to some mothers. Others just smiled or thought, *The old dimwit is as crazy as a coot and harmless as a newborn baby.*

It was Mrs. Shapiro who said, "Maybe he doesn't read the Bible yet. Maybe someone told him that his Jesus painted feet rather than washing them. God will get him. And his Jesus too. Oy."

On this day, the old man's voice even overpowered the old yenta's squeak of a complaint as he pushed his creaky cart past her house.

It even overpowered the thousand-piglet squeals of the large wooden wheels of his creaking, my-back-hurts, very old multicolored wooden pushcart that held all his paints.

Yes, Mr. John Shiverick's singing even overpowered the rattle of the four-foot-high wheel's perimeters, which were protected by heavy gauge tin as they rattled over the cobblestone streets.

Mrs. O'Malley, who at times was given to certain earthly leanings, thought the noise of the tin-covered cartwheels as being similar to two skeletons copulating on a tin roof during a thunder and lightning storm. And just in case someone overheard her thoughts, she then crossed herself to erase her off-color offering.

His voice even rose above what he considered the thieves-on-the-cross groans, which were actually the groans from the old wooden extension ladders hitched to the sides of his pushcart. His voice soared above the noises of a crowded trolley in the push-shove action of the many cans of house paints stored within the cart's cavity.

The cart with its long ladders appeared as a fire wagon to the kids who trailed along a vision enhanced by great sanguine splashes of red paint that dominated the battle of colors on the cart. The old man was a larger-than-life white stallion pushing onward rather than an old fireplug of a horse pulling the fire wagon.

They followed him, positive as the fact that God made big red apples, that this heroic figure, whose white hair appeared to join the wind-whipped clouds above when they looked up at him, was the ghost of a heroic firefighter long gone. He was none other to them than a flame-fighting poltergeist of the past who had saved many lives—children, old women, cats, dogs, tigers, lions, even the mice that pulled the thorns out of the lions' paws.

They didn't always visualize him as a fire chief and his pushcart and rattling ladders as a fire truck.

The children at other times saw Mr. Shiverick as a friendly Indian chief who saved the paint cart that made the transition from fire wagon to Conestoga wagon, along with its "go west, young man, go west" settlers, from a great prairie fire. The would-be frontiersmen were later returned to their log cabins and brownstones in the northeast by the good Chief Shiverick and his braves, the wild but tiny-person band that followed him, the kids themselves. The chief and braves were rewarded by the thankful settlers with Sugar Daddys, mint juleps, Devil Dogs, bull's-eyes, Baby Ruths, and other sweet delights that would make a rock salivate.

Mr. Shiverick's wearing of many hats meant the children drifted between being firefighting volunteers and a band of cowboys and cowgirls who prevented the bad wild Indians from igniting settlers' log cabins. At times, in their minds, they joined the wild Indians in igniting a cabin, if it was the cabin of a hated bully or mean teacher.

They knew destiny, whatever that was, selected them as his firefighting volunteers, heroes one and all, who marched to a different drummer—both fire and Indian chief, Mr. John Shiverick.

The mothers charged with keeping their kids in footwear believed their children marched to a different bummer. It certainly was a bummer that their shoes were not only sloshed with paint but also with paint hues that would make Picasso's color selections appear to all be in charcoal. On seeing the ornate paints used on the shoes, the mothers wondered most of all who would have a house painted in such gaudy colors, *Does the old self-styled Rembrandt only paint the wagons of Gypsies?*

The extension ladders' wooden rungs were bent by the weather and the stress of the old man's and his sons' weight over many years of climbing. The ladders could reach up four stories, higher than any ladder in the town of Rockledge. And certainly higher than any ladder the Rockledge Fire Department owned.

He had built the extension, the fourth level, himself. The Rockledge Fire Department kept three runners available to the old man's house in case of a fire in one of the town's four-story buildings.

When the Rockledge Shoe Factory caught fire, the wooden cart and its ladders appeared at the fire scene with the old man pushing, not even breathing heavy, and the three young firefighters panting like short-legged dogs chasing a speeding Model T Ford.

There were a few, tongue partially in cheek, who believed that someday Mr. Shiverick would build a ladder that would reach heaven. Most townspeople had said he couldn't build an extension ladder that could reach four stories into the sky, "It can't be done."

They, those naysayers, being those who did not know the old man and of his great belief that everyone had a God-given ability to accomplish anything and everything, if he or she believed in the Almighty who granted such graces.

His actual paint cart, instead of being loaded with firefighting equipment, housed a multitude of paints, oils, alcohol, thinners, lead mixtures, and the variety of brushes a housepainter artiste needed, so it had to be kept a distance from the fire.

The children believed the old man's empty paint pails were water Buckets to form a bucket brigade but were shooed off by police at each and every fire.

There were other goodies in the cart as the frugal old man had a waste-not-want-not attitude and thought, *God never wastes . . . Waste not . . . want not . . .*

The cart housed a perfectly good old work shoe and optimist that he was; John Shiverick was certain that someday he would find a passable mate for the shoe. He would present the pair of shoes to the town's only indigent person, or town bum as labeled in some circles, who had declared he could not work as he did not have work shoes.

Perhaps Mr. John Shiverick would come across a World War I veteran who had lost a leg in action and present the perfectly good work shoe to him as a show of gratitude for the soldier's service to a country that stamped on its coins "In God We Trust." Of course it would have to be a veteran who lost his left leg, as it was a right shoe. Also of course the foot and shoe size compatibility was important.

His cart not only contained the perfectly usable work shoe, but it also housed a discarded brassiere that he felt could be utilized as a Baltimore oriole nest in an emergency, such as a high wind tearing a hanging nest free from its mother tree, leaving the oriole babies without a home. Although he had not been a Boy Scout, he was still of the be-prepared ilk. Make that *very* prepared ilk.

The cart also played sheath to a hunting knife without a handle as well as a half of a handheld sharpening stone, with which a person without such a stone could sharpen his jackknife if he was careful.

At times, being frugal meant spending more than most would spend in certain cases. An example was his paintbrush selection, which included several that were made from the hair shaved from a rare pig known only in China and which cost a pretty penny.

These brushes, combined with his ability to keep them in rhythm with the Lord's word, appeared to converse with the very wood that drank deeply of his even, generous, God given . . . strokes.

Mr. John Shiverick, at times, was even known to push his paint cart beyond the Rockledge borders to Melrose, Medford, Malden, Winchester, Woburn, and Stoneham. If a Protestant church was poor and humble and in need of God's paint job.

It was not a free ride for the parishioners of these churches he painted. They had to pitch in; otherwise, why did God give them hands? Their scraping and sanding had to pass his inspection, as did the feathering of the chipped areas, before receiving his God-guided finishing touch.

On inspection of a parishioner's sanding job—if the old man's eyebrows only allowed the lower section of his clear sky-blue eyes to appear—it was best that the sander return to his efforts.

More than one pastor gave him the call from far beyond Middlesex County, believing he could possibly finagle a free or far less costly paint job for his church with just the right-practiced approach. After all, if this man painted for free, he perhaps could have only the brilliance of a five-watt bulb.

The call for help was either by mail or word of mouth, as Mr. John Shiverick's words, "No devil's instrument of a telephone would ever enter my house! A house of the Lord's," were known three-countywide.

If a free John Shiverick church painting could be secured, it could mean a surplus within the parish budget. The surplus, if applied correctly, could mean new pew cushions, a more joyous parish Christmas party, an increase in the stipend of the pastor, or even a new car as big and black and shiny as that or even bigger than that of Father Kennelly, pastor of Holy Is the Rose Catholic Church.

Father Kennelly truly believed his chariot should certainly be able to get him to the heavenly host faster than a black Protestant's faded gray Hudson driven by Pastor Huot of the First Congregational Church. The good father also knew deep in his heart that a black Protestant couldn't get into heaven even if he was, like in the breakfast cereal advertisement, "Shot from guns."

This the-old-man-can-be-had approach was rather a less-than-godly action on the part of some Protestant pastors. It called for cunning, as a wealthy congregation and its richly appointed interior cherry woodwork had to be kept out of the old painter's view. Thus, the pews were covered with painter's drop cloths, and it was indicated the parish would shortly be painting the interior.

The devil's word was out, and those armed with the knowledge that the old housepainter could be had, that he would charge a pittance or nothing at all for the painting of God's house, sought to seek advantage, even to the point of feeding this old Christian to the work lions.

Many parishes were truly needy, as there wasn't a lot of money for church painting in these days of the early thirties when a dime would get you both a cup of coffee and a bun. Or it could buy you the *Wall Street Journal* and a good-after-dinner five-cent cigar, if you were a big thinker.

If you had a dime.

Rumor in the town of Rockledge had it, a rumor promoted by the Protestant population, that a young priest from Somerville tried to convince the old man that his church was really a Protestant parish, and thus he should get the special rate—the no-charge rate.

The good father, when he determined the old painter was not senile, had abandoned this first tack, then, sailing a second tack into the wind, tried to convince the old gent that although the church really was Catholic, it would shortly be changing to Protestant; but even if it didn't, didn't they have the same God? (The young priest kept his fingers crossed behind his back on that one.) Finger crossing took words out of the lie category. Thus, under one God, they were under one roof. And shouldn't the walls under that one roof be painted? Free?

He had learned to cross his fingers behind his back when fibbing to the monks in the seminary. Later, he learned that by a slightly obtuse reasoning, he indeed could go to confession, confess to himself, and ask himself for forgiveness. Which he granted. But only after some self-chastisement thoughts, *What a naughty . . . little boy . . . I've been . . .*

The young priest wasn't seeking a wage increase nor a big black Buick when he asked for a free paint job. He asked the old man's help after realizing his parish's paint looked like a giant albino with scabies. And there was no way the bishop of Boston would allocate the funds for painting the church. Why should he? Hadn't the young priest rooted for Harvard's football team, a black Protestant, blue-blooded WASP school to defeat Boston College despite the knowledge the bishop had played for BC? The truth was the young priest had played for Harvard, a secret he had to keep if he was to keep his post in the Boston diocese.

But the young priest was willing to put aside his pride as his church had deteriorated to the point where no self-respecting termite would stop for a snack there, even if starving.

The young priest was also in disfavor with the pastor of Holy Is the Rose as he had the ill fortune of having his back to a mirror while lying with crossed fingers.

"So will you paint my church?" the young priest asked the old man.

"Have the pope sell one of his rings," was the old man's answer. But then feeling guilty about his uncalled-for remark, he added, "I will talk to Mr. O'Brien about painting your church. Lord knows he certainly is going to need a boost so he won't head downstairs to the devil's basement when that demon drink finally calls him home. And I already have one work shoe toward having a pair for him someday. You can call any park bench in Rockledge and get him."

"Please sleep on my request," the young priest asked the old man, "and I will telephone you tomorrow."

"My home is the house of the Lord. It does not have the devil's device that encourages idle talk and tale-telling by wagging and tainted tongues, promoting idle waste and gossip over God's given air."

Mr. John Shiverick turned to walk off.

"Then I'll reach you by smoke signals, carrier pigeon, jungle drums."

—

"You would be better off attempting to reach our Jesus by prayer. He was a carpenter and thus knew many painters, some who surely are out of work."

"No wonder you Protestants are a disappearing breed in Boston."

"Episcopalian, I'm an Episcopalian, the King's very own church," Mr. John Shiverick corrected.

"Episcopalian, piss-in-the-pail again, whatever," the frustrated young priest, who had played a very aggressive running guard on the Harvard University football team and was also known for his trash-talking decades before it became popular in sports, blurted out.

On this note, the old painter considered giving the young whippersnapper in black a caning. And he could. Everyone knew that Mr. John Shiverick always had a good switch on the side of his pushcart, much like a white-hatted cowboy of the old West had a Winchester carbine cased on the saddle of his trusty pinto pony or piebald stallion.

His switch could lash out with lightning speed "like a terrible swift sword," those who had felt its sting had said.

Among the kills of his switch that were painted on his pushcart fuselage, much like the enemy plane kills painted on the side of the Red Baron's biplane during the war to end all wars, World War I, were several stick paintings of caned boys who, while following the cart, used the Lord's name in vain. And felt the cleansing fire taught to the tune of the hickory stick.

Mr. John Shiverick considered the young priest for a moment. "Oh, wayward young boy caught in popish captivity, I will pray for your soul."

Instead of caning the young man of the cloth, Mr. John Shiverick used another terrible swift sword, his tongue, and continued his further chastisement of him with the words, "Surely, Sears and Roebuck has lowered its standards in selling ordinations. Despite all this, agape to you, young sir."

The young priest had to turn away to stifle his smile, and a thought entered his mind, *Too bad you're a protestant . . . old man . . . We could use you . . . on our . . . side . . . Which is God's . . . only side . . .*

No one in Rockledge ever tried to verify or disprove the rumor of the exchange between the young man of God and the old man of God that day, as it was too good a tale to tatter. And while it did not need any enhancement, they got it anyway.

The old man did not look back as the young priest disappeared in his old Studebaker, its fenders flapping like an injured bird, and thought, *Good riddance . . . to bad rubbish . . .*

And he pushed off, the great cartwheels doing their clog dance on the cobblestone.

On this day, the day that God has made, John Shiverick needed no delays or detours. He was on the way to his God-given task, to paint the church and parsonage of All Saints' Episcopal Church, one of the three churches he attended each and every Sunday. He attended the First Congregational immediately following the Episcopal service. Then Sunday afternoons, even in the hell's heat of summer and witch's tit cold of winter, with gout-pained foot, rheumatic-racked knees, and sciatica-tormented buttocks, he took the twelve-mile walk to Boston's North End to the great stone cathedral and dreamed of the great cathedrals of England and the masons who built them.

There was little breath left for singing during these Boston-bound afternoon treks, but there was enough for a low humming of "Nearer My God to Thee."

On this special day, he sang louder than he ever had, even louder than when his sons Matthew, Mark, Luke, and John were born. He sang louder than the tin-clad wooden wheels managed to clack against cobblestones. While the kids sang out, and the dogs barked the good bark.

This was the day of days. A day that God had made. A day to sing until his voice vibrated the very gates of heaven with its joy. *This was the day . . . that God hath made . . . thank you . . . savior . . . Lord God . . .*

And the kids, those heroic firefighters, fighters of bad Indians, those Christian lads heading to the Crusades, those young tykes who wanted their shoes painted, also realized it was a special day.

For it was the day that Mr. John Shiverick's first grandson was born, son of Charity Shiverick DaSilva.

The boy . . . my grandson . . . named John . . . as in John Shiverick . . . as in John the Baptist . . . the apostle John . . . John of gaunt . . .

Truly, God had smiled on the old man. He had known that God had a reason for taking his first son, John, home to heaven at birth. His second son was then also named John. Then there followed the birth of sons Matthew, Mark, and Luke. None entered the clergy. God moves . . . in strange ways . . . at times . . .

The daughters that followed, Faith, Hope, and Charity, couldn't enter the cloth. Although Hope, the closest thing to a hell-raiser in the family, would tell her gasping sisters when frustrated with their father, "He wants religion? I'll become a nun!" Then the mock anger left her face, and she roared with laughter, hoisting her skirt slightly to do an Irish high step! "There, old man. Take that!" Then she looked around quickly to make sure the person who she wanted to take that wasn't there. Or she'd get it. Get it royally. The switch to the open palm despite being an adult.

And Charity had laughed at her sister. Despite covering her mouth to stifle her laugh, she still believed she would burn in hell for her blasphemous laughter.

Although she hadn't laughed, Faith wondered whether it would somehow be known to her father that she laughed, and that she too would burn with her sister in hell.

Here on this day God had made was John the baby, reborn as the son of Charity that very morning. A baby he, John Shiverick, now dedicated to God and church. His final chance to claim his own flesh and blood for the cloth.

No matter that the boy carried a black Catholic surname—DaSilva—rather than Shiverick . . . the boy will become a minister . . . God works in strange . . . ways . . .

Thinking such thoughts, he rang out in his heldentenor voice, "for I cherish the old ruggggged crossssss!"

It felt good to be in God's good graces and cautioned himself, *But don't ride too high . . . on . . . the high horse . . . with too straight a back . . . sitting on an upright . . . corncob . . . believing it was a throne . . .*

"Do you mind ceasing that racket? You're disturbing the peace." It was the old mother superior of St. Rose's parish, who always charged out with the speed and striking ability of the Light Brigade, to face this heathen down when his clanger of a voice rang through her belfry, especially when she recognized that some of the children from her Parish Grammar School were among his followers.

She knew, as God was her witness, the old man through some evil pact with the devil had increased his voice to a Wagnerian, chalice-shattering crescendo. Besides that, he purposely failed to grease his monkey squeals cartwheels when he realized his path on a given day carried him directly past St. Rose Parish.

He often sang to himself as he passed by, "Knick-knack . . . paddy whack . . . give the dog a bone . . . this old man is traveling home . . ."

One day, she saw him even jump in the air and click his heels as he pushed his cart by.

"Cease. Desist! You old he-devil, you old, you old . . . something or other." She blessed herself after using her personal expletive, "something or other."

The phrase did leave a variety of interpretations.

He greeted her in return, "Hark, surely, it is Attila the Nun." She gave the old coot credit on that one. She even told the sisters that served under her about his Attila the Nun pun and covered her face to stifle her laughter. The young nuns hoped she did not note the fact that they might agree with the old man.

"I hope that heathen attitude makes your day, evil old . . . something . . . or . . . other . . ."

She crossed herself immediately after her bad thoughts.

"Thank you for the blessing, Sister, every little bit helps." Mr. John Shiverick needed a day such as this. A grandson . . . John . . . and Attila the Nun nonplussed . . .

It hadn't been easy the past week.

He had discovered a pack of the devil's own playing cards in his home. The jacks looked like Mephistopheles, the queens like harlots. The king of clubs, like the pope.

Worse than the devil's own calling cards appearing in his home, God's home, was the fact that no one would face up to their ownership.

And with good reason. Mr. John Shiverick did not understand the power of his terrible swift sword. No one would willingly kneel and present their neck for severing, a severing accomplished by a word or worse a look. Thus the cards ended up without parents.

Hadn't this very week his very own daughters turned on him, practically demanding indoor plumbing with the words, "Father, no one else in Rockledge has to walk out into the cold and snow to an outhouse or bath in a basin in the kitchen."

Hadn't his daughters, also this week, declared their need for shades and curtains on the windows?

The sisters had turned a deaf ear to their father's thunder of Thor words, "The good Lord does not want man to defecate in the very home in which he sets a dinner table."

This relatively timid timbre of the indoor plumbing refusal turned to a bolt of lightning when the subject of considering the covering of the windows with curtains and shades came up. "May God strike me dead if I ever have the unholy audacity to try to block out his heavenly light!"

As Mr. John Shiverick started up his cart, almost burning tin as he traveled past the mother superior, the old nun on seeing the old man lost in thought and believing he was thinking up another insult, chose the best defense is an attack theory, and warned, "If you continue this racket I'll sic Officer Bulldog O'Toole on you, you black . . . you black . . . protestant . . ."

"That toothless old bloodhound is too lazy to scratch a flea on the tip of his tail."

"A pox on you," Sister Superior blessed herself, having called down the pox.

—

But the worries about Officer O'Toole or a pox were the last thoughts on Mr. John Shiverick's mind on this day.

His new grandson, John, was his destiny, his life forever after, his only thought, and he raised his voice in praise and pushed aside such mundane sounds as the horn of a Model A flivver that nearly ran him down but which he believed was sending a friendly greeting, even after the driver yelled out the window in a happy voice, "Get off the street, you old featherhead." Road rage, 1932 vintage.

Mr. John Shiverick barely heard the fire siren voice of Mrs. Burris calling out the names of her nine sons and four daughters, urging them to run home quickly, as the Friday fish was to be served.

He thought, *Only a black Catholic . . . would have thirteen children . . . The thirteenth . . . the traitor . . . at the last supper . . .*

Town rumor had it Mrs. Matilda Burris's call to her husband, Sean, once shattered the glass of bitters he was hoisting high in Patsy's Pub, some five blocks north of the Burris home, just over the Woburn line. Nobody believed this glass-shattering tale, but it was a great story worthy of continuation and embellishment, especially at Patsy's, where a shattered glass was kept in a place of honor at eye level on the central shelf, where the good stuff was on display but rarely ordered.

The old housepainter listened to Mrs. Burris's voice as she called off each of the thirteen names rather than a simple "Come and get it!" and wondered whether all multimothers were born with the roll-call talents of a drill sergeant.

Even the barking dogs that first lollygagged toward his singing and the call of his cart started to lope, then canter, getting completely caught up in the excitement, some chasing their tails as a whirling dervish, while the short-legged dogs reached in a full gallop before catching up to the old man and his paint cart, where they were all well received. We are all . . . God's . . . creatures . . .

But try as they might, the baying of the happy baying hounds could not drown out the old man's singing, despite the fact his voice was strained through a giant, pure-white mustache that would have done a walrus proud.

The kids came from everywhere, even the Burris brothers, who chose the paint cart happening over supper and the keen competition it brought with each serving. This was no easy choice, being late for supper, when you considered their competition at the table meant the family had the skinniest ants in Rockledge.

Different offerings drew the kids to Mr. John Shiverick, not only away from supper, but also away from the last at bats of the pickup baseball game, a game of bore a hole, bore a hole, right through the sugar bowl. Away from games of jack stones and hopscotch and mibs and away from playing dolls and holding little girls' tea parties.

They loved the clatter and clack of the wheels on the cobblestones, the dancing dogs the old man attracted. They loved clicking their sticks in the thick wooden spokes of the giant cartwheels and the reward of wheel click sounds far superior to clattering a stick along a picket fence.

The cartwheels sounded much like the clack-o-clack of those wheels of fortune that came with the carnival that came to town every Fourth of July. The carnival, where the girls watched in awe as the boys peeked under the sideshow tent whose front bore a colorful painting of a woman dressed in less than what was allowed at a public beach. They studied the colorful poster that advertised "Cleo, Queen of the Cooch" and thought . . . cooch . . . oh so terrible . . .

And wondered what cooch meant. Some felt their first tiny stirrings.

Even the shaking of the Queen of the Cooch could not compare with the old man's eyebrow battle between the evil raven and the doves of peace, for as the old man sang, his white eyebrows attacked the black hair that connected them over the bridge of his nose.

The brows were the pure white of new-fallen snow, their line of demarcation as black as looking into a cave of coal. Or into the devil's very heart.

The children loved the battle between good and evil despite the fact that the battle of the brows always ended the same way, the pure white winning, as the knitting of his brows smothered the dark-haired sea monster with foam.

The doves always, always obliterated the raven.

But as good as things were, the singing old man, the clattering of the pushcart, the dancing dogs, the battle of the brows, the ghost of a heroic firefighter . . . the most goodish thing . . . by their thinking, and their highest hope was that the old man would choose their shoes to paint on this day.

He had such bright colors. And their parents would be so dancing mad at the old man that they'd forgot to be angry at their kids for having their shoes painted and forget to send them to bed without supper.

The girls would hop, skip, and jump barefooted, beseeching him to paint their toes the colors of the rainbow.

His mood on this day was such that they knew as sure as God made little green caterpillars, they could plan on two, three, four colors and not dark blues and blacks, but rather reds, oranges, and yellows and bright greens, the color of new spring leaves, maybe pinks, with polka dots and stripes, all the colors of the clowns that came to town with the Shrine Circus once a year. And they chanted the poem they had learned from their fourth-grade teacher with a little rearrangement of the words, "We want new shoes, blue shoes, pretty pointed-toe shoes—not fat shoes, flat shoes, scuff-'em-on-the-mat shoes, that's the kind they buy."

One parent, Mrs. Nicolea Arcodemis, had gone to Officer Niko Nicodemis and sought the old man's arrest. "He destroyed private property, my son's shoes!"

Officer Nicodemis asked, "And what would you have me do, Mrs. Arcodemis, bring him in on a charge of painting a shoe?"

"And what color was it painted?" Judge Mickey O'Shaunnessey, would surely ask first. And then his honor would ask second, "What's next, Officer Nicodemis? Which painter will ye be bringing before me next— Mr. Rembrandt himself?'"

"The old man is a crazy," she insisted.

"Aye (Officer Nicodemis loved to switch to an Irish accent when informing a citizen that things were out of his hands), that I realize, Mrs. Arcodemis, but there are real crimes out there to solve, serious ones. Someone tied a can to the tail of Mrs. Burris's dog, Pooper. And someone let the air out of the tires of Rockledge's only police cruiser just the other day. What if someone was speeding that day? You can't chase a speeder in a police car with a flat tire, now can you? And you surely can't bring a dog, especially one like Pooper, under control when a can is tied to his tail. Now can you?"

"He's a crazy old coot."

"Ah yes, aye, me good lady (all the Rockledge police were Irish, except Officer Nicodemis, so his lilt came easily), but he's a harmless crazy quite different from most of them who love God more than a good pint. You know most God-fearing people start all the wars in the world, Mrs. Arcodemis. Them Christians. But this one just wants to paint shoes."

"I'm telling your mother, my sister, that you are a shirker of police duties."

"You'll have to call long distance, dear aunt. Mother has been dead some twenty years."

"Probably driven to her death by a son who shirked his duties."

The police officer patted the little woman on the head, with the words, "Now don't go telling no Catholic or Protestants, for that matter, that I said that bit about Christians starting wars."

He was glad she didn't pursue her purpose of having the old painter arrested as he was perhaps a little afraid of the old man. At very least, he felt some trepidation. *What if the old coot . . . painted my shoes . . . before*

I could bring him in? Now that would be a fine . . . kettle of fish . . . me . . . showing up at the station . . . shoes painted . . . The chief would ask, "Did you arrest him before . . . or after . . . he painted . . . your shoes?"

Besides, how could he arrest the old man on this day: The old man was very, very happy. "Aye, certainly for sure, to arrest a happy man is a crime in itself."

Officer Nicodemis, having seen enough unhappiness in connection with the duties of his chosen profession, in his wisdom, always hesitated to step in the way of happiness. Besides, if he arrested Mr. John Shiverick, he would have to spend his day off in court. And without pay, yet . . . and what if the old man . . . is really dangerous?

Aye. Indeed, Mr. John Shiverick was happy. Aye. There was another John the Baptist born, and on this very day, he sang, "This is the day that God hath made."

The old man vowed that from this day forth and every year thereafter on this date, he would paint the old wooden church, All Saints' Episcopal Church, the Church of England, all by himself. Let his sons find their own churches to paint for free, if so inclined . . . and best they be . . . so inclined . . .

The painting of All Saints' was to be his thank you to God for God's gift to him.

Mr. John Shiverick felt so good on this twelfth day of August 1931; he did something he had never done before.

He painted the four paws of that dog claimed by no one and called by all Flea Bag. Yes, painted the paws four different colors—red, yellow, orange, and a brilliant green he had mixed himself.

And in front of his royal audience of kids, he renamed Flea Bag Emmett the Eminent.

Yes, Mr. Shiverick, king of Rockledge, named the dog Emmett the Eminent in honor of the famous Emmett Doughnut Bellwelter, the world's most eminent comic and poet laureate, a rare combination of skills to say the least.

And the kids chanted, "Emmett, Emmett! Emmett the Eminent. Emmett for president! Emmett for pope!"

The new Emmett liked the attention; it was so different from the usual kick and curse he received.

Some say that it made a difference in the old hound's life right up until the day he died some four weeks later.

Some said Emmett stepped proudly from that day on, and some even gave him a second name, Brightstepper. The old dog with the brightly painted toes liked that too.

Mrs. Arcodemis claimed that the old man was a murderer, that the dog died of lead poisoning. Despite the fact Brightstepper was pushing twenty. And had been hit by a baker's dozen car.

She pretty much kept her allegation to herself. She didn't want to anger the old man. He would probably paint her son's trousers. Or the kids, those wild Indians, would probably stick blackberry briars on her flapping sheets.

Regardless, the dog had little doubt—no, make that no doubt—that he was something special from that day of the painted paws on.

Just as old Mr. John Shiverick knew this was a special day.

He was blessed by God, sure as God made little spring peepers.

Thank you, Lord . . . maker of heaven . . . and earth . . . and giver of John . . . to all . . .

Mrs. Burris spotted the old man talking to himself and thought, *The old buzzard must have . . . money in the bank . . . talking to himself . . . that . . . way.*

CHAPTER 2

PIE—AUGUST 13, 1932

The potato pickers, on all fours, like thick-legged workhorses with hands, dug into the furrows with their fingers for the potatoes that hid there, sometimes between sharp rocks or even an occasional Indian arrowhead that would slice a hand as quickly as a filleting knife flayed a cod.

When cut, the pickers did not worry about stemming the tide of blood, as the blood had difficulty making it through the dirt that caked their hands. Their fingers were worn to stubs, and if you did not look closely, you could mistake them for the very potatoes they picked.

The dust stirred up between their fingers hung in particles collecting in their nose, coating their tongue, lining their mouths so that at times, air had to be sucked in, like sipping milk through a crushed straw.

The potato pickers did not turn their heads to watch the old man approaching. They knew better. It could be a dangerous interlude, looking up from their work at Pie, a name bastardized from *pai*, which means "father."

Instead, they stole cautious glances back between their legs as he strode the several hundred feet from the farm to his potato fields below.

Pie's strides across the furrows were greater than usual. As always, he was without socks, but the dirt that colored his feet and ankles gave the appearance that he indeed wore socks the same color as the dust that choked the air and those who breathed it.

Everyone called him Pie, "father," a cruel joke on themselves. Strange, calling him father. The workers, most with only falsified papers hidden away by the old man, thought of him less as a father and more as walking death. A few of the more imaginative thought of him as offal-covered hog's balls.

The tongue of the old man's belt stuck out several inches in front of him after it was pulled through the buckle. It was longer than usual on this day, as he had hitched it up several notches. To what he considered made him flamboyant, whatever flamboyant meant. He had heard it at the Portuguese-American Club used by some snotty young Cape Verdes who liked to mix big snotty English words into his conversations mostly in Portuguese.

He felt that the swaying belt tongue appeared as the bowsprit on a tall rum-running, three-master cutting through a choppy sea heading for adventure and offered a phallic appearance to his swagger.

But there were no romantics working Pie's fields; thus, other than by himself, it was unappreciated.

The workers saw the belt tongue as nothing poetic. They saw it as a whip that would lash their backs or to grind their faces into the earth's maw. Each man and woman dreamed of receiving their proper papers someday. Once free of the falsified ones in Pie's possession, they would make him pay, pay more for his laughter at them than the belt, the kick. But they knew this would never happen. Even the young and strong were afraid of the unknown, which the old man personified.

To the younger women, his swaying belt was truly phallic. His gait was such that the belt tongue was thrust in front of him, like a spear to be plunged into warm flesh of someone considered more an enemy than a partner in passion. The down and dirty appeal of the phallic symbol was accompanied by fear, especially when only viewed in the shadow on the soil as the old man stood over them. Sex by a leather dirk.

The belt, taken up another notch as he approached his workers, elongated the air-licking tongue. Why not flaunt it on this day? He had a new grandson! And sure as the devil spread young girls' legs, he had made this new grandson, John Anthony Shiverick DaSilva. The John could be dropped and the Shiverick sliced away, he thought, *Like the head . . . severed from a newborn billie goat . . . a worthless . . . milkless . . . birth . . . sum na bitch . . . fuccum grandson . . . he Tony . . . like me . . . Pai . . . no fuccum John . . . he . . . Tony . . . me . . .*

One more notch was hitched up, causing the belt to cut into his gut, a cut that would have brought great pain to anyone else. But to Pie, it made him feel more phallic, and why not . . . Pai fuccum all . . . father my tribe . . .

The workers did not have to worry about his catching them sneaking their glances on this day. They would not be cuffed nor would any of their seventeen cents an hour pay be docked, despite the fact Pie begrudged the seventeen cents rate. Hadn't he worked for a nickel an hour when he came over from the Azores ten years before? Didn't he buy this land and build his farmhouse and barns and sheds with those nickels? Pai's own hands . . . no fuccum money . . . only Pai's . . . fuccum bankers . . . fuckar thieves . . . only worse . . . fuccum lawyers . . .

He thought that even Goda, who was so black she had a bluish tint, much like blue anthracite coal, was not worth her hourly scale.

Pie paid the blue-black Cape Verdi—fuccum she devil—more than double what the others were paid, thirty-five cents an hour. She received this handsome stipend not because she outworked even the strongest of the men, which she did; she received the extra money because she could provide a service they couldn't.

She should have been working for six cents an hour, or for nothing, he believed. Hadn't he, Pai, paid good money for her, nearly two hundred dollars, to have her smuggled into this country on a passport and papers he provided, papers now in his property . . . No pay . . . no pay . . . Goda owe Pai . . . all owe Pai . . .

But there would be no checking on work ethics or whether the farm help earned their pay on this day. He did not have to show his power with his belt, a kick, the threat of being without a job, the threat of being returned to Portugal for lack of papers.

His power was his new grandson, living proof of the strength that steamed out of his loins into M'ae's years before, was still alive. Now M'ae old . . . no Pai old . . .

But Mie was loved with the desperate dedication that Pie was hated with.

This same steam was now building up into a shrill whistle in the spout of the teapot he called his bonitas rinoceronte chorizo—his pretty rhinoceros hot sausage—that simmered there in his pants in the potato field.

Pie fixed his eyes on Goda, a glance of steel, molten, unblinking dart points. The male workers stared into the dust below them. Hating Pie for yet another reason, wishing they had the power to have their way with Goda.

The women stared into the sky, wondering what it would be like. To hear this man call their name instead of Goda and then clap his hands together, a signal not to waste time. A signal to crawl to his feet and then get up and follow when he turned his back and walked off. They would sneer at him and return to their work. They would thrust a trowel into his heart after he did them. Or would they?

Goda felt Pie's eyes on her like the suctions of an octopus, prying her legs apart like tentacles prying open a bivalve. The tentacles turning to testicles in her sun-boiled imagination in which she saw them drop into her silken purse like gold nuggets.

Her eyes roamed to a distant meadow where a bull, alone in the field, charged about, pawed the ground, then ambled in such a manner that its pride and joy swung from side to side like a hammock of lust.

The sweat of her efforts in the soil had drenched her dress, the one sewn from the best of the flowered sacks that the grain was delivered in to the farm.

Until Goda arrived earlier this year, the women argued and sometimes fought over who would have second pick of the flowered grain bags after Pie's favorite daughter, Alameida Antonina, had made her choice.

But no longer did Alameida Antonina receive first choice from among the lovely flowered sacks that smelled sweetly of the fresh grain that they had held. And she no longer bothered to check the sacks when the grain was delivered to determine which she would choose. She did not want the women laughing at her. Second choice, after a *puta* . . . *puta* . . .

Goda now not only got first choice, but she also got to pick the first three flowered dresses to be.

Once, while making her choice with only Pie present, she had quickly cut out the bottom of the sack with a razor blade she kept taped beneath her left breast, kicked off her own clothing, and slipped into the cloth that a moment before held grain. Her thunderous breasts fought for freedom at the bodice while thighs as powerful as the thighs of the draught mare that dragged the heavy harrow through the soil each spring flexed and relaxed, testing the very staying power of the new hemline.

Remembering that first day, spittle dripped from Pie's lips, landing on the tongue tip of his belt and then dripping on to Goda's back.

He watched his spittle, joined by her sweat, drip down from her shoulder, to her spine, to the giant muscles of her buttocks that topped off her thighs, sweet scoops of chocolate ice cream on twin cones.

They both remembered that day. Her ink-black body laden with nipples blacker than giant aces of spades was dusted white with the sweet-smelling grain that had been housed in the sack moments earlier. He had drawn in the chalk that laced the blackboard body.

She did not have to glance up at the old man with the undulating belt to know why he was there on this day, the day of his grandson's birth. She waited for his hand clap, calling her to come on all fours, shoulders close

—

28

to the ground, ass high, like a cowering *cadella* bitch dog approaching its angry master. But she would not obey. Goda no go this day . . . He clap like . . . wings of chicken . . . head just cut off . . . Me no go . . . for clap . . . Goda no go . . .

The second clap of Pie's soil-hardened hands was like a rifle crack.

Goda stared at the ground for a moment. Pie had already turned away and was leaving.

It was a steaming day where heat waves boiled up from the baking dirt. The humidity hung like a noose around her neck; the lack of air choked at her. Too hot to . . . do . . . do it . . . Too hot to work . . . Perhaps could be good day . . . to no work . . . end fucky early . . . make Pie come quick . . . two seconds . . . I clap my hands . . . he come . . . like bolt of goosed lighting . . .

She was so close to the ground now that her body buried her sun shadow below her. Enough . . .

Her first moves were measured, like a big cat awakening in the sun. She started on all fours, then hunkered closer to the ground, moving like a panther on the prowl in the tall grass, her back arched, buttocks as powerful as a female lion's, tighter than a drum top, flexed and unflexed to jungle rhythm.

Assuming this stalking posture, her crotch hovered closer and closer to the hot soil, where the heat from inside her swapped like oven breath with the rising earth's.

Her breast expanded, slacked, expanded, working like bellows breathing glowing life into a farrier's fire.

She stared at the old man with the belt, smiled at his hoarse *seda*, silk. Pie offer Goda seda . . . silk . . . to Goda . . .

Goda slowly got to her feet, whispered, "Seda? Goda seguir, follow."

She has promised herself he'd never take her again. She had paid her debt, earned her wages. Worked the men into the ground, even the ones hot on her tail to be close to her source of steam.

But the day was hot. The promise was silk, silk that cooled a hot body. Silk that encased and invited. It was too much. The heat bugs, ticking off their rapid-fire milliseconds even appeared to be weakening. "Goda seguir."

Pie kicked the knee of a worker, an old man with wrinkles molded out of baked clay. "Follow. Seguir. Ocarina."

The old potato picker got painfully to his feet, following in a distance behind Pie and Goda, reached into his rear pocket, and pulled out his simple wind instrument, placed it to his sun-cracked lips, and played.

The ocarina's haunting notes followed the couple away from the field, its potatoes and its potato-fingered workers, and up the gentle hill.

"Seguir, follow," she whispered as throaty as distant thunder whispering to heat lightning, as she slowly closed the distance between her and Pie. "Goda seguir."

Pie spit in the air. The old ocarina player stopped, crouched down behind a boulder, rested his back against it, and closed his eyes, playing music so sorrowful that a feeding hyena would take time out to weep as the old man with the green eyes of a jungle cat and the powerful black woman with eyes of black lightning continued on until they were out of view of the potato field, out of view of the old ocarina player. But not out of range of the ocarina, whose musical pulse joined in the rapid trill of the cicadas, singing to the heat of the scalding sun.

Goda grasped her breasts in her hands, lifted them skyward like an Inca maiden offering her child up for sacrifice. "Sentir, silk feel."

"Sim. Yes."

He glanced at the potato field, checking to see whether any worker dared to change the marks he had made in the soil behind each one, marks that would determine the distance they covered while he was gone. He had dropped a raisin near each mark, unseen by the worker, just in case a line of picking was changed.

Once out of sight of the field, Pie led the way, moving swiftly to the cave that served as the hog's castle. He had dug the caves in a hardpan knoll and framed the doorjamb and lintel with large slabs of granite he had cut from a nearby hill.

Goda climbed the rail fence into the hog pen, her dress hoisted high on her thighs as the hogs—huge, highly intelligent animals—looked on in what appeared to be apparent stupidity. The curiosity in their small, mean, myopic-appearing eyes was veiled by thick lashes and hid the animals' full knowledge they were absolute kings of their domain.

Most of the time.

Pie sent the smaller animals squealing off by his daring to boot the nose of the largest of the beasts, the boss hog, Bog.

Despite the kick in the face, Bog was top hog in any pig pile; his ears were serrated from rips suffered while defending his status in the past. The look the hog gave the old man was one of pure, undiluted malevolence, a look of "your day will come."

Goda ducked under the lintel, her soaked skirt lifting high, displaying a thick patch of splayed ink-black hair, the briar patch set asunder as if visited by a wild zephyr.

"Sumna-na-bitch," the old man said, reaching for her.

She dodged his grasp and then glared at him, body set akimbo.

The cave was dark, except for the one stream of dust-and-pollen-streaked sunlight that slithered in over the offal.

"No touch," she said and attempted to exit the low-ceiling cave.

He started to take off his belt. She had felt it before and backed away from the exit.

"Carneiro," sheep, he ordered, bringing the belt high overhead, the buckle as the tip of the flail.

Goda turned away from him, dropped to all fours.

"Carneiro!" he ordered.

"Baaaaa."

He walked around to the front of her, undid his fly that was adorned by only two of the four buttons called for under the original job description. "A carne de porco."

She moved her shoulders from side to side, swaying on all fours, causing her breasts to swing like two girls jumping rope, her low-hanging dress front serving as the rope as it swung high, swung low. A sweet chariot.

She avoided his command by pushing her body forward, backward, all the time swaying from side to side, just brushing against him, like a dog brushing against its master's legs.

The old man watched as her breasts came to life, separate from the woman, individual voodoo dancers around the fire, nipples rouged by the fresh blood of the sacrificed chickens, glistening from the sweat of work and searing sun.

Her huge nipples protruded and throbbed, became the flashing black clones of her eyes.

Pie's chest and stomach had turns heaving like participants in a tug-of-war as he watched her breasts sway forward, backward, up, down, like a flying carousel horse.

And all the time, the sweet notes of the ocarina drifted in from the distance. The notes coming faster.

He shifted his feet in the muck that sucked at his shoes until he was directly over her.

Goda remained on all fours, glared up at him. "No. Goda do nothing."

With a single motion, he grabbed her arm, yanked her to her feet, and captured her wrists in his belt, then forced her down with his boot while tightening the tether until her entire body quivered in pain. Painfully trussed like a hog for market, she kicked jerkily like a horse thief that had plummeted through a trapdoor and was yanked up short by a hangman's noose.

—

He dragged her through the mud and hogwash, through the cave door, and into the sun.

She looked up as he raised his fist, a fist that had sledgehammered her before.

"No! No!" Goda cried as she rolled onto her back, and without a word, her body seemed to plead for mercy.

Yet somewhere in the darkest recesses of her mind and body, there was a demand that no mercy be given her.

Suddenly, it had become a pagan ritual

She reached down and scooped up a handful of mud and matted her hair with the offal until it was as wild as an African bushman's, stared him in the eyes through the madness, and insisted, "No! Goda say no!"

"Sim!" Yes! The old man plunged so powerfully that she skidded through the mud and offal, leaving a trail behind her much like the trail of a field-dressed deer being dragged through the snow.

Pie's grunts were echoed and reechoed by the hogs swaying in the background, squealing like unwashed ogling choirboys.

She fought him off. "No! No!" she insisted but continued to arch her back like a drawn bow not ready to release a giant nocked arrow.

"Vaca, cow, moo!" he grunted. Finished. "Vaca!"

Only the white of Goda's huge eyes could be seen in her face. Then the gleaming white of teeth set in a snarl. "No. No vaca."

He twisted her arm. "Vaca! *Vaca!*"

"Moooo."

He was positive that someday his new grandson, born on this very day, would dominate in such a way as to ensure that Pai's loins would live forever.

The old man felt good about that. He felt very good. And very young. Like he would be that way, young forever.

CHAPTER 3

THE CHRISTENING—
CHRISTMAS 1932

Charity cradled the five-month-old baby in her arms, as Tony, arm around her waist, smiled at her.

At this exact moment, he truly loved her, and only her.

For that matter, he always loved only her. Charity Shiverick DaSilva, mother of John Anthony Shiverick DaSilva. Yes, he loved her from the moment he first saw her.

But he did not make love to only her.

It wasn't that he was ever looking for others. But there was something about a quiet man. A quiet man, one who appeared not to think too much about himself. Or too little about himself. But always was himself. Kind. Caring. Strong. Weak. A paradox on parade.

Tony DaSilva was a man who always appeared perfectly tanned. He wasn't. The dark sugar brown of his skin gave that effect. Set in this calm face were the light-yellow-green eyes of a tiger. His eyes were emphasized by a boyish smile of teeth so even and white that when it broke, it broke like the sun coming up through the mystery of a morning mist.

And more than one woman closed her eyes and wrapped herself in that mist, disappeared in it, was enveloped by it, climbed to the heavens in it, and then was held high against the heavens just long enough to allow the sun to burn through and melt the wax in her wings.

And plunge her to earth to crash in a smoldering, praying, pleading state, visualizing him rising time after time like a nine-lived phoenix from the ashes.

Tony was positive that once he married Charity, it would end their flights of fancy, their scooping him up like a diving osprey sinking its talons into an unsuspecting salmon. So he could live an ordinary life. With one woman.

Like a goodly percentage of men, Tony found it easy to avoid temptation as long as temptation did not appear. Yet it did appear. But marriage to Charity, the one he loved, would end this thing that was so exciting at first, confusing next.

The Shivericks had stopped at the DaSilva Farm stand to buy corn and raspberries and maybe enjoy the temptation of Mie's homemade fudge, as long as it wasn't a Sunday. There were to be no temptations on Shiverick Sundays.

Tony was in the deep pit he'd dug and shored up with flat stones so he could drive cars over it and work beneath.

Someday he would have a real car lift. His own garage. He could fix anything mechanical, often not needing much more than a small roll of baling wire, a tin can, and tin snips, maybe a piece of rubber. Some said, "He could weld the rear ends of two skunks together without spilling a drop."

Thiff's garage would sneak cars up to Tony to work on at night, and Tony would return them before dawn so as Thiffault's golden coach pulled by white horses would not turn into a pumpkin pulled by a team of mice.

Tony could fix anything. Thiffault wouldn't tell anyone he wasn't doing the work, being more than happy to enjoy the words of satisfied customers. "Leave it to old Thiff to fix the unfixable. You old dog, you."

Thiffault had sworn Tony to secrecy and, as a bonus, let him have access to a potpourri pan of nuts and bolts he did not need.

Looking at Charity dressed in white, a white she had protected on all their dates, he thought of that day, the day he was in that pit on the farm. The first time he saw her.

Momentarily locked in the past, Tony looked around the church, confused. It's Johnny's . . . christening . . .

Then again, looking at Charity, his Charity, his wife, and their son, and back to those attending the christening, wanting to speak out, "I'm the happiest man on earth." But he would be embarrassed in front of his brothers, the Shiverick family, friends, and strangers. But he wanted to speak out. Like that day, the first time he saw her.

—

That first time. He was in the pit peering out from beneath Joe Jackson's old flivver. The mechanical brakes had been locking. And the spark was not providing that boost of electrical juice needed to start the Model T.

Jackson was called Shoeless, not after the old baseball player, but because he always wore the latest, most colorful, finest, and most expensive shoes available. Shoeless was as homely as an elephant's scrotum, but the women never saw his face as they put on their brakes on seeing his shoes. A man with shoes like that was a special man. A very special man. And his feet were large. Especially large. Many of the young girls giggled together about what large feet meant. Especially large, very large ones.

And of all things, whenever he was wearing a certain pair of colorful shoes, he had a full set of color-coordinated hubcaps to snap on his flivver, turning his car into a Rolls Royce of sorts. He had more than a dozen sets of hubcaps that matched the shoes of the day. Shoeless knew how to play his cards. If there was a girl he particularly wanted to get to know, he had a huge pair of shoes, too large for even his big feet. He stuffed cotton in the toes to make them fit. He would glance down at his shoes, and then up at the girl he particularly wanted to encourage, and smile. He laughed to himself. He knew that the girls knew what big feet meant. And that shoes with matching hubcaps would get their eyes where he wanted them. Off his face, homely as a baboon's ass, and onto his shoes.

Tony was under Joe Jackson's car that day. The car was wearing spring grass green and buttercup yellow hubcaps. Tony couldn't wait to see his matching shoes on this day. But then Charity stepped out of the Shiverick Hudson and into the sunlight.

The pain in Tony's chest was nearly unbearable. He could barely breathe. It was a pain similar to that he had given to many young women who had taken in his blue-black wavy hair, hair that shined like a raven's flapping wings in the sun. He drank of her smooth, light swan-feather soft skin; her frail body whose very underendowment thrilled him; so very different than the endowed boat-bow farm girls. The "Milkers," his brother Manny called those farm girls.

He took in Charity's jawline, drawn by an artist, smooth as a baby's ass.

The frailness of her chin, dainty as a lily of the valley blossom, was in stark contrast to his deep chin dimple that appeared to have been hewed out of oak by an adz.

He stood, peering out from beneath Shoeless's car; his lower jaw dropped like that of Charlie McCarthy when his ventriloquist master Edgar Bergen fell asleep at the switch.

He laughed out loud at his own idiocy and smiled openmouthedly.

—

It was his smile that caught Charity's eye, those strong white teeth, even as a deck of cards clacked against a tabletop to make them all even.

The smile was slow and gentle, but the teeth strong enough to tear apart a loaf of hard crusted Portuguese sour bread. His smile could flash as swiftly as a lightning stroke shredding the sky.

And Charity's heart was in the heavens this day. She did something no lady ever did, especially a Shiverick woman; she stared at him.

This tall, thin, elegant lady brought up on the Bible started to smile nervously, then stopped, devastated by the sweat she could feel forming along her hairline, on her upper lip, along the bottom of her brassiere, and she thought, *A good woman . . . just does not . . . stare . . . at a farmer . . . nor smile . . . I must tell myself this . . . Do not stare . . . or . . . smile . . .*

But she did, and now on this day, the lady and the farm boy were christening their firstborn, a son, John Anthony Shiverick DaSilva.

Tony remained in a state of shock; it was a year now that he and this woman were married. Had a child . . . How it had . . . happened . . . like a . . . miracle . . . Ma will light a candle . . . for our son . . . her grandson . . . Mie will light two candles . . . more . . .

The marriage had happened over both the objections of the people of the king of England and the people of the pope—John Shiverick and Pie DaSilva.

Tony was a black Catholic, a foreigner as well, whose blood was probably "grease" to John Shiverick. And she was a Boston baked beans Protestant bitch to Pie, with a skinny ass and cold tits made for a convent.

Yet here they stood. With only eyes for each other.

The Rev. Morganthaw Newhall, the very old pastor who headed up the Rockledge All Saints' Episcopal Church, the church of the king of England, dropped the baptismal water on the baby's head and then quickly dried it as if he feared he had drowned the little boy. And while doing so, the good reverend's Coke-bottle-thick glasses fell into the baptismal water.

Reverend Newhall ignored his glasses and turned to the baby, who looked something like a drowned rat, and dried the baby again with such gusto there was some tiny flame of fear in Charity's heart that he would rub the baby's scalp off. My Little Johnny already . . . suffered cradle cap . . . What if the good Reverend Mr. Newhall sets Little Johnny's eyebrows on fire . . . with the friction? Oh, you willie-nilly silly . . .

But hadn't she seen in the Boy Scout manual? Yes, she was planning for Johnny's joining the Scouts twelve years hence, where you could rub a stick real fast and start a fire in dry tinder. And wasn't the reverend rubbing real fast, and weren't her baby's fine eyebrows like tinder?

—

"Are you okay, Charity?"

She looked up into her husband's concerned eyes. "Yes, I was just thinking."

"I thought I smelled smoke."

Tony's words confused her. *What does he mean? Is it smoke from . . . my baby?* But before Charity could look around for help, from out of the blue, the forgetful old Episcopal pastor made the announcement of the completed baptism. Actually, it was more like the drone of a low-flying, crop-dusting biplane than an announcement.

His glasses were now back on his head but as crooked on his face as the rear bumper of a tail-ended car. A good pair of windshield wipers on the glasses would have helped ease his confusion, as dripping baptismal water stifled his clear thinking, "I now pronounce you man and wi—ah, I christen thee, John Antonio Shiverick DaSilva."

Hope poked Faith in the ribs as they stared at their new nephew, now held tight against their sister's tiny breast in a manner that appeared to be trying to protect the baby from catching fire, and nodded toward Tony, whispering, "Even in church, he's got a bulge in his pants."

Faith poked her back, eyes big "Where did you learn to talk that way? Father will hear you. And if he doesn't, God will hear you."

"Perhaps I'm wrong, and Charity's movie-star-faced husband has a scroll of the Scriptures tucked in his shorts. For safekeeping of the Holy Grail," Hope snickered.

"Oh. Sometimes my own sister frightens me."

But Mr. John Shiverick was deaf to worldly words and ways and stared opened eyed into space where he only saw God, a God smiling down on his grandson. A grandson that would carry the word of the Lord onward for him, for all to hear. He whispered to himself, "My grandson, the Rev. John Shiverick." He couldn't quite draw himself to say "DaSilva."

"Father is talking to himself," Hope said. "He must have money in the bank. Hey, maybe that isn't a sacred scroll in Tony's trousers. Maybe his money belt slipped. Hogs bring good money in today's market."

"Shush up. You just shush up now," Faith whispered.

"No one can hear me," Hope said aloud.

Her sister said, "There is nothing louder than a whisper in church."

"Except a fart," Hope said, pinching her nose closed.

"That's just about enough," Faith said, turning her back on her sister. "If Dad was dead he'd be turning over in his grave."

"Oh, you're too much, Faith. Just too much."

Manny, Tony's older brother, turned to their youngest brother Franchesko, "Sure, no one can hear her talkin' about Tony's tool! And

—

perhaps it's an innocent bulge and not a hard-on. Perhaps brother Tony has swiped the church chalice."

"I think our brother has just found a unique way to tell someone he loves her during a christening without saying it out loud. It's the first hard-on I've ever seen in church. At least in the front of the church," Franchesko said.

"That Hope sister of Charity's said something about 'a fart in church pew,'" Manny said, and they both laughed at the "phew in the pew" joke. They always joked in church, mostly because they didn't understand Mie's love for someone you can't see, and it made them nervous. Could the person they couldn't see see them? And jab their bandy asses with a pitchfork that would make the devil's pitchfork look like a pudding spoon?

The brothers didn't mind all that much, laughing at the same old jokes like "phew in the pew." Old jokes were much more comfortable than some of the modern jokes that could be mean and senselessly raunchy. Raunch was fine when it fit. Meanness never fit. It sucked. The brothers had punched many a mean one in the nose. Jokes to them were a laugh along, not something that sucked like a kid on a nanny goat.

All three brothers had a workable selection of curses that came in handy when you banged a thumb while nailing up barbed wire or when a milk cow stepped on a bare foot or when you got your foreskin caught in one of those dang-fangled new inventions that replaced the buttons on the fly of their overalls called the zipper.

But imagination was introduced into their swearing. Tony wasn't given much to cursing at all. In fact, he was quiet as a pismo clam when it came to the colorful word selection and left most of the cursing to his younger and older brothers.

Tony was a swear word inventor. His invention would replace any swear word that he wouldn't want Mine or his sister Alameida Antonina to hear.

The first time he got his downstairs personal property caught in his fly zipper, that first time he used the new fangled invention, he yelped, "Uninvited invention, teeth like a piranha!"

"Uninvited invention, you say! Your balls will bake like snowballs in hell for that type of talk," Manny had kidded.

Manny and Franchesko had slapped their knees with glee on that one. And every time Tony would use a weak-kneed invented swear word replacement for a good and healthy cuss, it would bring joy to his brothers and always their same knee slapping retort, "Your balls will burn like snowballs in hell."

The two brothers weren't all that outfitted with strong curse words out of respect for their mother. Mie would be heartbroken. They settled for curses like bat shit, rat shit, cat and gnat shit, and cursed them in English.

Not a lot of friends and never a stranger made fun of their pudding-soft swears. There was something about their ham-size farm-boy fists that did not invite laughs in the face.

When the word "motherfucker" came on the scene, they brought no joy to the DaSilva boys. And as often as not the "mother" offerings only drew the special attention of the Rough and tumble, or just add "or" tough, ham-handed farm boys.

They adored their tiny mother and her giant heart of a lioness and often wished they had the courage to tell her they did. But that would never happen. You just never, never ever, told your mother you loved her.

While they knew little about boxing or fighting, they could take a baker's dozen punches to the head and smile, just to get in one awkward but most effective sledgehammer little-brother-hits-like-a-mule connection.

And when the swing took, it would as often as not leave the mother mouther with a nose that looked like a potato deformed growing between stones in a rocky soil or with a well-closed eye that did not look unlike a road-killed sewer rat. The black eyes they gave were termed "two sirloins," as a single sirloin would not help to reduce the damage around the eye.

They understood the farm girl and the traveling salesmen, the virgin lamb that ran faster than the farmer in his knee boots jokes and the colorful language that accompanied such tales, such as "she had tits like a thirty-two-quart-a-day milking cow."

Not only did they not like certain city slicker motherfucker words, the city slicker jokes were also more often than not told too fast for them to understand. And MF was not only a never-ever swear, but it could also bring the utterer a punch in the mush.

And they felt the city boys didn't laugh like country boys. Country boys laughed as the joke was being told.

City boys wouldn't laugh until their joke was completed, as there was no story to the joke, only a punch line.

The country boys did not like the fact that the city fellas would ask, "You get it?" as if the country boy's brain was made of soy sorghum.

Yup, old jokes always made sense to them as you could start laughing before they were completed. Nothing wrong with that; that was the DaSilva brothers' philosophy. And it worked fine for them.

—

Of course they didn't know what the word "philosophy" meant. They all understood the words "common sense" and "fair" and "funny" and "Mie loves her little keeterzingers—her little children."

They had learned the meaning of the good words from Mie. And whenever she used these words, tears trickled down her cheeks, different kinds of tears, tears of laughter or love or hope or the thought that she wouldn't always be there to feed and hug them

But the DaSilva boys were doing all right in the old Episcopal church on this christening day, with its pew backs made of boards some twenty-four inches wide, similar to the ones they cut on the farm mill.

Mr. John Shiverick pledged not only to paint the old wooden church every two years as opposed to every five, but also to supply the paint as well, both labor and materials at no cost. And of course this enhanced his getting the date he wanted.

There were some in the town of Rockledge who believed asking for and receiving such a Christmas christening date was the evil eye work of a demented old devil.

But these opinions were kept within the confines of the opinion holder's home, partially out of awe of Mr. Shiverick's terrible swift sword and the fear that he was a true believer with a possible in upstairs.

Besides, his painting of the church for free meant they would not have to face a special tithe every time it needed a new coat.

Mr. John Shiverick had vowed he would paint the church every two years, which meant the church would always glow with the whiteness of heaven. And be enhanced with the earth green of shutters ten feet long. The bonus was that he would be so busy he would have less time to get into mischief.

Also, the Rockledge Episcopal Church—despite the fact that many outsiders to the church, including Catholics, Buddhist, Baptists, atheists, Adventists, holy rollers, whirling dervish, and deists—felt the parishioners there regularly starched their asses, had its share of free spirits.

And a true free spirit always backs his free-spirited brethren. The old man who pushed a paint cart in these days of the automobile and painted the shoes of children and the paws of pups and old dogs and who cursed telephones, indoor toilets, and window curtains alike qualified as a free spirit in anyone's book.

Although he wouldn't describe himself such. The only spirit he knew was the one he walked in, the spirit of the Lord.

Among the old man's backers who said, "If he wants a Christmas christening, let him have it," were the present children as well as those who had grown into young adults and had followed his pushcart to the promised Holy Land and fought the heathen devils with their wooded swords. And those then children who followed their good Indian chief as he rescued settlers from bad Indians. And those who had fought fierce fires behind the man who pushed the very fire wagon himself. They laughed, remembering those wonderful days. Despite time and their changing into trolley drivers and housewives, bankers and bums, the old man remained the same.

They had learned under his terrible swift sword to walk in the gait of a heavily armored steed, lances held high, to the Holy Land.

Some of the young All Saints' deacons as kids had worn pillowcases during the old man's yesteryear Crusades to the Holy Land, with head and armholes cut out and with the hand-painted blood-red Holy Crusade cross on the breast.

The children crusaders that followed Mr. Shiverick's paint cart often painted the red crosses of the crusaders on his wagon with tubes of lipstick uncovered in trash cans, thrown there by unhappy fathers who discovered the devil's own paint secreted in a teenage daughter's sock drawer, wrapped in the middle of a pair of socks folded together, or hidden in the hollow of a brass bed leg, as if their fathers had never hidden their secret stuff in brass beds.

Others painted their crosses with the juice of crushed wild raspberries discovered in the Big Woods behind the Shiverick home.

One lad had a real crusader's red cross banner, a flag borrowed from the clothesline of the gentleman who headed up the Rockledge Chapter of the Red Cross.

Many of these old-day crusaders and firefighters were now the adult parishioners who backed the old man's desire to have his grandson christened on Christmas day, even the ones who believed he was crazy as a coot but a harmless old loon.

Yes, the old man had detractors, but they hid mostly in the woodpile.

Those who would be critical of the old man's arranging for his grandson's christening on Christmas day were cautious not only of the now-mature adult parishioners who had attended the Crusades, but also of the new breed.

The new breed were those new, young whippersnapper crusaders, some third and a few fourth generation pushcart followers, who served under the old Indian and fire chief. The whippersnappers would drive a hollow reed lance into the unsuspecting groin of anyone they felt figured to do Mr. John Shiverick harm on his pushcart journey to the Holy Land.

The old gent ventured forth through ` snowball fights and the July burning of caterpillar nests that infested many trees.

—

Leaving the scene of burning caterpillar nests and watching the incinerated caterpillar paratroopers fall to earth was no easy decision.

These were the ones who backed anything the old man desired, especially when their parents termed Mr. Shiverick as "crazy" because that would have made them crazy too. The young ones considered tying their parents to an anthill and covering them with honey after their parents called Mr. Shiverick blasphemous, whatever that meant, and declared the old man should be burned at the stake. Well, the young kids understood a burned steak; they'd witnessed them at July Fourth cookouts.

The youngest didn't want their leader and friend "burned as a steak."

Even the older ones weren't sure what the word "blasphemy" meant, but they were as certain as God made little pink peas that the old man wasn't guilty of it.

These modern-day kids of the 1930s were not quick to cower. After all, weren't they the ones who rode their bikes through burning piles of autumn leaves that stuck in their spokes and left a firestorm meteor trail behind them.

Shades of Buck Rogers and things to come.

Regardless of the exhilaration of such circus daredevil feats of riding through burning leaves or watching incinerated caterpillars burn earthward, they would leave there to follow the hymn singer.

They sang along with him, "Onward, Christian soldiers, marching as to war, with the cross of Jesus marching on before," while at the same time "Fireman! Save my child!" rang like fire bells in the back of their heads.

Some of the more talented bike riders—the freewheeling dealers—turned their bikes into air-pawing crusaders' steeds by setting their bikes back on the rear wheel, towering over those lackeys riding their broomstick plugs and those poor Christian peasants who trudged to the Holy Land on foot. Yup, Mr. Shiverick had legions defending his God-given right to have his grandson christened on this holiest of days.

Who would dare—what parent, name one—to cross these young tartars when they chanted their thoughts of "Leave Mr. Shiverick be. Leave Mr. Shiverick be. Or else!"

If the tartars were forced to go to war to protect their battle-worn old knight in tarnished armor, they would. Despite the fact they were no longer kids, they would once again don their knight helmets made of Wheaties boxes painted silver, carry their garbage can cover shields, and wield their wooden picket fence slat swords.

Sure, there was no shortage of enemies of the old man, but they backed off, if not in the face of the very young, surely in the face of senior citizens, years shy of Mr. Shiverick's ninety-something. Had he not been painting houses (as well as shoes) and leading the good against evil for six-plus decades?

So a critic voicing an opinion against him, such as on the Christmas christening, could find the old man defended by a doctor, lawyer, firefighter, bum, butcher, free spirit, Freemason, certified freeloader, certified public accountant, a person who counted on his fingers, town father, or a cutter of doughnut holes.

Rumor had it that the chairman of the Rockledge Board of Selectmen had a pair of painted kid's shoes, one orange, the other green, on his mantel along with trophies for being the outstanding baseball player of his graduating class, a Silver Beaver Award for his thirty years dedicated to scouting, a Phi Kappa Phi pin mounted alongside his navy aviator's wings, not to mention a small copper bust of Abraham Lincoln he was awarded for having grown the outstanding beard in the town's bicentennial celebration, a beard that many believed led to his being elected a town father.

He was one regal, award winning, codger of a selectman. Yet his painted shoes were most treasured.

So the loved and respected Mr. Shiverick's backing came from far and near. Low and high.

Then there were others who defended the right for others to "march to a different bummer" and others who declared, "The old goat is harmless as a mad hare. Leave him be."

Thus there were no pickets, as some planned, outside the church on this Christmas christening.

Mie DaSilva, most people anglicized her name from M'ae, looked across the church at the Rev. Mr. Morganthaw Newhall.

He was outfitted in the Episcopalian garments that looked suspiciously like those of a Catholic priest, and she felt that perhaps she could live with her new grandson's being christened here. Although it made her cry. She crossed that big heart housed in her little body and looked heavenward. Tears streaming down her soft, old, baby cheeks.

But catching a glance at Mr. Shiverick, who stared at the English in his grandson, she wondered whether her being here in a Protestant church, reversed collared clergyman or not, was in reality a threat to the pope and the Catholic church and Rome, wherever it was, for she was not a woman of great learning.

She blessed herself, small tears again moisturizing her soft brown eyes.

And wondered what would happen to her new grandson, being raised by persons of a religion that did not confess their sins. *Oh . . . keeterzinger . . . please, little dear one . . . be safe from on high . . . Lord . . . do*

—

not let this baby . . . be judged . . . a sinner . . . for he know not . . . what . . . they do . . .

How could he ever be saved? How could her new Portuguese grandson ever get to heaven?

She blessed herself again, ending the blessing by placing her hand inside her dress top, between the second and third buttons, found her beads, and recited the Rosary through her shaking fingers.

Hope nudged Faith's ribs with her elbow and nodded toward Mie. "Look, the little lady is adjusting her bra. Must be some sort of Catholic ritual of pretend breast-feeding. I heard she has been an active wet nurse for thirty years. That's a lot of milk over the dam."

"Enough, Hope."

Mine looked at the two sisters, smiled a smile so gentle that even Hope's hard-hearted Hanna and hilarious heart softened.

Mie swore to God she would burn a candle all the days of her life for the baby. His candle would be centered among the hundreds she kept burning, creating a forest fire setting for her holy statues housed in that small room at the farm, the room that Pie never ventured into unless it was to light one of his black stogies off a holy candle.

He returned many times to relight the same cigar, smoking it until its stub threatened to burn the tip of his nose, often chewing a chaw of tobacco while he smoked, a rare talent, even among the spittoon set. He was uneasy in the room. But glad she spent many hours there in prayer, doing her thing. *So I can do my thing . . . inside some young things . . .*

Despite his approval of Mie's many hours there, Pie did not like the fact she spent so much time making the candles out of the various animal fats always available on the farm. Her time could be better spent slopping the hogs, weeding the raspberries, feeding him, cooking, and planting. Despite his feelings, the number of her candles increased.

They burned not only for family and friends, alive and dead, but also for the man who ran the country store, as she had heard of certain meanness and smallness that made up his character, such as kneading stale bread with water to make it appear fresh or resting his belly against the scale to increase the weight of the cut of beef being sold.

They burned for others of his ilk as well. They burned for a wide spectrum. It meant a lot of candle replacements. Thus, there were times she did not have time to wash Pie's feet, as she often did as he played solitaire at the kitchen table.

She would be lighting candles as Pie played the sodden cards between dishes that littered the table, muttering to himself, "Sumna-a-bitch. Sumna-a-bitch," celebration words for good cards, for poor cards.

—

Hope poked her sister in the ribs again as the Rev. Morganthaw Newhall chanted, "I christen thee in the name of the Father, the Son, and the Holy Ghost," and nodded toward Tony, as if to say, "Pay attention. This is important," as Tony, on hearing the holy words, looked away from the Reverend Mr. Newhall and turned his look lovingly on Charity and his new son.

Manny nudged Franchesco. "They look like Lorenzo Jones and his lovable wife, Belle." He had heard the radio soap several times down at Thiffault's Garage. There were no radios at the farm. Pie made it known that if you have time to listen to the radio, you have time to work. The brothers preferred to go without the radio and were left wondering what their fellow farm boys hanging round Thiffault's were talking about when they talked of the Captain Midnight secret decoder. "Ha, ha, ha-haaah, only the Shadow Knows and the Kingfisher, the Green Hornet, Jack, Doc, and Reggie.

All eyes were on Charity, Tony, and Baby John as the final towel was applied to his head.

All eyes except Pie's, whose eyes were glazed, wondering what the womb of Mary looked like. He wiped his mouth with the back of his hand, leering skyward.

Hope nodded her head toward Pie, toward Tony, and then at their father, and their frail, elegant sister Charity, and whispered to Faith, "That poor little baby. Our poor little new nephew has to carry the burden of an elongated English conscience and elongated Portuguese genitalia throughout life. Oh, Johnny."

"Amen," the Reverend Mr. Newhall ended, making sure John Shiverick noticed that he held his hands over the baby's head until every last drop of holy water anointed him.

CHAPTER 4

THE FARM—1940

The matador was fearless as he stared into the bull's eyes, tomato-size eyes that bulged with red frightening ferocity, eyes with veins like a road map, eyes so bloodshot they looked like they were bleeding through the thick early July dust that coated them.

School had just ended. Nine-year-old Johnny DaSilva had jogged, walked, tossed stones into the water lily reflection pools of the rich, and encouraged stray dogs to follow him during his eighteen miles of travel from Rockledge to the farm.

The first time he had covered the eighteen miles on foot, he was only seven, only a boy. It seemed to be a great distance. But later, as a man of nine, as past adventures were remembered and future ones dreamed of, the trip was floated along on the waters of expectation. In years to come, he would walk, jog, do the Boy Scout's pace, run through wind, rain, and snow with a away-we-go enthusiasm.

It was the cousins' first full week of working on the farm. The pay was low, but Johnny and cousins Dinkie and Pointer Gouveira expected a full cornucopia of adventure. Plus! Adventure can make up for lack of funds. Their combined thinking was "You can survive with low coinage . . . but only if you have . . . high adventure . . .

Their pay was two cents an hour. And the workday was from dawn to six in the afternoon. "A glide," according to Johnny, "if you think of the fun we can have after work."

And here it was. Their very next day after school ended for the summer.

Adventure.

Waiting. Staring the three boys in the face. A bull! Ready to fight . . . a duel to the death . . .

Although the opposition was not exactly a bull, it certainly was a dangerous substitute and much like the brave bulls used in Spain and Portugal bullfights. Big bad eyes. Well, not exactly bad. Long tail. Hooves.

Johnny taped his worn dungarees tight to his legs, miraculously turning them into skintight toreador pants. He wished the dull cotton was a bright and shiny silk. And in his mind's eye, they were a bright-blue and gold silk. He was Sol coming to earth.

With the tight pants, there was less fear the bull would snag them, dragging its tormentor to the ground to complete the goring. *Someday . . . I will earn enough money . . . to buy my own toreador pants . . . so very tight . . . that it would seem they were . . . painted on me . . .*

It would take a while to buy a pair of the matador pants as Pie's opinion of his two-cents-an-hour pay scale for his young grandsons was "too fuc-um much."

Their pay, given grudgingly in greasy pennies for sixty hours in the sun-scorched field, wasn't one you wanted to blow in sixty seconds on Bulls-Eyes, Bit-O-Honey, Squirrel Nuts, or other candies, nor pay for your adventures such as movies, Ferris wheel rides, Western flyer sleds, or Columbia bicycles. You made adventures that didn't steal your hard-earned pay. You invented adventures. In many sizes and shapes.

The cousins' no-small-thinkers first adventure was a big one. As the oldest of the three, ten-year-old Dink said, "A bullfight! We must have a bullfight. The idea is to keell zee bull, before zee bull kills you."

They had been building up their courage to fight the bull by sneaking a swig of the cider on the back of the farm's pantry shelf, that cloudy jar that was fermenting like the base of a farting cow's tail.

They jockeyed to see who would have the honor of facing the bull first. But on seeing their red-eyed adversary in the blood, the jockeying shifted gears into reverse, and the brothers Gouveira voted that Johnny get first shot at the honor. "After all, you're our guest," Dink said.

"Ya, you're our guest," Pointer echoed.

Despite being drafted, the new matador appeared as fearless as any four-foot-tall boy shaking in his boots while standing in the presence of a fire-breathing animal could appear.

In their eyes, their bull had obviously strop sharpened its horns.

Dink had claimed top-dog billing in their pecking order despite the fact Johnnie was to face El Toro first because of his age, although he was the smallest of the three.

Johnny, who provided nicknames for all his friends, named him Dinkie. "You're Dinkie because you're the smallest and because you're always tugging on your dink. You pick one. Or both."

Dink countered that he was nicknamed Dinkie, "Because my dink is huge. Huge with a big H. Bigger than a bull's." And he gave a couple tugs on his pecker through his pants, an action he accompanied with a bell clanging noise. "Ding dong. Ding dong long. I've got the clanger of a bull."

Johnny felt bad that his cousin felt bad about being nicknamed Dinkie, but it had to stay that way as after presenting a friend with a nickname, he accompanied this with a "black, black, no take-see back" oath and then touched something black, thus sealing it for eternity. He could actually visualize his cousin's gravestone. "Here lies Dink. He tugged it until it was pink."

Johnny tried to soothe his cousin's hurt, informing him that a great man was named Dinkie. "I think it was Dinkie Doo."

"He was the father of the professional baseball players' ritual in the batter's box—the rearranging of their private parts, more often than not in front of thousands of cheering fans."

Johnny never figured out whether the fans were cheering for their favorite hitter or for his efforts of rearranging his dick in his shorts.

But Johnny lost his battle to soothe Dink by chiming in, "Hickory, dickory, dock, a mouse ran up your cock. It took one smell and ran like hell, hickory, dickory, dock."

Dink lost it. "You A.H. horse's patootie!"

Johnny tried another angle to soothe his cousin after baptizing him Dink. The three cousins had been playing baseball in a cow pasture with a baseball so heavily laden with black tape to hold it together that it weighed more than a rock of similar size when a black Packard that appeared so long to the kids they felt it should have had railroad box car numbers on its side rather than number plates stopped.

The Packard had those shiny spare wheel covers situated inside the front fenders. The wheel covers had chrome mirrors perched on top of them.

The stranger in the Packard with the winged-lady-holding-a-wheel hood ornament watched them take turns hitting while he polished off his grinder. He had told the grinder shop owner, "You damned ginnies can make pepperoni hot enough to make a polar bear's balls sweat during a January swim."

The deli owner knew his sandwich's revenge would take some of the sting out of the comment of the guy who ordered the submarine.

The Packard driver had made his comment about the clerk's sandwich-making ability as a compliment. It fell short. On seeing the look of doubt on the clerk's face, he tried again with what he considered a compliment. "You wops sure can make a good grinder."

He obviously failed as the sandwich maker said, "Ba fan gul," then added, "here it is in English—fung gu to you too," then turned his back on him, hoisted his right leg high, and farted.

Johnny told Dink he was positive the man in the Packard was either a professional baseball player or, better yet, a scout for the Boston Braves and that he was obviously interested in Dink's hitting. "Not everyone can hit a baseball soaked in cow flops as far as you can."

"Nah, ya full of it," Dink said. "They'd never bring no guy like me whose pants are covered with grass stains to play for the Boston Bees in the Bee I live."

Johnny went over to the Packard. "Hey, mister, are you a baseball scout?"

"Would any of you kids like a piece of candy and a ride in a Packard? Maybe that cute kid, the little one."

"Look, mister, hang around while we hit a few, and then I'll give you a signal, yes or no."

Johnny returned to their cow-flop-laden field of dreams and told Dink, "I told you he was a big league scout. He heard about you. He'll return to the Bees and share his observation of your hitting. And when you get to the bigs, remember free tickets behind the dugout for Pointer and me.

"And remember how to relax before thousands of fans when at bat. Just grope yourself. Like you and your dick owned the world. Like you and your dork will be the next president of the United States. Start groping."

Dink groped himself.

Johnny turned and smiled at the man in the Packard.

"He's here for you, Dink," Johnny said."

"Oh, man, you are so full of what makes the grass grow green."

Dink puffed up, glanced at the man in the Packard, who was smiling the fox-looking-at-the-chicken smile. Johnny lobbed the ball to Dink, who swung so hard he screwed himself into the ground, driving the ball into the deep outfield. Then he turned and smiled at the man in the Packard. The man blew him a kiss.

Johnny gave him the signal he didn't expect to the candy-and-ride invitation, a middle finger extended stiff from among its folded brethren.

The Packard burned rubber, leaving the scene as Johnny pretended to write down his plate registration number.

—

"You're all set, Dink. I signaled him that you're number one. He's off to the Bee Hive, I mean Brave's Field, to draw up your contract."

"Liar, liar," Dink said and tossed the baseball at Johnny, but it flew over his head and landed in a fresh cow flop still seething with bees and horseflies enjoying a five-star meal.

"You get it,"

"No, you get it."

"You get it."

"You get it. You threw it."

"We'll pick it out of the field after Pie spreads the pile," Pointer said, fearful his brother and his cousin would appoint him as a committee of one to search the dung pile for the ball.

"You have to get it," Johnny said to Dink, "'cause that scout saw you hit that dinger, and someday there will be a statue in Brave's Field center field of you holding that very ball while scratching your other two. It will be like the Babe Ruth plaque in center field in Yankee Stadium."

"Could I have my statue in Fenway Park? I like the Red Sox more betterer."

"Sure. I think there were two big league scouts in that Packard. One from the Bees and the other from the Sox."

"Hey, you guys with the big dinks got the balls."

Dink was satisfied with his new nickname on that day.

Pointer, who was a month younger than Johnny, was nicknamed by his cousin because of his propensity to point at his brother or cousin or anyone in or out of the area, for that matter, wordlessly but definitely indicating he did it, a knee-jerk self-survival motion it seemed he could not conquer. Even if he got kicked in the ass a little later for his pointing a finger of guilt.

Regardless, both Johnny and Dink believed that despite his yellow-bellied sapsucker squealing, Pointer was still one of the three Musketeers. "All for one." Sort of. "And one for all."

Dink said, "Da tree of us is Les Trois Moose-go-teers."

"I didn't know you spoke French," a surprised Johnny had said at the time.

"I speak all the languages except Greek."

"Sprecken de deutsche?"

"Datsa Gleek to me."

"Oy. Oy-fa-zoi."

"That's Greek to me too."

"Sure."

But on this day, there were nearing the bull ring, not the baseball stadium.

The bull was in Mr. Osterhouse's cow pasture.

"Come on, Sissy Blue," Dink said to his cousin. "Climb the fence and conk El Toro between the eyes with your sword and get this bullfight on the road."

Johnny looked closely at the wooden sword, a slat torn from the pride and joy, white picket fence of Farmer Osterhouse. What if old man . . . Osterhouse . . . recognizes it?

The Osterhouse farm was ramshackle, only a few remnants of chalky paint remaining of its drunken, wailing walls, complete with broken shutters that screamed painfully in the wind, but the fence received top-shelf treatment from the old farmer who believed deeply that first impressions were important.

The picket fence received better treatment than his wife or children, better even than his favorite dog, Dog, thus named because of Farmer Osterhouse's lack of imagination.

Johnny's matador sword was forged just the night before, during that grand moment when the Osterhouse farm dogs slept like, well, like the milk-fed fleabag farm dogs they were, completely exhausted, resting from doing nothing all day.

The three cousins had pried the fence slat free oh so very carefully. Old man Osterhouse was known to not only have a shotgun loaded with rock salt, but also a double barrel one at that. "One for each cheek," Johnny said.

Rumor had it that one barrel was loaded with rock salt while the second tube contain a concoction of nails, screws, staples, salt, and other angry hornets of what Dink termed "ass-biting potential."

"Quiet" was supposed to be the word. But the slat groaned as its tough, forged nails held firm. The wood and nail moans were that of a coffin cover being lowered over their faces. Terrifying.

Johnny finally pulled it free, after pretending the sword had been embedded in stone and others had failed before him. The picket was perfect with which to kill zee bull.

Although now, as Johnny looked into the bloodshot eyes of what he truly believed was an insane bull, his wooden sword did not appear to be made of the right stuff.

The longer he stood frozen in his cow-pasture bull ring, the more the creature in front of him appeared more and more like a demented fire-breathing dragon and with real bad breath to boot.

It did not appear one single bit afraid of the boys' terrible swift sword. No, not one bit. Johnny wondered where that terrible swift sword that Grandfather Shiverick so often sang of was . . . that inspired fear . . . and admiration . . .

He wondered how long he could put off the moment of truth.

"I've gotta shoot Kelly," Johnny said, squeezing the top of his thighs together to prove to his cousins that indeed the bullfight had to be called off because he had to go pee . . . a real wicked whiz . . . even Noah didn't have to . . . go this bad . . . after drinking rainwater . . . for forty days . . . and nights . . . game called on count of . . . rain . . .

"Come on," Dink said, "Don't delay. The wicked whiz is dead."

Surely, his cousins wouldn't expect him to proceed when he had to leak so bad that he was moving like a flamenco dancer with fire ants in his tight pants, ants that kept falling out, and he had to stomp.

Johnny was ready to throw in the cape until Dink's grin told him how much pleasure his quitting would give him.

"Sound the trumpets!" Johnny said. He was ready for the start of the bullfight.

But it was the bugle call of Mother Nature that was even greater. "I have to shoot Kelly first!"

"Kelly," of course, was what Uncle Matt Shiverick called urine or piss in the vernacular.

"What better name for a bloody piddle than naming it after an Irishman. Kelly and horse water are one," Uncle Matt had said to himself while cutting wood, steadied by Johnny, with an old bucksaw.

Johnny had been shocked that his uncle used a swear word. No one ever dared to curse. Even at the Irish.

While "bloody" and "piddle" meant little to him, he knew from listening in when the big people talked that his uncle Luke Shiverick received a hide tanning when he used the word "bloody" as a kid.

"Yellow belly, yellow belly, yellow-bellied sapsucker," Dink chanted.

"Ya, yellow belly, yellow belly sapsucker," Pointer said, pointing first at Johnny and then at the bull.

Johnny bent over and picked a yellow buttercup, held it under his chin, and challenged his cousins, "Does it show yellow under my chin?"

"Yes," Dink said.

"Liar, liar, pants on fire. All that yellow under my chin means I like butter."

"Cut the bull, get it, cut the bull," Dink said, "and clock El Toro with the flat of your sword. Be Manolete, the greatest bullfighter of all time."

Johnny lifted a bright-red fighting cape in front of his face, peered over the top of it at El Toro. Johnny realized that he was fearless yet wondered why his knees were working like a sewing machine.

The cape had been borrowed early that morning from a clothesline. At 4:00 a.m. to be exact. Before the borrowing, the cape had been a set of fire-red long underwear complete with trapdoor so you wouldn't have to peel off the entire garment in the icebox cold of the March wind outhouse when nature called. Often, the corncobs or pages from the Sears and Roebuck catalog felt like slabs of ice when applied between the buttocks' cheeks. The long johns turned bullfighter's cape had prior to the purloining, been worn year-round by Mr. Thiffault of Thiffault's Garage fame. He was a man of pride and well-being, not taken to enjoying the theft of personal effects.

"You've got all the goods you need to face a brave bull," Dink said, "now do your thing. Be the brave cuspidor," which Dink believed was Spanish for matador.

Yes, Thiffault wore the long johns year-round, including July and August. The only daylight they breathed was when they were hung out to air once a week, usually on windy night to aid the air cleansing, and a full moon, just in case a prankster might consider them fair game. But none would dare. Thiffault was a man of great pride and well-being, not to mention an ample medicine-ball shape and weighty stomach. He could swing his stomach like a tomahawk and bowl over any snot-nosed kid that was enjoying a lippy day.

The good man Thiffault had gone to the clothesline the next morning to claim his long johns, only to find them *missing*!

He felt like he had been . . . well, violated.

The thieves had stolen something that was not only very personal and well loved, but what was also destined to be a family heirloom someday. Known far and wide for his lack of generosity, Thiffault was of the waste not, want not school and planned to will the red long johns with the trapdoor to a young niece by the name of Matilda.

The young girl had declined to sit on his knee when invited there, uttering the words, "I can tell by the smell you're not feeling well."

This led to her uncle informing her that it was just as well she did not sit on his knee as there was little doubt in his mind she was an ice ass. And would be willed the long johns while other nieces and nephews would get it all. "It all" being what everyone believed was plenty, plus.

He felt that whoever did this dirty deed, the swiping of the beloved piece of underclothing, was as sick and lowdown as the Osterhouse farm

—
53

cat, Meow, that defecated in its own food dish, certainly a strange leaning for something as supposedly clean as a cat.

Thiffault considered that the sickest and meanest thing concerning the theft was the note.

The note was pinned where his beloved long johns had hung only hours, perhaps minutes, before.

It read, "That highland goat was feeling fine, ate three red shirts right off the line, and that's not all, it ate your long johns too. Then barfed and died! The goat and your red lovelies will be buried together. signed—The Long John Kidnappers, in cooperation with the Chelmsford Board of Health."

Thiffault told everyone who came into the store that he would send the note to the FBI to be studied by handwriting experts. Dink, a Righty, had written the note left-handed while wearing gloves), and if the perpetrator did not come forward, he would pay the penalty, time in the pen. The big house. When this failed, he offered a reward, to be announced after the culprit was captured, which, of course, he never planned to pay.

It was the scuffle of the bull's hoof against the earth that returned Johnny's attention to the beast.

This caused Dink and Pointer to move a good distances behind the beast, out of its eyesight. Out of sight, out of mind, he hoped.

Johnny, cape in position, sword ready to smote the bull between its bulging now-throbbing orbs, chose his action. Strike swiftly, terribly! He brought the slat sword downward with a "*whack*" right between the eyes of the bull.

The mighty blow didn't even make the old exhausted Betty Boop, the farm's oldest, friendliest cow, blink.

In fact, the old milker appeared to like it, and while she failed to smile, she did take on a look of contentment.

"Whack her! Whack the bull's titingers!" Dink cried, pointing to the cow's udders.

Johnny stared at the huge old udders only inches from the ground. His thought process drifted back to a joke he had heard his uncle Manny crack. "Why doesn't a cow . . . grow as tall as a tree? Because its roots . . . don't touch the ground."

He felt the animal's warm breath on his face.

His bull, the wild pride of the Pampas, Betty Boop, was trying to kiss him, or at least lick his face. But stopped her romantic approach and instead fell sound asleep while standing up.

He looked under the beast he faced. What had been a great set of bull balls in his imagination just moments before, mountain oysters of Alps proportion, changed into a foursome of timid tits.

Now that he looked, he could make out the bra Pie had made for the cow to keep Betty Boop from dragging her long hangers against the sharp stones that jutted up around the farm.

Actually, the cow's mighty omega tits were held high by a brace of bras. Pie had elongated the bra straps by stitching them to old machine webbing from the abandoned sawmill on the banks of Mill River. The strap was fitted around Betty's back and appeared to do the Herculean act. Her roots didn't touch the ground.

Looking at the mill webbing, Johnny remembered the first water snake he shot near the sawmill with his father's old .22, the one with the blueing worn away and the bare metal showing. "Always keep your gun clean as a whistle," his father had said. Later, he would forget this and pay the price. And a black snake swam away without a shot being taken at it.

They were fishing for pout at the time. They always brought the gun. Only shooting the head off the snake counted. A hit anywhere else on the snake was a miss.

The webbing was a bright-reddish color and tied over Betty Boop's hips and gave the old slower-than-slow-motion cow the appearance of having racing car stripes painted on her in the wrong direction. Which was appropriate.

The transition from mighty bull to moo cow left Johnny in a stunned state. Looking at the jury-rigged bras, his mind drifted back in time like a leaf slowly tumbling and yawing its way to earth to another old joke. "What's the strongest thing . . . in the world? A brassiere . . . It holds up two milk factories."

The twin bras ended the titty nicks Betty had suffered. Blood in the milk didn't help sell. Any more than a blood spot in an egg. But you can candle an egg. You can't candle an udder. Blood on any food, except a good and rare, still-mooing New York strip steak was unacceptable.

Blood was a turnoff to city folks. Not so to country folks. Pie always drank the steaming warm blood of a freshly slaughtered pig or goat.

It was city folks that bought the eggs at the farm stand, so Pie made the cousins candle the eggs twice before they hit the stand. The farm stand sold eggs, raspberries, corn, potatoes, and Mine's homemade fudge and served as a moneymaker along with the bulk milk from the cows and the rich goats' milk sold to the TB sanatorium. No milk today. It was a bullfight. A slow coming one.

The cow's attempt to lick Johnny's face caused its horns to move closer to his face. But he couldn't move. The horns . . . look . . . so . . . sharp.

Johnny was mesmerized by the transition of his bull to cow and now back again. *I won't . . . panic . . . I don't . . . panic . . .*

Hadn't he faced a horrible death at the hands of Pie . . . because of . . . the goat milk caper?

The goat milk thing—the old man had warned the three grandsons, "No fuc-cum put-tum milk bucket behind goat. Put-um to side."

He had never told them *why* the bucket was to go to the side. So it was an unreal demand but laden with the very real dangers of any of Pie's commands. They wondered if the old man demanded this placement as he didn't want the cows to kick them in the face if they milked behind the animals. Fat chance he'd worry about them getting kicked in the face.

Despite the fact, more than one milking farmer looked like a National Hockey League player missing their front teeth or, worse, from a kick from a cow or goat.

Betty Boop the cow had only lowered her head to eat grass, not to charge.

Johnny didn't know this. *Oh shucks . . . the brave bull has lowered its head . . . all the better to . . . rip out . . . my guts . . .*

But he told himself he had handled other death situations. Yes. Such as the goat milk caper.

Johnny had believed it was easier to have the milk pail behind the cow or goat and shoot the milk backward into the bucket rather than the awkward shooting to the side that Pie demanded and which also exhausted the wrists. Dink had said on milking five cows to the side, "I feel like I've been whacking off five days."

Johnny's mind flashed back to his bovine bull whose head was lower now like a cowcatcher on a train but, in reverse, a human catcher; he was about to be plowed aside or under. Had Pie sent the cow to kill him?

He had seen a newspaper picture where a man was scooped up on the horns of a bull and shaken like a rag doll until his stuffing that appeared red and green despite the black-and-white image vomited from his body. Betty Boop had honed her horns for years on the hard woods that were allowed to survive in the pasture to provide shade for the cows during the dog days of August.

She was the only cow that hadn't had her horns burned off with molten hot metal bars by Pie. She was so gentle; she was no threat. It was Mie who stepped in in Betty's behalf. She believed the cow was too gentle to need dehorning. Mie had seen butterflies, even a hornet, land on her horns, her nose, a fly on her eye, and she hadn't reacted. Betty's horn tips were now swaying back and forth, as if she was watching a tennis match in slow motion. The boys, before declaring the gentle old cow was a mad bull, had watched her as Betty waltzed about in such a romantic way they were certain that in Dink's words, "She can't wait to titty-pulling time."

Charity, while not a city girl, was far from a country girl and had warned Johnny, "Animals are unpredictable. And that's what makes the more gentle ones even more dangerous as you're not prepared. Always be prepared for the worst." His father had added a phrase. "Always be prepared for the worst, son, but expect the best." Johnny, confident in his ability to think and move faster than a speeding bullet didn't worry all that much about things.

Hadn't his quickness of wit saved the day in the past, twice in fact, in the goat shed? Wouldn't this quickness of wit save the day in the bull arena where Betty Boop ate hay so incompetently and slowly that Johnny feared her mouth would stall during a chomp? Yet deep in his nine-year-old heart, he just knew she was fueling up her strength. *The better to . . . gore me . . . to shreds . . .* He could visualize his young balls hanging on her horns like ornaments on a Christmas tree, but he believed there was no substitute for quick wits.

The first time they escaped harm's way in the goat shed was when the three cousins competed in an aerial battle to see who would be Eddie Rickenbacker, the World War I fighter ace. The title "ace" was earned by shooting down five or more enemy aircraft. Ace had a ring to it even finer than the dinner bell Mie (she was called both Mie and Mine now) rang to call them from the fields to a meal of pickled pork chops, tomartsoboule, and her homemade ice cream melting on a blueberry pie hot out of the oven, the same oven where the homemade bread nearly always cooling on the window shelf came from.

Anyway, the Nazi planes and pilots they called the "Bloody Blotch Fokker" pilots, letting their tongue roll on the potentially dirty word if used right—"Fokker"—that buzzed and dove in the goat shed, were none other in reality than the flies that called the shed home.

But until the day they could actually fly real planes against the enemies of their country, flies in place of planes would have to do as the enemy. At first, their dogfights were just that. They'd be flying the bright-red planes that aces flew. Pretend. They would swoop down on an unsuspecting dog and kick its ass, not enough to hurt it but enough to make it take the same evasive action a Fokker—God they loved that word—pilot would take. "Gottem!" Pointer cried out as the stream of goat milk, gunfire direct from a goat tit, hit the first fly on the wall. "Got the Fokker!" Dink and Johnny followed up with quick "gotchas," and within moments, they each were sitting on four kills. But the Red Baron, a giant botfly that had strayed from the horse shed, could not be downed despite taking a fusillade of direct-hit goat milk rounds.

"I got the bot!" Pointer claimed several times.

"Why's he still flying?" his brother asked.

"I say old chap," Johnny said in an accusing clipped English accent, "why is the bloody blotch still about?"

"The sucker just doesn't know he's dead yet. As soon as he realizes it, he'll crash," Pointer said, firing several long bursts of goat milk into the air.

"Stop! Stop firing!" Johnny said. "We'll be too low on milk to pass Pie's check."

"God help us!" Pointer said. "The pails will not have enough milk. It's youse guys' fault." A quick glance showed the shortage of goat milk.

Pointer took off for the hills, "It's youse guys' fault."

Dink handled the situation better. The situation meaning his escape from a brutal cuffing from their grandfather for the milk pails being too low.

Dink looked at Johnny, raised his nose in a most snooty fashion, and told his cousin, "I have better things to do than play milkmaid to an old Portagee." He pivoted and then walked off at a haughty gait. Once outside the goat shed, he took off, hell-bent for election.

Johnny thought Dink's haughty ass looked silly. Putting on the ritz . . . and all . . . Fact is . . . his tail looks like the butt wagging on . . . the pathway news film . . . showing ill-douche . . . Mussolini . . . walking away from the camera . . . watching his fascist planes . . . strafing Ethiopian soldiers . . . defending their sacred soil . . . by chucking spears . . . at the Italian triplanes . . .

"You know your ass looks like Mussolini's, Dink," Johnny called after him. And while it did appear somewhat like the haughty wagging duck ass of Il Duce, Dink took the stand that the best defense is an attack and yelled back, "Your ass is grass!" and disappeared.

Johnny turned his head to address his own rear end. "You hear that, ass? You're grass." His ass didn't answer, although he had tried to expel a fart but had to settle for a flatulent sound he made by squeezing air out of his cheek with his lips puckered up. A hint of humor helped when you were helplessly terrified.

And the bottom line was there was not enough milk in the pails. And this left Johnny alone to present the pails for inspection. He had a plan where he could limit his milk inspection to a single cuff rather than being killed.

When the old man found the pails not full, Pie's cupped hand, the size and hardness of a coconut cut in half, could cause an explosion that filled a boy's brain with a burst of lightning that could make his throat well up with choking bile.

Johnny showed up in the living room, a pail of milk in each hand.

The old man looked up from his playing cards, prepared to make the milk inspection.

On seeing his glance, Johnny started to do a little jig, loosey-goosey like a puppet on a string, whistling, smiling silly, like an idiot monkey that got into a nearby poppy field and ended up flopping and bopping.

He had heard his uncle Matt Shiverick one time tell his brothers how he dealt with the dangerous crazies that approach him while he's doing his milk route in South Boston. "The only thing the crazy bar-stards are afraid of is some nut cake crazier than they are. Fruitcakes are invariably afraid of nut cakes."

Pie watched the jig for a moment, flexed to give Johnny a backhander, but instead returned to his cards, pretending Johnny didn't exist but wondering why he was acting like the coo coos that hung around by the Rialto theater in Lowell.

Johnny continued his jerky-jerky puppet dance until he saw his grandfather peek under one pile of cards, pick out the one he needed to continue his game of solitaire, and took the moment to walk away without a single near-crippling cuff from his grandfather.

He had Houdini-ed himself free on that day. *It sure was a better choice . . . than my trying . . . to lead him in a prayer . . . of forgiveness . . .*

And he would escape the mad bull on this day as well and best he did, as a good goring or even an unintentional step on his toes by the docile seven-hundred-pound-plus Betty Boop could weld his skin and bones to his tired and tattered Keds.

But he had guts and brains. *And I could . . . jump high buildings . . . with a single . . . bound . . . if I had . . . to . . .*

The second goat milk caper proved more dangerous than the first one. He knew his grandfather would not buy another nuttier than a fruitcake jig. Plus the old man might not have to cheat while playing solitaire if he was stopped.

Following Johnny's close-cuffing escape, the days of firefights with Fokker goat shed flies were a thing of the past. The RAF and Yank fighter planes were all grounded.

Johnny had his cousins' stories of great torture by his grandfather when the milker appeared with the milk level too low.

No one denied, Johnny had quick wits.

—

On this particular day, Johnny had failed to follow Pie's orders. "Put-um fuc-cum pail to side when milk-a-da fuc-cum goatez. No fuc-cum behind."

Pie never explained *why* concerning the pail to the side bit, and try as he may, Johnny couldn't think of a good reason to do so. To milk with the pail behind the goat was so much easier on the wrist, so much more accurate.

Oh, little foolish one.

Johnny, from the time he milked that first goat the summer before, had a strange feeling about touching the private parts of an animal, touching the private parts of any creature, a female creature at that.

But Pie convinced him. "Tit. Take tit!" Grabbing the goat's tit and yanking painfully on it. And then taking his open right palm and cocking it over his left shoulder. And as much as he wanted to feel of the warm-tit, both Dink and Pointer had declared while touching themselves, "It just doesn't get any better than this." Johnny never touched himself.

He didn't buy into what his little buddies said, "If you beat your haddock in the attic, you'll need glasses. Thick ones. And hair will grow in your palm. Thick hair."

What stopped him from touching the spot that could make you feel wonderful were the words of Grandfather Shiverick: "if you do something not natural, God will sear the guilty hand off at the wrist with a bolt of lightning."

Johnny had fearful thoughts. *What if God missed . . . and it didn't come off . . . and instead . . . my hand was seared to . . . my private . . . forever?* And then he would have to walk around for everyone to see what type of crime resulted in such a punishment. Didn't they cut the hands off . . . thieves . . . in Baghdad . . . for all to see . . . and know?

But he sure wanted to know if it was as good as his friends said.

Grandfather Shiverick had also told the boy when he was four years old that God would fire a bright dart from the sun into his eyes, blinding him, if he ever looked at a woman with lust. Johnny had sworn he would never look at a woman, wondering what lust was and why anyone would want to look at a woman.

Johnny was four when his grandfather took it on himself to speak to Johnny for God.

He had peed all over his shorts, the toilet seat, the floor when his "it-thing" hardened one day while he was sitting on the toilet, reading the water stains in the ceiling. One stain appeared to be a girl, an older woman, maybe twelve or thirteen, complete with, well, complete with that which he had never viewed, those things in front of their bodies. "Breasts,"

—

he had murmured aloud. Then rushed into the bathroom and washed his tongue with that cow's tongue, sandpaper-rough homemade lye soap his Grandmother Shiverick made for the family.

He knew from that day on that he must never try to pee when suffering what he termed a "stiffie," a word description he believed far superior to the ongoing title given by his friends to such a prominence—a "woodie."

He took his first stiffie on as a real guilt complex, and for a good month, he peed no hands. And discovered it definitely is easier to ride a bicycle no hands than peeing no hands. He finally got tired of wiping off the toilet seat, his shoes, and, one time, the medicine cabinet mirror and went to guiding his stream with two hands. You just can't be too sure . . . when dealing with . . . inaccurate streams . . . or . . . stiffies . . .

Johnny decided touching a goat's, ah, stalactites—that's what Dink like to call 'statistics' to milk it was not the same as touching himself or a girl. He had never done it. Touched someone like a girl. He wondered if you started . . . things . . . by touching the tip of the girl's nose with the tip of your little finger . . . or what . . . How did you kiss a girl . . . on the lips? You couldn't reach her . . . lips . . . cuz . . . your noses would hit first . . . He was glad his nose was small. Perhaps he would meet a girl with a small nose.

Anyway, the second happening in the goat shed took place a short while after their goat milk, aerial dogfight episode.

Pointer had the milk pail behind the goat on this day. His wrist was tired.

Johnny and Dink were milking to the side as instructed. You never knew when Pie would appear out of the goat shit or cobwebs that drifted like Dante's shades everywhere in the musty shed.

They were thunderstruck and watched helpless, first in awe, then in panic, as the ass of Pointer's goat opened like the fearful eye of an awakening cyclops, and the goat turds, shaped like the marbles they liked to shoot playing mibs, came tumbling out like coins from a slot machine that rang up three jackpot lemons.

There were, however, no accompanying jackpot flashing lights and bells. Just the stink of sheer fear from the three boys. Goat scat is relatively odor free. So is rabbit scat.

They started picking the scat out of the milk with the speed of a brace of hungry bears pawing blueberries off the most lush bush of the swamp.

But the milk in this one bucket was stained.

They emptied the bucket behind the goat shed, washed it, and returned to the two pails of clean milk.

—

"Johnny, you tell Pie you did it," Pointer pleaded, "and I'll give you my big glassy, the boulder with the cat's eye in it." The one Pointer wouldn't risk when they were shooting peewees, mibs, or aggies.

Johnny looked at Pointer, understood he was really petrified with fear . . . but then again . . . anyone . . . with a brain . . . would be . . . scared silly . . .

"I'm scared shitless," Dink said.

They tried dividing the goat milk among the three pails, but each was a third short.

"We could milk Betty Boop to fill 'em," Dink offered.

"She's milked," Johnny said. "Mie milked her earlier. Anyway, Pie can smell the difference in milk."

"We could run away and join the navy," Pointer said.

"He'd find us and feed us to sharks," Dink lamented.

"Get three rocks about this size," Johnny said, forming his hands to about the size of a football. "Wash 'em good. Real good. Our lives depend on them."

"Why?" Pointer asked.

"Do it!"

They did.

"Now what?" Dink asked, no longer reluctant to give up the leadership of his gang.

"Fill the pails until all three are even."

They did.

"What now?" Dink asked.

"Watch."

Johnny lowered the stones into the pails, bringing each up to the milk level expected by Pie.

Now the boys were separated from the men.

They had to get past Pie's inspection and then empty them in the bulk goat milk vat.

There was no room for appearing nervous.

"Pointer," Johnny said, "why don't you stay outside, and, and ah, make sure no bad guys sneak up and try to rat on us to Pie."

"Yah. Good idea. That's important stuff," Pointer said and disappeared like a will-o'-the-wisp.

"You up to carrying a pail for inspection?" Johnny asked Dink.

"Do ducks shit in their drinking water? No sweat," Dink said, puffing out his chest like a pouter pigeon.

When they came into the living room, Pie was playing solitaire with cards so worn the eyes of the kings, queens, and jacks were missing.

The old man not only drew new eyes for the face cards, but he also drew nipples on where he figured the queen's teats would be.

Johnny stood in front of the old man with two buckets. Dink was behind him with the third pail. For a while. As when Johnny looked behind him for support, the pail stood alone.

Pie's eyes were like darts with glowing tips beneath his heavy brows.

The old man's hand lashed out.

Johnny ducked.

But when he straightened, his grandfather's hand was on his head, mussing his hair. "Fuccum good move."

My god . . . Pie doesn't feel good . . . He's . . . dying . . .

What Johnny didn't know was that Pie was going to have a visit that evening from the lady from Lowell city that they had seen him hand money to, green stuff, on two different occasions.

To this day, Johnny didn't know how they managed to disappear before Pie's eyes lugging three pails of milk, complete with rocks in them. Only when he was at the bulk milk vat did he dare to breathe.

"How? How did I do it?" he asked himself aloud, still shaking. Then after looking over his shoulder and not finding Pie standing over him with an ax, he answered himself in a voice three steps up the ain't-I-great ladder, "Only the Shadow knows."

He lifted the first bucket and started to empty it, breathing calmly for the first time since the goat shit hit the can, when the stone in the bottom of the bucket thundered into the large storage vat.

The rocks . . . oh god . . . Please, God, help me . . .

Did his grandfather hear? Would the ax fall? The ax . . .

He'd heard the story about the time his father had answered his grandfather back as a young boy. He ran up the stairs and hid behind the door in his room, pushing a dresser against it, and was holding it closed when the ax wielded by Pie came shattering through the door, smashing the bureau he had pushed against it.

He waited. Unable to breathe. The world had stopped. Nothing.

The stone had hit the vat at the exact moment Pie had swept the cards that had failed him off the table despite several jump starts with peeks under the solitaire piles and had given a thunderous opinion of their traitorous failure with "Fuc cardas cheat Pie," and he kicked his spittoon against the wall, a three-point boot in any league. Pie had little patience with cheats of any kind but especially with cards that cheated him.

Dink and Pointer, huddling outside the window, only heard something about Pie being cheated, "Johnny got caught!" and their sneakers burned rubber as they headed out like jackrabbits with a promise.

—

Johnny removed the rocks from two remaining buckets and poured the milk into the vat with shaking hands, fearful that an invisible rock would sound a Big Ben chime that would bring the old man running.

Johnny located his cousins hiding behind a bush in the dark. He led them to the cold cellar where they would not be seen.

He couldn't stop his hands from shaking. He remembered the day that his cousins and he were hiding behind the couch listening to the brothers Tony, Manny, and Franchesco, talking about "thumping their tubs."

"Yah, I do it before having sex. It makes it last longer," Manny said tongue in cheek.

Franchesco said, "I do it both before and after."

"Guess I have to put in my two cents worth," Tony said. "You remember old Thiffault's kid, Mendon?"

"Yah. He had some MS disease, multiplied scleer-roasted or somethin'," Manny said, "that made his whole body do St. Vitus's Dance, like a bluefish on featherlight line."

"Right," Tony said, except when he was twanging his banjo, and his grip on his pork chop was as steady as a Steady Eddy. And this was the time he wanted it to be herky-jerky. But he had steadied his hand through sheer willpower."

Johnny's hands kept shaking until he thought, *If Mendon can do it . . . I can . . . This is more important than . . . even . . . what Mendon . . . was doing . . . stopping fear . . .*

And his hands stopped shaking.

But the sweat kept pouring down his forehead. He rested his head against the cool earth of the cold cellar walls. A large hole had been dug in the dirt side of the storage shed, and it was lined with cakes of ice and straw.

The straw had been cut in the last cutting of fall while the hundreds of ice blocks had been cut from Mill River that past winter. The blocks were dragged out of the water and across the ice by the old plow horses, whose steaming nostrils blotted out their homeward route.

But they would know the route home if they were dropped off in New York City. The horses needed no direction over the snow-covered hills and fields to the farm no more than a baby needs street signs to find its mother's bosom.

The ice was stored in the skeletal remains of an icehouse that was built on cool underground rocks and was further protected by the shade of the giant elms.

With luck, some of the ice would survive well into the summer.

The cousins had always wondered how long the ice would last. They had made plans before the summer was over to sleep there in the icehouse and make igloos out of the stacked ice that was left. Rags, the farm's giant white mongrel, would make a perfect polar bear. Maybe they could catch a couple farm rats, toss them onto the ice blocks, and yell, "The seals are in!" and try to harpoon them.

As Johnny poured the last of the milk into the vat, he thought of when he sat with his cousins under the sweet-smelling lilac bush, nibbling the tiny yellow buds centered in the colored violet flowers, trying to cool off from six hours of grubbing in the hot soil for potatoes, and planning their Eskimo adventure.

"Won't it be cool when we have an igloo?" Pointer asked.

"Eskimos give you their wives when you go to visit them. That's cool," Dink said, very knowingly.

"I don't ever plan to get married," Johnny said, "so why should I marry someone else's wife?"

"Dummy, you don't marry them. You use them."

"Like for what?"

"You'll die a virgin, a darn virgin. Never will know a woman," Pointer said.

What in heck is . . . a . . . virgin? Johnny only thought the question. To ask it would be to admit that he was some sort of a city bumpkin and that Dink was a sharp country mouse.

"A virgin is someone that never gets laid. The lowest of the low."

The milk vat cooled his forehead. The milk had been poured. He had gotten away with the caper. Now Johnny stood silent, trying to work up the courage to return to the outdoors through the kitchen. What if Pie heard . . . the stones . . . was waiting with . . . the ax . . . or worse . . . the coconut fists?

Johnny stood in the dark, behind the door leading into the kitchen, watching the old man sitting in the rickety chair, playing solitaire.

The boy surveyed the room. It was eleven steps across. And he'd be out the door.

He was so close that he could see the cards being played by his grandfather. The old man was in a bad mood. Without Mie around, she was removing corn from the crib for the cows, he would have to pick up the cards himself.

Johnny could see the queen of clubs, even her pinpoint eyes drawn in by the old man's pen. It was the one card that had not been scattered on the floor. He could even see the two black dots Pie had drawn on the queen's breast, giving her nipples . . . weird . . .

—

Pie had also added something to the card besides the crudely sketched-in tits. He had blackened in two triangles, apex to apex, where the two-headed queen's crotches met. The faces of the queens appeared to leer down at the old man's work.

Finally, Pie picked up the cards and spread them out as he remembered them, keeping the queen in his hand. There was no red king to place in the one vacant spot. The old man looked at the card and back at the board several times. Johnny could see there was no play. It would be a very dangerous time for him to walk past him.

Pie made one last check for a play. None. He looked around the room. Seeing no one, he started peeking under the six stacks of face-down cards until Johnny saw him uncover a red king, which was moved into the empty space and was suddenly face up. He played the black queen on it.

Now it was just a matter of playing the cards out. He had won. Again. *Good fucum play . . . good fucum . . .*

Time to celebrate with a chaw and a hawk. He bit off a hunk of chewing tobacco from the larger square. Chomped on it like a crocodile chomping on a fresh-killed zebra. The stream of tobacco he spit flew through the air and hit smack in the middle of the spittoon. He smiled. There was something about perfection that he enjoyed.

Johnny moved from behind the door, into the kitchen, looked approvingly at his grandfather's winning efforts, and was away. And into the safety of the dark. *Thank you, dear God . . .*

Two dark shapes appeared out of the pitch black and jumped on Johnny. Rolled him to the ground. Clapping him on the back. Yelling, "We did it! We did it!" Johnny joined in. They clapped and hugged each other like a band of banshees, wild Indians hooting and hollering. They had got the rock-filled milk pails past their grandfather.

The celebration was, in reality, whistling past the graveyard, as they could not completely stop the shivering with their thoughts. "What if he had . . . caught . . . us? But he hadn't." And close calls only count in horseshoes.

Johnny was a survivor.

This thought returned him to the present, where survival abilities were needed again.

The bull.

He still stood before the murderous bull. He had hoped this horrific, murderous, fire-breathing vision had gone away.

While Betty Boop was a kindly cow on slower, more soporific days, today she was El Toro, the brave bull, with balls of brass. At least to Johnny. She didn't move.

—

"*Whack her*! Whack the bull's titingers! Teta, teta!" Dink demanded. "Whack her tetas! Whack her tits."

El Toro's razor-honed horns were so close to Johnny' face that he was sure they reflected in his eyes. Was it better to have the horns at this level and perhaps lose his eyes or have the horns lower and risk disembowelment or, worse, loss of what his Rockledge friend Righty Minichelli, called cajones?

Johnny didn't see Betty Boop standing soft eyed and gentle in front of him, chewing her cud. He saw a bull that he had to kill before it killed him. He knew if he killed the beast, he had to cut off its tail as a symbol of victory; everyone expected it, demanded it, before it was dragged throughout the city and then cut up and given to the poor. That's the way it's . . . done . . . iggy . . . yuck. Betty appeared to agree as her soft, long-lashed eyes settled on his.

And if the bull won? Would the bull cut off his, Johnny's, "thing" in place of a tail and have him dragged through the streets to feed the poor? *Oh Jesus . . . Oh good Jesus . . . Good Jesus H. Christ . . . Don't swear, John . . . Oh darn . . .*

"Whack her tits. Whack her tits hard. She'll fight," Dink said.

Johnny just stood staring into the Betty Boop's huge soft eyes, with those long fluttering eyelashes. Her bad breath had flown the coop, and now she had the sweet-sour smell of the grass she was munching.

"Whack her, Johnny, or I will," Dink said, picking up a board, taking aim at the cow's udders. "I'll make her charge. Get your cape to stop her horns!"

"Don't hurt her!" But Johnny's words were too late.

His words did cause Dink to change his Babe Ruthian swing from the udder bag to the cow's butt.

Johnny knew he was about to lose his eyes to her horns.

The flat of the board hit with a splat.

The big beast didn't spring forward.

Betty instead looked at Johnny. His long johns fighting cape. His terrible swift sword of slat. Then she peered at the grass on the other side of the fence. It looked so delicious that she salivated.

But this wasn't the end of the bullfight. The message delivered by the whack on her tail took time to travel the length of her body to the kindly but dim-witted brain, but when the pain arrived, the cow's eyes crossed, and not with pleasure.

Betty stared for a brief moment, her eyes crossing at a large horsefly that used the broad space between her eyes as a landing strip. Betty Boop couldn't quite see it. Yet knew it was there. Tap-dancing. She tried to

—

reach it with her tail, figuring it caused the pain in her brain. She took a moment wondering why her tail wasn't longer. Her eyes straightened.

And when her eyes straightened, she bolted forward. In reality, it was a tiny, little jump. Far short of making it to Johnny.

Johnny threw up his cape. Actually tried to hide behind it, fell over backward, and landed in a relatively fresh cow flop. Which was bad enough, but the flock of yellow bees feasting there took umbrage and bit his butt to high heaven and back. He let out a howl. A howl that led the brothers to believe their cousin was indeed gored, gored terribly, possibly his belly guts were hanging out like a long link of sausages. Like the links Pie made immediately after slaughtering a hog, making the casings out of the intestinal track.

And the brothers took off for the high hills, hell-bent for election.

A half hour later, Johnny found his cousins on the distant edge of the farm, dueling with hollow reeds they had snapped off at the brook during their flight.

Pretending they hadn't left him bleeding and dying in the bull ring.

Johnny gave them the look.

They returned a who-me look. Then both ignored their cousin.

That is until Johnny held up the brave bull's tail.

Well, it wasn't the entire tail, only a piece of the brush tip from the end of Betty Boop's tail. He had cut it off with his jackknife, a difficult job as it was wagging like a friendly dog's tail, the result of Johnny's soothing words to the confused little darlin' cow.

"Wow! Wow ka-zow. Wowie. Wowie kaa-zowie!" Pointer exclaimed as his eyes did an Eddie Cantor sing-along bouncing-ball act as he looked at the tail.

"That's nothing," Dink said, fearful the tail could mean he had lost the leadership of the three musketeers to his cousin. He immediately made plans to con the kid cousin out of the bull's tail. *That will . . . make me smarter . . .*

He thought of bribes. He would give Johnny all the giant strawberries he filched from Osterhouse's strawberry patch. They didn't dare swipe from the farm patch, positive that Pie counted everyone of them. And as long as he had that ax, nothing doing.

Some said the killing ax he used on the farm animals he slaughtered with gusto was the sharpest in the world. Others said it was the dullest. Both made you wince.

Dink thought perhaps he'd give Johnny a puff on the pipe he made with a reed inserted in a hollowed-out chestnut and stuffed with dry weeds, some of which were more exotic than others. Nah. The pipe was the signal that he was *the* man, *the* leader. Yes . . . the man in demand . . . the man with the hand . . . on the pipe . . .

No one else his age smoked, let alone a pipe.

He'd thought of the threat, *I'll tell Pie who cut Betty's Boop's tail off*, but he could never stoop that low to squealing. Maybe he'd threaten that he could keep Pointer from telling, that is unless he got the bull's tail.

But Johnny had . . . king-size . . . King Kong . . . caa-hones . . . yoo mung gus . . . happy hangers . . . have a ball . . . take two . . . they're small . . .

But Dink knew he'd think of something.

As it turned out, he didn't have to do anything. He merely was handed the tail when Johnny got bored with it, and it started to stink. It was drying out, getting brittle, but was still quite a coup to have the tail. It was sort of a lion's tail magic wand, like the ones witch doctors used in the jungle to strike fear into men's hearts. Or win a maiden's heart.

He would only use it on girls when Johnny wasn't around. To show to the guys from the other side of town. Maybe he would even use it as a mustache to get older girls to not run away from him laughing. Or to pretend to tickle them under the chin but let it slip and instead tickle their titties.

Eventually, Dink got bored with the tail and made arrangement to transfer ownership to Pointer because he loved his brother, and besides, he wanted Pointer's favorite boulder in trade, that giant marble with the cat's eye.

While the bullfight was the Three Muskateers' hour, even greater than the rocks-in-the-goat-milk-pail caper, the greatest event of the summer on the farm was yet to come. The bucking bronco ride.

That isn't to say there weren't slow periods, making it at times a very somnolent summer. But the sleepy time days were of short duration. There was just too much imagination and energy involved.

And the sleepy time days were not that tough to take. They made a raft, complete with pine bough beds and a fireplace constructed on a piece of tin borrowed from the roof of a dilapidated barn. Throw in a cache of homemade Portuguese sausages, both hot and sweet, donated by Mine and sweet corn, whose tassels were used to make grandiose pirates' mustachios. They wore the Pirate's mustachio when they confiscated apples, peaches, pumpkins, and pears gathered from sundry farms, during night stores capers. They told each other they planned to pay the aggrieved after making their fortunes in Hollywood, alongside of Jimmy Cagne playing for the Red Sox alongside of that new kid, Ted Williams, or finding sunken Spanish galleons laden with gold. Their word was their bond.

—

The raft was perfect for drift trolling. They set out their fishing lines with green leaper frogs, wiggly worms, crayfish, and shiners. The longer they went without a bite, the better. It meant more snoozing in the noonday sun and munching goodies. Having belching and farting contests. If you could get off a blast of a belch accompanied by a flying fart at the same time. Well, you were just King Tut.

They didn't worry about not waking up when a pickerel or pout or perch hit as the lines were tied to their toes. These short breaks were needed to recover from work in the boiling fields, tedious work that could often be done with the eyes closed. And to rest up for better things, adventures in which a kid could truly exhaust himself.

For their final adventure of the summer, they needed their eyes open. Wide. They would need their eye teeth looking and wisdom teeth thinking. It was bucking bronco time!

And the bronco would not be a Sissy Blue-Shoes, like lovable Betty Boop, the wild bull they fought to start off a summer of newly discovered courage.

No Bouncing Betty of the bobbing boobs.

The bronco to do the bucking was Bog the Hog.

Bog was the king of the barnyard. King of the beasts would be more fitting. *The* beast.

The hog was flat out a crocodile with tusklike teeth. Its ears were more tattered than a Civil War battalion's battle colors. Great rips and bites shredded the ears, but anyone who thought the scars were symbols of defeat were sadly mistaken. They were victories.

Even Bog's pure white eye was a war won, as the eye's tormentor was shredded like wheat before a thresher.

Everyone's favorite when betting a buck on one hog against another was Bog, a traveling pit bull brought from farm to farm to face all takers. Bog was so mean it was rumored that when he did not have an opponent to rip, he would bite his own ass and hold on until something better came along.

There were no cockfights among the farmers. They were illegal. But as Old Farmer Osterhouse had pointed out, "There tain't no laws that say against a hog fighting a hog."

In one case, Bog actually faced off with a pit bull. The good farmer Osterhouse owned such a dog and had bought himself a couple hundred acres of land with his winnings with that animal he lovingly named the Pits.

It was said the farmer, who, if he had to chose between his wife and daughters against the dog, would have to bring in a couple women from outside to do the cooking and cleaning.

There were a lot of greasy green bills that changed hands the day of the Pits against Bog fight. Some of the green had a smattering of substance on them, a sniff of chicken shit, perhaps a stain of cow dung, some even a hint of horse manure on them, depending what the betting farmer's morning chores were. All had the sweat off honest brows. Bog was sort of minding his own business when Pits and his fans arrived at the farm.

Just about that time, the small-town police chief Hector McDougall cited the law to Pie and those in attendance. He said, "Hogs and dogs come under the same law that governs cockfights and are illegal."

"Who givum fuc-cum good happy merda," Pie snarled.

Well, to remain police chief all these years, the chief had adopted an if-you can't-beat-them-join-them attitude, and that he did. And he put a couple bucks on both the Pits and Bog; that way, he was on both sides. And wasn't betting because he would have the same amount of money he started with

So the stage was set; the chief, to quote Pie, didn't give a fuc-cum, good happy shit, either. He had done his job. Citing the law. The town didn't have a lockup anyhow.

Bog was ready to rock and roll. He had been primed earlier that day when he was tossed in with one of Pie's fighting cocks, a mean bird injured in a previous fight but still had plenty of the cajones with which all roosters are brought into this earth. It had the makings of an interesting comparison of styles.

It took Bog about six seconds to render it.

Bog, in disdain, paid little or no attention to the mastiff as it came under the fence, figuring it was just another farm dog that did not realize the penalty paid for entering his domain.

Bog discovered quickly that the Pits was not a bashful tail between the legs doggie. It tore across the garbage-strewn hog pen like a mink after a field mouse slashed at Bog's eyes, ripping off what would pass as an eyebrow on a human, and then quickly retreated to listen to the squealing of the pained hog.

The Pits made the mistake of thinking that Bog's squeals were the death throes and rushed in again and commenced to clamp his teeth into Bog's balls. Clamped with all the tenacity his ilk is known for.

Now any animal thus approached, including the most fearless of men, would howl and head for the hills.

But Bog was not just any animal. And certainly not a candy striper.

The giant hog managed to move his massive body in such a manner that he could grab the Pits' rear section and rip it off.

A tribute to the pit bull's makeup was the fact that even when its hind section was missing, its front end remained clamped in the hog's haunch until the Pits finally packed it in.

They say Farmer Osterhouse cried that day.

And why not? He lost fifty acres to Pie alone, to say nothing about what he lost to other farmers and such other sundry persons who knew of Bog's, well, bad manners.

On this day, the day chosen as rodeo day, the cousins approached the bucking bronco of their choice with much more caution than they had approached their wild bull, Betty.

Johnny and the cousins knew this hog's history. Its background was black enough, but when you added imagination and the fact the beast had one white eye, well, that can get to you. Even if you have already killed a bull.

"He's nothing but a bucking bronco," Dink said, not looking Bog in the eye. They stopped a few feet short of the stone fence that served as Bog's coliseum. The stiff giant needlelike hairs on the animal's back looked more and more like the mane of a hungry lion, and they felt more and more like Christians. The hog slopped on a five-star menu of chicken bones, rotted oranges, soggy bread, gristle, hair, feathers, and live mice that came too close to Bog as they fed on tidbits there, as well as stale baking soda crackers that were smeared with rancid peanut butter.

Bog's good eye watched the food, both eating it and slaughtering it at the same time, ignoring the three boys.

They felt it was the blind eye, the white one, that watched their every move. And maybe it did. Who knows?

When they started out for the rodeo, they felt, and with good reason, that Bog would be the "greatest fucken bucker of all times."

Their first bronco, rode just a week ago, was a young billy goat and a disappointment. When Johnny had climbed on its back, the only action he got was a sorrowful "baaaaa." Johnny got off the little kid when Dink said, "Let me at him." But after the little billy looked at him, Dink said, "He's not worth the time."

For all general purposes, the billy was a no-show; that is until after the contest, when Pointer was taking his mocking bows for Johnny's efforts. The goat butted his bony ass, sending him "piss spout over tea kettle," according to the story Dink told the kids down at Thiff's that night.

When they set out from the farm for the rodeo, Pointer headed his finger in the direction of Johnny, remembering the sissy ride of the young billy, and said "I'll go first. This calls for a younger man."

"I'll go first. I'm the oldest," Dink said.

"I killed the bull and will bust the bronc," Johnny said.

Then they saw Bog the Hog up close, shredding a giant head of cabbage that looked to them too much like a human head to leave them feeling real comfortable.

"Maybe we should buck up to see who goes first," Dink said. "Everyone should have a chance."

There was no argument.

"Ya, we'll buck up to decide who goes first," Pointer mandated after his cousin and brother said bucking up was the way to go.

But they had to change methods as all three did not throw their fingers, odd or even, at the same time. Pointer had held back with the words, "Darn, I guess that disqualifies me."

"The three of us will draw straws. See who gets the short end of the stick then," Dink said.

But his brother pointed at Dink's hand, having spotted the palming of the quarter-inch piece of straw. "No fairs."

Even the court of last resorts failed to get a volunteer to go first. They were calling each other chicken, holding their fists against each other and moving their elbows back and forth in a wing flapping motion.

"Hey, this would make a good dance," Dink said. But the dancing stopped when Bog gave a belch of distain.

They had seen what Bog had done to the fighting rooster Pie had tossed into the coliseum. Heard about the Pits having his ass torn off and the horrible rumor about the baby.

Johnny wanted a distance spitting contest, short man goes first.

Pointer claimed, "No fairs. You not only can whistle better with those chipped teeth, but you can also spit further."

They gave a stab at who could spit the farthest when Johnny showed the chipped teeth had been capped.

But the rules kept changing as the spitting contest went along with what would have been winning spits. The winners were challenged with claims that ranged from "The headwind blew it back," "No fairs using Kentucky windage (they'd heard that term when Manny, Tony, and Francisco were shooting .22s at a Carnation milk can set up on a fence post out fifty yards.) They'd spit on their forefinger to pick up the direction and strength of the wind and then make an adjustment of the aim to the left or right, up or down to compensate."

When Dink spit further than his brother, Pointer accused, "Cheat, you juiced up with gum." And he did a "cheat, cheat, can't beat" song and dance around his brother.

"I've got it. We'll put three names in a hat and draw," Dink said, happy with his brilliant decision, tapping the side of his head. "Kidneys."

He took out a stub of a pencil, scribbled on three small pieces of bark from a blowdown white birch, and put them in his pocket. "Pull one."

"I'm not going in your pocket," Johnny said. "Tiny Tim might bite."

"Up your giggly with a meat hook. You draw, Pointer."

Pointer reached in his brother's pocket and drew out a piece of bark. It had Johnny's name on it.

"Darn it. You've got all the luck, Johnny. You get to go first."

Dink broke up the two pieces of undrawn bark in his pocket. They also had Johnny's name on them.

Johnny looked at his cousin, disappointed.

"What gives?" Dink asked.

Johnny didn't answer.

Dink knew that Johnny knew that his name was on all three pieces of bark.

Johnny drew a circle in the dirt with a stick. "We'll do it this way."

"Ho, what goes here?" Dink asked, thinking it was one of those step-across-this-line, knock-the-chip-off-my-shoulder, for-two-cents-I'd challenges.

Johnny rounded up three ants and placed them in the middle of the circle and pointed at each one. "Dink's, Pointer's, mine. Whoever's ant is last to get out of the circle rides Bog first."

"Can you stomp the other guy's ant?" Pointer asked.

"Nah. But you are allowed to slow the other guys down by hawking a lunger on it, but you have to be outside the circle when you spit," Johnny said.

The sheer brilliance of the contest received nods of approval from the cousins.

They liked it. And their expectorations hit the ants with uncanny accuracy, and why not with some of Pie's spittoon chromosomes slip sliding around inside their little spitters.

And their power and accuracy got better.

Johnny even took a moment out to show off his accuracy, knocking a small sweat bee out of the air. No easy task with his front teeth filled.

Dink spit with the power of a camel, but he was prone to scatter. Pointer was a chin dribbler.

Meanwhile, back in the ant arena, Johnny's ant was getting it from two sources. The cousins were both taking aim, ready, fire at his little fella, a courageous but a slow-moving short-legged, tiny, and perhaps slow-thinking ant. It was laden with goo, but it was an ant with the heart of an elephant and kept on trucking.

Unless Dink's and Pointer's racehorse ants got stuck into one of those conical traps where the ant lions lay in wait at the bottom, invisible just under a thin layer of sand, it was hopeless.

As there were none of the traps where the more the ant tries to climb out, the more it slips downward and into the hidden and waiting maw of the ant lion. A sort of Poe-like "The Pit and the Pendulum" contraption.

Despite its great will, Johnny's ant was the last one out, meaning Johnny would be the first bucking bronco rider . . . Oh hurrah . . . hurrah for sure . . .

But the heroic tiny one lucked out. While Dink and Pointer stomped their little racehorses after the race, Johnny had no such plans.

"What gives?" Dink asked, watching Johnny dry off his ant. "Don't forget to get under the arms."

Johnny said, "I set the ant free with a 'Get *the*.' Hey, I'm a poet, and I know it."

"Yah, your feet are Longfellows."

It was zero hour. And the time to end all small talk. Johnny climbed over the stone wall into Bog's pen. The other hogs kept in a nearby enclosure to protect them from Bog looked up from their orange peel and onion skin dining just long enough to give an opinionated snort. You could tell they had all crossed tusks with Bog as all, without exception, appeared to be in need of cosmetic surgery. Even the females nearby had paid the price; none would have won a Ms. Piggy contest, although one moved its curly tail in a good imitation of Mae West.

While Bog's reputation among the hogs was a badass one, among humans, it was even worse. People wondered why the animal was allowed to live.

Bog was an oldie as hogs go, and hogs go into pork chops, fatback, bacon, and brush bristles pretty early on.

While Pie loved the hog's downright meanness, nay, make that cruelty, that alone wouldn't have saved him from the shave and a haircut and blowtorching the bristles off, followed by a boiling bath that all pigs and such are destined for.

It was Bog's porker, his little pig pecker, that saved him in the long run.

He had great genes despite the pit-bull-tattered testicles.

—

Bog flat ass fathered the fattest little piglet porkers for the market.

Manny DaSilva said Bog's pecker was a sledgehammer, like the one at the fair that sends a bell-ringing rocket, past the words "tee hee," "weakling," "have you tried Wheaties," past "nice try" to the room at the top that proclaimed, "He's man's he man!"

So Bog was one of those rare animals that many humans wished they were, both a lover and a fighter. But you can't have everything. No one wanted to be that ugly.

Now the giant boar was going to have a chance to go beyond lover, fighter; he would have his time as a bucking bronco.

As Johnny prepared to step down from the top of the stone wall and into the ring, he hesitated a moment, feeling more and more like a Christian being ushered upstairs to the part of the coliseum where the tigers' and lions' lyrics sang "chow down" and where the rabid fans waited, thumbs itching to turn downward.

It was at this point that Dink called out, "Remember the Osterhouse baby."

"You bat shit prick without a human body," Johnny, who never swore, well, practically never, called out.

Johnny had put that story far back in his mind.

The story that Johnny had heard, told in the banshee wails of old Portuguese women dressed in black from top to bottom, was that Bog had not only killed the Osterhouse baby, but also eaten it as well. Oh my god . . . please strike me . . . with lightning . . . before I step down . . .

The story was told on the front porches of many a farm, most often during lightning storms.

It seems that Osterhouse's wife, his fourth, had brought her new baby, a sickly boy, to Mie for breast-feeding.

Grandmother DaSilva was a wet nurse. And the women of the town and beyond believed she only drank goat milk and only ate goat cheese, the very products Pie sold to the TB Sanatoriums to cure the hopeless tuberculosis patients.

As the story went, Farmer Osterhouse had wanted a big strong son that could run the farm so he could spend the remainder of his life repairing and painting his prized picket fence. His new wife was so thin that if she had straw where her feet were, she could pass as a broom.

Despite the fact the little and fourth Mrs. Osterhouse dared to express the opinion that "if a good Dutch baby is breast-fed by that old woman, it could turn out to be Portagee, dirty and dark," the old farmer insisted knowing only Mie's goat-milk-laden breast could change his son into a man.

—

The young woman had walked the mile from her house to the DaSilva Farm distraught. The story had it that she sat down a short distance from the farmhouse, resting her back and head against the hog pen. She cried softly as she looked at the son she placed on the warm ground beside her.

She laughed as the curious hogs gathered nearby, so curious, stupid, slow, and harmless, even that giant one with the white eye.

Then she closed her eyes as the sun warmed her face and smiled again. And she napped.

Story had it that her screams brought the workers from the distant fields. Even brought a fisherman from Mill Pond more than a mile away.

The story had it the fisherman ran the mile from the pond, which really was a river, down Boston Road in his chest waders, no mean task. The fisherman was no kid and was nearly stone deaf to boot.

The baby had just disappeared.

There were no answers.

Although there were plenty of whispers that followed for years and many a knowing and terrified glance was cast toward the farm where the giant white-eyed hog reigned.

That was the story most oft told.

Although mothers and aunts told their children that Gypsies stole the baby boy. That he lived happily ever after. Became king of the Gypsies. That he grew up to be beautiful, not ugly and covered with warts, like Old Farmer Osterhouse.

Young boys bought the first story, the one they overheard from their listening positions beneath the porch during lightning storms.

But Johnny DaSilva wasn't to be a boy much longer, at least a live boy. He was appointed by the gods that select fools for such events. In this case, a bronc buster. *Please help me, God . . . I'll never swear . . . again . . . and I never choked my goose . . . with my own hand . . . like Pointer . . . claimed . . . the lousy little . . . turkey fart . . . I'm sorry I said . . . fart . . .*

He thought of the old Chinese proverb. How did it go . . . to complete the journey . . . the first step must . . . be . . . taken . . .

He tightened the three bandannas hitched around his waist, which replaced the less colorful piece of hay-baling twine that usually held up his dungarees.

There was no shortage of bandannas around the farm. If you couldn't wipe the sweat out of your eyes, you couldn't see your work.

The three yippee-aye-yay-kai-yay cowboys all had bandanna neckerchiefs.

Cowboy hats didn't come that easy, so they had to settle for the old bowler hat they had found doing nothing special on the head of Farmer Osterhouse's scarecrow.

It looked like the real McCoy. Something a cowboy would wear. If he was a mad dog killer.

And they had the Boy Scout campaign hat, complete with tenderfoot badge that had been doing nothing hanging on the handlebars of a parked bike.

Dink wore that Boy Scout cowboy hat, assuming control during that short duration when he planned to be the first bronc rider. But he didn't give it up after Johnny lost the ant race and won the chance to face Bog.

Johnny's cowboy hat was made out of a paper bag with a cardboard pie plate brim, the middle cut out and pulled down over the bag.

It was okay, except the bag had housed sweets and had a few ants wandering about in it.

The bowler fell off Pointer's head and into Bog's domain.

"It belongs to you, boy," Pointer said, talking to the hog.

Johnny tied a piece of leather, the tongue of a long discarded belt, around Pointer's forehead and stuck a turkey feather in it and called him Tonto.

Pointer didn't buy the Tonto bit. He wanted to be a cowboy rather than some redskin. He was about to rebel when Dink told him, "Injuns don't have to break broncs, stupid."

Pointer nodded, "Ugh," meaning "yes," he approved of his transition from a pale-eyed gringo to a proud Indian chief.

Johnny smiled down at his cousin and mussed his hair. "King-O-Sarvy christen *the* Chief Scalp-a-Skunk."

"Funny fellow, Punchanello," Pointer said, brushing his hair back.

"Funny as a rubber crotch," Dink said. And they all laughed.

They had heard their uncle Manny say "Funny as a rubber crotch" and seen the three brothers, Tony, Francesco, and Manny, slap their thighs with glee.

"A rubber crotch," Dink repeated. "Bouncy, bouncy ballie, I lost the head of my dolly."

The frivolity was over. It was high noon, and the moment of truth was upon them. At least upon Buckskin Johnny. Johnny the brave. His entire demeanor showed his cousins that nothing in this world cowered him. *I'm . . . scared . . . shitless . . .*

"Burn rubber!" Dink yelled.

Johnny bolted off the wall and bounded onto Bog's back.

They knew they wouldn't have to tell Bog to burn rubber. Bog burned rubber in battle better than any of the young Turks down at the Flying Red Horse Sunoco Station, where they burned out, peeling rubber, showing off for the city girls that stopped at Thiffault's garage on occasion, to check out whether there were any cute farm boys.

But Bog didn't budge.

The three boys stared in wonderment.

Johnny appeared to be the only one who didn't mind.

"I'll fix his ass," Dink volunteered, picking up a broken fence board and, with a swing, made that much more efficient after a summer of hard farm labor, swatted the giant beast on its curly tail, compressing it so it appeared to be driven up Bog's buttocks.

Bog didn't buck. He just couldn't figure out what was what. He was the purveyor of pain, not others. He did onto others, not others onto him. The hog was dumbfounded as to where his antagonist was.

It was at this point that Johnny, with screwed-up courage, put the boots to the hog's ribs. Bog looked around and suddenly knew from whence doth the pain cometh.

Flexing its body as it turned its head, the hog sunk its tusks into Johnny's calf, piercing the flesh and muscle, sending fat squirting out of the wound, baring what appeared to be a glistening white splinter of bone, sending a searing message to Johnny's brain.

His scream would shatter good crystal for a half mile.

"Shit up! Shit the shut up! Shut the shit up. Pie will hear you," Dink said. Pointer just ran.

Pie arrived moments later, the tongue of his belt slashing the air in front of him.

Johnny was trying to stop the bleeding by sticking his fingers in the holes in his leg.

Bog stood a short distance away, looking at him, not in an unkindly manner. His action had put things into proper balance.

Pie took the board out of Dink's hands; the boy hadn't moved a hair since he whacked the hog with it.

The old man turned the board on edge, lifted it high over his head, hovering over Johnny, and brought it down with the finality of a guillotine blade.

Johnny put his hands over his head to protect himself.

No need.

Pie's swing caught the intended target—the bridge of Bog's snout.

The giant hog's legs stiffened like those of a coffee table, its good eye glazed, rolled out of its head, leaving both eyes pure white, while blood and snot spilled out of its nostrils and mouth like faucets of fire.

Too strong to die immediately, it stood marching stiff legged, marching in place, a true soldier, until Pie sent it to its back with a kick to the stomach more sickening than the edge of the board had provided.

The hog quivered on its back, its legs pistoning into the air in its death throes.

The glaze left its eyes for a brief moment. But now its good eye was covered with blood and swill.

While the white eye was pure as snow.

Johnny worked free from the suction of the mud and hogwash, looked at his grandfather with the look a drowning person would give to the lifeguard that rescued him. "Thank . . . thank you, Grandpa."

Pie smiled at the boy.

And then hit him with a smashing cupped hand roundhouse that crashed into his skull.

The smash didn't knock him down.

It triggered motion, motion that became a dash for life. Yet despite the speed that only terror can provide, he found himself in the show position behind the win and place positions of Dink and Pointer. The three headed over the hill.

Johnny, still at a combined speed of Zephyr and Miriam, managed to pull up beside them despite their head start.

They glanced at his torn leg, fast-flying botflies sticking in the blood, and said to his cousins, whose eyes rolled until only the white showed. "It's my piss-cutting end of a rodeo career."

"Oh good Jesus," Pointer moaned.

"Amen," Dink pontificated, minus the usual pomposity, and crossed himself.

Johnny crossed his Protestant heart. *Don't . . . let Grandfather . . . Shiverick . . . see . . . this . . .*

They only stopped when they were high in the hills above the farm and could look down.

There was no trail of dust below, no galloping Pie, a posse of one.

Pie knew they would have to return for supplies. They would be his. He had discovered why his hogs looked thin despite his increasing their food. *Shits fuckum ride Pie's hogs . . . fuckum shits . . .*

They knew they couldn't return to the farm.

Bog the breeder hog was dead. And for all purposes, they had killed it.

They sat on the variety of stumps that were offered by Mother Nature. Surely understanding they would starve this very night. Or be slaughtered in their sleep.

Then they remembered the old oak. And its hollow, created when it lost a large limb to heavy snow two winters past.

Investigation showed their cache was still there. A king-size can of Friend's Beans, a can of tuna, a can of pineapple.

The loaf of Mie's homemade bread and a dozen of her gingersnaps that had also been secreted there were nothing more than thankful little mouse turds.

They'd stored the staples weeks earlier for a rafting trip to the Dry Tortugas. They had planned the trip after Johnny read about them in the adventures of Richard Haliburton.

They had planned to join the Pirate Laffitte.

And planned to secrete plenty of stores for the trip. But they ate all the food that night, finishing off by flicking mouse turds at each other.

To survive the final days of summer without returning to the farm, they visited local fruit trees, cornfields, and blueberry patches and made other night store visits to the windows of local farmhouses where they took into custody the blueberry and apple pies, fig squares and oatmeal cookies cooling there. Of course before they did this, they made themselves cardboard sheriff's stars and declared the cooked were "the enemy of the people" that had to be taken into custody.

Of course later, when they made their millions, they would pay those who owned the cooked goods before confiscation in gold and double the value. They were not crooks nor cheapskates.

They ate the pies and cakes and cookies and figs first then washed them down with the beans, tuna, and pineapple on the spot.

Their feeding frenzies were similar to that of a pack of piranhas smelling blood. Luckily, summer was coming to an end. Farm women were no longer cooling their cooking by open windows.

No matter. They did not have time to make it to the Tortugas. But their worry wasn't the Tortugas this night. It was whether Pie would sneak up while they slept and slit their throats.

"What about the cans?" Johnny asked. They had saved empty cans to hold water during rain-wept days at sea heading to the Tortugas. Johnny had told them, "We'll save cans to collect water at sea, 'cause Mr. Haliburton said man can live for a long time without food but only a day or two without water. He sailed a junk, don't know if it was a Ford or a levee' Chevy across the China sea, or somethin'."

—

"There's probably not enough time left this summer to make it to the Tortugas," Pointer lamented.

"Lafitte will have to plunder and pillage without us until we get there next summer," Johnny said, brushing off some of the matter that stuck to him during his adventure in the hog pen.

"God, Johnny, you stink," Dink said. "A good elephant fart would relieve the air."

"Thanks."

"Maybe China is closer than the Dry Tortoises," Pointer said. "I love chop sewer, chop suey." He had eaten his share of the beans that night with two twigs he used as chopsticks.

Johnny smiled at Dink, who was now slanting his eyes with his forefingers, reciting singsong, "Chinky, chinky Chinaman, One Hung Low."

They all laughed.

Pointer laughed so hard he cut one and started Johnny and Dinkie singing, "Beans, beans, the musical fruit."

"The more you eat the more you toot."

"The more you toot the better you feel."

"And then you're ready for another meal."

"Of beans, beans the musical fruit, the more you eat the more you toot."

They slept in the woods that night, curled up close to each other, just in case the makers of the strange night noises chose to attack, but the owls and tree frogs and such appeared content to remain in their trees.

Until they finally slept.

The cousins.

The friends.

It was a combination of the morning sun, the stiffness from using the ground for a bed, a rock for a pillow, and the desire for what had been their farm fare breakfast all summer of three fried eggs, four chunks of linguica, five pancakes soaked in syrup, and as much pure cream, udder warm, as their stomachs could stomach that brought them around.

"Let's head downhill for the Roman orgy," Johnny said, not knowing what an orgy was but knowing it involved naked women feeding reclining men grapes.

"Pie will kill us," Pointer said.

"Then we sally forth and conquer the crops of the robber baron!" Johnny said, waving his sword in the direction of Farmer Osterhouse's vineyards. "We're off!"

—

So off they galloped on steeds of pretense, swatting themselves on the hind quarter, for wont of a real stallion's flanks, with a giddyup from Pointer.

A hearty "Hi, ho Silver" from Dink.

"On, Pegasus, my winged one," Johnny commanded his starry steed.

And thus the three Musketeers galloped wild and proud to the vineyards, then on to the blueberry patches where they pillaged until their tummies ached.

They took no prisoners, eating all.

And they galloped back to their hideout in the hills where they again sprawled on their backs, soaking the last of the summer sun, holding thick bunches of grapes over their heads, nipping off the bottoms ones, stuffing their faces Roman gladiator style.

"Bring on the wenches," Johnny said.

"Adjustables?" Pointer asked.

"No, monkey."

They were fearless warriors, well, nearly fearless, as while they pretended such, not one of this troika was about to show up at the farm for dinner the balance of this summer.

Back at the farm, the old man ate with lust, certain he would inherit the sexual prowess of his meal as well as the fearlessness of Bog.

The boys felt the old man's presence high on their hidden hill that night.

The three boys weren't sure of exactly what fear was or even if such a thing existed. But they knew something was there, always to do with Pie.

But the moon was full, and Johnny relieved the tension with the sorrowful bay of a coyote. The three set their voices to the air, listened as their wild tones climbed skyward to the full moon. They watched as the embers of their fire joined the swirling dance of fireflies and disappeared among the stars.

The campfire blinked its last blinks.

"Some summer."

"Ya."

"Ya."

"One for all, all for one."

"Ya."

CHAPTER 5

THE OLD EASTWARD-HO SCHOOL—1937-1943

The old Eastward-Ho School was different from the other schools in Rockledge.

North, South, and West Schools were located in the more densely populated areas of town.

There were no farms, unless you count backyard and truck gardens and the town's one piggery. The three more cosmopolitan sections often referred to the Eastward-Ho area as the Home of the Hays—as in hayseed.

Even school superintendent Jacob Morse was not sure that he should use his gas allowance to travel the three miles from his office in the Rockledge Town Hall, where he, along with his lone secretary of thirty years, Ms. Miriah Mulch, were the final decision makers on school matters.

He considered himself a benevolent despot, and Ms. Mulch, his queen, a bandy-legged Cleopatra whom he had lusted after for thirty years, a fact he denied to himself. He did not actually lust after her but rather mooned over her for three decades, from the days she was a leggy young thing full of spring to the present, where sciatica had her walking sideways like a crab. Which aroused him no end.

The herky-jerky walk actually accented her good points—calves that appeared to be pumping blood to other parts of her body—and he thought, without knowing it, that the ankle bones connected to the knee bone, the knee bones connected to the thigh bone, the thigh bone is connected to the, and so on until the part of the body that demanded the greatest blood flow is reached. Her sciatica stroll also seemed to bring new life to a buttocks that had failed to get the word that other parts of her body had received and had no sag whatsoever.

His feelings, which he addressed only in the dark recess of his mind, were illicit.

His thoughts were difficult to face. *I have imagined . . . therefore . . . I have lusted . . . definitely illicit thoughts.*

These feelings started that day he entered his office and found his new secretary of three weeks leaning over the desk to reach some attendance sheets. Until that day he had only viewed her ankles and personally could handle the sight of their sliminess, a sliminess that matched her patrician-thin neck.

But the sight that day of the hem of her skirt hoisted nearly knee-high, displaying fluid, flexed calves of unimaginative power, had disconcerted him. Her thighs as powerful as . . . those of a wild mare . . . like that Russian wrote . . .

"Thighs like a wild mare," he said aloud, startling himself.

Which book was that description used in? He knew it so well—thighs like those of a wild mare's. It was one of those Russian epics.

Regardless of epics, he was disconcerted that day. And he was upset, thinking about the triangular shadow at the apex of those thighs.

And thus, Ms. Mulch, who, unbeknownst to all, had a very close friend of the same sex, actually made the final decisions on the programs and spending on education in the Town of Rockledge. Strange as it might seem. The boys at Coogan's Pool Parlor called this type of ruling, whether in the presidential office or the kitchen, as "rule by the power of the crotch," man's rule of thumb and survival since Adam wondered what Eve kept under her fig leaf.

Although she was always careful, so very careful not to let him know that he didn't have the final say-so. No man can . . . survive that . . .

Her friend had informed her on that point.

The final say-so was important when a contract was coming up that involved construction in which both Ms. Mulch's and her friend's brothers were involved. Her brother was dearer to her than even her friend. As often as not, the brothers' low bid was mere pennies lower than next lowest. Certainly, there was no hanky-panky here. The bids were sealed.

Ms. Mulch and her brother had never played doctor when they were kids. There was a mother-son relationship here, stronger even than their sister-brother closeness. She had raised him when their mother died of scarlet fever. The father, a cowardly male, had fled the scene posthaste.

If the contract was important enough and needed to be peeked at while unattended on the superintendent's desk, there was a good chance that she would lean further across the desk to reach paperwork, thus providing a chance for those powerful thighs to make a cameo appearance. She had discovered his peek-a-boo leanings by mistake. She had caught his eyes reflected in that gold calendar holder as she had bent over to pick up a piece of paper that had missed the basket. At first she was put out. He had no right. She had told her friend about this disgusting action on Superitendent Morse's part. *Viewing me . . . of all the . . . of all the nasty nerve . . . trying to see . . . what is mine . . . yours . . .*

Her friend laughed, told her to make a man's weakness her strength. Then they discussed their brothers, then their private selves, and that what went on behind closed doors was no one's business.

Ms. Mulch felt rather bad whenever this ploy was employed, as the school head was not a bad person, just a weak one . . . a male thing.

Also, when placing herself on partial display, she felt a swing of guilt, as if being unfaithful to her special friend. What she didn't know was that her special person liked nothing more than to display that white band of flesh between silk stocking top and panties to the more powerful men in her office. Then, catching them looking, she smiled. Little did they know was that smile was saying something else . . . eat crow . . . And that she was a natural blonde.

Parents went along with Superitendent Morse's decisions, as the Parent-Teacher Association had not been invented as yet. And the School Committee, feeling no pressure from parents because of the lack of a PTA, were more than willing to go along with his professional training. He had not one, but two master's degrees.

The teachers went along for the ride because he was given to recommending teachers' raise requests in a make-peace-not-war philosophy. It was not worth upsetting his queasy stomach by fighting such a large group.

It was a lot easier to let someone else make a decision, claim credit for successes, and let Ms. Mulch fend off detractors.

But failures were few as since only a small percentage of the citizens of Rockledge had a college education. How were they, the mass, to question someone smarter than them?

The mission of the superintendent was relatively simple—make sure a prim and proper education went to the handful of students who would go on to college and make sure the balance did not commit a crime or get pregnant. Perhaps some would become electricians or plumbers. He hoped to accomplish the latter with a minimum of school expenditure so more could be spent on prizes of his thinking, the college bound. The future bankers, doctors, lawyers . . . Indian chiefs . . . No . . . not Indian chiefs . . . What am I thinking?

There wasn't a lot of money in Rockledge, a town of just under twelve thousand. Times were tough. Although few realized it, other than Roger Bapson, the stock market was committing suicide, and those with big bucks settled in Brookline and Winchester and Newton, not Rockledge.

Times were so tight that the usually kindly population felt some animosity, although they wouldn't admit it. Mrs. Burris was dropping babies, like leaflets from an autumn sky, and that they had to support.

Although some return to the taxpayers was realized through the enjoyment of speculating whom the various fathers of her children could be.

While this little old lady in the shoe, Mrs. Burris couldn't immediately remember the name of a certain child at certain times, she surely loved them all. Teddy didn't mind being called Jackie, nor did Jackie mind being called Teddy, as long as there was a hot dog in the frying pan for each that evening. Rather than using a name at a time, she would call each "my wild Indian."

Mrs. Burris even loved her two youngest, whom at times appeared to have invented the words "double trouble."

Rhesus Burris was thus nicknamed by Johnny as his hair was the bright rufous red of a swinging rhesus monkey's ass, and Boattail was nicknamed thus as he was blessed with the blue-black hair of the strutting, ass-wagging, tuxedo wearing, boattail crackle.

Despite the great range of color of hair in the Burris kids, never a rumor of any hanky-panky circulated. The kids clothes were always clean. She worked sixty hours a week, not nearly enough to support her kids, and was endowed with a mustache that would have made Groucho Marx jealous.

She also had the dark, laughing, rolling, wild eyes of the comedian. Seemingly not a combo to entice a wayward milkman or iceman.

Actually she had nothing to laugh about, and her Seven League Boot travels could be attributed to the fact that she had so many children she didn't know what to do. Some thought, *A touch left of center.*

Superintendent Morse, with Ms. Mulch's endorsement, felt it a sworn duty that education funds not be spent in great amounts on those unblessed families such as the Burrises and the DaSilvas; these students would never know the insides of a college.

The children's and parents' reward would be the knowledge that most of the parents never made it past the sixth grade. There was a chance, actually a good chance, that their kids would make it to the ninth or even the tenth grade, depending on when they reached the age of sixteen.

Rhesus, Boattail, and other friends who would join the gang later were nicknamed by Johnny DaSilva, who took it on himself to take over where the baptizing priest or minister left off.

He even went beyond the pale of friendship to present nicknames to others who weren't close friends. The timid James Bull, a baker who owned a shop, James's Doughnuts, was Ferdinand the Friendly Bull. Johnny hoped that all kids of the future would also know of a nickname. The nicknames did not denote bullying; to the contrary, it was shared humor and an honor to have a nickname.

Johnny wanted to name the shop Ferdinand's Cow Cakes but kept this to himself, as he didn't want to offend the man who on occasion was known to give away a broken doughnut to anyone who would sweep his front steps, pick up the alley, and say, "Please." Make that "Pretty please" when Ferdinand was feeling a mite powerful as lord of the doughnuts.

Johnny's nicknames were never meant to be mean and were accepted with great joy by those who realized a nickname was a badge of belonging. This allowed them to stand above the company of the multitudes of other Richards and Roberts, sans nicknames, of the world.

Johnny was not given a nickname. Rhesus and Boattail Burris took care of that.

They figured it was only fitting that the lord of imagination be the only kid in town without one.

Rhesus, at first, said he wanted to call Johnny the John, the Two Seater, Shithouse, Toilet, Crapper, Outhouse, or even Poop Chute, as these were all nicknames for the john, as in "I've gotta go to the john."

Giving him no name was great stuff, treating the king like a pauper.

Rockledge was fifteen miles north of Boston as the trolley travels, yet there was only one black family in the town. It was in the Eastward-Ho section.

Why blacks boycotted Rockledge was never figured out other than they suspected they would not have been welcomed. They were wrong on that one.

The one black family in town was welcomed warmly because it was more than top shelf. The Yanders kids were among the brightest, most athletic, best looking, and unassuming kids in town, certainly credentials that would make many dislike them.

"Not one bit uppity like some of those little burr-headed turds are," according to Officer Kelly, who was not particularly known for his ethnic benevolence.

He knew the hidden voices that later ran off laughing after tossing a rotten tomato at him from out of the dark were not those of the Yanders. "Hey, hey, Officer Kelly, we knows your mutter's got a pimple on her belly."

"You little ginny and kike shits! Mic monsters!"

He hated calling Irish kids mics, but they deserved it. He believed when someone was a piece of shit they weren't of Irish pride, but were mics. *Surely, he thought, This proves . . . that Officer Kelly here . . . is not . . . biased . . .*

He would continue his ethnic tirade with, "I know your whore mothers, you chink turds!" At times, Officer Kelly forgot there were no Chinese families in Rockledge.

He would have given chase, but he knew if he caught one of them little buggers, he'd have to give them a kick in the arse so hard they could wear their pucker hole as a necklace. Then . . . me own ass . . . will hit . . . the baloney slicer . . .

It would be his own chief who would call him on the carpet. "Kelly, you thick mic, you kicked the son of the chairman of the board of selectmen in the arse."

The chief knew the parents themselves, concerning the boots to the bottom, had indicated, "If they deserve it, serve it."

Cuffs to the back of the head were okay in public, but using a wise ass's ass as a football was okay only when there were no witnesses, and they weren't the kids of the selectman.

Worse for Officer Kelly having to go before the chief was the fact that a kick could mean that the fantastic spit shine on his black gumshoes that he worked on for hours while hiding out at the fire station would be smudged.

His best friend, McNulty, claimed Kelly had shined his shoes to mirror quality so he could look up the dresses of the pantyless ladies of the night that occasionally strayed from Boston to Rockledge, escaping the sweeps in the big city following the complaints of the wife of a Baptist minister or some other shocked proper Bostonian who witnessed a man being propositioned in Boston Commons while she was visiting Filene's Basement.

Mrs. Yanders, a shy woman, also made the most fantastic strawberry shortcake and bread pudding imaginable complete with lemon sauce. And all the kids, and their parents for that matter, were always welcome to join in even on a ruse. "Have you seen my son, Joseph, Mrs. Yanders? I'm so worried about him."

"Please come in."

Sometimes there was fried chicken for those kids when one happened to be on the scene, and it was shared with the visitors, even if it had been on the Yanders family dinner menu for later that day.

Aside from being good people, the citizens of Rockledge in their wisdom realized that you do not blacken the character of the hand that feeds you, unless you are stupid and hate fried chicken and strawberry shortcake and bread pudding complete with lemon sauce.

Mr. Yanders hit baseballs to the kids using a heavy fungo bat. He made the baseball travel greater distances than anyone they knew; the fly balls were high cans of corn that even their own dads couldn't hit. The town kids wondered why he wasn't playing for the Red Sox.

Johnny told his friends, "Mr. Yanders can hit even further than Jimmy Foxx." This impressed everyone as all the kids knew Jimmy Foxx was Johnny's favorite player. They knew that Johnny, who could scale a baseball card with the best of them, would never risk his Jimmy Foxx in a closest-to-the-wall, winner-takes-all contest, especially with Rhesus or Boattail, who had an uncanny ability to win when an important card was up for grabs.

One day Rhesus asked Mr. Yanders why he didn't play for the Sox.

Mr. Yanders smiled at the little boy with the hair the color of a banty rooster, closed his eyes, and whispered, "Maybe someday. Maybe someday when Tim makes me a grandfather, our kind will get to play. We Americans don't always rush things. Maybe it's better that way. I don't know. But when we get there, we will get there big time."

Then he hit a fungo that climbed and climbed, a stroke some later claimed brought rain down from the clouds it disappeared in. "Yes, maybe someday a Yanders will make it. Perhaps Tim's son or his son's son might get a chance. In the meantime, I guess we'll have to wait a bit."

Johnny looked at him strangely. *What does . . . someday . . . mean?*

And the young boy felt sad, for what reason he wasn't sure.

"Why not now?" Johnny asked later as the boys watched the black man walk away.

"It's his color," Rhesus whispered.

Johnny whispered back, "What are you talking about? Don't people spend good money at Revere Beach to try and get the color of the Yanders. The Yanders get it for nothing. And get to wear it all year."

The Yanders rarely thought of their color since they moved to Rockledge but were well reminded of their shade when they traveled to Chelsea or Southie, especially South Boston, where kids, on spotting them, would sing, "Southie, Southie, my hometown, Eli Yale! Now get the hell out 'cuz you're brown. Brown like poo. And that won't do. So vamboo. Which means git. Go. Go on git go."

The kids of Chelsea were more direct. When spotting people of the Yanders' shade, they weren't given much to singing.

A red mickey was the answer. The brick would be tossed through a windshield or at a woolly head, sufficing as an invitation to "enjoy gitting while the gitting is good."

That's why the Yanders held close to the Eastward-Ho section of town. Tim, their oldest, was happy there. There were no fights to be fought. Because you couldn't win, especially if you won.

The Eastward-Ho kids didn't consider themselves hayseeds or anything but lucky. In fact, they didn't even think about how lucky they were. They just enjoyed their luck without question. Open country. Green. Woods and fields. It was just "how sweet it is, sweet as sassafras."

They had the Big Woods that housed the town's only giant oaks. The oaks served as mighty masts of their tall ships. The maple trees' propeller seeds could be split at the base and worn on the nose like airplane wings with nostrils.

They even had duels, airplane wing to airplane wing. First off the ground. They were both the planes and pilots. Arms outspread as wings, mouths providing the motor power. "Verinn! Verinn! Vroom! They flew wingtip to wingtip. Fingertip to fingertip. Peeling off. Diving. Barrel rolls in the Big Tree rather than the clouds. Climbing, diving. Wing guns rattling."

They rode the limbs that served as a bucking bronco, Flash Gordon's spaceship, the tall mast of a LaFitte the Pirate marauding three master.

Then out of the Big Tree into the tall maples where they climbed to the highest point and release winged seeds that drifted to the ground, parachutists, the boys became Screaming Eagles. Then the race was on, whose winged seed remained airborne in a light wind while the others fell earthward in tight circles. Then into the saplings; they flew the trees, swinging, swaying high, wide, and handsome, a Pole-killing Stuka dive-bomber in their sights. Their mouths rattled their wing guns' shots! On occasion, one of the gang's Stuka blaster got to be the wing squadron leader by letting fly with a string of farts, bullets that set every other kid pilot's throat into a sour jealousy. Each claimed to be World War I flying ace Eddie Rickenbacker downing the Red Baron Von Richthofen himself.

The birches and poplars were more limber than the young oaks and were best for swinging. Frost's Birches never knew such action. And you could take the thick end of the propeller blade seeds, split it, and clamped it on your nose, thus looking like a kid lucky enough to have a praying mantis as a permanent nose adornment, a prelude to later-day gold nose rings.

There were reeds for spear tossing. And plenty of poison ivy to rub on your arm if you were tired of going to school. Of course no poison ivy was rubbed on the throwing arm. Who could ask for anything more? Surely not a kid full of piss and vinegar!

In the Big Woods beside the Big Tree was Murphy's Swamp, good not only for the highbush blueberries that could make a rock salivate. The high bushes were havens for sunning black snakes, which provided fun games as such as snake races as well as cruel sports such as snap the snake, which would send the guts of a particularly aggressive reptile spewing out its mouth, never failing to set everyone agog with gagging and leaving some of the gang tossing their cookies.

The Big Woods provided fun and games all year round. In the spring, they would capture green leapers with those lovely long Marlene Dietrich legs. Each boy placed his leaper inside a circle drawn in the dirt, and on "go," the frogs would be released. The first greenie that jumped the perimeter was top frog. All the owners of the also-ran frogs had to hold out their palms and hold their contestant until it released its sticky pee that perhaps lead to warts.

One day Mrs. Burris witnessed the boys in the distance with their palms extended and asked Rhesus for an explanation. She figured they were playing some boys' games where they read each other's palms.

Rhesus, rather than explaining that his friends were waiting for the frog to pee in their hands, agreed with his mother that they were giving a sort of palm reading as she would not tolerate even a hint of any off-color action.

Then not satisfied with such a simple answer, Rhesus told his mother they were pretending they were young priests on Palm Sunday. He thought, *If that doesn't get me . . . a double dessert tonight . . . nothing will . . .*

You could find spring peepers and tree frogs that also sang like Marlene Deitrich.

While the green leapers were best for frog-jumping contests, the peepers made for some great sing-alongs just before dusk.

When anyone discovered one of the hard-to-find peepers, they would cup its back legs in their hand, leaving the body and head to hang out, and stare into its eyes and sing, "Jeepers, creepers, where'd you get those peepers? Gosh oh golly, where'd you get those eyes?"

Then they would tickle their tummies until they sang their splendid spring song.

The bullfrogs had love-hate relationships with the boys. They provided great targets for their slingshots. When luck was with a shooter and a bullfrog was conked, knocked cross-eyed silly, the kids would go to great lengths to revive it. "Don't want a dead frog on my conscience," Johnny said.

"Yah," Rhesus echoed. "Their relatives can be vengeful. They'll get toads to piss all over you, and you'll have warts everywhere, including on your hamus-alabamus of a dickie bird." On the credit side of the bullfrog balance sheet, the kids loved to watch them snap up the injured insects they tossed in front of them.

But it was the green leapers that were special. They drew little girls whose pigtails were just meant for pulling, little girls loaded with latent motherly instincts. The girls treated the frogs as if they were their children, stroking them as a mother would stroke the hair of a child. This, at times, caused the girls to contently purr. The sounds of their purring made the boys tingle, and they did not know why. It was very upsetting as the boy was the king and thus should be in charge.

It wasn't until the boys and girls became teenagers that they had any inkling the feline purring was. And why.

Some of the boys, Johnny included, often wished they could be stroked in the same way the frogs were stroked. But then he couldn't understand why anyone, especially himself, would want to be a frog . . . even if there was . . . a . . . kissing princess . . . around . . .

There was a second group of little girls who followed them around trying to get the boys to holster their slingshots and not shoot at the frogs. Fat chance! When failing, they made noises to frighten the target bullfrogs to the safety of the mud below. The boys wondered why they didn't mind their own business. And go play paper dolls.

Rhesus taunted these girls with, "Ya-yaaah, you protect toads because you look like a toad."

The boys could outrun the save-the-toad girls or else would lead them to a dark section of the Big Woods, where the girls would stop and turn around and retreat. There were times that the purring girls were sort of nice to have around. But they weren't sure exactly why. And the boys ran slower for these girls. And had high hopes they were not frightened by the dark woodlands.

The little girls that protected frogs hated Rhesus the most, which was interesting as they hated each and every one of the boys a lot. They thought.

Both the purrers and the protectors hated Johnny the least. It was those emerald eyes set in the tanned face that made him appear like one of the big, wild animals, but a gentle one, that they would like to make purr and perhaps enjoy a purr alongside.

If all else failed, Rhesus had a coup de grace that would send the groups of girls scurrying off. He chased them with a toad squeezed in his hand until its eyes bulged and it sort of cawed like a tiny crow, while he chanted in a croaking voice, "Warts, warts, lots of warts. Warts on nose and lips and twats."

"What does he mean 'warts'?" one girl asked.

"Toads pee on you and give you warts, dummy," were the words of wisdom from Romola DaSilva, Johnny's thinner-than-a-rail sister who refused to run when chased. "And I'm telling Mrs. Burris he used the word 'twat.' And if he puts a toad near me, I'll give the toad warts!"

She more than likely would have had a centipede put down the back of her blouse for her effrontery, but she was Johnny's sister.

Also in the back of Rhesus's mind was that even if Johnny didn't intervene, Romola could make things miserable for him. An inner sense told him that her bite was as bad as her bark. Although there was no sign that this was true. She often cried, but only after she was out of their sight and after a boy who didn't know she was Johnny's sister called her "Skinny Minnie with the meatball eyes."

When Johnny received reports of such incidents, he always set out on a search and destroy mission.

After a successful revenge sortie, he would return home and try to force-feed sugar into his sister to put a little meat on her bones like their ma was always trying to do.

Johnny would protect his sister against a fire-breathing dragon. But he wouldn't say hello to her in front of friends. After all, she was a little sister, and all little sisters were considered yuck.

The Eastward-Ho boys, when not swinging from birches, also had a plethora of oaks to supply acorns for nut fights. No other section of town could match this hatch, and often raider groups invaded Eastward-Ho, hoping to build ammo supplies. As often as not they were driven back by the Eastward-Ho superior nut firepower.

The young maple saplings were designed in tree heaven by young boys that wanted to play aerial games of tag—bending tree to tree, leaping tree to tree, wild as a colony of spider monkeys who had sat on a fire ant hill by mistake.

The Eastward-Ho end of town had rock piles tumbled by Mother Nature like dice from a Yatzee cup, perfect for cowboy gunfights that carried from boulder to boulder.

There were natural dirt mounds on which to play king of the hill. The mounds were created by farmers that years before simply emptied their refuse in the woods and by Mother Nature, who, through the years, enhanced them by dropping several feet of softening needles and leaves on top.

There were long-abandoned farm fields for games of baseball, capture the flag, and "Red Rover, Red Rover, let Righty Minichelli come over." There was even a cow pasture for dung toss fights and buffalo chip scaling contests.

The quiet earth of the pasture would allow you to sneak up on your best friend and plant a tam, otherwise known as a "fresh cow flop" on his head.

The girls thought the boys were "wild and crazy guys, nitwits to be avoided," but it sure was fun to watch them. And look down on their low lives.

There was also a section of the woods that had small stones and sand pebbles almost as round as a bead that you could use for shooting aggies, mibs, or marbles. If you couldn't afford the glass marbles, you could buy for a penny a peewee or a nickel for a boulder.

Not always did a kid have the penny to make an aggie purchase, and if he did, it was lost in the first contest. The sand pebbles came in awfully handy. They were recognized as fair exchange, two for one real aggie if they were nearly round. Of course even the roundest of pebbles would not be accepted to shoot against a cat's eye or other real-beauty marble.

If a small kid lost all his marbles, he could "owe-sy" and pay off later, but not in sand pebbles, only in baseball cards. A kind of loan sharking.

Other fair owe-sy exchanges involved large balls of string or the tinfoil from the inside of cigarette packages or gum wrappers or a large, soft-eyed field mouse you could carry in your shirt pocket to draw attention or a can of red wigglers hand dug from a dung pile for fishing.

The owe-sy system probably was the forerunner of the credit card system.

It was rough paying up later on, as interest was added, and you couldn't palm off a Catfish Meckovitch for a Jim Tabor or a Jim Tabor for a Jimmy Foxx.

The true value of the Red Sox's new kid on the block, Ted Williams, was unknown. But they all knew he could hit!

Murphy's Swamp in the winter proved a training ground for some of the finest stick handlers playing ice hockey in the greater Boston area.

You not only had to get around your opponent but also around the army of swamp maples that grew through the ice as well as little kids

—

running a slalom course between the trees with their flexible flyer sleds or just playing tag and slip, sliding away on leather soles and heels.

Then there were those wise little kids, future wise guys, who hid behind trees and stepped into a puck dribbler, yelling, "You were hit by Eddie Shore!" or "You were diddled by Dit Clapper!" Then ran away over rocky turf where the skaters could not follow, unless they were really pissed.

Some of the Murphy's Swamp stick handlers got to participate in the Greater Boston Interscholastic Hockey League, the oldest high school league in the country. Some got to lug the rubber for Boston College, Northeastern, Harvard, or Boston University.

In Rockledge it wasn't who would win the Boston Bean Pot but rather which team would win with a former Rockledge High puck handler leading the way.

The dessert of living in the Eastward-Ho section was to the east of the grade school. A kid could just follow his nose over a nearby knoll, and there was Pat Pastori's piggery.

The kids of the east end of town and the piglets were made for each other.

Chasing them in the hogwash of their pen was great. Johnny was the leader, having had experienced Bog the Hog, thus the little squealers of Pastori's were tame as nursing puppies.

Their little dancing, curly tails provided year-round fun. In the winter they would be pig-napped, brought to the school yard, and released in the snow. There their broken field running left the squealing, diving, boy would-be tacklers looking like abominable snowmen. A few tomboys ended up looking like snow princesses. And in some of the pig piles of would-be tacklers in the snow was the first experience of a boy touching a girl.

The piglet chasers had difficulty explaining to their teachers and then to their mothers not only how they got their clothes down to their longies soaked, but also why they smelled of offal.

The pigs, even the piglets, always made it back to the piggery, and why not, that's where chow down was. Their filet mignon garbarge was served, and the milk-filled stalactite tits of their mother sows provided them with their personal soda fountains. There was also the Lorelei lure of the squeals of feeding brethren and wind-wafted odors, which proved a strong homing device.

Pat Pastori often pondered why a particular piglet would be thinner than its siblings, a little less secure, even looking over its shoulder at times. These particular piglets were a little more skilled in their broken field

—

running than their brethren, getting first to the fresh pails of slop delivered that day. Even more of a mystery to Pat Pastori was why one piglet had the number 31 painted on its back. Why was it bigger than its siblings? Why did he have one little oinker too many? Had he counted his piglet crop wrong?

Number 31 was a salute to Johnny's pig prowess, which he parlayed not only into a monetary reward one January, but also into one perky pig as well. The greased pig contest was one of the highlights of the annual Rockledge Winter Carnival. A porker was set free on the ice and the lucky shoe-glad kid who captured it not only collected thirty-one bucks in nickels as a reward but also got to keep the pig.

Everyone had been betting on Rhesus and Boattail Burris in the greased pig contest. And why not? Hadn't Boattail poked tacks through a set of gloves to get a better grip. It would have worked, but when the pig felt the sting of the tacks, it burned rubber with a squeal that sent Boattail slip sliding away to fall unceremoniously on his tail feathers, causing his corduroys to whistle a noise Righty Minichelli said sounded somewhat like "soweeee!"

Rhesus was even more ingenious than his older brother. He had sewed together a pair of trousers and a shirt out of burlap and somehow taped sandpaper to the insides of the sleeves and pant legs. This boy not only understood the importance of a buck, but also how to make one as well. Everyone in Rockledge understood but left it unsaid that Rhesus would prove one day to be Rockledge's first millionaire. That is unless Boattail beat him to it or they both ended up in reform school.

Rhesus was the odds on favorite.

The result of his sandpaper was often the pig that escaped was a little smoother and was more difficult to grab.

The young animal showed its heels to all, well, almost all. The hoofed pig spun its wheels on the ice a number of times but not as badly as its pursuers who followed like a swarm of bees heading to the honey tree. It lost half of those trying to catch it when it signaled for a right turn and hung a left instead.

Johnny didn't give chase. He stood still, off from the others, bent over, his legs apart and bowed, with his arms cupped inside his legs, forming what could look like an escape tunnel to a animal being chased by what appeared to half the town.

Johnny was a human Venus flytrap.

With everything on the ice in movement, the pig opted to escape through the only unmoving thing, Johnny the tunnel.

And Johnny was thirty-one dollars worth of nickels and almost one pig wealthier. Number 31 the oinker inherited by Pat Pastori was returned to the farm.

Twenty-five bucks went to his mother, and four went into the collection plate at church that Sunday. It drew the attention of the collector, a Mr. Bingham, who wondered whether he should return the money, obviously ill-gotten gains, considering the large amount was given by a boy with holes in his stockings and snot wipes on his sleeve because the family could not afford handkerchiefs. This was the boy with wax in his ears sometimes who put in a paltry two cents each Sunday, cupping it in such a way that interested bystanders could not determine how much had been given.

Mr. Bingham knew. The boy couldn't cup four dollars from his sight. Mr. Bingham had seen other hand cuppers give as little as a nickel. And it was he who uncovered Johnny's two cents donations and muttered to himself, "What can God buy for two cents?"

But the pious collector recanted, thinking, *A buck is a buck . . . Sometimes God works . . . in strange . . . ways . . .*

Johnny's last buck bought candy bars for him and his friends to pig out on. He told his buddies, "We're having a pig out! Get it? Pig out."

He also bought an apple for his latest possession, the pig. This was the first time any apple he was involved with wasn't pilfered.

He forgot to save fifty cents to buy ten Dr. Peppers for the gang. How about three Pepsis? Johnny called for a collection with the words, "We need tonic."

Righty had three cents. Tim Yanders took two shiny pennies from his penny loafers. Rhesus was broke but managed to come up with four passing-by big kid when he offered up his cat's eye boulder, an unbelievably low price.

Rhesus said, "You guys can pay me back later for what I coughed up." He was as thirsty as a Sahara sand dry martini.

They managed three king-sized Pepsis but did not chug-a-lug-alugga as suggested in the commercial. Very definitive lines of demarcation were scratched on the bottle. Joseph Fats Tolland, a mathematics genius and the skinniest one in the gang, had figured out the shares in drams by using his slide rule, fluid displacement measurement, and repeated fillings of the soda bottles in his lab. He also had figured out shares on Coke, Dr. Pepper (yuck), Moxie (double yuck), and Hires.

Drinkers were cautioned as they approached their demarcation lines and reminded of the penalties of a violation of trust. "Your ass will be grass and drop-kicked over the moon."

The slow sippers drove those waiting their turn crazy.

When the tonics were finished and the hint of chin whiskers wiped, only then did they sing, "Pepsi Cola hits the spot. Twelve full ounces, that's a lot, twice as much for a nickel too. Pepsi Cola is the drink for you. Trickel, trickel, trickel, nickel, trickle, trickle, trickle. yah-dah, da-dat."

All that candy, the three bottles of soda and Johnnie still had a buck left. Days like this do not come along that often, and he toasted, "Eat, drink, and be merry!"

"One for all, all for one!" Righty offered.

And as many as could meet the call to arms, burped the good burp. Rhesus accented the belches with a lively two-step, a hoisted leg, and a fart of high octave.

A vote of the gang decided how Johnny's last buck was to be used. More making merry.

It would be the purchase to be made by an older boy, Piggy, who had quit school with the words "School don't teach ya nuttin'. The streets does. Ya know how much I make on these books? Tons!"

He turned the purchase, a collection of ink drawings that, when flipped, set the main characters into sexual acrobatic motion, over to Boattail.

Piggy looked to both sides and whispered, "You didn't get it from me. You tell, your ass will be grass, and I'll mow it with this." He flashed an old Boy Scout knife with a broken blade for emphasis. It made no matter to Piggy that all the boys knew he couldn't fight his way out of paper bag with a scalpel in each hand.

The pages of Piggy's purchase were flicked by Boattail, greeting the boys with ink drawings of Ms. Olive Oyl performing acrobatics on Popeye the Sailor Man. This was a different Popeye in action than cartoons they viewed at the Rockledge Theater.

"My good god!" Righty Minichelli exclaimed. "That thing between her legs where a pecker is supposed to be looks like a Wimpy burger."

"You dumb duck," Boattail said, "it's Wimpy's face."

"It looks more like Bluto's. What's it doing there?" Fats asked.

"Maybe it is a Wimpy burger," Skinny said. "He appears to be munching it."

"Can't be a hamburger. There's ain't no onions on it," Rhesus said.

None of the boys knew the answer to exactly what that fur face between Ms. Oyl's thighs meant.

Although Rhesus, who didn't know either, said, "Perhaps he's checking for echoes."

A shocked Johnny exclaimed, "Even the sheep on the farm didn't do those things!

Righty said, "Some of it's gotta be a mistake. Or Billy the boy artist that did it didn't know nothin' about men and women."

Skinny Potts, testing to make sure his rotund stomach was still there above his belt, sort of like a large chest, confessed, "I saw my mother and father doing something. I believe it was it they were doing. Big people don't do nothing with their mouths. Except say 'you have to push your belly to one side or the other.' They didn't even kiss lips let alone all that other stuff."

"My mother and father don't do it, at all. That I know for sure. My dad is a knight of Malta," Soupy said.

Rhesus flipped through the booklet a second time, spinning the pages slower. Still, Olive Oyl's mouth ended up on Popeye's down there, making it squirt until some of the squirt came out both his ears, and cats lapped it up.

"Maybe she was a plumber and was just getting Mr. Popeye's pipes unplugged," Fats said. "I heard my father tell my mother one time she'd better get with it one of these nights. His pipes were getting rusty."

"Maybe it was how Popeye got that bad eye he always squinted. Or got the wax out of his ears," Rhesus said.

"Well," Skinny Potts, whose chubby face appeared to be five moons in a conga line, said, "We're practically in junior high. We should know something about what's going on here. Perhaps she was just hungry."

They all looked at him questioningly.

"Yes, we should know about what's what," Skinny finished. "I mean, it looks like more work than emptying the trash and not even as much fun."

"The thing I don't understand is why Popeye kept saying, 'You are even better than spinach, Ms. Oyl,'" Soupy said.

Johnny couldn't figure out why he hadn't vetoed this purchase. It was his dollar. "Why did you guys want to buy this puke?" *It's a cop-out . . . to blame my buddies . . . I was curious . . . too . . . but Ma could have used . . . that buck . . . and what about Grandpa Shiverick's . . . terrible swift sword?*

Things had been tight since his father had gone to work in the Sun Shipyard in Chester, Pennsylvania. A dollar was big-time spending. There had been no work in Massachusetts. He was one of the few men who had a job. Most of Johnny's uncles were with the Civilian Conservation Corps or with the Works in Progress Administration. The WPA built roads, and the CCC planted trees around the reservoirs. President Franklin Delano Roosevelt put the people to work, doing something useful at the same time.

Johnny's dad didn't send much of his pay home, saying in his soft-spoken way that it was difficult to support two places to live.

His aunt Hope had told his mother when they thought he wasn't listening, "He's doing something I don't like. Letting his kids go hungry. Wearing fancy duds."

"Tony always liked to look nice," Charity said.

Johnny noticed his mother looked down when she said this.

"How much can your soul let you spend on your own clothes when the soles of your kids' shoes look like a talking duck?"

"Tony's saving for a Packard so he can drive home and visit me and the kids. He wants to see Johnny, Romola, and James every weekend, not just once in a while."

"He can take a bus or drive home in an old Hudson. They're giving them away these days," Hope said. "Everyone wants a Zephyr or Plymouth with that fancy sailboat hood ornament."

"He has pride. Besides, he needs a big car. He wants to be a chauffeur for some rich family in Brookline or Newton."

"The rich families have their own cars."

"But they have people drive them."

"Why?"

"Look, Sis, Tony and I are doing just fine. And things are getting better. Thank you," replied Charity.

Hope said, "Getting better means the family cuts so many corners that life is a circle where you end up chasing your own tail."

One cut corner involved making the conversion from kerosene to coal for the black iron stove in the DaSilva kitchen. Although a small kerosene stove was kept in the kitchen as well just in case.

Coal was cheap, mostly because it was free.

All Johnny had to do was to head down to the railroad yard turntable located in a large round house where the big engines that came to the end of the line got a merry-go-round ride that would face them back to Boston. Johnny's dad loved to say, "Run for the roundhouse, Nellie. They can't corner you there!" And his mother would say, "Tony, you shouldn't be talking that way in front of a child."

Johnny had his coal collection program down pat. He would merely curse the engineers, "Rat scat!" and their coalmen high above, spit at them, do a menacing Indian dance, and black meteors rained down from above.

He got the idea one time while walking Romola and James along the tracks.

It was the day he nicknamed James "Jazz." The new name was the result of the fart noises his little brother loved to make with his mouth.

—

The resonance coming from between his buckteeth was greatly enhanced when accompanied by flatulent noises realized by squeezing his left arm against his body as he formed a cup with his right hand under his left armpit. Some bragged to kids from other towns that this little kid from their hometown, Rockledge, could actually play music with his fart noises.

Jazz was some sort of a hero. For the most part, big kids ignored little kids, but in Jazz's case, the big kids would call him over and tell him, "Fart through your teeth, kid."

He could do just that and more, playing "God Bless America" with his armpit. And where have you seen that lately? Johnny told little brother that if he kept improving, he was going to get him a monkey and a tin cup.

His mother threatened to tan Jazz's butt with a coat hanger for making the noises.

One time she actually gave Jazz a whack on the knuckles and read the riot act, "You'd best clean up your act, young man, you and those filthy noises. Someday you'll go number two right in your mouth while you're doing those noises. Would serve you right."

That thought cured Jazz of making that special mouth noise for more than a week.

Johnny, in defending Jazz from a second clothes-hanger whack, told her, "James loves music. He's only trying to make jazz music. One of the important instruments in a jazz band is the tuba. Those are tuba noises." Thus, Jazz was born out of James.

Johnny kept his fingers crossed behind his back while telling his mother of his brother's love of music. "It's not really a lie . . . Ma . . . Jazz doesn't have many toys . . . actually none 'cept the whistle I carved him . . . and fart noises . . . make him happy . . . real happy . . . I'll get Jazz, James, not to play his tuber in front of company or at church, Ma."

"You've always been a good boy, Johnny, never getting in no trouble. Always take good care of your sister and brother. Keep James out of trouble. Protect your sister with your life. Your mother can take good care of herself, so don't worry there. But 'course, always remember, don't forget what I've always told you. If I get hit by a car, make sure my underwear's clean. Don't take no peek while under there. No peeking. But I know you won't forget. You've always been a good boy, Johnny."

But, Ma . . . I'm not a good boy . . . the Olive Oyl thing . . .

The free coal was the result of Johnny walking Romola and Jazz down to the roundhouse so they could watch the railroad workers turn the engines on the giant turntables.

While the family didn't have Ouija boards or monopoly games, there were still a lot of ways to enjoy yourself. Although if you had a Ouija, you could use the spirits to secure other toys.

While Johnny felt that you did not have to have a gaggle of dolls with giant blue eyes and golden hair or a battalion of shield-holding Ethiopian soldiers to be happy, he didn't have good luck convincing his siblings of this.

It was a little much at times to not have toys or enough food.

Romola, instigated by the echoes in her roiling stomach that sounded like thunder in the valley to her, occasionally indicated she would like just a little bit more to eat. Johnny looked at his sister, then asked his mother, "Is there a little more food?"

Their mother would say, unable to face her children because of a tear in her eye, "Darn dust. Forget your selfish self for one moment. Think of the starving children in Ethiopia."

Johnny wondered what his mother was talking about as the little lead Ethiopian soldiers that Skinny Potts played with looked quite healthy. They were healthy enough to be warlike, armed with spears and shields. Also, Pathé News showed Ethiopian soldiers and tribesmen throwing their spears at the biplanes of the invading Italian army that was strafing them. You have to be . . . pretty healthy . . . to throw spears . . . at airplanes . . . but probably . . . not too smart.

Johnny felt sad that his mother didn't understand he wasn't asking for himself, but rather for Romola and Jazz.

Charity had turned away to rub a tear from her eye that this time wasn't caused by dust and surprised them by cursing, "Darn onions."

"Ma . . . you're so silly . . . We didn't . . . have no . . . onions for supper . . ."

The free coal was the result of his walking his brother and sister home after showing them the roundhouse. He repeated his father's saying for the benefit of Jazz and Romola, "If you're ever chased by bad guys and there are no cops around to help you, run to the roundhouse. They can't corner you there."

"I don't get it," Jazz said.

Johnny mussed his hair and gently pushed them into the house. Safely behind their front door, he told them, "Lock the door and don't wake up Ma. She's gotta work tomorrow."

There was no lock, only a bent nail that could be turned from the casing to the door. He heard it scratch into place, checked the door with a slight push, and then headed to the railroad tracks.

—

It called for ultra careful walking between the tracks leading to the roundhouse. There were those who did not read the sign in the passenger car toilets which asked, "Please do not flush toilets until the train leaves station and gathers speed!"

The toilets were direct drops to the ground beneath the speeding trains.

At high speeds, when the poop hit the tracks, it would hit with a "splat" that pretty much thinned it out like a soup kitchen gruel.

When the train was going slowly and those who couldn't read or cared less about barefoot boys walking the tracks flushed, a soft pile could be waiting to ambush the barefoot or sneaker-wearing walker in the dark.

His friends walked the tracks for a different reason, one that could pay big dividends. The biggest payoff was the discovery of a dynamite cap, a red package with four soft metal legs that could be bent and clamped to the tracks that had been left behind by workers. They were powerful enough when placed in a coded sequence of several caps to not only alert the engineer in a loud and fast-moving train of danger ahead, but also packed with enough dynamite to blow a hand off. Or at least a couple fingers.

The biggest dividend in walking the tracks was when you could claim your balance, walked a rail a prescribed distance under a certain time, making you champ. If you did it during a lightning storm, that made you special. One rumor track walkers of several generations kept alive was that lightning hit the rail during one walk, melting the sneakers off the feet of the walker.

You had to have reliable witnesses or one that could be bribed with a couple licks on a Sugar Daddy before claiming to be titan of the tracks.

It was walking a rail rather than the railroad ties that gave a kid good balance, balance to be used later while lugging the old pigskin along the sidelines, or deke a hockey goalie out of his jocks with a Houdini move of head, stick, and puck.

But Johnny's mission to the engines, those sleeping, fire-eating dragons, was more earthy than finding a dynamite cap to frighten the unholy bejesus out of a passing girl or claiming to be a champion walker with a one-track mind.

As Johnny approached the roundhouse, he kept in the dark shadows of the early evening. The engine crew from the last North Station to Rockledge train always hung around a little late, sipping a cool one, bullshitting and giving each other a good zing.

It was important to jump out and surprise the trainmen, these knights of the round table riding their coal-breathing dragons. Jumping out of the dark, Johnny screamed, "Ya mother wears army boots!" Then after thumbing his nose at the railroad men, he would add, "and ya sister wears jockey shorts!"

Within moments, the railroad men were throwing coal at him as he "Yaa-yaaared!"

When the action got slow, Johnny would peg a piece back, getting things started again.

The firefights would end as quickly as they started; the battlefield littered with the black bombs when it was time to chug their engine into the roundhouse.

The nuggets, while coal black, were gold to the boy collecting the heat for his home.

After the battle of the dragon warriors, he would travel to the nearby Dillons Coal Company, where he would collect small pieces of blue anthracite that could occasionally be found on the ground by the coal chute where they loaded up the coal trucks.

Johnny liked collecting the blue anthracite that tumbled over the edge of the slide. Its color was like that of a bluebird he had once seen in an abandoned apple orchard as he jogged the twenty miles to his grandparents farm.

It disturbed him that the railroad men who tossed the raven-black coal hated him. He would like to operate a big steam engine himself someday. *Oh . . . to . . . ride the magic . . . dragon . . .* He'd even be willing to serve as a coal man and shovel coal for years to get his chance at the throttle.

What he didn't understand was that the coal-tossing engineers did not hate him nor want to hit and hurt him. To the contrary, their exchanges among themselves were "The little guy's got the balls of a bull," "Gotta love that little turd." And they made sure that enough angry coal was tossed at him to get the family through one more frigid night. They showed heart by hiding their heart. "The little pecker whacker is willing to take a few bumps on the squash for that one last lump of coal."

But they wished the little shit and his little turd friends would stop hopping rides as the Boston-bound train started to chug out on its first run out of Rockledge just minutes before school started. The railroad men tried to reschedule the first run earlier as the kids would head to school early under any conditions.

They hitched their ride a short while after the customers boarded, and when it hadn't picked up real speed jumped off before the train got up too much of a head of steam. One day Johnny and Righty didn't jump in time and ended up with a five-mile walk from Malden, where the train stopped to pick up passengers. Then it was back to Rockledge, where they got a detention for being late for school.

Rhesus had had the closest train hopping call. One day he decided to jump off despite the speed the train had attained and ended up skinning his ass on the clinkers that lined the tracks. But this wasn't near as bad as the ass skinning his mother gave him as she pulled cinders out of his tail, knowing full well where they came from. The cinder surgery hurt almost as much as her crying because of the damage to his only go-to-school trousers.

Boattail was less than sympathetic for his little brother, as the entire gang's credo was "don't get caught." His report to the guys stung as much as the cinders. "Rhesus's ass was skun better than one of those mule skinners skinning the asses of that Borax twenty-mule team. *Yes!*"

Righty said once he was sure Rhesus wasn't killed, "Now his red hair and butt both look like a monkey's ass."

Boattail, for weeks, commented, "My monkey-assed little brother couldn't fart for weeks without crying. His ass was so sore he couldn't cut the cheese. And we all know my little monkey brother likes to fart. It's the love of his life. Gives him a feeling of power."

Rhesus was down at heart with his brother ragging him in front of his friends. They had hung tough together through so many incidents.

"Sometimes Rhesus sounds like a howitzer letting fly. Other times like a sousaphone with the runs. It hurts when you have a rare and beautiful talent like little brother and it deserts you. Sometimes he can come up with flatulence that sounds like 'Rev-vet!' a noise better than any old bullfrog could croak. Makes a brother proud."

Talk of his rare talent, taking his sore asshole out of the conversation perked Rhesus up, and he held his hand up for a little love potion celebration. He spread his fingers in an open leg V, and brother Boattail gave him a middle finger in the crotch of the V.

With the fingers' sex act completed, peace was restored; the ragging had come to an end. He had paid his penance. And the gang had cured him of risking his life jumping off fast-moving trains.

Eastward-Ho housed a plethora of Lorelei offerings that left them all fun fulfilled, but that didn't mean that the gang was free of worries.

While chasing Pat Pastori's piglets running in the clouds of heaven here on earth, there was the best of the best—free doughnut holes. If you were a boy and funny or a girl and cute, there was a good chance you'd get a couple free doughnut holes from Danny the Doughnut Man. He was a great and beloved young god down from the mountains according to all the kids. Danny the Doughtnut Man considered all young ones funny or

—

cute, and all were eligible for these rewards. "Danny for president," "Danny for God," "Yvonne deCarlo for Danny," were their cries of thanks.

The kids noticed that Danny not only managed to have more doughnut holes than doughnuts, but also and glory of all glories, he had parts of broken doughnuts for the skinny kids and skinny dogs. And that was okay with everyone, the skinny kids and dogs getting more. It was okay, "Or else!"

Danny was what heroes were made of. And the kids hoped that he would live forever and stay at the Bigos Bakery. Danny enjoyed being a hero. But it never went to his head as he was shy. He just liked kids. He remembered being one himself, although he was now eighteen years old.

He didn't stay around forever. He was drafted when a thing called World War II broke out.

His greatness, which he surely would have gladly given up, was brought to the forefront when he was killed later in some place most had never heard of. Sicily. Or something. Sounded like a girl's name to the gang.

Soupy Campbell figured, "He must of got some Eye-talian angry in a pizza parlor or something." No one laughed.

That wasn't true. Danny was killed when his squad leader told his men to "Get up. Move forward."

Danny was the only one who got up, but like the others, he didn't move forward.

A goodly spray of German machine gun bullets drove him back into the ditch. Alone. And he wondered where the kids were, wanting his doughnut holes. Kids . . . doughnut holes . . . free . . . from Danny . . . the Doughnut Man . . . who will give . . . the doughnut holes . . . to the . . . kids . . .

Danny Bigos knew his brother too well. Dirk started selling the holes.

"How in hell do you sell a hole?" Righty lamented.

The kids who had enjoyed the freebies of Danny the Doughnut Man swear they could feel him turning over in his grave when Dirk ran his first doughnut hole sale.

They were furious. The gang did not understand it was the early start of the soon to come, absolutely nothin' for nothin' era.

They tried to sabotage the sale of holes by putting a sign on the bakery window one night that read, "We know what Dirk the Dirty uses for chocolate chips. Check your baby's diaper."

This was followed with a sign a few nights later that stated, "Those aren't raisins in the raisin cookies. Check the rabbit's cage."

The Bigos Bakery sales went down, but only for a couple weeks, as the odors of fresh-baked goods proved too much for the those who lived by the philosophy "follow your nose to your stomach."

But the kids didn't buy any, even on the rare occasions when they could afford them. Not one single doughnut.

Their abstinence was both paying homage to their hero and in a hopeless fight against things to come, "nuttin' for nuttin.'"

Yes, it was a sign of the times. And the free doughnut holes died with Danny.

When they brought Danny home in a flag-draped casket and then eventually to the Heather Hill Cemetery, Johnny, Tim Yanders, Righty, Soupy, Boattail, Skinny, Fats, Rhesus, and all the rest hid behind a hedge and watched. As the firing squad fired its salute into the air, the boys lifted the doughnut holes they had baked themselves, and despite their less-than-desirable taste, they saluted Danny by gulping them down dry throats with wet eyes.

As they lowered Danny the Doughnut Man into his last resting place, Soupy summed it up with the words, "I wish it was Dirk."

Rhesus put the period at the end of Soupy's declaration. "Yah, the doughnut-hole-selling prick. They should lower him into the hole."

Later, the Big Woods gang had a song they sang whenever Dirk stood by the screen door watching them pass by. He tried to figure out which kid might have put the signs up.

Dirk couldn't figure out why they sang silently. If he could, he would have heard. "Dirk's got plenty of nothin' and nothin's plenty for him. Goodbye, Mr. Nothing."

Then they headed to the Big Woods where they carved "Danny the Doughnut Man, Forever" on the surface of a giant smooth-barked beech tree. It took a long time and a lot of hands to carve that much into the beech, which was a constant Indian companion to the Big Tree, a chestnut, in the Big Woods. The Big Tree was the boys' pie in the sky, home away from home.

The beech was Danny's tree.

The Big Woods Gang used other trees to carve their names and fames. "Fats—1941," "Soupy sort of likes Dina," "Science teacher Mr. Price is a prick!" "Guess who?" "Down with Nazis and the other rats, Johnny."

The Big Woods housed in the Eastward-Ho section was a good place to live and play during World War II. It got you away from all the crying and cursing of the adults when they thought the kids weren't around.

The Japs and Nazi rats who bombed London and the rest of the world wouldn't dare drop any bombs there. Not in the Big Woods with Johnny and Tim, Righty, Soupy, Rhesus. Scoff, Fats, Skinny. Boattail and the boys defending their sacred soil.

Climbing the Big Tree in the open field near the peak of the Big Woods allowed an overview of the warplanes buzzing like avenging Green Hornets over Boston: the P-38 Lightning, B-17 Flying Fortresses, B-24 Liberators, F4U Corsairs, Hell Divers, Wildcats, Brewster Buffaloes, and Bobcats that circled overhead and into formations before heading "over there, over there. The yanks are coming, a drum drum drumming, over there." At least those were the words the boys sang.

The Big Tree had made the transformation from a Flash Gordon spaceship and the Pirate Dirker Dow Dee raiding schooner to a Lightning, to a Sherman tank, a PT Boat.

They walked the miles to Boston, where they hid in the bushes close to Boston Harbor and watched the destroyers and troop ships, battle ships and more troop ships, cruisers and even more troop ships forming up. Many of the Liberty Ships were made right there in the Boston Navy Yard.

Watching from the tall grass, Johnny wondered why his father couldn't work here instead of Pennsylvania, even though he said he was a foreman getting a higher pay there.

On returning to Rockledge, a soldier, home on leave to the Eastward-Ho section of town, his chest adorned with a colorful garden of ribbons, caught them spying him from the bushes and asked them if they were Nazis.

Johnny stood up, puffed up his chest, and said, "No. We're Nazi killers. As soon as they let us sign up. What's that ribbon for, Seargent?"

The soldier mussed up Johnny's hair. "Buck private, son, buck ass private Bumper Murphy, and that's for a battle I had in T-Town, Tiajuana, Mexico. I call it C-Town with an emphasis on what the C, as in cunny. For now let C stand for cunning. Someday a long way away. You'll have your chance. Perhaps too soon."

"Wow!" the boys exclaimed as one.

Johnny said, "You can bet your bippy we're cunning enough to get over there. We're all cunny."

Johnny became a leader because of his dual citizenship, his ability to come up with nicknames, and for what they suspected was a pugilistic prowess. While they weren't afraid of him, the gang did think he was a little crazy as no one was too big for him, even if it meant a beating for him. He made them pay.

He had not only fought a ninth grader when he was only in the fifth grade after the older boy called his brother Jazz a "Buck-tooth little root eater." He continued to fight the larger boy even after his butt had been kicked to the tune of two black eyes, a bloody nose, and a cut lip.

The older boy, exhausted, had called it quits with these words, "The little punk ain't no fighter. So this don't count as no fight. My farter said he'd kick my ass so hard I could wear it as a necklace if I beat up someone so bad that I could go to reform school. So I ain't gonna kick this shrimp's ass no more"

"You're yellow," Johnny said.

The ninth grader said, "You're lucky I didn't hear you call me yellow you little piss pot." But according to firsthand reports of Johnny's fight managers, "The big kid evacuated the scene real fast after their boy called him yellow."

Johnny's family moved from the South School end of town to Eastward-Ho Elementary School when he was in the fourth grade.

The transfer came when Charity and Tony left their fourth-story apartment in the south end. It was the highest building in the town and had housed shoe shop workers for nearly a century before all the shoe factories were shut down. Shoes could be made cheaper someplace else.

They ended up in a house so old that the floor joists were trees that had one side flattened by an adz. Being the second oldest house in the town was like being left at the altar. There was no plaque on the housefront announcing how old it was nor was there any of the upkeep that such a historical plaque brings with it.

Johnny found himself among strangers at Eastward-Ho School.

The new DaSilva house was the second oldest home in Rockledge, that is until the oldest, which had been fully restored at great price thirty years before, was torn down to build a school.

The town had failed to save the famous old house, a stop on the underground railroad for escaped slaves en route to Canada. "It's wartime. No time for fancy stuff." It also declined to recognize Johnny's new home as the oldest house in Rockledge. It was desolate and "just plain shabby" according to some.

The chairman of the board of selectmen, Will Iverson, in executive session, had declared, "It looks too much like a smaller version of our poor house to put a plaque on it." Will's folks, according to the Gospel of Will Iverson, were at Plymouth Rock to greet the passengers on the Mayflower.

When Johnny's father learned of Iverson's remarks via Will's son, Will the Fifth, and then from Johnny, Tony told his son, "They are Johnnies-Come-Lately. Tell them your people came over on the Pinta.

—

Joseph Abbott seconded the motion not to invest in the DaSilva family rental, which cost the family twenty-two dollars a month rent, due on the first day of the month, no excuses accepted "'cause moving them dirt-poor Portagees out would be impossible with all those Liberals out there hiding in the bush, just waiting to attack us working people that pays the bills."

Selectman Abbott said, "The kindest thing we could do for that house would be to shoot the sick old critter behind the ear and plow it under." He scratched his head after taking his stand, wondering just where the house was located. He didn't get around all that much.

True, the house had been involved in a long and lingering illness. The ridgeline looked like a humpback whale suffering a slipped disc while the floor sills were as punk as a pileated woodpecker's abode in a hundred-year-old cedar stump.

The sides of the coal bin in the cellar had collapsed many years before, and the coal and bulging wooden side gave the appearance of an old coal mine collier pony.

The cedar shingle siding was wafer thin, and the rotten puttied windows rattled like teeth.

No one had enough mercy in his soul to put the ghost of a house out of its misery. At least not while its owner, a deacon at the Rockledge Congregational Church, could find a P.T. Barnum. "One is born every minute," live one to rent it. Besides, they just don't shoot houses, do they?

Two of the thirteen hallway steps leading to the second floor just weren't there. And best those traveling them remember it was the fourth and ninth stairs that were missing. Or else they would be introduced quite quickly to skinned shins, or worse, an injury that would keep boy or girl, man or woman, singing a couple octaves higher.

There was no central heat unless you considered the small cast iron coal stove in the kitchen as central heat.

It could only provide enough heat for the kitchen and then only if the doors were closed and the temperatures didn't hover near zero. Like all old folks, the stove had its backers—those people who enjoyed the most wonderful soft and golden offerings toasted on the red hot iron stove lid. No toaster, even if you waited for "Kingdom Come," according to Charity, would ever be able to duplicate the golden hue and softness of its toast.

The water faucets in the kitchen and upstairs bathroom were left running all winter, the speed and amount of water was governed by the expected temperature that night. Otherwise, they'd freeze tight as a nun's knees.

Weather was monitored and predicted by the reading of the forming frost thickness, as well as patterns, on the window panes. For a real accurate temperature prediction, a small glass donkey with a heavy string tail was used. It was kept on an outside sill that could be seen from the kitchen. If the donkey's tail was wet, rain was predicted. If it was flapping like a loose house shutter in a mystery movie, expect winds. If housing a snowflake or two, well, that speaks for itself. If dry as a bone, it would be a warm day. If frozen, the donkey's tail predicted cold weather.

A few old sayings were also used to monitor weather and to determine how fast the faucets would be allowed to run to combat freezing. "Red sky at night, sailor's delight. Red in the morning, sailor's take warning."

Also, the word of old folks with rheumatism or arthritis were as good as a weather word carved in stone. "The shoulder hurts, Pa. Gonna rain."

"Lower back hurts, Ma. Gonna snow some soon. Most likely, sooner than not," if both Ma's lower and upper back ached.

"You sure your back hurts, Ma? I was gonna do some shopping tomorrow. Perhaps it's your butt that hurts and it's only that god-awful sciatica."

"Nope, Pa, 'taint sciatica. I know my ass from my elbow. Don't you go telling me I don't know my own God-given body."

But Johnny and his mother pretty much depended on either reading the window pane or the donkey's tail.

Johnny and his little brother Jazz, six years old and six years younger than big brother; and sister, Romola "Romy," nine years old, often slept in the same bed in an effort to keep warm. That is until Romy got a little older, and it was decided that such a thing is just not done, not in Rockledge, and especially not in the Shiverick family.

Also in bed with them was the object of their affection, Rags, a mostly mongrel with a little Alaskan spitz mixed in. Many a ruse was used to lure the dog into a position where he warmed the feet of the person doing the luring.

Jazz, despite being the youngest, had won his share of dog time. He was a cute one. Once he rubbed a piece of bacon over the socks he wore to bed, but he had to pay the price. During the night, Rags had chewed off a chunk of sock, and Jazz had cold toes, double-timing it to school the next day. His mother, looking out the window, said to no one special, "Never seen James so anxious to get to school."

They all wore socks to bed just in case they weren't honored by the foot-warming Rags on a particular night.

—

There was plenty of amusement in the bedroom despite the fact the family radio remained in the kitchen. When their mother came up to bed, she brought it upstairs with her.

Not because she wanted to listen to music in bed. Charity just didn't want anyone sneaking downstairs and listening to one of those crazy late-night radio shows or soaking up all the heat that would be needed the next morning when they all made a beeline for the kitchen and the coal stove. Any extra opening of the door in the heated kitchen means a loss of heat.

The bedroom ceiling was stained as the result of a myriad of roof leaks. The stains took on many shapes, some of them crazy shapes. They were fun. Some sinister and frightening were more fun.

The streetlight across the way always flickered, turning the ceiling stains into old-time silent movies. The stuttering light set the jungle tiger, the mad dogs, the dragons, and dancers on the ceiling into life. Later, as Johnny got older, some of the hovering, back-hunching shapes took on more exotic meanings. Once he tried to rid himself off by wiping his hand across his forehead in a mind sweeping effort. He found that, in the words of his uncle Manny, such an effort "didn't do diddly shit," and the shape became more real, more painful down below.

There was a different silent movie every night because the shapes changed every night, thanks to ever-blooming imaginations. The dragon the night before was an alligator the next. The dog became, of all things, a pussy cat. The giant dancing, prancing horse turned into an amoeba. How do you figure that one out?

The rat-face boy always stayed the same night after night. Well, not really. Johnny wanted to help him, had taken a gray crayon, and tried to smudge in features that would make him a regular kid. And perhaps even a prince someday. It was a difficult effort as the water stains took on a different appearance as light changed when you stood on the bed, face closer to the ceiling. *How did that painter guy . . . do all that painting stuff . . . way up high . . . on his back . . . in the cistern chapel . . . where the pope lives?*

But the rat-face boy still looked sickly, hungry, and appeared to be getting sicklier and hungrier. Johnny checked him out several times a night, hoping for the best. *I'm sorry . . . Hang tough . . . I'll keep . . . try . . . ing . . .*

Johnny had more important assignments than helping out this rain-stain boy on the ceiling.

Charity named her eldest son to one of the highest positions a young man can hold. When he was seven, she told him as seriously as if making him a Knight of the Garter, "Your little brother and your sister are yours to protect forever. Your mother will not always be here."

He looked at his mother—she appeared so serious—and wondered, not understanding, *What do you . . . mean . . . Ma? You'll always be . . . here . . .*

The seven-year-old did understand he was to pound the poo out of anyone picking on Jazz or Romy.

It was simple for Johnny to use his God-given skill of nicknaming friends, relatives, teachers, cops, cats, and dogs.

Romy was easy. She was always wandering, roaming.

He named her Roamin' Through the Gloamin'. His little sis was a dusk walker.

Charity and the kids would sit around the black iron stove when the weather was most frightful outside, even too cold to venture to a Rags-warmed bed until they had built body heat as high as it would go. Singing helped. Sometimes Romola would do a stilted, skinny-legged jitterbug to "Beat me, Daddy, eight to the bar," the clattering of her too-large feet sounding more like a clog dance than a jitterbug.

Most often they would sing, "Pardon me, boy, is that the Chattanooga Choo-Choo? Track 29! Boy, you can give me a shine," complete with all the train noises. The chugging songs served to keep you warmer than most others as you chugged along with the singing, moving your arms like railroad engine pistols that moved the great steel wheels.

Charity would rock Jazz in her arms, as the family got closer and closer to the stove and to each other, combining their heat. Soon they could hardly stay awake.

And Charity would whisper to Johnny, "Why don't you take Rags and warm your bed a bit now. The kids and my bed is all set."

"It's okay, Ma."

"Well, here we go. Ready, on your mark, get set, go!" Then it was a dash up the unlit stairs. *Don't forget . . . four . . . and nine . . . they just aren't there . . .*

Johnny always wondered how Rags, who couldn't count, always avoided the two missing stairs. *Dogs can see in the . . . dark . . . that must be it . . .*

Charity, more often than not, ran up the stairs with her youngest son sound asleep in her frail arms.

Johnny's voice cautioned, "Four and nine! Don't drop him down a hole."

Then feeling silly playing father of the family, he added, "Unless you alert me and I can watch."

Johnny and Jazz kept the dog-heated bed warm while Charity and Romola prayed on their knees beside the bed. They would slip into bed as the boys slipped out so the heat wouldn't be lost.

And then the boys prayed on their knees. In the bitter cold, Johnny wrapped himself around his little brother, and they looked like a mother kangaroo and her joey in prayer. Charity would end the daily prayer session from the bed, always ending with the words, "Please help my beautiful children to remember to skip over stairs four and nine and in all ways take care of themselves and each other."

It seemed like a reasonable request and was granted most of the time. Although a painful or plaintive wail greeted her at times that indicated the prayer wasn't answered. She wondered what her crime was that led to the injury, real or imagined.

Some caution had to be exercised when giving a thankful kiss to Rags, the heating system. He had what an orthodontist would term an "underbite," not to mention "bad breath," a term their mother dropped on them when they forgot to brush their teeth.

The underbite was such that there must have been a bulldog among Rags' Heinz 57 Varieties in the family tree.

Jazz often bragged that "Rags has buckteeth on the bottom, and I've got them on the top, so he should be my bed warmer all the time. Besides, I'm little and get cold easier."

Johnny would often give up his dog time and assure his brother, "Your teeth will be fine. I'll take care of that."

"Will you take care of Rags's teeth too?"

"Yup."

"Will you pull my teeth backward with a vise on my teeth?"

"Yup, and I'll get you the best dentist in the world to operate the vise."

"Until you do, you don't have to fight for me. I can fight for me."

"Sure, pip squeak. Can the chatter."

Jazz got the Mortimer Snerd razing even from those who really didn't want to hurt him but felt it was fun to get a laugh.

Uncle Luke Shiverick liked to say, "Little James here could chew corn through a picket fence."

"Don't listen to your uncle. He don't know nothing. We'll get those teeth as white and even as a picket fence," Johnny said.

"Right through a picket fence," Uncle Luke said.

"You know, Uncle Luke, there's a half a horse out there complete with a head that could use you as its missing body part," Johnny said with spunk that delighted his uncle.

"John Shiverick DaSilva! How dare you speak to your uncle that way!" his mother said, reaching for her punishing broom. And it wasn't going to be the whisk end to the navel she planned on using. "You were not brought up that way." It would be the wooden handle to the head.

"Now you hold up, Sis," Luke said, "the boy's right. He's a gutsy little guy. Besides, it's well known in this family that your brother Luke is indeed a horse's ass."

"Luke Shiverick! You didn't learn to curse in this family."

Luke barely stepped aside as she jabbed the whisk end of the broom toward Johnny's stomach, but before he could finish his "Ha, you miss . . ." Charity caught him beside the head with the knob end.

"Oh, good Jesu . . . jeepers," Johnny said, feeling the knot that was already starting to grow on his forehead, reminding himself not to curse around the kids again. Unless little sis wasn't about . . .

Luke looked on his little sister Charity from his six-foot-two frame, puckered his lower lip, fluttered his eyes, and said, "I'm telling Ma."

"You silly darn fool," she said.

"Watch that 'darn' swearing."

They both started laughing as they grabbed each other in a family bear hug.

"Hug over." Charity turned to Johnny. "You've never answered back to an adult before. Come here."

He hesitated, wondering what "terrible swift sword" action she planned. He was prepared to duck as she had built up an abnormal strength on her thin frame from lugging flat stacks of boxes to the folding machine at the box factory.

He saw her hand coming up, but it was too late to duck.

His mother's hand fluttered, stopped, and then landed gently on his forehead.

"Just as I suspected, the boy's running a fever," she said, kissing his forehead. "That explains everything."

Johnny placed his own hand on his forehead. It was cool. *My gosh . . . she's so . . . ashamed of me . . . she fibbed . . .*

And while he was ashamed that he made his mother ashamed, he was happy to escape the big-time punishment that answering back called for. The stab, butt, slash of a bayonet instructor.

This big-time punishment was taught to the tune of the hickory stick. Every kid between Eastward-Ho to South Boston, rich or poor, who felt his oats to the point he showed disrespect to an elder got it.

The kids waited at suppertime while the elders ate. Then they fed. Little did they know that when they were adults, the kids would dine first.

—

In severe cases, adult hands were first folded in prayer for the soul saving of the young miscreant and then the hickory stick, broom, or whatever stick would swing into action, serving as an exclamation point on the prayer that preached "spare the rod, spoil the child."

If Charity was really hurt by the actions of one of her children and wanted to hurt deeply in return, she'd tell them, "You don't love your home. We're going back to the apartments."

Johnny, Jazz, and Romy hated the anthill apartment and loved their home, even the lattice showing through the plaster like the ribs of an horse dying on its feet. They loved their smiling hallway stairs with the two missing teeth.

They loved it more than their new friends from the Eastward-Ho section loved their homes with their carpets and ceiling lights, their homes where you could actually throw a switch to turn on a light rather than standing on a chair and turning a bulb. The homes of their friends had those new fangled refrigerators, and they didn't have to lug blocks of ice from the ice delivery truck to the icebox.

It was cheaper to have Johnny carry the ice from the truck to the icebox, wrapped in newspaper so it wouldn't slip, than having the iceman bring it in. Hey, if you carried the ice in five times, that was five cents, of which a penny was yours. Of course that penny reward, two chewy candy mint juleps in tummy money, involved lifting the heavy panful of melted ice water from beneath the icebox and emptying it down the sink.

As often as not, the water would slosh, meaning one cold assed stomach.

The card placed in the window signaled the iceman to "cometh" as a stop and drop was needed. It had the prices, facing in the four directions of the compass, printed on it—fifteen cents, twenty-five cents, thirty-five cents, fifty cents. Whichever price was facing upward informed the carrier what size block of ice was needed.

Johnny, Romy, and Jazz felt a little uneasy when friends came to their house. Not because they feared that if a friend had to go to the bathroom, he or she would forget about stairs four and nine being missing. Not because their bathroom was unheated in the winter and they could freeze their little tail sections. It was the rumors about the house. That during the Civil War, it had been part of the underground railroad.

They heard this from new friends that were from old families.

When Johnny asked Tim Yanders why the older people in town were more afraid of the underground railroad than the younger ones, he said, "You know."

"No."

"People are afraid that someday a huge black steam train run by ghost engineers, black men outfitted in white sheets, would rise up from the ashes in the cellar and take their town from them. People are afraid of things they do not know or understand. And I don't understand. I heard my father tell my mother that people feared the Underground Railroad and who it brought here. Making their house less valuable."

When Tim gave his explanation, he looked down at his feet rather than at Johnny, an unusual action for a young boy who was brought up to look people in the eye.

Then his coffee-cocoa colored forehead broke out in small beads of sweat. "The underground railroad was something that took place in people's homes to hide runaway slaves from the South until they could help travel them up to Canada."

"What's a slave?" Romy asked.

"It's a man that got stolen from his people," Tim said.

"No one would steal Jazz, would they?"

"Nah," Johnny said, "he'd be too much trouble."

"They wouldn't want me cuz of my teeth," the little boy said.

"Why would someone steal people? Why would they do that anyway?" Romy asked.

"Money. Power. Meanness. Fear. Who knows?" Tim said, taking his eyes off the floor and looking down into the young girl's eyes.

"Is a slave one of those people they stole from Tarzan and chained together by the ankles and made them row big boats to America?" Jazz asked. "I saw what they did when the good guys' boat came close to the boat they were chained in. They tossed them over the side, all chained together, and the bad guys who did this went home mad because they had to do the rowing."

"Sounds about right," Tim said, smiling.

Jazz smiled back.

"You know you're one handsome lad when you smile. Most people are, but you more so," Tim said to Jazz.

"I would have helped them get to Canada."

"I know."

Tim helped Johnny work on his house when somehow Charity found a few extra pennies to nail this and that. Grandfather Shiverick always had paint leftover, a clean brush he didn't need any longer, and a helping hand as well.

Later, at some point, their home started to look a lot better than the low rent they paid. When the landlord, on seeing the improvements, discovered just what a little jewel he had, the rent exploded to seventy dollars a month, exactly half of Charity's month's pay.

When they moved into the new house, it meant a new school, no more South School. At least that's what everyone thought except Johnny.

Four days in a row he walked from Eastward-Ho School some five miles back to the South School and his old friends, only to be returned to Eastward-Ho by the truant officer.

On the fifth day, the truant officer, Billy Boyle, enlisted four kids, with a bribe of a nigger baby each, those wonderful little men made of licorice and sugar, and a mint julep, that misty chewable of chewables. Billy Boyle believed that all Johnny needed to feel like he belonged at Eastward-Ho was to have a little tussle.

What a temptation bribe combo! The nigger baby was the best of the best, and the mint julep would capture its flavor, and the licorice-sugar marriage would linger on.

All they had to do was make Johnny feel the comradeship that can come from a good fair fight.

"Don't hurt him none. Don't want to get called before the school board. Just make him uncomfortable," Billy Boyle said.

It was Marco deLisio, the biggest kid in the class, who had the best idea for a 'no injury yet uncomfortable dealing' that would make Johnny not want to return to the South School. "I'll rub fresh dog caca in his face. Now how about the nigger babies and the mint juleps?"

They were handed over and disappeared in a flash. The only evidence of their existence was the black juices running down the corners of their mouths and the attempts to free the sticky mint juleps from the roofs of their mouths. After the officer left and the bribes were eaten and Johnny arrived on the scene, three of the kids left, figuring by the look in Johnny's eyes that he had the four of them outnumbered.

Marco stayed. He was a kid whose maturation was three years beyond his age.

"Look, south end snot," he said to Johnny, "we don't need no girlie wimps here," Marco said, placing a wood chip on his shoulder with the words, "Knock it off!"

"For two cents I would!"

"I don't have no two cents. Will ya mother wears army boots do to get sissy-prissy moving?"

Johnny wanted to say, "Ya mother has a mustache," but didn't. Both Grandma Mie and Grandma Shiverick tickled his cheek with their old-woman fuzz. A mean mustache statement to this big kid would be one against these two little women whom he loved and loved to be hugged by.

—

Despite his loving of hugs, he often thought, *I'm too big a boy . . . to be hugged . . . Grammy Shiverick . . . Grammy Mie . . .* These hugs were the happiest moments of each day to Johnny as he looked at the chip on Marco's shoulder. Johnny remembered his father's words, "Do onto others before they do onto you."

Johnny checked the chip again. It appeared to be laughing at him. *Big guy . . . wants to do onto me . . . a fist in the face . . .*

His father had not condoned fighting but added, "If the other kid swings first, well, he's asking for something. And it would be generous to give it to him at this point. Do you understand?"

So maybe a bad word to this big kid would get him to swing first.

But then Johnny remembered the words of Thumper's mother in the *Bambi* movie telling her long and lop-eared little son, "If you can't say something nice, don't say anything at all."

So he let it go by simply blowing the chip off the larger boy's shoulder.

Johnny fell over backward from Marco's push, a well-aimed punch to Johnny's throat.

Johnny's eyes crossed for a moment, causing Marco to smile at the smaller boy and the crowd of kids that had gathered. "Look at his eyes. They must see a fly on the tip of his nose."

It was Marco's turn for crossed eyes. It was a short sort of punch to the tip of the Marco's nose from Johnny's small fist, which was folded into a two-fingered noogie.

Johnny was completely confused when Marco headed homeward, crying.

And Johnny started to head homeward to the South School. But the kids that had gathered were looking at him in a strange way. Sort of like he wasn't a bad guy. He hadn't planned to stay at the new school when he arrived there but liked the looks the Eastward-Ho kids were giving him. But maybe he should just let them admire him and leave a little later.

Marco returned to the school a bit later and, to his credit and true to the code of the kids, never squealed on Johnny. Also, he didn't like the idea of the word getting around the school grounds that he cried after getting a punch in the nose from a runt. Maybe he could tell the kids Johnny had secreted sand between his clenched fist fingers, and it got in his eyes. Nah. He'd just make Johnny the right-hand man in his gang later on. Johnny had no plans to join Marco's nonexistent gang at Eastward-Ho School.

It was lunchtime, and a free-for-all sort of football game started up. The ball was thrown in the air, and whoever caught it was chased by the rest of the boys until flattened. In turn, the fallen gladiator had to toss the ball into the air, and the kid who caught it became the next victim. There was no such game at the South School. The entire school yard was hot topped.

Johnny stood on the sidelines, watching and thinking how great it would be to have the ball with the whole world chasing him. But he was an outsider. Anyway, he would be heading back to the South School as soon as the watchful eye of the lunch teacher wandered away.

A runt that the other kids called Manny Minichelli tossed Johnny the ball and yelled, "Come on!"

Johnny nodded no, and Manny called him Yellow belly.

Everyone stopped frozen in space, looked at the newcomer, the outsider, the gauntlet tossed in his face.

Johnny stepped toward his challenger, stopped, and remembered Grammy Shiverick and her words. "Sticks and stones will break your bones . . . but names will never . . . hurt me."

The little boy with the large dark Mama Mia eyes followed up, "Ya smelly yellow belly."

It hurt. But Johnny already felt that he had violated the codes of his grandmothers when he punched Marco and did not make a move.

When Mrs. Minichelli's little boy added, "Hey, ya smelly yellow belly with meatball eyes, your gran-mudder wears army boots. And has a mustache," it bit hard.

Johnny pretty much felt that while names couldn't hurt him, he wasn't going to stand by and let them be hurled at his Grandmother Mie and Grandmother Shiverick.

Then Minichelli tossed in, "All kids from the South School are yellow as dog pee in the snow."

To heck with . . . sticks and stones . . . Johnny ran at his little tormentor hell-bent for election!

He met him more than halfway, and the two bumped bellies like little dancing bears who both wanted to lead. They rolled on the ground, locked in what else—bear hugs. The circle of boys and girls closed in. The Eastward-Ho boys rooted for their schoolmate in the rumble with the new kid from Southie. The girls covered their eyes partially and called for an end to the fight but mostly not meaning it. Besides, the new boy was sort of cute.

As they rolled and tumbled and tussled, Johnny could see they all cheered for the boy Johnny would later nickname Righty.

One tiny girl with eyes the color blue he had seen in a National Geographic picture photo of waters on an island some place far away seemed to be for him. She pointed at Johnny and, despite being ostracized by the other girls, yelled to him, "Do good! Do good, you!"

—

The two combatants continued until exhaustion and ended up bear-hugging each other. A tie game. They just lay there. Breathing in each other's face. Both staring into space.

Johnny spotted one little girl poke his only cheerleader during the fight, the blue-eyed girl, and scolded her with the words, "Bernadette, you must not cheer for an outsider. You've always been a bad girl."

Bernadette . . .

Before the two boys recovered from their exhaustion and could return to combat, they were lifted off the ground by the scruffs of their necks, surely by some sort of supergiant.

It was five-foot-tall, thin-as-a-willow Ms. Kelly, the fifth-grade teacher and school principal. She hoisted them upright and marched them back to the school on their tiptoes. Their tiptoe arrangement was the result of Ms. Kelly shifting her hands from their necks to their sideburns and lifting upward.

They stopped their fighting and everything else at this point. Ms. Kelly was careful. She wanted to show the power of authority yet not embarrass them beyond repair. The little woman held their faces close together. Johnny whispered to Righty Minichelli, "You've got a good right. Like that new boxer, Joe Louis."

They had little choice in their journey back to the school. Although they dragged their feet, leaving the little woman sweaty and hoping her wig wouldn't fall off. Scarlet fever had been unkind to her, but she had lived while her twin sister had died when it struck.

The kids knew she wore a wig and wanted it to fall off. They had found out her secret after Soupy Campbell had asked his father why Ms. Kelly had no eyebrows, only black pencil marks. Mr. Campbell informed his son, "Ms. Kelly had scarlet fever when she was a kid, and the poor child lost all her hair. In all fairness, don't tell the other kids."

Fairness . . . to a teacher . . . one that slaps your palm . . . Come on . . . He didn't have the courage to mock her. He had no death wish, but he did pass the word and muttered under his breath whenever she scolded him, "This little wiggy went to market. This little wiggy stayed home . . ."

Meanwhile, Johnny's and Righty's sideburns-tug trip back to the school was completed, and the gathering was now in the school basement.

"Hand!"

Johnny watched as his opponent held his hand out, palm up.

"Who's at fault?"

"Me," the Mama-Mia-eyed little boy said.

"Me," Johnny said.

"Hold your hand out too," she said, turning her attention to Johnny.

He held out his hand, palm up. *Is she giving us . . . candy . . . or what?*

Ms. Kelly truly believed that discipline was a holy grail if the children of the world were to survive. This day shortly to become a holy day, a sort of Palm Sunday.

The ninety-eight-pound woman brought the solid oak ruler down flat on Righty's hand first with all the formality and the finality of the switch being thrown on an electric chair.

The resounding "splat!" sounded much like a belly flop off a diving high board.

"It didn't hurt," he said, choking back the tears.

"Well, we'll see what we can do about that, young man."

This time the ruler was raised higher and brought down on an angle so as the steel edge would hit first.

The crack of the ruler against the boy's palm sounded like a rifle shot.

The tears streamed down his cheeks. "That hurt even fewer."

"Less," the mighty mite teacher corrected.

"It hurt even less." But his words were not truly convincing.

"Well, we can correct that," she said. There was little doubt that to the tiny teacher, standing Madame Tussauds-like beside the guillotine waiting to collect heads, that the ruler's edge must now line up with the boy's thumb knuckle rather than his palm, like the machine's falling blade, and it was aimed at the helpless thumb knuckle, and she brought the ruler downward with the finality of the hand controlled by the hooded head that released the guillotine blade.

But before the ruler's metal edge could reach the Achilles' heel of the hand, its downward swing stopped in midair when Johnny's words hit her. "Hey, don't I get a turn?"

All the kids thought he was crazier than a coot. Except Righty. *Why's the Southie kid . . . doing this . . . for me?*

The swoosh of the ruler scything downward was further emphasized by the stunned silence of the young onlookers.

Johnny grabbed the avenging tool out of her hand and snapped it over his knee.

A no-no act of courage and sheer, undiluted stupidity if you read the eyes of the audience. An act of immeasurable folly if you read Ms. Kelly's.

It was a toss-up who was most astounded: the teacher, the class, or Johnny.

There was no question who was the most gratified, hands down. It was Righty.

All were locked in a high holy-day-in-hell tableau.

—

Johnny was first to break the spell, a move that showed indeed that he was more than a Greek god coming off the mountain to save a mortal. He showed that indeed he was a mortal.

Johnny broke and ran.

But fast as he was, Ms. Kelly amazed all, her short legs pumping in a roadrunner blur, quickly closing the distance and about to pounce, when a tiny voice of a girl cut through the air, drawing the attention of the avenging angel of a teacher, thus allowing Johnny's escape.

"Ms. Kelly! Ms. Kelly! Has a pimple on her belly. Squeeze it and out comes jelly." The little blue-eyed girl, Bernadette Clarkson, did not have the chance to actually complete the word "jelly."

She immediately became the focus point of the latest stare and glare of the teacher who was surprised, not so much for the sheer impudence, but by the fact the little girl rarely spoke, even when spoken to. Ms. Kelly had discussed with the school board in executive session whether they could look into what might be happening in the Clarkson home. One board member, Mr. Vandehaben, asked Ms. Kelly if she was lacking in things to do with her time. Ms. Kelly asked if he condoned a father taking his daughter to bed.

While Johnny and then Righty had taken off like big-assed birds, Bernadette had flown the coop like a tiny-tailed chickadee.

Righty was headed to Chilly Brook, his favorite hideout during the hot, dog days of summer.

Johnny was on his heels.

Bernadette trailed them, keeping a respectable distance behind.

Righty arrived at his secret escape spot, one he had hidden in from even the best of friends in the past. Yet he had looked back over his shoulder a number of times to make sure Johnny was still following.

He plunged his sore right hand, made tender from tossing it at Johnny and from Ms. Kelly's iron ruler, into the cool water of the hidden spring.

Bernadette stood away out of sight in the shadows of a low-hanging pine tree.

Righty watched, wordless, until declaring, "It didn't hurt, not even a little."

"I know."

"You shoulda stayed out of it. I was going to grab the ruler myself."

"I know."

"And I woulda rapped her hand."

"Sure. I should of minded my own Ps and Qs."

"Ya."

"Ya."

"Thanks anyway. Actually, thanks for nothin', but thanks anyway."

Johnny, who had missed Ms. Kelly's licks with her numbered piece of oak corrector of bad boys when he grabbed the measurement stick, said, "My hand didn't hurt at all."

They both burst out laughing.

Then they turned when they heard a girl's laugh.

It was Bernadette.

"What's a girl doing here!" Righty asked, sending her running by the tone of his voice. "Ya see her run! Did you see her sweater? Those bumps. They look like breasts. Only smaller."

"My name's Johnny. Johnny DaSilva. What's yours?"

"Americo."

"Americo, Americo, God shed his grace on thee. And from thy . . ."

"Americo Minichelli."

"I'm going to name you Righty because you've got a great one. Who was that girl?"

"Bernadette something. She's poor. I heard someone say that her father uses her."

"I'm not poor," Johnny said.

"Doesn't matter none with a friend."

Johnny looked at the boy who led him to his secret spot. It . . . doesn't . . . matter . . . with a . . . friend . . .

It was at that moment Johnny decided to stay at Eastward-Ho and not go back to his South School.

The two sat in silence for some time.

"What do you mean 'uses,'" Johnny asked.

"What do ya think?" Righty asked.

"We better go back and face the music, Righty."

"Righty?"

"Ya, I give friends nicknames."

"All my brothers are lefties. Port siders. I'm the only righty. A starboard sider."

"Then actually you're a double righty. But I'll call you a single righty. All right, Righty?"

"Sure."

"We'd better get back."

A short while later, they entered their classroom.

Ms. Kelly did not look up, appeared to be speaking to her desktop. "Well, well, is that Peck's bad boys I hear? But then no one is really bad. Most likely just had bad experiences. Sometimes bad things happen. But we can learn from them. And good things can happen."

—

She looked up and smiled at her class. "Does anyone here know this is free cookie day?"

No one knew there was such a day as free cookie day. It had never existed. But Ms. Kelly believed that sometimes it is good to celebrate the results of a real bad moment. And turn it around. When she had lost her hair as a young girl, she had shaved the hair off her favorite doll, Nan, and then made all colors and lengths and just all kinds of wigs for her. She still had Nan. She brought her out once in a great while, and while she bedecked her doll in them, she also put on the ones she had made for herself. Of course she had to wear the same gray one to school . . . and into the . . . real world . . . every day. This was a given.

The regular cookie time, which was midmorning every day, most certainly served as an early introduction to the coffee break and included a small bottle of milk, chocolate or white.

But it meant having a penny for the two cookies and two cents for the milk. And while most of the class partook, there were those without the three cents.

On this day, the entire class not only had a cookie but also a milk as well. And those that had had the three cents got to take it home or perhaps buy bull's-eyes, that wonderful target shaped carmel wrapped around white sugar. The white part melted in your mouth. The chewy carmel lasted longer and could be licked off the back of your front teeth where it often stuck.

When no one was looking, Ms. Kelly placed a dollar bill in the cookie and milk fund. *So much for my retirement . . .*

By lunchtime, they were all hungry again.

Johnny didn't have a lunch with him, and he hadn't left it at the South School, where he had started that morning. Hunger had him eating the slice of bread with a thin layer of peanut butter and a tiny sprinkle of sugar for energy on the way to school.

Righty tore his sandwich that contained odors as wonderful as the colors that bedecked it in half, no easy task, as it was loaded with several layers of homemade Italian meats, Limburger cheese, garlic, and onion. Righty's fingerprints were in the soft Italian bread sandwich he attempted to hand to Johnny.

"I don't take nuttin' for nuttin'," Johnny said.

"You can owe me."

"Okay." Johnny couldn't believe his good fortune, but immediately after the first bite, he turned to his new friend and said, "I'll pay you back. For sure."

He took another bite and commented, "Jeepers crow, the sandwich smells like what my uncle Francesco DaSilva calls a French whorehouse on fire in July."

"What the heck is a French whorehouse on fire?"

"Jeepers crow. I don't know. My uncle Francesco says that whenever my dad and my uncle Manny make a garlic and Limburger cheese Dagwood Bumstead submarine. Or cut one."

"Cut one?"

"You know. Cuts the cheese. Lets one fly. Who cuttre' la boola formaggio."

"You speak French, Johnny?"

"A little bit. Oooh cuttre' boola formaggio means 'who cut the cheese.'"

When Johnny finished his half sandwich, Tim Yanders leaned over to Johnny. "Dessert? Have a nigger baby." He handed Johnny one of the little licorice men you got two for a penny for down at Flaherty's Corner Store.

"Thanks. I'll pay you back, ah . . ."

"Tim. Tim Yanders. That was really something you did. Not many will try to correct a wrong."

"A wrong?"

"Tim means the ruler and all that. He doesn't believe in corporal punishment," the tall girl answered, then looked away. Johnny turned and stared into the most beautiful face he had ever seen. Steel gray eyes, the color of a shark in shallow silver waters. "My name is Yelena." She held out her hand, palm down. "A lady never shows an open palm to a gentleman."

Johnny didn't know whether he was to shake the hand, kiss the back of the hand, or slip a diamond ring on all the fingers of this beautiful girl, so he dipped her finger in his ink well.

"Well, that's different," she said. "*U*sually the boys try to dip my pigtails in their ink wells."

"I've got baseball cards," Johnny told Righty and Tim, trying to change the subject, completely unsure of what his follow up to dipping Yelena's finger in the inkwell should be.

The three boys showed each other their baseball cards, King Kong Keller of the hated Yankees, Stan Spence of the Washington Senators, Johnny Mize of the Giants, Pee Wee Reese, Pistol Pete Reiser, and Ducky Medwick of the Brooklyn Dodgers.

Johnny loved Pistol Pete, who was always running into walls trying to catch fly balls "because I've gotta have 'em."

Yelena wasn't about to lose center stage to a bunch of bent and grungy baseball cards and took a final shot that would keep her status as ruler-mistress of all she surveys. "Someday a woman will be president."

—

"They can't," Righty said, "'cause they can only be president twenty-seven days a month."

"What do you mean by that?" the beautiful little girl asked.

"I don't know? I heard my brother Pretty Lefty say it."

Yelena huffed off. "For every good man, there is a good woman—in front of him!"

Johnny learned that Tim's father played baseball in something called the Negro League, and Johnny asked him, "Did he ever play with Babe Ruth or Jim Tabor?"

"Nah, they played in some other league," Tim answered with a soft smile.

Johnny thought that Tim's smile held some kind of mystery behind it, something that Johnny didn't understand. Much like the mystery Yelena's eyes held. *Like that picture painting . . . of moaner lee sa . . . in the museum . . . on that field day . . .*

Righty's father wanted him to be Joe DiMaggio.

His father had told him, "Be prouda your name. Here we are all Americans. Is a beautiful-ah country to come-ah to. Be-a prouda. Be-a prouda. America-co."

All the Minichelli kids were proud to be Americans. Johnny liked that. They all saw the movies. America won all the wars. The cowboys beat the Indians, except for that sissy with the long, curly blond hair, General Custer. But rumor had it that the Indians had snuck into Custer's camp and filled all the troopers rifles with blanks. *Rotten redskins . . . arrow flynn shoulda played Custer . . .*

All the boys wanted to join the Scouts and wear an American flag on their sleeves, pledge allegiance to their country, carry a jackknife, wear a uniform like a soldier, salute, and all that good stuff. A lot joined. Some didn't.

Johnny couldn't afford the neckerchief, let alone a uniform. Soupy had a kit bag full of allergies so his mother wouldn't let him be in the field as much as scouting required. Scoff Burns's father, Bummy, told his son, "Scouts are a great spot for those fudge-packing queers to do their recruiting. Anyone touches my kid, or anyone's kids for that matter, is gonna have ta answer to your old man."

Even the kids that couldn't join the Scouts and get to wear a uniform still wanted to be heroes. Hey, who wouldn't with the Jap rats and Nazi nerd turds killing kids and women and pet puppies and all that stuff. Hadn't they seen dead horses on the Pathé News at the movie house, their legs stiff, up in the air? Of course they'd kill puppies on purpose.

Anyone, rich or poor, could become a hero. Wasn't this America? Of course the kids weren't exactly sure what a hero was.

All the Minichelli kids were born in the United States, except Big Lefty. He was born in Italy, in a place called Monte Casino, and proud of it. Big Lefty was proud to be an American. He wasn't exactly sure why. But he didn't have to know why. He was the link.

Righty was proud of Italy too. And why not? The movies showed they held duels when someone did someone else wrong. They didn't duel like the Germans with those skinny sabers whose duels ended when one combatant suffered a badge of honor slice on the cheek. In Italy, according to the movies, they dueled with double-barrel shotguns.

The kids didn't have sawed off double-barrel shotguns to enjoy Corsican duels of honor, but they did have plenty of hollow reeds that made outstanding en garde swords. They had pilfered, borrowed, garbage can lids that made great shields, ignoring the fact that the dueling counts did not use shields.

Later on as they got bigger and stronger, they would duel like the big kids with cudgels, hard oak, and elm sticks three or four feet long.

They would stand on a log cudgel to cudgel and try to push each other off ala Robin Hood and Big John.

When the log spanned a fast-flowing brook, it was the greatest as someone always got their ass wet.

They felt their oats. If Charles Atlas could pull a railroad engine, surely Johnny DaSilva, Righty Minichelli, and Tim Yandero could pull an engine, the coal car, the passenger cars, and a caboose as well. They didn't start off as ninety-eight-pound weaklings in whose face bullies kicked sand. They started out with the moose muscle structure that most young boys were positive they possessed. Wasn't Charles Atlas old? Perhaps even thirty. Certainly old enough to die. Weren't they young. Young enough to fly.

You bet your bottom dollar, little Buster Brown.

They often asked each other not only how people lived past thirty, but also why.

But then Johnny thought of Grandma Mie and Grandma Shiverick and how they pulled him to their bosoms when they knew he was hurting. How they knew when he was hurting, he never knew, as nothing could make him cry. Nothing! But somehow they knew.

And they knew when he needed a cent or two for penny candy.

Grandma Shiverick would lament, "Where are my glasses? I surely would give a whole penny to anyone who could find them."

Well, he was the only one in the room and soon was a penny richer with his words, "Grammy, they're on your forehead!"

And Mie, even tinier than Grandma Shiverick's five foot even, would hand him a piece of homemade fudge with the words, "Make too much fudge, what I do with it? Will someone help me?"

"I will, Grammy."

She would pat him on the head. Smile. "Tanka yoo, Keetazinger." Oh, how he wished he knew what Keetazinger meant.

I'll . . . kill . . . anyone who makes fun of her talk . . . And Johnny knew why people had to live past thirty . . . but only the good ones . . .

School lunch period delivered some painful moments for Johnny, when hunger bounced back and forth like a tennis ball between his stomach.

It was at this lunch period, while sharing a sandwhich that smelled like-a-French-whorehouse-on-fire sandwich with Righty and a nigger baby with Tim, that the three became as close as Huck and Tom and Mr. Twain.

Bonded forever.

They were perfectly positive that they would live forever, bouncing back and forth between the ages of nine and twenty-nine.

They knew this despite the fact that their Captain Midnight Secret Decoders, the badge with the turning dial that could be pointed to different letters, dictated from the voice on the radio, "Turn your Secret Decoder to seven, to four, to . . ." and when decoded, there was the warning "Be very careful, or else . . ."

Despite having to return to the schoolwork each day, the Eastward-Ho School years were great days for the Big Woods gang. Ah yes, my friends, they believed they'd never end. At first they trickled, then tumbled down.

Despite the fact they wanted to go into the seventh grade, which was housed in a "big kids" junior-senior high school, there was something scary about leaving the fun and comfort of a school where they were the upper classmen and going to the bottom of the pile they had already once scraped up through.

While most of the memories were good as they neared the end of the school year, they heard horror tales from older brothers at the junior-senior high school and, at times, became schizoid scared.

Johnny did not fear going up to the big school. His friends would go with him. Although there was no denying Eastward-Ho had been great fun, except at lunchtime.

Lunchtime was when Johnny nibbled his folded-over sandwich the peanut butter was was so thin, it looked like a slice of bread with five o'clock shadow. That was easy enough to survive. He'd had had plenty of practice. What wasn't quite so easy was when a friend with too many sandwiches held up a roast beef or tuna sandwich three inches thick and asked, "Anyone want this?" and not receiving an answer would make a one-handed toss into the nearest waste barrel.

Johnny always felt like diving into the container, mouth first. He never did.

While the government provided free peanut butter and cheese and flour for the unemployed of the Great Depression, there were some, like his mother, who refused charity and brought her three kids up to do likewise with these words, "There is always a way when you love God because he loves you. Where there's a will, there's a way."

The Rockledge Lodge of Elks left a fantastic fruit basket complete with a plump turkey, grapes so juicy they looked ready to burst, and crisp Macintosh apples so biting they could have been snapping turtles on their steps at Thanksgiving time at home.

The Elks left off three baskets on each holiday to those they considered the poorest families in town. The DaSilvas, the Burrises, and the Clarksons. Bernadette and her younger sisters were in the same boat as Johnny; their father was also a traveling man.

The Elks considered awarding a fourth basket that Thanksgiving, but it was not given away as the only other needy family involved a divorced woman. The feeling was "She made her own bed, let her sleep in it."

The day they left the Thanksgiving basket on the DaSilva front porch found Johnny peeking through the curtains with more than passing interest. He had never seen such a feast. Not even when he sat in the top of the Parson family's swaying cherry tree, scooping mouthfuls of the big bings into a maw, feeling not unlike a baleen whale feasting on plankton, joyfully spitting the pits high into the air. It was wonderful to feast at heights that no one else would chance.

When Charity spotted the basket from the Elks, she was out the door "faster than a fart with a hurricane for a tail wind," according to her brother Matthew, who witnessed the entire episode. He was on the Elks's basket delivery committee.

Charity kicked the basket off the porch, scattering the contents, and then limping, chased the escaping and befuddled Elk's car and crew for several blocks, wailing, "We are not poor. We are not poor!" ending with a small sob that only she heard, "We are not poor . . ."

—

On returning, she saw Johnny staring at the scattered feast. He barely heard her whispered words, "We're not poor."

"I know, Ma." *I know . . . Ma . . .*

Though he could not help but think of what a replacement the basket would have been for their planned special Thanksgiving treat—three thin slices of chicken roll, one for Johnny, one for Romola, and one for Jazz. Charity said she didn't particularly like chicken.

She had also told her sisters and brothers, in answer to their question, "Yes, of course, we're all set for Thanksgiving."

One of the things that left Johnny confused was spotting the welfare line that doubled twice around the poor farm, where the free goods of the Great Depression were dispensed.

He was proud that neither his mother or he waited in such a line, but his hunger pains were tripled, as if a rock crab like the one he saw eating a small fish alive at the ocean was inside his stomach.

He had felt a thin stream of saliva as he watched those in line look down at the ground as they received their allotment of the rich, creamy peanut butter. *It could be . . . spread . . . so thick . . .*

Only that morning, he had watched an old woman smear peanut butter in the large drilled hole of her bird feeder and wondered whether any would be left there after dark. *Come on . . . forget that poo scat shit thinking . . . Anyone up there . . . forgive me for talking that way . . .*

Mr. Jonathan, who had just checked out his supply of the dole, didn't want the flour, his drunken wife couldn't bake anyway. *Just as well*, he thought, *she'd probably set the house on fire.* And that would be the end of his beer can collection. A collection that would be his future as someday he would open a beer can museum.

"Johnny, come here, boy."

"Yes, sir, Mr. Jonathan."

"Here, lad, take this home to your mother. Lord knows you poor folks can use it."

Rather than insult the man's good heart, Johnny reluctantly took the flour and jogged off.

He lugged the package like a football, dodging the defensive lineman oak trees in the Big Woods, dashing zigzag through the secondary poplars on the shortcut home. He dreamed of how fresh-baked bread would taste. If he gave it to Grandma Shiverick, she would bake bread for him and Romola and Jazz. *Yes . . .*

"Hey, what you got there?" Skinny Potts asked accusingly, knowing full well the difference between the white package with the bright yellow center bought at the market and the plain brown welfare packaging.

The other boys looked up from the pickup football game in the Big Field.

"That's that free stuff for the poor," Skinny said.

"Uh-uh. I just got it to, ah, mark out our football field."

He punctured the floor bag and chalked out the lines of the field, taking ten giant steps to mark out the ten yards needed for first downs. "There."

Johnny then got into the game and kicked ass royally! There is something about rock crabs gnawing on a pinched-tight belly that can make a man mean, even an eleven-year-old man. But he was disappointed. Skinny had not carried the ball. He wanted to make that fat tummy of his friend ache like his. There is something about a head driven into a navel at such speeds that it doesn't stop until it reaches the backbone.

All good things come to an end, and his football game did. He had to get home and check in. He was setting pins at the poolroom then also set pins in a bowling alley that night.

But he had to wait for that one last play. The score was seventy-one to seventy, and his team had to make the goal line stand to win.

The ball was centered to Skinny Potts, the heavyweight of his gang. He carried the ball through the middle of the line.

Johnny leaped into the hole and sank his unhelmeted head deep into Skinny's most generous belly.

Skinny went down with an "Iyay!" Then jumped up and ran home sobbing, "Prick, prick."

Johnny hoped he wasn't hurt. He was sure he felt his head ricochet off Skinny's backbone. After receiving congratulations from teammates, he went behind the Big Tree and threw up. His tackle had sent blue lightning through every bone in his body. The trouble with tossing his cookies was that there were no cookies to toss. His stomach was Old Mother Hubbard's Cubbard, which was also bare. In between barfs, his mind wandered. He had a concussion. *Old Mother Hubbard . . . went to the cupboard . . . to get her . . . poor daughter . . . a dress . . . When she got there . . . the cupboard was bare . . . and so was her daughter . . . I guess . . . sorry . . .*

He felt he had met the standards of Grandfather Shiverick. "Be proud, but be not an ego pagan on a high horse."

Guess I'm . . . pukin' proud . . . that I'll do . . .

When he got home, Skinny told his mother, a woman of great ampleness, that Johnny had hurt him, perhaps even broken his spine, on purpose.

—

Mrs. Potts thundered to the DaSilva abode, where she was met by Charity. She glared at the skinny Charity and demanded, "You and your skin and bones ragtag gang of gangsters will apologize. Now!"

Johnny hid behind the kitchen door and peeked out through the crack.

Charity stared at the large blazing woman, startled and open mouthed.

Mrs. Potts had built up an entourage of curious mothers, kids, and puppy dogs as she had trucked to the DaSilva home. The group greeted the large lady's demands with a light smattering of applause.

Mrs. Potts could see that the bone thin Charity was no match and thought Charity had to be a coward. "Besides, if your ragamuffin ever touches my little boy again, I'll just take the baseball bat that I keep behind my bedroom door to him and then to you"

It was at this point that Charity stepped toward her aggressor.

"Don't take a single step more, or I'll come back with my bat and beat the dust off you like a rug."

Charity, looking like a thread-thin Ollie in front of the robust Stanley of Oliver and Hardy movie fame, started shaking with such anger that much to her chagrin, a lightning flash of flatulence escaped her, a release more easily made on an empty stomach than a full one.

The fart stopped all action, forming a tableau of openmouthed onlookers and participants.

"The power, the sheer bigness of the unscheduled flatulence, actually inflated the back of her dress like a hot air balloon fast-fed with helium," according to an eyewitness.

From out of the poignant silence of the still movie frozen in tableau came the sweetest of smiles and the soft voice of Charity. "I hope that satisfies your needs, Mrs. Potts. It does mine. Now please leave while I'm still a lady."

The light applause Mrs. Potts had received earlier from the followers was replaced by a "Hip, hip, hurrah!" started by Johnny from behind the door and echoed by the gaping group. "Hip-hip, hurrrr-ray!" This caused Mrs. Potts to pivot and posthaste leave the scene of battle, like a retreating caboose railway car.

Some later referred to the incident as "the saga of the farting folk hero."

The report of the incident around the town set shock waves in the Shiverick family. Uncle Matthew felt they registered high on the Richter Earthquake Scale. He was proud of his little sis.

Grandfather Shiverick blamed the devil for this incident on the input of the DaSilva family and told Charity to pray for forgiveness.

Perhaps this out-of-character action can best be explained by the knowledge, that while Johnny, Jazz, and Roma had small rock crabs chewing their underfed innards, Charity has a colony of crabs gnawing hungrily and mercilessly in her. A hungry stomach is even more given to such power releases than an overindulged one.

Johnny made his escape during the confusion that followed the incident and made his way to work.

When he got home that night from setting candlepins at Coogan's Pool Room and Bowling Alley, he was greeted by the whisk end of his mother's broom. Poor timing.

There are times in a young boy's life that he finds himself with more talent to be in the wrong place at the right time than is natural.

As proof in Johnny's case, there was the Soupy Campbell caper.

Johnny's friend had not been given the Soupy moniker because of his last name, Campbell, as in Campbell's Soup.

He got it as a result of one of the most talked about happenings in Rockledge.

Soupy's God-given name was George Ira Campbell III. His father was a banker, a deacon, a colonel in the Salvation Army, and hit cleanup despite a .190 batting average for the bank's softball team. The plans were that George Ira Campbell III would follow in his very large footsteps.

This was not to be the inheriting of a royal cloak, at least in Rockledge, after the "incident."

Johnny and George Ira were walking to school through the Big Woods one warm early June day when they discovered a skunk sunning and sound asleep on a large flat rock.

George Ira, not one of the Eastward-Ho School folk heroes at that point, was always on the lookout for ways to join the hallowed gang. Something brave, sort of like what Johnny and Tim Yanders were known for. Even Righty the runt was thought of as brave following the ruler incident.

George Ira turned to Johnny and said, "Rhesus told me that if you grab a skunk by the tail real fast and lift upward, its body weight will close its pucker hole, and it can't spray you."

"Don't believe it."

"No, I don't. But I believe what Boattail said, 'Dead men tell no tales,' which, when translated, means dead skunks can't pee."

Johnny watched dumbfounded as George Ira picked up a large, flat stone and slowly approached the skunk.

—

"Best to let sleeping dogs lay," Johnny told his friend, repeating one of the many wisdoms Grandma Shiverick offered between kisses and hugs and pennies for finding her eyeglasses.

As George Ira continued tiptoeing toward the woods pussy, Johnny had a sinking feeling in his stomach and was struck speechless when his friend lifted the flat stone over his head and did the . . . unthinkable . . .

The flattened body of the squashed skunk twitched like the live wires of an unended utility pole, but instead of spitting sparks, it released a fine, all-finding spray.

Although Johnny's mind froze when George Ira entered the hallowed halls, his feet weren't frozen.

After George Ira hit the low road; Johnny hit the high road.

George Ira III was pissed on from top to bottom, toe, knee, chest, nut.

But the coup de grace in an incident that would guarantee he would never be president of the Rockledge Bank was that George Ira continued on to school, where he was greeted by neither open arms or nostrils by an unsympathetic teacher and longtime school chums who abandoned him like a fart in church.

He was sent home for several days.

Reports from Hayden's Grocery Store were that his mother bought an even one hundred cans of tomato soup for George Ira III to bath in.

What followed was the birth of Soupy, Soupy Campbell.

Even after he smelled like a soup kitchen rather than pole cat juiced kid, friends just would not walk with him. He was suspect. What if he found another sleeping skunk while they were with him. There was a fear afoot that took some time for all to overcome.

Johnny was the first to talk and walk with him. Others eventually followed. After all, he had entered the hallowed hall of fame of Eastward-Ho, a legend before his time. Through the back door, of course. A pole cat's rear door.

What truly ended Soupy's solitary confinement and cruel greetings of "Here comes Flower," "There goes Flower" was a betcha-don't-dare gauntlet picked up by one Herve Hopalong Cassidy Harrison.

Actually there was more involved than just a dare. It also involved a financial transfer of ten cents to anyone who would swallow a live grasshopper. Rhesus had put up the dime for the bet. Unbeknownst to his cohorts and camp followers, he had a number of bets with older kids that he could get someone to swallow a grasshopper.

Herve had no interest in gaining status with the Eastward-Ho gang; he did have interest in the dime.

Rhesus came up with the ten cents.

Soupy whispered to Herve that he would throw in his jackknife, the one that only had one broken blade. The knife was one complete with a compass in the butt end of the handle and a can opener secreted in with the large and smaller cutting blades. It also housed a thin plastic needle for picking your teeth, which made it kind of cool. To pick your teeth like a gangster—well, it didn't get much better than that. Soupy rarely removed the knife from the case sewed in near the top of his high-laced right boot. Soupy hoped that if someone, anyone, ate a grasshopper it would help take him out of the limelight of being the kid the skunk pissed on.

The knife and the dime settled any qualms Herve might have had about swallowing such a green critter. All you had to do was close your eyes, pinch your nose, and gulp quick. Real quick.

"No gulping," Fats said.

"You gotta chew," Boattail said.

"No holding your ears so you can't hear it scream," Rhesus said.

Herve was wavering.

Soupy flashed his knife, utilizing the sun for reflection.

Herve moved with the swiftness with which only the terrified can move. Not only did he plop the grasshopper into his mouth, but also chewed on it as well. Everyone in attendance reported it was like that "in Concord and in Lexington" thing, when that first crunch-crack chew was heard. It was a shot heard around the world.

Thus, Johnny christened Herve "Hopalong Cassidy" on the spot.

And just that quickly, Soupy became yesterday's news.

Later Johnny told Jazz and Roma about the grasshopper swallowing, and the three of them recited one of their favorite pieces of poetry, "High up, over the tops of the feathery grasses, the grasshoppers hop.

"They won't eat their supper, and they will not obey, their grasshopper mothers and fathers who say, 'Now listen, my children, now this must stop. Now's the time your last hop is to be hopped. Now come eat your supper, and go to your beds.'

"But the little green grasshoppers shake their green heads.

"'No. No,' the naughty ones say. All we have time to do now is to play.

"If we get hungry we'll nip at a fly or nibble a petal as we go by.

"If we get tired, we'll snuggle up tight and sleep in a blue bell overnight.

"But no, not now. Now we must hop.

"And nobody, nobody, can make us stop!"

Charity, having overheard her children, quietly told them, "Perhaps little Mr. Herve was hungry, like many of the unfortunates of this Great

Depression. God will make sure it will end shortly with the help of Mr. Roosevelt."

"But, Ma," Johnny said, "his father owns the bank."

"Even so, some understanding, some kindness is called for here."

"Understanding? Ma, he used the ten cents to buy a creampuff and ate it in front of us. Smirking like a bullfrog that just swallowed a dragonfly. And he never brushed his teeth before eating it, and worse, he didn't brush afterward," Johnny reported.

"I wish I had a creampuff," Roma said.

Charity, who never swore, shocked her children with, "Wish in one hand, do crap cakes in the other."

Johnny looked at his mother, his eyes open like an owl's. *Crap . . . cakes . . . crap cakes . . .*

It was only years later they understood that she was saying," If you wish in one hand and don't follow it up with work, you get only scat in the other hand."

When she realized she had cursed in front of her children, she said angrily, "See what you've done! You've made your mother curse. And don't you go running to your grandfather telling him. And don't dream without planning to work for it."

Fulfilling wishes took a lot of forms, some very trying. Delivering the morning newspaper was one. The family didn't own an alarm clock.

When Johnny first got his route, Charity and he would only half sleep in order to make sure he was ready to roll at 4:00 a.m.

Eventually they woke up at this time automatically. Although once he started setting candlepins in the poolroom bowling alleys, his mental alarm clock started to fall to fatigue.

Uncle John Shiverick, who delivered milk for Hoods on the cobblestone streets of Boston in the early morning, came to his rescue.

Johnny each night tied a string to his toe when he went to bed, then dropped the weighted end of the string out his second-story window. Each morning when his uncle headed into Boston to do his route, he'd give the string a yank. But this meant getting up at 3:30 instead of 4:00.

Johnny's part of the bargain with his uncle was to help him deliver his milk on Saturdays.

He loved his uncle's old clippity-cloppity horse, Creepin' Moses. The sound of its hooves on the cobblestones, "clippity clop, clippity clop," meant he could close his eyes while walking behind the horse, just following its beat.

Johnny marveled at the miracle that Creepin' Moses knew the milk route, stopping outside customers' apartments, bypassing those who did

—

not purchase the Hoods's products. The old clopper knew the route as well as the milkman, walking by those apartments that got their milk from Whitings Milk Co. or got no milk at all.

A couple of times, Uncle John debated with Creepin' Moses about the horse going by one of those look-alike brownstone apartments only to learn the old clop was right and he was wrong.

Uncle John would muss up his nephew's hair at such a time, telling him, "The Creator makes us all divine in some special way."

Johnny loved his ramrod-straight uncle, his craggy brow, so much like his grandfather Shiverick's. He also appeared to walk tall, his head in the heavens. But he loved him most of all when his uncle would throw a steaming horse bun at him. It meant he now belonged to what passed for the adult world.

His uncle would allow him to carve a chunk of frozen cream forced out of the bottles' expanding contents as a reward at the end of the route. As the milk froze, it forced the cover up sometimes as high as an inch or two. This was a king's ransom.

His uncle explained that this was not a major larceny, that certain particular customers wanted their delivery neatly packaged with all the contents within the confines of bottle and cap. Plus, Johnny helped to save a life as the particular unknown cream buyer "had heart problems and shouldn't have that much rich stuff."

The freezing mornings were tough on his teeth. The cold would get in the cracks worse than any dental drill in the world. Often in the freezing predawn blackness, before delivering his papers, he forced heated wax between his teeth, into the cracks and cavities, so the cold couldn't penetrate.

He didn't use the wax when he helped his uncle on his milk route. When the bitter cold winds caused his teeth to ache, Johnny only had to hold his cheeks up against the soft, warm muzzle of Creepin' Moses to ease the pain. He loved the horse's warmth and hay-sweet breath. It was nothing like Rag's dog breath, but he loved his pooch no less for it.

Creepin' Moses sort of liked Johnny's bad teeth warming as well.

Johnny often thought his rapport with the horse was special, very special, sort of like that between Elizabeth Taylor and Flicker. He knew a girl who had the blue eyes of the sky, like that young girl on the screen. *Who . . . was it the beautiful Yelena? It must be . . . No . . . her eyes were . . . gray . . . with a promise of . . . rain . . .*

Yelena's eyes were the steel gray of a shark's belly and as penetrating as that of the unblinking shark.

There were times when he questioned this rapport with the old milk horse, like the time he bent over, exposing the upper part of his cold butt to the brittle wind off the Charles River, and he suffered a horse bite.

"Holy Moses! Holy good Moses!"

He laughed at his unintended joke.

Nearly all the time, his work was work. Except when his uncle John tossed a fresh horse bun at him. Or when he warmed his face on Creeping Moses' muzzle.

Going to school and after school with his friends was his escape.

There were tons of friends. Tim Yanders. Righty Minichelli.

There were Bobby "Butt Burner" Burnham, the first in the gang to puff on a cig.

Then there was Dickie "Dick Tracy" McDermott, whose uncle was a cop; fat "Skinny" Potts, whose pot belly tired him quickly; and if anyone in the gang was to get caught stealing cherries, it was the Thin Man.

The real Thin Man was Fats Tolland; a good wind would blow him away.

Rhesus said, "Fats doesn't dare to fart. He'll end up on the moon."

There were the brothers two, Rhesus and Boattail.

And of course, Scoff Burke. Johnny nicknamed them all. Scoff was thus named because of his inability to leave other kids' stuff alone.

But they all felt Scoff meant no harm. As long as he gave the purloined stuff back.

There was always a pickup baseball game going at the Eastward-Ho School field. Teams were chosen by tossing the bat. One kid would toss the bat in the air and a second would grab it. Then they would have turns moving their hands up the bat. The last hand to fit against the knob got first pick.

When the ponds weren't frozen, the hockey players would join in a pickup basketball game. During one such game, Scoff, who also told windies, said the Boston pro basketball team, he didn't know its name, had picked up a center that was six foot two.

He almost got laughed off the court. The giant wrestler, the Swedish Angel, was six three. No one grew that tall. Except the oak trees.

Righty proved this with the statement. "They couldn't bend over to tie their sneakers. 'Nuff said."

Baseball presented the most problems. There was always a basketball available or at least a volleyball or even a beach ball for a pickup game of basketball. A wooden block could serve as a puck when your last puck slid off the ice into open water. The wooden puck was used until some lucky kid caught a stray shot at a Boston Bruins or Pics game.

—

If the football wouldn't hold air any longer, you could stuff it with rags; and if your wrist was strong enough, you could still toss a spiral.

But baseball.

Baseballs would come apart at the seams. In midair. Before your eyes. The string unwinding as the ball sallied forth.

There were a lot of days like that where they all gathered around the pitching mound, trying to figure out how to hold their baseball together. When a cover was knocked off, the ball of string was then taped with a layer of black tape. The tape in turn was taped and retaped as the bats whacked the ball dizzy.

Skinny Potts rarely connected, but when he got that belly swinging toward the pitcher in a centrifugal motion, he could really whack it and did the ball in on this day.

He really cranked one out, sending the ball flying skyward, leaving a tail of string that got longer as the ball carried far into the outfield.

When Burper Murphy finally caught up to the ball, it definitely was much smaller than when it was launched. It was not much more than the size of a pregnant golf ball. It looked like one of those shrunken heads you could buy at Halloween. He shivered at the thought and then went flying home. His fellow ballplayers thought he had to take a leak. Bad.

Well, when Burper dropped that shrunken head baseball like a hot rock, Johnny immediately renamed him Catfish.

The real Catfish was Catfish Meckovitch, who played right field for the Sox; a herring gull passed over Fenway Park during a game and dropped a catfish near him. But lucky Burper got the call to fame.

It was a great nickname.

Everyone wanted to be called Catfish.

Years later, a great pitcher came along by the name of Catfish Hunter, but he was a pretender to the throne. He got his name because he loved to fish for catfish, not because one was dropped on his head.

Meckovitch wasn't cut from the Hunter stardom cloth. He not only played second and third fiddle to the other two greats there in the outfield, Ted Williams and the Little Professor, Dom DiMaggio. Catfish also had to share right field with Tom McBride and Leon Culbertson. All five outfielders hit over .300 at one time. Tough to find work there.

Later in life, Johnny wondered why the song wasn't "Where have you gone Catfish Meckovitch?" rather than "Where have you gone Joe DiMaggio?" But then again, Johnny was a true lover of nicknames. *You can't compare . . . the name Joe . . . to . . . catfish . . .*

What was left of the baseball ended up in the hands of the catcher Scoff Burke. He said, "It's too small to play with," and started to put the remains in his pocket.

"No, you don't," Righty said, taking the ball and tagging out Skinny Potts, who slowed by his swaying bread basket and his mincing Babe Ruth home run trot, was just completing his round of the bases.

But they couldn't continue with the tiny ball.

Rhesus said he had a giant ball of string he had been collecting for years. "I'll sell some of the string, and we can wind it around the small ball."

"Nuts," said Righty, ending the game.

Rhesus defended his string with "Someday it will be the largest ball of string in the world. I'll make a fortune at the fairs and get to see the hoochie-coochie girls too."

"Yah, we can wrap some of his string around the ball to bulk it out," Fats said, thinking if he ingratiated himself to Rhesus, he would be invited to view the hoochie-coochie girls with him.

Rhesus, defending his want for an exchange of cash for some of his string, said "After all, this is my future, my fortune."

"Nothing doing. We're all broke, anyhow" Soupy said.

"Doesn't matter none, we don't have no tape to tape it back together," Righty said.

"We can scoop up some pine pitch from a wounded tree and stick the string together," Soupy said.

"Nah, someone's hand will stick to the ball, and he'll toss his arm out," Righty said. "Anyway, we ain't got no string."

"We can use our shoelaces," Johnny said, "and each one of us can go home and get a couple Band-Aids to tape it up."

His suggestion drew a few oohs and a few boos.

"Perhaps we should forget it," Tim said. "It's December, and you guys will be playing hockey pretty soon. And some of us playing basketball. Perhaps we should forget it."

Scoff, who had disappeared when the discussion of repairing the baseball started, was returning, running across the field toward them, speaking faster than the time he was grabbed at the Five and Ten when caught "borrowing" a Captain Marvel comic book.

He was completely out of breath, but his voice still boomed. "The Japs have invaded Pearl Harbor! The Japs have invaded Pearl Harbor!"

They gathered around Scoff, putting their arms around him to comfort him, wanting to aim their anger at whomever put their friend in this state of being completely unglued.

—

"What are Japs?" Righty asked.

"Who's Pearl Harbor?" Rhesus asked.

"You kids all have to get home and into your cellars. The Japs are coming." It was Bummy Burke, Scoff's dad.

"Who are the Japs?" Johnny asked.

"The Japs are sneaky little rat bastards who fucken' attacked fuckin' Pearl Harbor."

"What's Pearl Harbor?"

"It's some place where we Americans keeps a lot of our ships and other big boats," Bummy said.

"They attacked the Boston Navy Yard?" Skinny Potts asked. "My dad works there!"

"My dad works in the Sun Shipyard in Pennsylvania," Johnny said.

"Shut up, you kids. I've got the news," Bummy said. "The dirty rat Japs killed lots of American soldiers and sailors while they were sleeping. And sank all our ships and did all sorts of dirty shit. I'm joining the navy tomorrow to fight them."

"And I'm joining the army tomorrow morning and gonna fly a plane and bomb the Japs tomorrow afternoon," Scoff said proudly, puffing his chest out like a miniature Bummy Burke.

"It's the army for me. They get bayonets," Boattail said, thrusting an invisible bayonet through the air with such intensity it caused those nearby to duck.

Within weeks, the baseball cards of Red Ruffing, Dutch Leonard, Dixie Walker, King Kong Keller, and other heroes of the baseball diamond would be replaced with the new War Cards, whose squares of bubble gum, the same size as the card, tasted even worse than the gum that came with the baseball cards. The War Cards showed Japanese Zeros sweeping low and strafing schools and hospitals where kids and old women and sick people tumbled out of the windows, often missing a leg, or on fire.

The gang gathered in a tight circle for protection as Bummy continued, "What makes them dangerous is Japs are tiny and tough to see. They have slanted eyes so they can look under your window shade or the crack of your door."

The War Cards that came off the assembly line faster than tanks showed just how bad these Japs were. While many cards depicted airplanes with giant red circles painted on them, strafing schools and children playing kick ball during lunch, other cards showed little yellow men bayoneting nuns and priests.

Other War Cards with deeper meanings they did not quite understand but left them uneasy showed American nurses being carried off in torn

—

dresses by the same little bowlegged yellow men with evil leers on their faces.

"And they all got buckteeth," Bummy said, "so they can bite your head off, at least bite the heads of you little people kids."

Almost overnight, posters sprung up declaring, "Loose lips sink ships."

Small, red, white, and blue squares with blue stars inside them appeared in windows, with the number of stars announcing how many sons served their nation.

Older men wearing white helmets and armbands that read "CD" for civil defense, came around after dark and tapped on your window if any light was showing through and, in authoritative voice, whispered, "Turn 'em out in there. The enemy can see a match ten miles away at sea."

One civil defense volunteer tapped on the Minichelli window and informed them the enemy could see a cigarette miles at sea.

"Does it have to be lit?" Righty answered back.

"What are you, a spy?" the CD officer said. "Your kind better be careful. We heard of your Mr. Mussolini."

"I'm coming out after you, you turd shit," Righty said, starting for the door but was stopped by his brother Big Lefty. "It's okay, little brother. He don't know nothing."

Mothers and wives checked their mail each day, first searching for the larger, official-looking envelope from the government that when opened read, "We regret to inform you . . ." then looking for a V-mail letter from a loved one.

They were now in the seventh grade. Yelena started a junior high after-school knitting class. The Junior-Senior High principal thought it was such a good idea that he allowed their efforts to carry over into class.

They knitted wool squares that would later be sewed together into a shawl that American soldiers could wrap around their shoulders while they sat in their foxholes at night. The kids watching the Pathé News of the war searched for signs of their patchwork quilts without success.

More interest was shown in class when subjects alluded to the war. "What would the angle be for a mortar shell to travel two hundred yards, reaching a height of three hundred yards, and landing on a Nazi machine gun nest?" "Where is Hamburg, Germany?" "What ocean do our men have to travel to invade Japan?"

In history, Ms. Case told her class, "We must save gas, all kinds of fuel." "Tell your fathers not to burn rubber. The Japanese hordes have captured the rubber plantations! You remember our study of the rubber trees."

"Light travels faster than sound. A searchlight beam can catch an enemy ship before the sound of the ship's great guns reaches them," Ms. Sullivan said.

Ms. Kane started sniffing the air in class each morning to make sure no one had spilled kerosene when filling their heating stoves. "There are shortages. We must make sacrifices. Besides, I detest the smell."

One bitter cold morning, when the kerosene stove was reactivated in the DaSilva home, Johnny had spilled kerosene while lugging the five-gallon jug with one hand while trying to wrestle the battered and torn, saliva-soaked tennis ball free from old Rags who had it firmly clamped in his now nearly toothless old mouth.

Most of the spill was confined to his hands. And the odor remained despite repeated hand washings with the homemade lye soap they used when it appeared only when someone had come in contact with poison ivy.

Ms. O'Malley had smelled the kerosene in the class the first thing when she entered the room and demanded, "Would the unpatriotic one who is wasting fuel vital to our war effort please step forward and accept the deserved punishment. Which will be doubled as you know it makes me nauseous."

No answer. No one wanted to get whacked in the open palm by the leather-stropping strap her father had used to sharpen his razor before he died.

No one fessed up to having kerosene hands.

Ms. O'Malley started sniffing hands in the front row first.

Then the second.

As she neared the last row that housed Rhesus, Boattail, Righty, and Johnny, her nose was as hot as a hound on a hare. Her avenging hand started vibrating like a tuning fork, making the strap whip like a viper's tail.

Righty tried to hide his hands under his shirt. He knew they smelled of kerosene. He kicked his ass for not washing them after filling the jug that morning. Now he was going to catch it. Besides, his fried egg sandwich had tasted really bad to boot.

Ms. O'Malley was closing in fast on Righty, not unlike a turkey vulture closing in on carrion.

She was in front of Righty now. He jammed his kerosene-smelling hands deep into his pockets.

"No! It's me," Johnny said, standing up, extending his hands.

"So it's you who is the traitor, Mr. DaSilva! The one who would betray our brave fighting men."

Her first ruler whack cracked Johnny's knuckles before he could turn his hands palms up and absorb some of the fury on the fat of the hand. The strap sent horror messages to his brain, as the little woman's arm strength was imbued with red, white, and blue patriotic power. Johnny had once heard his uncle Manny DaSilva declare to his dad, following a Portuguese-American vs. Franco-American soccer game in which he was kicked you know where, "Nothing, nothing in the world hurts like a kick in the balls."

I never got . . . whacked . . . by my teacher . . . before . . . it's like wearing a glove . . . full of hornets . . .

Up to this point in his life, Johnny had never been kicked in the testicles.

On her third swing, Johnny committed a no-no. He removed his hand from the target scene, and the strap crashed against her upper leg with a hot sting her old-maid thighs had never known, even in her wildest dreams.

She uttered the words she would regret to her dying days, "God will get you, John DaSilva. He will get you good."

Better God get me . . . than your god-darned . . . razor ruler . . .

The teacher's words and whacks didn't end Johnny's physical and mental pain for the day.

Righty was waiting for him when school ended, and he stepped out the door onto the school grounds.

There would be no "Red Rover, Red Rover, let Johnny come over," "All-ee, all-ee in-free" game of Relievo. There would be no "Buck-Buck, how many fingers do I have up," or "Bore a hole, bore a hole right through the sugar bowl, and place it with a dot," for Johnny with Righty this afternoon.

There would be no game of catch or hitting pepper.

"What did you do that for?" Righty accused, showing why he was called Righty by following up with a right cross that set Johnny on the seat of his britches.

"I'll hate you the rest of my life. No one takes the tumble for Righty Minichelli." The words were very similar to ones Righty had heard Jimmy Cagney mutter while doing a little two-step dance that said he would take on the whole world.

The anger only lasted until the next morning when Johnny woke up to Righty's bouncing a tennis ball off Johnny's front steps and catching it in his mittened hand while he waited for his friend to come out. When Johnny finished delivering his newspaper each morning, he would catch fifteen minutes of nod and nap before heading to school.

Righty yelled through the window, "Let's go to school through the Big Woods!" a long cut that added nearly a mile to the trip.

No answer.

"Wanna chuck a few snowballs at old man Montgomery's cat?" Righty yelled through the window.

"Sure."

"It'll be fun," Righty said. "The cross-eyed sucker always seems to be meowing some sort of sticky ass yah-yah song that sounds like that sicko song, 'taught to the tune of the hickory stick.'"

Johnny had tied a scarf around his eyes. It had been bitter cold early that morning delivering the Boston papers plus the *Christian Science Monitor*. The driving snow hit his eyeballs like darts hitting a dartboard!

He rotated the scarf from around his snow-needled eyes to around his mouth as despite the fact that he had loaded his teeth with melted wax, the cold made them ache and throb until even his ears, balls, and eyeballs hurt like a flesh-tearing wet towel snap to a bare butt.

The cavities had appeared despite the morning after morning scrubbing of his teeth in the frosty cold water of their unheated bathroom. Only later did he learn that he could brush with salt or baking soda as they could not afford the expensive "Brusha, brusha, brusha, with the new Ipana."

He was going to lose the teeth. He knew it. He worked up the courage to go to good old Doc Jones and propose a payment program so he could have his teeth fixed, maybe save some.

Doc Jones agreed to keep an envelope with Johnny's name on it in his office.

Johnny would go to the office whenever he had a nickel or extra pennies, and they would be placed in the envelope. When the envelope totaled seventy-five cents, the cost of a filling, Doc Jones would fill one of the diseased teeth.

The problem was that several times before he could garner the seventy-five cents the tooth was too far gone, and the money was used to pull it.

It was a slow process, saving the money, and the tooth fairy was nonexistent.

Some of his funds earned setting candlepins at the poolroom and delivering the morning papers were pooled with his mother's box factory pay to help keep the house together, the house being the family.

His father, Tony, wrote how—with the war effort and all—work was picking up in the Sun Shipyard, and that as soon as he saved enough money for a car, he would be able to visit them on a lot more weekends.

—

Of course, he needed some extra gasoline rationing stamps to buy fuel. He said as soon as he had a car, he would have enough money to help them out at home.

They all wanted the car for him. His return trips home by train or bus were becoming fewer and fewer. He said travel for service men had top priority.

They all wanted him home, bad.

He hit fungoes to Johnny and Jazz, took them flounder fishing at Salem Willows, where they rented a boat and rowed out of sight of land where they not only caught more flounders than anyone else, but also bigger ones as well. Occasionally they caught mackerel or even a striped bass.

When they ran into a school of porgies, so thick they blackened the water, they would cast metal weights with homemade snagging hooks, hooking enough both for bait and for cooking. The scup were good but bony. You always had to have a slice of bread nearby in case you swallowed a bone. When this happened, you ate the bread, hoping it would wrap around the bone until it started to dissolve and could stick in your throat.

The porgy would be put on a big hook, and his father trolled the bait behind the boat Johnny rowed through the breathing ocean whose chest expanded and expired, and their little craft was lifted up and settled down.

At home, their father would hold Romola in the air one handed, and she would cry out, "I'm a bird! I'm a bird, Daddy. You're the strongest daddy in the world."

Then returning her feet back on the ground, he waltzed her around, telling her that she was the most beautiful girl in the world.

"Oh, Daddy. Waltz me around again, Willie!"

Until her daddy came home each time, she felt that on a beauty scale of one to ten, she was a minus two. But when he was home, she was an eleven. When the most beautiful man in The world told you that you were the most beautiful girl in the world, well, you went right off the scale.

Dressed in his perfectly tailored suits, she thought him "more handsome than Douglas Fairbanks Jr. and John Barrymore—combined!"

"I bought this suit just to wear for you, my Romola."

Charity wanted him to come home, even if it meant saving all his pay for a car. To hear him tell her she was the most beautiful woman in the world. To know that the man more handsome than Errol Flynn, Douglas Fairbanks Jr., John Barrymore, even more handsome than her favorite, Tyrone thought she was beautiful was so wonderful.

But most important, she needed a man, her husband, to hold her.

"You said I was most beautiful, Daddy, now you're telling Mama she is," Romola had said.

"You are, my little butterfly love. But I have enough love for you. Your mother. And the world. And beautiful flowers are many different shapes and colors. Come, a date, I'm buying ice cream."

They did not serve single scoops of ice cream at the farm stand in Westford. Nor doubles. Only triples. And only five cents.

The old farmer and his wife that made the ice cream told the DaSilva children, "If you can't handle a triple, give a couple licks to your favorite doggie."

"How did you find this place, Dad?" Johnny asked his father. "It's the greatest."

The Westford Farm Stand was the greatest. After dark, the farmer showed free outdoor movies on the side of his always-sparkling white barn. And the kids laughed when a cow inside the barn mooed at the moment a fair maiden waited for a kiss.

Their father was always so polite, Romola thought. When he thanked her uncle John Shiverick for the use of his Hudson, it was like a happening. She thought that her uncle John should be more thankful that her father borrowed it from him, rather than some stranger.

"Daddy, everyone loves you."

Johnny especially loved everything about his father, especially his teeth. White. Strong. Even. With that wonderful gold mine of a tooth in the back. It was the one and only cavity he ever had, and he wanted to treat it royally.

Johnny admired him even more than usual on this day, the coldest day of winter, as his own teeth hurt more than any time he could remember.

Actually, Johnny had wanted his teacher to whack his hand that morning in school. Only a new and anger-inflicted pain would make him forget, at least for a moment, the pain in his teeth.

Righty rapped the window and yelled, "Come on, Johnny, stop the darn thinking. We're gonna get the strap if we're late again. We can't even go though the Big Woods now."

The ruler wasn't near as bad as when his teacher gave a cruel and unusual punishment, prohibited under American jurisprudence, when you were late on consecutive days. She didn't realize how harsh her action was. She would stand with her face only inches from the face of the perpetrator and reward the perp with breath so bad, at least according to Rhesus, "It would gag a maggot."

Righty figured Johnny had a bad teeth morning. It had been freezing cold when he stepped out the door at seven. He could imagine what it had been like at 4:00 a.m. when Johnny started his route.

What the punished kids hated more than the ruler, strop, or even the bad breath was the fact their teacher would tell each and every one, each and every time, "I'm disciplining you because I care about yooo." The real problem is that the "yooo" in the discipline was always accompanied by spittle that made her halitosis stick to their clothing like fungus to a tree.

After one outstanding tanning by the teacher, Fats told his friends, "I'd rather have her not care and not have her whack me than have her care for me and whack the piss out of me." This drew nods of agreement from the Big Woods gang.

Righty could see Johnny through the window. His friend was stuffing warm wax in his teeth as fast as his mother melted the old stubs of candles from little olive-skinned Tony Cicardi's Tony's Grinders. He saved the stubs for Charity when they were burned almost even with their hosts, old Chianti bottles, whose sides were streaked with multicolor waxes, giving them the appearance of roly-poly tattooed men. Tony had worked in the box factory with Charity before he started his own pizza joint, Tony's. "Whatta else-sa. I call it? Mary? Ay?" The "ay" always punctuated with an open hand, palm up, and hunched-up shoulders. The yellow skin, tiny size and hunched shoulders gave him the appearance of a canary taking a shit, Righty had said.

But canary crapping or not, he made the best grinders in the world, grinders being heroes to New Yorkers, submarines on the coast.

Why grinders? They were called this only in Massachusetts. But then again, didn't those broad A people of Massachusetts call soda "tonic," and "don't they Paaark their kaars" rather than "Park their cars?"

When a Bay Stater visiting other parts of the country asked for a tonic, they were more often than not asked, "Hair tonic or nerve tonic?"

His wax job finished, Johnny hit the open door held by his mother, on the run.

It would mark the third day this week Righty and Johnny were late.

When their teacher's batting arm was sore, she would make them hold their hands out the window until they were nearly white with cold and reduce the number of whacks by 75 percent.

Their chests were pounding when they entered the classroom.

Skinny greeted them with a big smile. "We're in luck. Teach slipped on the ice and broke her hip."

—

Righty and Johnny and most of the class felt bad about this as they liked the little old woman. She was harsh, but she was fair. She always got her man, the right man who did wrong.

"She was like a Royal Canadian Mountie, sort of like Nelson Eddy. She always gets her man," Johnny once said.

A hum surrounded the room. The thin, flat-chested Chinese American substitute teacher, Ms. Sun May Loo, could not make out the hum, but it sounded strangely like her name was involved and believe they were saying "Teethless Loo" rather than "Titless Loo."

It was true; Ms. Loo did not have the prow of a wave-cutting destroyer. She was endowed with frontage more similar to that of a flat-nosed Boston terrier or a troop-landing barge.

She interpreted their drone incorrectly and muttered to herself, "I haf teef, thirty-two teef. No cavities."

Why should such a lovely youthful cameo of a face accented with the large almond liquid eyes of a whitetail doe need breasts? She actually appeared younger than some of her seventh-grade students.

The humming chant continued; substitute teachers always were, always will be, fair game. "Loo Loo, Titless Loo—the Jap!"

The young woman was becoming more and more confused. She placed the back of her hand against her forehead and nearly fainted.

"She's not a Jap."

It was Johnny.

"Speech, speech!" It was Rhesus.

"She is Chinese American. The Chinese have been fighting the Japanese for years. My uncle Luke Shiverick told me. His tale was that he served in the Flying Tigers. Our American pilots joined them in fighting the nips. Flying Tigers they call themselves. Tiger teeth are painted on the front of their planes. They wear leather jackets with both Chinese and American flags on their sleeves. In case they get shot down. Then the Chinese help them. But wearing the two flags if the Japs catch them, well, it ain't too good."

Then as if shot, he sat down so quickly; everyone was speechless. As was Johnny. He had never made a speech before.

He felt like standing again now that his speech-making cherry was broken. He wanted to tell the class he would rather have had a beating than see their teacher break her hip. That he had heard his aunt Hope say one day, "When an old person breaks their hip it signs their death warrant." *And she helped us . . . sew blankets . . . for our soldiers . . . and sailors . . .*

The class was well behaved now.

And the school vice principal, peeking through the small window in the classroom door, wondered whether all the kids had been stricken sick at the same time. Or if they were stunned by the perfection of the beauty of this tiny woman-child. Ms. Loo, that's her name.

Ms. Loo appeared to be lost in thought as the class labored over their papers. *I'll have to remember that Flying Tigers thing . . . in case . . . some class . . . in the future . . . gets out of hand . . . I'd love to be able to . . . rent that DaSilva . . . boy . . .*

Sports had always been the after-school activity. But now they had an additional one, an activity brought on by World War II.

Johnny and his gang ran wild in the streets, shouting, "Remember Pearl Harbor!" They all wanted to fight Jap rats. And who wouldn't. Even if the little yellow men didn't have thick glasses and buckteeth and slanted eyes, they had attacked Pearl Harbor.

Johnny had nearly squeezed the nose off Scoff Burke after Scoff had told Johnny's little brother Jazz, "You gotta be a Jap rat with your buckteeth!"

The Big Woods gang wondered how a Jap could be called a hero, but weren't their leaders called "Hero Hito" or something?

They sang about their own heroes. "Johnny Zero is a hero today." It seems he shot down one of those airplanes with the red circle on it, the one they called the Zero.

Then there was the story of Capt. Collin Kelly, who aimed his crippled Flying Fortress into a Japanese battleship, so brave the boys wanted to cry. It was easy to see Captain Kelly trying to hold the stick of the dying plane steady so his final breath on earth would allow him to sink this ship.

Johnny knew that he would be a Johnny Zero the very first he heard the song on the radio, "Johnny Zero is a hero today."

He would fly a P-47 Thunderbolt or P-38 Lightning. He would be both thunderbolt and lightning. *I'll send a son . . . of the rising sun . . . into the sea . . . with a clap of thunder . . . and a bolt of lightning . . . Johnny DaSilva . . . is a hero . . . today . . .*

He was proud that his thoughts were, well, poetic.

But a few weeks after Pearl Harbor, Johnny felt he had been shot down. The army recruiting officer told him he was too young to join the army air corps. "Way too young."

"I'll go to China and join the Flying Tigers," he threatened.

The recruiter smiled and told him, "Bring me back an order of rice and wonton soup."

"Up yours," he said slowly.

"I'm an officer in the . . ."

"Up yours, sir." Then he turned tail and ran as fast as he could. The final two miles, despite the shabby treatment by the recruiter, he sang, "Nothing can stop the army air corps." Those were the only words to the song that he knew. Later he knew words to a new song. "Off we go, into the wild blue yonder, climbing high into the sun. To live in fame or go down in flame."

There were other great things to chant during those war years. His grandfather Shiverick had told him there were only six things in this life that were certain or real: "God, the king of England, taxes, death, war, and politics."

The war chants of "Hitler is a shitler," "Off with your Toe-Joe," and "Loose lips sink ships" were joined by political chants "win with Wilkie" and "a cow's tail is long and silky, lift it up and you'll find Wilkie,'" "no third term," and "we can go far with FDR."

Pins with political slogans and pictures of the presidential candidates were swapped even-steven for the top of the kids' exchange rate—baseball cards.

After Johnny's experience going it alone, Righty, Tim, and Johnny swore they'd join up together, and then they'd have to take them. They marched in on the navy recruiter at the Boston Federal Building, demanding they be taken into the navy. The kindly old recruiter who looked a tad like Popeye the Sailor Man told them he'd add up their ages to see if they could make it. Their total age was thirty-nine, and Popeye told them, "Sorry, you're too old."

He got off easier than the army air corps recruiter who was nailed with an "Up yours."

"Swab jockey," Righty said.

"Right, swabbie," Johnny endorsed and nodded to Tim for his comment.

"We'll be back."

"Sometimes you're too nice," Righty said, giving Tim a noogie on his upper arm.

A week later they were at it again.

"I heard the Seabees will take anyone," Johnny said, "as long as they can build."

"Go home and play in your sandbox," was the recruiter's directive.

"There's too many cat turds like you in it," Johnny said, starting his dash before he finished the sentence.

"Good, good shot," Righty said as he and Tim caught up to Johnny and passed him because the old Sea Bee was closing the space between them. Later, safe in the Big Woods, they laughed until Righty actually peed himself, as they wondered how he could run so fast in those tight bell-bottomed trousers.

"Lucky he didn't have a woodie on. He would have strangled," Righty said.

"He ran like he had a bee up his butt," Johnny said.

Regardless, they still liked the old guy. He hung in there for a quarter mile. When he finally gave up the chase, they turned, saluted him, and sang out their prepuberty, patriotic young voices, "We're the Seabees of the navy. We can build, and we can fight."

"But we can't run," Righty sang. And they laughed some more until Tim said, "Stop. I'm hurting." He held his stomach as he tried to stop laughing.

The merchant marine was to be their final try.

"They ain't soldiers or sailors," Righty said.

"They lug guns and ammo and stuff to the fighters," Tim said. "That's good."

"Not good enough," Righty said.

"Their ships get torpedoed, and they have to swim in freezing waters," Johnny said, "and that ain't all. They have to fight off the sharks."

"That's good enough," Righty said.

But the union boss that signed up merchant marine applicants told them, "We don't got no more openings for admirals and that, and you're not tough enough for crew. Go learn something about whiskey and waa-waa women."

"You're funny as a rubber crotch," Johnny said.

"Good shot," Righty said as they ran away top speed. After all, their pursuer had a nose that looked like it was rearranged by a running motorboat prop.

"I can't figure it out," Tim said. "Instead of drafting guys who don't want to go, why not take us volunteers?"

It wasn't too long after Pearl Harbor that America declared war on Germany, giving the kids other song outlets besides "Johnny Zero is a hero today" and "the sky pilot said it. You gotta give him credit, for a son of a son of a gunner was he."

The leader of the Nazis, Adolph Hitler, was a guy with a little mustache like Charlie Chaplin with his hair combed over one side of his forehead.

"His hair is probably covering up a zit," Johnny said.

—

"Yah, his mustache covers up a hair lip," Righty said.

They loved to beat up Hitler. Whoever drew the short straw was to be Adolph Hitler. Adolph Hitler himself, which meant combing your hair down on one side of the forehead and holding a black comb on the upper lip with just enough showing to represent the black postage-stamp-size mustache.

The Hitler of the day had to sing "Sieg Heil. Sieg Heil" and goose-step about while everyone pounded him.

The Hitler-of-the-day reward was that he was allowed to sing the first verse alone before being joined by the Big Woods gang in the Nazi hail to victory—"Heil, heil, I spy Hitler at my door. If I had a submarine, I would bounce him off the bean, and there wouldn't be any Hitler anymore."

The singing of patriotic songs led to the changing of their kid games. No longer was it cowboys and Indians, a favorite. It was great as they had no trouble getting the gang to play either the cowboys or the Indians.

When they played war, it was impossible to get anyone to play a Nazi or Jap. Not even for a bribe of a Jimmy Foxx baseball card or a War Card.

Hopalong tried to get Johnny's brother, Jazz, despite Scoff's warning, to play a Jap, "Cuz he's got those big Jap buckteeth."

Scoff had warned him that Johnny had fixed his wagon. Johnny gave Hopalong a pink belly in front of their friends. He pinned him to the ground chest up and lifted his shirt upward from the waist, exposing his stomach. And then ever so gently, Johnny patted his belly and patted his belly and then patted it some more, faster and faster, until the soft pats turned the stomach a bright pink, a pink that burned like fire despite the relative softness of the hit.

But the war games ran thin at times without real humans to fight. They had made Nips and Nazis out of straw and cardboard, but it wasn't the same.

Besides, war was exhausting.

So they played cowboys and Indians. They could really get laid back. The cowboys drinking the beer and whiskey, the Indians, their firewater.

Tim was always an Indian, not because he appeared to be the color of Indians they had seen in National Geographic daguerreotypes, but because he carried himself like a great chief.

Johnny was always the sheriff, never by choice but by acclamation. He was the one they could always trust. Wasn't it up to him to check the lines on the back of the soda bottles that math genius Fats Tolland had marked out to make sure each gang member only drank as far as their allotment. There was never a complaint, and Johnny always drank last as they all sang, "Pepsi Cola, that's a lot, twice as much for a nickel too. Pepsi Cola is the drink for you. Chugger lugger, lugger, lugger, lugger, lugger, lug."

Rhesus and Boattail were always the bad guys; it sort of came natural to them. They had those great, weird, crooked, crazy smiles, not unlike a mad monkey spazzed out on an overripe banana or a parrot that partook of a bad seed.

Scoff Burke was a natural to run the saloon. His dad Bummy ran the Silver Dollar in Scollay Square, right near the Old Howard Burlesque House, that wonderful "Temple to the Tempted," as Johnny had named it.

Scoff told the gang, "I went to both the Old Howard and the casino. The casino was better. The women do more of that hoochie-coochie stuff."

"So what?" Righty said. "They must look funnier than us with those floppy things hanging from their body."

"You telling me you wouldn't like to see what Nookie Clarkson is growing on her upstairs?" Rhesus asked.

"Nah," Righty said.

"You're crazy.

"So?"

"Sew buttons on your fly."

Those words were nearly always used to end the discussion.

So Scoff went back to bartending, Tim to his tribe, Righty to the good guys, Rhesus and Boattail to the bad guys, and Johnny to his sheriffing.

So to hell with war. It was time to play cowboys and Indians. And be kids again. At least for a while.

The Big Woods Indians and cowboys got into the mood with war whoops and yippie-i-yay, kie-yaes.

Skinny Potts ran the stagecoach. It meant he could mostly sit. The bad guys loved to cut him off at the pass and hold him up (even the good guys, including the sheriff) would take a shot at a hold up since Skinny's pockets were almost always full of candy.

Romola was a dance-hall girl, Ms. Muffin and little Jazz was kid, as all cowboy movies had a dance-hall girl called Kitty and a kid called Kid.

Few of the kids went to the movies anymore. They had upped the ticket price from a dime to twelve cents. They either couldn't afford it or wouldn't pay it. But then the Rosie the riveter and other wartime employment plugged into the economy, and overnight, the ticket price went up to a quarter, and no one even blinked.

Their rifles were long sticks with a crotch at the end to fit into your shoulder that allowed you to take good aim. Sometimes a nail, if you were lucky enough to find one, was sunk into the end of the barrel and used as a gun sight. If you had a second nail, it could be the trigger.

—

The .45s were small triangles of wood they found at home construction sites. Perfect pistols.

Rhesus asked the gang, "Want to join a pistol club?"

"What do you do?"

"Drink beer till midnight and then piss to dawn."

That got him a bunch of slaps to the back of the head.

Their horses were either brooms or branches, although the very best horse was imagination.

They rode off into the hills. They rode off into the sunset and into the Big Woods, where they panned for little white stones in the tiny stream or mined for thin slices of silica in the small sandbank or embedded in a piece of ledge. "Dar's gold in dem dar hills!"

They would return to Dodge City and the Last Chance Saloon and their thirty-five pound dancing girl, Kitty, filthy rich, their gold burning holes in their pockets.

Scoff's Saloon was situated on the rear wall of the Burke's garage, where one of the boys, often Rhesus, ordered, "Bartender, set 'em up for everyone. And Kid, you go fetch Ms. Muffin. And why can't Bernadette be Ms. Love Muffin. I heard she can be a pretty fancy woman, one this dance hall could rightly use."

Gold, a white pebble, bought beer. Diamonds, a slice of silica, purchased whiskey.

The beer was water laced with some salt. Rhesus and Boattail could handle more beer than anyone.

But then again, they knew where the outside faucet of the Burke's house was hidden, behind a rhododendron and protected by an armada of sniffing bumblebees. Here they could wash the salt out of their mouths and swig clean water unbeknownst to their friends and start another round of beer, much to the admiration of their mates whose salt-laced mouths were puckered like feeding fish.

Herve Hopalong Harrison, along with Scoff, were the main whiskey drinkers. Hoppy was tops, as he had once seen his uncle the policeman tilt his head back and brag, "No one can huck one down like this good old boy."

Hopalong would order a whiskey with the words, "Think it's time to huck another one down."

It was too bad he already had a nickname as Huck would have been a natural.

The whiskey was water laced with pepper. While several tried a shot at whiskey, only Hopalong could smack his lips with pleasure after a swig. The others' best effort was a mighty sneeze. One thing for certain, during these salt-and-pepper beer-and-whiskey days, none of them had clogged sinuses.

It was Hopalong's day in the sun, the whiskey drinking. He hadn't been there in the sun since his grasshopper chawing days.

After he finished his hard drinking at Last Chance, his audience would watch him stagger out of the saloon, climb aboard his horse, and softly suggest, "Giddy-up, Whiskey, time to mosey on."

With his ten-gallon hat pulled low on his forehead covering his pepper-stung red eyes from onlookers, his parting words were "Gotta go fight redskins. They're using up all our firewater and pissing in the settlers' wells."

"Don't go stirring those Injuns up," Johnny cautioned.

"Remember the last time you did that, Whiskey Jack, Tim, ah, High Eagle, had you crying uncle when you didn't want him to scalp you with the piece of shale."

"I'm just goin' after the no-good ones."

"Okay. Happy trails to you, partner."

Later, good guys and bad guys, cowboys and Indians, would gather in the Big Woods on the Big Boulder and chew the jerky. Both boulder and woods visited years later weren't really as big as remembered during those days that they truly believed would never end.

Well, not everyone believed these days would never end. Tim Yanders's words when Boattail asked him why he planned to go to college were "You don't stay little people forever. You grow big."

But cowboys and Indians, the saloon and the giddyup was pretty much a temporary escape from a world that was centered on the war. Many an adult looked on and wished they could gallop into the Big Woods on stick horses.

There just was no escaping the war either during or after the fighting. There on the movie screen were John Payne, John Wayne, Van Johnson, Robert Walker, Richard Widmark, up there in fighter pilot goggles, marine raider camouflage, and army paratrooper jump boots.

The boys slowly moved out of their frontier days and to a war mode marching to the words, "Remember Pearl Harbor" or "Tramp, tramp, tramp the boys are marching. I spy Hitler at my door. If I had a submarine, I'd conk him off the bean, and there wouldn't be any Hitler anymore."

When they marched down Pond Street toward the Big Woods, Johnny would lead his group, pretending he was Grandpa Shiverick, singing "Start me with ten," and kids would fall in behind him. "Who are stout-hearted men?" More friends would escape from other fun and games or even chores and join him, "and I'll soon give you ten thousand more!"

—

Kids that the Big Woods gang barely knew joined in, waving their wooden swords, cap guns, sling shots, small triangles of wood representing pistols, an occasional air gun, or BB gun. Some just pointed their index finger straight out, the other three folded against their palm, with the thumb cocking their finger gun after each shot. "Pffffft!"

They traded what had been their horses to the Crusades, their cowboy horses, their pinto ponies, and roans and mustangs and appaloosas for jeeps, subs, fighter planes, tanks, and PT boats.

They came out of the trenches and marched "shoulder to shoulder, bolder and bolder . . ."

They ran up the boulder-strewn hill leading to the Big Woods, into the Big Field, where they charged an invisible enemy. Firing their tiny tree limb machine guns tossing their dirt clump grenades. Some fell heroically to the ground, seriously wounded, "I'm killed," but miraculously jumped up after a few seconds to fight on.

Being killed didn't last all that long. Then.

At times they were Jimmy Cagney or Pat O'Brien in *The Fighting 69th*, or Lew Ayers in *All Quiet on the Western Front*, or Gary Cooper in *Sergeant York*, who was everyone's favorite as he got to give turkey calls to lure Germans out of their trenches to be shot.

They weren't a pretend Fighting 69th.

They truly heard the chatter of the "bloody botch" machine guns, the explosion of enemy artillery around them eating up their comrades, the ones they didn't know.

They didn't have to be told to "Fix bayonets!" or to put on their gas masks, those giant eucalyptus leaves with eyes cut out of them, or camouflage faces, brown and green from mud and moss, neither of which hid their determined and fearless young faces.

While they had to depend on World War I movies for characters until the pictures could be updated to the present conflict, they couldn't make it into World War II fast enough.

The war to end all wars, World War I movies were fine at first.

There were no Japs in the old movies but one enemy, Germany, was still there. How come?

Although at times, the gang got confused between the spear pointed helmets of the kaiser's men and the earmuffed piss pots of Hitler's gangsters that they saw on the Pathé News.

But it didn't really matter whether they were Sgt. Bill Dane on *Bataan* or Sgt York in the Rhineland.

CHAPTER 6

MRS. MORTENSON

World War II made young boys want to get old fast so they could become soldiers.

Part of the transition of the kids was the graduation from Eastward-Ho Elementary to Rockledge Junior-Senior High School. This signaled that teenage time was upon them. There was the first manly removal by razor of hair on the upper lip for the boys: a great moment.

It was the crying time for the girls who discovered hair on and between their legs.

Then there were the first puffs of a Wings cigarette behind the school for both boys and girls. Each had its own hangout. One difference was that the boys saved the cards depicting airplanes tucked inside the package cellophane while the girls either tried out their power on boys by giving them their cards or their disdain for boys by tearing the cards in half.

There was also some sort of stirring that both girl and boy felt. It felt good and it felt painful. Stirrings that were very disturbing as they had no apparent basis.

They had been the big guys that final year at Eastward-Ho. At the junior-senior high school, they were the little guys, seventh graders at the bottom of the pile. They had gone from king of the hill to Humpty Dumpty.

Although they were allowed to hang out on the fringes of the big men of the upper class who realized that having hangers-on on didn't hurt their status and also provided background laughter to their jokes.

It gave the Big Woods gang a sniff of the good stuff to come. If only they could get older, faster.

At this level they were finally ready for . . . dirty jokes.

The grammar school jokes were funny at the time. They were funny a second time; later they laughed at how juvenile their jokes had been.

Johnny remembered the first one he ever heard, at least the first he understood.

They were jokes by his uncle Manny DaSilva about the woman with the cluttered clitoris and the one with the vulgar vulva. Johnny had a little idea what a clitoris and vulva were, but did not understand the one he heard come from his uncle while he peeked through the kitchen door where his father, Manny, and Francesco played cards. "You hear about the American that married the Chinese girl who didn't want to do it until they were married. So she made him into a lotus eater."

Johnny was positive about the word "clitoris." It was some sort of thesaurus.

He loved to look up words. Ms. O'Malley, way back in elementary school, had them learn three new words a week. He even remembered the first three. His favorites, lugubrious, ludicrous, lucrative. He had hoped at that time to become ludicrously lucrative so his ma would not have to be lugubrious about not having enough money for both the rent and food. He was proud as hell of that sentence. Maybe he could work with words, be a printer or something.

He was also positive that a vulva was a car that came from Norway or Sweden.

The first dirty joke he understood came from Righty when he first transferred from the South to the Eastward-Ho School.

Righty asked him, "Want to hear a dirty joke?" but without waiting for an okay, he said, "Two white horses fell in a mud puddle."

"It sounds like some young kid made it up."

A week later, Righty had another joke, a much more mature one. "What made the Little Red Tomato blush?" and without waiting for an "I don't know," Righty said, "She saw Mr. Green Pea."

The very first influx of jokes that greeted them in junior high was more mature and told only by the big kids, "You hear about the book *Tiger's Revenge* by Claude Balls or *Yellow Stream* by I. P. Freely?

"Then there was *Bloody Stump* by the great Russian author Bityacockoff and *Open Kimono* by I. C. Moore."

Suddenly the new kids felt pressure to come up with jokes. The presentations were pressure packed. If the joke was a dud, it was greeted by boos or, worse, silence, with the listeners giving a Colosseum-type thumbs down.

The first one to break through the joke barrier into the big time was Rhesus. With what seemed like a hundred sisters and brothers in a one bathroom house, he got a lot of shots . . . big deal . . . of his sisters rushing around in their underwear.

"What's the strongest thing in the world?"

Not receiving an answer, Rhesus said, "A brassiere, it holds up two milk factories."

It got more than a good laugh from the group of upper classmen; it got a thumbs-up from a senior.

Johnny couldn't figure out what was funny. *What in heck is a . . . bra . . . zee . . . air? What's it got to do . . . with a hoods or whitings milk . . . factories . . . because they had good . . . foundations . . . of their own?*

Righty told his friend what a brassiere was and what the milk factories referred to.

Oh my good . . . god . . . I'm spending too much time . . . playing sports . . . and . . . working . . .

Soupy was next to get a schoolyard lunchtime thumbs-up. Holding his index fingers at the corners of his eyes and lifting them upward to give himself an oriental look and in his very best imitation of a Chinese voice, said, "Confucius say, 'Woman who fly in airplane upside down will have crack up.' Ah, so."

"What's so funny about a plane crashing with a woman in it?" Righty asked.

"You are an ah, so, a flaming one," the all-knowing Boattail said to Righty, giving him a friendly shove.

"So solly. So fluckin' solly. You plick Boattail."

Now they all laughed, even Righty. There is just something about a slight Italian accent inherited from Italian-born parents combined with a Japanese inflection.

Soupy wanted to get in on the laugh wagon and chanted, head cocking from side to side as he walked, "Clickity-clack, went her crack, as she walked down the railroad track." He got a thumbs down from his Roman friends of the Big Woods Colosseum and immediately became the resident Christian, Scoff and Fats the lions. Soupy laughed as they chewed his ear and the back of his neck.

"You know Chinese girls' down below," Righty said with authority, "well, it goes sideways instead of up and down like American women."

"How do you know?" Rhesus demanded, figuring Righty was impinging on his status as resident doctor, which he claimed he had played with numerous patients, and was resident sex fiend. The claim was backed up by a smile one would expect from a lecherous orangutan.

"A guy who saw Nookie's told me."

"Who in hell is Nookie?"

"Bernadette Clarkson."

"Who saw her thing."

"Everybody."

"Did you?"

"Naw."

"So how do you know a China women's stuff down there, her thing, grows sideways?"

"The Chinaman's son, who starches my dad's white shirts, told him. And then he wanted a nickel when I said, 'Prove it.'"

"It's probably the truth," well-known mathematics genius Fats Tolland said, "I overheard a couple math teachers talking about Ms. Timmons, the senior's math teacher. They said she is so deep into geometry that her nether part is slanted in on an obtuse angle like Ms. Loo's."

Johnny was confused by the talk about female parts that he knew nothing about and apparently his friends knew everything about.

Johnny truly believed that it was a search for knowledge rather than sexual curiosity that turned part of his mind from the joy of sports and the exhaustion of setting pins late at night and delivering papers in the early morning to this area of darkness.

First it was Mrs. Mortenson, a friend of the Shiverick family, then Mrs. Scranton, who was a customer on his paper route, that filled in a few pages of his then empty life log on ladies.

His efforts started at 4:15 a.m. with his folding of the papers to put in the paper bag that hung over the handlebars of his Western Flyer. The bike was the gift of Aunt Hope, who said, "You can pay me back later as you deliver more papers. Don't worry. It's not a handout. You can tell your ma that."

It was Johnny's pride and joy, that red and white beauty with the balloon tires, and the tank between the bars of the body that housed a horn and extras such as the modern-looking headlight on top of the front fender, the bell on the handlebars, the mud flaps, the wire newspaper carrier that rode on top the front wheel.

The papers were folded in different shapes, always with a little tuck at the end that kept it locked in.

The shorter tosses were merely folded in half. Longer ones called for a tighter folding, to just about the size of a stick of dynamite. The long throws were folded into a very tight triangle. And they would sail.

—

Mrs. Mortenson was a different case. She was a family friend. It was while she was visiting with Johnny's mother and aunts, Faith and Hope, having a morning cup of tea when the incident took place. Actually it was a half cup of tea and half cup of milk. "That's the way we English drink it," Faith said.

Hope gave her a highfalutin "Ta ta."

Faith, Hope, and Charity agreed that tea kept them thin, but Mrs. Mortenson disagreed and started a little combination tap dance and slide-together-step waltz while singing, "It's sin, sin, sin, that keeps you mighty thin," as she reached into the fruit bowl that always centered the giant oak lion's paw table.

Johnny peeked from behind the pantry door where he had been searching for one of Grandma Shiverick's homemade gingersnaps, which she often forgot to put away, knowing of his searches.

Mrs. Mortenson had picked out two grapefruits and stuck them inside the top of her dress to the delight of the sisters, who feigned shock.

Johnny had never seen his mother and aunts act so giddy. *Why . . . what's . . . with the . . . the grapefruits?*

Mrs. Mortenson's dance had lost its embarrassed overtones, more and more so as what had been grapefruits now appeared to be her giant breasts, which flowed in great circles, first to one side and then the other. She changed the action of her shoulders, and now they soared upward to her shoulders and down to her navel.

Johnny thought it was hilarious until Mrs. Mortenson started cupping the grapefruits in her hands as she danced, lifting one upward, then the other, then pushing both to one side and then the other. Then squeezing them together, throwing her head back, eyes closed, lashes fluttering. Giving them a super squeeze, and in her best Mae West voice moaned, "Here's juice in your eyes, Big Boy."

It was then she spotted Johnny through the tiny slits of her closed eyes. She was the only one that saw him peeking through the opening between the door and the door casing.

She did not stop her dance when she saw him. Instead she opened her eyes wide, then slowly closed them and smiled to herself.

He saw a piece of spittle form on her lips dangle . . . onto her breasts. The grapefruits had fallen out. What remained in their place were plentiful and dark protrusions appearing in the center of each. The sisters laughed and buried their faces in their hands. Johnny didn't laugh.

His eyes burned, watered. *It's the real ones . . . those must be . . . grapes . . . sprouting on their . . . tips . . . At last . . . I've seen some . . . I won't tell . . . anyone, Mrs. Mortenson . . .*

—

He felt a warmth and strangeness that he didn't understand. He squeezed his legs together, bunching up the contents in the crotch of his shorts painfully. Yet good painful.

She stuck her hand inside her dress top, slowly rearranging her breasts then cupped them, jumping on her toes to make them move like little girls jumping rope.

Then she laughed uproariously, supposedly with her friends. She stooped, picked up the grapefruits. Rolled them toward the open door of the pantry. "Strike one." She laughed. "It looks like one pin standing." The sisters roared, not realizing she could see Johnny's erection through the crack in the door.

"You missed your calling," Faith said.

Johnny used the opportunity to slink out of the pantry, carefully opening the screen door and closing it just as carefully before making his escape to the Big Woods.

Even in the cool air, out of the confines of the closeness of the pantry, he still felt a disturbing warmth. A warmth different than that of working a farm field at high noon or running the bases on a steaming July day.

The sensation bothered him for some time. *Why?*

The next time he had that feeling was when he was delivering the *Christian Science Monitor* to Mrs. Scranton.

He had always wondered if she was one of those very religious persons, like a nun or the pope or even like his grandfather Shiverick. She must be . . . Otherwise why would she take a paper named . . . Christian? If she's a Christian . . . like Grandpa . . . she's a good . . . woman . . .

That Christmas she gave him a dollar tip and spoke her first words to him, "Here's a little something extra for you to put in the collection plate at church. You are getting to be such a big young man."

He wanted to save the dollar for his dentist so he could try to save one of his aching teeth. Or rather add it to the pennies he saved under his mattress to have the dentist straighten Jazz's protruding teeth.

He ended up placing it in the collection plate that Sunday.

While she didn't tip the rest of the year, Mrs. Scranton always gave him a big smile when she paid for the paper with the words, "I always like to give a smile as a little something extra. It just goes to prove the best things in life are free. You're growing into such a tall young man."

On the morning of the errant newspaper toss, he walked quietly along her porch so as not to creak the boards and wake her up, but he didn't have to worry about waking her this morning.

She was awake. And he could see her dark shadow as she walked toward the refrigerator.

—

Then the refrigerator door was opened. Its light turned on. At first all he saw was her arm reaching in for the milk bottle, but when she lifted her head backward and drank from the bottle, he saw the refrigerator light on her body. It danced on her as she partially opened and closed the door, displaying her in an old-time jerky-frame silent movie.

She had a white sheer covering on. All he could think of was mosquito netting. Transparent. *Oh god . . . you can . . . see . . . through it . . .*

Her breasts appeared to expand, like circus balloons being inflated by an invisible milkman as she drank the milk. *Will they burst . . . if she . . . drinks . . . the whole thing?*

He could see the dark tips. The color and shape of the acorns he fired from his slingshot. As she guzzled the milk, head way back, her hair hanging and swishing like a mare's tail, her breasts seemed to continue to swell. And he wanted to help the invisible milkman inflate them. *Could you inflate her . . . through those . . . acorn tips? What would they . . . taste like? Would they burn?*

Johnny knew he was just supposed to walk away. *Walk away . . . dear God . . . help me . . . walk away . . .* He turned away, but only partially, glancing back he held his hands over his eyes, but peeked through his fingers.

He could now see that under the gauze she had panties on. He had seen panties hanging from clotheslines, but this was different. *She's wearing them . . .*

But here they were. The panties. With someone, a woman, Mrs. Scranton, the *Christian Science Monitor* woman, in them.

They were stretched across her hips, transparent like the gauze that stretched tight against her chest. There was a deep darkness down there. Like a tiny inverted fir tree.

He started to leave. Didn't. *I'm a . . . rotten . . . sick dog . . . Please Lord . . . help me . . . to leave . . . Help me . . . oooh . . .*

Johnny watched as a small strange smile formed on Mrs. Scranton's face, an inner smile that froze him. He was certain she did not know he was there. The smile was tender, clean, like the smile of an angel. Almost.

She knew he was there, almost gave her thoughts away by speaking out loud. "The cute little . . . puppy . . . with the bulging pants . . . Shame on you . . . naughty puppy . . ."

Johnny had only seen such a smile on a face once before.

It was in an art appreciation book. A woman called Mona Lisa wore it. He had felt strange then, but the way she was clothed was as if she had been outfitted at a store where nuns bought their clothes. Her smile served as her wimple.

—

Now Mrs. Scranton's smile changed to that of a cougar salivating over the rabbit hooked on its claws quivering. It was the very same type of smile Mrs. Mortenson had when she spotted Johnny behind the pantry door as she did her dance of the seven veils and two grapefruits.

Then her smile changed again as she stretched under the light of the now fully open refrigerator door, like a sleepy milk-fed cat, arms bent backward overhead, causing her breasts to stampede. Their wet black noses the size of half dollars, galloped down on him. Apocalypse now.

He knew she couldn't see him there in the deep shadows.

She leaned back further, thrusting her hips forward, causing a dark forest fire of hair to appear at the crotch that formed a large triangle about the size of a nicely folded man's dark silk handkerchief.

He couldn't walk away now, a lynch pin hog tied him despite his sure knowledge that he would burn in hell forever for taking advantage of a woman's privacy. Her right to drink from a milk bottle, to innocently stretch away her sleep. *Without some pervert . . . like me . . . taking advantage of . . . her . . . moments of innocence . . .*

He worried that the whistling of his corduroy trousers would be heard. He squeezed his knees and thighs tighter together, faster and faster, like two sticks being rubbed together to start a fire.

His tried to will his legs the strength to move him from the window, out of the darkness. *Should I knock on the door . . . and . . . confess?*

He couldn't knock on the door in the condition he suffered. *She will be able . . . to see . . . the condition . . . I'm in . . .*

He was on fire. He tried to think of the time he broke through the rubber ice at Bucket Pond, his shivering, how tiny he was down there when he took off the icy clothes. About the size of his little finger and as wrinkled as the old nun who always yelled at his grandfather Shiverick and chanted that he would "burn in hell for a thousand eternities."

Johnny knew he should roll in the snow. Or hack a hole through the ice at Bucket Pond and immerse his private part in it. Or swim under the ice. Stay there. *Until God forgives me . . . or I drown in my own . . . scum . . .*

Despite the self-initiated frigid thoughts and winter cold, he still felt like all the heat bugs of July were rubbing their legs together, their ink-black pinpoint eyes getting ever smaller and brighter until the leg rubbing caused them to hiss out a high-pitched siren drone of pain.

Johnny was shocked, frightened that perhaps God had paralyzed him for his sin. He had stopped and moved to a place in the dark so he could again stare through the window, watching Mrs. Scranton.

She appeared to be rubbing between her legs. Perhaps it was like scratching your ribs when you first wake up.

—

Now. It was him rubbing himself.

Had the rubbing made him grow even more? Was his it watching her too. *Is it as sinister as me? Maybe I just have to . . . pee . . .*

Sometimes when he held his piss while playing baseball or in church, it grew down there. A piss hard-on, the guys called them.

But it never burned.

Johnny watched as Mrs. Scranton cupped her breasts, thrusting them upward, causing them to spill sideways out of the gauze, coming to rest in her armpits. Like the five ball in the corner . . . pocket . . .

What was she doing? Is it a religious . . . exercise? Maybe . . .

She saw him!

She held up her right hand, palm up, and moved her index finger back and forth. Beckoning him.

She was going to arrest him. *She's going to . . . call the police . . . call my mother . . . call Grandfather Shiverick . . . call God . . . to have me put away . . . forever . . .*

He turned and ran, ran with only the speed fear can deliver.

Mrs. Scranton's Mona Lisa smile changed. The slow, sleepy smile was still there, but her lower lip pouted forward. Then her eyes closed slowly, as one hand dropped down, located the top of her panties, slid slowly downward to that dark area between her legs to her tiny uncared-for penilelike erection, the beak of a small bird seeking to sup.

She cursed aloud as she cared for her needs, "The frightened little shit." *Just as well . . . a lady could go to jail . . . for touching young shit . . .*

Then she moaned and rested her head against the refrigerator.

Close to its interior light. The light exposed the aging deep lines that surrounded her eyes, the erosion of her upper lip that made her lip to appear like wave lines left in the sand by a receding tide. Her chin had started to sag. Someday it will hang . . . like an oriole's nest . . . She released a pathetic cry.

She saw this reflection in the kitchen clock mirror. *I must remember . . . to hold my chin high . . . let them think that I'm . . . haughty . . . yes . . . let them think that I'm haughty . . .*

She fitted herself against the refrigerator handle. And muttered to herself as she set up a rhythm against the handle, almost snarling, "That filthy little boy. Taking advantage of a poor unprotected woman. Doesn't he know what God does to people like him? I'm sure his young thing was much too small anyway. The filthy little dog. And me, practically a virgin."

Her moan was not so much one of released passion as it was of pent-up despair.

As was Johnny's in the dark of a nearby bush.

CHAPTER 7

WE POKE ALONG NO LONGER

Uncle Sam sent the Shiverick and DaSilva uncles home from the Civilian Conservation Corps so they could turn to Uncle Sam and be among the first to battle in World War II. Their CCC loden uniforms They wore in their conservation work projects were traded for navy blue, army brown; and marine corps red, white, and blue.

With the outbreak of World War II, Johnny's uncles returned home from the alphabet outfits—the CCC, the WPA. The Civilian Conservation Corps planted trees around watersheds while the Works in Progress Agency built new roads. The work programs of President Roosevelt weren't needed now. The workers were needed on other projects.

There was war work, building tanks, and ships and planes. And ambulances. And coffins. There was too much work for too few men. Things like production lines and women welders like Rosy the Riveter were about to be invented.

Men from all walks of work were needed to man the tanks, ships, and planes, and then transport the young broken bodies home. The unemployed were first ready to go, followed by those exploding with patriotism and draftees.

It was easy for the CCC young men to adjust to the uniforms of the various services. They had been wearing the green of the CCC for several years. WPA workers found it a pleasure to get away from the work overalls and signs stating, "Another WPA Program in Action" and into the rainbow of military uniforms.

A short while earlier, they were doing what the few rich or working termed "pretend work," fulfilling the mocking slogan of the WPA—"We Poke Along," but many of the "New Deal" projects were to last for decades.

Despite the success of the Roosevelt programs, many wore the "No Third Term" political button and insisted "the Roosevelt efforts were programs that didn't work." They were projects "where the shovels wore the loafers."

What was forgotten by FDR's opponent was that the CCC and WPA workers voted, as did their families, and he was a shoo-in.

When Johnny visited the CCC camp of Manny, Francesco, and Johnny's father, he was proud of how they looked in their forest-green uniforms, planting their trees in straight rows that appeared to be legions of soldiers.

The pup tents, lean-tos and rough cabins they pitched or built to live in were very romantic to Johnny. They were much like those movies of the The Fighting 69th and The Charge of the Light Brigade and tintype photos of the Union troops waiting to fight at Gettysburg. He could hardly wait to join them. Meanwhile, he would sleep in Righty Minichelli's Boy Scout tent.

The Shivericks, Matt, Mark, Luke, and even old John built roads for the WPA. Johnny saw them covered with dirt and dust from the pick swinging and the smashing of the steel point into rock-hard soil and old tarmac roads that spewed tar spitballs into the air. The pick swings often would strike a no-give rock, sending shivers up their arms into their heads. Their shovels were often worked to the point where the blade edges were broken or cracked, giving them the appearance of uncared-for teeth.

The boys and men of the WPA were in great condition for digging foxholes, battle ditches, and gun abutments to fight from and slit trenches to shit in.

The Shiverick and DaSilva men joined up to fight Hitler and Hirohito to "crush the Krauts," "cut the nuts off the Nips."

Posters sprung up everywhere—"Loose Lips Sink Ships," "The Yanks Are Coming," "Uncle Sam Wants You!"

Popping up first were the old films of Pat O'Brien and Jimmy Cagney, Gary Cooper, and Lew Ayres, heroes in The Fighting 69th, Sergeant York, All Quiet on the Western Front.

Later the World War I epics were replaced by World War II flicks with John Wayne, Robert Taylor, Henry Fonda, and Jimmy Stewart in From Here to Eternity, Bataan, Guadalcanal Diary, Back to Bataan, Battle of the Bulge, Twelve O'Clock High.

Many of the 4F movie stars that played the hero parts at times had to be killed on film to point out what sorry ass bad guys the enemy were. Those selected to fall in battle only did so after taking ten to a hundred enemy with them. When critically wounded, the results were nice, clean wounds. The movie stars wounded were that they got to make a speech before dying, rather than screaming out of control, cursing God and their mothers for bearing them, their guts slithering out of their bellies like slimy green and blue snakes. And of course, those on the screen got to get wounded over and over again. There weren't enough stars to go around as many were off fighting.

A few of the actors played the part of a hero leading an army, yelling to their men, "Follow me, men!" before actually going off to war. There was no more playacting, and most were fighting as buck-ass privates. They found themselves as not only a single ant, but also as a frightened lone ant in a warring colony where multiples moved forward over you, then marched backward over you carrying the dead and wounded.

They tried to make themselves as small as an ant, as quiet as a pismo clam when the chef selected the next batch for chowder. As often as not, some little bowlegged guy, helmet almost falling over his eyes, gave a lunatic yell through the smoke and thunder, "Follow me, men!" And they did.

Some calls to action weren't quite so romantic—"We've got no choice. Come on." "Keep your bandy asses down. Don't shit your pants."

Most didn't feel like men, rather they felt like frightened little children that wished they were in the arms of their mothers being rocked as they listened to the crooning, "Rock-a-by baby, on the treetop, when the wind blows, the cradle will rock."

All they knew was they didn't want to "fall down, cradle and all." Often they thought as they moved out, not believing they were actually walking into machine gun and artillery fire that could rip them to pieces or evaporate them, *Asshole . . . asshole plus one . . . I'm coming . . . but not up front . . . maybe . . . if I keep this guy between me . . . and the bullets . . .*

Often they believed the thud they heard was a bullet hitting that guy advancing in front of them until they worked up the courage to look down and saw the blood pouring from what was a navel. A navel that was once connected to their umbilical cord that had been attached to their mother. *Ma . . . please help . . . me . . .*

If a movie star made it home from combat to make movies again, he promised God he never again would speak the words, "Follow me, men" or make a long romantic speech when taking a nice, clean movie star bullet to the shoulder. Rather than blinding, boiling shrapnel to the eyes or cleaned

—

away genitalia when a Bouncing Betty land mine was stepped on and sprung crotch high.

The war movies were very uplifting in that the Nazi and Nips were stacked up like cord wood, their blood running like sap in the spring, while we were careful to limit our dead hero numbers to two best friends hugging each other in their final minutes.

No one wondered why a Japanese soldier came out of flame-thrower-torched caves burning alive while our movie stars got to light up a Camel cigarette, write a letter to Mom, and then fantasize about dying in the arms of their old girlfriends, who, in some cases, were out with their new boyfriend. It was never decided whether going over or remaining home was more painful and called for greater sacrifices.

This was important, that the young moviegoers realize that their hero wasn't really killed and that he would indeed fight again. The hero star was needed to recruit young men to replace the suddenly old young men or suddenly dead young men.

It just didn't pay to have someone among the potential recruit crowd whispering, "I thought he was killed in *Back to Bataan*."

Patriotic songs were on the lips of all the kids. "Praise the Lord and pass the ammunition. Praise the Lord, I ain't a goin' fishin'. Praise the Lord and pass the ammunition, and we'll all stay free. The tail gunner said it. You've gotta give him credit, for a son of a gun of a gunner was he." Even the clergy was allowed to man a Flying Fortress gun turret and mow down the enemy as long as they said, "Praise the Lord."

These were the movies and songs Johnny and his friends saw, heard, and sang. They didn't see the tiny ant soldiers with slithering intestines, other ants with blood and shit-covered boots marching in their faces, with some heading to the front going "baaaa" and those dying in no-man's-land, crying "Maaaaa."

The kids liked their own songs rather than the ones on the radio. More marching action. "Tramp, tramp, tramp the boys are marching, I spy Hitler at my door. If I had a submarine, I would bonk him off the bean, and there wouldn't be any Hitler anymore." Little thought was given to how much size and strength would be needed to bonk Hitler off the bean with a submarine. For Christ sakes, John Wayne couldn't even accomplish such a feat. *Or . . . could . . . he . . .*

Who had time to question why? The kids just wanted to do or die after hearing the radio voice sing, "Johnny zero got a zero today."

The kids had their own ditties. "There's a German in the grass, with a bullet up his ass. Pull it out, pull it out, pull it out. Pull it out. Leave it in."

When they ran out of navy and army songs, they roamed far afield. "Salvation Army, Salvation Army, put a nickel on the drum, save another drunken bum—Salvation Armeeeeeee."

Johnny didn't like his friends singing the Salvation Army ditty but knew they meant nothing by it. They knew it rhymed and was great for marching about.

Salvation Army . . . He had stood tall and proud with his grandfather Shiverick on the winter wind-whipped street corners. He pictured his grandfather in his blue, nearly black, Salvation Army uniform with the red piping and that great cap, sort of like the marine corps dress blues, standing straight and tall, a soldier of the Lord. When his friends sang "put a nickel on the drum," he thought of other songs he'd rather sing and sometimes sang to himself, "Stand up . . . stand up for Jesus . . . ye soldiers of the . . . cross . . ."

Other times when they sang, "Put a nickel on the drum," he would say, "Knock it off," and they did. And no one knew why they stopped, not even Johnny.

Perhaps they had seen the old man looking skyward as he rang the "Please give," "Thank you," Salvation Army handbell; perhaps it was out of respect to the memory that he had painted their shoes a bright blue or buttercup yellow when they were the cobblestone kids that followed his paint cart as he sang, "For I cherish the old rugged cross," and they had pounded their tin can drums and cymbal trash can covers.

And then again, perhaps they stopped singing, "Help another drunken bum," as Johnny had a reputation besides that of not being a trouble maker, he had the fastest fists in town.

Few passed without depositing a coin in the black pot that hung there on the tripod where Grandfather Shiverick stood. It wasn't only that most realized the charity was one of the good ones. There was the vintage of the white-haired old man with the fierce eyes set further on fire by the craggy eyebrows that hung down like icicles. His giant flowing mustache appeared to be trying to take off, wing heavenward, as he sang, "Onward Christian soldiers, marching as to war, with the cross of Jesus, going on before." While he soared like Icarus, his mustache wax didn't melt; he did not fall to earth.

Johnny had the feeling at times that his grandfather was an Icarus that not only would reach the heavens, but would also soar higher. Past God himself . . .

But Johnny recanted this higher-than-heaven feeling. *I don't want to . . . piss God off . . .*

His grandfather did all the pissing off that was needed. A hard glare was sent to the well-dressed, portly passerby who pretended to be reaching for a coin but who, at the last moment, diverted his view in the opposite direction and kept his hands in pockets that were obviously lined with fishhooks.

The Salvation Army colonel had talked to him about glaring at nongivers, and there was his reported "You'll burn in hell" aimed at the Beau Brummel, who flashed a big bill, pretended to insert it in the bucket in front of an admiring audience, but who, at the last moment, palmed it and later return it to his wallet.

But the old man didn't mend his ways. So the colonel let it drop. After all, the old man raised more money than any ten of God's goody-two-shoes soldiers combined.

The colonel determined the final result, alms for the poor, was the goal. And it was better not to look a gift horse in the mouth than to accuse him of a hee-haw.

The old man, when someone walked by the swinging pot without making even a penny donation and couldn't even look him in the face, would chime, "Thank you brother, sister." Once stung such, the nondonors either made their exodus from the store by another door or gave, even if it was the two bits they planned to use for a sip of suds at Dooligan's on the way home.

Whenever Johnny heard a Salvation Army handbell calling from a swinging donation pot, he would gravitate in that direction.

When it was his grandfather, he would slip quietly up to him and take the old man's age-spot littered hand. He never forgot the gentle squeeze of the powerful yet tender hands, the hands that held the forty-foot wooden ladder straight up into the air, keeping the top from touching the freshly painted house.

Grandfather Shiverick would hold the ladder steady as Johnny climbed upward, with the wet paintbrush in one hand, to put that dab on the small area that had been missed, that very highest point secreted in the apex of the gable end where no one would ever see the bare spot.

Johnny had told his grandfather, "No one will see it there, Grandfather."

"I would."

Johnny couldn't have felt any safer if he was a dove in the hands of the Savior as he climbed upward on that wooden ladder, its rungs bowing slightly even under his lightweight.

He felt like he was climbing to heaven although he realized that it would be a little more natural if he worried about shitting his pants, as

—

174

the high end of the ladder etched Foucault pendulum circles in the sky, showing indeed the earth's rotation.

There were times the ladder top caused his brush strokes to go wild in the air like the baton of an insane maestro while it moved as if it was being held down below by an exhausted Whirling Dervish. *Grandfather . . . would never let me . . . fall . . . steady . . . steady . . . We did it, Grandfather . . . We did it . . .*

One night after one of these high-in-the-sky gable touch-ups, Johnny's dad, home from the Sun Shipyard for the weekend, looked in on his son. He saw the boy on his knees praying softly to God.

Tony gently closed the door and went down the dark stairs, carefully feeling with his foot for the two missing steps.

"I'm worried about our son," he said to his Charity. "I think he prays too much. I hope the world doesn't take advantage of him."

"I wish all fathers had the same he-prays-too-much worry," she replied.

Johnny always was so very proud whenever he had the chance to go to the top of the ladder and do a touch-up. He trusted his grandfather; his grandfather trusted him.

The only time Johnny was prouder than being on the ladder top, sometimes with grown-ups oohing and aahing far below, was when standing with his grandfather as the old man's Salvation Army bell beckoned givers, his voice clearer than the bell itself, or in church where Mr. John Shiverick's God-propelled voice rattled the single church chandelier as he sang his favorite, "For I cherish the Old Rugged Cross" in a voice that boiled out of the bowels of hell and raised itself to the heavens.

His singing even snapped old Mrs. Stronson out of her legendary narcolepsy in the rear row of pews. Rumor in town had it that her sleep was so deep that the town medical examiner had once declared her legally dead.

Johnny always found his grandfather in the same pew on the aisle end. He would walk up and gently take his hand, not looking up until he felt the gentle squeeze from the huge hand.

Then he would peer upward and see the song tearing its way through the giant white mustache like lightning splitting the clouds. *Someday . . . I will sing . . . that way . . .*

And he would someday sport such a grand white mustache. And the kids will . . . wish . . . they could grow something like . . . this . . . And he would twirl his fingers on both ends of the mustache that wasn't there.

Concentration in church wasn't a given. Johnny would at times vacillate between the world of God and the vision of angels and cherubs

—

at his side or to visions of a long-legged, blue-eyed, red-headed Maureen O'Hara or a sloe-eyed, dark-eyed Yvonne DiCarlo. Then he felt a sort of heavenly stirring involving very different kinds of angels. The movie stars' faces and long legs, in helter-skelter fashion, took turns providing different bodies for Mrs. Scranton, always a pew away.

Maureen's and Yvonne's heads would be on Mrs. Scranton's body. While the movie stars' bodies moved in the stuttering fashion of the year's dead silent movie, the true female parishioner's body had the slow, undulating rhythm of a brook trout marking time in slow waters with the slight movements of its tail.

Both sides of this two-faced angel coin slithered across his body, one side leaving him lightheaded with love for God and the other leaving him in a condition down below.

If his mother or aunts spotted it, it would lead to a caning that would have made an old teacher's ruler raps seem like love taps.

He wondered what these diametrically opposite feelings were all about. The angels made sense. God made sense. He had been taught this all his life. He remembered just how early he was taught about God. It was even before, as a small boy, he had giggled at his first fart, or at least the first he remembered, and hoped that he would be able to do more of them in the future. More rapid. Louder. Perhaps even some farts in Technicolor. Until someday he would learn to throw his farts like some can throw their voices. Then he could always get a seat in a diner. Or even better, be good enough to fart in church and then throw it in the direction of some grown-up who had been snooty to him. I couldn't do it . . . Grandpa Shiverick . . . would be ashamed of . . . me . . . but it would be fun . . .

The other feeling left him unsure. He knew nothing about it, that thinking of Maureen O'Hara in a torn pirate blouse, a skirt where a pirate's sword caused a slit that showed a leg as slender yet as muscular as a wild mustang mare.

Following such disturbing church thoughts, he often returned home and climbed the stairs in a quandary. Forgetting the missing stairs, his feet skipped out of memory, and he flopped on his back in his bed where he tossed and turned. The angels and the provocative ladies battled it out among the water stains in the ceiling.

His aunt Hope had turned to Faith in church one day during one of Johnny's wonder moments. "Did you see what I saw?"

"No."

"Good." *I feel so sorry for Johnnie . . . with Portuguese genitalia . . . and English conscience . . . trousers wetter than a tomcat . . . that fell in a brook . . .*

His first such incident in church left him completely confused. Was this the high point of his young life, a true challenge to win out over evil. Or was it some kind of low point?

He pictured Grandfather Shiverick singing to God, and then God and his grandfather looking down on him and smiling as he waved his conductor's baton for the old man and the heavenly choir. It was like walking in the clouds. *Seraphims . . . and cherubims . . . holding my hands . . .*

But what's with the baton . . . in my hand . . . changing to my pecker . . . in church . . . sick . . . sick, sick . . . help melees . . .

The rhythm and pulsations of the church's old wooden pipe organ seemed to have caught up with Mrs. Scranton as well on that day. The *Christian Science Monitor* lady was across the aisle from Johnny. Two rows down. Moving very slowly to the music.

She never seemed to pulsate like that when he handed her the only Monitor on his morning paper route.

Mrs. Scranton was certainly pulsating this church day.

She raised her hands high over her head, reaching for heaven, pulling the top of her dress taunt against her breasts, palms outspread, standing almost on tiptoes. The calves of her legs flexed and unflexed to the rhythm of the organ, an organ that had taken on a Haitian quality. Her buttocks penetrated by a Voodoo pin had brought them to life as wild as the helplessly quivering thighs of a mare in heat.

She had told him once when she counted out the five nickels to pay for her *Christian Science Monitor* weekly bill, "Twenty one cents for the paper, and four cents for the nice little Christian young man who delivers it."

Johnny watched her slender fingers, the nails deep red, as she slowly dropped the coins into his open palm that day. Touching the middle of his palm with her finger nail as she dropped each coin. Her fingernail felt like a spike being driven through his palm. *Oh . . . Jesus . . . she's a . . . holy lady . . .*

Now here he was in church, watching her. Feeling different down there. *Me . . . the nice Christian young man . . . who delivers . . . it . . . the paper . . .*

It was on that day that she dropped the coins in near-stop-time slow motion into his palm that she confessed that even on icy days, she made her way to church, a two-mile walk, to listen to his grandfather singing. "His voice is driven by bellows and pipes that indeed at times appear cowers the organ itself. Causing something to enter deep inside. Something heavenly."

—

It was her holy movements that battled the old man's voice for Johnny's attention that day, leaving the preachings of the Reverend Mr. Newhall a weak third.

The steam from the church's old radiators appeared to be the spewings of the devil's own heat.

The radiator cranked and groaned and often rumbled like a string of bowel-deep movements of peristalsis.

Johnny tried to put the radiator rousers out of his mind. *I'm mired deep enough . . . as is . . .*

Putting the whoopee cushion noises out of his mind wasn't that easy when his cousin Dink Gouveira attended church with him. Dink did not provide the slightest effort to hide the mile-wide shit-eating grin when the radiator's releases gave birth in his imagination.

Dink willed that Johnny also think of flatulence on these days, farts, past, present, and future. While Johnnie fought Dink's lead, in the back of his mind, he understood it was a way to speed the lagging church service by.

Dink, Pointer, and he had great names for their variety of releases from the simple "There's a stinger-singer for you" to "Who released the purple poots-en-popper."

Whatever the title, the fart was followed by certain rituals, such as calling out to each other, "I one it."

"I two it."

"I three it."

"I four it."

"I five it."

"I six it."

"I seven it."

Never, never, ever did the person whose turn it was declare, "I eight it." But there was always a volunteer to say, "You ate it. You ate the fart."

Johnny had no problem tempting his good Catholic cousins Dink and Pointer to attend the Protestant sermons as the Reverend Mr. Newhall, while scurrying to the high point of his sermon, was at times wont to flatulence.

The cousins loved this. In fact, they were once given to applause, which drew some very heavy looks in their direction.

They loved the looks. And they loved to inform Johnny that their pastor, Father Lavasseleur, never farted during his sermon at St. Paul's. And not only that, he never burped, even after doing in half the decanter of wine used in Communion.

Johnny had retorted, "How would you know if he did the dirty noises? Priests burp and fart in Latin."

—

While Dink and Pointer got their kicks on Route 66, from the Reverend Mr. Newhall's Protestant gaseous sermons and body functions, Johnny got his Catholic kicks on another level.

Egged on by his cousins, he would go to confession and confess the most outlandish things he could think of. "Forgive me, Father, for I have sinned. I farted in the bathtub. And then broke the bubbles with my mouth."

Johnnie wasn't sure if the owner of the voice in the confessional was deaf or just didn't listen. "Go and sin no more, my son."

"Do you mean go and fart no more, Father?" That usually brought the owner of the voice to life. He recognized the voice of this antagonist.

"My son, get your Protestant evil ass out of here before I come out of this confessional and render your backside to the point of needing realignment."

That didn't frighten him. But if the priest said, "I'm telling your grandfather Shiverick," then the fear of the Lord was installed.

At other times, he would confess to watching his cousins, which he would name in full Christian sequence, abuse themselves down below, while he did not participate, "Because I am a Protestant."

Following such sessions, Johnny would confess to his cousins, Pointer and Dink, the words that he had confessed to the priest.

This was nearly always followed by their pinning Johnny down and giving him an Indian burn, which carried ten times the heat of a pink belly. The pink belly was the gentle slapping of the stomach until it got warm, perhaps even hot if you had a good imagination.

The Indian burn involved a harsh knuckle rubbing until the burning sensation of the activated scalp molecules felt like a house on fire.

But Johnny wasn't thinking of Dink and Pointer guffawing at the Protestant Reverend Mr. Newhall nor his cornball confessions to the Catholic priest, Father Lavasseleur, on this day.

His main feature in church was Mrs. Scranton's swaying and sashaying buttocks and flexing calves.

Johnny felt doubly guilty. First for his thoughts. And then because this was the church his grandfather scraped and painted the entire exterior of including the steeple as a gift to God every three years.

He knew he couldn't continue to sneak glances at Mrs. Scranton. It wasn't right. Besides, he was bound to get caught.

When he was little, he wiled away parts of the service by forming the shape of a church by clamping his small fists together into a church shape, then forming his two index fingers into a steeple and chant to himself, "Here is the church and here is the steeple, open it up and here are the people." Then the fist church and steeple fingers would disappear, and in their place were flittering fingers, serving as the little people. He would try to put Mrs. Scranton out of his thoughts with "Here is the church, here is the steeple."

But it didn't work.

Watching the *Christian Science Monitor* lady, he felt that he was not worthy to be one of the little people beneath the steeple. *Get thee devil from my sight . . . Oh please . . . get thee . . .*

He clamped his hands over his eyes so as not to watch this woman.

Yet through the darkness of his hands, he could still see her, standing on her tiptoes, hands extended to heaven, the calves of her legs flexing and unflexing, her buttocks swaying in a sweet, hot harmony to the music. And the picture of her standing in her dark kitchen, opening and closing her refrigerator door, causing her to dance beneath her invisible night gown as if in an old-fashioned silent movie.

The church music rose to a crescendo, and he took a peek through his fingers just in time to see in that split second that Mrs. Scranton was completely entranced, her head lolling from side to side as if her neck was broken. She turned her head in his direction. He could only see the white of her eyes that rolled upward. Like the woman in that voodoo movie.

Then with eyes closed, she had smiled on him. *I know she . . . did . . .*

He was ashamed of the wetness that anointed him. *God forgive me . . . I wish I was a . . . real Catholic . . . and could be forgiven . . . with a . . . go-and-sin-no-more . . . confession . . .*

CHAPTER 8

TELL IT TO THE MARINES

Before Johnny could go tell the marines that he wanted to join up, his uncles Matthew and Mark Shiverick beat him to signing up for the service.

The day after Pearl Harbor, the brothers joined the navy together after talking with a navy recruiter in the Rockledge five-and-ten-cent store.

"Come on, men," the chief petty officer said. "Join your U.S. Navy and help sink the Rising Sun."

Brother Luke earlier had run off immediately when hearing about the raid of Pearl Harbor and joined the army. He explained to his family that night, "Why fool around? The recruiting sergeant said I could get at 'em right away without wasting a lot of time training."

Johnny didn't get to see his uncle Luke off as he left the next day without fanfare or goodbye.

Johnny took the trolley with Uncles Matthew and Mark to Boston's North Station from which they walked to the Federal Building. It was from where they would head to Great Lakes and boot camp.

Johnny said his goodbyes there, but added, "I'll be with you real soon. The navy is part of the marine corps. The recruiting sergeant told me."

Mark had mussed his hair. Matthew squeezed his nose and then pulled gently, showing Johnny his fist with his thumb sticking out between his index and middle fingers, leaving the thumb looking like a nose with a fingernail in, and said, "They won't take you without a nose. Anchors away." And his uncles were gone.

Johnny walked the twelve miles back to Rockledge rotating between singing "Anchors Away," "The Marine Corps Hymn," and "Those caissons keep rolling along. For its high, high yee, in the field artillery." Then he lapsed into silence, singing only in his heart "Onward Christian Soldiers" and crying softly. *Please . . . God . . . take care of all my uncles . . .*

Grandfather Shiverick said goodbye to his sons back in Rockledge, giving each "God save the king, and may God be with you."

John, who tried to join the army with his brother Luke, was labeled "too old" despite pulling a page from his father, Mr. John Shiverick the elder, and threatening "eternal damnation" if they didn't accept him.

The recruiters had laughed at the threat. They might have thought twice about this if the threat of everlasting damnation had come from John the younger's father.

Later that week, Johnny walked into Boston with his uncle John, who had learned about the Seabees.

His uncle John told him the Seabees of the navy would take anyone who was in the construction profession, regardless of age, and that he would be able to fight too.

"I know, Uncle John. I know the Seabees song too. We're the Seabees of the navy. We can build, and we can fight. And I know the coast guard song too. Semper Paratus is our guide."

His uncle smiled down on him. "You take care of your mother and don't let no Japs sneak up on Rockledge."

"I won't. We sharpened sticks and are going to the Big Tree in the Big Woods, look south toward Boston. One if by land and two if by sea."

His uncle had convinced the recruiter that house painting was part of the building trade. He had also told the recruiter he knew heavy equipment. He didn't reveal that his heavy equipment knowledge was on how to hoist a three-story-high extension ladder.

As his uncle John entered the Federal Building, he waved to him. "And watch out for your Grandmother Shiverick too. If I know Dad, he'll manage to join the English army, probably as a general."

Johnny's walk home saw him trip several times as he looked skyward, trying to see the faces of his uncles in the cloud outlines.

"We're the Seabees of the navy. We can build, and we can fight."

He sang the song over and over and, at one point, was positive he saw the Sea Bee arm patch—a bee in a navy uniform, a shovel in one hand and rifle in the other.

Then he sang to all his uncles, "Over hill, over dale, we will hit the dusty trail, as those caissons go rolling along. Anchors away, my boys. We can build, and we can fight from the halls of Montezuma," all the time wondering whether the fake mustache he was making out of hair he "borrowed" from the tail of a neighbor's Labrador retriever would help him to age quickly. "You take a leg from some old table. You take an arm from some old chair. And from a horse you take some hair . . ."

His uncle John's last words to Johnny were "The first chance I get I'll get me a transfer to the marines."

Johnny had told him he would be there beside him real soon, and tiny tears formed in his eyes. "Musta caught a bug in the eye, but it won't stop me none from sighting down the Enfield the marines will issue me."

His uncle had rubbed his eye also. "Musta caught a bug too."

His uncle John proved true to his word. He learned the heavy equipment of the Seabees in nothing flat and was given a chief's rating for his skills. He kept his promise to himself, and somehow they sure didn't know how at home he swapped his chief's rating and giant bulldozer blade for a marine corps buck private rating and a handheld entrenching tool.

But his career didn't last all that long. The Second Marine Division was going ashore. Pops Shiverick had his four-man fire team running toward the cover of a stand of palm trees when the young men he called my little children were shredded like rag dolls by a withering Japanese fire patterned months before.

None of the fire spits struck the old buck private as he surged forward. *Why the young . . . Lord? Why take the . . . young?*

Moments later, a Japanese mortar round struck the base of a giant palm tree the Moment he was running toward it.

Marine buck-ass private John Shiverick, age forty-four, saw the explosion at the base of the tree and hit the deck, his head coming to rest against a coral rock. The rock felt cool on his exertion and sun-boiled face. The truncated tree slammed down on his head, nearly tearing off his jaw, leaving it hanging from his face like a broken door hanging from only its lower hinge.

His first day of combat was his last. After a month on a hospital ship and six months in a naval hospital, he would head home. A marine corps private first class with magnets and repaired muscles working his jaw open and shut.

Meanwhile, Matthew and Mark had tried to get assigned to the same ship. Nothing doing. The navy didn't want brothers dying together. A rule they forgot when they allowed the five Sullivan brothers to serve on the same vessel, and all five were lost.

Matt ended up on a tin can, a destroyer that ran interference for the Liberty Ships on the Murmansk Run to the Barents Sea. The bitter cold was nearly as dangerous as the mines, and the German U-Boats picked them off like little tin bear setups at a carnival shooting gallery. The biggest difference between the two was that the little tin bears did not bleed or freeze to death in the Barents sea or sink hopeless beneath the waves. The little target on the bruin's arm flashed bright, and the carnival bears did an about-face, ambling in the opposite direction.

Meanwhile, the Shiverick women were popping rivets and welding the plates that made up these vessels.

Matt was aboard a minesweeper searching for the mines his brother's "can" was trying to avoid. Neither realized the other was so close.

Matt saw the explosion that racked the destroyer, his brother's ship, sending it shuddering to the bottom in minutes. The mine exploded amidships, and the shrapnel tore off both Mark's hands. When they pulled him aboard a rescue boat, one of the sailors said, "This is the guy that was swimming like a seal!"

Brother John arrived home much sooner with his Rube Goldberg magnet jaws than brother Matt would make it with his set of "claws," as he called them.

When Matt finally made it home, claws and all, the first thing he did was chase Johnny, who again had suffered something in his eyes, a cinder, declaring, "You'll make a mighty fine meal for a lobster, me matey," an action that swiftly cleared up the cinders.

"Fine and dandy with the lobster bit, show off," his brother John said, "but try this one on for size," and commenced to hang a heavy set of keys and a small steak knife from the magnetized roof of his mouth.

Grandmother Shiverick was glad to have two of her sons home. *Just two more, Lord . . . please . . . Thank you . . .*

During World War I, the war to end all wars, Grandmother Shiverick's younger Devil Dog brother, Charlie Henniger, who had discarded his gas mask as excess baggage, had suffocated in the poisonous gas that writhed through the trenches like an unseen serpent, and as fast as his little legs would take him, he could not outrun the green devil.

The oil painting of Great Uncle Charlie Henniger was Johnny's most favorite picture in the world. It did not show that he was barely five feet tall. What it showed was a cocky young man in his dress marine blue jacket with the red piping and the high leather neck that was to help ward off sword strokes. It hung in the little room that had been Little Charlie's. A small candle kept an eternal light as nephews and nieces picked up the torch.

The painting of Charlie, complete with the warlike glint in his eyes that only a very small man can conjure up, his cropped hair brushed straight up to its half inch in height, was just below that of a painting of a peaceful, long-haired, and gentle Jesus.

On a second wall, a picture of the president of the United States hung just below that of the king of England.

Sometimes after Grandmother Shiverick talked to Jesus, she would talk with her brother. She didn't really know the king or the president and held her tongue here.

When Ruth Shiverick was asked by Mr. Shiverick if she was talking to Charlie when she exited the room, the very old woman would say, "Heavens, no. I was talking to Jesus, dear. Little Charlie is dead."

One day she came out of her room as Johnny was staring out the old multipane window at the small flat stone in the backyard.

There were simple scratchings on it that Johnny had done with a small sharp stone. "Pal, a pal to the end." He had helped his uncle Matt bury the family dog, and the two of them had erected the monument.

His grandmother placed her tiny age-spotted hand on his hand, looked into the distance, and said softly, "Don't be sad, Little John," then crooned, "we'll all be together in the great beyond. The great by and by."

He had only heard that croon once before. Mostly her tone was "I wonder what little boy I'm going to get to eat my homemade apple pie," as if anything other than a homemade pie or bread would make it into the house.

Sometimes Grandma Shiverick would say, "I'd gladly give three pennies to any little boy who could find my eye glasses."

"Gramma! They're on your forehead!"

"Well, I'll be a devil's uncle."

"Grammy."

"Yes."

"You keep the pennies, in case you lose them again and I'm not here. And you have to pay a reward to some other little boy."

The first time he heard his Grandmother's crooning, he was only a kid, seven years old, not the thirteen-year-old he was now.

He had rushed to her side as giant oaks crashed to the ground behind him. Trees he had caused to fall and power lines he had caused to explode.

It was 1938, and he had been playing kick the can with some kids from the South School.

It was his chance to be a hero. The kids that were on his team had all been captured. They could only be freed if he kicked the can that sat in the middle of the intersection of Pond and Pine Streets.

He made his charge through the enemy, the protectors of the can—deking left, head faking right, like a Boston Bruin forward skating in on a

Montreal Canadian goalie, and then the straight-away burst, watching his imprisoned teammates watch him with their my-hero smiles.

He unloaded his foot on the can, an empty Campbell's Soup can with its jagged top sticking its tongue out. The kick would have been a three-pointer from fifty-five yards out. It soared high into the air. While not hawk eye, certainly Rockin' Robin high.

And then the transformer on the nearest utility pole exploded in a shower of sparks and powerful bolts that shot skyward.

"Johnny did it!" was the cry from every mouth, tin can prisoners and guards alike, as the giant sparks showered downward.

They ran homeward, barely ahead of the trees that fell behind them.

Although Johnny's kick received credit for the first bad breath of the approaching hurricane, in reality, the electric burst was caused by a tree that had fallen on a power line a mile away. The voltage had traveled at the speed of light toward the transformer near where the South School boys played. The surge arrived at the transformer there at the same time the soup can soared sky high.

"Johnny did it!" was the cry of the boys.

They wanted to make sure God got the right guy.

Thus forsaken by man, in this case, by boy and God alike, Johnny was certain that one of the hundreds of giant trees would crush him before he could get to Grandma's house.

God surely had loosed the lightning of his terrible swift sword on Johnny for kicking the can into the transformer.

And what a swath that sword cut, that Sturm und Drang, storm and stress, the hurricane of 1938. There were enough trees down every fifty feet of street to build an ark.

None swatted Johnny like the fly he was, and he made it to Grandmother's house. She took him in her arms and sat down in the old wicker rocking chair and rocked and crooned. Rocked and crooned. Old Pal, the dog beneath the scratched stone, was at their feet then.

The warmth of her old bosom that smelled of apple pie and cinnamon was a safe harbor in which this little ship lost at sea swayed gently at anchor.

"I didn't mean to do it, Grandma. I caused the trees to fall."

"You didn't do it, dear. It's just God's reminder that some of us just get too big for our britches at times."

Was I too big for my britches . . . thinking horrible thoughts . . . although I can't . . . remember what the horrible thoughts . . . were . . .

As he got older, he had a better handle on what his bad thoughts were. *About Mrs. Christian Science Monitor . . . Mrs. Scranton . . . in church . . .*

I bulged . . . and tried to hide it with my bible . . . and with the morning paper . . . and later . . . I had to clean the white spots in my pants . . .

His grandmother felt him shiver, wrapped the shawl higher around his shoulders.

"Grammy."

"What, dear?"

"Don't be afraid. I'll protect you." And he closed his eyes to her crooning, and slept. As the mighty trees continued to fall, one of which thundered down onto the roof over their heads.

"I know you will, dear."

The thunder of the tree on the overhead roof did not stop him from sleeping. It did jump-start a nightmare. His mother's face was close to his, accusing, "What's this, young man?" She had just made her nightly inspection of his corduroy knickers, the ones he had worn in church. There was a stain, a dried white stain, Mrs. Scranton's stain.

He already considered these pants traitors for several reasons. First, he was the only boy in the class still wearing knickers. Two, they whistled while he walked, so he walked like a cowboy who had spent a month in the saddle, but then his legs got tired from his bowlegged walking. But when he walked normal, his thighs came together, and the pants whistled.

When a classmate heard the whistle, he would always point and say, "Gottcha. Whistling warbler." Then the entire class would look, some stared, some even laughed. Except Yelena Smoltz. She just gave Johnny a soft smile that read, "What do you expect from little children?" She was unlike any of the other children. Certainly not like Johnny.

Now the corduroy knickers had betrayed him again, this time during his nightmare in the hurricane. "What's this, young man?" It wasn't a question. It was a demand. His trousers were being held inside out and the dried chalky white on the inside of the fly displayed like a badge of disgrace.

"I cannot tell a lie," Johnny said. *Oh I wish I . . . was a . . . Catholic . . . and I could lie . . . and then confess to a priest . . . go and sin no more . . . and be done with it . . .*

"I'm talking to you, Mr. John Shiverick too-big-for-his-trousers DaSilva, you lumpen. What is the story?" Still not a question. Still a demand.

"The art teacher, Mrs. Baker, was at the school, and we made paste and used it with some newspaper to make papier-mâché dolls. And it was messy."

"I could ask how the paste got on the inside of your trousers."

"It happened when I was going to the bathroom."

—

"I'm sending you down to your father. March right down there and face the music."

He marched off, his lips moving silently. *March right down . . . to a John Philip Sousa march . . . March right down . . .*

"Are you talking back to me under your breath, young man? You better not be unless you have three fannies. 'Cause one or two won't be enough for the spankings you'll get. Tony! Can you hear me?"

"Do bears go in the woods?"

"He's your son. It's up to you. I can't handle him. He has white spots in his pants and lied about them. Said it was artwork of some sort, and I think he was answering back under his breath as well."

Johnny headed down the stairs, full tilt. He didn't want his mother leading him down while pulling up on his sideburns. Panic set in. *Do they know about me . . . and Mrs. Scranton? Do they know? She takes the . . . Christian Science Monitor . . . She's innocent . . . honest Injun . . .* Johnny knew Indians never spoke with forked tongue. *Like I do . . . can they read minds? Do my parents know about . . . Mrs. Mortenson . . . her grapefruit dance? It was my fault . . . for looking . . .*

He knew he had to be careful when heading down the stairs in a panic. Stairs four and nine were missing.

Thirteen stairs . . . five down . . . then four . . . is my . . . rit me tic right . . . Uncle Matt's milk horse could count better . . .

The old horse, Hoodsie, that pulled the old, Hoods's milk wagon could count. *Milk at this house . . . not the next three . . . milk at the next two . . . skip this tenement . . .*

Johnny wondered how Hoodsie could keep count with the noise of his tattered and torn hooves on Boston's cobblestone streets clattering like two skeletons screwing on a tin roof. Not that the horse was some sort of Einstein. If a widow died and her house was to be skipped, it took several days for Hoodsie to relearn his numbers. Then again, Johnny had thought, *Hoodsie doesn't have . . . all that many . . . fingers and toes . . . to count on . . .*

There were times Johnny was happy as his imagination wandered. It made him laugh. Other times he worried. *Am I all right . . . upstairs . . . or has the tenant . . . run off and left it . . . empty?*

Now it was worry time. His father had a punishment he couldn't survive.

Neither his mother's threats, often accompanied by the waving of a wire coat hanger or his old Eastward-Ho vice principal's ruler whacks, not to the open palm as administered by his kindergarten teacher, but the embarrassing and resounding whacks to the butt could compare to what his father did.

Of course the ruler whacks to the butt were bad, especially with the teacher's denouement. "Hope you didn't suffer brain damage."

He entered the small room that passed as the living room. His father sat in a chair, a calm look on his face.

Opposite him was a second wooden chair, vacant. Johnny called the empty chair the punishment chair, the electric chair.

Johnny sat in it, facing his father, who was looking into his eyes.

Johnny tried to match the look. One of complete calm. There was no accusation. No threat. What was the look? He could never figure it out. *It's . . . sort of like . . . he expects . . . good things . . . of me . . .*

How long they looked into each other's eyes, Johnny didn't know. Was it a minute. Or an hour. A month before he looked down? Just for a moment.

When he looked up, all he saw was his father's back. He was walking out of the room.

And that was Johnny's punishment. Killed . . . my heart killed . . . for creaming my jeans . . .

After Johnny went back up to his room, Charity turned to her husband, "Now what do you think of your son?"

"I think we'd better get him out of knickers and into long pants. He's a young man."

"You're no help." She gave him a push on the shoulder. "I've got work to do."

"Save some strength for love."

"Is that the only thing ever in your mind?"

"No. Sometimes I think of grouse hunting behind a good bird dog. Having a fine filet mignon. A drink of Madeira. Dozing by the fireplace."

"That's nice."

"And once I'm well rested—*amor* my amabilidade belleza, my lovliness, love from your amante, your lover boy. Commercio. Commercio!"

"Oh, you're incorrigible. I know you're talking fresh. I just feel it."

Tony sang to his wife, grabbed her, waltzed her around Willy Nilly style—flouncing, singing, "Amor, amor, amor. Commercio. Oh membro! Membro!" *Love . . . love . . . love . . . sex . . . my member . . . my member . . .*

"Oh, Tony, when are you going to grow up."

"Never."

No, 1938 wasn't a particularly good year for Johnny. Starting with the hurricane and then the explosion in the corduroy knickers, in church, of all things. Pal had died. He remembered the first shovelful of dirt his uncle Matt had thrown into the dog's grave that covered the bright-red kerchief he had tied around Pal's neck. A single piece of dirt had stuck on the dog's open eye. Johnny had shut both eyes before they placed him in the grave. *Why had it . . . opened?*

Even after the thick white fur of the Alaskan spitz was completely covered, he could still see the speck of dirt on his friend's eye, and that look that asked the boy, "Why didn't you remove it?"

No, it wasn't a particularly good year for Johnny.

Although he slept tight, obeying his grandmother's words, as the Hurricane of 1938 raved and ranted and cursed outside, "Sleep tight, don't let the bedbugs bite."

And hadn't he been a big man with his promise, "Don't worry, Grammy, I'll protect you."

The little man did not quite understand that it was his grandmother who was doing the rocking and crooning.

The nightmare of his mother holding his white-stained trousers in his face demanding an answer, retired, replaced with soft sounds of crooning, the smell of hot apple pie and cinnamon, the feel of a loving, breathing bosom that enhanced the slow rocking of the chair. Johnny had slept (sleep tight, don't let the bedbugs bite) as homes were swept off the shoreline and across Boston Harbor, several with entire families clinging to the chimneys and roof shingles. Giant trees crushed Packards and Plymouths and Hudsons alike, paying no more heed to the passengers inside than the cost of the car itself.

The storm wasn't hidden by curtains and shades. Grandfather Shiverick had not allowed curtains or shades in the house. "If the good Lord wanted man in the dark he would not have invented the sun."

Nearly three years had passed. The fallen great oaks of the hurricane of '38 had been dismembered by mere mortals using arm power to operate their gap-toothed bucksaws. Not only had Hitler begun his annihilation of millions of Jews, Gypsies, and Poles. The physically and mentally lame, with the goal of ending up with a race where everyone had blue eyes, except himself.

To show how the world had changed Mr. John Shiverick had not only acquiesced to the pressure of his daughters and to the civil defense corps and installed both curtains and shades, but he also became a CD warden, making sure others obeyed the blackouts.

It was up to him not only to make sure that the blackout would keep German planes from finding Boston, but also to do his part to ensure Hitler would feel the terrible swift sword of the Lord, not to mention the king of England.

Not a single peep of light could escape in any home or there was an authoritative tap from a gentleman of age outfitted in a white helmet and wearing an armband. Both announcing "CD."

The world was at war. German, Japanese, and Italian armies were taking whatever they wanted nearly at will, as nations trained their common, everyday, run-of-the-mill citizens to try and stop them.

American boys trained with stick rifles and stone grenades. There were not enough rifles to go around, but eventually, sticks and stones would break their bones.

Johnny watched the small banners pop up in the windows of the people he delivered his morning papers to. More each day. A blue star announced how many sons or daughters were serving. It was set in a white square with a thick red banner around it.

Other stars would be making their appearance shortly. Gold stars, announcing that someone in the family had made the supreme sacrifice.

One day he saw his first gold star. It looked like gold inside the red border. The morning light was poor. It was in the window of the *Christian Science Monitor* lady.

He felt horrible for Mrs. Scranton. She had lost a son not much older than Johnny. She aged overnight. And seeing Johnny didn't help . . . And I had those . . . thoughts . . . *How . . . could . . . ? Oooh . . .*

There was also a gold star in the Keefe home. Was it Tommy? He was such a wonderful guard on the football team, just last year. *So skinny . . . so tough . . . nah . . . It's not Tommy . . . Nothing can happen to anyone that tough . . . Hasn't . . . he said as much . . . himself . . . You can't kill steel . . . When the goin gets tough . . . the tough get going . . . Hadn't he played with broken ribs . . . not telling anyone . . . until he passed . . . out? It couldn't be Tommy . . .*

Mrs. Keefe had two sons. Timmy was a big strapping boy. Powerful. Like a bull. The girls always wanted to feel his muscles, and this made him blush. He didn't play football. The coach had told him, "Gentle giant, go home," and lamented that he couldn't put Tommy's heart in Timmy's body. Maybe it was Timmy. The gold star.

He looked to see if perhaps the gold star had a name in it.

"Oooh." *Both stars were . . . gold . . . They had gone off . . . together . . . part of the activated 102nd Infantry Division, the Yankee Division, the Y/D, Massachusetts National Guard.*

Johnny could feel the bile welling up in his throat.

His throat felt clogged, sour, and he fought against throwing up. He had had no breakfast and the night before it had been hot dog Scutch, a made-up name for a soup that contained potatoes and a hot dog cut into small pieces. The family was holding back a bit so it could buy a chicken for Sunday and still pay the rent.

His mother could have made a few extra dollars. She had the gasoline rationing stamps the government had issued and wasn't using the Model A that was up on blocks. There were plenty of offers and bids on them by new friends and long-lost relatives. "That's not the idea of rationing," she said. Some cursed her. Others were much nicer and just turned their backs on her and strode away without a word.

Johnny believed the slight hunger pangs were worth her not selling out, rationing stamps for money or food. Come on . . .

The hunger was bearable. They would have chicken next Sunday. That was a promise. *When Dad starts sending money home . . . from the Sun Shipyard . . .* He was a riveter there, at Chester, Pennsylvania. He had to set up a home away from home first before helping here. Keeping two homes was expensive.

One thing Johnny found out looking at the two gold stars, hurt overcomes hunger.

Tommy . . . remember how you let . . . me . . . carry your jersey and . . . shoulder pads . . . from the football field . . . to the school after practice? You were going to be . . . the smallest lineman in professional football . . .

Johnny remembered the picture Mrs. Keefe had shown him of her two sons in their army uniforms. The giant helmet hung so low on Tommy's tiny head; he looked like a little baby bird in an upside-down nest.

The helmet looked so small on Timmy's large head, a handsome and gentle Denny Dimwit. Mrs. Keefe, a large woman, tall and wide, had laughed at the photo with Johnny. "Timmy's me. Big Tim. Tommy was always so small, so fierce. We called his dad, God rest his unholy soul, Tiny Tim. God bless my Tiny Tim, my own personal scrooge."

Tommy had been the reason Johnny had gone out for the football team.

"Ya no smaller than me," he had said, "and look at me. If they knock me down, I bite their ferkin' foot."

"Aren't you afraid of getting athlete's fo . . . ah, athlete's tongue."

"Ya can't be funny, Johnnie, if you plan to be a guard. Little guys that play guard can't be funny. You want everyone on that football field looking over their shoulder for you not because they think you're funny. They're looking because they fear you're going to hit them so hard with your helmet that your head will go up their arse and your nose come out their dingus."

Were Tommy and Timmy . . . together . . . when . . .

He couldn't bring himself to think the rest of it.

—

The small flags in the windows announcing how many were serving, how many would never serve again, replaced the black crepes of yesteryear that announced the deaths of young ones to scarlet fever, measles, and chicken pox. New serums and inoculations took care of those diseases. There apparently are no medical cures for war.

"Don't ever be no pismo clam or no pismire." Tommy had told him." Put your helmet right into the knees. Slam your helmet into their crotch. Never knew no one whose balls were stronger than a head."

No one knew what Tommy meant by "pismo clam" or "pismire." He had discovered the words in the dictionary while he looked for dirty words. And he wasn't about to tell anyone one what pismo or pismire meant, but they sure sounded great.

He knew that no one would look it up in the dictionary. First, they didn't give two rats' asses. Second, they didn't know how to spell either.

"I won't be either, Tommy—piss Moe or piss Minnie."

"Good. Then you can be a guard like me but not as good. But a tough, darn good guard. One they look over their shoulders for, especially the big guys."

"Can I get hurt real bad by a big guy?"

"Pismo. Pismire. Didn't I tell you not to be one of them? The big guys are the ones that gotta worry about getting hurt. Remember, if a big guy knocks you down, he's an asshole first class knocking down a little guy. A little guy knocks him down, he's an asshole, second class."

"Tommy, now that I'm gonna be a guard what's a pismo clam?"

"I never telled nobody that, but wait, I'm heading out to kick ass. Kick the ass of that dickshit eater, Hitler. So you carry the big word of the little guy. Pismo. Pismire."

"I'll do it." *You'll be proud . . . Tommy . . .*

"A pismo is a clam that just lays around on the beach and doesn't do nuttin'. Pismire is an ant piss type of termite. Understand."

"Yes. Understand."

"Yup. Okay, get your rear into gear and remember what I told you. Set up those trash cans in the alley behind the supermarket, tackle them, block them, dent their asses. Make 'em rattle like the Tinman was thumping Dorothy on a tin roof. Bite the tackle opposite you like Toto bit the Tinman's ass when he saw his girlfriend riding that pile of junk."

"Yes. *Yes!*"

"And when your trash cans start looking over their shoulder, you ain't no pismo nor pismire. You're the man. *The man.* You're a running guard."

Johnny had done the trash cans. He wanted to tell Tommy about one special can. The one he filled with rocks.

—

I'll show him . . . instead . . .

"Gotta bug out. Remember. No pismo clam. No pismire." And Tommy was gone. Forever.

He remembered Turtle Poulidakis, Rhesus and Boattail's little brother.

Turtle was no agile swinging monkey like Rhesus, nor no speedy brain, motormouth like Boattail.

Turtle was Turtle.

Until the two gold stars appeared in the window, Johnny really never knew one other person real close that died.

Anthony "Turtle" Poulidakis. Johnny loved the little cement block because Turtle would let Johnny tackle him for hours.

He remembered going to the Poulidakis house and asking Mrs. Poulidakis if Turtle could come out and play.

She had peered suspiciously down her nose at him, her face hidden mostly by the door. She was the suspicious one. Some of the kids suspected she was a spy because she was so dark, had some kind of slant to the eyes. And when a kid knocked on the door, she always remained partially hidden behind it.

Hadn't the United States government, in one of its posters, the one beside the "Loose Lips Sink Ships" one hanging at the post office, said, "There could be a spy behind every door."

Of course no one ever talked about her being a spy around Turtle unless they were cruisin' for a bruisin'.

Little did those who suspected her of being a combination of Axis Sally and Tokyo Rose realize that she remained partially hidden behind the door in the dark as she was ashamed of the busted nose and the swollen lip. Which were mostly the result of her stepping in the way when her husband, who had muscles on his muscles much like a Rhodesian ridgeback, was trying to pummel his sons.

Turtle had one thought, *Someday . . . I'll . . . get 'em . . . fix his wagon . . . real good . . .* Letting Johnny pound him with tackles and blocks helped him get ready for the day of reckoning.

Yes, it would be a safe guess that anyone who hinted she was a spy would have ended up looking like Alfred E. Neumann.

"My little boy Ant-tony no playa with you anymore, ever," she had told Johnny on that day. And then closed the door.

It was then he saw the black crepe that had replaced the "Warning, Whooping Cough" sign put up by the Board of Health when the doctor had reported young Anthony Poulidakis had the whooping cough.

It was the last crepe Johnny could remember on a Rockledge door. Medicine had come to town and the dancing, hocus-pocus-selling medicine man moved on.

Turtle had been so slow doing everything. He was always the last one in during the bare ass swims at Duck Pond. He was always caught by Mrs. Pippen' as he was the last one over the fence during a raid of the Pippen plum tree. Everyone in the class fell asleep including the teacher, No Doze Dennison, when he gave his oral topic in social studies.

Turtle . . . how did you die . . . so fast?

Mr. Pouliadakis, in a ridotto, a masquerade attempt to cover up what everyone in town knew, that he sucker shot his own wife, used to toss stolen candy to all the kids as he rode his bike with the fat tires home after finishing his day's work cutting meat at the A&P Market.

It never entered his mind to save a couple pieces of candy for his own son. Why should he? He knew the Turtle was too slow to cut the firewood, nor caught and killed any rabbits in the snares he put out.

Without tasting his supper, he would say to his wife, "What kine of sheet iss diss?" But he never waited for an answer. He had an answer for her. A mere backhander if she was lucky.

His ouzo drinking buddy, Bedigosian, said, "Pouliadakis's not so bad. He cried when he learned Anthony had died."

Johnny told him, "That's a crock of happy bullshit."

When Bedizosian, built like a lowland gorilla, lifted his hand threateningly, Johnny said, "I wouldn't."

He didn't.

"Besides," Johnny said, "your armpits smell like Gorgonzola."

This time when Bedizosian raised his hand, Johnny ran like hell's fire were chasing him as he wasn't sure what he meant when he had threatened him with "I wouldn't" as if he was some sort of karate expert or hired killer.

When Johnny had come to call on Turtle, not knowing that Turtle couldn't come out and play "no more," Mrs. Poulidakis stood even further behind the door, where the darkness was even deeper. The busted nose and swollen lip were now irritated by the new flow of salt from her eyes. She had never cried for herself. Only for her son.

Rhesus and Boattail had been hiding in a bush near the door as Johnny talked with Mrs. Pouliadakis, and they joined him as he walked away.

The three friends walked in silence, heads down, to the Big Woods, where they climbed the Big Tree.

Boattail told Johnny, "The man in the black suit will come to Turtle's house and take all the blood out of his body with a giant needle. He'll wear giant rubber gloves. I seen him do it when my grandfather died."

"And then after he got Turtle's blood," Rhesus said, "they put some other gunk in him with another needle that looked sort of like a chalking gun."

"Honest," Boattail said. It was the first time he had ever used the word "honest," as he felt that when he spoke, everyone believed and that the listeners should kiss his ring. If only he had one other than the White Owl cigar band he wore when he was lucky to discover a wrapper on the street.

"And then the guy in the black suit will dress Turtle in his go-to-church good suit," Rhesus said,"

"Then they comb his hair," Boattail said, "and his cowlick will keep popping up stifflike, like a cow's tail when it's letting a cow flop."

"And they will put some powder on his face, like he was a woman," Rhesus said.

"Or a clown," his brother added.

They sneaked Johnny into the house when they saw their mother go upstairs for a nap. They were going to let him look at Turtle in the casket for a nickel each, all powdered and hair slicked down, except for that piece that was like the tail of a cow letting fly.

"She went to a back room for a nap," Rhesus said. "We could sneak up the stairs and talk with Turtle. Though he won't be able to talk back."

"If he does, I'm running like hell."

Rhesus opened the front door quietly, and they entered, standing for several moments, looking up the stairs at the door to their dead friend's bedroom.

Johnny looked at the stairs. *Wonder if . . . four and nine . . . are . . . missing . . .*

The three of them stood beside Turtle's bed. The two brothers looked at Johnny to see how he would react.

"I've never seen a dead person before," Johnny said.

"I did. My grandfather. And saw one in the newspaper too," Rhesus said.

"That's not the real thing," his brother said, "as I saw lots of dead people in the papers."

Johnny looked at Turtle. He had never seen him in a suit. "It sure doesn't look like Turtle."

"Nah, it ain't," Boattail said. "He's kaput. His real stuff is on its way to heaven Ma said."

"Hope he goes there a little faster than usual," Johnny said, "or we'll all beat him there." *He sure doesn't . . . look like . . . little Turtle . . .*

"We could sneak kids in and let them touch him for a nickel," Rhesus said.

"Cut that out! Stinkhead," his older brother demanded. "We gotta get a dime for that. A lot of risk here. A nickel doesn't buy you a good cigar nowadays."

"He looks so small," Johnny said.

They all looked close.

"Ya," Rhesus said. And cried.

"Cut that out!" his big brother said. "Dam sissy"—and he cried—"I don't want him to go either."

Johnny cried too. It was the first dead person he ever saw. *Never even saw one . . . in the papers . . .*

Even if Johnny had wanted to touch Turtle, and he didn't. He wouldn't have. *I gotta save . . . every penny to get Jazz's teeth fixed.*

He was tired of fighting bigger kids, even good friends, that called Jazz Bucky Beaver, Mortimer Snerd, and Thumb Sucker.

Rhesus came the closest of his friends to feel five from Johnny. Johnny had his fingers rolled into a square knot fist and the knuckle sandwich loaded and cocked. Johnny knew how to toss them. Don't wind up or come from the side. Just a short straight one. With a little snap of the wrist just before the target was to feel five.

"Your little brother can eat corn through a picket fence with a muzzle on," the rufous-headed Rhesus had said, not meanly, but as a statement of fact after Johnny had won his Brooklyn Dodger's Pee Wee Reese and Pistol Pete Reiser, the Gold Dust Twins, cards.

Actually, Rhesus loved Jazz, even with a little hint of admiration for his high scale on the bite-o-meter. And the fact "the little turd swung at me."

Rhesus wondered whether perhaps he could make two bits on a bet with someone that indeed Jazz could perform the task. He'd give the kid a nickel. Well, perhaps two cents.

Rhesus also looked at Johnny's fist with a certain amount of admiration. "Don't fire it, Johnny. You could cut your hand."

Johnny looked at his friend quizzically. "What? Cut my hand?"

"I've got a glass jaw," Rhesus said, complete with a shit eating grin that could have bulldozed a marine latrine clean.

"Ah, I'm not gonna hit you. I know you miss Turtle too."

"I heard your uncle John Shiverick got hit," Boattail said.

—

"Yes." Then he added, "He got shot in the face." "Shot in the face" sounded so romantic especially when they had all heard about Red Sloan, who had got shot in the ass twice. The second wound to the buttocks meant he had to wear a colostomy bag. Yet despite having such a painful wound, physically and mentally, he managed to run down Dozie Delmontea, the fastest halfback on the football team. The Doz, showing off for his buddies, chanted, "Red, Red, shit the bed, wiped it up with gingerbread. Heard you hadta pin your Purple Heart on your purple arse."

Red ran down the Dozer,

Dozer had a double nickname as he not only ran with the speed and power of a bulldozer; he also was always asleep in class.

But sore ass and all, Red Sloan gave Dozie a boot that had his friends holding both hands directly over their heads, signaling the field goal kick was good.

The longer the war went on, the more the old men who were the young boys the year before realized there were no good wounds. If they were slight, it was back to the front. If shot in the foot, there was an investigation. If they were serious, they weren't funny. Even the shot in the ass.

Anyway, unbeknownst to all except family, Uncle John's face wounds were the result of a coconut tree collapsing after its base was hit by an artillery round and the falling tree batted his head into the corral. While not the result of getting shot in the face, it was a legitimate wound. It just was a wound that could make some idiot laugh.

It was ironic that Uncle John was the last of the four Shiverick brothers to join and the first to get wounded and get home.

John not only finagled a transfer from the Seabees to the marines but also was made a five-stripe gunny sergeant.

Everyone figured it was with his terrible eyes that all the Shiverick boys and girls, except Charity, had helped him to get the transfer and the stripes.

Older than all the enlisted grunts he served with, he not only survived the nickname Pops but also made it a battle cry. "Try and catch up with Pops, boys!"

And he led the charge up the beach, hoping to come face-to-face with one of those six-foot, Royal Japanese Marines who would be screaming "Banzai!" which roughly interpreted by marines as "eat rising sun steel," "melican co-sucker!" The jarheads only laughed at the Nips'pidgin English after reducing their size with their BAR, a Browning automatic rifle, or their KA-BAR knife.

The marines answered the Nipponese with "nip on these" and squeezed their balls. Often after knocking down a charging Japanese soldier, they would yell out, "No tickee, no laundry," not giving two healthy shits that it was a Chinese saying adopted from the Chinatowns of Boston and San Francisco.

It didn't come about. This face-to-face thing for John Shiverick the Younger.

A spray of machine gun fire that kicked up spits of sand in front of him changed his John Wayne-like "follow Pops" charge up the beach.

As the Japanese machine gun fire blasted up sharp spits of coral that approached him moving faster than a rabbit with a promise, John Shiverick III swore for the first time in his life, "Damned Zulus!" and hit the deck.

The problem was the deck for him was a volcanic rock about the size of a semi-inflated football.

As his face neared the coral, he admired its iridescent color just before his jaw hit the rock. It hurt like the time he had got winterbalm on his balls during a football game. The coach asked him after the game, "Why can't you run like that every game?"

After that, he kept a small vial tucked in his hip pads just in case his Rockledge football team needed a touchdown against hated opponents such as Reading or Winchester. He was happy, although he wouldn't admit it, that both Reading and Winchester got so far ahead that a lone touchdown wouldn't amount to a hill of beans, and he didn't have to break the vial and apply the balm.

It was the Japanese mortar round that hit the base of the coconut tree located thirty feet in front of him and the rock his face rested on. It severed the tree from its earthbound roots, causing it to crash down on the back of his head; that did what he later named the dirty deed.

He looked at his teeth strewn around the sand in front of him and the two canines that, for some reason, embedded in the coral. He wondered, *Can I save 'em . . . and they can stick 'em back in . . . or maybe they will make great . . . watch fobs . . .* Then suddenly, the funny left him; he pissed his pants and passed out.

Hurt as hurt, it still was a trip home that many of his comrades would have paid the ticket price for.

Not John Shiverick III.

He had been asked, because he was the John III, whether his father was John Jr.

The old housepainter was not junior.

He and Mrs. Shiverick had lost their firstborn, John Jr. Thus, when another son came along, he was also named John. He became John III. And nearly became John the last. But when he finally would cash in his chips, the record keeper at the Lindenwood Cemetery would have some questions to ask about two brothers named John.

"Tell you what," Boattail had said to Johnny, "you get your uncle John to hold up a set of keys with the roof of his mouth with those magnets they put in there, and I'll let you touch Turtle for free. But your uncle has gotta perform for me. I can get a nickel from each kid in the audience to see the keys hanging. I can get a dime if he can hang his old KA-BAR knife from the roof of his mouth."

"You know what, Boattail, when horse's asses were being manufactured in heaven," Johnny said, "the good Lord must have wanted one perfect one. Voila! Boattail. The perfect, pure, unadulterated, undiluted horse's ass. You piss me off."

"Better pissed off than pissed on."

The only real-life marine Johnny ever knew was his uncle. Except for the uncle he never knew, Little Charlie in the painting, wearing the dress blues with the leather neck on the jacket who was killed in Belleau Wood during World War I.

On returning home after his discharge from the navy hospital, his uncle John appeared outfitted in a khaki shirt that had pressed pleats down the pockets that you could shave with. His royal blue trousers had a blood-red stripe down the side and were held up by a khaki belt with a gold buckle that was complete with an eagle sitting on top of the world with an anchor in its talons. The buckle shined as bright as the sun on the pure white cap with the black spit-shined visor.

When he had taken off the cap at breakfast that morning at Grandma Shiverick's, his closely cropped steel hair shone like ten thousand fixed bayonets.

It was a twelve-mile walk from Rockledge to Boston and the Federal Building, but twelve miles can go fast when you do the Boy Scout pace, run fifty, walk fifty. He had said his hellos to his returning uncle and then headed to the Federal Building.

"What can I do for you, son?" the marine corps recruiting officer asked Johnny.

"I want to join up. Now."

"Why?" the dress-blues-clad recruiter asked, looking down at the fourteen-year-old who he could see was trying to hide the fact he was standing on his tiptoes. He tried to suppress a smile.

"I wanna fight Japs."

"How old are you, boy?"

"Twenty-four." He purposely hadn't shaved and attempted to make the some twenty-odd whiskers that dotted his face look like twenty-thousand by adding small ink dots and soot to his chin and upper lip. He had figured that to say that he was eighteen wasn't enough. Hadn't someone said giant lies are easier to believe than midget ones? Everyone tells small ones . . . and don't get . . . believed . . .

"Jeez, you don't look a day over twenty-three," the recruiter said, staring into the youth's glaring eyes.

Johnny then looked at his feet, being nearly without practice in the lying profession. "Okay, I confess, I'm only seventeen. But I'll be eighteen next week."

"Look, son, you've still got a couple years to be a kid. Why do you want to fight Japs when you're just a kid?"

"They shot my uncle in the face."

"That's not good enough for me to get some twelve-year-old shot in the face."

"I'm fourte—!"

"I know."

Johnny looked at his feet again and then slowly brought his head up and looked into the recruiter's eyes. "They killed Timmy and Tommy. Tommy let me carry his shoulder pads. Timmy was almost as gentle as my two grandmothers."

"I understand," the recruiter said, mussing Johnny's hair.

"Don't ever do that." *Ever* . . . "I'm not a kid." *Not no more* . . . "I'm joining up." He tried to push the recruiter aside but was surprised at the stoic strength of mind and body he felt. *Holy mackerel . . . I'm glad he doesn't play tackle . . . for Melrose . . . or Reading . . .*

Johnny still tried to force his way forward. "I'm signing up."

This time the recruiter gave him a shove, that set his rotator cuffs rotating counterclockwise.

"Don't ever do that again. Push me." *Ever* . . . "You peckerwood." Johnny didn't know where he got the word or what it meant, but to the sergeant with the slight y'all drawl, "peckerwood" was a Yankee slap that deserved a slap back.

He gave the boy a forward and backward slap that stung pride more than cheek.

The recruiter never saw the short right, with the wrist snap just before it sunk into his stomach.

Johnny was stunned that the recruiter had barely grunted. Only the reddening of his face above the khaki collars with the black marine corps

—

eagle, anchor, and ball on them divulged his impending anger. The neck flexed. The top button popped. It appeared the chest and biceps were going to burst the shirt like a lobster snapping out of its shell prior to growing a larger casing.

"That's enough of this good happy horseshit!" The recruiter placed his giant hand on Johnny's face and pushed him gently backward.

Johnny lost his balance and bump assed down the granite steps of the Federal Building.

The boy stared into the now-amused eyes of the recruiter. "I'll be back."

"I know you will. When you come back in four years, I'll sign your ass up with pleasure. The corps can use that blackberry briars-in-the-skivvies meanness."

Johnny walked away slowly. The recruiter's voice followed as he dredged up superlatives. It had been a slow day. So why not? "Ya, kid, y'all (his peckerwood jab at Johnny) must of swiped the balls off a brass monkey. Yah, the corps named a cap after you, you little pisscutter." It would be a good six years and several hundred masturbations before Johnny knew what a pisscutter was, and then he wished he had never found out.

"Boy, when those Kentucky DIs get your little Yankee doodle ass, they're going to be in for a surprise. Y'all's brass balls are going to be used as Christmas tree ornaments. Your peckerwood tail assembly will be in for a surprise too. You betcha. Your ass will be grass."

Johnny looked back at the recruiter. *Why the old grunt likes me?* Johnny smiled. Johnny gave him his middle finger.

The recruiter gave him his little finger. "You don't deserve the best, boy."

Johnny gave him the middle digit finger on both hands.

The recruiter stared.

Johnny glared. *All right . . . all right . . . we speak . . . the same . . . language . . .*

"Just call me General Doug with the big corncob pipe!" he yelled back at the recruiter. "I shall return." *And piss in your . . . canteen . . .*

CHAPTER 9

FRIENDS—ONE HIS DAD?

The start of World War II meant hurrah for those volunteering to fight their new enemy and hurrah for the fact that suddenly there were jobs everywhere.

They were called defense jobs, the building of a war machine.

Johnny hoped they soon would be called offense jobs. *Those B-24 liberators . . . and the B-17 flying fortresses . . . and our tanks and tin cans . . . are made to . . . kick ass . . . kick ass big time*

Often as he walked through the Big Woods alone, when no one would hear his singing, he bellowed forth, saluting, marching, "Thanks to the Yanks, the men in the tanks, in the ships, in the planes on the shore!"

He always loved descriptive adjectives, and at the top of this love list were now "Flying Fortress," "Liberator," and "Tin Can." He was on top of the nickname game. He had nicknamed nearly every friend he had. Righty. Rhesus. Dink. Soupy.

He got into the naming business because he loved the use of words and his imagination when using them in combination. Words, titles, descriptions—he thought so many failed to fit the subject. *Hey . . . a doctor's business . . . called a practice . . . Give me a break . . . my little pecker . . . called a private . . . why not call it . . . a general?*

His word questioning gave him openings to tease his friends who were going to have their tonsils or adenoids out. "Oh, gee, they're going to practice on you."

Johnny told his friends he would never go to a doctor who had a practice, only go to one that had a perfection.

It made sense. Now if he could only convince doctors to change their medical perfection.

He figured it would be easier yet still near impossible to get a medical man to change the title from medical practice to medical perfection than to get a lawyer to change his job description from law practice to law perfection. The lawyer most certainly would say . . . "I object . . . boy . . . I love talking to . . . myself . . ."

That's why he questioned the words "have to" when his father said, "I have to stay at the Sun Shipyard in Pennsylvania, son. I started there when no one else would have me. I can't just up and shift to the Boston Navy Yard. They probably wouldn't hire me anyway."

"You can get a job in Rockledge. We're called the Shoe Town. They manufacture brogans for dogfaces and boondockers for Jungle Bunnies."

While his father could not change job locations, those who had worn the WPA brown and CCC leaf green were changing into army khaki, navy blue, and marine green.

Those who had been in the CCC, WPA, or on the welfare rolls and hadn't gone off to war had all the overtime they could handle. Some even held two full-time jobs. The money was there. The jobs everywhere.

The farmer-shoeshine boy slogan—make hay while the sun shines— was the word. Everyone in the country was in a badass, kick-ass mood and knew their American fighting men—their sons, fathers, cousins, uncles, friends—were the world's finest fighters.

Everyone forgot that the enemy had been training for years with real automatic weapons, real airplanes, and very real tanks and live ammunition.

Their families and friends were now training with broom sticks for rifles and with cutout cardboard tanks placed over an old Model A, pointing their fingers and saying "bang." Shouting "bang!" as if their finger was a large caliber gun.

At first, old World War I songs were dredged out. "Over there, over there, the Yanks are coming, the Yanks are coming, and they won't be back till it's over, over there." "It's a long way to Tipperary. It's a long, long way to go."

Johnny was surprised to find Tipperary was in Ireland and not at the door to Berlin. *Did our soldiers . . . stop . . . to pick up their . . . four-leaf clovers . . . there?*

But the World War I "Over there, over there, the Yanks are coming, a drum, drum drumming everywhere." Often they only knew part of the songs but gladly made up the balance as they went along, then replaced, with the new World War II lyrics. "Johnny Zero got a zero today," and suddenly the broomsticks were replaced with Springfield and Enfield rifles, Browning automatic rifles, the BAR. The old World War I biplane gave way to the P-40 Tiger Shark, the P-51 Mustang and the P-38 Lightning, a plane with twin birds-of-prey, falconlike bodies.

Johnny and all his friends knew it would be over fast. Faster than greased lightning . . . I won't get a chance to get in it . . .

He knew they would all be singing "When Johnny comes marching home again, hurrah, hurrah. We'll give him a hearty welcome then. Hurrah. Hurrah. The men will shout, the girls will pout, the ladies they will all give out."

Johnny's father promised he would return home from the Sun Shipyard in Pennsylvania and work in the Boston Navy Yard as soon as he put enough money away to buy a car. So he could commute from Rockledge into Boston.

"I understand, Dad." *But, Dad . . . the yellow peril . . . goes right into . . . Boston . . . you know . . .*

Johnny had hopped the yellow trolley more than once. He was always careful not to sit on the large light that was fore and aft on the electric car that ran attached to sparking overhead wires and careful to hug low to its roof when up top so as not to get electrocuted. Hadn't his mother always said, "If you die through your own stupidity, I'll . . . I'll kill you!" Then she would turn away. Hiding her tear from him. She had a remarkable ability to drop a single tear, then buck up her courage, and turn the valve off before any flow started.

Charity told Tony, "If you don't want to take the Boston trolley to the navy yard, we can take my brother John's old Hudson off the blocks."

"My family isn't going to ride in an old Hudson when there are still some Packards out there being sold by families with sons gone to war. And the Yellow Peril is going to slip off the tracks one of these days and slide right into Duck Pond. And ruin all the balicky-bare swimming for the kids."

"Please don't use that kind of language in front of our kids."

"You know what the Yellow Peril is like. Anyone who has rattled inside it feels like a set of dice being rattled in a crap game tossing cup."

"Please don't use that kind of language in front of me."

The Yellow Peril was the combination of a work of art—a piece of beauty, a comet flight—and horror show, moving like an electrocuted elephant in its last throes.

It rattled through the sheepfold woods, sparks flying, swaying like a burred bull shooting out of its chocks at a rodeo. Other times it had the gait of a dog whose back was broken in collision with an automobile.

—

Johnny's mind turned to Duck Pond as he listened to his father talk of the trolley and its relationship to the pond.

The trolley ran alongside Duck Pond, where Johnny and his friends often swam naked amid their hoots and hollers, a covey of jabberwocking jaybirds, gloriously happy in their nonsense.

They sunned on a high outcropping of rocks, and when they heard the groan and moan of the Peril, they would dive into the water as swiftly as possible before anyone aboard could recognize them.

Rhesus always waited until the trolley was parallel to the rock, then covering his face with a smear of scooped mud so he couldn't be identified, he would do an all-exposing combination dive, starting out with a beautiful swan dive and ending with a frog plop, belly flop.

The swan part was a thing of beauty, arms outspread, back arched, head high. The frog plop meant knees bent, legs and arms outspread, leaving him looking like a football goal post.

Rhesus never understood how word got back to his father after one such dive, a report that would lead to a beating not only for him, but also his mother as well, for defending him.

What Rhesus didn't know was that an unfavorite aunt who had tanned his ass more than once and enjoyed it when he was a small snort nose rather than the medium-size snot nose he had grown into, recognized his tail assembly in that split second when he hung still on high, just before transforming from a swan into a frog.

She had screamed, "That's my sister's kid's bare ass there!"

Rhesus's father, his ketchup-colored hair bristling, told his wife, "Everyone in Rockledge will think we all have small donks set in penal colonies surrounded by a red ring."

While only Rhesus did his special dive when the trolley came along, they all had special Olympic dives they did for each other's amusement and scoring.

Hopalong (thus named by Johnny for his on-a-dare swallowing of a live grasshopper) Hufton earned a lowly two, on a scale of one to ten, for his Flying Flatulence dive, which simply involved his diving off their pet rock, jutting his butt out, and letting fly a fart. In secret, he planned a dive that would get him a twelve on a scale of one to ten. He would toss a doughnut into the air, get his bare body airborne, thrust his pecker at the doughnut, and announce the dive's title while still airborne, "Taking a flying fuck at a rolling doughnut."

Actually, Hoppalong's low score was not because of poor execution; his arse had formed a perfect arch. The dungeon level score was because his fart was a fraud. One of the judges detected that he made the noise through his flaccid lips, rather than it coming from the promised land.

Hopalong Hufton never really understood why he was scored so low for his dive. Even with the fake fart. He broke up his French and typing classes with his Bronx cheer-type fart, a noise not unlike that emitted by a male woodcock during its mating season. The little bird with the big nose gave off the Bronx cheer "prent phart" at the top of its climb, just before plunging earthward, only to pull up a few inches short of plowing itself deep into the alder-run mud.

Fat Burns, Scoff's younger brother, would throw his skinny body into the air, his legs flailing as if he was on a high-speed tread mill, his right hand pumping the air as he pretended to masturbate. Just before he hit the water with a resounding belly flop, Fats would let out a wonderful cry of sexual agony, "Aaaaah!"

His entitled Flog-the-hog dive got high points, mostly nines, because of the high risk of injuring his member during the belly flop.

Soupy Campbell told Fats, "We'd all give you perfect tens, Fats, but anyone can beat their meat while airborne. Anyway, with all your ribs showing, you look more like a harp with Zeppo Marx strumming you than a man thumping his tub."

"Why don't you try it if it's so easy, skunk piss."

Soupy struck first with a cheer, "Hit him high, hit him low, come on Rockledge, let's go," then switched to "Ain't it great to beat your meat on the Mississippi mud."

Righty Minichelli did a dive he entitled the Pink Ass, a reverse belly flop. Instead of landing with a splat on his stomach, which left the designated area looking as red as a red ant's ass, Righty did an incomplete jackknife, causing him to land flat on his bare butt, leaving his ass looking like the coals in a smoldering campfire. The dive was usually worth a seven but the pinker his tail, the higher his score. Righty always surfaced ass first, claiming it was his dick of a snorkel that served as a keel.

Righty encouraged the gang's hefty friend, Skinny Potts, to give his Pink Ass dive a try. Which he did.

But Righty forgot to tell Skinny to protect his testicles by cupping his hand over them right before the splat landing.

As the fates would have it, Skinny's unprotected balls were bashed, much to the delight of all except Skinny, of course. He didn't talk to Righty for a week. Just about the length of time it took his testicles to come from beneath his armpits where they were hiding and return to their proper storage area.

—

Skinny did get a big ten with the generosity of points and an outpouring of the glee at seeing their friend with the mashed balls, crying out to God, "Kill me, God! Put me out of my misery."

Up until Skinny's "Kill me God!" the Big Woods gang figured no one would ever best the nine given the Red Baron's biplane dive of the brothers Rhesus and Boattail. Boattail's hairdo, a pompadour that was combed back on the sides, formed a duck's ass in the rear. Other times, if the duck's ass wasn't formed and the hair went straight back, it looked like the stern of a canoe.

Somehow the brothers executed the biplane, their asses shining like the sun setting over the waters of Martha's vineyard, ran down the slanted surface of the gang's giant pet boulder Rocky, on which they all had sunned and supped. They got airborne in such a way that their bodies touched, chest to back, arms outspread, voila! The biplane.

But it didn't end there. While airborne, Rhesus, who formed the top section, spoke in what he imagined was the German accent of the Red Baron, "Ya, das shootten us downeth, and my nutsagopooffen."

Meanwhile, Boattail provided the voice of the English flyer who was locked in aerial combat with the Red Baron. "I say, nutsafooffen my bloody arse, you barsted bloke. I dam well Gatlinged your balls off!"

All this conversation in a thirty-foot free fall was not an easy transmission.

The dive itself would have drawn only an eight, but the German and English imitations, according to Johnny, sounded like a farting contest between the tailpipes of a Porsche and a Harley and gained them the extra point.

Despite the fact it did not score all that high, a seven, nearly everyone's favorite, was Soupy Campbell's the Death of the Diving Duck.

The Soup was an outstanding diver—from backflips, somersaults, jackknifes, gainers, twists, swans, rolls, you name it.

His swan dive, in particular, was a thing of beauty—ankles together, back arched, arms outspread, neck extended, head haughty.

The fact that his skin was milk white didn't hurt his swan dive's overall excellence one little bit. The gang was used to giving the rotten raspberries to all their friends' attempts at anything. Rarely did they give out with an appreciative ooh or an ah, but the Soup's dives did gain one or the other occasionally.

His invention of the Dive of the Dead Duck came about completely by accident and on the spur of a moment.

The Soup was at the high point of his swan dive off Rocky, a lovely Leda of Leda and the Swans, a Leda with a penis, when a loud bang echoed in the nearby woods. Someone was shooting squirrels with a 10 gauge, a shotgun, which under certain conditions, could sound like a clap of thunder in a canyon.

On hearing the shotgun retort, the midair-hanging Soupy buckled like a dead duck, folded his swan wings, and plunged straight down, emitting a Donald-Duck-type "oh boy."

After hitting the water, he floated on his back, the bottom of his feet facing skyward.

Laughter pealed off Rocky's back as the boys laughed so hard it hurt.

The tears streamed down Skinny's face as the bare-assed boy held his stomach and sobbed, "I'm just glad I don't have pants on. I would have pissed them.

They forgot to score the dive, except for Rhesus who visited the smooth-barked birch that served as a scoreboard over the years, and scraped in, "Campbell, Dive of the Dead Duck—seven."

Johnny, blessed with the Ted Williams's batting eye, those keen eyes that could see the stitching on a big league curve ball and read "Spalding" on its hide while it traveled at ninety-plus miles per hour, spotted something the others hadn't. The seven on the birch tree scoreboard wanted the dive scored at an eleven on a scale of one to ten.

What Johnny spotted as Soupy made the transition from swan dive to the Dive of the Dead Duck was that his eyes fluttered as he folded like a mallard hit by both barrels full of number four waterfowl shot. He did that wonderful arabesque and fluttered earthward, dead as a duck. Johnny remembered Righty's words as he looked at Rhesus's seven score on the birch. "My good God, he could make a rock cry." Righty had blown his mooselike nose, adding a goose honk to the situation, breaking up the gang one more time.

Those were the days these friends thought would never end. Those were the days. Those were the days, my friend.

They had celebrated the Dead Duck Dive with a twenty-gun salute as they moved over Rocky's stony back toward the air and then water, with Fat's war cry, "Last one in kisses his teacher's ass!" Then they were all airborne, landing with a cannonade of splashes below.

They floated on their backs, spitting duck pond water high in the air—spouter whales, they.

When an occasional hard-on rose to the occasion, the owner floated high in the water and the carrier of said stiffy proudly proclaimed, "Periscope up."

Boattail, a regular fish, always dove to the bottom when he heard the cry "Up periscope," scooped up a handful of pebbles, surfaced, and tried to sink the sub. He was usually successful, as there is something about pebbles tossed at a protruding penis that can be very deflating.

Johnny was another deep diver who could hold his breath like a field mouse hiding behind a leaf from a roaming farm cat. He sought a heavily clawed crayfish to instigate some real abandon ship action from the wearer of the periscope.

Those hardy mariners who remained periscope up despite the pebble bombardment, gave up and hoisted the white flag when Johnny sounded and collected hands full of crayfish from the underwater crevices at Rocky's base.

If Johnny managed to sneak up on the surfaced submarine and place a crayfish with dueling claws on the flesh-deck of the human submarine, the "I give up, kamarades" could be heard all the way from Duck Pond in Rockledge to Frankfurt, Germany.

It was during one of these Duck Pond moments that Johnny's father, looking for his son to tell him he was home, came upon the scene.

"Cheezit!" Rhesus boomed. "Johnny's old man is here."

Those in the water sounded, their white butts looking like the smooth heads of a pod of dolphins. Those on Rocky covered their private parts with anything handy, a branch, a handkerchief that had old Christmas hard candy hoarded in for a high moment, a soup can full of worms for fishing.

Their fright and flight stopped when they spotted Johnny's father spazzed out with tears of laughter streaming down his face. After he put it back together enough to use his voice, he yelled to his son, "Johnny, save some of those crawdads for bass fishing tonight! Full moon coming. The bucketmouths will be hitting. Grab some night crawlers and some of those little red cider worms for catfish and crappies. Tomorrow we're heading to Salem Willows for flounder and haddock. I'm renting a dory. You can drop over the side, grab a couple lobsters. I know where the bugs hide out. See you guys." Then as an afterthought, he said, "Keep your finger on it, guys."

Johnny was surprised by his dad's "Keep your finger on it." *Where did he learn that? That saying belongs to us . . . kids . . .*

"Nice guy, your old man. For an adult," Rhesus said.

"Scratch your bandy blue butt," Johnny said. "My pa's younger than yours."

"Mine's older than God," Rhesus said, "a real Methuselah. So your dad can be an old man. Besides I enjoy having a bandy ass as it powers that randy root of mine. Anyways, sticks and stones will break my bones, but names will never hurt me." Then pointing at himself, the rufous-headed Rhesus added, "I'm a shithead. See. It didn't hurt me."

—

"Fuck off," Boattail said to his brother. "You're no blood of mine. Ma bought you from traveling Gypsies for a dented old bed pan she was throwing out. So piss off."

Johnny got everyone's attention away from the brothers when he scaled a flat stone across the flat waters of Duck Pond and yelled "Eleven!" Johnny always had a flat stone in his pocket for scaling on water or hot top. Once he claimed a seventeen, a total under question by Rhesus, who said, "Prove it."

There were certain supplies the various friends always carried in their pockets, like Johnny's flat rocks, Fat's hard Christmas candy wrapped in and stuck to a handkerchief that would turn the stomach of a septic tank, Boattail always had a deck of miniature playing cards. And then there was Scoff, whose inventory depended on his pickings on that day. Nothing was off limits to his light fingers—cigars, bras, shoelaces, flashlight batteries, chewing gum, things acquired with all the ambition and courage of an old claim jumper in the Black Hills of the Dakotas.

Scoff had shown up at a show-and-tell day when he was in the third grade. He had forgotten to bring something to explain. When his name was called, he fished in his pocket as he hemmed and hawed, searching for anything. He was relatively new at the art of acquiring property without proper title at that age and his cupboard was nearly bare.

Johnny could tell that his friend did not have much in the way of showing and telling and wondered what he could do to help him, but his pockets only produced an old Juicy Fruit wrapper. So he just watched as Scoff fished around in his pockets chanting, "Old Mother Hubbard went to the cupboard to get her poor daughter a dress. When she got there, the cupboard was bare . . . and so was her daughter . . . I guess."

Johnny nearly always carried fishing line wrapped around a stick and a can full of hooks, but not on this day.

Scoff did have a River Runt, a red and white deep-diving plug used in bass fishing, but its treble hook was caught in his pocket lining. To make matters worse, the tip of one hook was slightly embedded in his foreskin, which cowered beneath his trousers. No taking the River Runt out for this show and tell.

It hurt more than getting caught in the zipper of his fly. There wasn't a man alive at the time of the invention of the zipper only a couple years before who wouldn't understand this feeling of helplessness.

Hadn't Johnny, in a philosophical mode when his foreskin got hung up after a distance-pissing contest in the Big Woods, waxed, "Every man must give up a pound of flesh to the toothy beast during his lifetime." *Sure . . . sort of like Grandma Shiverick . . . telling Ma . . . after she caught me eating dirt . . . when I was a little kid . . . Charity . . . every child . . . has to eat a . . . peck of dirt . . . before he dies . . .'*

Everyone in the class could see Ms. Feeny's eyes narrowing, her pupils changing to black BB pellets, especially Scoff, who watched to see if she went for the top-right drawer of her desk, where her hand-rapping ruler was sheathed. *If she makes a move . . . I'm out of here . . .*

It was then he felt the tampon he had rescued from the purse of one of the teachers at lunchtime the day before. The lunch monitor had put her hand in the middle of his back and pushed, "Keep moving. Take a seat." He made a move all right and had the tampon in his pocket to prove it.

The funny thing was that Scoff had no idea what it was or what it was for.

He pulled it from his pocket, placed it on the show and tell table in front of Ms. Feeny, who nearly fainted, but somehow between fanning her heart and giving a God-help-me roll of her eyes, managed a set of worrying words to Scoff. "This better be good. Pray tell what that is you have, and why you have it!"

"My dad uses it to clean the barrels of his side by side shotgun."

Ms. Feeny's sigh of relief sounded like the dying breath of a beached pilot whale.

The gang all understood what the pain was when a zipper sunk its teeth into an unwary frankfurter, everyone except Johnny, who was still wearing trousers with the button fly.

His mother explained to him that he was still wearing the old-fashion button-fly pants with the words "Waste not, want not." Charity really meant "We just can't afford any new clothes at this point."

One problem was the longer the button-fly trousers were worn, the bigger the exhausted buttonhole became. The bigger the buttonhole, the bigger the replacement button, until some, usually rescued from a woman's discarded coat, were as big as a half dollar, and the buttons could even be mismatched, one pearl, one hardened cardboard, one's "Button, button, whose got the button" search came up short.

As much of an unwanted attention getter that the big buttons were, they were better than the too-small buttons for the too-big buttonhole.

Button slippage, as often as not, often meant a cry from a friend, "The barn door is open. The horse will get away."

Righty, without looking down and drawing attention to the fact, would warn Johnny that buttons on his fly were undone by softly asking him, "Does it pay to advertise."

On this day, the day of the River Runt, Johnny gave Scoff forty feet of line from his stick, and Scoff wrapped the line around the bottom half of a Moxi soda bottle tied on the River Runt on to terminal end. Then using the Moxie neck as a fishing reel handle, he cast it out.

Ten casts later, he landed a smallmouth bass that was swimming near the surface.

Then Johnny, using a second length of line, took a lunker largemouth that was cruising for a bruising and eating little fish, then spotted the crayfish walking in circles on the bottom. Its legs on one side had been snipped off so it couldn't hide under a rock.

Skinny Potts, using a worm he had discovered in his half-eaten apple, asked Johnny for line and a hook.

As he rigged his setup using a small stone as a sinker, he asked, "Who knows what is worse than finding a worm in your apple?" Then he sulked when Soupy had the answer. "Half a worm? God, Skinny, that's older than yesterday's turd."

Skinny landed a hornpout, that wide-mouthed ugly of the bottom fish world, and asked, "Who's gonna take it off the hook?"

No one answered. But using the superior-thinking apparatus humans, even kid types, are imbued with, Skinny separated it from the line by bashing it with a sharp rock.

Jackknives popped out, cooking sticks cut, fuzz sticks to start a fire were whittled, and soon a rip snorting fire was snapping, and the fish were being cooked.

Johnny, in his best Tonto voice, grunted, "White man, build big fire, not only burn venison but Injun see fire, scalp white man. Indian make small fire, cook venison. And whiteman no find where Indian cook. Indian keep scalp."

"Gheeze, Johnny, you sure ensure that Tonto and Pocahontas will keep their jobs," Fats said, his skinny face breaking out in a skinny smile.

As the fates would have it, Scoff discovered both a pepper and a salt shaker in his back pocket and found a loaf of uncut Italian bread wrapped in a red bandanna that was always tied to a stick he carried endlessly over his shoulder, full of finds.

They tore the bread in pieces, setting up a pecking order, careful to have the one with the dirtiest hands tear last.

They made fish sandwiches and used the bones to pick their teeth.

"You know," Righty said, "you can't kill a hornpout. I caught a catfish once and buried it in the sand on shore because it gave me some sort of evil eye that hornpout can give you. It's sort of a voodoo doll.

"I dug it up three days later, and it was still alive. And it still gave me the evil eye. So I put it back in the water. You don't take no chances around a pout, I'll tell you."

—

"You ever watch them in a frying pan?" Fats asked. "You cut their head off, skin 'em out, toss them in a hot pan, and they wiggle and swim and move. You know they're escaping somehow, and that they'll get you eventually."

"How can they give you the evil eye," Righty asked, "when they don't got no head?" A statement, not a question.

Johnny said, "After you scrape all the meat off its head and paint it black with bright-red and bright-blue designs and tie a leather through its eyeballs, you've got a good-luck Indian necklace. One that keeps off evil eyes, animal, human. Subhuman. Even monsters. The only thing better is the head of a snapping turtle necklace. It not only wards off evil spirits, but it also brings good luck."

"Can it get you laid?" Rhesus asked with his wide-assed grin.

"No, better than that."

"Tain't nothin' better than getting a little ass. I like ass-bestus. It helps put out your fire," Rhesus said, his smile now swallowing his ears.

"Nope, better than Nookie," Johnny said.

"How do you know about Nookie, oh vestal virgin."

Ignoring Rhesus, Johnny said, "I put on my snapping turtle's head necklace for the first time. I dropped by the bakery to try and scrounge a whole doughnut rather than just a hole from Danny the Doughnut Man. He looked sternly at me and said, 'Ain't got no doughnut holes today.' His boss had given him hell for breaking some doughnuts on purpose to give out to the kids after he ran out of holes.

"I said, 'Thanks anyways.' No wise remarks like 'thanks for nothing.' As I turned to walk away, I rubbed my good-luck snapping turtle head necklace. Danny the Doughnut Man called my name. I turned, and he handed me the biggest honey-dipped doughnut ever invented. Not a hole. And not broken.

"But I didn't eat it all. No way. You have to share with your charm. I held a piece of the doughnut down below my neck, and that turtle head snapped off a bite."

"Man," Boattail said, "if bullshit was money, you'd be a millionaire."

"And if brains were dynamite, you wouldn't have enough to blow your nose."

"Old stuff, Johnny, real antique," Rhesus said, jumping in to defend his brother.

The pitter-patter, carefree chatter, the fish cooked on a stick, fish caught by the kids, complete with salt and pepper, and Italian bread torn by hand, the sun, the balicky-bare Olympic diving, oh yes.

Yes, those were the days, my friend.

—

Johnny, who had learned about the outdoors from his father, managed to teach his buddies about fishing, animals, trees, and even flowers—no, devil's paintbrushes were not those housepainters trying to edge Grandfather Shiverick out of contracts.

They learned if you drank water that flowed out of a cedar swamp, it could drive you insane. That certain wild plant bulbs tasted like potatoes when roasted on the same stick as the largemouth and pout.

Whenever Tony took the bus or train from his shipyard in Chester, Pennsylvania, to Rockledge, Massachusetts, father and son would fish Mill Pond in Chelmsford. They always caught fish—pickerel, bass, crappie, yellow and white perch.

When fishing was slow, they went to the sites they had prepared the past winter. Johnny and his dad dragged large limbs and brush onto the ice. The pile would sink in the spring thaw, setting up the hiding spots for the small prey and hunting spots for the predators.

Then they made small maps on birch bark and hid them in tree hollows. On the slow summer fishing days, they would take out the map and find their underwater pile where the fish congregated to hide from the sun and predators.

At night, Tony taught Johnny to toss a big boulder in the water with a "kerplunk!"

"'Cause, son, bullheads are curious fish. They'll come to investigate. And they'll discover that ball of worms on your hook. When you feel them stripping line, let 'am run with it. They are just mouthing it. When the line stops stripping, set that hook because they're chewing that cud of worms. Those fish not only hit the food they see, but they also answer telephone calls. Like the boulder in the water when we fish cats. You remember how I told you to get the blackfish taugs in the ocean to come to you so you could spear them?"

"Yes. Catch one on those green crabs, dive down, crack it apart with a rock. The taug will hear the cracking. They will also get the smell of crab dinner on the drift. And they will come a runnin', bug eyed and bucktoothed as an old lady reading her card and yelling, 'Bingo!"

"You've got it."

Then one day, his father wasn't there when the train from Chester arrived in Rockledge. He swore he would be.

Johnny kept looking back down the tracks, although he knew this was the last train of the day.

Then he heard the horn. A happy horn, and some guy in a shiny black Packard with whitewalls as wide as the center strip on a superhighway and with spare tires set in shiny black and chrome metal protectors housed in

—

the front fenders. There were blinding silver mirrors on top, both spares, but the hood ornament, a silver-winged lady, arms outstretched, was the pièce de résistance.

Johnny couldn't take his eyes off it. He had grown to love the image of an elegant Packard, seeing it through the eyes of his father. *Someday . . .*

The lady of the Packard hood was even more elegant than the three-mast sailing ships that graced the Plymouth hoods.

The Packard's horn blasted again. *Who is it?*

An arm appeared out the window, motioned him to "come on over here. Don't shilly shally."

I don't . . . trot trot to Boston . . . to buy a fat pig . . . home again . . . home again . . . jiggidy jig . . . let the rich snob . . . come to me . . .

The arm was replaced by a head that appeared out the open window. "Johnny!"

"Dad!" Johnny leaped a tall building with a single bound. Faster than a speeding . . . bullet . . . "Dad? Whose?"

"Mine. Hop in. We're going to the farm."

They didn't drive up the driveway to his parents' old farmhouse that had not been painted since it was built forty years before. Farmhouses don't get painted when there are cows to milk, apple trees to prune, potatoes to plant, corn to harvest, and goat tits to put bag balm on.

They parked down at the entrance to the dirt driveway. "Don't want to get dust on this beauty."

"You'd better believe it, Dad."

Tony opened the trunk of the Packard, pulled out a new South Bend fishing rod with a Pfleuger reel, and handed it to his son. He had a matching one.

The two headed away from the farm, past the underground hog havens, over the first small hill behind it. Without any type of word or signal, they both stopped and turned their sight backward to the Packard. They turned to each other. And smiled.

Then they were off again, uphill, into the woods toward Mill Pond.

"Beat you to that stand of reeds," his father challenged, and when Johnny shot out in front of him, Tony grabbed his belt and pulled him backward using the action to slingshot himself forward.

Despite Tony's great lead, they ended up neck and neck at the reeds that stood guard around a small vernal pool.

His father placed his left hand on his hip, held his right arm out in front of him assuming a dueler's stance, and then flicked his fishing rod at Johnny. "En garde!" Then jumping forward, both feet off the ground at the same time, he stabbed the tip of his rod into Johnny's stomach, "Touché"

—

Johnny grabbed his stomach, fell to the ground, moaning a fake "Oooooh. I'm dead."

"Don't get any sand in your reel," his father instructed, helping his dead son to his feet.

They started out again toward the sandpit that was hidden two knolls further.

They hiked up the shoulder of the pit, keeping away from the edge where a number of trees hung precariously on the top border as the settling sand tried to pull them down and under.

"Over here," his father beckoned as he searched between two slabs of Rock that had been knifed out of the soil millions of years before. "I hid 'em here when I was a kid."

Johnny looked as his father pulled out two sheets of tin used for shed roofs. "What are they?"

"Take a look," his father said, putting one piece of metal on the edge of the sandpit, standing on it, and then getting it into motion downhill by shifting his weight forward and back like a car trying to escape from its slippery snow prison.

Then he was off, "Giddy-up!" snow-tinning down the sandy slope, trailing a wake of sand like a pursuing avalanche.

Johnny followed on his steed of metal. "Yippe-aye-yeah-ki-yeah!"

Their painful plunge into thorns at the bottom became bearable when they discovered their tormentors were dressed in wild raspberries. They plunked down in the warm sand, scooping the berries of the bush with both hands, and shoveled the sweet fruits of their labor into their mouths.

"We have to leave some for the whitetails," Tony said, "as of all the various foods and trace elements a deer needs for a high and thick rack, nothing approaches wild raspberries."

Sated, they struggled up from their warm sand beds and walked slowly through the berry patch and into an aspen stand held prisoner by clumps of white pine that invaded onward, beating their competition, the hardwoods, oak, maple, walnut, to the open areas.

"When you walk through the poplars—"

"Dad, you said the last time that these trees were aspens."

"Aspens, poplars, cottonwood, all the same tree," the father told the son, "like mountain lions have the name cougar, catamaran, panther. Same family."

"Wow."

"It is all *wow* in the outdoors."

Johnny loved the clear, calm way his father enunciated his words. *Wow . . .*

"Why do we always stop in the aspens, Dad?"

"Ruffed grouse feed in the aspens. Then hide in the nearby pine trees. If you keep walking, they think you do not see them, but if you stop, they're not sure. They get nervous. Panic. And fly. Playing those Gene Krupa drums they call wings. That's how you hunt old Ruff when you don't have a bird dog. Make them nervous."

"Why are they called rough? Are they rough and tough birds?"

Tony put his arm around his son as they walked. "It is r-u-f-f, short for cuffed, not r-o-u-g-h. A ruff is one of those round stiff collars the dandies wore in Europe a hundred years ago. Old Ruff grouse has a similar wheel-shaped collar around its neck. Come on. Onward to Mill Pond." Tony set off at a jog. Johnny caught up to him and then ran abreast. They moved easily, almost effortless, as they extended their strides.

"Deer," his father said.

"Antelope," Johnny said, upping the pace.

"Elk."

"Wapiti."

"Samee-samee," his dad said.

"Then—cheetaaaaah!" Johnny said, streaking forward.

"Hey," his father said, out of breath, catching up to his son, "this is supposed to be fun."

"Tortoise," Johnny said in a slow-motion voice that matched the speed he downshifted into.

His father laughed, making a flying tackle on his son.

They lay there, out of breath, laughing. Then on their feet, loped slowly through a large field of ragweed, milkweed, and goldenrod that opened into occasional small open patches that housed devil's paintbrush, toothwort, thistle, and Queen Ann's Lace. "Hey . . . Dad . . . Queen Ann . . . had a ruff . . ."

They slowed to a walk in the wild flowers as the sun warmed their faces, eyes closed, faces tilted upward.

The sudden coolness caused them to open their eyes. They had reached the edge of the field and were out of the full sunlight and into the shadows of the trees. Then into the woods, where the sunlight filtered in. A slight breeze moved the maple leaves whose reds and oranges and yellows were being swiftly colored in, making the two joggers dizzy within nature's cosmos, turning their surroundings into an old-fashioned silent movie in full color.

"Let's turn it on. Let's run," Johnny said, setting off at a full canter.

His father legged it beside him, singing a Jamaican tune, "Run, run, run, when you see a prit-tee wu-mon. Run, run, run, when you see a prit-tee wu-mon." *No way can I run . . . run, run . . . when I see a pretty . . . woo mon . . .* Tony could feel a warm stirring in his crotch as his penis swung forward, back in rhythm to his running motion. He closed his eyes, changed his running style, swaying slightly at the hips to cause his cock to sashay to one side and then the other, cutting a swath through smiling women, naked smiling women.

Tony thought of his brother, Manny, and his American dream. *My dream is a bathroom rug of tits . . . that I could do a . . . breaststroke through . . . sucker suckee . . . on the way . . . to the tub . . .*

Johnny snapped off dead pine limbs underfoot as he ran.

"Run like a whitetail doe," Tony said, now tit sated. "They never snap a dry limb. They put each hoof on soft earth."

The boy put on a burst of speed. "I was made for speed" *Oh . . . sure . . . slew foot . . .* "So see you later, alligator."

"In a while, crocodile."

Johnny was happy his father knew all the kid calls, forgetting that Tony was a kid once himself.

They ran through the woods, and they ran through the hills, and they ran through the rims, and they ran through the rills.

"Here!" Johnny said, stopping on their smooth, round rock on the edge of Mill Pond, which in reality was a very slow-moving river, actually a brook that had been dammed up. *Our spot . . .*

The fact that they had traveled through heavy woods without taking a bearing and came out at *their* rock did not surprise either father or son. To the contrary, if they had not come out at the rock, they would have been surprised.

Tony tied a heavy stone and a jagged stick to the end of a long piece of rope and tossed it far into the river. He slowly retrieved it.

He enjoyed Johnny's unasked question as to what he was doing. "Guess?"

"Well, when you throw the big boulder in the water at night, it's because the catfish are curious and will come runnin', running." He wanted to pronounce his g's as his father did. "But you said the boulder hitting the water during the day doesn't seem to make them curious. So why?"

"What you are doing on the retrieve is stirring up the bottom. Setting all the goodies free. To get the little yum-yums out of their beds in the mud. Putting them into the stream of things. Putting them on the menu of every hungry fish from here to Timbuktu."

"After we catch some white perch for eating, can I dive for lures? Can we stay and do some bass fishin', fishing, after dark?"

"Why not."

They were some fifty feet above the dam, an area where many species of fish congregated to feast on the food being carried downstream. Just before the dam, about eight feet underwater, was a pile of sandbags left there from when the brook was first stopped up and diverted while the dam was constructed. Fishermen who ran their lures too deep often got them hooked on the burlap and lost them. The former sandbag dam was a Christmas tree of Daredevyles, runts, deep divers, flatfish. The only ones immune from the lure-swiping burlap were the crazy crawlers, jitterbugs, and other pitter-patter surface lures.

"Should be plenty there. And you might make yourself four bits. There might be a twenty-five-pound snapper down there. Your grandfather pays two cents a pound for snapping turtle meat. That's weight without the shell."

"Does that count the head and legs?"

"The legs, not the head. Use the head to make lucky necklaces to sell to those people in Lowell, the ones from Haiti."

"Looks like the water's still. You always said we need a little surface wind ripple to catch fish. Do you think Grammy DaSilva baked bread? Grammy's bread with Nana Shiverick's homemade beans and bread pudding! I could eat a rock."

"Hey, hey, hey. Whoa up, Silver. Are we going to cut bait, or are we going to fish?"

They baited their hooks with the selection of insects, worms, and slugs they picked from under rocks and off the bottoms of leafs near their fishing rock.

Johnny had a pile of smoldering leaves that he kept night crawlers in, picked off the local golf greens on dew-sopped nights, plus a good collection of red wigglers dug out of an old manure pile. He had caught a mouse to use bass fishing, planning to tie the mouse to a little twig, hook tied to its body, and float it out into the water. And then when it was out a way, he'd pull the mouse off its raft and into the water. The swimming mouse would attract the biggest bucketmouth bass.

The problem is Johnny had made the mistake of naming it Ping Pong Paddles because of its ears. He hadn't listened to his Nana Shiverick, who told him you never name any live animal you plan to raise for food or bait. Never.

His grandmother, who was in charge of killing the chickens and rabbits that were used for table fare, named one bunny buck with ears feathered more than the others Indian Feather Ears.

It lived to an old age, he-man of the hutch, a furry cock of the loft.

Ping Pong Paddles had no such long life. Johnny had made a home in a shoe box for the mouse that lived on cheeses collected for Johnny by Scoff—"No questions asked."

Johnny had not informed his mother of the bait turned pet, and when she spotted the mouse making its rounds of Johnny's room, she flattened it with her broom.

"I think your grandmother DaSilva will have bread out of the oven when we show up with a string of pout for her. She seems to have a sixth sense about when her son and grandson's noses are sniffing the air and fills it with the smells of bread and apple pie and—da da—homemade ice cream!"

"Whoa up, Dad. Are we going to fish or cut bait?"

"Touché."

They caught bass, largemouth, and smallmouth, even a few of those red-eyed rock bass and even pretend bass, the crappie that calls itself the calico bass.

The dark settled in, and although the thought of Nana DaSilva's homemade bread and homemade peanut butter was a strong lure, the lure of catching a stringer of hornpout and maybe one of those bucketmouth bass that sleep all day and only eat at night was too strong.

"You prepare the stink bait?" Tony asked his son.

"Yup, just the way the pout like it. Gourmet. Giant rotting night crawlers that I picked off the greens at Unicorn Golf Course. And rotting shrimp the fish market tossed out. I left the whole kit-and-caboodle hanging in an onion bag on the clothesline. Two days in the sun. P-U. Whew!"

"Any problems with your mother?"

"Nah. But I had to beat off a couple tomcats that chose our bait-to-be over a female cat as it started to ferment. There could have been a problem with the little red wigglers I pulled out of Gramma DaSilva's cider pressings. I put 'em, them, in the icebox so they wouldn't spoil. But the worms got out of the Hoods Dixie cup they were in and got all over the box. Lucky I was the first one to spot them."

"Great. But are you sure the night crawlers smell as ripe as your sneakers in July?"

"Worse. We won't even have to hook the pout. When they get a whiff, they'll just commit chop suicide to get at them."

"Good. Do they wiggle like Dorothy Lamour in a sarong and two cups of Jell-O doing the tango?"

"Yup."

Tony clapped his son on the back. "Then we can count our hornpout before they hatch."

Johnny looked at his dad. Looked away. Smiled. I'd rather joke with you, Dad . . . than have a mustie . . . at the spa . . .

Often Johnny stared up at the ceiling in the dark of his bedroom, evenings dreaming of the strawberry ice cream and soda water concoction. The five cents needed to purchase one didn't come along that often.

"Dad, the Red Sox named their right fielder Catfish Mekovitch because a herring gull dropped a hornpout out of its mouth, right beside Mekovitch in Fenway. I wonder if those *Globe and Post* sportswriters know their fish. If they did, his name would be Hornpout Mekovitch."

"Let's toss 'em out and stand by to direct traffic," his father said as they cast their baits into the slow-moving stream.

They felt their worm ball bait sink to the bottom, and it wasn't more than a hop, skip, and a jump before they both felt their stink baits being mouthed by the bottom-feeding whisker wearers and then being carried off.

As darkness deepened they landed pout after pout, tossing them behind them in the tall grass to be rounded up later.

"Dad, can we take the raft Pointer, Dink, and I made out tomorrow? We can catch pickerel. I caught a bunch of green leapers that will drive them crazy. And we can bring the .22 and shoot water snakes."

"Sounds good to me."

"Can we shoot tires first? I carried twenty-three old tires to the top of the sandpit hill up in the Farm Woods. And put deer and bear and rabbit and grouse drawings on cardboard I wedged inside the tire center. I also drew in some Jap rats. And Nazi storm trooper rats. And Mooso-leanie faced rats."

"Sounds great, mate."

"And I found a new section to roll them down the hill. They'll bounce like a deer running," the boy said, getting more and more excited.

"Fan-tas-tic!"

"And I'll bring the bow you made me. I made a whole batch of new arrows. And we can shoot with them too."

"This will be all snap shooting. Reaction," Tony said, "not like shooting woodchucks as they sun in the field. No time for breathe in, let half it out, and then a slow squeeze, like you were squeezing a lemon in your hand. How did you do on chucks this summer?"

"All the farmers wanted me and Dink and Pointer. Ah, Dink, Pointer, and me. Groundhogs all over the place. We did good. Pie made fodder out of them to feed the pigs. I think he made sausage too. But plenty of farmers opened their fields to us. Even Old Farmer Osterhouse after he had to put down a horse that stepped in a chuckhole and broke its leg. She was carrying foal too."

"Chucks are bad news. How well did you do shooting at the tires with the bow? They're tough enough with a rifle. With a bow they could be impossible."

"Nah. After shooting ruffed grouse with a .22 and a bow, the tires are slow. Bow. Slow. I'm a poet. And don't know it."

"Yah, your feet show it. They are long fellows."

"Got the big feet from you, Dad. I don't have to wear snowshoes in the winter to walk on top."

"Yah, that's why the army wouldn't take me. They couldn't find combat boots to fit your old dad."

Johnny knew that if his dad got to face the bad guys, they'd pay big time. *Big time . . . . they'd . . . pay . . .*

He knew it wasn't the size of his father's feet that kept him out of the army. His mother had told him his father's work in the Sun Shipyard was vital to the war effort. "We need ships, and he is a little too old."

"So wasn't Uncle John Shiverick, and he got in," Johnny had said.

"That's enough of that, young man. Because your father is gentle doesn't mean he isn't brave. He would go in a second if they thought they would take him, but he's proud. Too proud to fail to get in. He's really just a little too old, older than your uncle John Shiverick, and look what happens when you're old and try and go fight. You get shot like your uncle. A young man could have dodged those bullets. Do you want your father shot because he is too old? No, of course you don't."

"I know, Dad's brave, Ma." *I wish he could lend . . . me a few years . . . just enough so we could go to fight . . . together . . . Dad could carry the .22 . . . I could bring my bow . . . become a sniper . . . No Jap rat . . . would see a puff from a sniper rifle . . . and shoot me . . . out of my tree . . . then I'd . . . I'd scalp . . . 'em . . .*

"What are you thinking about, dear?" his mother had asked him at that time.

"Ah, that I need a, a haircut." He wondered if his crossed fingers meant that he hadn't actually lied to his mother. *If I was a . . . Catholic . . . I could go to confession . . . and . . . it . . . wouldn't . . . be . . . a lie . . .*

After his conversation with his mother then, he had wondered what it would be like to be a Catholic. *Please . . . dear Lord . . . don't let Grandfather . . . Shiverick . . . read my mind . . .*

Johnny had wondered whether he would have hit for a higher batting average if he was allowed to cross himself before each at bat. But Ted

Williams didn't cross himself. Was Ted Catholic? Nah . . . his mother was with the . . . Salvation Army . . .

He had sung softly to himself, "Salvation Army, Salvation Army, put a nickel on the drum, save another drunken bum. Salvation Armeeee."

"What are you singing?" his mother had asked.

He crossed his fingers on both hands behind his back. "An army song. I want to join the army. I was singing onward Christian soldiers." *Forgive me . . . Mother . . . for . . . I have . . . sinned . . .*

When his mother had turned away, he crossed himself. *What in heck . . . did . . . I . . . do?*

The Salvation Army was his mother's favorite charity. She had told him many times, "The army people are humble. They are bankers and school superintendents, mill workers, shoemakers. Even some millionaires who take a few pennies and treat you like you gave a million. They give it all to the poor and ask nothing in return."

"Forget the army thing, Johnny. You are much too young. You want to end up like your uncle. Without a jaw, sticking keys to the roof of his mouth for kids' amusement."

"But if Dad and me went in the army together, we could end it fast and bring everyone home. Uncles Matt, Luke, and Mark Shiverick and Uncles Manny and Francesco. And—"

"Enough. I won't hear it." She looked down at her son. Parted his hair gently in the middle. "You look like alfalfa, your hair parted in the middle, freckles and all."

"Aunt Hope said I look like Tom Sawyer and that Jazz looks like Huck Finn with his buckteeth and all. I didn't like that about Jazz and told her so."

"You don't ever talk back to an adult."

"Even if I'm right?"

"Even if you're right."

"I'll talk to your aunt. It was unkind. And she isn't an unkind person."

Johnny often thought about his father and he ending the war. *No one can shoot . . . like us . . .*

If they ended the war, he wouldn't have to deliver his morning papers with his head down. He wouldn't have to look at customers' windows to see if one of the blue stars had been replaced by a gold star. *Why does there . . . have to be . . . wars?*

"Yes, your feet are long fellows." It was his father's voice. "You still with me? You drifted off."

"Do any snipers carry bows and arrows?"

"I don't really know."

"They could."

"Perhaps."

"I know they could. I heard that natives in the jungle in the Philippines killed Japanese with blow guns."

"I'm sure a sniper could carry a bow and arrow if he could shoot like you."

Johnny could feel his chest expanding, tightening on hearing his father's words.

They stood in silence, man and boy, looking at each other, alone at their secret fishing hole.

"What's that racket back there? Those hornpout still kicking. They should be pretty well played out by now," Tony said.

Johnny went into the deep grass to see why the pout were causing a ruckus.

The one remaining fish had a good reason for raising ruckus. Only its head was sticking out of the mouth of the giant black water snake that had swallowed the fish one by one as they were tossed backward into the grass. The fish's eyes bulged in fear. The snake's were as focused and steely as the head of a nail.

"Guess we'll just have your grandmother cook up the bass we've got on the stringer," Tony said.

"I'll kill that darn snake with a rock!"

"Nah. It was just doing what comes naturally. It was our mistake," his father said, pulling the stringer of bass out of the water, where they were left to stay fresh. The bass on the bottom of the stringer wasn't much use. They could see its tail had been eaten off by the snapping turtle that released it at the surface and swam off into the dark waters.

"Want to play Indians and Indians later?" Johnny asked, tossing the stringer of bass over his shoulder.

"How about tomorrow. When we can see the signs. We can play it on the way to the raft and pickerel fishing."

Most of the time they played Indians and Indians as they knew the Indians were more skilled than the cowboys and settlers.

One would hide, the other seek, searching for scuffed leaves where the one who hid failed to heel and toe or for a snapped twig carelessly stepped on.

His father always took off like a big-assed bird when it was his time to hide. "Make your decision and move out. He who hesitates is lost."

Johnny always wondered whether his father would find one of his favorite hiding spots and hide there. That's why when he was the seeker, he never checked his own hiding spots, fearful his father would be watching him from a cloistered treetop and discover his hideaway.

—

Johnny's favorites were the giant rotted stump that he hid inside, closing the opening with a large sheet of birch bark and in between the large open pages of ledge, which his friends always shied away from because it served as the house for porcupines, coyotes, snakes, and, some suspected, a passing cougar or even a sleepy bear.

He had discovered the giant stump hideout quite by mistake. He had seen steam escaping from one of the many woodpecker holes in the stump one winter, and sure enough, a careful, peek see turned up a sleeping bear sow and her two cubs. He had retreated posthaste when he mistook her snorting snore as a growl.

The discovery of the ledge hideout was another lucky discovery. One steamy summer day, he had been sitting on a boulder when he noticed one section of the ledge that steadily dripped water from a hidden spring. When he threaded the shale to secure more of an outpouring for a drink, he found it hollow behind its fascia.

If his father had discovered him rather easily in several games in a row of Indians and Indians, he used the hiding place in the most secret corner of his bag of tricks. He had seen a movie when he was young where a good Indian hiding from bad ones had lowered himself into a swamp and breathed through a reed.

His dad had spotted him. *But too good . . . to say . . . I gotcha . . .* His father had turned and walked off, still in search.

He learned from his father during these times. Tony explained to him that the reason he had discovered his son's hiding place was because a crow or blue jay or red squirrel would caw, squawk, or chatter, giving the young intruder hell. "You have to hide from them as well as me," he had told Johnny.

The boy learned the red squirrels were the worst of the finks, keeping up their continuous and rapid fire. "He's here, he's here, he's here."

And if you tossed a stick to drive it away, you'd only pissed the feisty fellow off, and it would turn its chatter into machine-gun staccato, its tail as active as a gunner's trigger finger.

There were other things to watch for, even a weed could give you away.

Once Johnny, being pursued closely by his father, had crawled inside a punk, rotting log. He figured his father would never dream that he would hide inside a log with red ants all over the outside of it. He had forgotten they would be inside as well but had bitten his tongue as the ants bit him, including one that crawled up his nostril and another over his right eye. He sensed his father nearing.

His father had spotted the dry ragweed that had been snapped off near the opening of the log. Then saw the thinnest line of a heel drag where Johnny had forced himself inside.

Tony plunked himself on the log, trying to get his rear end to transmit to his hiding son inside it that he had no idea Johnny was there.

Tony wanted to get up immediately as the single-minded red ants found the opening at his belt line. Half were creeping and crawling up his backbone while the rest were heading down his buttocks for a little dining.

Tony was having these kinds of visitations on top the log. Johnny, inside, was infested with the ants, centipedes, along with a possible passing snake or cold-snooted, star-nosed mole. He thought to himself, *Wonder how long . . . the tough little turd . . . can take it . . .*

It was a bite on the balls that got Tony moving on.

He walked out a distance, then hid. He'd wait until his son left the log then pounce on him with a "gotcha!"

It didn't work. Johnny punched armholes in the log and crawled off into the high grass, looking like an alligator with its butt bobbed.

Tony waited in his hiding spot, but no Johnny. Finally he left his cover and investigated. Not only was his son missing, so was the log.

"I'll be damned."

His son was learning survival. He would not be as easy to trick as he was when he was a young boy and hid in the open field, out of his sight.

Tony would yell out, "Stand up! I see you!" Although he couldn't see the hiding boy.

And the young boy would stand up. Figuring his dad somehow did see him. *Fathers . . . do not . . . lie . . .*

Even later, when he learned he had been tricked, Johnny didn't think of his father's subterfuge as lying. It was strategy.

Johnny, in the full bloom of gullibility, was convinced of this. Like the mouse who believed the cat that said, "All I want is to have you enjoy the smell of the cheese on my breath" was an upright citizen.

The boy was learning, and Tony did not beat his son down. To the contrary, as each learning incident took place for Johnny, Tony felt the closeness growing. Fathers do not compete with sons. They were becoming equals—Indians chasing Indians.

Not all of Johnny's education by his father involved the outdoors.

The boy had hints of education about the indoors.

The main difference was that Tony knowingly taught Johnny about the outdoors, and unknowingly taught him about the indoor aspects of life.

Tony finally had agreed to go for a job interview at the Bowdoin Square Garage, just off Boston's Scully Square.

He asked Johnny to get him a pair of his work shoes from his closet.

The work boots stood like a tall tree among the variety of dress shoes that ran from wing tips to patent leather.

They were neatly arranged, like soldiers in parade formation. The variety of dress suits, jackets, and shirts were all perfectly spaced above the shoes they would go best with.

Tony told his son he had bought the nice clothing for Johnny. That they were his as soon as he grew into them. Johnny felt the silk in one particular suit and dreamed of it replacing his whistling corduroys or dungarees, which the vice principal of Rockledge High had told him, "Can *not* be worn to school."

He secured the steel-toed and steel-arched boots and brought them to his dad, who was reading *Field & Stream* at the kitchen table while his mother stacked pancakes on his plate. She didn't have much time for cooking. Her two specialities were pancakes cooked on the hot surface of the black iron stove in the morning and hot dogs boiled at night.

Tony ladled the maple syrup Johnny had tapped from trees in the Big Woods and boiled over an open fire there. He was surprised how much of his tapping it took to boil down to a couple spoonfuls, but it was fun tapping nature. Carving and hollowing out the spigots, making birch bark buckets, tying the sheets of bark together with roots he had pulled out of the ground and split, and then sealing the seams with pine pitch.

He had learned maple sugaring from his grandfather Shiverick, who sugared off, cut wood, and prayed all winter long when house painting was shelved for the season. At first his grandfather had used an old plow horse he had swapped for a house painting. Then he discovered an old one-lung John Deere tractor abandoned at the dump, fixed it with baling wire and a heavy-duty *Carnation Evaporated* milk can that he reshaped. The forlorn and abandoned girdles he found at the dump, usually secreted in a nondescript container that even the elite of dump pickers would overlook, were cut up into the various seals needed to prevent leakage of fluids or power.

The old man often lamented to his grandson that he missed the old horse. "In the sugaring woods, you can whistle, and a horse will come to you. You can whistle 'til the moon turns blue and a tractor won't budge one inch."

Johnny watched closely as his father spread the syrup he had tapped and boiled, hoping there was enough for his father.

"Hope it goes well at the interview. It's at the Bowdoin Square Garage?" Charity said, "I'm sure you know more about cars than anyone there."

"Hope so. But I'm not sure it will pay like defense work. I can always go back to the Sun Shipyard. I kept a small apartment in Chester."

"Maybe you could place a taxi sign on the roof of your Packard. I know they get good tips. Better than I get on my paper route during Christmas," Johnny said hopefully.

"On the roof of my Packard? I don't think it would work," his father said, "besides, someone would always be trying to steal such a beautiful vehicle. Someday it will be yours. I better be heading into Boston."

"You going alone?" Charity asked.

"I'm a big boy now," her husband said.

"I didn't mean anything by that."

"Come on, Johnny. We'll go see about that mechanic's job for your father."

The drive into Boston was a lot faster in the Packard than hopping a ride on the rear light of the Yellow Peril or crouching low on the trolley's roof with sparks showering down on your back and head. Sometimes there would be as many as four or five of his gang on the roof and an additional buddy sitting on the rear light.

Their goal was always the same. The Boston Commons. To watch and listen to the guys who made speeches while standing on their soapboxes. Some were dressed like U.S. senators and called each other, with great respect, senator.

Several of them had snuck into the State House on the upper north end of the Common and listened to a real, live debate between real live state senators.

Johnny believed the Boston Common senators would do a better job than the ones inside the State House. They seemed to have more common sense and definitely appeared more sincere, or was "honest" the word the boy was trying to think of?

Not all the Boston Commons senators wore ascots, which often were napkins or place settings that if checked closely might say "Hotel Statler." Some were dressed as cowboys, many outfitted as clergy, and one outfitted himself quite nicely as a burlesque queen, but a final touch seemed to be missing there.

Some said the most interesting things. "Senator Henry Cabot of the Cabot Lodges squats to pee."

A smattering of cheering.

"And doesn't have the common sense of an ally cat to scratch dirt over it."

A much larger volume of cheering accompanied by head nodding.

Eloquence was most often the order of the day. "Just because we are running out of space to dump our refuse, we cannot allow dumping in the Grand Canyon—it will be full in ten years."

"Eros is God."

"God is everywhere. All around us. In this grand common. In the air. In my shorts."

"If God really so loved man, why hadn't he put our peckers where our noses are and our noses where our peckers are. Thereby we could screw and whiff at the same time. And with the nose down there, no man would have the unmitigated gall to blame another for his flatulence."

"The pope is Polish."

"The world ends January 32!"

"All you gawking fools can go to Erebus. You're not good enough at being bad to go to Hades."

"I never use soap and water and have never been sick a day in my life. That has to tell you something."

"Yes, sir, Mr. Senator. You stink!"

Johnny backed away from the man as he approached him. *Yes . . . no one gets close enough to you . . . to give you . . . their . . . cold . . .*

The only ones that the Rockledge boys considered ridiculous and potentially dangerous enough to taunt were the animal rights people.

"Hey, lady, you've got hamburg juice coming out of the side of your mouth," Rhesus said to a well-dressed middle-aged woman.

"Mister, you've got on leather shoes and belt," Boattail said.

"You don't sleep on a goose down pillow, do you, fella?" Soupy asked.

"Scientific tests prove that plants have feelings, register pain, joy. What do you eat, rocks?" Righty asked.

Fats, whose skinny ass had a love affair with Joe and Nemo's hot dogs, was most the volatile. "Fess up, Mr. Oog the fella, do you eat rocks or cocks?"

And Righty had grabbed his crotch and smiled at the speaker who believed a monkey's rights came before cancer research. Righty had lost a younger sister, Josephina, to the disease.

They could work themselves into a lather, either agreeing or disagreeing with the speakers or just being amazed at the wonderment of the acts. And asking themselves what these people did to eat and sleep and purchase their senator's clothing, Indian headdress, strippers G-string.

Johnny had told his friends, "I recognize that one guy. He was on the front page of the *Post* I delivered this week. He's some sort of brain surgeon at Boston General. Honest."

Boattail tapped Johnny on the side of the head. "Sure. And he worked on you."

When worn out with the excitement of listening to and watching the soapbox kings, popes, presidents, Indian chiefs, males dressed as female strippers, and monkey rights people, they would rest and regain their energy by riding the swan boats. Looking skyward, they hoped to see a passing pigeon's droppings on a bald man's pate or on a stuck-up lady's nose so her eyes would have to cross view it.

Then refortified in spirit, they would walk across the Common to the New-York-style deli to refortify in body.

The aromas in the deli were worth the price of admission, breads, cheeses, gingers, olive oil, cheesecake, and onions.

There were, of all things, homemade Boston baked beans; and although it was a New York style deli, there wasn't a pot of Manhattan clam chowder. Bostonians would not sit for such an insult.

Their noses were as active as a hutch full of feeding and mating rabbits, as they sniffed the great variety of bagels that ran the gauntlet, from A to Z, Z to A, and then sideways.

The deli was an exotic foreign country to them as they took in, owl-eyed, the great and exotic combinations of sandwiches—Reubens, corned beef on rye, and a cornucopia of homemade meats and cheeses that would cudgel the stomach of a camel.

The deli operator, a kindly appearing old man, one day invited the boys to "stop drooling on the counter and screw out of here."

It was strange that it was the gentlest of them, Skinny Potts, who had picked up the bulky roll and bounced it off the deli king's potbelly.

They were amazed how swiftly the short, fat man could run. And how persistent he was. They figured he would tire within the first fifty feet. But he nearly caught Rhesus, who had lollygagged on the end of the escaping pack of friends to bait their pursuer.

The deli manager managed to grab Rhesus by the belt and was reeling him in when Rhesus, who could fart on command, let a ripper fly, thus gaining his freedom.

Rhesus, after his fear wore off behind the safety of the State House steps, told his panting companions he had saved them all by willing the fart on command, that caused their pursuer to give up the chase.

Taking on the posture of the soapbox orators they had enjoyed earlier, Rhesus said, "I wasn't about to let that giant turn my friends into Aunt Sallies and get themselves bopped. Not only that, I don't know whether any of you saw me will that bird turd on the nose of Ms. Snotnose on the Swan Boats."

—

Boattail knocked his brother off the soapbox with, "You didn't will no fart on that guy. He just scared the living shit out of you."

The boys, rocked with laughter, slid down the wall in pain, grabbing their stomachs, already stretched to the breaking point by seeing and smelling, unable to afford the foods in the deli.

Rhesus wasn't one to stay down for the ten count and started to pontificate again when a new hero arrived on the scene. A big-time, bigger-than-life, real-life hero. It was Scoff, his arms full of deli goodies. "Just scoffed this stuff up while everyone was watching the foot race."

"Hey, you swiped that stuff," Soupy said in a holier-than-thou tone, still in the mode from the Eastward School days—trying to put attention on others so they would forget his polecat sandwich, the sleeping skunk he crushed between two rocks.

"Nah, I didn't. I just borrowed it. When I make my first million, I'll pay him back."

"You paid the mean old grinch of a grouch back, in spades," Righty said.

They munched and crunched the ill-gotten gains, food made tastier by the fact it was ill-gotten.

And Soupy didn't have to pay second fiddle to anyone in the food-downing race despite his accusing "You swiped that stuff," although he did look down when Johnny smiled at him.

After they finished eating, they decided to sit on the State House front steps and make burp noises as the various state senators and representatives exited.

"Another vote for you senator."

"Have a good dinner, your honor."

"Still eating at the public trough, governor."

"Hey, look at the Packard coming this way, "Rhesus said.

"It's my dad," Johnny said. "He's going to be in charge of the Bowdoin Square Garage."

Tony pulled up in the Packard and, leaning over, opened the passenger door for Johnny. "Hi, kids. Come on, Johnny."

As the car pulled off, Skinny said, "I always thought Johnny was poor."

"Lucky you waited until he was gone," Righty said. "If there is one word that he hates after 'mother f,' it's the word 'poor.'"

Heads turned again, this time, older ones, street wise ones, that knew the status symbol of a Packard.

"He's gotta be a pimp."

"Nah. A pol. Probably the governor."

"Mafioso." The bystander that offered that opinion quickly looked around to make sure no one heard his words.

"Maybe he owns one of those Chinatown restaurants."

"Where's his pigtail."

"You don't need no pigtail to own a Chinese restaurant."

"In a pig's ass you don't."

"In a pig's ass, in a pig's ass. What are you, some kind of fudge-packer queer?"

"I'll pack your ass. I'm guessing the guy driving the Packard inherited his dough. look at his clothes. Class and cash."

"Maybe he's a priest."

Johnny had never been in Bowdoin Square before.

The Bowdoin Square Garage, the building he hoped would bring his father closer to home, looked impressive. He was proud his father was going to be in charge of all the mechanics inside fixing so many cars.

His father drove through the small square. "I'll be able to get a better parking spot a little way from here."

Johnny saw the sign "Scully Square." He had heard something about Scully Square. *What was it?*

Scully was the home of the nation's two most famous burlesque houses—The Old Howard and the Casino. Such skirt-waving operations were only fitting for a flag waving city. "One if by land, two if by sea, 1 on the opposite shore shall be." Viva Barbara Freitchie! "Shoot if you must this old gray head but spare my country's flag," she said.

Tony parked the Packard under a streetlight only a short distance from a corner restaurant, Joey's. It served as an unofficial, second-level outpost of the police department.

Walking beat patrolmen, an occasional meandering motorcycle cop, one on horseback and even a supervisor in a cruiser, would stop there for a cup of the hottest, strongest, foulest coffee in the world, a cup of Joe that some cops were certain the chef had shit in.

The coffee gave them something to talk about. So did the well-endowed waitress who wiped the countertop farthest from her with a bar rag with the greatest set of tits running a neck-and-neck race to the finish line that would excite even those who did not play the ponies.

Besides all this, the waitress was a natural in the sense of a ballplayer with great hand-eye coordination. She moved her valentine-shaped ass to the exact cadence of her gum chewing. A must-see for every cop in the precinct. Joey, the owner liked this despite the fact they frightened off some of the less-than-law-abiding citizens of Scully. And some forgot to pay for their hamburg. The police contingent meant there were no visits

—

from those offering protection or an occasional gun-waving druggie who wanted to tap the funds Joey made on his numbers game.

Thus, it was Tony's chosen parking spot when he visited Scully. He understood that his wide whitewall tires, the elegant chrome mirrors on the spare tire discs mounted in the front fenders, and the wonderful flying lady that adorned the Packard hood had a better chance of survival with cops in the vicinity, even if they were more dedicated to the mathematical formula comparing the ratio of the chewing of gum to the movement of the sweet swinging ass of the waitress.

Another officer said that her breasts fell under the formula I=PRT. "And I don't mean interest equals price times rate times time. I mean Interest equals priority ripe tits."

"Jesus, I'm working with Einstein," his supervising officer said. "I'm gonna hafta watch my job."

"Wait a sec," Tony said to his son and disappeared into Joey's.

He returned within minutes and handed Johnny a brace of Captain Marvel and Batman comic books and a Milky Way. "The interview could be an hour or more; they don't want to hire a supervisor that can't cut it. So enjoy, grab a nap. I'll be back as soon as I can. Have the patience and silence of an Indian, oh young running buck."

"Yes, Buck in Rut."

They both pounded their left breast with their right fist.

Tony mussed his son's hair.

"Indians don't do that. They scalp."

Tony pivoted and walked off.

Johnny watched his father cross the road, admiring how he stepped with the heel-and-toe walk of a stalking Indian. The heel was placed softly on the ground first, and the toe then lowered slowly so as to stop the stepping action and retract the foot if it felt a dry twig beneath it that could snap and give away the position of the walker. *Dad . . . you'd be a . . . Mohegan . . . soft walker . . .*

Tony crossed the road, walked along the sidewalk in the dark, and walked in the front door of a building that Johnny couldn't make out. But it gave no indication it was the Bowdoin Square Garage.

Johnny dug into Batman. He would have preferred a Richard Haliburton true adventure book. They hardly sold 380-page hardcover books in places like Joey's.

He glanced up from the comic book every few minutes to take in the inhabitants and visitors to Scully Square, whose lifeblood was more than interesting and were like peanuts roasted in the shell, and only one of which just could not satisfy.

—

It was then he saw a familiar figure exit the building his father had entered ten minutes before. Johnny had been taught to look at both the forest and the trees. And to look at the openings between the trees and to look for the openings between the trees. The figure was the only one who placed his heel down first then the toe, as if wanting to be certain his foot would not snap a twig that would give away his presence. But there were no twigs nor trees in the wild forest of Scully.

The figure was slumped, collar up, shoulders forward, head down, not a single thing familiar about his father's demeanor. Except? *That soft step . . . a silent stepper . . . but why slumped? Are you okay . . . Dad?*

Maybe his father was sick, injured.

Johnny let himself out of the car and headed into the flow of the crowd. Despite his ability to take high-speed long steps through the darkened woods and avoid the hardwood branches that sought to crack his skull and the briars, and while they had no animosity toward him, they still reached out to rip his hands, face, buggy whip his eyes. He had trouble moving through the sidewalk people of Scully, people of important destinations avoiding the mindlessness of the rude, the sick, the powerful, and the mad. Meandering was nearly impossible. Johnny was pummeled with the same callousness of humans as he was with the branches and briars of the nighttime woods.

He looked skyward for openings, like in the woods at night, small strips of sky meant openings in which to run in the dark.

But there was no sky. There were three huge dirty opaque balls—O'Mean's Hock Shop, a giant glittering coin; the Silver Dollar Cafe, a huge blinking marquis that announced Burlesque at its best; the Casino, a glance down a side street, another of Boston's small squares, a sign which announced "Brattle Book Store" in big print, "Brattle Square."

The flow led back into Scully Square, at least according to a sign that announced the Scully Square Pool Parlor for Gentlemen.

Checking overhead hadn't worked. He was still blocked, with an efficiency that would make any professional football offensive lineman smile at nearly every turn in his efforts to pick up speed in the crowd and perhaps gain on his father.

And there he was, through the many legs that served as trees in the forest called the crowd, a soft stepper. His father.

He was going to call out. But didn't. The steps were more deliberate, and Johnny could read them. The Indian hunter had spotted his prey. The step became more stealthy. Determined.

His father stepped up to a ticket booth. *Why wouldn't . . . he . . . take me . . . to the movies . . . with him . . .*

—

235

It looked for a moment like his father was doing an old-fashioned dance in the flickering light of an old silent movie.

It was the stuttering neon light in the overhead marquis that announced "Old Howard House of Burlesque."

His father went inside.

After several minutes, Johnny walked out of the shadows and into the foyer of the house. Behind protective glass were colored, life-sized prints of the dancers and baggy pants comedians. The women's nipples were covered with small circles of cloth. He wondered how they were held on. If he knew their name, pasties, he would have known the secret. Fancy sequined loin clothes were cut far below their navels. The signs announced the ladies were Peaches, Queen of the Shake; Ann Corio; Tillie, the Titan of the Tassels.

The baggy pants of the comedians were held high, pecs high, by whatever passed for pectorals among the relatively unathletic gentlemen. The pants were held up by brightly colored suspenders, belts, neckties, bras, garter belts, and other sundry adornments.

Johnny's eyes returned to Ann Corio. It wasn't her nearly naked body as much as the eyes that stared into your very soul. His father was inside there. Being stared at. Staring. *Why?*

The swinging doors set in motion by young men, old men, and all ages in between revealed swift second glances of the stage, much like the swiftly flipped pages of Betty Boop ink drawings revealing Ms. Boop in very compromising positions, somewhat like naked yoga.

His first glance came up with a large blonde woman who appeared to be falling asleep, legs spread wide, swinging a tassel that was attached to her left breast. The next opening of the door and the tassel on her right breast was swinging clockwise in coordination with the left.

The third door opening, initiated by a man that looked to Johnny surprisingly like Skinny of Laurel and Hardy fame, also involved a burst of applause, vocal as well as by hand, as the tassels now swung toward each other, one clockwise, one counterclockwise.

The next door opening was by a rather large gentleman that, as the fate would have it, looked somewhat like Fats. *But Hardy . . . is . . . long . . . dead . . .*

The applause, now more vocal than by hand, was thunderous, as the dancer's tassels had changed directions and, instead of swinging in, were swinging out, sending the large flaccid breasts out to the side, like large flat hands giving turn signals.

Then she was pinched off the stage by a baggy-pants comedian who returned center stage, gave a giant toothless gumming of a smile, and was joined by two very tall women who shuffled onto the stage like circus elephants holding each other's tails. The blonde's face had all the character of a sponge used to clean the toilet bowl. She was that blase. The brunette was uneasy. She looked like Mrs. Mortenson. While she was uneasy on stage, there was an air of expectation, her not wanting to expose herself yet craving to display herself to a gang of strangers and not knowing why.

They were situated on each side of the comedian, who held out the waist of, first, the blonde, then the brunette's skirts.

He looked up, looked the blonde in the eye, then the brunette, and then knowingly at the audience, and smiled that more-than-toothless smile—"Ya gotta eat."

The blonde closed her eyes and appeared to release a snore. The brunette shuffled her feet uneasily. Like a mare in heat in her stall. Mrs. Mortenson . . .

"Hey, you! Kid! Slip your rear into gear, and get your horny little ass out of here!"

The ticket seller had stepped out of his booth just long enough to send Johnny shuffling off, not out of fear but out of shame. It was a shame he knew he would not only carry for himself but also for his father. *Why? Why . . . couldn't . . . I . . . have been a . . . Catholic . . . and leave this . . . this feeling . . . at the ticket booth . . . the confessional . . . Oh why, oh why . . . did I ever leave . . . Wyoming?*

He had difficulty finding the Packard. His travels took him through Scully, Bowdoin, Brattle Squares. It was getting dark, and he wasn't running like an Indian but rather like a frightened kid. The branches were cracking his skull, the briars ripping his eyes.

Had the Packard been stolen? Oh god . . .

Car lights shined in his face with the glare of a criminal being questioned, horns blared the anger of a disturbed hornet; the elbows were so bad that if they were administered during a Bruin's hockey game, it would have led to an intent to injure penalty rather than a simple elbowing one. What passed for music rumbled out of door after door, causing eardrums to beat like a trash barrel being pummeled by a sledgehammer.

Out of this great unfumigated mass of humanity came an old woman, perhaps at one time someone's well-loved grandmother. He thought 'help at last' as she approached him.

Johnny stared at her in panic. *I don't have any . . . money to give you . . . Grammy . . .* He felt awful; he had grandmothers of his own.

The old woman's face was powdered the solid white of a Kabuki performer, her mouth a bright-red slash as if she had just bit the head off a bunny. Her voice appeared to come out of her blood-red eyes and leered

—

at him, her breath that of a neglected garbage bucket. "Like to put your candy money to good use, my little one."

Johnny put his head down and rammed into the crowd that hardly felt a difference in its indifferent rhythm.

When he broke into the clear, there it was, the Packard.

He saw his father as he slipped into the same side door he had slipped out of hours before.

Johnny managed to seat himself in the car just as his father came out the front door of the building.

"They liked me," he told his son as he slid behind the wheel, "but they're not hiring. Would you like a cone or a Joe and Nemo?"

"I think I'll skip it." *Dad . . .*

He didn't take his eyes off the beautiful flying lady Packard hood ornament on the return trip to Rockledge.

The next time he saw the ornament, it was parked in front of his house. And he was shining it.

The older jerk kids who had taunted him with "Poor, poor lives in a sewer" would now know that they were the poor ones. *Poor jerks . . . they'd . . . want a ride in . . . the . . . Packard . . .* "No way, jerks."

Johnny had been very careful that morning, knowing he would be shining the sedan. And there would be onlookers.

He had pulled the heels of his socks down to the arch of his feet, making sure the holes would not pop out when he was working and whipping the shining shammy on the glistening hood. *Pardon me, boy . . . is that the Chattanooga Choo-Choo . . . Track 29 . . . Gonna give me a . . . shine . . .* The cloth popped on the hood with a snap of a bullwhip.

And he shuffled his feet so the soles of his shoes would not flap. He had put fresh cardboard inside that morning. He always felt up when he used a Wheaties, Breakfast of Champions cardboard cutout for the shoes. But if the soul flapped, all would be lost, as whenever it flip-flopped, it was like a tongue chanting, "Poorer boy, the boy is poorer, lives his life in a sewer." *I'll whip all your asses . . . someday . . .*

And why not? Wasn't he saving a few cents each week to purchase that Charles Atlas? Don't be a ninety-eight-pound weakling, 'course. *No one kicks sand . . . in my face . . . but they do . . .* At least the big wise guys did. He couldn't even fight them, as with their long arms, they merely had pushed him away.

The snap of the shining rag kept bringing him back to the pleasant task at hand. Shining his Packard.

Johnny walked, bowling his legs like a cowboy's so the wales of his corduroy pants wouldn't whistle. He had told the wise guys his father owned a horse farm in the country and that he rode so much he was like John Wayne, always in the saddle even while on the ground.

One of the big wise guys said, "You sure you're not bowlegged? Cuz you have one of those giant Portagee slongs hanging between them."

He didn't want to wear corduroys. No one else was wearing them anymore. The leftovers were cheapest on the market.

Johnny wanted to buy himself chinos like all the guys wore and maybe brown and white bucks. And penny loafers with the shiny penny inserts.

He was making money, good money, between his morning paper route, setting pins, diving for golf balls, doing odd jobs like moving that heavy stove up four flights. But there never was enough leftover.

A couple dollars to his mother because he hated to see her cry when Jazz said he was hungry. Roma would never say that. She would rather die. She just looked skinny as a blade of hay that was short changed by the fertilizer spreader.

Then there was the occasional Baby Ruth bar for Jazz. And the wax teeth he bought his little brother on a fairly regular basis, which he could wear until Johnny could save enough to have his Huck Finn protruders filled and buy braces to pull them in.

Jazz had told Johnny to use his own money on himself, that he had a friend that said he had pliers, and they could pull them out. He had tried tying a string to a tooth and slamming the door, but the string broke. And Jazz had that feeling of the doomed man whose hangman's noose snapped when the trapdoor was tripped.

And he had bought Roma the dress. The dress in the window that looked so much like the dress Johnny had drawn and colored to outfit the paper doll he had designed and cut out for her from a piece of cardboard his mother had brought home from the box factory.

"This ain't no charity," his younger sister said. "I don't take no charity." She looked threatening at Johnny.

"No way. No way. When we get some sugar, you can make me some fudge. That would pay off any debt in this world."

"I've been getting some of those little blocks of sugar in the restaurant. I have nineteen of them so far."

"You're not stealing them?" Johnny asked seriously.

"Of course not. Ma would kill me. I just ask the people at the counter if they're gonna use their sugar in their coffee, and when they say no, I hold out my hand. They paid for them."

"What about taking no charity, Roma? Ma would surely kill you."

"I do a little tap dance for the ladies. And for the gentleman, I wiggle my ears," Roma said.

—

Johnny looked at his sister. Thinner than the soup . . . at the . . . poor farm . . . "Do you say thank you?"

"'Course. Ma would kill us if we didn't. I do a curtsy."

Johnny looked at the bony knobs she called knees, smiled, and said, "You don't go showing any more of that fine leg than you have to."

Roma looked down shyly and pushed her palm at him with an "oh." And she blushed.

Johnny . . . why don't you say nice things to your . . . sister . . . more often?

"Why don't you be nice to me like this all the time?" she asked, looking up at him.

Because you're . . . my . . . sister . . . "Because you have so many things about you deserving of compliment."

Jazz played "Hearts and Flowers" on an invisible violin while Roma sang to Johnny, "And the farmer took another load away."

Johnny pulled her pigtail. "I wish there was an inkwell around so I could dunk your oinker's tail in it. I'll dunk Sadie's"

"Give me back Sadie," Roma threatened. Sadie was a Raggedy Ann doll. A true Raggedy doll. Johnny had made it for Roma. It was her first doll. He didn't have access to buttons, so he took two off the fly of his corduroy trousers and wore his shirt outside his pants. Her dress was made out of material salvaged from the fancy-dancy grain bags of the day. The DaSilva sisters got first choice, first choice being after Pie took the fanciest of the grain bags so Goda could make herself a dress. The old man was careful not to give enough material that she could make the neck high or the hemline low. Johnny had used fishing line he had got out of a tree where an errant cast by a fisherman had left it for thread. He made a sewing needle by boring a hole in the thick end of a thorn.

Raggedy Ann's body was made out of goat skin Johnny had yanked out of the mouth of the most brutal of the farm's hogs, Moag, son of Bog.

Pie always beheaded the billy goats at birth and tossed them to the hogs that snorted in fierce delight.

When Johnny asked him why, the old man had grabbed him by the scuff of the neck and lifted him off the ground. "No give-um fuckum milk."

The doll's hair was the real prize. Old Farmer Osterhouse raised show horses that he transported out to the western end of the state where they were entered in the Eastern States, Tri-County, and Cummington Fairs.

Johnny undertook a midnight shopping spree in the Osterhouse barn, where he clipped the finest hair from the finest prize horse.

"Would you really take Sadie back? Are you an Indian giver?"

"Yes."

"Then give me an Indian."

"Say you're sorry for that and-the-farmer-took-another-load-away ditty."

Roma looked at the doll and looked at the scowl on her brother's face. "No."

"Atta girl," Johnny said, messing up her hair, snapping the elastic band that held one of the pig tails. "I wouldn't dip your pigtail in an ink well. It would probably pollute it, kill all the octopus and other little ink makers hidden there."

"Why don't you write stories?" Jazz asked his brother.

"Mostly because teachers are always whacking your hand for lying."

"No one whacks your hand," Jazz said proudly.

"That's for sure."

Jazz smiled at his brother, his teeth looking like an attacking pit bull.

Gotta put a few more cents . . . in that envelope . . . for the . . . doc . . .

Johnny couldn't imagine how the price of a filling could go from thirty-five cents to a whole dollar. And braces! They would cost him an arm and a leg. A hundred dollars. *That's . . . sick . . . Wonder if I could sell . . . more of my . . . blood . . . under a second . . . name . . . without getting . . . caught . . .*

Doc Jones kept two different envelopes for Johnny. One for fillings for Jazz, Roma, and himself, and a second to get Jazz's teeth straightened.

The good doctor, commenting on straightening Jazz's teeth, told Johnny, "No way are you going to save enough, not in ten lifetimes."

"How much if we don't have him end up looking like Tyrone Power. Say, maybe just like Pete Lorre."

"I notice the number of Indian heads going into the envelopes is diminishing," the dentist said, resealing the envelopes and sliding them into his desk drawer. He held the money for Johnny as it gave him a chance to swap Lincoln head pennies for the rapidly disappearing Indian heads garnered on his paper route.

Johnny daydreamed about the money going into the envelopes, what it would buy. *French fries . . . taffy apples . . . sausage at the fair . . . with fried red and green peppers . . . and onions . . . and cotton candy . . . and hot dogs . . . with relish and mustard . . . and ketchup . . . and diced onions . . . and horse radish . . . and . . . oooh . . .*

And the dream ended, either in pain as the gastric salivation juices bottomed out in his belly, leaving him with the feeling someone had put him on an acid HIV, or in guilt that he would put his stomach above his brother's teeth.

—

The teeth had to be fixed. His right hand was sore from whacking the teeth-like-a-picket-fence wise guys.

Charity bought the food for the week and then locked it up in the food closet so it wouldn't all disappear in one day.

Her security method had to keep changing. First, a latch and lock were put on the outside of the two matching food closet doors. But Johnny, through experimentation, discovered the doors could be pulled out just far enough so that he could reach his bony arm inside and reach the most forward of the guarded foods.

Charity, on discovering that the coming Saturday's food was gone, also discovered how he had managed to get his arm in.

So she put a little latch on the inside of the doors so they could not be pulled out.

Johnny then used a coat hanger to undo the inside latch, pulled the locked doors toward him, and reached in.

Charity, on discovering Friday's designated food missing, came up with double and triple locks inside and out the closet doors that appeared foolproof, and she was quite proud that she had foiled her criminally adaptable son.

She apparently did not understand the workings of a tool called the screwdriver.

A hungry Johnny used such a tool to take the hinges off one door, remove just enough to quell his hunger, and then screwed the hinges back on.

Charity could not figure out how he accomplished this grand theft but decided she would lock the front door and not give him a key.

So he entered through an unlocked window.

She locked all the windows.

Johnny discovered that by pounding his palm continuously at the wooden apex of the pane closest to the lock, it would move the thinnest of hairs each time; but with enough perseverance to defeat the Chinese water torture, he could open the lock and let himself in.

On discovering her son's latest sortie, Charity did what she should have done at the beginning to stop him from raiding the meager food storage. She wept, which was bad enough, but she wept softly. An onlooker, such as her son, might not even realize she was crying if it wasn't for the ever-so-slight quiver of the shoulders.

His hunger never again was such that he would invade the dark recesses of the food closet. Johnny considered occasionally taking one of those offered sandwiches that were thrown unclaimed into the school lunch trash barrels. He didn't. *Shit shit shit . . .*

Charity considered taking the Elks's Thanksgiving basket rather than using it for kicking practice.

She didn't. *Oh god . . . please forgive me . . .*

As Johnny put aside pennies for his mother to run the house and for Jazz's teeth, tiny black dots, like ink dots, appeared on his almost-too-white teeth. The ink dots grew into a jagged lace, similar to the ice on the edge of a freezing waterfall, but the lace was not snow white.

On the coldest of morning, when giant oak trees moaned and elms snapped under the weight of ice storms, he melted wax and forced it into his teeth to cut back on the pain.

He used salt and baking powder and brushed his teeth with his index finger.

When a tooth hurt like a foreskin caught in a zipper, he would put aside his deposit in Jazz's envelope or his mother's hand and go to Doc Jones.

The good doctor filled Johnny's teeth, cash only, for a dollar-twenty rather than the going price of a buck and two bits.

He informed Johnny of the break he was giving him, adding, "A little charity never hurt anyone. Good works can be rewarded on earth. Cash only."

"All in Indian head pennies still?"

"Of course. How else could I cover such losses. Wish investments never hurt anyone. You have to build for tomorrow. If you have any Indian heads left over, a lad could do worse than setting them aside for a rainy day."

"That will be fifty dollars, please, financial advice."

Johnny's eyes widened.

"Just joshing," Doc Jones said.

"Oh." *You're as funny as a . . . fart in church . . .*

"I don't charge for financial advice. I'm not a lower-than-whale scat lawyer. The piranhas. They bill you even when they are on the crapper. Crapper isn't a swear word. John Crapper invented the toilet as we know it today. Anyway, they bill you while sitting on the Crapper, big C, reading their life history—Superman comics."

"Yes, sir." *You're about as funny as a . . . piranha in your . . . bathtub water . . .*

"Did you say something?"

"No, sir, I was just thinking."

"Good boy. Thinking never hurt anyone. Of course the poor shouldn't think. It gets everyone in trouble. No, the poor shouldn't think. No offense meant. Anyway, you're a bright young lad. No digging ditches for you. You could be, well, anything. You could be the guy standing over the ditch, telling them what to do. That will be half your first week's pay for job placement efforts. Just kidding. I mean you would never tell anyone that it's a combination of salt and baking soda that makes your teeth so white. Out would go my teeth cleaning business. I would have to charge you for profit lost. I wouldn't, though. Can't stand the thought of hiring one of those sleaziest lawyers."

"I won't tell anyone."

"And the tartar, little Tovarich, comrade, and don't go telling anyone that Jones is a shortening of my, of the name Jonavitchka. Don't tell anyone about your tartar correction method. I would have to sue. Just kidding. And besides, if they used your method, our highways could disappear. The least bad thing that would happen would be damage to cars driving the potholed roads."

Johnny, while trying to find a substance that could be stuffed into a tooth cavity to relieve the ache, a pliable material much like the melted wax he used in the winter, discovered the hot tar he scooped out of the shining black of the roadway for toothache relief, when chewed, removed the tartar.

Charity had asked her husband if he could "send a little extra," and Tony said he "would try, but the expenses of the Packard and driving home leave things spread a little thin."

Charity had taken on a waitressing job nights, catching a bite on the fly after finishing up at the box factory.

She was stretched as thin as telephone wire strung between two poles leaning away from each other, nearly to the point where her frail body hummed.

CHAPTER 10

THE NEW MILLIONAIRES

There were a million ways to make a million bucks other than diving bare ass for golf balls.

Rhesus and Boattail had told their friends this a million times as they flipped shiny coins in the air, asking, "Anyone wanna match? Make a quick buck in a game of chance!"

If Rhesus flipped a dime in the air, caught it in his right hand, flipped it over onto his left wrist, keeping it covered with his right hand, and you said, "Ya, I'll match. Heads!"

Invariably, it would turn up tails, and Rhesus had doubled his dime. Some thought he had an unusual amount of luck as he always won.

Actually, at age thirteen, he had learned to remove the chance factor and, in doing so, removed luck by replacing it with skill.

Sheer, unadulterated skill. With eyes as sharp as a monkey on the lookout for hungry cheetahs and hands even faster, he would scoop his flipped coin out of the air as the midair call was made; and while it was cupped in his palm being moved through the air toward his wrist, he would spot the position heads was in and make the midair adjustment needed to win. Suddenly, the Rhesus was the predator, the cheater.

Johnny caught on to the action but was on the horns of a dilemma. Do you fink on a friend or stand by and watch other friends cheated?

"Rhesus, you better knock off your coin flips with our friends. Just flip with the rich kids in the highlands," he said.

"Don't be a Goody Two-shoes. I'm just working my way through divinity school."

"You're going to have to get there via Melrose Highlands, not Rockledge."

"You gonna stop me."

"Perhaps."

"You and whose army?"

"Just me, myself, and I."

"Perhaps we'll give it a try, little buddy boy," Rhesus said, his red crew cut bristling like a banty rooster.

"Perhaps you'd better think about it."

"Well, maybe we'll just scale baseball cards against the wall," Rhesus said.

"Fair enough," Johnny said, not knowing just how wrong his words were.

The gang lined up, with the winner selecting the value of the cards to be scaled.

"Closest to the wall takes all," Rhesus said, bowing low, inviting his friends to scale first. Each had a card of equal value to the Bobby Doerr Red Sox card.

Going against Doerr were Nellie Fox of the White Sox, Snuffy Sternweis and Scooter Rizzuto of the hated Yankees, Al Kaline of the Tigers.

With only Rhesus left to scale, Johnny was closest to the wall, with his Johnny Pesky less than three inches away.

Rhesus's card glided through the air with the grace and stability of a P-38 Lightning coming in on a strafing run, settling within an inch of the wall. He raked in his opponents' cards with all the finess of a Las Vegas croupier.

Rhesus had the hands, a combination of a baton-wielding maestro of the Boston Symphony and a cutpurse. His touch, of course, was enhanced by the fact several cards enjoyed more doctoring than the spitball of Dizzy Dean.

He had split the end of his cards, inserted a small piece of metal for stability and glide ability, and then glued the cards back together.

"Okay, I'm putting Joe D, the Dimage, the Yankee Clipper," Rhesus said. "Let's see your Hank Greenberg and Jimmy Foxx."

"I'm putting up the Kid, the Splendid Splinter, Ted Williams," Johnny said.

"I don't want no draft dodgers," Rhesus said.

"What are you talking about?" Johnny said. "He's a marine pilot."

"Oh yah, my dad said he's a teacher. Teaches guys to fly. He was drafted."

"The marines don't draft," Johnny said.

"Ya ass drafts."

And they all scaled several times, and Rhesus took all the cards, including Johnny's Splendid Splinter, Boo Ferris, Jim Tabor, Mort Cooper.

Johnny's last card was Pete Grey, the one armed outfielder of the Pittsburgh Pirates. Grey would catch the ball, toss it in the air, flip off his glove, catch the ball, and toss it home, swifter than any of the gang could swipe an apple off an apple cart.

While not trained from birth, the Rockledge boys learned to swipe apples off venders' carts by seeing the best in action—the boys of South Boston and Somerville when they ventured into their turf for sandlot, no uniform football games.

They walked the eleven miles to play the Somerville boys on Dillboy Field, where they climbed the cement walls and tussled when the field was empty. Then they traveled on to face the Southie boys at their South Boston football field of rocks and broken bottles.

The ragtag Rockledge players used cardboard stuffed in the shoulders for pads and wool watch caps stuffed with rags for helmets.

On the return home, they often drifted a few miles sideways to take on any Melrose, Medford, or Malden teams that might be itching for action. The Rockledge small towners always got their asses kicked on the scoreboard but made out better when bloody noses and black eyes were added up.

Johnny, minus his change and several cards from scaling, decided perhaps he could collect more money for Jazz's choppers and help his ma to buy food by working rather than gambling.

The coup de grace of his gambling career came when he lost Pete Grey and then his very favorite Catfish Meckovitch. He shared duty there with other right fielders Tom McBride and Leon Culbertson. All three batted more than .300 but could not gain their own spot in the outfield as Terrible Ted Williams and Dom DiMaggio, Joe's little brother, owned left and center.

The headstone that was finally placed over the grave of the riverboat gambler Johnny DaSilva was the game of glassies, which involved only the top-shelf marbles.

Rhesus and Boattail dragged their fingers, nearly pushing the aggie into the hole. It paid off as their marble bags were full of the biggest boulders and most beautiful cat's eyes.

When accused, the brothers denied the dragsy charges, declaring the ditches allegedly dug holeward by their fingers were actually the trails left in the soil by a South American strain of snails that could not be seen by the human eye.

It was tough to argue the point because as Dick Tracy put it, "None of us have a clue about South American snails."

"Hey, we can't even see the little buggers," Soupy said.

"We can work to make money," Johnny finally volunteered to Righty, although all the gang hated that four-letter word, "work," as Hopalong said, "It just royally fucks up playing."

Johnny and Righty split from the group, with Righty claiming, "There's a million ways to make a million bucks."

"Name one."

"One."

"Gimme one."

"One."

"Are you some sort of goofball?" Johnny asked, shoving Righty's shoulder.

"Yah, I'm one."

"Jesus, Lord in heaven," Johnny said.

"Don't be a fuckhead, Johnny, using the Lord's name in vain, especially when it looks like rain and lightning comes with it."

Righty looked skyward, rolled his eyes, and crossed himself, just as a clap of thunder rocked the sky.

"I wish I was Catholic. You get to cross your heart all the time. It evens helps you to get a hit in the ball game."

"And the cool guys make a cross in the dirt at home plate when they're at bat.

The rain and lightning blasted through the clouds, shaking the earth, blinding them.

Righty crossed his heart repeatedly, picking up speed as the bolts of lightning came more often and the air filled with the acid smell of the lightning.

Johnny crossed his heart when he thought Righty wasn't looking.

"I saw that Johnny. If a Protestant does that, he burns in hell. You can't even buy your way into purgatory like us Catholics can. Don't ever do it near me. I could get killed by the same bolt of lightning God means for you."

"Well, what am I to do? I'm shit-ass scared of lightning," Johnny said.

"The only thing you can do is what all Protestants do when they're scared, and that's shit your pants."

"I'm practically a Catholic," Johnny said. "I'm an Episcopalian."

"I don't care if you're one of those piss-in-the-pail aliens or not, don't cross your heart near me during a lightning storm."

"Some buddy."

"Hey, Johnny, I'd lay down my life for you like Sergeant York did for Jimmy Cagney, but you can't expect me to get hit by lighting for you and have my ass turned to acid because you got to bless yourself like a Catholic in front of God, who we all know is Catholic, instead of just shitting your pants like scared prot-tis-tants do, even your ones that piss in the pail."

Luckily, the rains stopped as suddenly as they started as each was calling the other loony.

"A rainbow," Johnny said, pointing skyward.

"Make a wish."

"I wish we could make a million so I could fix Jazz's teeth and help my ma buy food. And I wish your brother fighting Hitler over there is safe."

"And that he gets laid. He said Italian girls, real Italians, not like the fake ones we grow in this country, love American soldiers, especially ones that speak Italian and will do hot things for a cigarette. They will even marry you for a week for a pair of silk stockings.

"Ma said in his last letter he was near Monte Casino, where he was born before Ma and Pa and he came from Italy to become a citizen of Rockledge. And that would be like a miracle if he met a nice girl, one that didn't do it for a cigarette, and gave her a pair of silk stockings and married her."

Johnny wished there were silk stockings again in America, but the paratroops needed the silk for their parachutes, so there were no silk stockings. Maybe someday he would "hit the silk" with paratroopers dropping into Germany. He heard his uncle Manny say he was going to join the paratroopers as when they talked about a jump, it meant into the air or on a woman.

American women painted their own stockings on with a brown dye. And he had to paint the seams down the back of his aunts' legs as they couldn't reach back there, and he hated it.

He hated painting Mrs. Mortenson's seams even more. He was afraid of her since that day long ago, when he was just a kid, and she put the two grapefruits under her sweater, looked right at him, and smiled when he blushed and turned red.

He had tried to walk away when she said, "Harry hasn't come home from work yet, and I need my seams painted on. You're thirteen, a man now, and a steady hand can paint a straight seam."

"And there's a dime in it for you if you paint a good seam."

She handed him two bottles, one with the light tan that the entire stocking was painted on with and a smaller bottle containing a darker dye for painting the seam.

"Use the light color if I missed anything back there and the dark for the line. I'll just stand on this box so you won't have to bend over. Well, perhaps even while I'm standing on the box, you'd be better off kneeling. Your line drawing will be much straighter if you are at eye level."

Johnny first filled in the couple small areas she had missed on her calves.

"I better stand with my legs apart so they won't smear each other. Did you get that area where my dress is up high?" she asked, hoisting her skirt slightly.

Johnny wondered how she knew she had missed an area under her dress and in back of her. He tried to color in the missed spot with his eyes closed.

"If I wanted to hire a blind person to paint a straight line, I would have hired Ms. Helen Keller. She's a genius. Please open your eyes like a nice boy."

She opened her legs ever so slightly, her calves flexing in the new position as her high heels placed a different pressure on the muscles.

He stared at her ankles where the ribbons from the shoe tops wound around her ankles twice before ending with a single circle at her calves.

"You can do it right if you watch what you're doing," she said, smiling down at him.

He finally looked up. She had painted to within a few inches of where the top of her legs came together and formed a V. The white area led to a pair of panties as creamy white as her skin.

He thought of the mornings he helped his uncle John deliver milk on the cobblestone streets of Boston. He had never gotten tired of hearing the clippity-clop of the old milk horse. It knew every house where milk was delivered. And would stop there waiting for them to catch up and take the milk for the house before it moved on to the next customer.

In the freezing weather, he would come across milk delivered by the Whiting milkman. He used a truck. Why, Johnny couldn't figure out, as a truck wouldn't stop at each customer's house. Or come when you whistled.

The milk often froze in the wagon before it was delivered, and the cream would sometimes be an inch or more out of the bottle. So pure, so white. He would carve part of the cream from the bottle and let it melt in his mouth.

That area above Mrs. Mortenson's painted-on silk stockings and just below her panties looked like that frozen cream. And he wondered whether it would taste the same if allowed to melt in his mouth.

But then the beauty of this first view of the white above the woman's silk stockings and just below the panties became a dark and dangerous area—as there, licking out below the elastic of the panties surrounding the inner thighs, was black hair, tufts of it, like a wildfire. It was sort of like their cooking campfire in the Big Woods that got away from them and became a wildfire out of control, and they were in danger.

And he felt like that day when the fire got out of control, and they ran in panic, not understanding the danger but knowing that trouble approached.

And they had hidden, Johnny, Righty, Fats, as they watched firemen, packs of water on their backs, spray the edge of the wildfire, leaving it wet.

Like the wetness that appeared to be forming at the V of Mrs. Mortenson's panties. He moved his face closer to see if it was wetness.

"What's going on down there, young man?"

Her voice made him jump. He hit his forehead on the apex of her crotch. It was wet, but it didn't hurt like the time he was caught hiding in the box factory on top of the boxes piled high, watching how hard his mother worked in the steam below, knowing he had to get her out of there.

Mrs. Mortenson said, "Perhaps it's too much to ask of such a young person to paint a straight line in such poor light where you can't see anything. Am I right? Of course I'm right. You don't expect me to pay for services not rendered, do you? Of course not."

Johnny started to walk away.

"Wait. Perhaps I should give you a dime. We don't want anyone to know that you can't paint a straight line. We don't want anyone to know, and there's nothing like the cold sweet and sticky taste of a Charleston Chew cooled in the icebox to seal one's lips to secrets."

She took her fingers and made a child's motion sealing her lips and smiled at Johnny until he made such a lip sealing motion.

No, his banging his head against Mrs. Mortenson's crotch did not give the same physical pain that took place after the foreman at the box factory where his mother worked spotted him. But there was a pain deep inside him, in the hollow part of his stomach.

The foreman had spotted him and yelled, "What's going on up there, young man?"

His voice had made Johnny jump. He hit his head on the I beam in the ceiling. It was a different type of bump.

The man's voice was less kindly than Mrs. Mortenson's.

—

251

When he came out, the foreman had kicked his ass hard, but Johnny was soothed somewhat by his words, "Ya lucky I'm not telling your ma. Charity would kick you tumble ass over.

"Fact, she'd kick your ass till the cows come home if she learned you were probably pulling your stiffy up there. What would people think who got their gift in a box covered with stiffy stains?

"And the FBI can check on you. Stiffy stains are like fingerprints. There are no two sets of fingerprints or stiffy stains alike."

Johnny reported the foreman's threat that stiffy stains could be checked like DNA and asked, "Righty? Is this true?"

"Ya."

"I hope your brother Big Lefty meets an eye-tal-yan girl while fighting over there and gives her some real silk stockings. Painting them on is dangerous. He could be the first guy in history to get a Purple Heart for a war-caused crotch injury," Johnny said.

"You saying we can't make a million painting silk stockings on?" asked Righty.

"Yup. Too dangerous."

"Just as well, with our luck making a buck, some fat woman would probably fart on us.

"I'd kill anyone who'd fart on me."

"You couldn't kill no one, "Righty said. "Best if we go into the painting business that we put some sort of cork stopper up their butt so they can't let one fly on us."

"Fat women can really let fly. What if they blasted that cork out of their tail, and it hit someone in the eye."

"I wonder if it would sound like someone opening a bottle of champagne when the cork blew. There'd be some pretty disappointed winos coming to investigate."

An old man interrupted their conversation, "Hey, you two kids want to earn two bits each? Sure you do. Don't you? Of course. Where else could two fine young businessmen like yourself earn such a fortune in a few seconds. All ya gotta do is lug this little stove up a flight of stairs.

"It's an ark. Noah could of got four of everything aboard if his ark was that size," Johnny said.

Their eyes followed the path the old man pointed in. "A flight of stairs," Righty said, "it's so high we'll get a nosebleed. Hey, it's so high we could get a period or something."

"Hey, young men, it's too much for little boys what wears short pants to carry a stove upstairs, but you men have long pants on, and they're not even corduroys. Then again, if you don't need money. But then again, we all need money. You can never have too much. It makes the world go round. And square. And in a triangle. No doubt 'bout dat."

"We'll take it." *Four bits to lug a lousy stove, a dream*, Johnny thought.

He wondered whether the stove was too wide for the rickety flights of stairs and too high to make the semicircle turns at each landing.

Someday he would ask his grandfather Shiverick to rent his pushcart and block and tackle used to haul the paint ladders skyward. Then Righty and he could really haul some freight, would really be movers.

If you got a quarter to move a stove, you could get a couple bucks to move a whole house. Then someday they'd have one of those giant moving trucks.

"Yup, we'll move it," he told the old man. "Where's the apartment?"

Old man Mancini pointed up.

The two young boys couldn't see where he was pointing as the boiling sun that followed the flash storm poured down, causing them to squint and sweat before they even lifted a finger. They didn't have to see. They'd just lug it upward until the old man told them they were there.

"The top flight. The fifth floor," the old man said. "And remember you agreed. Twenty-five cents. Don't cheat an old man. You wouldn't cheat an old man?"

"That's more than one flight," Righty said.

"Not if you're one of those flying dinosaurs.

"It's five flights," Johnny counted.

"You're not trying to cheat an old man, are you, son."

"No, sir," Johnny said.

"Not for all the money in the world," Righty answered.

The old man smiled. "You've got a deal. Shake on it. A man's word is his bond."

They shook. It was their first contract. They were movers, movers and groovers. And would soon be rich. Four bits. Two bits each.

The steps were not only steep and narrow, meaning they constantly skinned their knuckles gripping the heavy stove, but several were also broken or missing, and the combination of the great effort on the steaming boiled potato of a day and looking down through a missing step left them both weak and dizzy.

But you didn't get a chance to make a quarter every day, a quarter each. Signed and sealed with a handshake. A man's bond, a deal, a contract.

A couple times they'd nearly lost it as hands grew sweaty and fingers numb.

Johnny, at the bottom of the stove, pushed until he thought his entire backbone would be compressed accordion-like into sandwich size.

Righty at the top tugged until he was positive his arms would be ripped out of their sockets.

At last they were there, five flights up.

Twenty-five minutes, a penny a minute. *This was indeed America,* Johnny thought. A man can become a millionaire.

"Well, thank you very much, young men. You've made an old man happy. Very happy. I feel like giving you a nickel each. A whole nickel each. Do you know how much that is? A fortune today. In my day, a king's ransom, a king's ransom. Do you know how much a nickel is?"

"Yes," Righty said. "It isn't a quarter."

"Take it or leave it. Those are your two choices. You certainly aren't going to lug it down five flights."

"We certainly aren't," Johnny said, turning to Righty as he smiled while looking over the edge of the railing at the ground far below.

Righty smiled back.

"You wouldn't," the old man said.

Their smiles got bigger.

"Fifty cents. Fifty cents each! I know it was a horrible hard lug."

It was a lot of money for Jazz's teeth. He could see his little brother smiling, his mouth like piano keys, ivory without those little black keys in between. And he could buy his mother three loaves of bread for the family.

Johnny grabbed the edge of the stove and Righty the other side. Not a word was spoken as they lifted the stove.

"A dollar! A dollar each!" the stove owner screamed as they released the stove.

For such a heavy stove, it appeared to take a long time before it hit. It was sort of in slow motion, as it went from being a big object to being a small stove that became even smaller as it shattered.

Their moving career moved on.

And the two boys did too, posthaste, like little-ass birds with their tail feathers on fire.

Later, after hearing the stove caper, Rhesus told Johnny, "The big bucks are in water lilies, not breaking your back lugging stoves to the top of the Empire State Building. We sell them to the rich in Mellon Highlands. And they like long stems, three or four feet long."

"And we throw in a few that haven't bloomed yet. Rich people like to see them pop. It makes them think they are growing them," Boattail added, picking up the speed of his speech as they tried to recruit Johnny for a chore they little liked.

—

254

Not to be outdistanced, Rhesus machine-gunned, "And they put them in silver bowls on long tables with white scarves."

"Doilies, dummy, and the rich people don't believe in killing anything, not even bugs. They capture the bugs in a bottle that are swimming around and crawling on the water lilies, and then they dump the bugs where poor people live. I saw them dump some bugs in your yard, Johnny," Rhesus said, crossing his heart to prove he was telling the truth.

Johnny wondered why the two brothers needed a partner as they never shared, not even with each other if they could help it. The exception was that they shared punches to the face. They were always losing their tempers and belting each other.

But beware of someone else hitting one of them; then they had a monkey biting their wiener and a bird pecking out their eyes.

"Why do you need me?"

"Because we're the pearl divers. Rhesus and me dive to the bottom, grab the water lily roots, and swim them to the surface. The only thing you have to do is swim around, enjoying yourself with a beautiful necklace of lilies around your neck like some Hawaiian prince while me and my brudder risk our lives diving to the bottom of the sea."

What he didn't say was that he and Rhesus were scared shitless of water snakes.

"What do I do?"

"Nuthin' except collect lots of money while me and Boattail do all the work."

"Then why do I have to go with you? Can't you just give me the money?" Johnny laughed.

"All you gutter do is swim along on the surface, and we drape the long stems around your neck and rest them on your back," Boattail said.

"And then you get a cent for every water lily we sell. You can make thirty cents in nuthin' flat," Rhesus said, reaching into his pocket and pulling out his hand filled with quarters and half dollars.

Boattail reached deep in his pocket, and pulled out a wad of bills that was actually a wad of paper cut to bill size with a dollar bill on the outside. "Watdaya say, partner?"

"You're on," Johnny said, a big smile swallowing his sunburned ears as he thought of the money and the great ways to use it.

Within minutes, they were walking through the woods toward Buckman's Pond, which had a water surface rarely seen as it was a haven of wild water lilies that covered its surface like aurora borealis crowding out the evening sky.

On the way to Buckman's, Rhesus caught a swallowtail butterfly, ripped off its wings, and stuck them to his cheeks. "Bozo the Clown," he said as he did a prance dance around the wingless butterfly whose body shuddered as it attempted to fly.

"Let's haul ass," Boattail said, and the two brothers stepped up their pace on the path that narrowed the deeper it got into the woods. The sound of cars faded among the warm stirrings of the leaves moved by the heat, hailed by the heat bugs that rubbed their legs together with the frenzy of a franc-making whore in a Paris house of ill repute.

Johnny watched as they disappeared and then tore two thin leafs off an aspen tree. Surely the way they spun in the wind, appearing like wind chimes dancing with a ballerina would serve as wings for the swallowtail.

He dipped the stems in pine pitch and affixed them to the butterfly's body.

The butterfly tried desperately to return to the air but only managed to tear off the Rube Goldberg wings and get its body stuck in the pitch Johnny had used to glue them on.

It lay unmoving until the pincers of the first red ant on the scene bit.

Johnny quickly ground the butterfly and red ant under heel. *There's . . . no other way . . .*

He took what remained of the butterfly in his hand, wondering where the winged beauty, which moments before was as lovely as the wild violet it was resting on, went.

He dug a small hole with a stick, placed the insect in it, and turned a small slice of shale into a grave marker. He located the violet the butterfly had landed on and put it beside the grave.

He remembered Rhesus's words. "The rich people . . . don't believe . . . in killing things . . ."

They were like his father's words when he went off to war, not uttered critically but rather in a "this is the way things are." "The rich people don't kill people. They send the poor."

He remembered the rich woman who had asked his uncle Manny, who had just returned home proud as a peacock from a deer hunt, his thirteenth straight year of chasing whitetails, with his first buck ever, "How could you kill such a beautiful thing in cold blood. Degenerate!"

Uncle Manny didn't know what a degenerate was but did know he wouldn't want that woman to even call him a great guy and said, "Ma'am, you're wearing a fur coat, leather shoes, belt, gloves, and purse and probably heading for a fillet mignon at some fancy-ass restaurant. That steak was a soft-eyed moo cow before your hired killer hit it in the head with a sledgehammer and skinned it alive, ripping out its heart and putting it still pounding on a table with a hundred other still pounding hearts. Get real."

"No more!" the woman had commanded.

"One more, ma'am. The rich always hire the poor to do their dirty work."

"You smell awful," she said, turning away.

Johnny remembered saying, "Yah, but my uncle can wash. You are ugly and mean and can't wash away those things."

The slap on the side of the head made Johnnie's brain scream as flashes of red and white fought to dominate the pain, and he stared at his uncle who said, "You never learned, no way, from your father or us uncles to talk sass to a lady."

"You did."

"Ya, but I earned the right." Then his uncle, hands the size of the mitt of a knuckleball catcher, messed up Johnny's hair. "But thanks for sticking up for blood."

The woman changed her glare from Manny to Johnny.

"Don't waste your looks, ma'am. You ain't got none to spare, and eating all that domestic meat full of chemicals and coloring and salt won't help them none, "Johnny said, then turning to his uncle, "I'm sorry I forgot, but only because I forgot she was a lady."

The slipper she threw barely missed his head.

"Thanks, ma'am. Could I have the other? We could use them velvet slippers to slop the hogs."

"You unadulterated pig, my husband will find you and fix you."

"Have him work on your ass first. Seems we busted that pretty good."

Johnny kicked over the shale gravestone of the butterfly, ground his heel into the grave. "The rich treat bugs better than us. And they don't have to put wax in their teeth on winter days."

He caught up to Rhesus and Boattail as he came over the top of the giant boulder that served as the northern boundary of Buckman's.

He wished that, rather than entering the murky water of Buckman's, he was on the big boulder they dove off at Duck Pond, water so clear they could spot the crayfish around the rocks below.

"I didn't bring a suit," Johnny said.

"Don't need one," Rhesus said. "You can troll your dick for snapping turtles and make two cents a pound if they take it. 'Course it will be a small turtle as the bait is small."

Johnnie wasn't afraid of turtles but didn't know the pond was loaded with water snakes, and that was why Johnny was a partner, so to speak.

"Do what I do," Rhesus said, stripping off his T-shirt and wrapping it around him, making him appear to be in a giant diaper.

Johnny laughed.

Boattail knew better.

Rhesus got red around the ears when Johnny laughed at him. "What's bugging your ass?"

"You look like My Hat My Gandi, one of those guys from India that sits on nails while he's wearing a diaper and then lets the cows come into the house 'cause they like cow shit on the floor."

"Oh ya," Rhesus said, taking a step toward Johnny. "I know you're gonna run for it and lose the water lilies if something scares you,"

"I won't run no matter what," Johnny said.

"Don't shit me," Rhesus threatened.

"I couldn't shit you. You're too big a turd."

"You're not our partner no more," Rhesus said.

Boattail swam to his brother and whispered, "Tons of water snakes today."

"We'll give you one last chance," Rhesus said, diving to the bottom, his My Hat My Ghandi diaper mushrooming full of air as he sounded.

The two brothers repeatedly dove, dug the lilies' roots free, returned to the surface, and wrapped them around Johnny's neck as he swam on the surface.

The lily stems grabbing his ankles and legs along with the weight of the ever-increasing number around his neck and draped over his back made it difficult to catch his breath, and he swam lower and lower in the water, wondering if he could make it.

Rhesus saw Johnny getting lower and lower in the water. "Don't let none slip off your back, or else."

"Oh yah."

"Yah."

"Ya mother wears army boots."

"Ya mother didn't have no kids that lived."

"Oh yah," Rhesus said, putting a lily petal on his shoulder. There was a shortage of chips in the middle of Buckmans. "Knock it off."

"Both you knock it off," Boattail ordered. "We've got big bucks to make."

Johnny trailed after them, the long stems of the water lilies grabbing his ankles and legs and arms, making it more and more exhausting to swim, but he followed them as they headed to the thickest patch of lilies.

"Ya gotta promise, no matter what, you won't drop the lilies and run," Boattail said, looking into Johnny's eyes.

"Or swim for it," Rhesus added.

"I swear on the army boots you said my mother wears," Johnny said, as he slipped beneath the murky surface, swallowing a mouthful of the bitter cedar-stained water. Johnny knew he could make it. Just knew it. But he wasn't making it, and he started slowly to sink from the weight.

That was when the large black water snake that had been hiding in the lilies around Johnny's neck made itself known, eye to eye, and Johnny pressed the starter button on the 150 horsepower outboard that was strapped to his ass for such emergencies, and his bow, lilies and all, lifted high out of the water.

In telling the tale to the gang later, Boattail swore, "He never touched the water. He was so high above the surface you could read 'Pan Am Airlines' on his side."

"The coast guard tried to catch him," Rhesus added.

"He walked on water, just coming up a hair short of parting the waters," Boattail said.

"And he didn't lose a single lily," Rhesus said.

"And that was one skinny kid after that snake scared the living shit out of him," Boattail said.

"But we made him one rich man," Rhesus said.

And that they did.

They sold more than a hundred of the white beauties, and Johnny had nearly a buck and a quarter in change in his pocket later that afternoon.

The two brothers visited houses on the both sides of the street, returning to Johnny when they needed to restock.

While getting a new batch of flowers, Rhesus whispered to Johnny, "Keep an eye on Boattail. He's a dirty bird. If he puts any of the money into his left pocket, you tell me."

Boattail sideslipped to Johnny as his brother headed out. "Johnny, keep an eye on Rhesus. He's as sneaky as a monkey swiping pennies out of a blind man's cup. If he appears to be scratching his ankle, watch close to make sure he isn't dropping dimes into his sock. Tell me if he does. I can't stand a cheat."

Moments later, Boattail was knocking on another door.

The lady that greeted him towered over him, and he looked up into the great face of a horse, complete with wide nostrils, and he wondered whether he could see her brains and was concentrating so that she had to ask a second time, "How much is each lily?"

"Twenty cents each. We risk our lives diving for them. I've already lost five partners to sharks."

"There are no sharks in our fresh water."

"Ya, well, they said the same thing, and you see what happened to them."

"How much if I purchase two dozen?"

"I can give you a bargain, twenty-five cents each."

"Is this a flimflam, twenty cents for one, twenty-five cents if I purchase two dozen?"

"Yah, well, when you get two dozen, you go top shelf. Bigger flowers. Longer stems. Longer life."

"No."

"We sell the short-stemmed ones to your neighbors that don't have the high class you got."

"How many did Mrs. Vanderpoel purchase?" she asked, nodding across the street.

"Three dozen."

"Give me four dozen. Four dozen of the ones that cost thirty cents each."

Boattail ran back to Johnny. "Put the stem stretcher on two dozen more. The old broad is giving us ten cents each!"

Sold out, the three boys returned down Franklin Street, heading from Mellon Highlands to the Big Woods, where the gang would meet at dusk to discuss the day.

On this day, much of the discussion was about Johnny's ability to outswim a water snake without ever touching the water.

The money felt good in Johnny's pocket, but he couldn't help wonder how many more of Jazz's teeth he could get fixed, maybe even his own if Boattail's left pocket didn't appear to be much fuller than the right and if Rhesus didn't appear to have water on the ankles, like Mrs. Murphy, who suffered terrible water each time she had one of her seventeen kids. Some were even Mr. Murphy's. When Mr. Murphy wasn't around, they referred to her as Pat Murphy's pig.

"Hey, there's a bum! Sleeping in the grass over there," Rhesus said. "Let's get 'em."

"They've always got big bucks," Boattail said. "The bastards steal and mooch and all that crap."

"We can't steal his money," Johnny said.

"We're not stealing. Bums is rich. We're just like Robin Hood. Take from the rich, the bum, and give to the poor, us," Boattail said.

"Nah, nothin' doin'," Johnny said, sticking out his jaw to the much bigger Boattail.

"He might have a million bucks on him. Maybe even a ten spot. We got to get it before he hides it in a mattress or a tin can."

"Nothin' doin'."

"Hey, either we take it or someone else does. He's drunk and sick and rich," Boattail said.

"You can get your mother out of the box factory. Maybe buy her new army boots," Rhesus said.

"Nah."

"Hey, you can fix your horse-toothed brother, Jazz, so he can't eat corn through a picket fe—"

Johnny's shove ended the sentence short of "fence," sending Rhesus to the ground.

Johnny stood over him, kicked dirt in his face, glaring at Rhesus, whose even white teeth smiled through the dirt.

"My ma works seventy hours a week in the box factory so Jazz and me can get our teeth fixed."

Boattail offered his hand to his brother to lift him off the ground but pulled his hand back just before Rhesus reached it, causing him to fall backward into the dust for a second time. "Didn't I tell you, stupid, not to trust no one that offered a helping hand."

Then turning to Johnny, Boattail said, "Just take all the money in Rhesus's pockets. He keeps his millions back at the ranch. Go get that too 'cause people like you don't pay any taxes. You just get welfare."

Boattail told Johnny, "We give you the biggest cut, and you want more. You ain't no patriot."

"Nah, you ain't no patriot," Rhesus said. "Where were you on December 7, 1941, when the Jap rats raped Ms. Pearl Harbor! Hey, there's another bum sleeping over there."

"We can get his dough. Bums got millions," his brother said.

"We can't swipe his money," Johnny said.

"You either love your mutter and baby brudder or not," Rhesus said, "or do you want her to work herself to death and let your brudder's teeth all fall out?"

Boattail slid onto his stomach. "Keep low in the weeds, or your ass is grass. The drunken bum could get you. Or old O'Toole, the cop, will get you for grand larceny."

Johnny crept slowly toward the bum. It seemed like a mile, yet as slowly as he crept, the bum seemed to be getting closer, larger, his beard appeared to be the tough, blue-black stubble of the guy in the oh-so-tough-but-oh-so-gentle Bardol Oil ad. Johnny could see his beard had more white in it than black.

The bum's breathing rattled like that of the strangle victim he had heard on the Inner Sanctum radio show the night before.

—

Johnny was close enough to touch him now. His cheeks were sunken in to the point where Johnny was certain they touched each other inside his toothless mouth.

Each drawn breath caused his lips to suck in like a bottom-feeding carp. His exhales made his lips flutter and make fart noises like the kids in his class accomplished by cupping their hand under their armpit and moving the elbow and arm sharply down, forcing the trapped air out in a realistic Bronx cheer of flatulence.

He crept closer, trying to figure out how to get the millions out of the bum's pockets.

He glanced back at the brothers. The closer he had gotten to the prey, the more they backed up and prepared to run.

Then he was within inches of the sourness of the bum's breath, a sourness that smelled of sickness and not just of wine sucked out of the discarded wine bottles.

His hand investigated the back pockets but only felt a buttocks that confirmed Johnny's feelings that the bum was indeed starving to death. Nothing there.

And the front pockets, thighs so thin he feared he would snap them off if he were even a little rough.

There was a coin deep down. That was all. Perhaps a . . . gold piece . . .

It was a penny, an old one. There were thin shiny lines scratched into it. Johnny had to hold it close to read the scratches. Yup, sure as shit, the scratches said, "Lucky penny."

Johnny reached in his pocket, took out his water lily money, looked at it sadly, and, using the gum he has been chewing, he attached his earnings to the lucky penny and stuffed half it in the bum's pocket.

"And what in holy mother of God are you doing!"

Johnny looked up. It was the great hulk, which, if it had a headlight, could pass for the train boxcar; it was O'Toole the cop.

They knew O'Toole could kick a kid's ass further than any cop on the force and realized they stood in shit up to their nostrils when O'Toole's face spread in a broad grin and he scuffed his hobnail boot like an angry bull.

"Oh shit," Johnny said, then shot off away from the giant cop with the words "And they're off and runnin'."

He kept running until he was sitting on the big boulder in the Big Woods, alone, glancing downhill to see if O'Toole had sniffed out the fear spores he had left.

Finally feeling safe, he lay on his back, watching the clouds scud slowly by thinking not backward on how he'd lost all his money but rather how he could make enough to get Jazz's teeth fixed.

His uncle Manny had told him he could marry a rich woman.

"Why would they want to marry me?"

"You've got the gift," Manny told him.

"What gift?"

"You got the dimples in the cheeks and chin and that slong of a swinging chorizo. You're hung like Mighty Joe Young."

"I don't get it."

"It's a gift from God, an entitlement to all us DaSilvas. And you've got both dimples and dong. You've either got it or you ain't."

Johnny said he had overheard Mrs. Mortenson tell one of his aunts, "It's not what you got but how you use it."

"If any woman ever says that to you, you tell her what your uncle Manny tells you. "Ya, but what if you've got it and know how to use it too?"

Johnny just wasn't sure what his uncle was telling him.

It had been one strange pisser of a day. Being chased by a water snake and a cop and giving his money away. None were of any great joy of any kind.

While Johnny didn't think he could ever marry for money, he would, just to get Jazz's teeth fixed and Ma out of the box factory.

Scoff Burns, whose mother also worked in the box factory, said all the bosses there were trying to take a shot at his and Johnny's mothers.

Johnny couldn't figure out why anyone would aim a gun at his mother, want to take a shot at her. *I'd kill anyone . . . that tried to . . . hurt . . . Ma . . .*

But killing someone who would shoot his mother wasn't his problem now.

Rhesus and Boattail were swiftly approaching him, followed in a hundred yards by a still-trucking Officer O'Toole, yelling after them with a broad Irish Boston, "You little bar-stards!"

But that was the officer's last huff, and he sat down on a stump, exhausted.

On seeing O'Toole had packed it in, Rhesus hid in heavy brush and yelled down, "Hey, Adam and Eve were Irish!"

"You little piss-ant bar-stards! I'll boot your arseholes until you wear them as necklaces!"

It was Boattail's turn to yell down from his concealment behind a giant oak, "O'Toole, Adam and Eve were Irish! They met in the Garden of Eden with both wearing fig leaves. Eve lifted Adam's fig leaf and said O'Toole."

Rhesus chirped in, "Adam picked up Eve's fig leaf and said O'Hare."

Officer O'Toole had heard this mocked at him before out of dark alleys, off rooftops, and even chanted so low at the early mass that unaccustomed ears thought it was a lovely Latin offering.

But rather than getting immune to it, it pissed him off more each time.

"I'm pissed off!" he yelled up to the mocking voices.

Chapter 11

SUMMERTIME

When Johnny was eight, he was a bronco buster and matador and saw his first killing when Pie hit Bog the Hog across the nose with a two-by-four after it bit Johnny as he was attempting to break the wild horse hog.

Making a million dollars with schemes only kids could invent didn't take up the gang's entire summer of 1939.

But making money was secondary by 1944. Johnny was thirteen and had graduated from kid stuff. He was a man and wanted to sign up in the marines, join Merrill's Marauders, and kill Jap rats—and sing "From the Halls of Montezuma to the shores of Tripoli, we will fight our country's battles . . ."

But there were other considerations, such as joining the army air force and shooting down Jap Zeros from his F42 Corsair or blowing German Mess of Shits from the sky with the flashing guns of his P-38 Lightning when they tried to bomb London town, where his grandfather Shiverick was born.

Johnny and his fellow Big Tree squadron members would keep the Krauts away from London and the Nips from returning and finishing off the rest of America's Pearl Harbor fleet.

While he was a marine raider or army air force fighter pilot, he still was a kid who walked around with his fly partially open due to the fact he was missing two buttons on his corduroy trousers, which the whistling knickers drew attention to.

He was too busy daydreaming to notice. He was across the world with adventurer Richard Haliburton swimming the Hellespoint and, wow, hiding among the harem women of some crazy sheik. The latter was a sort of dangerous adventure as his head could roll, cut off by one of those Eunuch guys who were always angry because they had had their balls cut off and couldn't ball any of the sheik's ladies.

Whenever Righty caught Johnny with his fly wide open, he asked his friend, "Trolling for queers?" an interesting question, as they did not have the slightest inkling as to what a homosexual was. All Johnny knew was that the American Indians prized medicine men, witch doctors, and other tribal members who marched to a different tom-tom.

Johnny's imagination ran wild much of the time, and he visualized a medicine man stomping his bell laden feet in dance, singing, "Yipsee doodle, I flipped my noodle, I don't need a truss anymore, my rupture's gone, my rupture's gone . . ."

His aunt Hope had a different approach to her nephew's open fly jaunts. She would discreetly inform him, "Someone's barn door is open, and his little pony might escape."

He didn't notice his fly was open in the summer as he enjoyed the cooling effect; it was different in the winter when the north wind blew.

He received unwanted guidance from aunts and uncles who believed in the hard-nose, soft-heart approach in dealing with those they loved.

It was Uncle Luke who encouraged him not to wipe his nose on his sleeve by accusing him of spending twenty-four years in the navy where you got to wear a stripe or hash mark for every four years of service.

Johnny had six nose wipes, hash marks on his right sleeve without having spent a day in the navy. Uncle Luke said that was against regulations. He presented his nephew with a dark-blue hanky with an anchor design on one corner with the words, "John, remember a dark-blue hanky is best because you can spot your past wipes. Now you take a white hanky, same color as your nose wipe, you could end up wiping your nose on past booger runs."

It always interested Johnny as to what luck was, and the hanky would involve luck later the same day. He was carving a fuzz stick up in the Big Woods behind Grandma Shiverick's after the long jog back to Rockledge from the farm. He was proud of his fuzz stick knowledge and hoped to eventually start a fire by rubbing two sticks together at high speed. Both methods involved use of a little pine pitch, dry birch strips, tiny tinder, and a lot of muscle power.

The long run between his favorite spots was easy. He used the Boy Scout running credo, run fifty feet, walk fifty feet. On this day, the run had left him with a hunger that left his stomach feeling like a rat was gnawing inside him, and the cupboard at home was bare.

He had had a chance to end his empty stomach song as his aunt Hope had offered him a hamburger as he looked "starved, like one of those kids in Ethiopia."

He declined, as he understood that his mother would be hurt to think that anyone would believe one of her children went hungry. Besides, he wondered where Ethiopia was, and it took his mind off himself. Instead, he buttoned the top button on his fly as it made his belt line tighter and roped in the stomach, cutting the pain.

But luck in the Big Woods was with him, unluckily for a cottontail sunning itself, whose eyes closed after a good chew of wild alfalfa, a mistake for an animal at the top of the predator food chain in which stealth every moment meant staying alive.

The slingshot and knife were part of his person, like his nose, eyes, ears, and hands.

He decided not to use the slingshot as Kelly the cop had spotted it earlier hanging from Johnny's back pocket and commented accusingly, "Carved another notch on the handle for that recent broken window at the South School!"

"I didn't do it, Officer Kelly."

"Nope, ye lad didn't, did ye!" The sentence wasn't finished before he learned something by the oh-sure tone of the officer—no one sounds more guilty than an innocent person denying a crime.

Johnny also learned that Officer Kelly could give the quickest kick in the ass going. "And go tell ya ma Officer Kelly kicked your arse, and she'll boot it over the moon. And that cow up there will sing 'Hi diddle diddle, the cat and the fiddle' to your arse. And that cow will drop one of its bossy waffles on your arse 'cause you're constipated. Constipation affects your brain. Otherwise you wouldn't try and feed any tomfoolery to me. Anyway, the cow on the moon would know you couldn't go to the toilet so it would go for you in your knickers, me boy."

After the smoke cleared in his brain, Kelly could kick so hard your ass would clatter upward into your cerebrum, according to Boattail. Boattail had the town record for Kelly kicks despite his plea to Kelly, "Kick Rhesus, he's smaller and will fly higher."

Boattail got his brother a good boot, as Kelly had to know whether indeed the smaller Rhesus did fly higher. But Boattail was always a favorite kick for Kelly ever since he had found Kelly sleeping on a park bench with his shoes off and had put fresh dog crap in the toes of his shoes.

But that was Johnny's last denial. Pleading innocent seals a guilty verdict. So it was best to confess and run.

Johnny remembered the day Coo-Coo Kenefic, thus called Coo Coo not because of others thinking him crazy, although he was suspect as he got all As, except in gym, on his report card. He was called Coo Coo because he raised and raced pigeons. He had homing birds, tumblers, fantails, and could they coo. Johnny thought of the birds. *Could they coo . . . Could they coo . . . and could they . . . could they coo coo coo? Has anybody seen my girl . . . five foot two . . . eyes of blue . . .*

Coo Coo had dyed his birds bright colors so no one could steal them. Then he whispered to the birds that it was possible that a bank robber, a Jesse James, or an Al Capone could be lurking behind a tree waiting to birdnap them. He whispered so no human ears could hear, as he didn't want anyone to think he was crazy. Yet he had no trouble conjuring up the vision of a Greek Charles Atlas clone gone bad stepping out, an ouzo in hand, demanding Coo's pigeons, in Germanic voice, "Hall right, put your vings up. Do not let out a peep. Not even a coo."

The reason Coo Coo thought everyone wanted to steal from him was he stole from everyone. He swiped anything. A pencil, a cookie, a scarf. One time he swiped a Kotex from a little girl in the fourth grade, Leanna Burr, who had a nosebleed and was using it as a nostril stuffer.

Her twin brother, Lonnie, who hated being a twin, convinced her she was starting her friend down below, "Just like Ma."

Leanna nearly suffocated when she forced the Kotex up her nostrils to prove him wrong. One day Coo Coo swiped two cents off the teacher's desk. Rhesus had collected the two cents for cookie money and placed it on the desk. When the teacher returned from the teachers' room and found the money missing, she asked, "Who took the money off my desk?"

Everyone in the class, with the exception of Coo Coo, broke out in a guilty sweat while the perpetrator had the look of a choirboy who had spent his last penny buying ice cream for the poor.

So Johnny pretty much believed the best bet was not to declare you were innocent, a move that would mark you guilty. The best bet was to confess and run or tell the accuser "screw you" and then run.

His uncle Manny DaSilva also had occasional comments on Johnny's wiping his nose on his sleeve.

Like the day he asked his nephew if he strangled anacondas and "chalked the snake up on your fuselage, oh Flying Tiger."

Manny said every time he shot a whitetail buck, he carved a small notch on the neck of his old Winchester .30-30.

And while Johnny didn't have a gun, he did have hands and could use them to strangle an anaconda and then mark his kill on his sleeve by blowing his nose there.

Actually, Johnny didn't know what an anaconda was, and Uncle Manny explained, "It's like a python, except its teeth are in its arse. You think it's slithering away while all the time it's coming toward you until, *wham*! Its ass bites you. And turns you into a turd."

"Ah, come on."

"I shit thee not. Hey, you're a man now. You're ready for man jokes. Leg pullin'. If you can get someone to believe a big lie, a real big one, well, you might be the next Adolph Hitler. You're not ready for no girl jokes yet, but man jokes. Ya."

"Really?"

"I hope you're not being sarcastic with your 'really?' Girl jokes can get a young guy like you in trouble as you start to wonder what we're talking about. Wondering about where certain parts are and what you do with them. Nah, you're not ready for that yet. That's how you get headaches."

"Really?"

"But you're ready for the hunting camp jokes. Good stuff, jokes like when me and your dad and your uncle Francisco go to our deer camp up in Charlemont. One day, your dad saw a bear running through the swamp toward him. He swore it wanted to kill him. The poor son-of-a-bitching bear only wanted to haul his ass to save its bear butt from Francisco, who was swamp stomping, hoping to get a deer running toward us."

"Really?"

"But no, Tony wouldn't run or gun, even though he knew bears were killers as the bear rolled its bloodshot eyes at him. Sure it did. Your dad was really going to give up hunting. What fun would that be without all the brothers at camp? None at all.

"Anyway, camp jokes—Francisco told this story about the little rabbit that was sitting on a log letting a crap when this bear came along and plunked its ass down on the log beside the rabbit and dropped a dump over the edge of the log.

"The bear asked the rabbit, 'Mr. Rabbit, does shit stick to your fur?'

"'Nah,' the rabbit said, and the bear grabbed the rabbit and wiped his ass with it."

"Yah? So?" Johnny asked.

"Yah, what? You're supposed to laugh. Your dad laughed, like you were 'posed to. And the happy ending was that your dad wasn't afraid of bears no more."

"And I thought I wanted to go to deer camp with you guys."

—

"Look, stop wiping your goddamned nose on your sleeve if you didn't kill no anacondas!" Manny said, walking off with pretended hufffiness.

As usual, Johnny had jogged the fourteen miles from Rockledge to Chelmsford; it was a cakewalk. Hey, he'd done it in the middle of winter while it was snowing like hell. It was a Christmas storm. He had jogged to the farm thinking perhaps there would be some sort of Christmas gift for him.

He got a gift from Mine, not exactly what he had hoped for, a Bowie knife or leather hunting boots that laced to just below the knees. Instead, she had given him a set of rosary beads and a crucifix.

He wondered whether one of those priests in the high Episcopal Church wore that Catholic stuff. They didn't in his church. But if they transferred to the high church, he could get away with wearing it on the ruse that he was preparing to be an Episcopal pastor.

Being a pastor didn't seem like it would be a lot of fun. Well, maybe at a church supper when spaghetti was being served—it would be funny to have someone say, "Pass the pasta, Pastor."

Grandfather Shiverick always took him to the 9:00 a.m. service at the Episcopal Church.

Johnny, when he was young, wondered if the Episcopal Church was named for Christians who pissed in pails or were some sort of pissin' pals or somethin'.

Right after that early service, his grandfather would take his hand, and they'd move out, just making the 10:30 service at the Methodist Church across town.

It was at the giant cathedral in Boston in the afternoon. It was here Johnny feared he was a sinner as the cathedral was so grandiose and his mental sexual meandering grandiose as they were accompanied and encouraged by a huge organ with pipes fifteen feet high.

He was awfully damned happy he wasn't a Catholic and would have to confess his thoughts.

The early morning Episcopal service had been as staid as an old woman's whalebone corset stay. Everyone nodding approval of the minister's monotone, those not quite hearing it nodding the most animatedly.

The Methodist Church was built on boredom. The old-fashioned Pilgrim pole with a foxtail on one end used to tickle the noses of the giggling girls would have been right at home there.

As would the ball on the other end used to bop the sleeping boys.

The pastor tolerated the closed eyes, believing they were the result of the holy visions he had conjured up.

—

After the two services, grandfather and grandson barely had time to make it home for a cool drink of homemade lemonade and pick up one of those loaves of still-warm homemade bread, which they nibbled as they walked the ten miles into that big boss, Boston Cathedral.

The two didn't pay a lot of attention to Grandma Shiverick's words as she took the bread out of the brick oven with the warning, "Let it cool first. It can burn your tonsils and give you a stomachache if you eat it hot."

She smiled as she wiped her hands on her apron, kissed the top of Johnny's head, knowing full well as soon as they got around the corner they would start their attack on the still-steaming loaf. She smiled to herself and was happy that she smelled of just-baked bread.

One Sunday, as the old man and his grandson headed to their third service of the day, which Johnny thought of as the Boston Tea Party, the result of overtaxation, he was informed that the Boston service would be followed by an even more special occasion. That evening they would attend a special service for the elderly at the Congo Church.

Johnny wondered about calling the Congregational Church "Congo." There are no natives there . . . no coconuts . . . not even a monkey . . . and he hoped that after touching all four bases, the churches, he would be allowed to return to the dugout and listen to "The Shadow" on the radio—"only the shadow knows." Followed by demoniacal laughter. That laughter made Johnny happy; the Shadow was a good guy.

He knew he wanted to be a good guy. Not quite as good as Henry Aldrich whose radio show started with his mother's call, "Henry! Henry Aldrich!" And Henry always answered, "Coming, Mother." It was Rhesus who said, "Ya, Henry was coming, and so wasn't Bernadette."

Johnny remembered listening from a hiding spot as his uncle Manny told jokes. His favorite, recited in a Jewish voice, was "Abbie, what are you and your sister doing out there?" "Fucking Mama", "That's nice. Don't fight."

As they neared the Boston Cathedral that day, his grandfather, spotting the exhaustion in his grandson's eyes, said, "You cannot get too much of God, who never rests," his blue eyes misting as he petted Johnny on the head. He wet his hand with his tongue and slicked down the boy's cowlick. Fervent emotion activated the old man's huge white dove eyebrows. But it was all too much for Johnny; that is until he spotted Mrs. Mortenson, who, for some unknown reason, was sitting in the row across the aisle from them, and for reasons he did not understand, he could not get enough of her.

She sang to God on the highest with more stretching and straining than Johnny had ever seen her do at their little Episcopal Church.

—

Her calves already flexed in high heels flexed even more as she stretched to high heaven, causing her silk stockings to appear so sheer against her legs that they appeared naked and then caused her dress to stretch tight across her 'high derriere shelf' buttocks.

On this day, she had a circular rhythm of worship whose centrifugal force thrust her groin upward and forward. He noticed her smile at a parishioner who appreciated her holiness.

Why doesn't she . . . smile at me? I appreciate . . . her holiness . . . everything . . .

Her rhythm meant stretching high with her weight first on one calf, then the other with the right calf and the right buttocks flexing first, then the left calf and the left buttocks following the lead. Then her outreach to her savior went even more heavenward and caused her dress to rise and tighten even higher on her rear and bind tight against her breasts that appeared like the prows of a brace of racing boats busting through the heavy waves.

Johnny looked closer at her. *Did I see . . . pink . . .*

She appeared now to be pleading with some pagan God in hell rather than a holy one in heaven.

Her legs, her breast, her buttocks all appeared to burst in different directions, like wayward, windward waves that eventually managed to come together as a giant exploding wave.

The boy was frantic, attempting not to look at her, his eyes first nearly crossing and then rolling upward, leaving mostly the whites showing. It was when her eyes fluttered like butterflies caught in a swirling dust devil and then closed as she swung her head from side to side like an out-of-control sailboat caught yawing in wave troughs that he cried out, "God help me!"

Grandfather Shiverick looked lovingly at his grandson who was obviously caught up in the great Cathedral's holiness, calling out to God. The old man drank in the looks of holy admiration this God-given boy received from several of the parishioners that made them wish that their offspring could be more like him.

Mrs. Mortenson smiled at him when he called out, but her smile was different than that of the admiring parishioners.

"Now, my son, you understand how no Catholic priest chanting in a foreign language to a false God could stir such emotions as an Episcopalian can."

Johnny did not understand his grandfather's words as he didn't his grandmother Dasilva's tears in her eyes as she said her rosary beads before her small statues of Jesus and Mary.

Whenever she saw him come through the door of the farm, tears streamed down her face of a thousand wrinkles, her face that Johnny felt looked like the world's oldest and most lovable pixie.

On this day she hugged him tight as she lit not one, but two candles for him. He could smell the bacon fat in with the wax and lard of the farm-made candles, and the food odors made him realize how hungry he was.

Mie always knew when a little boy was hungry, especially after he had jogged miles to get there. Within moments, she handed him a fried linguica sandwich on bacon-laced lard smeared on homemade cinnamon-raisin bread heated to a golden brown on the black iron stove and cider heated just right, as it always was.

Johnny knew he couldn't wear the rosary beads and crucifix in Rockledge despite his feeling that when he came to bat during a baseball game, he would have God-given confidence, especially with a crossing of the heart thrown in. He also knew he couldn't, as it would kill his grandfather Shiverick.

Being a Catholic was out. His English grandparents wanted him to be an ordained minister. And he'd never seen a minister with rosary beads on. Perhaps he could tell everyone they were some sort of worry beads. Nah. He never lied. He hated lies. The only time he'd lie was to save Jazz or even his sister. Rarely he'd lie to save his own ass, as there were different roundabout ways to tell the truth. It was that the truth was a lot easier to deal with. You could always remember the truth. It never changed. It was always the same.

And the truth, as much as he loved his grandmother DaSilva, was his grandfather Shiverick's Protestant one.

When his grandfather Shiverick asked him how anyone could follow a religion where the leaders thought that only they could talk to directly to God, he had no answers.

And was asked how you could follow a religion where the priests not only talked in a foreign language, Latin or somethin', and preached in church with their backs to the congregation.

When he asked his grandson if he could believe in a church where people didn't go to hell if they were bad but instead they went to purgatory where they could be bought out of their sins and then go to heaven, Johnny shrugged his shoulders and thought, *It could be a good deal* . . .

And when if a little baby died before it was baptized it couldn't get into heaven, he had no answer for his grandfather but thought, *Sure, I just bet God would say to a baby, "Sorry you can't get into heaven . . . you cute little tyke . . . my priests didn't wet your head . . ."*

—

273

If Catholics were evil, how could his grandfather explain Mie, who, along with Grandmother Shiverick, was among the most loving people in the world, so kind that you knew that heaven was burying your head in her apron, smelling the fresh-baked bread, the blueberries picked that morning and kept in the apron until there were enough for blueberries on the cereal, and for blueberry muffins that left your teeth wonderfully blue, like you had swallowed the blue of the ocean and the sky and wore them as a smile.

There were other unanswered questions. Not just about Catholics. Why were the Seventh-day Adventists so good, so kind to him when he went to the New England Sanatorium after those angry bees bit him. He had disturbed their nest as he knocked down small dead trees with his Indian tomahawk, a perfectly shaped root he was positive was a war club an Indian chief had left there just for him to discover some hundred years later. He suffered many stings all over his body as his hands were fighting to keep the bees off Jazz, who ran ahead of him.

The funny part was that when they wanted bees, they couldn't find them.

Johnny's father years before had taken him to search for honeybees that would lead them to the honey tree.

The next day, father and son set out for the field and woods.

They had a small box in which they trapped one of the honeybees feeding on wild clover and golden rod. His father held the bee as Johnny rubbed a bright-blue powder on its rear end.

Then after his father handed Johnny the compass to read the bee's path, he released it. "Get the reading, get the reading!" his father had called out in glee. "It's making a beeline for the honey tree."

"North, northeast," Johnny replied, proud that the Boy Scouts had taught him to read a compass.

The two, father and son, ran lightly through the woods, occasionally sneaking a glance at each other, smiling, then returning to the compass reading.

How far had they run, a hundred feet? One hundred miles? Then they heard a drone like a distant airplane.

"*Bees!* The *honey tree!*" They exulted in unison.

They closed the distance between them and the droning bees. "There it is!" they called out again in one voice, and there was the swarm blackening a hole in an old oak where a limb once grew.

Johnny looked for the bee with the blue bottom. He wanted to thank it for finding them the honey tree.

"Quickly, gather the dry wood." Within moments, a fire was popping.

"The ferns!"

They threw the green ferns on the fire, then the hemlock and pine, and soon smoke billowed from the fire.

They quickly fanned it toward the honeybee hole.

And one by one the bees fell to the ground, overcome. Johnny looked for the bee with the blue bottom. Perhaps he could save it. "Quick, the honey bag!"

Johnny reached into his shirt and pulled out a canvas cloth as his father reached deep into the honey hole and scooped, removing his arm and hand covered with honey.

Father and son scraped the honey into the canvas with flat wooden sticks they had carved earlier, a procedure they did several times, and then they turned and ran laughing along the path. Their running bodies had carved through the ragweed and clover following the blue-bottom bee.

They grabbed off hunks of honey and ate the gobs as they ran, laughing, eating, and laughing, laughing and eating.

Johnny felt as good as the day when he and Grandfather Shiverick walked to the Boston Cathedral pulling off hunks of the steaming, freshly baked bread. Johnny looked skyward. Thank you, God . . . for bread and honey . . . Thank you, Dad . . . Thank you, Granddad . . . for my daily bread . . . and honey!

As they ran through the woods, his father appeared, disappeared, and reappeared repeatedly, and Johnny shivered, wondering why his father had to live and work so far away when work and the honey tree were also here where they lived, lived waiting for him.

The dead tree bees that had bit Johnny earlier leaving him in pain and sending him to the Seventh-day Adventist Sanatorium were long forgotten. But not the kindness of the people who strangely celebrated the Sabbath on Saturdays. Yes, the Seventh-day Adventists had been so kind. *So very kind . . . they were almost loving . . . taking care of me . . .*

He wanted Jazz to enjoy a honey tree hunt like he had. It seemed like their father didn't come home as much, didn't have time to take Jazz on his first honey hunt.

His experience with bees was so different. One full of pain, the other of joy. Jazz had the pain with Johnny, and Johnny wanted him to enjoy the . . . honey heaven side of the coin . . .

Although he loved Grandfather Shiverick and believed everything he said, Seventh-day Adventists and their nurses, so pale due to their no-meat diets, and kind, like Mine and Grandma Shiverick, could not be of an evil religion.

And certainly if Mine worshiped a Catholic God, it could only be a good one.

Sometimes it hurt horribly in the head and stomach thinking about what was right.

And how could you explain if he wasn't a Jew, why was he circumcised?

Izaac Levine said only Jews got circumcised and asked Johnny if he had saved his foreskin.

When he said no, Izaac asked him, "Why not?"

"I was only just born and don't have a hint of what happened to it. Why would you save it?"

Izaac had told him with those giant open and honest brown eyes, "Because you give your foreskin to the prettiest Jewish girl you know."

"Why?"

"She puts it under her pillow and wishes for the whole thing."

"Why?"

"Come back when you grow up, little boy."

"What's cookin' here," Johnny asked.

"Bacon, wanna strip," Izaac said, doing a burlesque movement that saw him unbuttoning his shirt.

"Forget it."

"That's the difference between those of Jewish persuasion and everyone else. We know when to circumcise and what to do with it. No wonder we're the chosen people."

"Chosen? You're the last one chosen at our pickup games."

"So?"

"Sew buttons on your fly," Johnny answered, "You are the last one to get picked or play."

"So what when I'm chosen? Someday I'll own the team. And I'll make myself captain and bat cleanup. And pitch a no-hitter. And you'll warm the bench."

Thinking of Mie and the candles, he wondered if the two were still burning. It had been more than a year since she had given him the rosary beads and crucifix. Sometimes in the dark, he took them from their hiding place inside the post on his brass bed. The top unscrewed from the post and offered a hollow for hiding—everything. Even the note he had written to Dotty Dean, that tiny girl who got all A pluses, not to mention a double promotion.

He had never mailed it to her; the words were mostly borrowed from a song. "I wish I had a paper doll I could call my own, a doll that other fellows would not steal. I wish you were my paper doll. I would give you

—
276

lots of good stuff, including my giant aggie with the blue cat's eye in it. Good stuff from a good honest and good boy just like Henry Aldrich and a Scout who goes to church and likes you an awful lot. I know I shouldn't say that last thing to you until we get married. Signed the Mystery Man."

"Ma, I'm gonna run to Gramma DaSilva's."

"Don't go getting hit by no cars, Johnny. You're all I've got for a man of the house to protect us from burglars."

He thought, *Sure she needs protection . . . Geez, that bayonet drill she pulled with her broom on that poor thief trying to hold someone up near our house . . . the poor beggar cried for the police to stop her . . .*

The would-be thief wanted her arrested for assault.

Officer Kelly said, "Oh sure, the little woman with the broom and the big bad guy with the knife." Officer Kelly started him toward the lockup with a swift boot in the arse.

And how about that hockey practice that time? She had told him to come right home after practice. But he had joined a pickup game and stayed until after dark. She wanted him home so he could get a bite to eat before going to set pins at the Sundown Bowling Alley.

He had just passed the puck to Rhesus who had "deked the goalie out of his jock" when her voice filtered down to him, "Johnny DaSilva, you come right home before I come after you."

He didn't answer despite several warnings.

On her fifth demand, he finally said, "Go on home, Ma."

"That's it."

Suddenly she was on the ice, wearing a pair of leather-soled loafers, slip sliding away; but armed with that terrible swift sword of a broom, she managed to corral what Johnny knew was one of the fastest, trickiest skaters he ever knew—himself.

And she had whacked him with that broom all the way up the street, black with night, except for the sparks that flew from his skates as he ran homeward over the blacktop road.

Some thought the sparks were from her bayonet—broom.

"Ya, Ma, don't worry. No car is going to hit me. I'll be back to protect you from the bad guys."

The farm was deserted as he trotted into the circular gravel driveway.

The cows were congregated under the large tree in the middle of the pasture, not moving in the heat; not even a cud was chewed. *It's going to rain . . .*

Then he saw the goats and the one Billy whose whiskers did a dance as he chewed. *A combo of Ma's dancing broom . . . and Granddad Shiverick's dancing eyebrows . . .*

Johnny thought, *The goats are too blah to baa* . . . "Corny."

Completely pooped out, Snore, the farm dog, escaped the heat by trying to crawl its lazy body into the shade but failing to complete the crawl he fell asleep in the hot driveway dust.

His eyes were open as usual and did not even twitch as a fly walked across his left eye. If his eye had been a globe of the world, the fly would have ventured from South America, to Great Britain, and finally to Norway.

Only the cicadas sung their happiness of the heat, their back legs vibrating their song with the ooooph-pazaaz of an erotic tuning fork that also spouted the time.

Mine wasn't weeding or picking the blueberries in the breakfast patch just below the kitchen window.

Of course not. It was that once a month that Manny presented her with the treat of all treats; he took her shopping at the Big Bear in Boston, the big city. But she didn't know what to buy as they grew everything they needed on the farm—apples, potatoes, beef and pork and chicken and homemade salt bread and chorizo and linguica. Then she made yellow soap so strong it not only threatened to kill the clothes it washed if they didn't come clean, but it also blew away any poison ivy the family came in contact with. She pickled the different meats, included pig's feet, which were put in a wooden barrel filled with layers of brine with the meats separated by layers of wax.

Mine made jellies and jams the supermarkets were yet to invent, concoctions that would make a rock salivate.

Pie made dandelion wine from the root, the leaf, and the flower. He made potato wine, white lightning, that caused threatening storms across his brow.

All the grandchildren had their turn in the grape barrel, crushing grapes until their legs were red and blue up to their knees, argyles of nature.

Pie kept a cask of wine beside his bed. The left side. The right side had his pinball machine, a machine with a small hole carved out in one corner so he could insert a coat hanger and bang the bumpers until the free games rung up. Under his mattress were the pictures of the whores doing it with donkeys, black giants, midgets, guys who had two heads, three peckers.

Over all of Pie's Mephistopheles maze, Jesus's blood trickled down his forehead from his crown of thorns, down his side where the spear had pierced, and hung on the cross smiling down.

In his back-and-forth life between the farm and Big Woods, there was camping out, most often in the Big Woods, where they set up their tents made of old rain slickers, and sneaking out bedroom windows when the rest of the family had gone to sleep. It was always exciting to take a roll call to see who made it out without waking their families each night, sort of like taking a roll call after a fierce military battle where everyone knew there would be casualties.

When the school year ended, a new life began for Johnny and his cousins, Pointer and Dink, and that was working on the farm. A slow way to make a million as their efforts went unpaid for, except in meals. Then there was work after the farmwork; it was for old man Osterhouse.

The old Dutchman paid ten cents an hour. Dink got eleven cents after farmer Osterhouse realized he could drive the old one-lunged John Deere tractor.

Pointer and Johnny couldn't understand why Dink got more for doing easier work.

Where the cousins slept meant little or nothing to Pie as long as they were in the farm fields by dawn.

When they slept in the woods surrounding the farm, there were no tents over their heads, only stars.

They had long deserted the summer bonds of their no-bounce-to-the-ounce racks on the farm.

If a little rain fell, they left their open sky and crawled under a lean-to they made out of several layers of pine boughs that wicked the water off.

The going was tight under the lean-to.

"Get your rotten butt out of my face," Dink said to Johnny, giving him a two-knuckle noogie to the collarbone that left an egg-sized welt on the bone.

Johnny grabbed his cousin's sideburns and lifted until the side of his face burst into flames.

Pointer jumped on Johnny. "Leave my brother alone, you shit."

"I'm your cousin."

"You cousin shit, you," Pointer said, trying to give Johnny an Indian burn on the nape of the neck until the friction burned, reddened the skin, and broke it.

Dink picked up his brother and tossed him into the top of the lean-to, causing it to collapse and causing them to collapse into a fit of laughter.

"I'm starved," Pointer said. "It's youse guys fault. You're older than me and should know better than to let us starve."

"I could eat week-old roadkill," Dink said.

—

"Hey, we didn't eat all the good stuff Mine brought us last night," Johnny said. "Can you imagine our little tiny grandmother walking through the black woods to our camp. Not afraid of bears or ghosts or nothing," Johnny said.

"I pity any bears that crossed her path," Dink said.

"Good idea stashing her stuff in the hollow under the rock so the raccoons couldn't get it," Pointer said as he lifted the rock and pulled out the food.

"Good idea the rock bit," Johnny told Dink.

"Yah," Dink said, brushing off the ants that were having a teddy-bear-like picnic, handing a linguica and egg sandwich between thick slices of Portuguese sour bread, a pickled pork chop, and a piece of apple pie to each and then munching on his own share, which turned out surprisingly equal, considering the hunger of each.

"We're starved," Pointer minced through a mouthful of pie.

"You mean we're saved," Dink said, correcting his brother with a pork chop in his mouth.

"I can't help thinking of Mine coming through the woods in the dark and rain," Johnny said, "we've got to get the statue for her."

The three had no trouble conjuring up a picture of the Holy Virgin, all three feet of her, standing among Mine's candles, with their grandmother's tears streaming down her cheeks, her eyes as loving as those of a mother monkey looking at her new baby.

They had spotted the religious statue they were going to steal while looking through the closed shutters of a camp used as a priest's retreat.

"We've gotta be careful," Dink said, "so I'll be boss. We'll kick in the front door. Pointer will go in and grab the Holy Mother. Johnny will stand by the front door with a stick in case the cops come."

"What will you be doing?" his brother asked.

"I'm the brains. And also got the best eyes. I'll hide in the bush to see if anyone's coming."

The caper called for poling their raft up stream until they reached the camp, mostly visited by Monsignor Micowalski.

They'd cover the raft with a tree limb and crawl up to the camp to see if anyone was there. If the shutters were closed and bolted, they were in like Flynn.

"We gotta be careful. Religious people give out hard punishment," Dink said.

"And cruel," Pointer added.

"I don't care nothing about that as long as he doesn't make me say no Hail Marys. My grandfather Shiverick would kill me, or worse, he'd look directly at me," Johnny said. "He just doesn't like that smoke and bell ringing and other hokeypokey."

They made further plans as they walked through the morning farm woods to Mill Pond, taking time out only to investigate where in hell those little ruffed grouse chicks disappeared to.

The cuddle of chicks was following their mother when the boys happened onto them.

The mother started dragging her wing like she was seriously injured, her eyes fluttering like a fan dancer's all the time.

They followed her for a couple steps and then turned their interest back to the chicks.

They weren't there.

It was Johnny who spotted the one leaf among all those dead-still ones move ever so slightly.

He got down on the ground, turned his head sideways, and looked under the leaf and spotted the tiny chick with the leaf stem in its beak. It had grabbed the leaf and rolled over on its back, covering itself with it.

He looked around under other leaves. Other chicks had grabbed the stems of leafs in their beaks, slid over onto their backs, pulling the leaves over themselves, successfully disappearing. Almost.

Johnny jumped to his feet, anxious to share his discovery only to see his cousins taking Bobby-Doerr-like swings at the flying grasshoppers with their Louisville Slugger maple branches.

"What did you see?" Dink asked, taking a last rip at his little green-winged baseball.

"Ah, nothin'."

"Oh?" Dink said, preparing to take a look for himself.

"Oh, just some sort of scorpion, an' red ants, and stuff."

"We'll mosey on, partners," Dink said, slapping the butt of his imaginary stallion and galloping off.

Arriving at their secret cove, they removed the pine branches that covered *The*, their raft. They thought it was the cat's meow when they built the raft then named it *The*.

Johnny had held the bottle of Hires Root Beer high in preparation of the christening and launching that day.

"Hey, be careful you don't break that bottle of champagne when you christen *The*."

"Don't worry, I'm as thirsty as you are."

"I'll say the words," Dink said. "I'm the oldest."

"You always get to say the words," his brother protested.

—

"That's cuz I'm always the oldest. Ready! I christen the *The*." They laughed.

"The what?" Johnny said, coming in on cue. They laughed again.

"The *The*," Dink said. They laughed, slapping their thighs.

"Don't stutter, little sailor boy," Pointer said. They laughed until it hurt. The Three Musketeers dissolved into Shemp, Curly, and Moe, twinking noses, slapping heads, tickling ribs.

But only for the time being, as within moments Johnny and Pointer were sinking their poles into the mud, Pointer nearly getting pulled overboard when the mud declined to give up his pole. Johnny had grabbed his cousin with one hand and the mud-stuck pole with the other.

"I'll keep watch on the poop deck," Dink said.

Johnny chimed, "Oh me, oh my, oh mutter, me farter's on the poop deck."

Pointer hoisted his leg and let fly. "Gaseous indigestion."

Mistake. He had no place to run and hide as he was pounded by his shipmates until he completed his three the-mail-must-get-through whistle three times and knocked on wood, which in this case was the logs that made up *The*'s deck, where he was pounded too as he attempted to complete his trinity to escape.

Completing his salvation with the third knock on wood, he crossed himself in thanks to God and lamented, "I don't know why I do this. I cross myself every time I come to bat, yet the Protestants get more hits. It ain't right."

"'Ain't' ain't in the dictionary," his brother said.

"It should be," Pointer countered.

They covered the mile upstream relatively swiftly despite taking time out to throw sticks at painted turtles sunning on a flat rock, having a piss for distance contest, and Johnny diving after a snapping turtle he spotted. Pie paid a penny a pound for this soup on the swim despite the fact trying to collect could be hazardous to your health.

This lost time was more than made up for by upping the cadence to the Volga Boat Song.

There were certain delays, perhaps on purpose, a splinter in a hand, a twisted ankle, and other things that could abort the mission as they neared their hit and gave more thought to getting caught.

While none had ever done time, despite the fact they were in their young teens and considered themselves hardened criminals, Dink and Pointer had spent more than the better part of an entire morning in the cellar as punishment for stealing a hymnal from the Congregational church.

Johnny had been a young Sioux brave captured by a Cavalry made up of older boys during a game of Cowboys and Indians. They tied him to a tree and left him. He vowed he would never be tied down again, never imprisoned.

The problem was that no one, including Pointer, wanted to be the one to suggest they turn back. After all, Mine had enough candles to protect them.

So they poled until they could see the priests' camp through the alders that lined the river.

Now the poling was silent as they headed to the bank. They tied up and covered their craft with branches, as they had planned. All was going well except they were still a hundred feet from the camp, and it was all open ground.

"We can't go through the woods anymore," Dink said. "The old heathen thinned out all the trees. Priests don't trust anyone."

"Probably cut the clearing so no Protestants can sneak through," Pointer added, rolling his eyes at Johnny.

"He probably thinned them out so the squirrels could watch him when he shit in the woods," Dink said.

"We gotta go by water. The swamp brook goes right behind the camp," Johnny said.

"How?"

Johnny said, "Simple, I saw it in the movies once. A guy escaped from jail, swam through a swamp right beneath the noses of the guards and bloodhounds while he was breathing through a reed,"

The cat-o'-nine-tails were quickly cut to the proper size, and minutes later, they were submerged, face up, reeds in mouth, and swam upstream, underwater. They lasted all of ten seconds, the time it took them to realize they couldn't get enough air through the tube, and surfaced sputtering.

"How in unholy heaven did baby Moses survive in the bulrushes?" Dink challenged.

"He wasn't in Pamplona. Get it," Johnny said, "the bull-rushes."

"Do we get any butter and salt with that corn?" Pointer asked.

"Cut the corn, you two. Father Ski will hear us."

"He can't hear us. He's got his head up his housekeeper's skirt," Pointer said quite proudly because his coming into smut repartee had been a slow one. He had been slowed down by his brother either slapping him for talking dirty or Dink's throwing in the punch line and taking credit for it before Pointer could finish it off. But that's what you get for being a younger brother.

—

A combination breaststroke and dog paddle close to the bank got them to their destination swiftly. However, they came to a "Stop" sign in the form of a water snake that swam from beneath the bank.

They swiftly climbed out of the water into the tall grass at the top of the bank.

The shutters were bolted closed; no one was there.

But they had to be sure.

"Johnny, you sneak through the grass and check out the place."

"Why me?"

"If I had Pointer do it and he got killed or something worse, Ma would kill me."

Johnny crept through grass as slowly as molasses creeping down an elephant's leg and wondered, *What would molasses . . . be doing . . . on an elephant's leg?*

Molasses. He loved the time he conned his goody-two-shoes sister into holding her tongue and repeating after him, "Molasses on the table," and seeing the expression on her face when it came out "My ass is on the table."

Those were the good old days, when he was in his own home when he could fight with his sister for being his sister and then fight any of the freaks who called her toothpick legs or skinny Minnie with the meatball eyes.

The crawl toward the camp was slow, and Johnny knew for certain that Father Ski was aiming a shotgun at his eyes this very minute and thought, *They'd never charge . . . a priest . . . with murder . . .*

He asked himself what Custer's men at Little Big Horn asked themselves. *What am I doin' here? General Custer . . . General Custer Dink . . . No way . . . General Dink got me . . . here at little big horn . . .*

He didn't want to look. Father Ski would shoot out his eyes. He closed his eyes as if doing so would make them bullet proof and crept forward.

He kept them closed. Luckily, he had taken a compass bearing on the camp.

Then he heard the bang, felt the shot. Right in the forehead, between the eyes. Except it wasn't a shotgun blast; he had crept headfirst into the floor of the front porch.

It hurt bad, but he took consolation from the fact that a shotgun blast would have hurt more.

There wasn't a sound inside the camp. It was as quiet as a church mouse. He wanted to laugh at his pun, but Father Ski still could be in there with his terrible swift shotgun.

—

I'm close enough now . . . He can't see my head . . . and shoot my eyes out . . . but he could blow my ass off . . .

He lowered his tail. How would he sit on that Indian motorcycle when he was sixteen without an ass? How could he sit in that plane waiting with his fellow paratroopers to jump into Berlin and onto Hitler's schicklegrubber back. And could a man give it to a girl without having an ass backing up his best?

"General Custer, what am I doin' here?" he wanted to ask aloud.

It stayed quiet as he waited, and his boredom became stronger than his fear. He signaled his cousins to come on down.

Five minutes later, he saw the grass move.

Jesus, was it them? Or Father Ski? Or some sort of freak alligator that someone paid seventy-five cents for when it was a six-inch-long baby and later flushed down the toilet and into a swamp where it grew into a kid-eating giant.

Then he saw Pointer. He was being pushed forward by his brother. "What's what?" Dink asked.

"What am I doin' here," Johnny asked.

"Whaddaya got, the shakes?" Dink asked.

"Sure, hubba hubba, ding ding," Johnny answered. That should show he wasn't scared. He got up and checked the shutters. "We can't get through these things."

"Well, we'd better beat it then," Dink said.

"What you got, the shakes?" Johnny mimicked.

"Oh sure, hubba hubba, ding ding. But better we beat it. We can't get in."

"What about Mine?" Pointer said, amazed at himself that he wasn't gone with the wind at the first suggestion they mosey on home, pronto.

"You're right, "Johnny said, and he could actually feel his spurs digging into the sides of his horse as he tried to catch up with the blond, long-haired idiot Custer, who was up ahead, waving his sword like he thought it was a hot damned Gatling gun.

"Yah," Dink said, more than a twidget unhappy, "but what do we do?"

"I got it," Johnny said, "up on the rooftops, ho, ho, ho."

"Have you flipped your noodle?" Dink asked.

"Up on the rooftop, ho, ho, ho," Johnny sang again, pointing at the big fieldstone chimney in the center of the camp's roof. "All we need is to get a fallen tree to use as a ladder."

They went into the dark woods in search of a tree they could lean onto the roof and climb.

Coming from the bright light into the dark left them momentarily blind, a good time to take a leak while their eyes adjusted. Johnny, on his knees, was shooting Kelly inches from what appeared to be a dark and rotten stump.

As his stream hit the stump, it appeared to move. Boy, that's potent piss I piddle . . . bringing a dead stump . . . to life . . .

It was mostly a dead stump he was leaking on, but what appeared to be part of it was actually a sleeping porcupine he was showering.

When he discovered its quills inches from his "dingus," another name they had thought up, he let out a scream. It was the scream of one who realizes what the pain would be if the two main characters came into play. He also could picture himself being rafted to the hospital, followed by a fast push on a gurney with a snootful, so to speak, of quills in his private, with his friends and all the pretty girls in his class looking on while his mother prayed for him.

Luckily, the porky didn't take immediate umbrage, mostly because of its love of salt. When he later told the story to his cousins, he enhanced it to "And I think it enjoyed me pissing on its head."

"That's nothing you enjoy," Pointer said in defense of the porcupine.

"I don't know," Dink said, "you're stupid enough. We'll leak on your head and see if you like it."

"You try it and I'll tell Ma."

"You spoil everything." Dink laughed.

Johnny didn't join in. He was still shaking from the close encounter of the worst kind.

They found the perfect tree to use as a ladder, a fallen pine, with several broken limbs that could serve as steps. Before you could say "think it over, boys," they were walking along the roof peak.

"What do we do now?" Dink asked.

"Who wants to know?" Johnny countered, stalling, needing the time to think. "What we do first is rip this screen off the top of this smoke stack. Then one of us, the smallest, ho, ho, ho, goes down the chimney, walks to the front door, and unlocks it. Then we get Mine's Mary statue."

"I don't like the idea," Pointer, by far the smallest, said. "Let's make it the biggest and strongest."

"Got the shakes, piss ant?" his brother said.

"Nah, that's my brains coming to the surface. No, I've got the guts."

Johnny and Dink both put their arms around him. No words were said.

They quietly helped him take his shirt off.

"You'd better go down feet first," Dink said.

—

"Nothin' doin'. If I got stuck, Father Ski could lop my head off," Pointer said, "if I was going head first down the chimney."

Things went good. His shoulders were narrow.

But things have to go good the entire trip down, and soon he found himself lodged in the narrow smoke trap. And he knew he was stuck immediately and started crying.

"Hey, don't be a baby crying," his brother said.

"You're gonna cry when I die and Ma finds out." He cried louder after using the word "die."

"We've gotta break in and pull him down," Johnny said.

"That would be breaking and entering, and we'd be in deep caca," Pointer said without thinking.

Within moments, Johnny and Dink were down the ladder and pounding on a shutter hinge with a rock and had the shutter hanging within moments.

Dink looked up the chimney, spotted his brother's eyes, wide and white in the pitch black. "We'll never fit up there."

"We have to try. I'll go."

"We can go for help."

"Pointer's head will burst with all the blood rushing to it."

Pointer's sobbing became more active.

All three boys knew he was going to die.

"I'm going for help," Dink said.

"His brains will leak out his ears," Johnny said.

On hearing this, Pointer's sobs became hopelessly pathetic.

Johnny looked up into the darkness. Pointer was stuck up more than twenty feet.

Johnny knew if he couldn't make it up, they both would die. And that Dink would kill himself rather than face his mother's fury.

"See if there is any cooking oil or butter," Johnny said.

Dink returned with a bottle of oil and said he would climb up, but Johnny wouldn't let him try. He took off his shirt, and he and Dink oiled him up.

Johnny started up, arms squeezed over his head with fingers gripping and pulling and bare toes digging into the stonework.

Then he saw the white of Pointer's eyes disappear. Squeezed tight.

And felt the tear hit him. A single tear from his cousin.

Johnny's shoulders were stuck. "I can make it. Push my feet, Dink."

But rather than push Johnny's feet upward, Dink pulled his cousin down, "He's my brudder," and started upward.

"I've got his head," he called down to Johnny.

"Great!" Johnny said.

"I'm stuck too."

"Oh great."

Johnny started up, climbing until he saw Dink's sneakers. "I'm gonna grab your feet. You grab Pointer's head, and every time I say pull, we pull."

Pointer's voice came down, "I'll have to push with my feet. My arms are stuck."

Three pulls and pushes later, all three realized they were going to die there.

Pointer would be first. He was upside down. Then Dink, he was getting the least air. Johnny would probably hang around for days, first hearing their cries, their last gasps, then smelling his cousins' rotting bodies. Finally it would be his turn to rot . . . alive.

"This will work," Johnny said. "We'll just go for an inch at a time. One for all. Pull! All for one. Pull!" They didn't budge an inch.

"Dinkster?"

"Yah?"

"I'm going to force myself upward."

"Great. I've got too much room here anyway," Dink replied.

"You bring your legs up as high as you can. I'll get my head against your feet. When I say three, I'll pull down with all my might, and you put all the power you've got in your legs pushing my head down with a single shot."

"I'm not sure. My legs may be dead."

"One . . . two . . . three!"

Dink pushed on Johnny's head.

The speed that Johnny shot down the chimney would more than match that of the guy shot from the cannon at the circus.

Johnny was free and ran out the door.

He found a length of rope in the shed, returned to the camp and to the icebox, where he found more oil, and headed up to the rooftop.

"Dinkster, Pointer!" he yelled down the chimney. "I'm gonna pour cooking oil down on you."

The oil was joined by the sweat from their bodies.

"Suck in your breath. See if you slide a bit more," Johnny said.

The rope was quickly lashed around Dink's legs by Johnny, who lowered himself down.

Johnny was down the tree ladder and again inside the fireplace. "All pull together. And pray."

And they all came tumbling down.

Dink turned to Johnny and said, "When I heard you leave the roof, I thought you were deserting us, you asshole."

"Up your giggy with a meat hook. If you guys died, there'd be no one dumber than me around."

"You're right," Dink said as Pointer mewed like a kitten crying for milk.

"Is Pointer still alive?" Johnny asked.

"I don't know if I'm alive or not, but the cheeks of my ass are killing me. Get me water, and I'll kiss your butt on Boston Commons on the swan boats at high noon," Pointer said with a dessert-sand voice.

"You're coming into your own," Dink said, "ass kissing."

"Great. I'm a success. Just before dying. Water!"

Johnny headed to the well where he checked the ratchet setup for lowering and lifting the water pail and was surprised with the ease the heavy pail came up.

Johnny was out the door, lashing the end of the rope to the spindle that lowered and lifted the bucket, and started cranking.

"Lit's git!" Dink said.

"Mine. The statue," Johnny said, heading back to the camp with Pointer following.

"Assholes!" Dink cried, following quickly on their tails.

The Holy Virgin was much heavier than expected and bulkier than a two-legged mule in their escape to the raft.

They didn't need a Volga Boat Song to make tracks on the water with their push poles. They hauled ass like a sixteen wheeler that burned out its brakes on a forty-five-degree grade.

They chanted away as they pole pumped, "We're the three Musketeers, the three assholes. All for one, one for all." Their courage now on a high.

They approached the farm, ending up hiding in the pitch dark and deep grass only feet from the window where Pie won every game of solitaire.

They wondered whether Pie would ever tire, turn out the lights, and go to bed and sleep!

For if he discovered them breaking into the house and Mine's holy room, he would break their wooden asses into little shit chips with his ax.

So it goes without saying, they were as quiet as the hungry mouse that licked the milk off the whiskers of the sleeping cat as they later lifted the kitchen window screen. They helped Johnny in with a boost, handed him the Holy Virgin, then accepted his hand to pull them in. They made their way toward the room with five hundred flickering candles, which, if true love can help, would save five hundred souls.

—

If they were thinking as they placed the Holy Virgin in the middle of the candles, they would have added three for themselves for luck.

They would need them.

But their fear stilled as they each thought of Mine discovering the Miracles of the candles the next day.

The three cousins had a very similar interest to that of the Big Tree Gang back in Rockledge.

While Dink and Pointer did not fly in the same squadrons in the Big Tree looking for Krauts and Nips to shoot down and then paint miniature kills on their fuselage of their P-38 Lightnings tree limbs, both were vitally interested and intrigued as to how the fuselage of a woman was constructed.

The dye was cast. The boys on the farm were once and for all going to learn where *it* really was, the "thing" women have "down there."

Was it on the bottom of the belly facing front or underneath, looking down?

They had finally completed the tunnel that led to the drop pit in the two-seater outhouse at the family's farm store where all the produce was sold.

Now was the time for all good men and the boys of wonder to keep an eye on the outhouse until a woman of almost any sort, as long as she was young, beautiful and built like a brick shithouse, came along. It was their day off, and the three cousins lay in the high grass overlooking the stand that smelled of fresh corn, homemade pies, and bread, and apples.

Then it happened; the woman that fit their Holy Trinity came along.

Pointer discovered her headed to that small wooden outhouse where initials were carved, Sears and Roebucks Catalogues read, checkers played by close friends on a board painted between seats.

They were up and headed to the tunnel entrance, hunkered low to the ground like attacking alligators, tails swishing.

Johnny had lost track of where Pie was, but he believed he had last seen the old man entering the goat shed, and thus they were unseen.

Pie sat back against the farm, a lilac behind each ear hidden by the bush, watching them.

Their faces were darkened with mud so they wouldn't shine. Then they heard a pig squeal in the distance and were sure their grandfather had left the goat shed and was in the distant hog pens.

—

No one went to the pen anymore except Pie. It was the last place Goda was seen.

Pie had told the police in smashed English that she had headed back to Cape Verdes, that she was tired of hiding from immigration authorities.

Police Chief Edward Evan, the only full-time cop in town and thus chief, said, "I don't think all the facts are out." This was the limit of the chief's knowledge and investigation. He believed the old man had something to do with the disappearance of the black woman who the observant chief believed has always appeared to be making off with a couple stolen watermelons under her blouse.

"Fuckum merdre."

The chief thought Pie was agreeing with him, that all the facts weren't out. He had thought long and hard before approaching the old man and now found it unsettling the way that Pie shifted the ax from hand to hand, all the time giving the chief a chewing tobacco stained smile.

The chief thought the old man's smile was similar to the looks of a recently used toilet bowl and shifted his feet each time the ax was shifted as if the two, ax and officer, were dancing partners.

Pie answered, "Fuckum merdre" to all questions, smiled wider, shifted the ax more often.

Chief Evan decided to come back with a couple volunteer deputies. He would have a deputy question him.

The cousins were certain their grandfather was at the hog pen. But they remained still just outside the tunnel entrance for reassurance.

Johnny sucked the little yellow center out of a purple lilac blossom draining its bitter sweetness. He saw a toad nearby. The toad was pretending Johnny didn't see him as he was snatched up. Johnny pulled a nearby buttercup out of the ground and held it beneath the frog's double chin to see if there was a reflection, proving that even toads liked butter.

The toad gave an opinion, but it wasn't whether it liked butter or not. It was its opinion of being held in Johnny's hand. It pissed in his hand.

One result was that it made Johnny's nose run. He wiped it with his hand but removed his pissed-on hand quickly. "Oh my god, what if I get warts on my nose?"

"Is it a go?" Pointer asked. "My little dirt devil is digging an ant trap."

"It's a go."

Then they heard the outhouse door close below them; the object of their affection had come and gone while they worked on their courage.

"There is no God," Dink said.

"It's Johnny's fault. He was chicken."

"There will be another day, me buckees. Sheath your swords."

Dink moaned and then asked, "Now what's buzzin' cousin?'"

Dink was the hep one, the first to wear pegged pants, comb his hair in a duck's ass, short on the top, long on the sides, brushed to the back of the head, with a finger tip pushing the hair in, forming the duck's ass.

They reminisced about the time Dink's duck's ass got Johnny's butt booted.

One of the big guys in Lowell, some sort of a Greek guy who had been shaving since he was three months old, had spit in the middle of Dink's duck's ass with the words, "Here's a little excream-mint for your asshole, asshole."

Johnny had belted the big guy on the jaw with the hopes he had broken his whiskers. Dink and Pointer were long gone before the big Greek was tanked.

The big guy got up and belted Johnny in the nuts and then grabbed him behind the head as he doubled over and pulled his head backward.

Much to the delight of the Big Guy's friends who chanted "Cut one, cut one," he swung Johnny's head into his ass, whacking him behind the ears as he did.

Seeing Johnny's plight and once a safe distance away, the cousins stopped and chanted "Hey, gleek, gleek, take a peek," and they dropped their pants and mooned.

"Hey, gleek's friend," Dink shouted, "beware of Greeks bearing Vaseline!"

The big guy shook his fist and released Johnny.

"Run, Johnny, run!" Pointer cried as the tormentor released him.

Johnny started to run, then circled back, and swung at his tormentor's boiler room, catching him in the balls. But as luck would have it, the blow that buckled the big guy caused his head to pound into Johnny's face, breaking his nose, leaving his teeth bleeding. The two faced off.

"Beat it, you little piece of shit," the big guy said, "while you're still breathing."

"I'm not leaving until I get to kick your ass," Johnny said, walking slowly toward the giant youth.

"Take ya fuckin' extra teeth ya got in your head and stick 'em in your ass, and then you'll have a nice smile at both ends."

Johnny smiled at that one. It was the smile that made the huge tormentor decide to move on, explaining to his buddies, "I didn't want to get any more of his blood on my clothes."

Back with his cousins, they enjoyed a triple hug as Pointer preened. "Guess we showed that big bucket of garbage something."

Dink was more appreciative of his cousin. "Johnny, you're somethin' else—the bowel movement of a cow, the cat's meow."

"And you're a poet. Your feet are Longfellows."

Pointer had to get his two cents in. "Ya, Dink's a poet, and he doesn't know-et."

Between work in the sun, napping in the shade, fishing on the water, they found time to wrestle and plan a successful future peek from their tunnel beneath the outhouse.

The goat shed was a favorite rendezvous spot when they returned from working different areas of the farm.

On this day, it was the usual topic. "You know it's just below the belly button," Johnny said. Both Nanny and Franny checked the three out on a regular basis, their pupils were shaped like gun slots rather than being round. They did not trust them.

Nanny had been mated so many times her tits dragged on the ground and became quite raw until the Three Musketeers visited midnight stores, in this case, the clothesline of Farmer Osterhouse. A large economy-sized bra hung out to dry on the line and at times gathered a smattering of pollen and dried cow flop flying flakes kicked into the air by the tractor that plowed it in.

They had hidden in the grass for nearly an hour, cranking up their courage before the great bra caper.

"How do you figure Farmer Osterhouse's wife has such giant titingers without being slumped over like the humpback of Notre Dame?" Pointer asked. "That bra could be mistaken for a giant hammock for napping Lilliputians."

"It's the cow flops that makes bubbies grow," Johnny ventured.

"That's why Nanny's tits are so big, dragging in the caa caa that way," Dink said.

"And that pollen stuff is made by the birds and bees. 'Nuff said there," Johnny added.

"Let's take it home and hang it high in the giant elm, and the orioles can make a nest," Pointer suggested.

"Nah, I promised it to Nanny," his brother said.

"What if old Ostie is waiting in the dark there, just waiting to paint our asses with both barrels of rock salt," Dink said, "and when it melts in your ass, you scream until you drive yourself crazy. Johnny, go get the bra for Nanny's sake."

Johnny ran like a broken field runner, like he did at those pickup games at Pomworth Park. It was his football coach who had switched him from halfback to guard with the words, "You're too mean to be a back.

Besides, you're also too skinny to make the team. I'm cutting you," words he would later change.

The broken field pattern differed as he neared his target. He hunkered low, and then with a grab like a peregrine snatching a sparrow out of the air, he had the bra! And returned safely.

His cousins joined him as they hooted and hollered all the way back to the farm and then to the goat shed.

By now Dink had taken charge of the trophy. The three sat on a bale of hay, looking at Nanny, who continued chewing, her jaw going side to side like a scythe as she looked back with that oh-oh look the boys loved.

"Nanny," Dink said, "we Three Musketeers have struck a blow against Nottingham sheriff Osterhouse and for the good of goats everywhere."

Johnny sang, "Bra, bra black sheep have you any milk? Yes, sir, yes, sir, two big bags full."

Dink and Pointer held Nanny's back legs in the air while Johnny slipped the bra over her legs and butt until the goat's tits were in the cups that formerly housed Mrs. Osterhouse's beaucoup boobs.

The three sat back and applauded each other.

"Wait!" Dink said. "How do we get the milk out?"

"No problem," Pointer said, taking his jackknife out of the T-shirt sleeve it had been rolled up in and cut out a hole at the tip of each cup. "There, the little dark-eyed beauties can look out the portholes and give milk as well."

They expected Pie would try to find out who was responsible for the caper and muster out corrective measures for such tomfoolery, but there was no punishment as Pie saw the savings in previously lost milk. The bra meant additional dimes from the TB sanatorium as well as savings in the cost of bag balm previously needed for bleeding tits.

It had set the old man's imagination in motion, and Nanny's daughter Franny, who drank her own milk, learned that imagination in the DaSilva family did not start with the younger generation.

He built a yoke and put it on the young milker's neck, making it impossible to get to her own spigots. Another female, Feducia, who also drank her own milk, was cured as Pie put a number of long hairpins in her nostrils.

The boys remembered the day he did it. It was one of the few times they saw him smile without having killed something.

He just stood back, admiring his work, nodding his head, repeating, "Fuckum. Fuckum. Fuckum-sumna-a-bitch. Now try-um steal milk from fuckum Pie."

Pie never figured why the milk production was down in the summer when his grandsons worked for him. Nor did he figure out that the little Japanese rising suns and Nazi swastikas scratched on the goat shed wall represented enemy planes shot down. The Jap Zeros and German Messerschmitts were flies that landed on the goat shed wall or were shot out of the air by bursts of goat milk gunfire.

Johnny, Dink, and Pointer formed a trio and sang, "Baa, baa black sheep," and then in unison, saluted the sky and gave a football chant, "Hurrah, hurrah, baa baa black sheep," honoring the famous World War II fighter squadron made up mostly of fighter pilots that flew to a different drummer.

It was glorious just how little it took to set them laughing. Those were the days.

"I know it's just below the belly button," Johnny said out of a clear sky.

"Bull tickey, you don't know nuffin'," Pointer said.

"Do."

"Don't."

"Do."

"Prove it."

"I saw."

"Saw what?"

"A woman, getting it."

"It?"

"What are you selling?" Dink interrupted.

"I saw. The woman's legs were way up in the air. She couldn't get them up if it was down low. "It" is high in the front, just below the belly button."

"Give me a break, snake. If a woman's thing was where you say, she couldn't sit on the toilet; she'd have to lay her belly on it. Shithouses would have to be a lot wider."

"I saw it."

"The thing!" Pointer asked, duly impressed.

"Nah; but you could tell where it was."

"Couldn't be," Dink said. "If it was there, a woman's belly button lint would always be wet, and it never is."

"How do you know?" Johnny said defensively.

"I've been around, clown. You can't shit me."

"I know, you're too big a turd."

Dink punched Johnny's arm playfully.

Johnny punched Dink's arm.

Pointer punched Johnny's arm. "You can't punch my arm."

"Hey, I'm your lovin' cousin."

Pointer punched Dink. "You can't punch my cousin."

Dink and Johnny both punched Pointer, and the three fell back laughing.

"Baaa," said Nanny.

"Baaa," Franny agreed, her baa a little strained because of the heavy yoke around her neck.

"If you saw someone doin' it, who were they?" Dink challenged.

"I don't know who the woman was."

"Okay, the guy doin' it."

"I can't squeal."

"Come on," Pointer said. "I'd tell."

"I'll just give his initials . . . Pie DaSilva."

The three fell back laughing again.

The boys noted the mother and sister goats didn't say baa to their latest frolic.

"Too good to laugh at our stuff, "Dink accused the goats.

"Nah, they're just sick of it," Johnny said, "but I'm telling you it's just below the belly button. I bet you a buck."

"You don't have a pot to piss in or a window to throw it out," Dink said.

"I will by the end of the summer."

"You're on."

"How we going to prove it?" was Pointer's question.

"The two seater," Dink said.

"We visit it again?" Johnny asked.

"Why not? Our tunnel is still there. Girls still use it."

"The more I thought about it," Dink said, "I don't want to be underneath some woman's drops."

"Simple." Pointer said, "We put a mirror on a stick and won't have to be directly under the drop zone. We cant it upward on an angle. We look up, and if we see "it," we know it's down low."

The next Sunday they found themselves hiding in the grass overlooking the farm stand and its two outhouse service, a two seater and a single seater.

Mine and her daughters ran the little food and fudge stand on Boston Road that was a favorite of city folks out for a day in the country.

"Why put the mirror at the two seater instead of the one seater beside it?" Johnny asked.

"A woman in the one seater is alert, afraid a rat or something will come up out of the dung dungeon. But two women sitting side by side, bullshitting, looking at the guys in their long johns in the Sears catalog and getting horny, thinking about if the guys wore them backwards and that big crapper serving as a back door for the longies was in the front and what they would see. They wouldn't know we were there in a million years."

"We have to be prepared for problems. What if they have the runs?" Pointer asked, truly concerned.

The tunnel had represented a lot of work. The dirt had to be dug, handed out the tunnel, and hid. Their efforts were made a little easier as they pretended they were breaking out of jail. Each day the hole was covered with a board, and a tree limb covered the board. Each day after dark, they dug.

Pointer had a new worry every day. He had taken to keeping himself pretty spiffy since he discovered that girls had been invented and worried constantly whether "it" was high, like Johnny thought, or low, like Dink believed. "Hell," he said, "they could even keep it in their back pocket or purse."

He knew better than that, but then again, he didn't know better. Not did his Dartanyan or Arhteroid.

What had again set them off, set them on fire, spontaneous combustion, was the hot stuff in Mickey Spillaine's "My Gun Is Quick" or was it "My Gun for Hire?" in which when the girl was naked, and Spillaine's words were "My blonde had a brunette base." And they thought he was the world's greatest author.

But was that base beneath the belly button or between the legs (or even hidden under the armpit)? Ah, that was the question.

They all agreed they had to know.

They agreed that any woman who had to go while visiting the stand was fair game. They didn't care if she was fat or thin, black or white, yellow or pink. Although they worried they wouldn't be able to see a black thing or what would be the story if the oriental thing was sideways, like their uncle Manny had claimed.

They didn't care if their target was young or old, rich or poor, but they agreed that if she appeared to have a bad case of gas, it was no go.

The first digging had been very slow, as it had to take place after dark until they were underground and out of sight. They had turns digging and hiding by the farm, ready to give an owl hoot if anyone left the house. Sitting by the front door just out of sight was the first method of watch, as Mine either prayed over her candles well into the night or worked until she fell asleep. She was so kindly that if she had been a dog she wouldn't have scratched, afraid to hurt a flea.

Pie was a different story. So they changed their watch setup to a branch high in a tree a short distance from the dining room window where

Pie played solitaire with a deck of cards so old and tired they were as floppy as pancakes, dirty pancakes.

It was Johnny's idea to set up a lookout in a tree. Pie wouldn't look up; the lookout could pretend he was in a ship's crow's nest at sea and that a warning owl call coming from a tree wouldn't be as suspect as coming from behind a two-foot-high bush.

The digging was slow, very slow, as there was little energy after a day of working fields so hot it burned their hands as they dug, planted, and weeded. But digging action picked up every time they talked about seeing a real woman's it. But by then they were so exuberant they wore themselves out digging with the renewed enthusiasm. They sometimes fell asleep in the tunnel.

They settled on Dink's idea of pacing themselves. "Let's pretend we're digging our way into a candy store or doughnut shop."

At times they pretended they were digging their way out of jail. That was pretty romantic, and they could take their sweet-ass old time as in their make believe they had all been convicted of burning Pie to death, by mistake, of course. All they had wanted to do set the hair on his ass on fire while he was sleeping, but it spread up the ravine to his pubic area, then up his belly to his chest, then under his arms, the hair on his head, and finally his eyebrows. Anyway, their life sentences without parole meant they didn't have to rush their digging.

Each night after calling it a day, they carefully covered the hole with a piece of board and then covered the board with brush. Then with branches, like they had learned in the Boy Scouts; they swept and roughed up the area around the entrance to make it look natural.

If during the day they spotted a particularly lovely lady whose chest strained against her blouse like a horse gone wild anxious to bolt out of the barn, leave the little farm store, and head to an outhouse, alone or with a friend on the same wee-wee wave length, you could bet your bottom dollar they would dig like a squirrel starving for a buried nut that night.

They were so busy digging nights they never noticed during the day that a pile of dry brush and a mixture of green leaves had appeared near the opening of their tunnel.

They had to shore up certain spots with pieces of wood borrowed from here and there as sections of the dirt ceiling often tumbled down on them.

All three started working the tunnel nights, now twenty feet long, as they figured a watch wasn't needed any longer. Each night for a month, Mie had prayed and worked herself to sleep while Pie won every single game of solitaire he played, smiling at each success, then headed upstairs, carrying the kerosene lantern he had played cards with Pie. The shadow he cast was grotesque and hung huge on the wall, the phallic tongue of his belt looking like a paddle that might have been used on the River Sty.

Night after night, the cousins heard Pie's rickety pinball machine racking up free games, the wine cask being tapped, then the grunts and noises of wild boars in a death struggle, Pie's snoring.

The eventful day was a late Sunday in August. Dink's thrust of the old rusty shovel they had borrowed broke through into space. Johnny had convinced his cousins, who did not need much convincing, that "borrowing with full intention of returning the shovel to its owner was perfectly acceptable."

He declaring, "Mr. Thoreau borrowed everything left lying around Walden Pond but always forgot to return it, and he was highly regarded."

They shouted with joy as the last shovel thrust sent the final section of wall tumbling into the liquids couched beneath the drop of the two seats.

They lay on their backs looking up at the seats, where they would soon see a real woman's real thing. And they smiled at each other and shook hands as best they could and kicked the air like happy puppies having their tummies scratched.

Dink said, "Something as beautiful as that hidden area deserves a better name than 'it.'"

"How about Fang," Pointer said. "I heard Uncle Manny describing one he saw to Uncle Francisco. He said it looked like it had some type of milk tooth or fierce fang protecting its cave. A clatterpuss or something like that."

"Uncle Francisco called it a pussy," Dink said. "I like that."

"I can leave or take cats," Johnny said. "I like dogs."

"Yah, me too," Pointer said, "but we can't call it a dog."

"I heard your father tell the others it looked like a taco," Dink said.

"Nah, we can't call it that, "Johnny said. "It sounds too much like something to eat."

"Look, let's forget it. We'll get one of those National Geographics at the library where they show those native women with nothing but banana leaves around their waists and see what they call everything."

"Hey, let's call that area the everything area," Johnny ventured. "It's everything to us."

They liked that.

Pointer, who left no bones about how much he loved to eat and planned to open his own bakery or candy factory, said, "Someday I'm going to bake a bagel that looks like you know what and call it an everything bagel."

"Who'd buy it?" Johnny asked.

"The same guy that eats tacos," Dink ventured.

"Anyway," he added, "let's haul ass. We're gonna need all our strength to enjoy looking up at all that moonshine. Besides, if you guys didn't notice, shit stinks," and he made a motion to throw Johnny into the stink pit.

"Don't even think it unless you want me to tear you a new rectum."

"Ya, you and whose army!"

"Me and mine," Johnny said as the three inched backward out of the tunnel toward the exit.

Dink said, "Tomorrow they'll be plenty of girls stopping and drinking Manny-made cold cider and eating Mine's spice doughnuts, then some ice-cold homemade root beer to wash it down and then . . ."

All three answered in unison, "They'll have to pee . . . Yippee, yippee."

God, those three loved each other and were proud of their project as the barnyard rooster that just did the giant swan that chased all strangers off the farm.

The next morning they loaded up with Mine's blueberry pancakes, spread the butter she had just churned the night before a quarter inch thick, then soaked them with the maple syrup they had helped boil down that spring, and amalgamated this with honey from the farm hives. Then they poured the rich cream skimmed from the cow's bulbous boiler room, closed their eyes, and nearly swooned.

Dink whispered to Johnny and Pointer, "I wonder if a woman chews her cud when you milk her?"

Johnny reminded his cousins how Goosie Lucy the cow had turned and looked at Johnny after his remark while milking, "Don't roll those big brown eyes at me."

Sunday was a day of rest, only at Mine's insistence, as Pie wanted them to put in at least a half day, eight hours or so.

But no, the four-foot-eight-inch-high little lady had her way.

After pigging out, they were on their way to the thick bushes where they could peer down on the farm stand.

"We've gotta be careful, "Pointer said, "that they don't do a plopper while we're looking up."

"Nah, they'll hold that big stuff till they get home and can take their sweet-ass old time and read one of those romance magazines," Johnny said. "All they'll do here is wet their whiskers. Besides they don't want to use a corncob or page out of Sears."

Then suddenly they were there. Two beautiful girls. "My god, they're twins," Pointer whispered.

"Doublemint, Doublemint, Doublemint Gum," Johnny sang, "double the bubble, double the fun." Then all three joined in the chorus, "Double the pleasure with Doublemint, Doublemint, Doublemint gum."

Their crawl to the tunnel entrance matched the speed of a buck rabbit with a promise.

They didn't even bother to look around as they pulled back the branches and the board that hid their tunnel and crawled through their hole to heaven.

Pie smiled down at them from the very tree they had kept watch on him from, thinking it was worth the trouble to haul his old body up that tree. It was easier getting down. He walked slowly toward the tunnel entrance as the boys crawled quietly through it toward the voices of the twins who squealed with the new found excitement of actually sitting side by side in an old-fashioned outhouse.

"I'm going to breathe deep to sniff them like a morning robin breathing the first sun up," Johnny said.

"Amen," Dink said, crossing himself, reminding Johnny his cousins were Catholics, but regardless were still A-OK.

But their deep breaths were not greeted by the perfumes of the young ladies seated above like royalty.

They were greeted by thick smoke and Pie's laugh, a laugh not unlike that of a hyena ripping apart a large-eyed roebuck in the pitch black.

Above, the old man used his jacket to fan the fire burning at the mouth of the boys' tunnel, adding dry wood for heat, greenery for smoke.

They were choking, forced forward to breathe, dropping into the wet slop of the drop beneath the now-vacant seats.

Pointer was smallest and stepped on Dink's and Johnny's shoulders to escape through the drop opening and then helped pull them to safety.

All three hightailed to Mill Pond, trying to outrun their own stink; thus failing, they shifted into overdrive until finally the three stood chin deep in water.

"I'll kill the old shit!" Dink said, coughing with exhaustion and smoke.

"I'll bury him alive in his own crap," Pointer added, trying to dig the smell of human scat out of his nostrils.

"Here's looking at you, kid," Johnny said with a smile, pretending he was looking up at a real woman's real thing. "To be or not to be . . . just below the belly button or way lower, that is still the question."

"We'll never know," Pointer said sorrowfully. "We'll never know." His eyes glistened slightly. A single tear dribbled down his cheek.

They decided to let it all hang out that night, forget about their aborted attempt at the outhouse.

—

After setting the fire, Pie had run from the start of the peek-a-boo tunnel down to the farm roadside stand where he set up shop in an easy chair located on the outside corner of the stand. He usually watched the customers come and go, kept an eye on the cigar box used as a cash register, made sure no one snitched berries out of the raspberry and blueberry boxes. He often took time out to rearrange them so it appeared the boxes were full, filling another box with his skimming.

But instead of watching the stand this day, he rearranged his chair so he faced the two-seater outhouse. Luckily, he had acted quickly as he was no sooner seated than the two ladies inside, sent flying by smoke and screaming youths from below, came flying out, adjusting their bloomers and dresses, but not before Pie got his bird's eye view of something, perhaps their private parts. It was only a quick peek, but then again the old man knew that "it" was indeed down low, actually upside down as that body part goes. The old man wondered what the view from the south was.

The three boys, covered with a slop that made their Wild West days riding Bog the Hog in the pigpen look sterile, came barreling out of the outhouse in an escape mode, only to come face-to-face with a wild-eyed Pie, grinning from ear to ear, screaming, "Merdre! Merdre! Shit! Shit!"

But the three thought Pie was screaming "Murder! Murder!" and took off for the big hill, not looking back once, for one single look back could mean a step lost, and a step lost could mean . . . murder.

On top of the hill, they set up camp, rolling blowdown logs together for seats, started a fire, and warmed up after their dip in Mill Pond. Work on a lean-to didn't start until the rain started. They dug up roots from the ground, clipping them free with their jackknifes, and tied a crossbar between two trees. They cut short but thick pines down to form the roof. It was slow work, and by the time they were finished, they were soaked again. They sat huddled in their hut, trying to sop up the heat from the fire that had more willpower than the rain that had slowed to light drizzle. The fire's willpower was fueled by a combination of the dead branches snapped from the lower limbs of the larger pines and the pine pitch collected from the oozing wounds of the trees.

"I'm so hungry I could eat a rat's ass," Dink lamented.

"I could eat a skunk's," his brother said.

"Why don't we sneak back to the fields and get some potatoes and raspberries and apples and . . ."

"Pie's waiting for us," Dink said. "You heard him, screaming 'murder, murder'!"

"You know," Pointer said, his eyes bigger than those of the great horned owl that had terrified them just at dark with its haunting cry, "some people think it wasn't the hogs that ate that baby years ago. Some people think Goda's disappearance was, well, Pie."

"Come on," Johnny said. "I read once where humans tasted worse than anything in the world. We're too muscular, and we're too salty or somethin'."

"Oh sure, what if people like Pie like to eat salty muscles," Pointer said, spreading his panic.

"Oh sure," Dink said.

"I read where you can eat ants and other bugs, and they can keep you alive for years," Johnny said.

"I ain't eating no ants," Dink said.

"Me either," his brother added. "One time I swallowed a mosquito by mistake. It was horrible. And it had bones in it."

"Let's go try and catch some catfish," Johnny said. "My father taught me how to call them in, like calling in the hogs, but without yelling sow-eeeeh?"

"What do you yell?" Dink asked.

"Do you have to put your head under water when you call them," Pointer asked," and what if you swallowed one of those water spiders?"

"We've gotta do somethin'," Dink said, "but sometimes you can fish all night without a single catfish. What's this 'sow-eeeeh' call for catfish? It's a fake."

"Nah. My dad said curiosity killed the cat, including the catfish. As soon as you get to the pout hole, you toss a big boulder in. Ka-plunk! They feel the vibrations, hear the sound. The boulder scares up some of the little animals and stuff that hide in the mud, and whamo! You've caught and killed a cat with its own curiosity."

"I'm too weak from hunger to pick up a boulder. Besides, you're full of what makes the grass grow green," Dink said.

"Hey, look at the pot calling the kettle black," Johnny said. "We're all still covered with some poo. Let's go out in the rain and use the ferns to clean off some more."

"The stuff is too sticky," Pointer said. "We'd need to be sandblasted."

"Hey, follow me," Johnny said, stripping off his clothes and heading out.

The cousins followed, not knowing where they were going or why they were bare, buck naked.

Johnny was already rolling in the sand in the farm gravel pit, scooping up handfuls of the sand, washing under his arms, his back, his legs, and his feet with it. Within moments, the three of them were like birds in a birdbath, sending sand flying in every direction.

—

Then they were trotting back to their campsite, buck naked except for the coating of sand all over their bodies that made them so wild looking they frightened themselves.

"Jeez, Dink," Johnny said, "you'd scare the living crap out of a constipated rock."

"Jeez, I hope I don't get poison ivory," Pointer said.

"Ivy. Ivory is a soap," Johnny said.

"I hope I get it real bad. And have to go to the hospital where they feed you as much as you want, and then when you're too tired to eat, they stick a thing in your arm and feed you some more. And I heard they could feed you ice cream through those tubes."

"Let's not talk about food," Pointer said, "okay? My stomach feels like a giant rat is eating it."

"We can go dive for snapping turtles," Johnny said, "and cook their meat on a stick and boil up some scalding turtle soup using its shell as a pot."

"How are you going to find a snapper under water in the dark. Be real, sla-meele," Dink said.

"You know where they had the sandbags near the Mill River Dam to hold the water back while they repaired it. When I dove looking for fishing lures hooked in the burlap, well, I discovered there were snappers hiding between the bags. We sneak up behind them in the dark and grab them."

"Yah, what if you grab the wrong end, and it bites your finger off?" Pointer challenged.

Dink said, "What if you do grab the rear end, and it shits on your hands. You'll get warts, just like you get when a toad pisses on your hands. Except these warts have little teeth in them, just like the snapper. And they bite and eat the inside of your fingers."

Johnny decided looking for snappers at night wasn't a good idea. He remembered the time he was searching for golf balls in the water hole at Bear Hill County Club. He had grabbed a snapper's head in the mud by mistake. He panicked, visualizing the turtle had grabbed him by his dangling dick. "Yah, forget it. Who wants warts with teeth."

Back at the camp, they huddled together in the lean-to. The fire was burning low. The rain had stopped.

"Rain's stopped," Pointer said.

"No shit, Dick Tracy," Dink said.

"I can still hear the thunder," Johnny said.

"Me too," Dink said.

"It's my stomach. Growling its hunger," Pointer said. "I hurt."

—

"Me too," his brother said.

"Me three," his cousin said.

They sat there, soaked to the bone. Miserable to the soul. Frightened. Then they heard a noise in the woods. Something big.

"Quick," Johnny whispered, "grab a stick, a stone."

Thus armed, they hid behind a tree as the night monster approached. The monster was barely a mouse's whisker taller than four feet. Mie's travels through the woods was made slowly, not only because of the pitch dark, but also because of her load of pies, linguica sandwiches, hot cider. She neared the opening between the trees. The boys raised their thick sticks and sharp rocks over their heads, ready to strike.

Mie, spotting the dying campfire, called low, "Kieterzingers, kieterzingers, little loved ones, where are you? Where are you?"

"Here, Grammy Mie, here, Mie," they all sang out, rushing to her side.

Her smile, even in the fading firelight, was that of a soft-eyed field mouse, a smile that called you from out of the rain to join her in the safety of the toadstool she was under. She was their smallest angel.

Each ate like hyenas over a fresh kill, glancing sideways at each other to see if they would try to grab what they were eating.

The stomach growls slowly turned to contented purrs, and each in turn came to their grandmother's open arms and was hugged, their heads resting on her loving bosom as she sang lowly, slowly, "Kieterzingers. Kieterzingers."

They didn't know what kieterzingers were, but they knew that they were well loved.

Each of the three pirates, previously the wild men of Borneo, had their own interpretation of what she was saying. Each cherished it as their very own, and that's what it was.

The four walked slowly through the woods toward the farm, stopping where the tree line ended and the farm fields started.

The three boys watched as the little woman walked into the dark toward the farm, not talking. Then when her shape disappeared out of their night vision, they returned slowly to their camp.

The fire was fed and once again became a flame-spitting dragon, and the transition from frightened and hungry kids to warm men of the world was again in osmosis. And again they wondered whether "it" was located just below the navel or down below.

"You know we've gotta do a couple things," Dink said. "First, we've got to make plans to see a real live one without having to dig a tunnel for a month. And second, we've gotta stop calling it 'it.' Any ideas?"

"If 'it' is down under," Johnny said, "we can call it Australia."

"I think I heard Uncle Manny say he was going out looking for some kitty or somethin' like that," Pointer said.

"Let's call it a puppy. Puppies are cute and playful and cuddly," Dink said.

"I heard the down unders are homely and not cute, and why would you cuddle one?" Pointer asked.

"Puppies is the name for the boobs," Johnny said, "at least according to Uncle Manny. One time when we were all down at the Bleachery Street Fourth of July fair in Lowell and a woman with big'uns walked by and Uncle Manny said, 'Look at those puppies trying to break free of their leash. Poor puppies. Puppies need petting.' And then he woofed at them."

"Johnny, I heard your dad call the bubbers of that German lady that don't speak no English snarling hounds."

"My father never said that. He's married to my mum, and don't you ever forget it, you dick head," Johnny said, getting up and approaching Dink.

"Come on, come on. Keep a cool stool," Dink said, standing up and mussing up his cousin's hair. "We don't have to name nuttin' until we actually see a real one."

"What if we never see a real one?" Pointer asked, fear showing in his eyes.

"What's in a name anywho?" Dink said.

"Plenty," Johnny said. "I get tired of calling my whacker a private. I think general would be better. Ain't that true."

"Ain't ain't in the dictionary," Dink said, "and besides I ain't renaming mine."

"Afraid yours would be called Mutt and mine Jeff?" Johnny asked.

Dink stood up and approached Johnny. "No one calls my wanger a Mutt."

"Keep a cool stool, drool," Johnny said, mussing up his cousin's hair.

"You keep a cool stool, ghoul," Dink said, mussing up Johnny's hair.

Pointer came up behind them and mussed both their hair, then combed his hair over one eye and made a Hitler mustache with his comb and said, "Seig Heil!"

Johnny started singing, "Oh, the führer says we are the master race," and his cousins joined in, "and we heil, heil right in the führer's face. If I had a submarine I would bounce him off the bean, and there wouldn't be any Hitler anymore."

"We gotta find a way to get into the war. They need us," Johnny said. "I'm already thirteen and haven't fought yet. Hitler and Tojo are killing innocent people and are bombing London. That's where my grandfather and grandmother Shiverick came from."

"I'm fourteen," Dink said proudly, "and they'll be taking me any day. I saw pictures on the news of Nazi soldiers, some wearing Iron Cross medals around their necks, who were fourteen, my age. I'll write you kids from Paris, where the girls will give me baths in perfume, scrub me down with their you know whats."

"Is that all you think about?" Johnny asked.

"Yup. No, wait a second. Sometimes I think of puppies. Yah, that Hitler fella can't be all bad. He's gonna get me to Paris."

"It's that Mussolini fella," Pointer said. "That no-goodnik is sending poison pizzas here. I haven't eaten a pizza since that time Uncle Manny came into Santori's Pizza Parlor and saved my life. I was just getting ready to put that first slice in my mouth when he grabbed the piece of pizza and told me about what Mussolini was doing, and then took the whole pizza from me, saying he was gonna bury it and that he'd kill that ginny bastard for trying to poison his favorite nephew. Me."

"You dick," Dink said, "he deked you, deked you out of your pants and pizza both, like Johnny did in that hockey game we watched him in when he deked the goalie out of his jock."

"Come on, you're my brother. Don't make me cry. Besides, Uncle Manny joined the army a short while later to get that ginny."

"Uncle Manny was drafted," Dink said.

"They almost didn't take him," Johnny added. "Seems he had a criminal record as he reportedly deked a hundred dumb kids out of their pizzas. He got fat."

"The army finally took him when they helped him to lose forty pounds," Dink said, "by cutting off that Portagee pecker of his."

"Pecker? You call our 'it' a pecker? Why?" Pointer asked.

Johnny and Dink sang, "The woodpecker pecked on the barnyard door, pecked and pecked till his pecker got sore."

"Wad-da-ya mean," Pointer asked, "don't they use their beak?"

"Hey, silly Sam," Dink said, "would you peck on a barnyard door with your mouth. No, of course not. You're my brudder. And thus a genius too."

"Woodpeckers are geniuses too," Johnny said. "They use that tough root between their legs, wood on wood, to peck with. Thus, their nom de plume 'woodpecker.'"

"Hot toddy," Dink said, "with your nom de plume crap."

Pointer was the first to lay back on the pine branch and ferns bed. "Man, am I tired. Look at those fireflies. We could capture them and put 'em in a bottle and have lights."

Dink was next down. "Look at those embers rising up. Hey, the sky is clearing."

Johnny settled in between his cousins. "Look, the fireflies are dancing with the embers."

"Yah."

"And both are dancing with the stars."

"Give me a break, laureate," Dink said. "Laureate, how do you like that for a two-bit word. You think you're the only one can read."

"I've got a great idea," Johnny said.

"I have too," Dink said. "Store it and let's sleep."

"Whooo!" the great horned called, causing them to jump.

"You asshole with the feather asshole, shut up," Dink said.

"Sometimes I want to bring my friend Righty from Rockledge up here to Chelmsford. He's never been in the country."

"We don't need no strangers," Dink said.

"He's my friend. His brother is fighting Hitler and Mussolini. And it ain't easy. He was born in Italy and is fighting his own people."

"The eye-talians ain't doin' no fightin'," Dink said. "Their newspapers carry ads—'Eye-talian rifles for sale; never fired. Only dropped once.'"

"Oh ya, Righty's an Italian and can whip your Portagee butt any day of the week and twice on Sunday. And whip it in spades. And his brother's just as tough. He could whip your ass, one hand tied behind his back."

"Yah!"

"Yah."

"Your mother wears army boots."

"Your mother gave birth to a worm."

"Yah"

"Yah."

"At least I can be used for fishing," Dink said. "You're useless. So kiss my ass."

"I wouldn't know where to start," Johnny said. "You're all ass. Anyway, are we all for sneaking that Holy Virgin for Mine into the house. When she sees it, she will know it's a miracle."

"Yah," Dink said.

"All for one," Pointer said, holding his hand up.

"All for one," his brother and cousin said as they all touched hands, "and one for all!"

CHAPTER 12

ONE LITTLE CANDLE

While Mine believed the appearance of the statue of the Holy Virgin in her Memorial Candle and Prayer Room was a miracle, her grandson Johnny ceased to believe in miracles, after all he'd be fourteen late that summer.

When he was eight, he wanted to be a bronc buster and a matador. Bog the Hog was his wild horse, but Bog was killed when Pie swung a two by four, as if driving a stake with a sledgehammer to hold the Big Top of the Circus up with such force the two-by-four splintered.

By the age of thirteen, the kid stuff was all over. He knew he was a man and wanted to sign up, get into the marines, join Merrill's Marauders and kill Jap rats—"From the Halls of Montezuma to the shores of . . ." or join the army air force and fly a P-38 Lightning and shoot down those Nazi Messofshits that was attacking London, where his grandfather Shiverick was born.

His trips to Boston in an attempt to sign up with the marine raiders or Screaming Eagle paratroopers or as a P-38 Lightning or P-47 Thunderbolt pilot all failed.

Then he heard about the Flying Tigers, Americans flying P-41s in China against the Jap rats. He wore leather jackets with the American and Chinese flags stitched on their sleeves as they tore into the Zeros in planes with shark's mouths and pierced eyes painted on the plane's cowling.

Johnny wanted to be one. He had seen a newspaper photo of an American standing besides his plane, a Flying Tiger. There were little

Japanese flags painted just beneath his cockpit canopy, denoting how many Nip planes he had shot down.

He'd heard that the Flying Tigers would take any American, any age, and teach them to fly And he was any age. He'd be one step ahead; he'd learn to know everything about the Chinese. "So when I meet General Clair Lee Chennault and General Chang, they would know that Johnny-me was a man they needed." He wondered how a general Flying Tiger could be named Clair Lee but guessed if you were really tough, you would want to be named after a girl so you could get into a lot of fights. Hope I don't say to the Chinese general, "No tickee, no laundree."

Right off the bat, he liked the leader of China's army; his wife looked just like General Douglas MacArthur's wife. He wondered whether all generals' wives looked alike.

When he thought about how to join the Flying Tigers, he would walk like a Tiger, think like a Tiger, and know what China is all about. This could cost a penny or two. He questioned his thoughts of bumming to China. Perhaps he would earn a million for his family first and then go.

Even before the war, he wanted to get to China. His uncle Matt Shiverick told him he could dig right through to the country. He had told Johnny this after his mother had informed her favorite brother that she was worried about her son. "Johnny just has so much energy it worries me sick."

Her brother said, "Don't worry, Sis. I'll have him dig to China."

Charity shrugged her shoulders and said more to herself than to her brother, "Dig to China?"

When his uncle told him that he indeed could dig his way to the Orient, Johnny started immediately. After all, would an uncle kid his nephew?

But he'd go now to the Flying Tigers. It meant redirecting some of the hard-earned money set aside from delivering the morning newspapers, setting pins at night, and diving for golf balls to fix his and Jazz's teeth, but mostly Jazz's. Ma didn't need as much help as the box factory had upped her pay because they were getting World War II top dollar like everyone else and were afraid they would lose their help to high-paying, high-profile Rosey the Riveter jobs. However, the price of rent and food had gone up, carrot on a sticklike, as wage scales became unbalanced.

He didn't have to save to fix Sis's teeth as they were as hard as her stare when she got the Skinny Minnie bit from what she called a puke face. When dealing with a puke face face-to-face, she was an up front, a ballsie Skinny Minnie.

Johnny smiled, thinking of his sister, so thin, she nearly always had to walk holding up her panties, an act she accomplished by pretending she was straightening out the waist of her dress. This was necessary because she was so thin they could slip off, and the elastic in her old clothing had grown weak.

If he used the money he was saving for Jazz's teeth, he would have to do something about his own teeth. Maybe he could chip away some of the cavities with a lobster pick or with a twist of needle-nose pliers to slow down the decaying. Jazz was tough. So tough, Johnny bragged to his friends that his little brother wouldn't cry if you stuffed raw onions up his nostrils. It might work, though. Johnny had even given thought at one time to becoming a dentist. Hadn't he figured out that by pouring melted candle wax into his cavities, it cut down on the pain he had suffered in the winter winds.

It was done. He used every cent to learn to eat Chinese food and more Chinese food. He knew this would work. Although he feared his eyes were starting to slant. Nah. Well, maybe just a little bit.

He became friendly with the little Chinese girl who served him. She would bring the unused rice to his table.

And soy sauce was plentiful.

Then that wonderful day, the fortune cookie read, "Yoo keep it up, mister, you see action."

That was good enough for Johnny.

He did see a type of Chinese action almost immediately. He ate so much Chinese food he got what Dink called, "The chinky Chinaman shits. They're worse than wiping your ass with a blowtorch."

While Johnny often questioned his cousin's medical prognoses, he knew he was right on the button with this one.

He knew he was going to die. Would they bury him standing up like they bury the Chinese? Or was it the Jews? Of was it the Chinese Jews. Oh shit!

And he did. And he did some more.

Despite his stomach woes, he continued to practice eating Chinese food and remained sick for a week until a fortune cookie read, "Yoo will come out well in the end."

That was it for the Flying Tigers when he ran out of money to eat rice.

But he had to get in! The Nazi rats, probably flying Jap Zeros, got his uncle Francesko dead.

He had joined up over the objections of his uncle Manny. Manny had been drafted early and already had been wounded twice.

—

Johnny's dad was against his efforts to sign up. "You're not even twenty-one." Tony knew better than to tell his son that he was only fourteen. His father's opinions still came from the faraway Sun Shipyard in Chester, Pennsylvania.

Tony reported to his son that President Roosevelt wouldn't let him fight as his making battleships was too important, more important than anything. This is what Johnny told his friends.

Tony told Johnny he tried to get Francheso to take a job at the Sun Shipyard with him. He didn't and look what happened. He got strafed dead by a German plane while attacking Hitler's hordes, according to Manny.

Actually, Franchesco was strafed while his trousers were off, his legs apart, as he crapped into a slit trench used as a latrine.

Tony told his young brother that he could get a job building destroyers, and he wouldn't have to go. That building ships was as important as lugging a rifle. "Plus, if you stay home, all the girls left behind will be after you."

"Really? Lots of girls! I'll start right away to grow a couple more dicks. Or maybe get a transplant from old Bog. Pie kept his pecker in vinegar."

Francesko went into the army with the parting words, "You know how I love hunting. But I heard the Nazi rats are tough to skin."

He landed that very June in a French place called Normandy. Along with his brother Manny.

Johnny couldn't understand how Uncle Manny could get shot by a bullet in the shoulder, then the leg, and a third time, shrapnel in the ribs, and was still fighting.

"Unfair," Johnny said aloud when the family was informed that he had been wounded for a third time. *And they won't . . . let me . . . have my turn . . . and replace him . . .*

The sliver of metal his uncle Manny took made him lose the use of his arms. Johnny guessed he wrote home with his teeth. "Or his pecker," Tony said, adding, "I guess I should have taken him duck hunting a few more times so he would learn the meaning of the word 'duck.'"

In his letter, Manny wrote that he would improve, that "there are still Nazi bastards out there. I want them."

Mine couldn't read.

So Johnny read her son's letter to her. "I'm fine here. I can't wait to get home. It will be pretty soon. But pretty soon could be a long while as they need me to fight these German guys (What he had actually written here was 'Why can't my officer bastards and doctor bastards tie me to the front of a tank and let the Nazi bastards get in some shooting practice so they can wing me a good one. But when they saw me tied on a tank, they'd run. They'd practice saying "Kamerade!" and putting their arms in the air instead of practicing shooting. And the wops, all they do is put their arms in the air and yell out "I gutta a cousin ina, Bostona.'")"

Mine looked up at her young grandson and smiled, a single tear streaming down her sun—and wind-weathered cheeks, loving him even more for his telling less than the hurtful truth his eyes leaked.

"Why we shoot Germans?" she asked softly as she pulled him to her bosom. "Mine's keiterzinger. Little kieterzinger." Johnny wondered what she was saying. He knew K was not a letter in the Portuguese alphabet. That was all he knew about the language.

He wished he had disobeyed his mother and learned Portuguese, but he had promised not to learn a foreign language and become a foreigner.

He had also promised never to date a Catholic girl. Or a girl who had already known a man. While he didn't understand what knowing a man meant or why dating a Catholic girl was bad or learning a foreign language was bad, he agreed.

Also, he had neither the time, money, inclination . . . or courage to ask for a date. That doesn't mean that wondering where "it" was located on a girl ever left him for more than a day or two. A promise to a mother is a promise, at least when you are looking her right in the eye when you make it. No bad girls for him.

A promise is a promise, and having your fingers crossed behind your back doesn't work so well here.

He regretted making the promises, but she worked so hard.

She was smart. Smarter than most mothers. He knew that because when she made him make a promise, she'd make sure there was a mirror behind him. There was none of that cross the fingers stuff taking place. He always tried to make sure there wasn't a mirror behind him when he made a promise, and if there was and he couldn't cross his fingers, he just crossed them in his mind and hoped this was as good as the real thing. It was just so much easier on everyone concerned to make a promise than to fight it.

Not sure whether thinking his fingers were crossed was good enough to ignore a promise, he wished he could cross his toes, but practice only made his toes hurt like hell.

Now he was watching Mine after having read or juxtaposed Manny's letter for her as she went into her prayer room.

It was so confusing; she was so good, so sweet he feared at times he could get cavities from her. *How could a Catholic . . . or a foreigner . . . who didn't speak American . . . be bad? But Ma is such a good person . . . It's so . . . confusing . . .*

—

Mine lit a new candle for her Manny, praying for his recovery from whatever happened and for him to come home quickly. She placed the candle beside the one she had lighted a year before for his protection.

Johnny thought the borrowed Virgin Mary that Dink, Pointer, and he had taken out on loan and they planned to give back someday appeared to be directing her soft smile on his grandmother.

He thought it might be nice to be a Catholic, although it didn't seem to get them any extra hits after crossing themselves at the plate when they came to bat. But that church seemed to let people get things off their minds, out of their hearts. *But who could . . . tell the truth . . . about bad stuff . . . to someone they didn't know?*

He and all his friends, without exception, even the altar boys who handed the cup to the priest so he could swill his booze and went to Christian doctrine classes, believed that to confess was the same as inviting a sore ass. Hey . . . if God wanted me to be punished . . . let him have his henchmen . . . hunt me down . . . Whoa . . . I'll burn in hell for that one . . .

Although Johnny thought it would be great stuff to go to a confessional, where the guy inside didn't know you, didn't know you weren't a Catholic, and didn't recognize you, then you could confess to all sorts of things—I stuck gum on the bum of a stray mutt and the dog died of forced constipation. My girl and I had sex while standing on our heads during a high mass. I let a fart, got up, and beat it before you priests set the Mafia on me.

His thoughts drifted between his imagination and his talking to himself. Being a Catholic could be fun, but some parts stink. Like Grandfather Shiverick asked, "How can anyone get between you and your talking to God with the claim that only they had the direct line?

"They talk in a foreign tongue so they can pretend they're talking to God while really laughing and making plans with the devil."

At times like this, his grandfather Shiverick's frown was ferocious and only softened when Grandma Shiverick wrapped her arms around his waist at just the spot the arms of her tiny body met his lanky one, a body as gaunt as Jesus on the cross. He had no problem conjuring up a picture of the Roman soldier taking his spear and piercing Jesus's side then going to that fourth cross, the one added just to the left of the two thieves, and piercing Grandfather Shiverick. He knew that was stupid, but it didn't prevent him from trying to catch his grandfather, just once, with his shirt off.

No chance. It was tough enough to catch him without a necktie. He wore his fedora, dress jacket, and tie, even while painting. Perhaps if I got up real early . . . some morning . . . but what would I do . . . if there really was a . . . spear scar in his side?

—

CHAPTER 13

A BEE WITH A BOIL

There was little doubt in anyone's mind that Pie was meaner than a bee with a boil on its backside.

But Johnny had to give credit where credit was due.

Each September, when he left the farm to go home and back to school, Pie would ruffle up his grandson's hair with only a hint of a mean tug and, with a nearly beatific smile, say, "An-toc-nee! Vipra casa, pouco merda domino, Asno." Then the old man would laugh, displaying teeth stronger and more yellow than the farm mule, a mouth that Manny had once said would "make a mule moan in a mouth-to-mouth biting contest." Of course he said this when his father wasn't around.

Johnny had always interpreted Pie's goodbye as "I love you, Little Johnny" despite the old man's always calling him Anthony and "come back soon."

It was a fair assumption on his part seeing that his grandfather was mussing up his hair, smiling, and Johnny knew that *casa* meant "home."

Pie, Johnny learned later in life, was actually saying, "Go home, little shithead, jackass." That was at least Manny's interpretation for him.

But while heading home that summer of 1945, Pie's goodbye was again misunderstood by Johnny, and he returned as loving a smile as he could muster up, which was 44/100 of a percent affection for his 99 and 44/100 percent unlovable grandfather.

Pie in turn misinterpreted his grandson's smile as some sort of I-put-one-over-on-you smirk, as no one smiled at Pie. The old man's rheumy eyes narrowed, and he changed his ruffling of Johnny's hair to

—

a violent jerk that yanked a large tuft out of his head, with the old man following up his action with the words, "Pie fuckum Jeroni-fucum-mo your hair!"

Johnny understood his grandfather's "Geronimo" as the hair was jumping out of his head like paratroopers shouting their war cry as they jumped out of the plane.

"I think I might have a touch of ring worm or somethin'," Johnny told his ma when she noticed the bald patch as he walked in the door after jogging the twenty miles from Chelmsford.

"You've outgrown ringworm. You're fourteen and going into the ninth grade. Let me see."

"Maybe it's ring-around-the-rosy worm," he said, avoiding her inspection.

"Stop acting like a child. You're the man of the family, with your father working and living in Pennsylvania. The Mosely kid has been picking on your sister all summer. He's your age. You'd better talk to him. He calls your sister 'alkin', talkin', skin and bones.'"

"She is."

"And calls Jazz a bucktoothed beaver rat."

"I'll fix his wagon," Johnny said, heading out the door he had just come through.

"Why can't you fight for your sister too?"

"I will. I'll fight him twice."

"Don't fight. Just pretend fight."

But he was gone.

It took him a while to find Teddy Mosely. He was in the poolroom, racking balls for the big kids, including Teddy's big brother Tommy. All the Mosely's, eight in all, had names beginning with T. Tommy smiled at his little brother as Johnny invited him outside into the ally. Tommy was five inches taller and twenty pounds heavier than his challenger.

"Turn the frosting on his cake to swill, Teddy," his brother smirked.

Righty came out from a corner where he was playing a pinball machine and followed Johnny, Teddy, and his Teddy followers up the stairs, onto the street, and then into the alley.

"What do you want?" Johnny asked his friend.

"I'll be your second," Righty said.

"What does that mean?"

"It means if you get killed or somethin', I finish the fight for you. I also check the dueling pistols to make sure they don't put no blanks in yours or dull the sword you have to fence with. And other stuff. Like making sure the merda mangiare, shit eater to you, doesn't have a roll of dimes clenched in his fist."

"Hey, all I want to do is punch this guy in the nose for calling my sister skin and bones."

"Well, she is," Teddy said, sticking his chin in the air, jutting out his lower jaw.

"I know, but you don't get to say it."

"Oh ya."

"Ya."

The larger boy knocked Johnny's hat off, the one that was just like the Red Sox one Ted Williams wore.

"Now you're asking for it," Johnny said as he bent over to pick it up.

But he never completed the pick up as Teddy Mosely's spit hit Johnny's forehead just about the time his fist caught Johnny in the eye with a well-practiced sucker punch that usually ended Teddy's battles before they started.

It was while Teddy was still smirking, turning his head from side to side to check out his friends' reaction, fists in front of his face in case his punch didn't take the sap out of Johnny's limbs, that Johnny let fly with a right that caught the bigger boy in the solar plexus, immediately removing all the air from his sails

"He hit Teddy in the nuts!" one of the bigger boy's backers yelled.

"Where's his nuts, in his belly button?" Righty challenged. "That's where Johnny hit 'em."

"Shut your ass, you ginny fuck."

"Get Tommy, get his brother. Johnny killed Teddy by hitting him in the balls."

Johnny watched as Teddy declined to get up, rubbing his stomach.

"Ya gotta get up, Mosely. You said Jazz had buckteeth too."

"Nah, I didn't."

"Ya, ya did."

"So!" Teddy's big brother was now on the scene, "This marine your ass will clean." While Tommy never served in the marines, he was more than happy to let everyone think he did. Tommy felt it might be a good time to sharpen up his fighting abilities. He had been practicing what he would say to the little Portagee as he headed up the poolroom stairs to the scene of his brother's demise, a Jap rat Portagee Pearl Harbor attack on little brud, if he had ever seen one.

While only in the tenth grade, he was eighteen, and most of his friends who had graduated that past June had already signed up or had been drafted, and he didn't mind saying he had signed up despite having his father and uncles visit the local draft board, a visit that not only would speed up his being drafted in the near future but also led to at least one of the uncles eventually getting drafted as well.

Righty had declared that Tommy had flunked the mental part of the draft proceedings, that is until he got bonzoed in the head with a golf ball hit off the baseball bat of another brother and went and took the IQ test again. The bash in the brain brought his intelligence quotient up seven points, and he passed.

Tommy, towering over Johnny, said, "I said *so*, piss ant." to Johnny who towered below him. "Go sew buttons on your fly," Johnny said. "This is between Teddy and me."

"Nah, anyone who hits my little brudder in the nuts when he ain't looking answers to me. Teddy and me ain't only brudders, we're blood brudders too. We cut our wrists and mixed the blood together. We're like the Corset-kin brudders. You cut one, the udder feels the pain."

Tommy knocked Johnny's Red Sox cap off again but didn't hit Johnny in the balls with his fist. Tommy saw Johnny keeping an eye on his right hand. Appearing to be ready when Tommy tossed the first one.

So in a multiple-choice world, instead of broadcasting his attack with his fists, Tommy head butted Johnny, then kneed him in the groin.

When Johnny doubled over, Tommy played a drum roll on his face, bloodying his nose and ear, then closed Johnny's eyes with what he believed was taps.

While Johnny could barely see through his swollen eyes, he could hear his tormentor's breathing. It was getting heavier.

"Okay, twerp, pack it in," Tommy said.

"What's the matter, Tommy? Am I beating your hands up too bad? Why don—"

Before Johnny could add the T to "don" Tommy dotted the smaller boy's I with a smash that left Johnny feeling like his eyeball had been mashed like a potato. He then grabbed Johnny's hand and bent his fingers nearly back to his forehand, an action that could make a rock sob.

"Take that, hand," Johnny said, smiling through bloody teeth.

"That's it," Tommy said. "This idiot's crazy."

He gave Johnny one last blast to the ear that left Johnny's head feeling like it was the clanger inside Big Ben and walked away.

"I'll give you twice as much the next time you say anything about my brother or sister, you piece of snake shit," Johnny said, following after the two brothers and their entourage.

Tommy turned and took a step toward Johnny.

—

Before Johnny could take a step toward his tormentor, Righty had his arms around him and led him off. "That's enough, Champ, let the horse's ass go look for the half a mare that bears his head."

Tommy slammed his open hands into Righty's ears, boxing them, staggering him. "You ginny assholes are all alike. You and piss ant hi-fuckin-ho DaSilva."

"I ain't no ginny," Johnny said.

"You're worse than the Mussolini wops that I'm gonna be killing next week when I join the commandos. You're a Portagee."

"What kind of geese don't fly?" Teddy chanted.

Tommy and friends answered in unison, "Port-o-geese!"

Johnny and Righty, holding each other up, moved on the group. The drummer, the flutist, they were missing the flag bearer.

Tommy led his gang away. "Come on, let's shoot a game of eight ball."

Righty looked at Johnny. "Hi-Ho, you've got the balls of a bull elephant." He barely heard himself as he cupped his hands over his ears, trying to relieve the blinding pain.

"You've got the cajones, not me," Johnny said. "When you grabbed me and led me away, I could have kissed you. I knew my face couldn't beat the crap out of his hands one more time."

They walked the three miles from the poolroom through the woods to Righty's home, stopping only to wash the blood off their faces and hold the flat, cold, wet stones of the brook against their faces to stem the swelling.

"You don't have to walk home with me, Johnny. I'm not dizzy anymore."

"Yah, but it's Friday, and your ma always has your eye-talian bread and calzones steaming in the pantry window. They're calling me, your ma's baking. 'Hey, Johnny DaSilva, come and eat me. I'm-a fresh-a, I'm-a hot-a. I'm-a melt in-na ya mouth-a.' I've only been away for two months at the farm, not two hundred years. I know on Fridays your bread will be calling me."

But the freshly baked bread wasn't in the pantry window.

Righty's mother, nearly as wide as she was short, was waiting in the doorway for him.

"I wasn't fighting' Mama. It's okay, Ma. My ears didn't get bashed. I got the flu in them. Or something."

She opened her arms for him, but he didn't move into them. Afraid she wasn't offering him Red Cross services but instead wanted him trapped within her maw; he obviously had been fighting.

"Your brother Americo got kill-ded ina Monte Casino."

"No, Ma, Big Lefty was born in Monte Casino."

—

"He was kill-ded in Monte Casino by the Germans. The American government army officer justa told me."

Righty went to her arms. They enveloped him. He turned from his mother's bosom to Johnny. "Don't let me cry, Johnny."

"I won't. You hug your mother. Let her cry. I'll see you tomorrow. We'll climb to the top of the Big Tree."

Johnny started walking off.

"Johnny."

"Ya?"

"I loved my Big Lefty."

"Ya. I know. We'll talk about it up top of the Big Tree. For now, you hug your ma."

When he got home, there was a note on the door, "I'm at Grandma's."

When he got to his grandmother's, everyone was there, all his aunts. All his uncles, except the ones fighting in the war. His cousins. Everyone.

Except his grandmother. She was coming out of the pantry with fresh fried doughnuts that still steamed.

"I'm sending everyone out in different directions," his uncle Mark said. "We'll find Dad. Don't worry, Ma."

"I know where he is," she said softly.

"Ma, the nurses said he had just disappeared from his hospital bed," Aunt Hope said.

"The doctor said after that fall, they figured close to fifty feet, from that ladder, he should have been killed dead. Everyone told him he was too old to be climbing no ladder. And painting the church for free. Again."

When Dad gives his word, he'll die with it," Aunt Faith said. "He nearly tore his lip off. His ear was hanging by a shred. Up a steeple. Painting for nothing."

"Your father wouldn't say he was painting for nothing," Johnny's grandmother said.

"Okay, listen up," his uncle Mark said. "You kids will head toward the zoo down Pond Street. Faith and Hope, toward the Square. You kids check the side of the roads and railroad tracks. He could have passed out."

"Never you mind, Mark. I know where he is."

Everyone towered over the little old lady, the matriarch of the Shiverick clan, her face showing all its Scotch, Irish, English, Indian traits, yet all appeared to be looking up at her.

She walked away, silently, down Pine Street.

"Where's she going?"

They followed and found out.

"Are you nearly done, John?"

—

"Just a couple last dabs, Ruth."

The old man, the old wooden ladder with its three extensions out, shivered in its own rickety height as he reached to the side of the steeple to apply that one last brush full of white paint.

"Send Johnny up. He has young eyes. He can see if I missed anything."

"That little boy isn't going up that ladder to that steeple," his mother said. "I forbid it."

"Ma, he's painting it for me," Johnny said, starting up.

At the top, the old man handed him the brush. "I can't get that one spot. Give me your hand and put your foot on the edge of the rung and lean out."

I'm scared . . . shitless, Johnny thought. All the way up the ladder, his sphincter puckered as swiftly and tightly as a guppy feeding on fish food.

Not a word was said as Johnny took the brush in one hand, his grandfather's hand in the other, his sphincter now user friendly, and leaned out, his entire body outside the balance of the ladder rungs, and painted.

The last spot covered, the two walked backward down the ladder, a rung at a time, together.

Then the family walked back together.

No one spoke. Except Ruth. "You're a silly old man, John Shiverick."

"You're a silly old woman, Ruth Shiverick."

Johnny hoped tons of their silliness coursed through his body. He was that proud . . . proud to the tenth power . . . squared . . . to infinity . . . That's a lot . . .

—

CHAPTER 14

IT COMES IN THREES

Johnny and Righty climbed to the highest point in the Big Tree, a point where the branches questioned their wisdom on supporting something, someone, on so frail an arm, a branch.

The two friends questioned their wisdom being so high on so frail a branch. They needed to be frightened.

But weren't.

They knew the Big Tree was their friend. To be trusted. The breeze made the treetop stir, and they swung like a Baltimore oriole's nest swings.

Without a word, they closed their eyes, faces tilted upward, their skin breathing in the warm sun.

The wind shifted back and forth, at times changing like two tides meeting each other, and now they turned in circles, in eddies of air.

"I know you feel bad for me, Johnny," Righty said, keeping his eyes closed.

"Ya, my little sister even hugged me when I left the house. She never hugs me. She did this time. She's so skinny."

"Ya, I know. I was there when the Mosely monkeys said that. When you shook all the branches of their family tree."

"Was Big Lefty skinny? He always wore that baggy stuff he called a Zoot Suit."

Righty didn't answer the question, only muttered, "Is."

"I didn't mean to say 'was.'"

"Yah, I know. I don't mean to say 'is.'"

"There's one more to go."

"Yah," Righty said, "with Big Lefty and then your grandfather Shiverick dying last night."

"They didn't even know he had a broken rib sticking him in the lungs. He figured if he told them he'd never get out to finish painting the inside of the church."

"It doesn't always have to happen in threes."

"I know."

"But it does," Righty said.

"It hurts."

"Do you think there's a heaven?"

"I don't know. Grandpa Shiverick believed there was a heaven. And a hell. And Grandma DaSilva thought there was a heaven and no hell. She thought everyone went to heaven. Bad guys and all. The difference is in heaven the bad guys listened. And became good."

"Do you think I'll see Big Lefty when I get there?"

"Of course. Everyone you love will be there. Smiling and talking about the good old times. And you get to scratch the ears of your old dogs that died. Grandma DaSilva said this. Mine said the smiles of everyone up there combined into a bright shiny sunburst that was God."

"That's nice. I want her to be right. My mother believes that. That's why she smiled at me even while her heart was broken. I believe your grandmother too, but what about her believing everyone gets there? To heaven. What about that son-of-a-bitch Hitler that killed my brother? And broke my mother's heart?"

"I think I go along with Grandfather Shiverick there. He thinks everyone with the devil in them, like Hitler and Mussolini and Hirohito, will burn in hell for eternity."

"I like that."

"You know what I like better than burning?"

"What?"

"What I heard my uncle Manny say. He said this rat guy died and went to hell where he met the devil. Who seemed like a pretty nice guy to the rat.

"The devil says to him, 'You can choose the door you want to go in to spend eternity.' Then the devil takes him past a door where everyone is screaming inside. Real hideous. The rat guy says, 'No thanks.'

"The devil takes him past another door where everyone is pleading, 'Please, no,' and there are all these moans. 'Nothing doing,' the rat says.

"Then the devil takes him to a door where the voices are chanting, 'Don't make a wave.' And the rat thinks this is great, the ocean, the sun, girls with their boobers hanging out complete with their owl-eye nipples, and says he'd take this door. 'Oh ya.'

"The devil smiles and let's him in. The rat finds himself immediately up to his lower lip in shit. Soupy shit. And he joins the others there, chanting forever, 'Don't make a wave. Don't make a wave.' And Hitler and Tojo and Mussolini are there."

"Ya."

"Then," Johnny said, "Big Lefty and all the good guys get one day a week to go down there to hell and make a fucking wave."

"I like that. Maybe I can visit with Big Lefty on that day and go down there with him. And make Typhoon waves. And even get to shovel some shit right into their mouths."

"And you could bring a dentist with you while you shoveled, and he'd say, 'Open wide,' and make sure they did."

"Ya," Righty said.

"But even better, you and me can get into the army or marines and slice their balls off with our bayonets or fly Spitfires for the English or Tiger planes for the Chinese. They take us young guys that our country won't take. Ya, maybe we can get into the Flying Tigers."

"Nah," Righty said, "they fight Japs. I want Germans. Especially Hitler. They fucked with the wrong person when they killed Big Lefty. And right where he was born."

Johnny leaned into Righty, massaged the back of his neck. Crooned softly as the wind again stirred their branch. "Rock-a-by baby, on the treetop . . ." and changed to a soft humming that joined the breeze song.

Both closed their eyes. For a minute. For an hour?

"I can't wait to see my brother again."

"I know. But don't rush it. That would piss Big Lefty off, just like the fly on the toilet seat."

"Yah. Let's go pike as soon as it gets dark. We'll have a condom-collecting contest first. The whole gang," Righty said.

"Yo, General Custer, sounds bad."

"Goody Two-shoes."

"Dance away my blues."

"Yah, like Ms. Sontag used to make us into poets in the fourth grade, and we chanted, 'New shoes, blues shoes, pretty pointed new shoes . . . but nah, fat shoes, flat shoes, scuff 'em on the mat shoes . . .'"

"That's the kind they'll buy," Johnny finished, adding, "my good happy horse poop, can you believe remembering this stuff from when we were nine?"

"We'll probably remember it forever."

—

"Remember how Ms. Sontag would give you hell and whack your hand with that ruler when she caught you chewing gum, and all the time she'd be munching on that giant piece of chocolate cake. Those were the days you could chew along with the teacher."

They started slowly down the tree.

Johnny said, "Did you hear what happened to Officer Donelly? He picked up the new beat patrolman in his cruiser and tells him he knew where they could get free hot dogs. When they got to the dog stand, Old Donut Donelly told the rookie to listen to the cruiser radio so they wouldn't get into trouble and said he'd bring back a hot dog with the works."

"Nah, I didn't hear that. So what? Cops always get freebies. Especially Old Donut. The front of his shirt has got more sugar and cinnamon on it than my mother's spice rack."

"Anyway, Donelly goes into the restaurant while the rookie cop listens to the cruiser radio for any important messages. Donelly gets the hot dog and slips a condom over it. And then, listen to this, covers it with mustard and relish and chopped onions and puts it back in the bun. The bastard. I love him!"

"You're shitin' me."

"Nah, you're too big a turd."

"Old crap. Come on. The rest of the story."

"Anyway, Donelly, the dork, the one who chased us out of Spot Pond that night we pissed in the water certain stink-people drink, he brings the hot dog back to the rookie with the big appetite. The rookie nearly kisses the lieutenant's sugar-shirt but doesn't. Only officers can kiss officers or somethin' like that. Anyway the new guy bites into it. But can't bite through the hot dog. So he pulls on it like a dog pulling on a blanket or somethin'. And guess what happens?"

"Jee-zuss, tell me. Or I'll piss my pants."

"The rubber slides off the hot dog and snaps into the rookie's face. Slapping mustard and all that other horseshit in his face. The rookie can't figure it out at first. Then he realizes he's got a condom hanging between his teeth. Covered with mustard, like some goddamned Greek has used it or something."

"Ya, ya? Go on. Although I'm pissin' my pants."

"The rookie roars like that lion that bit the mouse's balls when the mouse hurt him pulling out that splinter from his paw or somethin'. Donelly shits his pants in panic and gets out and runs down the highway. The rookie chases him in Donelly's cruiser, trying to run him over. But can't pick him off."

—

"Ya mean the fat bastard ran like a broken field runner. A halfback?" Righty asked.

"Nah, faster than that. He ran like a coward shitting his pants as the rookie comes close a couple times. And he doesn't get his cruiser back. The rookie drives it to the dump, tosses the keys in the trash, and flags a car down for a ride back to his beat."

"Just as well he didn't get the cruiser back. How would he explain how his cruiser seats were covered with his doughnut shit. Then?"

"Then Donelly commandeers some kid's bike and rides back to the station. But first he gets his pants cuff caught in the chain and falls on his ass."

"Wow."

"And Donelly has to tell the shift captain he lost his cruiser."

"Just like that naughty little kitten who lost his mitten and doesn't know where to find them. What else?"

"And Donelly's boss asks him how he lost a cruiser. Was he in the goddamned Battle of the Coral Sea?"

"Then what?"

"I don't know the rest. But I think they made the rookie chief of police, broke Donelly to dog catcher, later cutting off his balls and putting him on the pussy posse, the vice squad, harassing Rockledge's only hooker."

"So he's in charge of keeping our wiener cleaner. Remember Johnny when we were in the sixth grade and the big guys asked you to buy rubbers for them 'cause you looked older than they did."

"And they were scared. Yah."

"Rat's ass that was funny."

"Oh sure. Maybe for you. Not for me. I did just what they said. They said, 'Just go in, put the thirty-five cents on the counter. Cross your two forefingers, making an X, just like that cross on the box of rubbers. And look the guy right in the eye. And he'll give you the rubbers.'"

"Yah?"

"You were there."

"Yah. But I like to hear you tell it."

"Anyway. I go in. Put the money on the counter. Cross my fingers. And stare the big buy in the eye."

"Yah?"

"And he just stares back. This staring contest, like that garter snake and the mouse in the Big Woods that day. I wondered if he doesn't have any of that 'cross your fingers' brand And I say, 'Just give me any rubbers, then.' Finally, he says, with a roar that blows my eyebrows into my eyeballs, and that really hurts."

—

"You add stuff every time you tell this. It's great. The sayings."

"Anyway, I turn and run, like the hammers of hell are banging down on my butt, mistaking it for a nail. The big guys outside join me in hightailing it. Singing and dancing, clicking their heels. They think I got the rubbers. Finally we stopped, all out of breath. They asked me where the rubbers are, and I told them the guy was on to me. I had to vamoose."

"Yah, you had to vamoose, move your caboose."

"The big guys want to know where the rubbers are. And when I say I ain't got them, they want the money. And I tell them the money is back on the counter. The counter where I crossed my fingers in an X, just like on the box. And then that super asshole Merker jams his two fucken fingers up my nose."

"That was the wrong thing to do, Johnny."

"Yup. I nearly bit his thumb off. The son of a bitch didn't thumb no rides for a while."

"I feel a little better, Johnny, Merker's a touch hole of the highest order."

"Hey, he talks through his ass and farts through his mouth. He bragged he was some kind of a beach birth, born sideways or something, and they had to use a jackhammer to get him out. That's why he's so tough. It makes me sick to think of him. When I join the marine corps, I'm coming back and pound him into a puddle of piss."

"He always pounds you. More so after you bit his nose-picking finger."

"One day I'll pound him."

"You feel a lot better after we pike and condom count tonight."

"Yah. See you tonight outside the library. We can hide our books in the trash can in the ally. That's the only way I can get out on nights I'm not setting pins. My ma says I'm gonna be the first Shiverick or DaSilva to graduate from high school if it kills her."

"Hey, it could kill you. The teachers could, that's for sure. But you should be a writer with the crazy things you think up. It's like your brain is in a maze and keeps trying all these different routes. And if you write books, you don't need no school. Writers know nothing. But it doesn't bother them. They just make the crap up. Only doctors and dentists need to graduate from high school and go to college for a couple years as well. Anyway, I'll bring a book too. So your book won't be lonely in that garbage can."

"Yah. Okay, you send out the smoke signals, and I'll Paul Revere."

Righty sent out the smoke signals to the gang. He had a phone at home. But first he'd have to get the other three families on his party line off the line by picking up the mouthpiece and making fart noises into it.

—

The phone charges were never rung up when Righty called. Sally Pinkerton, an operator, had a crush on Righty. Sort of. But not really. She told her friends she loved his little meatball eyes. And didn't care if he was only a young kid. When her father got the third-hand news that his daughter had a crush on a little kid, her father read the riot act to her, "No girl of mine is gonna go with no ginzo."

And Sally Pinkerton told her father under her breath, "And no one is going to tell me who to go with and what I do."

"The library. At nine," Johnny said, running full bore to the houses of the members of the gang that didn't have phones. Pebbles were tossed at the windows, and when a face appeared, Johnny yelled out, "The English are coming! The English are coming! At nine. The library."

Rhesus and Boattail were first there to greet Johnny and Righty who were sitting on the big boulder. Those who arrived at the meeting place first got the best seats, the smooth areas. Those who were late had to sit on the sharp rocks, leaving them with the feeling they were sitting bare ass on ax heads. Then Fat and Hoppalong. And finally the rest.

"Got the rope, Fat?" Rhesus asked, assuming the position of boss as always.

"Yah."

"Better be strong enough," Boattail said, taking over the role of enforcer for his mob boss brother."

"You bet your butt," Fat said. "You know how slow I run. I don't want a rope that will break and have some lover boy run me down and pound the piss out of me."

"Righty, you got the pike?" Johnny asked. "I've got the Klaxon. That horn will blow the balls off a bull at a hundred yards."

"Yah. I've got the pike. Let's go."

"We gonna have a condom count before or after we pike?" Fats asked.

"Let's call the condom count off for tonight. I've been eating too much chop suey trying to get into the Flying Tigers."

"What the hell has chop suey got to do with collecting condoms?" Rhesus asked.

"Chopsticks, that's what."

"What?" Boattail asked.

"Hey, I eat Chink food five days a week with chopsticks, and how do you get those old condom rings onto the counting stick? By pushing them on with a small stick. Just like eating with chopsticks. I've had enough. Besides I want to take a swim in the reservoir after we pike."

"Why?"

"Johannson flunked me in French today and said don't come back. I hate French. Especially with some Swede teaching it. 'Yall, femme la port, sill voo plate.'"

"So why Spot Pond?"

"So I can let a leak there, knowing he'll be drinking it tomorrow morning."

"Hey," Rhesus said, "any id-jit can tock Frenchie. Polly voo francais, Chevrolet coupe, too jour, lamour, horse manure, for sure. And can count in frog—in dee twat mo cock sank."

"I know every language in the world except Greek," Boattail said.

"Abalagartsa y-oh," Righty said.

"That's Greek to me."

Righty held the tip of his thumb against the tips of his forefinger and middle finger with the remaining two fingers folded against his palm and moved his hand forward and back in the world wide Italian Hey-ah-whatsa-by-you-ah motion, translating his words "up your-ah asshole" to "Your-ra a nice-ah boya, Mr. Boattail."

"Hey ya," Rhesus said, extending his middle finger in Righty's direction in another international sign language. "Here comes-ah human ginny helicopter—wop-wop-wop, wop-wop-wop."

"I not knowah you speeka da Italiano," Righty said, bending his right arm in a forty-five-degree angle and slapping and holding the elbow with his left hand.

"Here's a kiss for you," Rhesus said, hoisting his left leg like a male dog visiting a fire hydrant and let fly with a fart that made a sound similar to a stepped on toad.

"That makes you man and wife," Johnny said. "You may kiss the bride, Rhesus."

"Barf," Rhesus said, "she didn't shave today."

"I'm too young to shave," Righty said.

"Hell, Righty," Johnny said. "You came out of the womb with a five o'clock shadow."

"How do you know?"

"Hey, who do you think smacked your ass."

"What do you think we paid the doctor to do? Why did you do it?"

"Hey, the doctor took one look at you and was too busy smacking your face to slap your ass."

"Cheeze, this is my best friend. With a friend like you, I don't need no enemas."

"Hey! Shut up!" Rhesus said. "There's the first car. It's Smith's cough drop, and the son of a bitch Timmy Smith must be attached to an oil rig the way the piston's punching that Chevy's fenders down on those wheels."

"We're not piking Smith's car," Fat said. "The son of a bitch is as crazy as a dog chasing its tail, and the middle of the dog stops suddenly, and the dog rams its own rear end up its own keester."

"Ya afraid," Rhesus said.

"The guy is captain of the football and wrestling teams because his head was x-rayed, and they found it devoid of brains," Hopalong said, joining Fats in opting for a car with someone who didn't have the power and weight to drive the fenders down onto the wheels. "Besides he's a senior and we're freshmen."

"He won't know any of us," Rhesus said, "except you, Hoppalong, 'cause we're going to tear off his Chevy's hood ornament and tie you in its place. And he'll be busy making a pretzel out of you."

"Hold it down. We're swinging into action," Johnny said, taking the rope in his hand, creeping and crawling out of the bush under Smith's cough drop car and tossing the top over its roof.

They waited in silence to determine whether Smith saw or heard the rope.

Nope. Righty crawled forward and tied the rope to the driver's door handle as Johnny tied the other end of the passenger's door.

Then the dangerous work, forcing the wooden wedges they had made into the bottom of the window so they couldn't be opened with great ease after the occupant discovered he couldn't open the tied-down doors.

Fat handed Johnny the Klaxon horn, and Johnny crept under the car and waited.

Rhesus and Boattail pulled the panties they had swiped off the clothesline over their heads after cutting out eyeholes for themselves and crawled up on the roof.

Then Fat, Hoppalong, and Righty did their stuff, jumping on the back fender, rocking the car in the opposite direction that Smith's sex thrusts were rocking it.

The two lovers in the car looked up, only to be greeted by the upside-down, panty-clad heads of the brothers hanging down from the car roof.

The brothers later reported at their critique later that night that Smith's and his girl's eyes appeared to be hard-boiled eggs gone insane, bopping along like the notes of a sing-along on the movie screen.

The two were frozen on the front seat.

That is until Johnny set off the Klaxon with an air blast that probably brought out the civil defense wardens for the entire Middlesex County.

Then they ran. Smith wasn't only strong and insane, but he was also a bully who enjoyed beating up on people's heads, especially little kids who couldn't fight back.

They heard Smith's roar through the closed windows. "I'll kill every son of a bitch in the school just to get the right one."

Certain Smith wasn't going to escape immediately, the boys stopped running just long enough to chant, "Sure cough drop. Do like the giant in the circus told his midget girlfriend to do, 'Kiss my nuts!'"

Smith's roar would have cowered a charging, bellowing bull elephant.

That was enough of that. The gang took off like a flock of big-ass birds.

All you could see was the top torsos as the gang ran for it, their legs pumping like roadrunners.

"I think I'll skip school tomorrow, just in case he recognized my butt," Johnny said.

And they laughed and clapped each other on the back and gave high fives and were so damned happy they forgot about heading into Spot Pond and pissing in Johannson's drinking water.

The best place in the world to be safe and celebrate was the Big Woods.

Actually, the Big Woods weren't that big, just a few acres between Pond and Pine Streets. They wouldn't find out how small their giant world of the Big Woods was until they returned home from future travel, college and war, those that did return.

Their Big Woods was only big in their minds and hearts. The woods at that time were huge. And the woods were theirs. That was all that mattered to them.

They lay on their backs near the Big Tree in the Big Woods, magic wands of grass in their mouths as they watched falling stars.

"That big one up there with the bright, bright tail, it's beautiful," Righty said. "It's my brother, Big Lefty. Bet you guys didn't know the Big Dipper was left handed. Hi, Americo."

They all closed their eyes. For different reasons. Laughter. Sadness. Both brought tears. And they didn't want any of their friends to see their eyes were glistening.

Big Lefty's star deserved to be the biggest, brightest.

They all knew Big Lefty. He always told the other big guys to "lay off. They're friends of Big Lefty."

CHAPTER 15

RAGS

Johnny and Jazz had asked their sister to come into their room that night.

A first.

She had been kept out with high walls, moats, dragons, and a variety of threats.

Books from Johnny's collection of Richard Haliburton's adventures and Edgar Rice Burroughs Tarzan series that he found discarded at the town dump were used as wedges under the bottom of the door. The brothers just opened enough pages and the cover to jam under their bedroom door to keep Romola from bursting in.

She tried and tried again to gain forced entry. She didn't know why she wanted in, other than the fact they wanted to keep her out.

Despite the fact a slight breeze could blow her away, she put her shoulder to the door, sometimes with such determination that the pages would double over on themselves. This made it not only impossible to get into their rooms from the outside, but also for them to get out until some engineering was completed. Johnny hated the damage to his books as he read and reread them.

They were his pride and joy.

Righty wasn't sure why he had to read books rather than practicing laying bricks to become a mason. His father, who carried a cement hod for a bricklayer, pointed out that he supported his seven kids, "Ana never gotta past thirda grade. A mason, he can support his kids like kings and still havea some money for a truck. Maybea an old truck but still a truck and all your own."

He told Righty and all the Lefties that he had plenty of pull with the union, and he'd get them jobs carrying hods too. Maybe one would be a bricklayer. He'd watched the bricklayers. They kept secrets, but he learned. He would teach the brightest brother, Santo, Big Lefty. He'd make the most money. They'd all make money. Take good care of their kids too, or he'd kick their coulo."

One day he told Righty and Johnny, "The old guy I hod for, he'sa froma Monte Casino too. He always gets da money for his chimneys. He teacha me. Other guys get acheat whena sometimes get no pay. Whata you gonna do. Take the chimney back? Anyway, when he finisha the job, he tells the customer da fireplace no work until theya pay in fulla.

"Some laughs. They say, 'Hey, whata you gonna do, take the chimney back?' They light da fire and da house fills with smoke. He tells dem, 'Pay, and it will worka in the morning.' They want it work right away. Nope. In da morning. They pay. Then that night he goesa upa on roof and lowers a stone on rope downa the chimney. You know why? 'Course you don't. You're justa kids. Wet behind the ears. Wipe your nose on your sleeve. Pick your ass. Anyhow, the stone breaka da glassa he cement into opening in flu-a. Guys likea him and meah, from casino, smarta, like the big bird who hoota, 'who-whoah.'"

Righty's dad loved all the sayings he picked up at work. It didn't matter whether he understood what they meant as long as he thought he knew. Of course you don't know. You've got a bird in the brain, not in the bush. "That'sa why you no know he put glass in flue, fireplace no work."

Anyway, Righty couldn't understand why Johnny searched the dump for hours on end, looking for books he hadn't read. He even bought some books, spending money on paper and ink instead of candy or toward new hockey skates or a baseball glove or even on shoes.

After all, Righty knew Johnny put newspaper in the shoes as the soles got thin, then changed over to cardboard as inserts when the holes in the soles started to appear, first as dime size, then as big as a fifty-cent piece.

He did something similar with the baseball glove he found at the dump, a big hole in the middle of the pocket. A piece of a purse made a perfect patch for the glove pocket.

Johnny showed up for the pickup hockey games at Buckman's wearing a giant pair of discarded skates he found in a trash can covered with rust. He got the rust off by rubbing the blades with pieces of shales he got out of the ledge in the Big Woods, where they sipped the water that trickled through the spring-fed thin layers of stone. He wore his sneakers under the skates to make them fit.

There was no fancy skating, but anyone who made fun of his sneaker-skates and the *Life* magazines he tied around his shins in place of shin pads paid the price, that is if they came close enough for him to work the magic of his hockey stick. He had been impressed by and always remembered Friar Tuck and his cudgel work on Robin Hood.

Then Righty wondered why, if he had to read or buy a book, why not Tom Sawyer or Huck Finn? Johnny told him that, "I live Huck and Tom's lives with the adventures me and the country cousins, Dink and Pointer, have during the summer. I could have written those Mark Twain books."

"Who is Mark Twain?" Righty had asked.

"He wrote the books."

"Well, how could you have written those Huck Finn books? You ain't found no bodies like Tom and Huck did. Besides if you found a body and it had money on it, a lot, would you keep it?"

"Nah. Maybe half. To help Ma. And another half to fix Jazz's teeth. And I'd give half to the church so I wouldn't go to hell. Anyway, bodies don't need money. How about you?"

"I'd keep a little to buy a truckload of candy," Righty said.

"A little bit? Sure. You spend a fortune on candy. You can eat enough sweets to melt the teeth of an alligator."

"See what I mean, Johnny, you otta be a writer. Whoda of thunk about rotting the teeth out of a gator. Only you."

"I'd rather be a reader and share other guy's adventures."

That's why many of his trips to the library hadn't ended in his hiding his books in garbage cans while he went off counting condoms in a contest to see who could get the most of the beadle skin rings on a stick within a certain time slot. Reading was an escape from holes in your shoes and wax in aching teeth.

That's why Johnny got mad as hell at Romola for putting her shoulder to the door, buckling the pages of his favorite Haliburton book. All the author's adventures were true, like the time he snuck into a harem and stayed with a whole bunch of women wrapped in kerchiefs who were owned by a guy who had some kind of sword called a some-omeat-a or something. And the harem had a whole bunch of guards with their tessies cut off so they couldn't mess with the women and would have killed Haliburton if they caught him.

When Johnny saw the book crumble, he went wild, wild as the time he nearly bit Merker's finger off after the jerk stuck his fingers up Johnny's nose.

—

Johnny carefully removed the book stop and pulled the door open with nearly enough anger to take it off its hinges. He could feel his fists rolling into a tight ball. She would pay.

When he finally got the door open and saw his sister, how thin she was, he was proud of her power. "Go to bed, Romola," he said, mussing up her hair, giving her a smile, "or I'll kill you."

"Give it your best shot."

"Look, you can have Rags," he said, stifling a smile.

The twelve-year-old girl with shoulders no wider than a crumbled copy of Haliburton, turned and called the spitz mongrel and perhaps many other breeds, "Rags, come."

Rags was the offspring of a who-dunnit mother, a notorious woman of the night, who, after all the dogs who had impatiently waited their turns took their shots, spotted a passing hound and said, "Et tu, Brute," calling it hither.

The ragbag Rags wasn't about to leave the warmth of and intoxicating sneaker odors of the brothers whose feet he had warmed and refused to jump to her from the bed it shared with Jazz and Johnny.

"Rags!"

"Romola, go to bed."

"No. I'll stand here forever. Rags! I'll kick your tail."

The little white dog, homelier than the asshole of a wart hog, understood the last call and jumped out of the bed and followed Romola, who shot back at Johnny, "And I'm keeping him 'til summer."

Johnny closed the door. "That's a long time."

"Johnny"

"Yah?"

"Her bedroom's cold," Jazz said.

"So's ours. Your feet can use Rags too."

"They're okay."

"She's got Ma to keep her warm," Johnny said.

"Ma won't come to bed until she listens to Arthur Godfrey."

"I was going to give her the dog. But didn't want to make it too easy. She's got to learn to stand up for herself. Who's going to protect her when I join the marines?"

"Me."

"Yah, I forgot. You and me, we always give Rags to Ma and Romy on the coldest nights, don't we? It's colder in Ma's room on the north side. The wind rattles the windows. 'Course the windows can't rattle right now. The frost on them is real thick. Remember when Ma's false teeth froze in the glass she was soaking them in."

"Yah. She cried," Jazz said, almost crying himself, thinking of his mother looking at the frozen teeth. But when she saw how sad her three children were, they were young then, she had smiled, a big toothless smile that made them laugh.

"Then after she laughed, she tried to whack us one, first saying she wasn't crying, and then saying that we're not allowed to laugh at her. Then she put the frozen glass of teeth against Rag's stomach to try and melt it, and Rags shivered so."

She had given them the toothless smile and pretended to be a clown and tried to hit them because she wasn't sure how to tell them she loved them. She felt she didn't deserve to say this. Wasn't it her fault that Jazz's teeth were rotting? And wasn't it her fault that Romola was thin as a toothpick? And wasn't it her fault Johnny came home so often with a black eye or bloody nose 'cause someone had called them Skinny Minnie or Bucktooth baboon?

No matter how long she worked there was never enough money for shoes and food both, and she had to decide which was most important at the time of need.

"You know what was more funny?" Johnny said to Jazz. "When she first got her false teeth. She hated them. She said, 'They're too even.' That was the same night I forgot to give Rags his water."

"Yah, and when Ma went to bed, she put her teeth in the glass of water."

"And Rags sneaked into her room and drank the water.

"And the glass fell on the floor, and Ma woke up just in time to see Rags grab her teeth and bite into them and chipping the two front ones. Guess he thought they looked like a bone or something. Remember Ma moaned, 'They look like they're false,' and she swung at you with the broom when you said, 'They are.'"

"Ya. I 'member. It's cold. Will you tell me a story, Johnny?"

"I just did. Besides we have to let Ramola play kadiddle with us tonight?"

"Never! Why?"

"She went to the eighth-grade dance," Johnny said.

"So?"

"And she's so skinny."

"Oh, the kids were talking about Romy. I heard these kids talking about some girl whose panties fell down while she was doing the jitterbug with this other girl. And everyone laughed," Jazz said.

"Who? I'll go get 'em now. I'll kill the bastards!"

"It's too late for us to kill anyone tonight."

—

"Who said anything about you killing someone?"

"She's my sister too."

Johnny opened the door and called down the hallway, "Hey, Romola, you already ruined Mr. Haliburton, and he was going to swim the Helispoint through a whole bunch of sharks, so you might as well come on here with Rags and Jazz and me and play ca-didle."

Johnny had heard that if you were walking with a girl at night and saw a car with one headlight out and you said "kadiddle!" before she did, you got to kiss her. But it probably wasn't true. He was nearly fourteen. Still hadn't kissed a girl and still didn't know whether 'it' was in the front or sort of underneath.

There was no kissing in the kadiddle that Jazz and he played on this night. Jazz's teeth ached, and he couldn't sleep. They didn't count sheep. They counted cars with a headlight out. The one who spotted one first and said kadiddle got a point.

"Okay, I'll play," she said, "but only because I'm sad."

"Why?" Johnny asked.

"Because."

They played kadiddle. It was difficult to determine at times whether there was one light or two, especially when two or three cars were in a line, as the frost on the window panes was nearly a quarter-inch thick in spots. Of course there was no frost in the area of the missing pane, which had been replaced by a piece of cardboard. And anyone caught moving the cardboard to get a better look at oncoming cars got his hair or his ear pulled.

Besides, Ma had told them not to damage the card, it wasn't just any old piece of cardboard. It was their ice card.

When the iceman and his old horse came clopping along, he would look up at the window; if the ice card was there, he'd deliver the ice for the icebox. The size of the piece of ice they wanted was determined by which side of the card was up, and whether the card read fifteen cents, twenty-five cents, or fifty cents. They didn't need the card in the winter as the house was unheated, except the kitchen.

After kadiddle, which Romola won, only after a Black Sox fix the brothers had agreed on because their sister was sad for the first time ever, they played water spots.

They'd stare up at the water stains in the ceiling, product of roof leaks, and try to make out pictures or patterns, which they pointed out to each other. "That's a horse with wings," "a dragon with three heads," "a racing car with Mauri Amsterdam driving," "there's the Awful Tower in Paris,

France," "look, up there in the corner, it's the Stashew of Lib-er-tee inside the boot of Italy,"

"Oh, Johnny you're the funniest brother in the world," Romola said.

You wouldn't think so . . . if you knew what I was looking at now . . . that big double leak spot . . . over in the corner . . . that looks like Mrs. Mortenson's melons . . . when she put . . . the grapefruits . . . under her sweater . . . and Aunts Faith and Hope laughed . . . And Johnny knew that somewhere down below, although he hadn't been able to make them out in the water stains yet, was a buttocks, flexing and unflexing, as she reached heavenward . . . Or was it Mrs. Scranton . . . on her toes, and the calves of her legs flexed, and she had looked over her shoulder at him. He could feel himself growing down there.

"You better go to your own bed, Romola. I'll carry Rags in for you."

The pounding on the front door stopped the three children in their tracks. It had to be late, too late for a visitor.

They heard their mother open the front door. "Yes?"

"I'm from the *Record*. Press. May we come in?"

It sounded like they heard the names of several papers that Johnny delivered each morning. Boston had the *Globe*, the *American*, the *Post*, the *Herald*, the *Record*, and the *Traveler*.

He could only hear parts of their questions and his mother's answers.

"Okay, Jazz, get into bed and shut up. I want you to put the pillow over your head. You too, Ramola. Close your ears. Now!"

The two younger children did this; they had never seen Johnny so absolutely demanding.

"You sound like Hitler," Romola said, walking down the darkened hallway, hands over ears, to the bed she shared with her mother.

The voices echoed up the stairwell in bits and pieces, not making sense, and echoed in Johnny's ears as he sat in the pitch-black stairwell that led downstairs. "Your husband . . . three children dead . . . their names are the same as your three children . . . Do you have any pictures of those dead kids . . . only your own children?"

He heard his mother's voice. "I don't believe any of you. Any of you."

"If you don't have any pictures of your husband's dead kids, do you have any pictures of your children here that we can use?"

"What? Get out! Get out, leave this moment, you sons of bitches."

Johnny had never heard his mother swear. Perhaps she had never sworn before this moment.

He slipped back to his bedroom. Romola was in his bed with Jazz and Rags. He crawled into between them and whispered, "Be quiet," despite the fact they weren't making a sound and were as quiet as if they had died and weren't breathing.

Johnny crooned, "Ture, a-lure, a lure-ah, hush now don't you cry," softly singing the only words he knew of the lullaby time after time. He wondered how his grandfather Shiverick could have said the Irishman's religion was that of the devil. Yet his grandfather had been a man of God. And he loved him.

"Ture, a-lure, a lure-ah, hush now don't you cry."

He sang long after his throat was dry as the hot July sand of Revere Beach. He sang until the sandman struck him down, long after his brother and sister were asleep.

They dreamed their dreams of the water stains in the ceiling. Jazz laughed at the clown with three asses and the cross-eyed lions. Romy was carried off by a young prince, who turned into an eagle that slid her out of his arms into his wings.

But on this night, the water stains were just that—water stains. Stains made by tears, his tears for his brother and sister and mother. Tears he knew would come but did not understand what fears caused them. What did the voices below mean? "Three kids dead." "Your husband." "Do you have pictures of your children."

He understood the next morning.

At the basement of the news store, on a long table where other newsboys also folded the papers they would be soon delivering, Johnny folded his papers into tight tricornered shapes, like the hats of the patriots of old.

The triangular-folded papers were for long touchdown tosses because they could be scaled to the most distant porches as he pedaled past.

Other papers were folded into the shape of dynamite sticks for shorter throws, screen passes.

The ones he simply dropped on the porch steps had only a single fold, quarterback sneaks.

No matter how they were folded—the triangle, the dynamite stick, the simple fold, the yet-to-be-folded papers—his face stared back at him. Time after time.

His face was there on the front page of paper after paper. Serious, the face of the man of the house. There were also photos of Romola, whose large dark eyes were those of a frightened doe. Jazz's face appeared as that of a fawn to Johnny, his lips held close together in a smile, hiding the teeth, those teeth, daring the world to take its best shot at him.

They were on the front pages of several papers that shared the theft of the pictures from the photo wall of loved ones in Charity's home the previous night.

Over the three photos were headlines, "ROCKLEDGE MAN'S DOUBLE LIFE UNCOVERED WITH DEATH OF THREE CHILDREN." "DOES LIFE END FOR LIVING THREE CHILDREN WITH DEATH OF ILLEGAL THREE?" "WILL ROCKLEDGE MAN THINK, 'OH, WELL, I HAVE THREE LEFT!'"

It was pointed out in the cutlines under each picture that those shown were not the dead children. They died with their babysitter, when soup extinguished the flames, the gas fumes killing them. However, they had the same names as his three legitimate children.

One story reported the words of a vice squad detective from the Chester, Pennsylvania, Daily Dutiful. "It seems the father believed it was simpler to name the two separate families alike, making his double life less complicated."

"You look at me just once and I'll kill you," Johnny told the paperboy folding his papers beside him.

"He's just like his old man, no good," a large boy whispered to his partner with a snicker.

Later that day, in the school library, Johnny overheard an upperclassman who was reading a paper secreted in his notebook say to no one in particular, "It's like DaSilva's father killed those little kids."

He never saw Johnny's fist flying toward his throat and went down like he was poleaxed.

"You're no good, you're just like your father," the male library assistant said, slapping Johnny's face.

He didn't feel the slap, but his teeth started throbbing. The winter wind, early that morning as he delivered hi papers had cut through the air like a buzz saw, causing the teeth that he had not yet had fixed to throb with a pain that shot into his eyes, through his head, and back into his teeth.

He didn't have the candle wax to melt and squeeze into the cavities to keep out the cold air while he rode his route and tossed his papers. He had cut his wax supply into three pieces the night before. Chewing wax cut their hunger, and he shared it with Jazz and Romola.

It didn't help to cut the hunger.

What did help was Romola making protruding wax teeth and declaring she was Hirohito and Jazz taking his forefingers and pulling up the corners of his eyes, smiling that bucktoothed smile, "Me Hirohito, you Jane."

—

"Me Tarzan," Johnny declared, pounding his chest, causing him to spit out his wax. It landed in front of Rags, who didn't know what to make of it.

And the three of them laughed.

Rags, not quite as hungry as the three of them, as each sneaked him a corner of their supper beneath the table, tried to chew Johnny's wax. But spit it out. The dog found it tasteless.

The wax was amalgamated with the wad of bubble gum Johnny that kept adding and kept stored on the bedpost when not in use.

This night it was in use as the ragamuffin dog decided to give the wax-and-gum combo a chewing. He was having difficulty as it stuck in his teeth, to the roof of his mouth, making his eyes partially cross and protrude like a goosed frog's.

Rags was the only dog they knew of whose eyes crossed when he was discombobbled. He was also the only dog whose nose turned from jet black to a pale pink when he was out chasing a bitch in heat. The local dog officer, Bim Boles, who had returned Rags home a number of times, noted this strange physical change and mumbled something like he "was glad his nose didn't change from pink to black when he was out taking care of someone or other."

Bim's words were meant for other ears, but Johnny had overheard them.

Bim always had the same lines.

Whenever Jazz came over to claim his dog, giving the bucktoothed Bim his bucktoothed smile, Bim would say, "You get away from me, boy (he liked to talk like some Southern redneck cop. Didn't know why. He disliked their disliking certain people), before you get me in trouble with your daddy. Tee hee."

Bim informed Johnny that laws were made to be strictly abided by, at all times, "Tee hee," with no exceptions. "Dogs are not allowed to run free in my town. Law says so. I'm positively pretty sure!"

Johnny wondered, when getting this serious talking to, why, if this was so, with laws saying so, that Bim never once issued a ticket to pretty ladies going astray of the dog leash law.

"And they all better have tags, tee hee," Bim would say. "The law says so. I don't make 'em. Just enforce 'em."

But Bim liked Rags. He was friendly and came when called while all the renegade dogs flew the coop.

So Rags allowed the dog officer to do his job according to law. It kept Bim busy as well as keeping Bim and Rags off the streets.

Every two years or so, a little pressure was put on Bim to bring in a number of dogs by the department head, old Chief Peter Martin, who

—

wore two pearl handled pistols on his hips in honor of General George Patton. A tough assignment when all the dogs in town, other than Rags, had no intention of being taken alive.

Need was the mother of invention for Bim when the chief said, "Time to round 'em up."

The bighearted, big-toothed dog officer merely cruised around town in his dog control wagon until he found a female in heat.

The captured bitch was tied in the back of the truck, the vehicle parked in a doggie neighborhood, and the rear door left open.

When the males got their whiff, all Bim had to do was stand by and direct traffic.

When the van was full, Officer Bim Boles headed back to the station and asked the chief what to do with the animals.

The chief knew there was no lockup for the dogs. He knew Bim knew it. And that he would have to tell Bim to release them in Woburn and let them work their way home.

But before the chief would let his dog officer off the hook so easily, he would always ask the same question, "How come there's no females in the group?"

"Had one. A real cutie. Some kind of poodle. You know how those French girls are. After. She. Had to let her go. She had a license. And a pretty momma." A strutter.

"Take 'em to Woburn. They'll find their way back to where they belong. Don't you go telling no one. Especially anyone from Woburn."

Delivering papers on this day that featured his, Jazz, and Romola's pictures on the front page was sad to the point of tears on his face which froze as he pedaled into the wind.

His sadness for himself was to change at the Bole's home. The blue star hanging in the window proudly proclaimed that dog officer Bim Boles brother, the second son of Elizabeth Boles, was serving his country. Tim's father, in a strange twist of fate, had died at Tim's birth, a heart attack.

Mrs. Boles had told Johnny earlier that her other son Terrence, that is Sgt. Terrence Boles, was a member of the U.S. Army fighting somewhere in the Pacific. She had told Johnny that Terrence had told her he was on some sort of paradise island, with palm trees and all, called Tinny-An. Now ain't that some funny name for an island, Tinny-An?

She had received word the day before that her son was not coming home, and she had replaced the blue star in the window with a gold star.

It didn't seem right to Johnny that a man could be killed while on some sort of paradise island, an island named Tinny-an.

—

Bim, who had studiously avoided the draft, later signed up after the young new chief, a 4F gung ho, ordered him to "put the law-breaking bastards out of their misery. Shoot 'em, drown 'em. Leave no survivors. Bring me back some dog ears for proof."

Bim never swore. Until this day. "Up your giggy with a meat hook."

"I'm the goddamned chief of this goddamned department and—"

"Then up your giggy with a meat hook, Chief!"

He turned in his badge, handgun, and quit.

People from Rockledge said Bim had joined up to avenge his brother's death. Had bribed a draft board member to overlook his flat feet.

It wasn't so. He joined because he wouldn't kill dogs for some gung ho police chief.

Tinian was a thing of the past for Bim, but there were other islands in the Pacific. Although some Japanese bullets had whipped through his pant legs and whistled past his ears, he never regretted telling that young shitbird in power that he would not kill a dog that didn't know no sin worse than tail wagging while pissing on a government-owned fire hydrant.

Many a scalding hot night he sat alone in his foxhole, bugs in his eyes and ears, sorry sores on his feet, terrified of the little yellow men less than a grenade's throw away. Little men with buckteeth like his own who looked for his wounded buddies out there in no-man's-land, making them scream out as the knife was put slowly into their stomachs and twisted. He saved his sanity by thinking about when he returned, a hero, he would run for selectman and fire that rat's ass 4F chief.

And Bim thought of Rags, his favorite, the friendliest, easiest to catch dog in town, that little white spitz mongrel with the dark liquid eyes that appeared to smile at him as he came to him.

As long as he thought of dogs wagging their tails, he would put off crawling out into the black no-man's-land where wounded screamed.

On this morning, as Johnny delivered the papers with his picture on the front page, he still found it in him to stare at the gold star that appeared on this day. He wondered if a man could die by someone just changing the color of a star on a white background, with a red and blue border around it. A short while later, Terrence's gold star had a blue one beside it—Bim's.

The paperboy with the aching teeth looked up at the last star of the night as the streetlights along Washington Street started blinking out one by one.

He remembered Bim's big-toothed smile, that of a modern-day Huck Finn. He remembered that when Jazz walked to the dog van to check if

Rags was bumming a ride home again, Bim would shoo him away. "I ain't your daddy, boy. Don't you go smiling that smile around me with those teeth. Tee hee." He loved a good joke. Time after time.

Then he'd laugh out loud. And Johnny and Jazz would laugh, not sure exactly why. Other than the fact Bim had laughed.

Now good guy Bim was out there some place, and Johnny knew he had to sign up. End this thing once and for all.

I gotta get there . . .

The gold star in the window got Johnny to thinking of Bim rather than Terrence. The dogs always knew Bim . . . was just doing his job . . . Some enjoyed the ride . . . it was like a get-together . . . every two months . . . or so . . .

Johnny had heard Bim telling anyone who would listen to his windies. "Don't worry none. Your dogs will be back from Woburn before night fall. Now don't go telling anyone from Woburn them are Rockledge dogs bumming home to here."

When some sweet little old lady asked him if he didn't feel cruel, catching and confining the dogs, he said, "No. Fact is they always loved smelling each other's assholes. Always. It must have been great. Life so simple that smelling each other's assholes was a big thing."

As fate would have it, after staying out of no-man's-land for some time, by thinking of those friendly dogs, no-man's-land came to him.

Bim saw the little man come through the mist. The Japanese soldier didn't see Bim at first.

"Hey, little buddy," Bim called out.

The soldier turned. "Why, you're not much bigger than a collie dog. Come on over to old Bim."

The Japanese soldier looked at Bim's big-toothed smile.

"Why I expect you're so friendly that your tail is goin' to start waggin' in a moment."

The Japanese soldier fired into his chest, knocking him backward. Bim took on a look of surprise. "Hell of a way for man's best friend to act."

He watched as the steam came out of the hole in his chest.

The Japanese soldier, a mere kid, came to his side. Rather than inserting and twisting a knife in the American's stomach, he wiped his forehead. Gave Bim a drink from his canteen. Took out a picture of an older woman and a young girl, his mother and sister.

Bim looked at the enemy. "That's mighty nice of you, little buddy. You and I didn't start this crap. I'm only here because I didn't want to put no dogs to sleep and collect their ears for some gung ho small-town police chief."

The Japanese soldier gave him a sad smile. Bim saw the giant buckteeth of the child warrior, and then Bim was dead. There was a second gold star in his mother's window.

There was only one gold star the day Johnny delivered the morning newspaper outlining his family history on page one, announcing that John, Romola, and James in Pennsylvania, where their dad worked in the Sun Shipyard, were dead.

Now Johnny wished that he, Romola, and Jazz in Rockledge, whose dad worked in the Chester, Pennsylvania, Sun Shipyard, were dead.

Somehow he knew, just knew, that the keeper of Rockledge's dog population would also die. *They've got to . . . take me . . .*

He looked at the pictures of his brother and sister and him as he set his final paper of the route on the doorsteps of the church that his grandfather Shiverick had painted as his gift to God for Johnny.

The good reverend was there before dawn every morning to greet the day with prayer.

This day he would have added prayers, but what to pray for?

Perhaps that no Boston paper would be delivered in Rockledge that day.

That the boy who delivered the paper wasn't the same boy on its front page.

The reverend wished he subscribed only to the *Christian Science Monitor*, that everyone in Rockledge subscribed only to the *Christian Science Monitor*.

Johnny watched as the Reverend Newhall read the front page of the *Boston Post*, dropped his hand to his side, slowly released his grip on the paper. He dropped his chin to his chest then looked skyward.

Johnny followed his glance. Here was one last star fighting the morning light, attempting to stay alive but died, to be reincarnated another day.

The star in the sky was gold, like the one that hung in the Boles window.

Poor Terrence.

Poor Bim.

Poor Rags would be sad.

Later that day.

"You and your brother and sister don't have to go to school today, Johnny," their mother said, "if you don't want to."

Jazz and Romola looked relieved, despite hanging their heads on their chest, like lovely flowers that had suddenly wilted.

"Yes, we do. We're going, "Johnny said.

"I knew," his mother said.

Romola and Jazz drew close to their brother and in unison said, "Yes. We are going."

Johnny wished both of them attended his school.

"If anyone says anything, just get me their names. I'll glue those assholes' assholes together with hot tar."

"Don't swear," his mother said.

"What about saying I'll fix the sons of bitches!"

"All right. You can curse, just this once. We'll all ask God to close his ears at the same time."

"Thanks, Ma."

CHAPTER 16

NUMBER NINE

"What are you talking about?" the equipment manager yelled into Johnny's face. "Football guards wear numbers in the sixties, tackles in the seventies, ends in the eighties. Quarterbacks wear single digit numbers."

"I want number nine."

"Yah, and I wanna shit ice cream," yelled Mo Hanley, the student manager, "and not just chocolate!"

Hanley, who towered over Johnny and in fact was bigger than all of the players on the team, gave Johnny a push with the words, "Shove off."

"I want nine."

"Listen, midget, shuffle on to Buffalo."

"I want number nine."

"Are you crusin' for a bruisin'?"

"See this finger? See this thumb? See this fist? You'd better run!" Johnny said, hoping Hanley would think he was funny or even better, think him crazy and give him number nine and leave him alone.

"Yah. I see your fist, DaSilva. It's got hair in the palm. Didn't your mother ever tell you about playing with yourself? You grow hair in the middle of your palm. You're a jerk off. A sick jerk. Like your father, the fucker. The baby killer."

Johnny, smiling upward at the giant, his eyes hidden from the manager by his eyebrows, reached upward and sunk his four fingers into the bottom part of the collar bone of his huge antagonist. He then anchored his hand with his thumb on the top of the collarbone and started with all the strength of someone who had milked goats and cows all summer to squeeze.

The pain caused the manager to slowly buckle to his knees. "You can have nine. You can have sixty-nine. Just stop the pain, no brain! I'm telling the coach."

Johnny released his grip.

The manager got to his feet and powered his knee upward, sinking it deep into Johnny's groin with the force of a steam engine piston, causing Johnny's eyes to glaze over.

Looking at the giant through opaque eyes, Johnny wondered why a person with so much size and power would be the manager rather than a fullback cheered by guys and girls alike.

"Why?"

Hanley had told all the players, "I'm not on the team because I'm too big for hick time ball. I'll play in college or start right out in the pros. I'd kill someone if I played at this pink dink level. Shrimps like you hickory dickery dorks are lucky that giants like me are gentle and not bullies."

It was sort of an interesting statement as Hanley had given Indian burns to the smaller players—the high-speed rubbing in one area by the butt of the hand until it felt like fire.

All this from this self-proclaimed nonbully.

Sometimes Hanley just used brute force, like the knee to the nuts he had just invested in Johnny's groin.

Johnny nearly went to his knees from the force of the blow, stopping short inches from the cement floor of the trainer's room.

He wanted to crumble to the ground so he could bring his knees to his chest to relieve the pain that exploded deep in his groin and short-circuited his brain, leaving him feeling like a hot wire was shoved in his ear. As the pain subsided, his stomach felt like he had swallowed goat puke.

"Kneel schea-meel. Kiss my ring. My thing," Hanley dictated.

"Up ya bucket. I kneel for no one and certainly not for a piece of second-hand shit."

"You're no good, DaSilva, just like your father and your skinny sister and bucktoothed brother. You're all piss ants." He tossed Johnny number sixty-three. "And the next time you give me lip, I'll break every finger on your hair-filled palm. Yah, come to think of it, I heard you're religious. Every day is Palm Sunday to you, jerk off."

The manager went into the trainer's room, rubbing his collarbone, muttering, "You're no fuckin' good. You're like the chrome on a lousy Ford, bad from the chromosomes up."

—

Johnny watched the broad back of his tormentor block out the doorway of the trainer's room and wondered. *Why . . . if Hanley's the biggest . . . and strongest . . . doesn't he come out . . . for the team? He could do some . . . bullying . . . the rules allow . . .*

Then suddenly Johnny knew the answer. *Coward . . .* "Hey, Hanley, you ape, I'm going to tear your ear off with my bare hands!"

Hanley ran to the door and slammed it. Johnny had discovered his weakness, his Achilles' heel. It was yellow. Hanley was a bully. Bullies cannot afford to ever lose in front of others; if they do they will never be able to bully again.

Hanley's voice came through the door, "I can't beat up no little pissers without getting in trouble. So take off."

With the door shut and the giant team manger out of sight, Johnny sank to his knees, rolled on his side, and pulled his knees to his chest. He still couldn't breathe and wondered how in hell he had got the breath out to call Hanley an ape, *God . . . it hurts . . . but I feel like apologizing . . . to every ape . . . in the world . . .*

Johnny heard the trainer's door open. A jersey was tossed out, number nine, and the door was closed.

As his hand closed around the jersey, Johnny felt an arm slide under his shoulder and help him up.

It was Righty. "What happened to you? You look like the little bear that ate the porridge that the big bear crapped a caca in."

"Get your hands off me. I don't need anyone."

"Sure. Sure sport. Relax. Pretend I'm not anyone. Pretend I'm the Shadow, and no one can see me helping you. What's with the number nine? That's for quarterbacks. Make Hanley give you something in the sixties."

"How come you're here to help me? Didn't you read the paper this morning?" Johnny asked.

"I read the paper. About your dad. Perhaps they will let him go into the army instead of jail," Righty said.

"So why are you sticking around me?"

"I was brung up on the farm and learned to like donkeys and other asslike creatures. Forget about your dad maybe having a choice of going into the army or jail. Let's get to the important stuff. What's with number nine?"

"You horse's petoochee. Ted Williams, Mr. Number Nine on the Red Sox, is now flying in the marines. They had a story on him, Mr. Red Sox, Ted Williams. His guts are even greater, even his hitting. One time he spit at the fans who booed him as he rounded the bases and then gave the finger to the press box fairies who used crummy words in their news crap about him. They followed his mother to San Diego, saying she begged money for the Salvation Army. My ma said that only the Salvation Army and the Shriners do any good for poor people."

"Oh yah, what about the pope? What about the Knights of Columbus, the Knights of Malta?"

"Ted is probably a secret Shriner."

"That's a reason to wear number nine?"

"It keeps the number out front of people."

"If you want to make a statement," Righty said, "make one like Bobby Doerr and wear number two. You see what he did. The Yankees' Joe Page dusted him off after Rudy York hit a home run just before him. It was close to Doerr's head."

"So?"

"Doerr didn't even blink and then followed up by laying down a bunt along the first baseline."

"So?"

"Sew buttons on your fly."

"I got pants with a zipper now."

"Sew zippers on your fly. Doerr lays a bunt a little way down the first baseline. A perfect one. A sure base hit. But Doerr stays in the batter's box. Waiting for Mr. Bean Ball Joe Page to field the ball. Page won't go near it. He knows when you get a quiet man mad, stand by. Doerr takes one look at Page who ain't movin' off the pitcher's mound. No, sir-ree. Then Doerr walks to first base. No one fields the ball until he gets there. Wear number two."

"Nah. I want to give the finger to the press, and then I'll kick the moo poo out of Joe Page. I want to give the finger to the press, to the crowd, to the world. Like Ted. I want nine."

"Well, why not settle to wear nine on your T-shirt under your football jersey."

"Yah! I'll do that too."

"And I'll draw a couple general's stars on your T-shirt shoulders," Righty said.

"You can't draw."

"Watdaya mean? I'm the best in the class."

"Let me see your hand."

"I'm not holding hands with you. I'm still pissed at you. Letting Hanley stuff you like an artichoke. Not hitting him with a chair. I'm pissed off."

"It's better to be pissed off than pissed on. Let me see your hand."

Righty held out his hand.

—

Johnny took it in his, opened Righty's palm, and looked at it. "Just as I thought. Hair. You jerk off."

Righty punched Johnny's shoulder. "Only on Sundays. What day's today?"

"Tuesday."

"And on Tuesday too. But mostly on Sundays."

Johnny smiled, punched Righty's shoulder, and said, "And then only during mass."

"Race you to the Spa," Righty said. "I've got fourteen cents. We both can get musties."

"Last one there is Hanley's dick." Johnny could only make that kind of bet knowing he was much faster than Righty, who, by his own admission, was slower than molasses sliding uphill.

"Hanley's dick probably looks like a one-eyed earthworm that worries."

"It's probably cross-eyed," Johnny said.

"He probably has a string attached to it so he can find it."

"I wonder if Hanley got that string I sent him."

"What string?" Righty asked, playing straight man.

"That string of farts."

They laughed. Cupped their hands under their armpits, brought their arm down with a squeezing motion that made the finest fart sounds in their class, perhaps the world.

As high school seniors they didn't have to run to make time to the Spa. They would flap their arms and fly for a mustie, a scoop of ice cream shot up with seltzer water. A short while later, they sat in the Spa, drinking and singing to their musties, "Heaven, I'm in heaven." Then they stared at each other and crossed their eyes.

The cheerleaders sat in a nearby booth with the cocaptains of the football team, the six-foot-three-inch quarterback and the two-hundred-and-thirty-eight-pound right tackle.

The Quarterback smiled at them and then nodded directing his friends' attention at Johnny and Righty. "Catch those two clowns."

The ladies thought Johnny was cute and that Righty was a hero as his brother had been killed fighting Hitler.

One cheerleader, Yelena, with the long blonde hair brushed until it shined like wheat in a windblown summer field, was the daughter of the richest man in town, Dr. Jacob Smoltz.

She had read about Johnny's father. The story had even made the *New York Times*. The Smoltz's were the only ones in town to subscribe to the

—

Times, along with the *Wall Street Journal,* the *Christian Science Monitor,* and the *Globe* for slumming.

Yelena caught Johnny's eyes for the slightest moment. *Oh, you DaSilva boy are beautiful . . . Oh . . . that jet black . . . curly hair . . . those light-green eyes . . . like a tiger . . . peering through the tall jungle grass . . . Wrong league . . . too bad . . .*

Johnny just knew she had read about his father having the choice of going in the army or to jail. She had read the original story, with Johnny's, Jazz's, and Romola's pictures. *She is thinking . . . I'm . . . no good . . .*

Yelena wondered if she should go out with him. *Just once . . . without Dad finding out . . .*

Her girlfriends said Johnny didn't date. Three of them, Sally Granville the snob, Nancy Degray the brain, and Vera Johnson the class president wanted Yelena to join them in forming a club to see which one could "cop Johnny's cherry."

Yelena declined.

The three ax ladies who planned to chop down Johnny's cherry tree called themselves "The Unholy Trinity Crotch Club."

Yelena wondered whether she could save this strange boy from being deflowered as a result of the contest. *A tender-hearted poetess . . . who could perhaps love him . . . forever . . . and ever . . . in dream world . . . not reality . . .*

If she could only get him invited to one of her friends' parties, a Halloween party. They would bob for apples and kiss underwater, like they were on a faraway island under a waterfall.

Of course Johnny, while a cherry, didn't always think like a working virgin. He couldn't possibly have told Yelena to mind her own business. He wanted to get laid, just once, and find out whether "it" was down below or in the front. Yes, if he had known that girls were competing for his body, he would have faked it, been a virgin for each one and any new members they picked up.

Rhesus had said that Johnnie was so horny that he wanted to be the male Nookie Clarkson.

Nookie was the class pump according to the guys. The word was that her cherry was pushed so far back she used it as a taillight.

It peeved Johnny off royally, really, when the guys told these stories about her.

She was quiet, the proverbial church mouse, except with eyes such a pale blue that to look into them was looking into an endless sky.

She reminded him of his sister Romola in that some seemed to like to pick on those they thought couldn't defend themselves. These gossips loved to tell stories about his sister. How skinny she was, couldn't go out in the wind, but they didn't pull that skinny crapola around Johnny. No one pulled it. Not anyone. Any size. Sure he might have the living happy horseshit kicked out of him by some, but they paid. A price higher than most were willing to pay to show off for their friends. The big guys could smack the bejesus out of Johnny, but they thought twice about making fun of her as he kept getting up and landed an occasional good one.

He would have liked to defend Bernadette; that was Nookie's real name and the one Johnny called her. He tried to speak with her. Look into the sky that was her eyes, trying to find what was behind their sadness, their beauty; but when you talked with her, she looked at the ground. Johnny wanted to tell her never to look to the ground, to kneel for anyone . . . anyone . . . He wondered what she would say if he told her never to kneel. He had discussed this with Righty and was very disappointed when his friend said, "She'd probably ask "if 'I don't kneel, how would I give my blow jobs?'"

The guys laughed when they used Nookie. She always cried when she did something for a boy. It wasn't a joyous yes cry. It was a soft crooning they said, sort of like a dying mourning dove.

Righty said, "Hey, Johnny, she only does it for friends. She doesn't have an enemy in the world."

"See you later, jerko bonzo," Johnny said and walked away.

Righty had called after him, "Hey! I'm sorry. Sometimes I fuck up trying to be funny."

"Why doesn't she ever smile?"

And here was Yelena, who always smiled, head of the cheerleaders and daughter of the great Dr. Jacob Smoltz, who treated presidents, dictators, and princes from all over the world so he could fix their eyes in Boston at the Massachusetts General Eye and Ear Hospital.

Here was his daughter smiling at him, Johnnie. Or was it a I-read-the-paper smirk he saw as he left the Spa.

He pushed through the crowd, trying to walk with his back straight, like a marine in dress blues just in case she was looking.

Instead, he walked with a slight limp. The cardboard he had stuffed in his shoes so no sharp stones would come through the openings in the soles had bent doubled when he had taken his shoes off while sitting in the Spa, and it hurt.

He walked with a shuffle, trying to keep the loose sole of his right shoe from flapping like a running dog's tongue.

He had put his chin on his chest rather than looking at her as he had walked out.

—

Seeing his chin on his chest, Yelena smiled again. *He likes me . . . Of course he does . . .* She wished she had a daisy and could prove he loved her. She'd pluck the petals off one by one. "He loves me. He loves me not. He loves me. He loves me not. He loves me, he loves me, he loves me."

The last petal would prove his love with its "He loves me." And she'd even cheat . . . revamp the petal-pulling rules . . . to make sure the petal plucking ended the way she wanted it to. She would pluck millions of the daisy petals and rosebuds . . . yes . . . rosebuds . . . and shower them softly about his bowed head. *He loves me . . . Yes . . . he loves me . . . Yes . . . yes he loves me . . .*

Seeing Yelena smiling again, Johnny was certain she was making fun of him.

He lifted his face and looked directly into her smoky gray eyes, his tiger hazel eyes narrowing, "You're no better than anyone else."

The two giant football players sitting with her started to get up with the tackle declaring, "I'll fix your ass so that you'll have to take a crap through your ears."

Yelena laid her hand on his huge arm. "It's okay. It's okay. I understand."

"No, you don't," Johnny said, closing the door behind him with finality, knowing he would never enter her world again.

She wanted to follow. He looked so much like a butterfly with an injured wing. A wing that never could be fixed. *Unless I kissed it . . . and made it better . . .*

Yelena wondered what it would be like to have your family splashed across the front pages of newspapers, the ones you had to deliver. To see your father held up to shame. To the best of her knowledge, Rockledge had never had a divorce. Or at least she had never heard of one.

She couldn't imagine her father being involved in such a scandal as Mr. DaSilva's. Holding his family up to ridicule. She couldn't imagine that. And three little children dying. *But that sweet boy . . . with the green eyes . . . snob he said . . . that was cute . . . "You're no better than me," he said . . . That's not entirely true . . . but things can change . . . with a little boost . . . from the right woman . . . What his father did with another woman . . . another family . . . states away . . . dying because of a gas stove . . . Thank God for my family . . .*

At that very moment, the good Dr. Smoltz, had his optic scope close to his favorite nurse's eye, holding it with his left hand, which was unusual, peering at her retina, which the bright light made look like a sliver of platinum.

"Nice, nice," he muttered, "a wondrous piece of God, the human body," his right hand, which moments before held his stethoscope, cupped her left breast.

"I hold you personally responsible for lefty being larger than righty, which I wanted to be the ace on my pitching staff," she said in mock concern.

She claimed a painful tightness in her chest, and he immediately put his ear to her now-bare breasts. He tried to listen to her increasing heartbeat as he titillated her with knowledge that doctors filed under medical background.

Despite the moment, he still felt a failure as he couldn't view her eyes, hold the stethoscope to her heart, and fondle her bosom. Something had to be given up. In this case, it was the stethoscope. He wished he had three hands.

Playing doctor as a kid had always been fun. But he had taken it past a little kid's dream, way past.

Meanwhile, down below, he prodded deep between her thighs with his penis working much like a tongue depressor against a set of lips that opened as did her swiftly widening pupils.

He didn't need the stethoscope as her heart pounded with the woofer wonders of a kettle drum at the Boston Pops on the Fourth July.

Nurse Fuzzy Wuzzy's "I'm coming!" was expounded with enough power to blow the swan boats off the water at the Boston Commons, finishing with a fiendish laugh. "I hope you won't bill me for clearing up my skin problems."

The good doctor exited the closet singing a Sousa march to himself, feeling patriotic, like he had done his duty. "She's a grand old bag. She's a high-flying bag!"

He grabbed a nurse, which happened to be his second shift girlfriend just coming on duty, and did a Cagney dance step or two with her. For the third time in a month, he whispered, "How can you tell the head nurse in a hospital?"

She answered with the dutiful laugh he expected, "By the fact the knees of her white stockings are dirty."

Yelena gave Johnny one last smile as he walked away from the Spa, wished that Johnny could know a real father, what a real husband could become, how successful, and that a professional like her daddy could still be generous, kind, and funny . . .

The first step in adopting Johnny would be to protect him from her friends who wanted to win their Unholy Trinity Crotch Club pin the tail on his donkey contest.

She thought, *Perhaps Dad could adopt this green-eyed boy for me . . . He could be my brother . . . and . . . we wouldn't have to do anything dirty . . . like Johnny's father did to women . . . but if Johnny is my brother . . . I can never marry him . . . just as well . . . I'll just . . . save him . . . and perhaps more . . . marriage . . .*

Later, in the front door of his house, he bounded up the stairs. Johnny wasn't thinking much of marriage and especially wasn't thinking about his sex life, although he was clutching his testicles for the second time that day. They rang with Hanley's induced Big Ben pain.

But there was to be a second clanging. He had miscounted the steps in his hallway as he flew up the stairs to his bedroom. One leg crashed down through the missing ninth step, sending his leg downward quicker than a Sir Isaac Newton law-of-gravity dropped apple. His groin came to rest on the riser of the missing tread.

He wanted to kill his father. He had had a second family far away. Three children named after Jazz and Romola, and they had died.

And he had to deliver the newspaper with the pictures of himself, Romola, and Jazz that the reporter had stolen. He was on the front page, leaving many to believe that it was him and Jazz and Romola who had died.

He pulled his leg from the stair hole and went to his knees, staying there for a very long time.

But he did get up.

CHAPTER 17

V-MAIL

That is, he wanted to kill him until he got that first V-mail from somewhere in Europe, where his father fought with the Ninety-fifth Victory Division.

His dad was a sniper of all things. *My old man . . . he played one . . . He plays knick knack . . . on his gun . . .* "Knick-knack, patty whack, give the dog a bone. My old man'll come tumbling home!"

Johnny remembered his father taking him to plink woodchucks on the farm with that old single-shot .22. Chuckholes could cause a horse to break a leg. Johnny marveled at how far his dad could hit one of the offending critters.

He remembered his father's smile after a long shot through open iron sights. "Had to use Kentucky windage mixed in with some plain old four-leaf clover guessing. Maybe I didn't hit it in the head, but there should be plenty of good meat leftover for a cookout for you and me in the hills tonight."

Tony not only got to be one of the three snipers who more often than not got to lead their unit into no-man's-land as point men; he also often got to lead the point, an honor that did not always last for any length of time. The idea of the point was to either spot the enemy or draw their fire before a company on the move committed itself.

His father's letters had large sections cut out or blacked out, censored so no secrets about the name of his outfit or its whereabouts could leak out.

Johnny understood the part where his father asked him to no longer write part of his letter in the Morse Code he was learning in

---

357

the Boy Scouts—da-dit-dit, dit, dit-da, da-dit-da; da-dit-dit, dit-da, da-dit—"Dear Dad," as Tony was asked by the company V-mail censor. "what's the code bit all about? You know you're already some sort of a spy suspect, being so old and all."

He hoped this guy was rattling his cage just for chuckles in an attempt to beat his boredom.

Tony carried the only bolt-action rifle in the company. It was the most accurate for sniping but did not carry the firepower of the M1, a semiautomatic. But like all equipment, there was a glitch—as the last shell was fired, the clip ejected with a zing that told the enemy you were temporarily empty.

Johnny wondered how many Nazis his father had killed. The fat sausage eaters had to look awful big compared to a woodchuck with only its head above the the grass and its fur matched the wild grasses to boot. He wondered whether his father put a notch on his rifle stock for everyone he killed, like a fighter pilot painting a miniature enemy flag on his plane's fuselage for each plane he shot down. *Dad would end up . . . with a matchstick . . . for a stock . . .*

His father only knew of one sure kill, although there were a couple of maybes.

The sure kill took place while his company was slogging through the outskirts of Metz. There was an old woman on the third floor, standing in the window, aiming something at his company.

The Able Company commander ordered, "Pick her off, DaSilva!"

"It looks like she only has a broom."

"Pick her off!"

Tony drew in a deep breath, letting it out slowly as he started the trigger squeeze, saw through his scope that she was wearing a dress made out of an old grain sack similar to the ones Mine wore on the farm.

He tried to change the vision of the old woman to that of a woodchuck, a chuck that dug holes in fields that broke horses' legs. And the horses had to be put down.

"Pick her off! She's getting ready to fire! Pick her off, damned you."

The CO's words exploded in his head as his rifle went off. And his scope filled with the red of her blood that invaded his eye.

She tumbled very gracefully for an old woman and fell to the ground.

The company medic Tony Kuber went to her side, felt the vein in her neck, and yelled back, "You really fucked up this time DaSilva, unless they are giving Bronze Stars for shooting old women with brooms!"

"Nice shot anyways," the company commander said. "It could have been a gun. She's only a Kraut lover one way or another."

The company moved on. No one stopped to inspect the dead woman. If they had, they would have discovered a German soldier dressed in drag, his sniper rifle nearby.

Johnny read his father's V-mails over and over, attempting to fill in the areas cut out or blacked out. He knew there would be no bragging. Doers just do . . .

He knew this from the day he asked his mother why his dad didn't show off the giant largemouth bass he had caught and stuffed and hung in the cellar.

Johnny decided he wouldn't join the marines and fight with the raiders, dress in dress blues, wear the dark-blue jacket with the gold buttons and the white belt and the light-blue trousers with the blood-red strip down the side.

Nor would he join up with the Flying Tigers, sitting back in the cockpit with the sheepskin collar of his leather jacket turned up, his white silk scarf flowing like a slipstream. The sleeve patches would show both the colors of China and the United States. His P-41 would have the tiger teeth and eyes painted on the fuselage.

No, he'd wear the dirt brown garb of the army. His shirt would have a blue patch on the sleeve with a red and white V as a background to a number nine, the Ninety-fifth Victory Division, his dad's. He would walk point with him. They would lead their company together. Taking the highest risk. They would be the only ones carrying bolt-action sniper rifles to protect each other. Share the same foxhole. And some night when he wasn't still angry with his father, he would tell him, "I forgive you . . ." *And some night . . . I will whisper on a cloud to Ma . . . "He is sorry, Ma . . . he did not mean to hurt us . . ." and she will whisper back to me . . . on a cloud, "If you can forgive him, son . . . I can . . . too . . ."*

The stock of his father's deer rifle, which he carved out of wood from an old apple tree on the farm, had so many downed whitetail buck notches it looked like something that helped fill Boot Hill.

His dad had sat beside him, proud as a peacock, when Johnny downed his first buck on Legate Hill in Charlemont with his single-shot 10-gauge cannon, the same one his father had used when he was a man-child deer hunter. Johnny was so small at the time that he had to hold onto his father's belt buckle as he was pulled along through the deep snow.

He wasn't sure when he fired whether or not he had knocked down the thirteen-point animal as the blunderbuss had knocked him over backward into the snow.

His dad had told Johnny's uncles, "Old Betsy knocked my boy piss end over tea kettle, and my boy had done the same to that old mossy back buck. A mountaintop roamer with thirteen points."

Thirteen was Johnny's chosen lucky number after that.

Tony had placed his arm around his son to steady his shuddering shoulders that day and told him, "I've never shot an animal large or small that I didn't feel a little like crying about. There is no shame in being able to put food on your family table. The wild animals, like your ridge runner here, have a chance to survive. Not like the cow or pig sitting in the meat counter down at the A and P. And wild animals don't walk around worrying about dying like most humans do. They live the day. The hunter takes his game fast. Otherwise, they die of old age, some other wild animal eating it while it is still alive. Or it starves slowly to death. Or gets sick and drags itself around, trying to escape what it doesn't understand. Look around. Nature is beautiful. But when a wild animal finishes enjoying it, Mother Nature is as cruel as any sadist out there. Yet its killing is done without any animosity."

His father had never talked at length with him. Most of their conversation was done with their eyes.

Tony sat quietly watching Johnny carve his first notch on the old shotgun stock as the sun set behind the hills, and dark approached swiftly. It was nearing five. It would be a long drag of such a huge animal in the dark, but his father did not rush him.

Johnny carved the notch beside the ones his dad had carved as a boy, marks now worn smooth.

"He's seen it all son. From the bright, breezy mountaintops to the dank, dark of the swamps below. He drank that clear bubbly water on the brooks in between. The same ones we got down on all fours to drink from. We drank with the wild ones.

"And he was a traveling salesman in the fall, during the rut, when he wandered high, wide, and handsome from mountaintop to mountaintop. And by the looks of him, he had some fights.

Just as well you got him. His muzzle's gray. His ribs are showing some. Got some scars probably from young bucks that got booted about when he was in his prime, and those same young ones are now in their prime, and he paid his final dues this fall. Each deer is born just once. Each deer only gets to die once. But we best be hauling butt. Just remember this old timer we're dragging out of here would rather go out like this, a warrior on his shield, than watching a bunch of coyotes having lunch out of his bread basket."

"You should of been a poet rather than fixing up cars."

—

360

"Your old dad is part poet, his feet are Longfellows."

Years later, when friend or foe called Johnny a poet because his feet were Longfellows, he thought of that mountain.

Now his dad was a soldier. Ninety-fifth Victory Division. A sniper. And Johnny, by hook or by crook, was going to join him. He could shoot. Could always shoot. He would bring the head of that thirteen-point buck to the recruiter's office. Tell them his dad was a sniper. The army would have to take him. Otherwise, President Franklin Delano Roosevelt would kick his ass so hard it would lasso his neck.

"Someone better take me!" *I'm getting pissed off . . . Hey . . . better getting pissed off . . . than getting pissed on . . .*

Even the Flying Tigers said he was too young despite the fact he had eaten enough Chinese food to suffer the Shanghai shits. Thinking of the oriental food, he sang, "They tried to sell me egg foo young, eggs foo young that wasn't egg foo young. They tried to tell us we ate egg foo young."

Later in life, Johnny believed the song "They tried to tell us we're too young" was derived from the old egg foo young song.

After singing the same words a number of times, he swung into the only other Chinese song he knew. "I, I, yie I, in China they do it for chili. Oh this is the first verse, it's worse than the last verse, so waltz me around again, Willy."

Even being bawdy didn't cheer him up.

The army recruiter had told him, "Forget it. You're too young. Best you better beat it out of here." He saw Johnny looking at the ribbons on his chest, his eyes stopping on the blue bar with a silver rifle on it.

"That's the Combat Infantry Badge, son. That's as high as a man can earn. I hope you never have to earn one."

"I want to earn one!"

"Move out, boy, or you'll earn one without your butt plate attached to your body."

Johnny returned to the army recruiter the next day. "My dad taught me to shoot the heads off swimming snakes, and my ma taught me all about bayonets with her broom."

"Sorry, son, but get your banty ass out of here."

"I can kick your sorry ass!"

"You probably could. But I'd call a cop, and he'd take all your lollypops away from you."

The navy recruiter had told him, "Go soak your feet in a bucket of salt water for a couple of years."

Just as well, the navy wouldn't take him. Hadn't Fat Burns's brother Tubber, home from navy boot camp, told the admiring kids that surrounded him to "join the army because sure as hell made little red devils you could piss yourself a dozen times before you could get those thirteen original states buttons undone. And not only that, that many buttons can ruin your love life. Before you get to the eleventh button, your girl has done a jarhead, two doggies, three flyboys, climbed a pear tree, and bit a partridge on the tail."

The marine corps recruiter told him, "Go soak your head in a bucket of shit."

Johnny had swung at him, but the guy with the hair a half inch long stuck a ham hock of a hand on his head and laughed. "Hey, take it easy. Maybe we can use you on the rifle range. If we run out of targets."

Johnny swung again, moving nothing but air around, and the recruiting seargent said, "Hey, take it easy, angel dog. You've got a few years to go before you can growl, snap, and bite. But when you stop nursing, I think we can use you. Here."

The recruiter removed a black eagle, anchor, and ball pin from his shirt collar and handed it to Johnny.

The young boy saluted.

The recruiting seargent turned away to keep from laughing, then turned back and saluted Johnny.

"Thank you. I'll earn this the hard way someday."

"I hope not, son."

Johnny walked home from Boston through Somerville, with a side trip to Dillboy Field, where he used to hop the fence to watch ball games. Cabbies would drive their hacks up on the sidewalk and let the kids climb up on the roofs and scale the high cement walls. Then it was through Medford and the Fellsway. With luck, a Yellow Peril would slow down to a walk when it wound around a sharp corner in the woods, allowing him to jump aboard the electric trolley.

If he couldn't hitch a ride, he'd make a side trip from Medford down into Melrose and sip the ice-cold well water of Crystal Springs. If dark fell early and he walked late, a bare-ass swim in Spot Pond, the region's standby water supply, wasn't out of the question.

The water was the best in the world.

Johnny always sipped the spring's water slowly, eyes closed, thinking, *A man could make a mint . . . selling this water . . . Nah . . . no one would ever pay for water. It's . . . free . . .*

His father, in his last V-mail, said he had visited Johnny's Uncle Manny in a Paris army hospital, where he was being treated for his fourth wound, the second to his unlucky left shoulder. Manny had asked for Johnny. Manny told his older brother, "Yah, they'll be sending me to the front again. Can you believe it? Why couldn't I have a million dollar wound, a couple of marching toes shot off, instead of all these two-bit ones? Maybe a stray bullet could take off my trigger finger. It wouldn't even affect my ass scratching. The first thing you ever told me was never to scratch your butt with the hand you eat with. I've been doing this fucken crap for four years. Four fucken years! And then if I lost a couple toes or my trigger finger, the fuckers would probably court-marshal me for self-inflicted wounds. Yah, I was only practicing the first four times, twice to the shoulder, once to the ribs, once to the thigh. Like I needed all that practice to shoot off a toe or finger."

The brothers had hugged, pounded each other's backs, two suddenly very old infantry men who, as kids, had fished and hunted together, with younger brother Franchesco tagging along. They had told traveling salesmen jokes about farm girls, wished they were back home with those guys who couldn't pass the physical, the 4F guys. Find 'em, feel 'em, fuck 'em, and forget 'em."

"Why couldn't we be as lucky as One Ball McKnight," Manny said.

"Franchesco always said that One Ball's testicle was in his eye socket, and that's why he had an eye for the girls. McKnight always told the girls, 'I'll keep an eye out for you.' Manny, was he a pig. A real oinker. He was a pig."

"That's what I loved about him."

They laughed until the tears streamed down their faces like a pair of Spanish onions were making whoopee in their eyes sockets.

Tony had to get back to his outfit and started out of the hospital room without saying goodbye, then backtracked until he was hugging his brother, and both at the same time said, "Keep your ass down," words that transposed, "Love you, brother boy."

They had never mentioned once that Franchesco was killed in Sicily by a stray America artillery round that did not even leave his dog tags. Keeping his ass down wouldn't have helped dodge the round as its gun crew didn't realize the Nazi army had left for the Italian mainland a day before.

Tony had to move carefully back to his outfit. His gunny could have gotten his ass in a sling by allowing him to sneak away from his company to visit Manny.

He chuckled as he ran through the Parisian streets, Manny's words still ringing in his ears, "Get one for me. And not a Kraut, dummy. Get one of those fancy Madame-O-Sells foo-foo girls."

—

"I'm married, brother. But I'll get one for you."
"Get one that's got a perfumed pussy."
"Okay."
"Get two. They're small."

CHAPTER 18

AN OLD POINT MAN

"Oh, my baby," Charity DaSilva cried to Johnny as he came through the door after football practice. "Oh, my baby."

She was holding a telegram in her hand.

Johnny looked at the blue star on the white background with the red border around it, hanging in the front window that he had hung there when his father went into the army. He knew his mother couldn't bring herself to do it.

"Oh, baby, you're the real man in the family now, forever."

Johnny hugged his mother for only the second time in his lifetime and went to the window. They would have to put up a gold star. He would not cry. He took down the blue star banner.

He just knew his father and his Able Company had fought bravely killing Nazis, perhaps one hundred for every one of the fighting Ninety-fifth who fell. He could visualize the men of Able, led by his father, Pvt. Tony DaSilva and Gen. George Patton.

His vision was clear: his dad charging into machine gun fire, his father climbing on a German tank, dropping a grenade through a machine gun slot. He looked at the blue star. He wouldn't cry now, maybe later in his bedroom. When Jazz or Romola weren't around and out of sight of his mother.

"I'll hang the gold star, Ma."

"No, no. Your father isn't dead. He's wounded. He's in a hospital in England some place. He was hit in the ankle and the shoulder . . . and the head."

After leaving Manny in the hospital, Tony had moved out with the Ninety-fifth steadily, always heading into the fire, like pieces of coal being used to stoke an inferno and with many of the men used as fuel turning into ashes.

The young men in his company, eighteen years old, twenty years old, just out of high school and college; twenty-five-year-olds who, a few short months ago, were working as ditch diggers and mechanics and salesmen, were now squad and even platoon leaders.

One dogface in Able had worked in the Sun Shipyard in Chester, Pennsylvania, a man who had believed he had the best of two worlds, until both worlds caved in on him and crushed him until he couldn't breathe—Johnny's dad.

The men of the Ninety-fifth had moved steadily toward the German border. Each day someone claimed he could smell sauerkraut cooking or bratwurst baking. "We'll be drinking that German bock beer before you know it!" "If I ever get to Berlin, give me a girl in my arms tonight."

They all advanced through mud and snow, many were buried under it. Some never were found.

Arthritis was settling into Tony's fingers, but for some odd reason, the trigger finger remained strangely free of the crippling pain. If only that finger would not twist, become deformed like the others were doing. His fingers had always looked bad. They at times looked like the very potatoes he dug by hand. His fingers became the very shape of the potatoes. If only that finger listened to the entire message before doing its deed . . . take a deep breath . . . slowly let it out . . . and then when it was halfway out . . . squeeze slowly . . .

If that finger would twist in agony like its brothers, maybe he would be sent back to battalion to cook or even fix jeeps. He'd soup one up, real royally, a jeep that would be a going concern for the officer that picked him as his chauffeur. A jeep full of poop and soup, just like the stock car he, Manny, and Franchesko had worked on. The only poor man's car that won a circuit race in a sport dominated by those cars with big bucks sponsors.

When they got home, they would soup a car that would shoot the moon, make them rich. Actually, Franchesko would only be with them in spirit, but that was okay. They would call it the Spirit of Franchesko, and it would get them off the farm.

Winning would be their revenge against these very stock cars that kept them poor. Kept them on the farm. There was no question; their cars were hot. Hot, hot, hot. Very hot. Winners, if they could have only afforded those expensive parts that were constantly blowing. They had needed a lot, especially the best tires.

The good thing about the finger was that it gave him something to look at as his outfit traveled through the battered towns where destroyed buildings looked like mouthfuls of broken and decayed teeth. They would have traveled through a great smoking maw, a maw that had eaten flesh for breakfast, lunch, and dinner, couldn't get enough.

The young tasted the most tender.

And now the remnants of many men from both sides were decaying in the gray teeth, belching forth a stench that could make you forget the maggots crawling in and out of what had once been the noses and mouths and eyes of living humans.

Tony remembered the eye sockets of a German youth, too young to fight other than in a schoolyard yet outfitted in full battle gear. The sockets that once held pale-blue eyes now housed balls of maggots as the long blond hair of the youth moved ever so slightly in the breeze.

How much longer must he look.

Tony's trigger finger would last as long as you could squeeze it. It was a betrayer. If it joined the others by becoming deformed, he would be taken from the front and away from hell.

He knew of men who had purposely blown off their trigger finger or shot off a toe and got to go home. But could you look at your buddies you left there? Could you look at your family and friends once home? And if you could look at them without avoiding their eyes, could you look at yourself?

But you'd be home. Home!

Tony's head throbbed as if someone, when he least expected it, drove twenty-penny spikes heated until molten into his temples.

Ah, but that finger, it could scoop the honey out of the jar that had been clutched in the hand of a dead school child he had trudged past only minutes before. Honey. He hadn't had honey since he raided the off-limits hives on the farm. That finger could still scoop those little sausages out of those little ration cans. They could dip into that wonderful fatty oil they sucked, like a baby sucking its mother's tit.

Tony thought of the calves on the farm, drinking the warm milk off their mothers, its whiteness running down the sides of their mouths. How many babies had Mine wet-nursed? He had watched them, gurgling, smiling, and burping. He tried to remember when she nursed him. He couldn't. He tried and tried but couldn't. So he looked at that finger. It was straight. "Goddamn it all to hell." I wish I could marry my beautiful finger, and we could head out tomorrow . . . no, today, for a honeymoon . . . to Niagara falls . . .

"You say somethin', DaSilva?"

"Nah, Sarge."

When he moved his neck, it sounded like stiff cellophane being crinkled. The snap, pop, and crackle sent short-circuit sparks of white hot pain via messages directly to his eyes. Everything hurt, including body parts that did not even exist.

But not that fucken finger. It could do anything. Always felt good. He could pick his nose with it. Never did. His entire body could be filthy with mud and lice, but he always took great pains to keep that trigger finger clean. It was for dipping into sausage cans or closing the eyes of a young trooper who had bought the farm before ever having a chance to live on one.

His trigger finger was as clean as his rifle. The socks rotted on his feet, his T-shirt was fetid, the seat of his pants smelled liked a Paris whorehouse on fire in the middle of July.

The pains that shot up his back were as if he was being struck with bolts of lightning finally exploding in his head. It wouldn't have been quite so bad if the pains arriving in his head weren't accompanied by the bang and crash of giant cymbals.

Of course there was a bright side to having such an all-American boy finger, a friendly finger with which he could actually scratch his head or the bottom of his feet. Oh, that ability to scratch was a pleasure he hoped he'd never loose. Anyone who has ever tried to scratch with a crooked, twisted arthritic finger knows it gives little to no pleasure.

But a real Jack Armstrong finger, one that could not only scratch your ass through those wool army pants and create that little bit of friction back there before finally finding the bull's-eyes, the actual asshole, and paying it homage. My god, it was almost as good as getting laid. In fact, it was better than getting laid, especially when you couldn't get laid.

The hips hurt, but it was a different hurt, not the sharp pain of a needle thrust under a fingernail or into an eyeball. It was deep and nagging, like a wife gone sour. The hip hurt wasn't a fierce pit bull tearing open your stomach. It was like someone's feisty little terrier, just clamping onto your intestines, intestines that just happened to be dragging in the filth at that particular time. A weak-mouthed terrier, not breaking the casings that contained the guts and crap. A terrier just applying enough pressure to block the intestines, damming up the shit and stink from passing. This message was slowly getting back to the brain. It was a constant reminder that indeed some place down inside, starting in the hips, real discomfort wanted to get much more mean.

Ah, if that finger, that funny finger, could talk, Tony could talk back to it.

Moses Long, the only black in Able Company, had been a cook back at battalion but, by being stubborn had worked his way to the front and now was Tony's fellow sniper and point man. He told him, "Mr. DaSilva, seems like you've been talking to that finger more and more."

Moses's use of the word "mister," as in "Mr. DaSilva," was two pronged.

Actually it was one prong and one compliment. This Moses, raised in the Bronx rather than the bulrushes, used the term "mister" like a deep South boy used the word "boy," and you knew what he meant—up yours, chitling child.

The compliment was due to the fact that DaSilva was much older than not only the company commander, but also the battalion commander as well. He kept up and asked no favor and was just about Moses's daddy's age. He didn't actually know that age, as he never knew his father. That's why sometimes when he called you mister, you could be in deep doo-doo.

Moses told Tony, "Mr. DaSilva, your talking to that finger ain't gonna get you no section eight and a trip home. You'd be better off letting me cut it off the next time a Big Betty gets lobbed into the company and spits its quicksilver through the air, zingin' and singin'. And I bet if I take a piece of your ear as well, they won't suspect no honky-tonk shit."

Tony had asked, "Why don't you let me take a piece of your finger and ear so you can go home?"

"Nothin' doin', Mr. DaSilva, I'm getting me some Nazis and some medals, so when I get home, I'm going to get some hero black and some hero white pussy. All the time I'll be eating free at one of those Jewish delis where the owners want to say thanks to me for kicking ass. I want a hero sandwich named after me. Give me a Hero Moses. Hero Moses would be loaded with layers of greasy chicken and soaked in more oil than a U-Boat that sucked up a depth charge. Then after I get me fat and sassy, I'm gonna head down to crackerville and call one of those lily skins. Hey, Mr. Boy, where you keep those nifty, shifty Georgia peaches?"

"Hey! Long! DaSilva! O'Mally get your tails over here."

It was the company commander.

"Here's the poop. The shit's gonna hit the fan. The Krauts aren't really overjoyed that the Ninety-fifth is going to knock on their door and go on in this afternoon. The men of Able Company are going to remember this day. Metz opens the door to Berlin. And you three are going to be the first through it. You're taking battalion point."

The three snipers all wished the CO would cut the shit. The big black man from the Bronx had really been kidding about wanting a hero sandwich named after him. The little red-haired Irish kid from Chicago wanted to be tough, but the freckles across his nose and cheeks kept getting in the way, and he actually wanted to talk a good battle, not fight it. The old farm boy from Chelmsford, Massachusetts, was almost too old to care, ready to die, but not wanting to.

Pep talks were no longer in vogue. "Let Ike, Chucky deGaulle, and Patton go first" was the thought of the day.

Tony thought about Chelmsford. And the farm, forgetting the crap words others tried to feed him. *Hey, DaSilva . . . no one in the fucking world . . . ever came from Chelmsford, Massachusetts . . . There ain't no such place . . . Everyone from bean state is from . . . baaars ton . . . but you're not from baaars ton . . . you don't paaark da kaar . . . or drink tonic . . . Do you guys really drink that stuff you're supposed to put in your hair . . . rather than soda?*

"Pay attention, DaSilva. Here's what. You guys are walking point for Able. Able is point for battalion. Battalion point for division. Division for the army. We're first! First!" the company commander said, wishing he had a pair of pearl handle pistols on his side. Of course he wasn't part of the three-man point.

Tony thought, *A pep talk? Please . . . cut the unholy shit . . .*

The CO continued, "When you draw that first fire in that valley between those two hills, just hit the ground, hug it. Stick your heads up your asses so they won't get blown off. And their snoring will let us know they're there. We move in. Clean 'em out. And you guys can come out of hibernation. Move it!"

"I'll take lead," Tony said.

"Cut the shit, old man," the little redhead said. "I'm gonna be the first into Germany."

"Forget it, you little piss cutter," Long said, grabbing him by the backpack and pulling him back. "You lead once we get you out of diapers. Mr. DaSilva can go first. He's nice and slow. And that's the way to go."

"Stow the crap and move out!" the company commander yelled up, pushing his helmet back on his head. "The Krauts will die of old age before we get to them."

The three men moved through the company in silence, none of the mud soldiers looking up from the butts or rations or letters. Fearing to look up as it could mean they would be picked as a replacement. They thought, *The poor bastards . . .*

The more honest ones thought, *Better them . . . the poor bastards . . .*

—

"At least they cheer the poor bastards heading from death's row to the chair," a seventeen-year-old buck-ass private from Tennessee, who had forged papers on his birth certificate, said to his buddy.

"Hey," he said, drawing the three point men's attention. He gave a thumbs-up.

"Ya," Long nodded.

"You asshole, Long, you could still be back at battalion cooking if you weren't dumber than an ox with the clap."

The company watched as the point moved out, the three getting smaller and smaller in the distance.

One dogface sang softly to himself, "So long, it's been good to know ya."

A lookout up the lone tree in the area yelled down to the CO, giving the three point men's progress toward the ravine through which the company, the battalion, the division had to pass when and if the point drew fire. Then the Americans would lay down their fire on the enemy.

"Hey, slow down, man," Long called up to Tony.

"If he went any slower, he'd stall," O'Mally said, his tough-guy act replaced with the understanding they were the chosen few. *I thought the chosen were Jews . . . wonder what the guys on the corner would say . . . if they saw me now . . .*

"Don't you go being no wise ass," Long said, smiling at the little redhead, wiping the sweat off his glistening forehead. *Don't want no shining target for no Kraut sniper . . . I wanna be a shining target for the best pootang that the Bronx got to offer . . . a real American hero . . . a real live American Negro hero . . .*

"Hey, Mr. DaSilva, how come you don't ask that finger of yours what those Nazis plan? What are you thinking?"

Thinking . . . I'm thinking Jazz is too young to know what happened to his dad. Oh, he looked so much like a real live Huck Finn when we were fishing . . . Romola knew something bad happened . . . She wasn't sure what . . . So thin . . . like her mother . . . I want to smother her with ice cream and chocolate and kisses . . . until she's as fat as a cat that got locked in the shed . . . with all the fresh cream buckets in it . . .

"You might not be talking to that finger out loud," the giant black man said, smiling, "but sure as hell you and that finger is doing some thinking."

It will be Johnny whose heart will be ripped out if I . . . don't make it . . . if I get home . . . When I get home . . . I'll tear open my chest . . . let my heart pound in Johnny's . . .

—
371

"We're through, we fuckin' through!" O'Mally shouted, looking back across the valley they had traveled through, without drawing fire.

"Yea, thought I walked through the Valley of Death, fearing all evil, shitting my pants, we got through!" Long said, grabbing Tony in a bear hug, lifting him off his feet, kissing his cheeks. "Man, this means we're gonna get home. We're really gonna get home."

Tony looked at his finger and smiled. "I'm going home to the farm. We didn't buy the farm, boys." *Charity . . . a nice new start . . . Johnny and Jazz and me . . . fishing . . . Mill Pond . . . Salem Willows . . . long strings of giant flounder . . . us smiling at the guys with a couple little ones . . . Romola eating ice cream . . . till I tell her she's getting too fat . . . her smiling at me . . . and Charity . . . maybe she will take me back . . . put me together again . . . the right way . . . put our family . . . back together again . . . without even having to call all the king's horses . . . all the king's men . . .*

They continued on to the high boulder, a signal point they had agreed on before they left the company. The big black man and the small redheaded boy climbed up. Waved back to the men of Able. "Come and get it!" Long cried.

"Come on, Tony," Long cried. "We did it."

Tony suddenly felt weak. The boulder was too great a climb. The giant black man from the Bronx and the little white man from the Loop held their rifles high over their heads and pumped them.

Spotting the signaling Long and O'Malley, the observer up the tree called down to the company commander, "The coast is clear. They're at the boulder." He took the powerful binoculars from his eyes, wondering why old man DaSilva didn't climb the boulder and celebrate.

They were going to enter Germany without a shot being fired. Celebration time. Yet the old man appeared to stare at his finger. *Why? Who gives a good shit? It's clear . . .*

"Able, move out. McKenna, you're platoon point."

"Johnson, you're squad, point," McKenna said."

The feeling was one of great joy as the 180-man company moved through the valley with a light-headedness. The three point man hadn't drawn fire.

The company was halfway across the ravine. Home stretch. Cabbage is ahead. Mother-in-law nagging in the rear. Then Beetlebomb. The race is over.

Then all hell broke loose!

The enfilade and defilade crossfire of the Mausers and machine guns of the hidden German battalion that had been lying in wait seared into Able Company. Mowing its men down like wheat before a reaper. Among those first to buy the farm were Long and O'Malley, who were hit so many times the firepower held them upright for several seconds.

The mortar rounds rained hell on top of the company, continuing long after not a single man of Fox Company moved or even moaned.

Tony, protected by the boulder, was frozen in time as the firestorm of death hailed down on his comrades. He stared wide-eyed like a child watching the Fourth of July fireworks.

The fireworks display turned into a horror movie. He was the kid in the front row, soaked with the blood of the actors on the screen before them. But they weren't actors. They were Long and O'Malley. Tony watched as their blood flowed into each other's, and he could tell one from the other.

When the firing finally stopped and the movie ended, Tony realized his friends and comrades of such a short while ago, a million years to be exact, were acting their last act.

Tony heard a moan by his feet.

It was Long. "My god, my good god, my good Christ almighty," the giant black man cried, crossing himself, forgetting he was a Beulah Baptist. His eyes closed slowly.

Tony looked at O'Malley. He appeared to have inherited additional freckles in death. They were spatterings of his own blood. His eyes stared into eternity. Steam rose from his open stomach, climbing, appearing to join the clouds.

Tony looked at the youth that wanted to be tough, his innocence the most dangerous sin of all.

Tony realized he was still standing and looked skyward in thanks.

The thanks was too early.

As the German troops moved out, one soldier fired a goodbye burst with the stray untargeted bullets tearing into Tony, taking off part of his skull bone, his left shoulder blade and hip, and the right heel, raking him from top to bottom, but leaving his trigger finger completely untouched.

German artillery and rocket fire drove the two American infantry companies held in reserve all the way back to battalion headquarters, almost to division, where they licked their wounds for twenty-four hours.

Was there another way to get to Metz?

Twenty-four hours later, the brass decided that the Valley of Death in front was the only way to go. You don't advance sideways unless you are a crab or a sidewinder rattlesnake. The battalion headed into the valley, not realizing it had been abandoned by the enemy.

The dead of Able had their dog tags removed and one placed between their teeth before they were slid into rubber body bags.

—

One medic looking for any sign of life moaned, "My god, they vaporized the entire company!"

A medic attempting to get a body into a bag said, "Wait a second! This one isn't stiff!"

He stopped, trying to get Pvt. Tony DaSilva into the body bag.

"Look, the poor bastard, what's left of him, has his trigger finger in his mouth, like he's trying to bite it off. How do you figure that one out?"

They rolled Tony onto a field stretcher and placed it on the hood of a jeep that picked its way across the shell-pocked field, a field that could pass as that of a giant adolescent, his face raw, pimply, and pocked and erupted, no longer worrying whether his date will see the scared complexion.

The field hospital was always a baby step behind the lines.

Tony was moved there while the doctors, like little Dutch boy medics stuck their fingers in the blood-leaking dike that was Tony.

Then it was across the channel by hospital ship to London for more treatment.

Next it was across the big pond and to the States and Walter Reed Hospital.

Finally he was at the Fort Devens hospital, less than thirty miles from both Rockledge and Chelmsford, halfway between the farm and Charity, a long way from the Sun Shipyard. And Metz.

Johnny replaced the blue star banner back in the window, letting the gold star that had been set to replace it fall to the floor.

CHAPTER 19

D-DAY

Actually, Johnny had been stepping up his program to get into the war for months.

What set him into double-time, hyper-high gear was the front page of the *Boston Morning Globe* he was delivering. He had heard a radio report before setting out on his route, "Because of D-day, Wonderland will not operate tonight. Wonderland, Revere." He didn't understand the radio report at first.

That was June 7, 1944.

The *Globe* headline read, "INVASION!"

And underneath . . .

> SUPREME HEADQUARTERS, ALLIED EXPEDITIONARY FORCE, June 6 (AP)—Allied forces landed in the Normandy area of Northwest France today and have thrust several miles inland against unexpectedly slight German opposition and with losses much smaller than had been anticipated.
>
> The grand assault, scheduled for yesterday but postponed until today because of bad weather, found the highly vaunted German defenses much less formidable in every department than had been feared.

Johnny read the report twice. *It better not end . . . before . . . I get into it . . .*

—

375

"Bullshit," Johnny told Righty, "slight opposition. Less formidable. My father and Uncle Manny and Franchesco DaSilva and Uncles Matt, Mark, and Luke Shiverick better be okay after that 'slight opposition' shit. Otherwise, I'll toss a grenade right through the editor's window. Nah. I'll toss it into their shithouse, and the explosion will cover them with their own writing."

He had lost confidence in news reporting ever since the papers had seen fit to substitute his, Romola's, and Jazz's pictures for the three dead children, half brothers and sister, of his father. Everyone was lying, and the papers were printing it as the god-awful truth.

They needed him there. D-day. Fighting the Germans and Japs and Ginnies, not the Righty and Big Lefty guineas, but those Mussolini bastards. He had cut out the headline "INVASION" and carried it in his wallet.

"Righty, they need me there."

"Yah, they need us. Waddaya gonna do? They don't know how tough we are."

Johnny knew that they especially needed him.

Grenade tossing with his right arm, he could throw a quarter-pound rock nearly the length of a football field. He learned to toss the rock fifty yards with his left arm. *Just in case . . . I get my right arm . . . blown off . . . Hey, what's the big loss? The hand is covered with hair anyway.*

Bayonet battles? Hadn't he surprised his mother when he parried her thrust, slash, butt in her last bayonet broom attack even after she surprised him in bed.

She had called up, "Get up and go to church."

He had called down, "Go away, Ma! I'm tired."

He had set pins the night before and delivered the Sunday papers early that morning . . . Good lord . . . they weighed a ton.

She wasn't sure whether it was the "Go away, Ma," or the "I'm tired" that set her off. She couldn't stand the thought that her baby was exhausted from work at any age. He should be just tired from play, but either way, anger or guilt, she bounded up the stairs, skipping over missing steps four and nine from long practices, and pried him out of the bed with the butt end of the broom, using the edge of the bed as a fulcrum. Despite being surprised, he was up and out of bed, parrying all the moves of her broom stab, slash, butt end!

She was always impressed by his defensive moves. *Never an aggressive return . . . Such a wonderful boy . . . How much my baby has improved in defending himself . . . but what in God's creation did he mean . . . when I put the broom under him . . . with his . . . "Long John here. I demand you lay down your cudgel."*

She was tired, too tired to go to church.

Charity never read Robin Hood. Reading the Bible was enough. A lot of words. If you finished reading it, you could read it again and again to get the words you hadn't committed to memory.

Regardless, she wasn't about to lay down her broom, bayonet, or cudgel—whatever in heaven a cudgel was—but knowing the days of winning duels were over, she went about sweeping his bedroom floor, as if this was the only reason she had bombed up the stairs to get her sleeping newsboy off to church. *We're all tired, my tired son . . . but we must work . . . and we especially must go to church . . . or go to the Hitlers and the heathens hell . . . where those who dared call us poor rot in hell . . . If we get tired . . . they win . . . we will never get that tired . . . My boy was so good . . . defending himself . . . one time using a toilet plunger . . . of all things . . .*

Shooting! Johnny was not only good at grenade tossing, bayonet thrusts, and parries, but how about his shooting?

He had had his cousins Dinkie and Pointer roll tires from the top of the farm sandbank and through the woods, bouncing and bounding like a whitetail buck.

The tires had cardboard circles cut to fit inside the tires' doughnut holes. The cardboard inserts had the faces of Hitler and Tojo and Mussolini drawn on them.

He banged away at them as they bounced downward, loading and reloading his single-shot bolt-action .22.

One time he got six shots off during a single Tojo tire roll down the hill through the woods. One shot was in Tojo's eye, a shot he claimed he took on purpose.

Checking the tires for hits was even better than the shooting when he found most of his shots had ripped through the cardboard. One had hit Hitler in the eye. He liked that.

Dink had missed all his shots at the head and upper body of Hitler in the insert but saved face when Johnny told him that the shots outside the tire had indeed shot the führer's balls off.

Pointer's favorite was the command, "Roll Benito!"

The favorite of all three was the Hitler insert where they had sketched a penis where Hitler's nose was supposed to be. After firing an entire box of cartridges and missing Hitler's donk, Johnny said, "Fix bayonets!"

The cousins took out their jackknives and opened the blades.

"Charge!" Pointer commanded. And Hitler's pecker was no more.

The brothers didn't give two good shits about joining up with their cousin to fight the Nazis and the Nips. They didn't know who Hitler was, but to shoot someone's dick off was a blast.

While Pointer and Dink had no quarrel with America's enemies, they loved to play invasion.

Their cousin filled an old army backpack and two heavy newspaper delivery bags with rocks and slipped their combat packs over their shoulders. They poled their raft out fifteen feet from shore to where it was about five feet deep and jumped in.

Johnny held the .22 high over his head; Dink and Pointer held their rifles carved out of apprehended boards from a house under construction over their heads as they yelled "Gung ho!" "Geronimo!" and "Hogland!" the name of the feared farmer who threatened to shoot them in the bony butts with two barrels full of rock the next time he caught them in his watermelon patch.

Johnny had jumped into a deep trough and not into shallow water like his cousins, and his rock-filled pack carried him to the bottom. He couldn't swim to the surface nor get the straps off his shoulders and started to panic as he swallowed his first mouthful of water.

He squatted on the bottom and then thrusted upward and grabbed a breath of air as he broke the surface, only to sink to the bottom again. He repeated the squat, thrust to the surface, breathe-and-sink routine nine times until he could finally stand with his head out of the water.

Then he was out of the water running through the weeds at the Japs yelling, "Banzai!" He bayoneted giant Japanese marines before they could complete hara-kiri on him. A kid could become a little confused after swallowing a couple gallons of swamp water and perhaps a couple blood suckers tossed in for good measure.

He always knew he would make it to shore, but if he failed to make it to the surface after a twenty count, he just knew Dinkie and Pointer would go over the side and remove the pack from his back so he could swim to shore.

The cousins were happy they did not have to become heroes as they both thought, *Heroes is pretty . . . dangerous shit . . . Oh ya . . .*

They were gloriously happy to join Johnny yelling "Banzai!" and bayoneting Japs that looked strangely like stumps and anthills. But they found it very realistic to stab an anthill and see the insects pour out like spilled blood.

After they caught their breath and carved their kills on their weapons, Dink claimed his gun was a submachine gun, Johnny tried to have them participate in some live fire.

—

"I'll run up from the shore while you guys hide in the bushes and fire the .22 over my head, like the real thing."

"Nothin' doin'," Dinkie said.

"If we shoot you between the eyes by mistake," Pointer added, "your ma would kill us. And you too."

"Yah, that broom of hers should be registered as a deadly weapon," Pointer said.

Deadly weapons—Johnny didn't have anyone to teach him karate. He had asked his uncle Luke, when he was home on leave, to teach him karate.

"Just in case I meet up with some Jap that does it. Karate. I can do it back."

"Do it first. Not back." Uncle Luke was more than happy to give advice. "First, when the little Nip assumes the stance and is laughing at you with his eyes and smiling that bucktoothed thing they do—do you know that Oriental women down there are sideways instead of up and down and—no wait. When the little Jap is standing there all fancy ready to whip your tail with that sneaky karate crap, kick him in the balls. Then pick up the nearest two-by-four you can find and whale the living gee-hoc-sa-fats out of him while he's clutching the family jewels."

Luke had left with a smile, turning back only to say, "You know your brother James looks like a Jap, with those buckteeth and all."

Johnny looked at his uncle, his face as blank as the ass of a cube of sugar. *You were always my unfavorite uncle . . .*

"Anyway, here's two bits, get him some wax teeth when Halloween comes around."

Johnny grabbed the coin as it spun through the air, flexed his arm to toss it hard enough to cut through his uncle's neck and come out his navel, but instead clamped his hand shut over it. *With another dime . . . I can get one of Jazz's teeth fixed . . . buy a box of twenty-two hornets . . . Nah . . . I'm gonna toss this coin . . . right through your . . . head . . .*

He clutched the coin tighter.

He heard his mother's voice. He was sure he heard her, although she wasn't there. *Toss it through his head . . . then go get it . . . and have one of Jazz's teeth fixed . . . but then of course, don't hurt Luke none . . . He's my brother . . . God fearing . . . but sort of giddy dumb at times . . . Can't help it . . . God made him goofy . . .*

Then again, Johnny didn't know that Uncle Luke was the one saving in an old shoe to buy that lapstrake dory he had seen being built in Kittybunk Port by the retired one-arm lobsterman. He planned to take Johnny and Jazz fishing after the war.

—

The old boat builder had told Luke, "Aaaa-ya, lost the arm, of all things, to a monkfish. That homely heathen of the sea what got the fishing rod on its head, and when it lures in them little fishes, it sucks them in. Just like he was pretending helpless in that net. Until I got close and he clamped on with those wicked teeth that goes in more directions than a fart in a changing sea breeze. Twernt the bite that did it. No, sir-rees. 'Twas the infection. Aaa-ya. I was so mad at that arm that when they cut it off, I saved it and then stuck it in one of my traps as bait. Friends told me it wouldn't work none. I said, 'Sure 'twill.' Worked just fine I'll tell ya. Aaa-ya. Trap was full as they get. Lobsters. Crabs. Moving round. Funny sight. A lobster and a crab trying to dance. One can only go forward and backward, other can only go sideways. Both want to lead. Best of all was one of them lobsters was resting in my hand, sure 'twas, I could of tickled its balls. Any-hoo, I figured that was a good way to finish a career. Ayaaaa-ya."

That's all Luke dreamed of, owning a Maine dory, made by a one-armed dory-building lobsterman that used the lost arm as bait. Luke thought about that dory nearly all the time, especially when he was being shot at. Nothing like dreaming about being in a dory, alone at sea, when someone is shooting up the crowd you're with.

That one-armed dory builder fit his idea of how things should be done.

Luke thought, *'Course no one will believe me . . . till they see that picture of the old gent with his missing arm around my shoulder . . . holding up that picture he took of the lobster holding on to the hand of that chewed-up arm . . . That will turn the ladies heads some . . . like the old dory builder said . . . Sure 'twill . . . ayaaa-ya . . .*

Funny part is no one realized old bachelor Luke liked the ladies. Never dated one. Figured they'd say no. But with that dory . . . they'd come a runnin . . . There would only be yes for him . . . there . . .

Luke wanted the dory, and he wanted a woman to call his own, real bad. The two were inseparable.

That's why it was going to be tough for anyone to understand Luke planned to turn his hard-got, dory-buying money in that old shoe over to Jazz's dentist to fix those teeth on his next leave.

Didn't want anyone to know about what he was doing. Two things. One, everyone would think God made him goofy because they knew he wanted that dory. And two, he didn't want anyone else in the family trying to get money from him. And he sure as holy heck didn't want all the bucktoothed kids in the world coming to him. The Bible said a man doesn't need praise for good works. And it was better to give than receive.

—

But at times he wondered, *Did God . . . work as hard to get it . . . that money . . . seems he didn't . . . have no respect for money . . . tipping all those money-changer tables over . . . but they hadn't worked hard . . . to get that hard-earned money . . . like I did . . .*

Luke had always been a bit bothered about buying the dory anyhow, wondering how a man could feel if he couldn't pull lobster traps with a winch and one arm but could build a dory. *Would it be safe? How in holy heck did he hold the nails . . . with his toes? Who knows? He could picture Jazz with the wax . . . couldn't wait to see the new teeth . . . would have liked to see him with the wax teeth first . . . Come on, Johnny . . . toss that coin . . . bang it off the back of my head . . .*

But he wouldn't get to see Jazz's teeth fixed. It seems the landing craft that was supposed to carry the marines ashore got hung up on a reef, and when Luke stepped into what he believed was shallow water, a radio on his back, a mortar baseplate on his chest . . . *No big deal . . . I can carry that along with the radio . . . It will be like a bulletproof vest . . . which I don't need as the Lord looks out for his children . . .*

The mortar man had caught a bullet in the eye as the craft headed shoreward. *Why did the damned fool have to peek over the gunnels?*

Then Luke was sinking to the bottom. *I'm going in singing to the Lord . . .* The ocean filling his mouth was entering his lungs. He sang in the deep silence, "For he loosed the fearful lightning of his terrible swift sword" *His truth is marching on . . .*

His last thought as he sank to the bottom of what turned out to be a fifteen-foot-deep first step was "Glory, glory, hell . . . His truth . . . is . . . Mother . . ."

Johnny thought of his battle to come; he would use his knee and a big stick, like Uncle Luke had told him. *Please God . . . protect Uncle Luke . . . He's as mean . . . as they come . . . but we can all use . . . a helping hand . . . Uncle Luke is . . . as mean as they come . . . he will live . . . forever . . .*

Not only was Johnny an expert with bayonet, gun, and a karate beat-the-shit-out-of expert; he was now also a man who could walk underwater. He knew Dink and Pointer would be surprised when he walked out from beneath the surface. Johnny was a strongman. He had found a cement block that he could do twenty biceps reps with in less than ten seconds.

He tried to look older than his thirteen years. To enhance his age, he had started shaving the mustache fuzz and the four chin hairs, sometimes as often as three times a day. He took to wearing an old soft hat.

"Tryna be a gangsta or somethin'?" Righty said.

While a little five o'clock shadow had set in, it wasn't all the result of shaving. He had enlisted Romola to rub just enough shoe polish into his chin and sideburns to look like a beard each time he tried to enlist.

He admired the army recruiting sergeants and navy chiefs that took a halfhearted swing at him or gave him a good swift kick in the ass, especially those who told him to come back soon.

He pretended to spit at those who called him boy or mussed his hair. *Funny thing about spitting at someone . . . whether it's a bully or a fruit cup . . . a cop on the beat or parish priest . . . friend or foe . . . it sure pisses everyone off . . . spitting on them . . . and I'll keep it as an answer . . . to bad vibes . . .*

He was getting tall to the point where he was nearly five foot nine. He had gained five inches in less than a year, three by growth and two by wearing the too large boots he found in a trash can and stuffed cardboard as lifts to further enhance his height.

"The cardboard won't work," Tim Yancy said, "if they measure you barefoot."

"I'll glue some cardboard to the bottom of my feet."

Johnny and Tim were scaling rocks across Duck Pond, seeing who could get the most skips.

Rhesus Eurasian took time out from shooting stones from his slingshot at bees that buzzed near his sweaty body to tell Johnny, "Nah, it wouldn't work."

"Any suggestions on Johnny's boot bottoms, Boattail?" Dick Tracy asked, "You've always got more on your imagination than a monkey with a piss hard-on."

"The only thing I've got to say, Detective Tracy, is that anything I say will be held against me. Boobies!"

"Thanks," Johnny said. "Any ideas, Fats?"

"Sure. The cow kicked Nellie in the belly in the barn just to see the old girl jump."

"Great."

"It is great. Isn't this better than going to school. It was my idea to skip," said Scoff Burns, trying to swipe a stick of Wrigley's Spearmint Chewing Gum sticking out of Skinny Potts's back pocket.

Johnny fingered his chin, felt the stubble of the several hairs he had managed to cultivate, "What do you think of these?" he asked.

"Unholy hay-seus," Rhesus said, his tiny face squeezed into a smile that closed his eyes and brought the corners of his mouth upward until they nearly made a complete circle by tying into the corners of his eyes. "You look like one of the fuckin' Smith Brothers."

"Yer cough," Boattail said. "Jeerrr cough. Jerk cough. Jerk off. Conjugation. Get it?"

"Now conjugate this," Dick Tracy said, grasping his crotch in his hand.

"Small, smaller, smallest," Boattail answered.

"Thanks." Dick Tracy sulked.

"Thanks to the Yanks, the men in the tanks, in the ships, in the planes, on the shore," Bobby Butt Burner Burnham sang, letting fly with one of his famous farts, which he topped off with a choirboy smile so heavenly that more often than not, an innocent party found himself being blamed for Bobby's stinkeroo.

"Let's take a skinny dip," Fats said, ripping off his shirt and running toward the big rock.

"Last one in is an old maid!" Righty yelled, catching up to and passing Fats Burns. He was christened Fats because fat burns, and not because he was so skinny that it looked at times as if his backbone would show through his rib cage.

"An old maid with the . . ." Rhesus said, cutting the sentence short and signing it with a clap of his hands as he dove off the boulder.

"Ya, like an old maid with the clap!" Fats yelled from the water.

Tim Yancy and Johnny followed, laughing, floating high, spitting whale spouts high into the air. "Why don't you join up with me, the army or marines, Tim?"

"Nah, all they let people with a different skin do is clean tables and serve meals."

"No such thing. I read there was one group of colored pilots flying P-38 Lightnings that shot down German planes that attacked our Flying Fortresses. You're smart enough to fly. Me, it's the infantry. Or I could get into a raider battalion and win a big medal like my father as all my uncles are doing, and I'll be important enough to send for you to fight beside me. I'll have a wheelbarrow full of medals, and I'll send for Righty too. And we will be in the same foxhole."

"Nah, they won't let us do it. There are guys from South Boston everywhere."

"You mean South Carolina and deeper South."

"I wish. But I mean South Boston."

"We'll pound their asses to powder."

"It just isn't this war anyway. My war is getting a doctor's degree. And leading my people so they can get doctor's degrees. Changing things that way. Fighting doesn't make any sense."

"That's pretty heavy stuff. I'll beat your butt to the rock!" Johnny dunked Tim's head under water and swam like a Merc motor was strapped to his ass. He couldn't help smiling when a short while later Tim passed him, smiling, waving backward. "Gotta catch it before you can beat it."

The big boulder, its top ledge twenty-five feet over the water, was warm.

They continued their stripping. Rhesus and Boattail, back on the boulder, snapped their shirts like whips at any bare ass within range.

"Yee ow!" Scoff screamed when the snapping end of Boattail's shirt passed by his buttocks and caught his testicles, long hangers that were a family tradition.

History had it that Scoff's great uncle, Fagan the First, and the modern founder of the clan of good guys who couldn't keep their hands off other people's property had been arrested in Spain for, of all things, stealing. History had it also that Fagan the First had been locked up with a bunch of his Irish buddies as one of the group had cut the balls off a fighting bull, so the story went.

They were released after being searched, and no balls were found, present or accounted for.

It wasn't until the fun fellows were a good distance from the lockup that Fagan the First popped the hidden bull testicles out of his cheeks.

As the history of the Fagan family goes, the bull's balls were handed on through the generations, with the latest recipient getting his big hangers snapped at by the wielders of the wet T-shirts.

Righty, coming out of the water and not wanting his butt stung, had scooped up a couple handfuls of crayfish and tossed the crawfdads and their snapping claws at the bare balls of the wet towel snappers, thus turning the favor of the fray over to the testicle protectors.

"Hey, hold on," Boattail said. "Those crawdads mean we can catch bass!"

"Yah," Rhesus said. "They are for bass!"

"You put down your T-shirts. I put down the cajone snappers."

The war of the balls ended as quickly as it had started as they whipped out their jackknifes and were carving fishing rods.

Johnny carved wooden fishhooks while Righty, Fats, and Scoff dug under the small roots of nearby bushes and cut down overhead grapevines and soon converted them into fishing line. The hooks were tied on. And soon the crayfish were crawling around the pond bottom, tied to the wooden hooks. Actually, they were crawling in circles.

The circle crawling was the result of Johnny's wisdom. "If we don't cut off the legs on one side, they'll crawl under rocks and into ledges, my father told me. This way they can't. The bass will find them."

Scoff yanked his pole into the air. A bass had nibbled at the crawdad.

—

"Let 'em run with it. Give 'em time to swallow it," Johnny said.

"What if it gets away?"

"It got away. All you did was yank the crawdad out of old bucketmouth's yap. Let him get it down into his stomach. And don't yank too hard. You'll pull everything out of the fish's mouth, and you'll lose it."

"Okay. Let him swallow it. Pull easy." Scoff checked the crawdad. It was still tied on tight; he spit on it for luck. "Why can't we put the hook through it?"

"If they don't get killed, we can release them. They'll grow new legs," Johnny said. "Anyway, if they fought the good fight and survived, they should be set free."

"I can buy that," Tim said. No one else got it.

"Hey, Johnny, I'm going to call you Nature Boy. You don't have a nickname," Scoff said. "How come?"

"Ya, how come?" Dick Tracy asked.

"Who do you think you are, Dick Tracy?" Righty asked Dick Tracy.

"Hey, how does it feel to be the only person in the world to be called Righty?" the boy detective asked.

"Knock it off," Johnny said. "I've got a nickname."

"Yah, what?" Dick Tracy asked.

"If I told you you'd know," Johnny said.

"No shit, Dick Tracy," Dick Tracy said.

Scoff yanked his pole back with all his might, pulling the fish out of the water, sending it flying high into the air and behind him. It was only hooked in the lip.

They caught more bass, smallmouths, and bucketmouths.

Righty collected dry twigs, stacked them, and then kneeling, lit them with a cigarette lighter he got out of Fat Burns trousers; he was the only one who smoked.

Naked, Righty knelt by the fire, fanning it with Fat's pants.

"Hey, I've got hot pants," the naked Fats, skinny as a rail, sang, as he danced around the fire.

"Hey, don't let your bush catch fire." Boattail laughed as the sparks flew between Righty's naked legs and crotch, making him jump into the air with a hoot and a holler.

"Don't worry about me and my hot sausage."

"Hey, Johnny, you're going in the army pretty soon, aren't ya?" Rhesus asked.

"Yah."

"You are gonna meet dirty girls that carry crabs. You know how they cure crabs in the army?"

—

"Nah."

"Well, they shave a path right through the middle of your pubic hairs."

"Yah?"

"Then they light one side on fire."

"So?"

"When the crabs try to run across the shaved area to the other side, the 4F-ers stab them with ice picks!"

"That's older than Methuselah's mustache," Johnny said.

The sun climbed high in the late-June sky, making their naked young bodies glisten, joining the heat of the fire to make them drowsy.

Johnny had gutted the bass, and they held them over the fire on the small maple limbs they had cut and skinned the bark off and cooked the bass until they sizzled.

"My dad said you only want to cook fish until its loses its translucency and turns white," Johnny said, removing his fish from the fire, blowing on it, breaking off a chunk and eating it with an "ahhh."

"Hey," Rhesus said, "looks good. Think I'll cook mine 'til it loses its translucency! What's translucency?"

Boattail pushed his squatting brother over with his foot.

"Daaah, wad da ya wanna be if you grow up?" Boattail asked. "An idjit."

"I want to be a good-looking woman so I can play with my tits," Rhesus said. "I love tits."

"Why doesn't a woman grow as tall as a tree?" Johnny asked.

They all laughed.

Everyone ate their fish, even Fat Burns, who hated fish.

And picked their teeth with the bones. And then ate dessert, the low-bush blueberries that had surrounded their giant boulder.

"Can you believe school's out tomorrow? What you guys gonna do this summer? I'm going to be a life guard," Fat Burns said, flexing his skinny biceps.

"You can't even swim," Scoff said.

"No matter. I've got the bod. I'll just sit there, way up high, looking down on you know what—girls—who'll looking up at this cool kid in the sunglasses."

"And if someone is drowning?"

"I'll send the peons."

"I'm helping my old man grow tomatoes this summer," Righty said. "He grows the biggest and juiciest in the world. And maybe he'll let me pick mushrooms this year.

"Why'd he wait so long to let you pick? Fraid you'd pick poison ones?" Scoff asked.

"Nah. 'Cause he's afraid I'll pick my nose while picking mushrooms. He hates that. One time he said he'd cut my fingers off if he caught me picking my nose and handling food."

"I don't know why," Scoff said. "Boattail, what are you and the Rhesus doing this summer? Got a job?"

"We'll make our bucks on water lilies. We dive for them at Buckman's and sell them to the rich bitches at the Highlands. Then we'll parlay that jack into a bundle playing a little blackjack behind the town hall."

"How about you, Johnny?" Boattail asked.

"I'm heading to the farm. I've got a rifle range in a sandpit there. As soon as I can get off seven shots and put them all in Hitler's face in a single tire roll, I know they'll take me. I want the bastards that shot my father and my uncles. I've saved all my money, and I've got twenty boxes of .22 longs. Hornets. I'm glad we skipped school today."

"Yah, but Landry found out our plans," Fats said, "and he said everyone that wasn't in school today or tomorrow will come back for a week."

"We'll bag him tonight. He'll skip tomorrow. He won't be able to face all our smiling faces," Rhesus said.

"Yah, we'll bag him," Fats said. "Who wants to spend an extra week in school?"

"I'm not spending any more time in school," Johnny said, staring into the fire. "I'm ready. As soon as I get that last shooting in."

"Hey, I hear the Yellow Peril comin'!" Scoff yelled, "Let's get."

One by one the naked boys dived from the top of the big rock into the water below, except Johnny, who was still staring into the fire.

Until the electric trolley was on the trestle that allowed its passengers to look down on the Big Boulder and the waters of Duck Pond.

Johnny jumped up too late on hearing the Yellow Peril, his nakedness in full view.

Well . . . make the most of it . . . a grand exit . . . And why not a grand exit? If someone recognizes him and tells his mother. Goodbye world . . .

He stood at full height, stretching up on his tiptoes, held his arms out to his side, and did a graceful swan dive, a ballet that only an airborn bird could perform. He did clamp his hands over his balls so they wouldn't slap against the water to end with an act very unlike a swan.

That evening he lost the bayonet battle with his mother. She ambushed him as he came through the door. She caught him with the bristle end of the broom, first in the stomach and then in the face, and again in the ass as he turned and ran. Her words chased him like a water snake after a field mouse, "Mr. Funny had to do a swan dive in front of everyone. The first time I've gone into Boston in five years, and my son is Mr. Dirty Funny. Well, I'm letting you know I got a picture, and I'm going to have it published in the *Boston American*. Front page."

Normally, Johnny didn't go for a bagging, but with the broom swipes still stinging his stomach, tender from too much sun, and with his ass six inches closer to the small of his back because of his mother's last swing, he doubly enjoyed the thought of tonight's planned bagging.

A short while later, Johnny and his friends were hiding in heavy lilacs a short distance from the home of Vice Principal Landry. "The punisher, an extra week in school."

The lilacs were picked as their waiting cover because of the aromatic atmosphere of their adventure.

Rhesus held the large paper bag as his brother crapped into it. Boattail didn't trust anyone else on such a mission.

The others each held the bag and then passed it on, a type of blood oath of brothership.

Boattail then tied a piece of clothesline around the top of the bag, string would not do, sealing in the goodies, and leaving a three-foot length hanging off.

They walked slowly in the shadows toward the vice principal's house. Peeking through the window, they saw the hated Landry sitting in his easy chair, the kitchen, reading and eating pizza.

"Pizza. He's just like a real person. Almost."

"I don't want to do it," Scoff said. "If we get caught, we get kicked out of school for good. If we can't go to school no more, we have to go to work."

"He's reading the sports section, eating pizza, just like some kind of human being," Fats said.

Rhesus set the bag down carefully on the top step, tied the rope end to the doorknob but held off lighting the bag on fire.

"He can keep us in school after it ends," Scoff said.

But no one lit the bag. They all looked at each other and to Johnny.

While they were looking to their leader, Boattail lit the bag on fire and said, "Johnny did it."

As Boattail lit the bag, Rhesus rang the door bell.

They were gone, back into the dark of the lilacs, by the time the vice principal yanked open the front door.

Experience told the vice principal to move quickly to the door if he was to recognize one of their skinny asses running away. Or even better, to have a chance to run one down. His bell was rung so often, and his answering the door was often greeted with some sort of a trick, but never a bagging.

He wasn't prepared for the burning bag he pulled into his living room on the door tether.

He started stamping on it to put out the fire, that is until he realized he was stomping. "Shit!"

The vice principal screamed with a shrillness that drilled through their heads, their hearts, "I will kill you! I will kill you little bastards!"

They didn't even think about their plan to yell out in unison as he stomped on the fire and the shit, "You've been bagged!"

They were terrified as they fled in silence to the high safety and dark of the Big Woods, where they peered into the dark many, many times, to see if the vice principal followed.

They drew consolation from the fact they were surely correct in assuming he wouldn't show up in school the next day.

Thus passed D-day, one of the biggest days in history.

And Johnny was headed to the farm, his rucksack full of boxes of .22 Hornet long rifle bullets.

He was positive if he could hit Hitler rolling down the sandbank on every shot that he could catch up to the D-day troops crossing France.

—

CHAPTER 20

SCHOOL IS OUT

His cousins knew Johnny would be arriving on this day, sure as the swallows come back to Capistrano, that old elephants went to their burial grounds and young bucks ride out the rut.

It was the last day of school.

Pointer and Dink sat under a big tree behind the bushes that overlooked the back door of the farm, back out of Pie's view, thus out of harm's way. This was the spot where they could discuss Pie's mood before they put their little asses on the line by being in his sight.

They knew Johnny would be there. He had walked and jogged the twenty-two miles at the start of each school vacation for a decade. Christmas, spring break, and the summer off.

It was always cold for Pointer and Dink when they had to wait to ambush their cousin during Christmas break but waiting for school to end and summer start was great stuff.

They knew as sure as the swallows come back to Capistrano that he would return to the farm.

It was a long wait but better than waiting for him at Christmas vacation when their dickie birds turned to icicles. Now they jumped out and grabbed Johnny, his smile so wide it nearly swallowed his ears.

"Made it. Jogged the jog."

Johnny never thumbed.

Dink told his cousin, "Mie won't let you in the house. You stink sweat."

"Ya, she will."

"No, she won't. She'd rather have a shit-covered hog from the farm trot in, "Dink said.

"Or a chicken with chicken shit on its feet running through the soup," Pointer added.

The three boys remembered the past Christmas vacation when Johnny came jogging in.

He was muddy from the cars splashing him. "Ya gotta clean up," Dink had said. "Strip down and wash in the snow, and we'll shake out your clothes."

It was the brothers' plan, thought about and laughed about for more than a month, to get Johnny to strip in the snow and then run off with his clothes, wishing him a merry Christmas as they ran.

Usually nothing surprised the cousins concerning Johnny, so they were in shivering amazement as Johnny stripped as bare assed as a skinned goose, rolled in the snow, and washed under his arms, his crotch.

"Your balls are gonna hide under your arms. You wash them with snow like that," Dink said, sidling up to Johnny's clothes.

"Don't worry," Johnny said, giving his private parts a little Indian burn, a swift rub that got the old ions and shit in the human electric field banging against each other for instant heat.

"Knock it off." Dink laughed. "You're gonna suffer a boner!"

"A woodie isn't suffering," Johnny said.

"How do you know?" Pointer said, pointing at Johnny's crotch. "You ain't never had one."

"If he did," Dink said, "he wouldn't know what to do with it. He'd probably think it was a rolling pin, and he'd make a piecrust or something with it."

"Or a banana pie," Dink said as his brother pointed at Johnny's shrinkage and laughed, beating their thighs and holding onto their stomachs, attempting to sing, "Itsy, bitsy spider went up the water spout," as Johnny cavorted in the snow like an oversexed, two-carrot snowman.

One carrot with steaming nostrils, and the other nonsteaming carrot suffering shrinkage. Life was just too good.

Dink and Pointer remembered the time Johnny had jogged to the farm through the snow. The sweat had frozen on his face, making him look like an iceman as they pointed at him, laughing, but they stopped laughing when they saw Johnny shivering, his teeth chattering.

Dink turned to Pointer. "He sounds like Sgt. Bill Dane's machine gun in *Bataan*."

"Nah, more like a million beavers working their little flat tails off cutting down trees."

They laughed. Halfhearted. Hadn't their uncles Tony, Manny, and Francisco, who lived in the woods cutting logs, trapping, hunting deer and ruffed grouse, picking mushrooms and even wild flowers told them that shivering was the body's last attempt at retaining its core heat, whatever in hell core heat was? And hadn't the uncles told them if the shivering failed to warm the body, death could follow.

They couldn't imagine life without their cousin. They remembered him getting gored by the wild bull, Betty Boop, and all of them digging underground toward the shithouse to try and discover whether a girl's "it" was up and down or sideways, "like the chinks claimed."

The more the cousins admired his long runs, the more the cousins rode his ass.

But now Johnny was shivering, and he needed help. If he didn't know it, they did. They knew his core heat could only be returned by a hot drink, which they didn't have, or the warmth of a human body.

They also knew he'd let his pecker freeze into an icicle and fall off before he'd ask for help from God or the devil, let alone his cousins.

Wordlessly, the two brothers dragged him into the little goat shed where the heat from the animals actually kept it warm in the dead of winter. Dink and Pointer stripped off their clothes and wrestled Johnny to the ground, sandwiching him between them, "Do you feel like a ball?" Dink asked his brother.

"Ya. Why?" Pointer asked.

"Cuz there's a prick between us."

Johnny struggled for a moment. But the heat from their bodies slowly brought his body temperature back.

Johnny realized what they were doing, what it meant to lose core body heat, but stuttered, "I bet—better not feel no stiff-stiff-stiffies from you guys."

"You should be so lucky," Dink said. "If your dick ever goes up again, you'd better shellac it."

"Ya, kiss my ass," Pointer said.

"Wouldn't know where to start. You're all ass," Johnny said. *The two dummies . . . they think they're . . . saving my life . . .*

"He seems better," Dink said.

"Ya."

The brothers released their cousin and made a dash for their clothes, but not quite fast enough as Johnny's snowballs hit home, turning their cold asses from pink to a bright red.

—

Pointer turned to hold up his hand in peace, and a snowball caught him in the testicles and he let out the bawl of a wounded bear and then started to cry.

Everything stopped. No one with a drop of Pie's badass blood ever shed a tear, at least not within a thousand miles of his home range.

Dink and Johnny knew the pain of the snowball to Pointer's already half-frozen nuts had to be like a bolt of lightning. While Pointer might point and declare, "He did it" at the raise of a fresh-cut cane branch, he had never cried. Never.

Looking at Pointer standing bare ass in the snow, tears streaming down his face, both Dink and Johnny turned away. They didn't want Pointer to see the pain in their eyes for him.

"Put on your clothes, crybaby," Dink said, picking up his own and pulling them on.

"I ain't crying, you flaming asshole," Pointer said. "It's the stars shining in my lovely eyes."

"It's daytime, idjit," his brother said. "No stars."

"You see 'em when you get hit in the cajones by a snowball, idjit."

"Oh, poor baby," Johnny said, planting a wet kiss on Pointer's check, then added with a spitting motion, "Pit-tooie."

"Is this love or you just fooling around?" Pointer asked.

"Foolin' around," Johnny said, turning to Dink. "He's okay."

"Ya, but he shouldn't ah cried."

"We'll just forget it."

"Ya."

The three headed to the cousins' house, only taking a few moments to glance though the window of the farm to see if Pie was cheating at solitaire, and then continuing on.

"We got big news," Dink said.

"Ya, we got laid," Pointer said.

"Sure. So didn't the linoleum," Johnny said.

"Truth," Dink said, "we wouldn't shit you on somethin' so important."

"Nah, we couldn't shit you. You're too big a turd," his brother added, "but we really got laid."

"Sure. The same old girl. Merry Palm."

"Nah. None of that twinky dink stuff," Pointer said.

"It was Goda," Dink said.

"She's older than God," Johnny said.

"Yah, but better," Dink said.

"Whoa! Don't stand near me, Dink. Sure as God made little green grasshoppers, there is a bolt of lightning coming your way."

"I bet she just squeezes your balls between her legs, and you don't know the difference." Pointer said.

"No way, Jose," Dink said.

"Oh sure," Johnny said.

Pointer said, "I tell you I got action. And not only that 'it' is not sideway or straight up and down. It's kinda like—just there. Sort of on the bottom of the belly or something."

"Why would she do it with you jerks? And not only that, but with those tits bigger than Betty Boop's, you couldn't get close enough to sink in the dagger," Johnny said.

"Listen," Dink said, grabbing his cousin by the top of the arms and hugging him close, looking him in the eyes. "Really. Cross my heart and hope to die. You've got to believe me. It was the real thing. My cannoli wobbler did the deed. If I lie, may all Mine's candles blow out. We really did. And ya right, her tits got in the way. Until she sort of tossed them back over her shoulder or somethin'. And then when I entered the dagger, she pulls them back over and rests them on my shoulders, like she was making me a general or a queen knighting me or somethin'."

"You're kidding."

"Nah. This is the real thing."

"The real thing," his brother added.

"Shut up. You little dipshit. You passed out doing it," Dink said to his brother.

"Ya, but only after I got it from her!" Pointer added, preening in sheer, undiluted joy.

"What a liar. Brother, liar, liar pants on fire." You passed out before you got it," Dink said.

Pointer said, "Funny thing is we had to give her a half-dollar each, like she wanted. But that's not the funny thing. Funny thing is she gave us both a nickel back for candy.

"Said something I didn't get—'Next time it will cost only a quarter. You good little big boys.'"

Dink chimed in, "Then she patted us both on the head and gave us the nickels and said we had sweet little pickles."

"Ya," Pointer said, "she said we had sweet pickles."

"Now you're the only one who hasn't got laid, Johnny, and don't even know where 'it' is," Dink said, words meant to lift him from runner-up to the high point of the pecking order.

"I don't give two good craps. I came here because I have all these boxes of .22s, and after I fire them off I'm joining the marines. I'll be fighting Japs and Krauts while you're here putting pickles into an old woman's pickle jar. God, she must be in her thirties. While she's patting your head, I'll be flying a P-40 Flying Tiger against the Jap rats and shaving off Hitler's mustache with my bayonet. You two little kids."

Johnny hated the fact they had done it and he hadn't. He had probably wanted to. But just couldn't. *I don't . . . know . . . why . . . someone is waiting . . . for me . . .*

They walked in the silence and dark toward the cousins' home.

Johnny was angry, cold-ass angry, and they knew it. He didn't like being last in anything. Even in a game he wouldn't play.

After a while, Dink spoke, "We can get you a little. Don't know whether it will cost you a dollar or perhaps five bucks you're so ugly."

"You invented ugly," Johnny said, giving his cousin a noogie and a two-knuckle punch to the biceps.

"Did a fly bite me, or is my ninety-eight-pound cousin still getting sand kicked in his face at the beach?" Dink said.

"Up your piggy with a meat hook."

"Ooooh, that hurts," Pointer said, rolling his eyes and then crossing them.

The three laughed, picking up the pace. Led by Johnny.

His aunt always had plenty of hot food. And always had fruit, even the fruits he could not steal off neighbors' trees. Johnny couldn't imagine someone having enough money to buy fruit. In the summer, it grew on trees. And was free. All you had to do was be able to climb a fence and a high tree. Climb down fast, jumping the last ten feet. And then run fast.

She always knew when Johnny was coming. School was over. Summer was starting. So even more food was added to her always-full cupboard.

Johnny always ate until he was full. She insisted. And then ate some more. And then some more.

He hoped his stomach wouldn't get so round that he wouldn't be able to shoot what was to be his semiautomatic marine-corps-issue M1 Rifle, which for now was actually an old, very old, single-shot bolt-action .22 caliber.

Aunt Anto, Johnny had trouble pronouncing her real name, Alameida-Antonina, just too many syllables, not to mention that he was also was missing two of his bottom front teeth.

Aunt Anto, who at times answered to Ant Ant as well as Aunt Anto, made all the mustard sandwiches he wanted. She wanted to fatten up his picket fence body, and he appeared to have an actual love affair or at least crush on this different type of sandwich. She didn't know the reason he lusted after the mustard and bread fare was that he could finagle them much easier than say a roast beef, ham an' rye, or turkey sandwich, which were costly.

The ever-present Johnny-bread special was also a reward to her nephew for his politeness and what appeared to be an aversion to the importance of fart and other childish humor leanings.

Aunt Anto truly believed she could wean her sons of their manufacturing of hay and toilet paper cigarettes to which at times they added a dash of pepper. And end their incessant talking to their private parts. This isn't even mentioning that she hoped she could end their farting up wind from her and then blaming their old dog Buster-Fazoo, who was named after an Italian swearword they didn't know the meaning of. They enjoyed the sound of the word, a sound they felt was second only to what appeared to their ears to be "baa fung goo." Her main aim in life was to stop Dink's and Pointer's talking to what she believed was their shoes.

Actually, her sons were holding the waistband of their trousers away from their bodies not to see down their pant legs and tunnel talk to their shoes. They were actually talking to their private parts.

On seeing a pretty lady walk on by, they would trouser peek at themselves and say in their talking to the dog voice, "Attaboy, sic her."

Then after the young lady walked by, they would sing words of love to their parts, "You must have been a beautiful baby 'cause you sure are beautiful now."

Luckily for Dink's and Pointer's tail section, Aunt Auto never caught them counting in their version of the French numbers down their trousers to the private area that often served as the center of their universe; it was a saying they repeated many times, a takeoff on *une, deux, trois*—"In, de, twat, mo cock sank."

It always gets dark very early in the New England gray skies of winter.

"Where do you three think you're going?" she asked the three boys after they tagged home plate and ate everything they believed was available and were ready to bug out.

She drew a semicircle in the air, told them to turn around and come back. "Your beans and linguica will be ready in just a few minutes." Their elephant trunk truffling on peanut butter and jam was just the warm up.

"Beans and linguica!" Dink said. "Johnny will be strafing us in his sleep all night!"

"We'll have to tie a string from his toe to the bedpost. Otherwise, he'll float off like a gas balloon at the circus," Pointer added.

Johnny had nothing to say, or at least in front of his aunt. He remembered his mother's words, "If I get any bad reports from up there,

I'll tan your hide like Bill Cody tanning one of his buffalo skins. If your aunt serves beans, I better not get any reports about you making some kind of mistake that makes people leave the room."

The best thing about his cousins' mother is she didn't make him cut each bean in half and then crush it to prevent gas back up and then the inevitable seepage followed by the explosions.

He also did not have to worry about the pain of a whipping by his aunt Hope Shiverick, as his uncle Matt Shiverick had alleged she'd perform, if he didn't cut each bean in half.

Johnny knew he was all right there, eating beans without first cutting them in half and crushing them, thus destroying their potential to overfill his gas tank. He knew he was okay as long as no mistakes took place at Aunt Anto Gouveira's home, but he wasn't into taking chances. He didn't fear any physical attack, such as his uncle Matt had led Johnny to believe his aunt Hope would render. He feared the loss of future bean suppers and the homemade bread that was used to sop up the bean and molasses juices from the plate. So Johnny brought a paper bag and an elastic with him whenever he traveled to his cousins home.

And when the gas buildup was too great a force to contain, he would excuse himself, head to the bathroom, and release gas into the paper bag. Then seal it shut by snapping an elastic band around the top several times. Then he would hide the brown bag and its terrible contents behind the throne of King John the Crapper to use again. Later, if the urge came up again, as it invariably did, and he'd carefully remove the elastic, and before there was any gaseous escape from the bag or his own emissions device, he'd clamp his butt over the open bag and let fly. The bag not only contained the odors that might result but also muffled the noise, which didn't sound unlike a boot being pulled out of the mud or worse someone stepping on a fat toad.

The bag worked. He never had an incident. Later, unbeknownst to anyone including Dink and Pointer from whom he never kept a secret except that of the brown bag, he would take the said bag into the dark of the night and destroy the evidence by setting it on fire. He was ever so careful to stand up wind from the blaze that burned a very bright blue rather than the natural orange of a paper bag burning. He didn't understand the bright blue flame, that is until his first chemistry class.

He often thought it would be great to put the bag under Dink's pillow some night so that when his head hit the sack, the bag would burst open.

But that would be like cutting off his face to spite his nose, or however the saying goes, since he slept in the same room. Plus the type of revenge his cousin would seek was quite disconcerting.

—

"Come on, Ma, we'll be back in a few minutes for supper," Dink pleaded.

"Yah, we're just gonna be those devils in baggy pants," his brother added.

"Okay. Whatever those devils in baggy pants means," she said, giving each a loving kick in the tail feathers.

"Those are the paratroopers, the devils in jumpsuits, the baggy pants," Johnny said, "jumping into Hitlerville. The three of us will be ready to jump out of Flying Tiger planes right into his lap."

Johnny started singing, and his cousins picked up the tune. "If I had a submarine, I would bonk him off the bean, and there wouldn't be any Hitler anymore."

"God help us," she said, crossing herself, turning away, pretending she had gotten flour that covered her apron in her eye. It was a trick to wipe away a tear that she learned from her mother, Mine, who could drum up a tear at any time by lighting up a candle or just looking lovingly at one of her grandchildren.

Dink dragged the old flexible flyer from the tumbled-down goat shed that not only housed the sled but also the truck tube for floating and fishing in the summer, the maul for splitting wood, and an old wind-up Victrola complete with the picture of a sad-looking dog on it.

They loved the sounds from the old giant tuber-horn speaker. Its rusty handle looked very similar to the one that Johnny's dad cranked up the old Model T Ford with to start it.

The shed also contained spilled moldy grain that was for the long-gone goat. The kernels stuck together in clumps that even the field mice wouldn't venture to eat. The shed also housed other absolutely worthless stuff that someday would bring a small fortune. Under a lone plank on the rickety floor was a section of the Sears Catalog, the section that showed women with "braz-e-airs" filled with what could pass for the globes in their history class with countries of the world, including Constantinople. Istanbul was Constantinople.

Johnny wondered each time Dink brought out this secret cache of sex for the three of them to enjoy, which part of this breast-globe was Rockledge. Where did Bernadette, he would never call her Nookie, Clarkson live? Nookie, according to the boys, had done it with everyone for ten towns around. Except for Johnny. He was usually setting pins at the bowling alley while his friends made their night rounds. She was gifted or plagued with Goda-size upper appendages. Everyone could see this despite her constant effort to hide them. That was like hiding the Grand Tetons in the middle of a desert. Actually, she hadn't done it with every

—

boy for ten towns around. It was just that nearly every boy claimed such action whether they had it or not so they could be part of the who-done-it gang.

It wasn't the breasts that Johnny thought about. It was her eyes, so very pale blue, that were like looking upward, not seeing the billowing cumulus clouds and viewing only the blueness of the sky.

Oh, he thought about her endowments. To not see them would be like living in the shadow of Mount McKinley and not knowing its mounds were there.

When her breasts drifted ghostlike through his imagination as he tried to keep warm in his bed on nights he didn't get Rags, her nipples often appeared as the soft blue of her eyes. Johnny was embarrassed with himself for taking unfair advantage of her. She could not defend against his visualizing. He most often tried not to see her breasts, tried to just look into the eyes. Sometimes it worked.

This night, the cousins were only after the sled for a quick slide before supper and didn't have time for a quickie peek see of the "linger-ray" section of the Sears and Rubber duck catalog.

Besides, it was too cold for their fingers even to take what they called their fingertip Braille walk over the bra and panty pages.

Just as well. What they didn't know was that while their uncle Manny was looking for worms in the rotting-warm planks of the floor, he discovered the catalog, hollowed out the middle, set a hair-trigger mouse trap in it, and carefully closed the cover. Manny had felt bad. After all he had got his sex training as much from the Sears catalog as from watching the farm animals do their thing. But it was too good an opportunity to play one on the little guys. And later he could ask the poor nephew who was first to open it where he got the sore finger.

However, he did feel bad about the shock when the trap hit home, but it did feel good to know that the Sears catalogue was a second-generation educator.

There was no lingering in ladies lingerie this night. They only had time for one slide before chow down. There was fresh snow. Missions to be flown. Parachute jumps to be made.

Dink was the pilot and was flat out on the flexible flyer. The two parachutists kneeled on his back as they pushed off down the dark snow-packed street.

Then they were there. The White Cliffs of Dover. They would jump down into the shore of England where German invaders had just landed. They would drive them back into the sea.

Johnny prepared for his jump, hoping his landing in the snow that lined the street side wouldn't be hiding a boulder or worse the sharp end of a stump. He needed to survive his jump so he could return to take the stick of his Flying Fortress, wing low over Dover, its glistening cliffs. There'll be bluebirds over . . . the white cliffs of dover . . . Tomorrow when the world is free . . . there'll be love and laughter . . . and peace ever after . . .

Then release his bombs on the German battleships retreating back to their Naziville homeland.

The sledding hill was steep. Johnny and Pointer were now standing, their feet on the edge of the sled.

They stared in silence as the sled sped through the chill-whipped air.

Pointer uttered the first word, "Whoa," and froze.

"Johnny, you're the jumpmaster," Dink said. "Give him a shove out the door."

Pointer said, "I'll tell you a joke if you don't push me off. Do you know why cows don't grow tall as trees? Its roots don't reach the ground."

"What corn!" Dink yelled through the wind as their sled picked up speed. "What did the farmer's daughter say when she woke up after napping in the field and found a cow standing over her? 'One at a time, boys.'"

Johnny sang, "The corn is as high as an elephant's fly, and it looks like its climbing clear up to the sky."

They were near the end of their run when Dink told Pointer, "The moment of truth, Babe Ruth, you go with a 'Geronimo.'"

"I'm too ca-cold to ya-yell."

"I'll yell for you," Johnny said, "and follow you right out."

Pointer looked his cousin in the eye, "You sure you'll follow?"

"Sure as God made bucketmouth bass for us to catch through the ice."

Pointer was frozen upright.

Johnny called out for him, but rather than Geronimo, he yelled out in the only sentence he knew in Portuguese, "Vai para a merda com as galinhas," roughly translated, "Go take a shit with the chickens."

Pointer, who had heard these words many times from Pie, laughed and jumped.

He hit the snowbank and bounced.

Johnny jumped, only getting out the word, "I'll" before hitting the snow and rolling. He had meant to sing, "I'll be seeing you in all the old familiar places that my heart embraces," but combat leaves most ends of things loose.

Johnny's war didn't have time to end in a combat jump onto the white cliffs of Dover to stem an invasion.

As he sat in the snow, he called out 'contact' as the four engines of the Flying Fortress clicked in, and the propellers swung into their whirling dervish of motion.

He gave a thumbs-up to his ground crew as his plane lifted off.

On the plane's fuselage, his imagination painted a picture of Yelena, her gray eyes intelligent and daring him to greatness. The background appeared to be blue sky, but a closer look would determine a pair of out-of-focus very blue eyes.

He had seen other women in bathing suits and less, such on the sides of the bombers in the newspapers and on the Pathé News at the movies. Betty Grable was a favorite with Rita Hayward not far behind.

President Franklin Delano Roosevelt would have a special plane for Johnny. One that he not only could drop bombs out of but also jettison special presents to the enemy far below. *First, I'll drop a bomb on Hitler's bean in Berlin . . . then a giant bottle of flaming relish on Hamburg . . . and a bad bun on Frankfurt . . . then let Colin Kelly take the stick while I bail out with my cousins . . . so we could slit the throats . . . of every lousy Kraut Tojo . . . Hirohito . . . Hitler sucker . . .*

Dink's yell brought Johnny out of his bombing run high overhead in Nazi land.

"Here comes Audie Murphy!" Dink said, charging at Johnny. "Hey, Johnny, I yelled that Indian's name when I parachuted out. So you didn't have to tell me to take a shit with the chickens. I yelled, 'Tonto!'"

They were on their feet, charging snowmen, Johnny yelling, "Let's get those Nazi rat storm troopers!" He charged a stand of small evergreens and flew though the air, tossing a cross body block at the pine troopers.

His I-fly-though-the-air-with-the-greatest-of-ease cross body block did not take the troopers down. In fact, he did not even get to them. His flight ended up against a solid oak, snow-covered stump, remnant of the tree that the town had taken down that fall.

He felt the blinding flash invade his brain and shatter his spine, and he knew that he was crippled for life. War can do that. How could he take care of his mother?

"Johnny," Dink's voice came at him from the long end of a tunnel, "you all right?"

"Ya, you all right, Johnny?" Pointer asked.

The two brothers approached the prone shape.

But Johnny felt the life coming back into his limbs. The battle wasn't over. He leaped to his feet and pelted them with snowballs.

—

"Knock off the snowball crap," Dink warned.

"Snowballs, bull, those are grenades! I pulled the pin. Let's get home to the homemade beans and apple pie!"

The three ran up the hill, the sled nipping at their heels, at near the speed they had flown down, Mercury-winged heels drawn by the Lorelei smell of the bubbling homemade beans, the sizzling popping fat of the Portuguese sausage, the steaming homemade bread soaked with butter so hot that it would kill you with the pain if eaten while still steaming. A minor sacrifice. The heat of the mouth-roof-burning pie would be cooled by ice cream. But there were problems concerning the pie. Which to have on the pie, ice cream or farm cheese? Decisions, decisions, decisions.

Hey, go all the way. Have both.

So went the devils in their baggy pants in an uphill battle to Ant Ant's kitchen and the hero medals.

They ate like combat veterans who had been on a monthlong K Rations diet. But then of course they always ate that way.

Then it was to Dink's and Pointer's room for a burping contest. The farting contest would be later when the beans clicked in.

Their mother was never allowed in, never allowed to look in. They insisted on this. They laid traps. If she went in when they weren't there, she could get a shock when she threw the switch as they had rammed a hairpin in it. Occasionally, they failed to remember to remove it with that tiny fishhook embedded in the split end of a wooden match and scotch taped tight. They hated that. When available, they would sometimes balance a small box of spiders on top of the door, a box rigged like a bouncing Betty in reverse.

A bouncing Betty was a personnel mine that when the unsuspecting foot soldier stepped on it, the spring loaded mine would bounce in the air and explode crotch high.

The box with the spiders in it was rigged to a mousetrap that was triggered by the opening door and fired the spiders through the air about hair high.

It worked, this uneasy truce.

They had to keep her out of their room.

Mostly because if she ever looked in, she would destroy them like they had destroyed the room. Among other things, the walls were embedded with copper BBs.

It had been Johnny's idea to string a wire from the high corner of the ceiling across to a lower point.

A Stuka dive-bomber, complete with swastikas on its gulled wings, could glide down on a coat hanger hook as the three of them opened up on it.

Their firing not only shredded the hated screaming devils of the hated Luftwaffer, but also shredded the wallpaper Johnny's aunt had hung herself lovingly for her little angels, carefully matching the flowers that broke on the seams.

The day's excitement wasn't over, at least for Johnny and Dink.

They waited until Pointer was asleep and then reached under the bed and pulled out a bottle of water.

Johnny poured a few drops on Pointer's forehead as Dink blessed him.

This was all that was needed to get Pointer swimming in his sleep.

They bit their tongues and squeezed back the tears of laughter as the sleeper went through a variety of swim strokes, the breaststroke, the sidestroke, and the dog paddle, which they liked best as the top half of Pointer's body moved upward and his hands went up and down like an insane piano player's.

Pointer called out in his swimming sleep, "Dink! Save me!" then was snoring again within minutes.

Dink and Johnny waited patiently until Pointer was out, and only then did they let out the painful laughing moan that sounded like that of a lonely Jack London Arctic wolf with a toe in a trap.

It hurt Johnny to laugh, a result of his coupling with the hardwood tree stump earlier that evening. He could visualize the hometown paper, the *Sentinel*. Johnny DaSilva suffers . . . combat wounds . . . fighting . . . for the country . . . he loves . . .

He kept his fingers crossed the paper wouldn't report that he had suffered the most physically and mentally painful wound imaginable.

He had tried but failed not to laugh at Pointer's sound asleep pet poodle dog paddle in the bed. But he did. And it did hurt.

I wonder how much it will hurt . . . when I practice my shooting . . . in the sandpit tomorrow . . . Hey, it can't hurt no more than Uncle Manny . . . getting shot all those times by the Nazis . . . probably by a Nazi officer firing one of those fancy pistols . . . the lunger . . . luger . . . or something like that . . . after I fire off all those twenty-twos . . . for bull's-eyes . . . They'll have to take me in the marines . . . or rangers . . . I'll get them dirty rats . . . Ya . . . it was Jimmy Cagney . . . with Pat O'Brien in the Fighting Sixty-ninth . . . Ya . . . Jimmy always called bad guys . . . dem dirty rats . . . You dirty rat . . . you killed my brother . . . Teacher hates it when I say dem and deese . . . Jimmy Cagney and me . . . singing . . . over there over there . . .

—

"The yanks are coming! The yanks are coming! And they won't be back until it's over, over there!"

Now we're there again . . . Dad . . . Uncle Manny . . . Uncle Matt . . . We'll wax their Nazi asses . . . and slide them down the razor blade shit chute . . . to hell . . .

Winter is long past. Summer is here, and "School is out!"

CHAPTER 21

LILLY BOLERO

Shoot the chute!

It was as steep as the hill they had gone sliding on the night before, but faster.

As while snow is fast stuff, the combination of sand and snow is ever faster stuff.

They were standing at the top of the farm sandpit cut into the hill until the hill was only topped with a section of grass and trees that looked like a poorly fit toupee.

The old barrel staves lined with tin bottoms and tied on with baling wire were still in good shape despite a half dozen years of being secreted in a dead oak, killed by lightning, and hollowed by woodpeckers and ants over the years.

"Who goes first?" Dink asked.

"Johnny," Pointer said, pointing at his cousin.

"Let's buck up," Johnny said.

"Nah, Dink always throws his fingers out after ours are out," Pointer said, scrunching his fingers up like a cripple and then tossing out the hand in the buck-up motion.

"Here's a fast finger for you," Dink said.

"Duck!" Johnny said. "He's flipping you a bird."

"Cheee, me own brudder. A boid yet," Pointer said in his best Leo Gorcey, Dead End Kids imitation.

"And away we go!" Johnny had tied on the tin bottom staves and pushed off. "Whoa-ee whoa whoa," but the rampaging stallions strapped

—
405

to his feet were not accepting whoas on the sand and ice that left a sound like teeth being painfully ground to dust.

He was going fine until one stave caught in the root of a white birch that had been washed overboard from the top of the hill and partially lost beneath the sand and snow. Johnny let out a scream as his body continued on despite the fact his leg definitely wanted to stay entwined in the black roots.

Johnny lay there, not daring to move. The white pain that had shot through the the base of his skull and down his spine settled in a tormented throbbing knee.

Is football gone forever? Bullshit . . . shucks . . . I can still hit harder on one leg than any one on the team could ever hit even if they had three legs . . . Oh my good loving god, it hurts . . .

"Are you hurt?" Pointer was looking down on his cousin, close to tears.

"I'll make a splint," Dink said. "I made one for a poor frog that broke its leg."

"Broke its leg, bull ticky," Johnny said. "You broke the leg of Tonto Tonelli's frog when he wasn't looking, just before the frog leaping contest."

"I saved it. Who put the tongue depressors on the leg and taped it on? Me. That's who." "Sure," Johnny said, trying to smile through the pain, remembering the frog leaping with a limp. "The poor thing starved to death after four days of swimming in circles."

"You ain't hurt. You're too dumb to be hurt."

"Do ya think he's not hurt?" Pointer asked his brother.

"Of course not. He's a phony baloney. Even if he lost the leg he could use that wanger to walk on."

Johnny's tongue was bleeding as he bit down, hoping to shut out the pain.

"Yah, you're faking it. We're screwing out of here," Dink said, setting out in a trot toward the farm.

"Yah, you're not hurt. Crybaby," Pointer said, trailing after his brother.

"Hey, who's gonna throw the tires?" Johnny called after them as he got to his feet.

But they were too far away to hear him.

The old bolt-action .22 rifle was leaning against the tree where they had left it.

Their shooting always followed their skiing down the sandpit slopes.

The box of ammunition was in the cloth bag he kept his marbles in.

He chambered a shell and started banging away at a black clump of dirt that had broken off above and had slid partway down the bank.

His first shots were squeezed off. No pulling the trigger. Just taking a deep breath, letting half it out slowly while closing the heel of the palm and the forefinger against each other. The secret was not to know the actual moment it was going off. That way there would be no flinch. Just cool as a cucumber, slow and easy on the draw.

The clod was hit dead on from the offhand, sitting, kneeling. Be careful in the prone . . . Don't get sand in the breach . . . or the end of the barrel . . .

Time for rapid fire! . . . Ready on the left . . . Ready on the right . . . Watch your targets . . . "Targets!" The clod disappeared before his eyes as he flipped the bolt open and quickly reloaded after each shot.

The shoulder he had injured the night before parachuting out of the flexible flyer and into Berlin didn't bother him. Wouldn't matter . . . I can shoot better with one arm than any one Nazi could shoot with three . . .

"This one's for Uncle Manny. You dirty rats! This one's for my dad. You crummy Krauts! This one's for my uncle Matt, you Jap rats!

"And this one's to save our people, my ma, Mic, Gramma Shiverick. To save our shores from the foreign devils. Loose lips sink ships!"

He looked around and found a stone about the shape and size of a baseball and tossed it high up the bank. It tumbled downward, bouncing, skidding, but his first two shots sent stone splinters flying. His hand was full of bullets that he would feed into his smoking gun and shatter the stone that had made the transition into a grenade lobbed down the hill at his advancing platoon.

In the excitement of loading and reloading, the shells spilled onto the sand.

The grenade was getting closer!

He picked up a shell from the ground. Its gray lead was ugly beside the brilliance of the silver casing that housed the gunpowder beneath the projectile. He inserted it in the chamber. It didn't want to fit. The grenade was getting closer. He forced the shell in. The grenade was within thirty feet. He tried to wish it back into a stone. But no. He could see the segments, the lovely pineapple design that would break into deadly flesh-eating slivers that would eat the air alive before slicing into him and his buddies.

The bolt didn't want to close. He forced it forward and down. The grinding sounded like the noise he heard at Revere Beach this past summer when he bit into the baloney sandwich that Fat Burns had garnished with beach sand.

Johnny muttered to himself, "One cool cat, this marine, paratrooper, P-38 Lightning fighter pilot, underwater demolition expert, ranger, raider." And thought, *The grenade is getting close . . . I can't miss . . . It will kill my me . . . I can't miss . . . It's a gimme . . . Boy, that sandwich was deadly with that sand in it . . . but at least Fats spent the entire afternoon in the water after I swiped his bathing suit . . . right off his body . . .*

Everything was in slow motion. The tumbling rock grenade was in his sights. He was right on. Right on. It was so clear. In slow motion. He squeezed. Right on!

The explosion was much too loud.

The grenade exploded in his face.

He was hit.

"Corpsman!"

He whispered for help. He was hit. But he wasn't no sissy crying for help.

His eyes stung. *Shrapnel . . . those Nazi rats . . . those dirty rats . . .*

Johnny looked up at the sky. He could see the shades lowering over his eyes. First, the blackness blocked off the top third of the eye. Then half his vision. Then he could only see out of the bottom of his eyes and only by looking downward.

Then blackness.

He opened his eyes wide. Nothing.

He pulled his eyelids upward. No vision. He was blind.

The grains of sand on the bullet had partially jammed the bolt, and the shell exploded in the chamber. Tiny silver and lead particles backfired into his face. The Nazi grenade . . .

He had to get back to the farm. He was getting cold.

An eclipse . . . Did I get caught in an eclipse . . . or the grenade . . . I didn't get it . . . I didn't get it . . . What about my buddies? I should have thrown myself on it . . . Gramma Shiverick . . . Gramma Mine . . . Yelena . . . Our shores aren't safe . . . Bernadette . . . I can't see . . . Oh god . . .

"I can't see!"

He had to find his way back to the farm. *How . . . Gotta find my gun . . . It will rust here . . . gotta get back to the farm . . . wind blowing out of the east . . . keep it to the back of my neck . . . the farm is west . . .*

He heard the faraway sound of cars traveling along Boston Road. Heading east. If he kept the sounds to his left, he could make his way back. And find the driveway to the farm. *Gramma Mine will fix me up . . . make me see again . . . She'll just rub garlic on my eyes . . . make them better . . . Grandma Shiverick will kiss them . . . and make them better . . . Dad will bayonet the Nazi rat that tossed the grenade . . . Mine will light a candle and make God make me see . . . and Grandpa, Mr. John Shiverick . . . will talk right to God for my eyes . . . No, wait . . . Granddad Shiverick is . . . is dead . . .*

—

*Wait . . . He's right there with him . . . He'll just tap God on the shoulder . . .
and squeeze those giant white eyebrows . . . down over his eyes . . . and tell
God . . . "You'd better fix Johnny's eyes, God . . . Yes, you just better . . . or
else . . . I will be . . . blind . . .*

He kept his right hand over his face as he traveled through the briars
and bush while he cupped his left ear with his other hand, allowing the
east breeze to register its soft-whispered directions on the back of the ear.
The cupping allowed him to catch the sound of the cars, even those with
the best tuned engines. He shuffled his feet along the ground so his toes
could pick up holes or obstacles before they tripped him up.

*It seems like a light-year since I started back . . . light-year . . . light . . . Let
there be light . . . Get the joke . . . asshole . . . It was you . . . me . . . who forced a
sand-covered shell into a gun chamber . . .*

He kept walking.

"It's the driveway. I made the driveway!"

Johnny walked the driveway, trying to remember its exact curve. Keep
the sound of gravel beneath his feet. *The farm's got to be about here . . .*

He turned, allowing the east wind to enter his ear, and headed north
to the house.

He found the front door and let himself in. He could hear Mine, Pie,
Uncle Franchesko, Goda. *I'll never see Goda's big bubbas . . . ever . . . I'll
learn braille . . . Hey, no football . . . I'll become a marathon runner . . . Rags
will run in front of me along the route . . . He'll have little bells tied to his
tail . . . I'll tell him he's a good boy . . . and the bell will ring . . . and just before
the finish line, Rags will come to heel so I can break the tape . . . and Tarzan
Brown will put the crown on my head . . . just like Jesus got crowned . . .
and Grandpa Mr. Shiverick will be so proud of the crown he'll paint Tarzan
Brown's running shoes bright orange . . . and Johnny Kelly and I will go have a
root beer together . . . Ya bells on Rags tail . . . tingle tingle . . . jingle jingle . . .
I'll run like hell behind my jingle bell . . . jingle bells jingle bells . . . jingle bell
dog . . .*

He felt his way along the hallway. And to the room. "I can't see."

They all looked at Johnny standing there in the doorway.

"Sure," his uncle said, "and birds can't fly."

"Home. Go home, go! Carsa," Pie said, motioning Johnny to head
home.

"He's hurt. Johnny's hurt," Pointer said.

Mine went to him, wringing her hands, taking him in her arms, and
pulled his head to her breast, purring, "Kieterzinger. Kieterzinger. Little
one."

Johnny wished he knew what the word meant. But then he felt the warmth of her bosom and heard the warmth her loving kieterzinger. He knew all was okay.

Except he couldn't see.

"I can't see."

Johnny felt his grandmother's arms wrap around him. He buried his face in the old woman's bosom, his warm tears streaming downward, runaway rivulets, washing through the dust of the morning's potato picking on her heaving chest.

His uncle Manny pulled Johnny away from Mine, held him by the shoulders until they were squared off, then drew back his coconut fist, muscled and gnarled from years of harsh farmwork out of the unforgiving earth, and aimed his punch directly between the boy's eyes. And threw it.

It was a flying fist that Johnny had seen thrown at a Lowell Lusitano Club-South Boston Shamrocks soccer match, after a cheap elbow shot was taken by a Boston fullback against his brother Tony. Manny's fist left part of the opponent soccer player's nose on one cheek and part on the other and led to an interesting knockdown, drag out fist fight between a farmer and the split-nosed jackhammer operator who threw numerous punches as he danced and pranced about. They all landed.

It was no match. The Boston brawler pummeled Manny. Manny shook off the blows like a dog shaking off water and then threw a second sledgehammer blow that put the rat-a-tat-tat dancer into the goal netting, leaving him hanging there like a fish in a gill net.

This was the same fist now traveling at a holy-shit speed toward Johnny's face. His uncle stopped his fist inches from his nephew's face. The fist displaced air around his face and left Johnny wondering what had taken place.

Johnny heard his uncle say ever so softly that Johnny thought he had lost his hearing, "He's blind."

"Kietazinger."

Johnny blacked out.

It was a soft, warm hand, a nurse's, and a song sung softly on the radio that welcomed him back to consciousness. "You say, Larue, Lilly Bolero, and just like that, quick as an arrow. You'll find your true love . . ."

The voice that sang was low and sad. Coming out of the faraway dark.

"How do you feel?" This voice was very near, the voice of a man, an old man, kindly but full of authority.

"I feel like I was playing blind man's bluff. They covered my eyes, and everyone poked at me. I hated it."

"This isn't blind man's bluff. You are in the Massachusetts General Hospital Eye and Ear Infirmary. You will be here for some time. Your eye has been injured. This is not play. You understand?" the old doctor said, squeezing the top of Johnny's arm with a hand as soft as the nurse's was but not near as warm.

"You've been hurt seriously. Your right eye."

"Then why couldn't I see out of my left?"

"It is sympathetic to its brother. The injury was traumatic. You've lost the whites of both eyes. The white holds your retina in place."

"The retina is important," Johnny asked, almost in a whisper, feeling a cold sweat break out along his forehead.

"Very."

The sweat seemed to be burning through his forehead, into his brain. How do those guys from India . . . wear those hot diapers on their heads . . . walk barefoot on those hot coals? "I'm boiling."

He felt the cool cloth on his forehead, felt the small soft hand of a woman brush his hair back, and heard a soft voice, "There. Is that better?"

Then the old man's voice, the stronger grip yet gentle, holding his wrist as if to keep him from moving. "Johnny, you have a piece of silver metal, a sliver from the shell, resting on your retina. And several small pieces of lead from the bullet imbedded in your eye."

"My .22 must have blown up. There must have been sand in the breech. I can't be hurt. I'm joining the marine corps this week. The Jap rats. The Nazi goose-stepping murderers."

He was placed by two sets of very soft hands onto some sort of bed. Now it was rolling. He could hear the rustle of the nurses' starched white uniforms. Another voice, very soft, said, "Try not to move.

"You must not struggle. Your forehead and shoulders and chest are being strapped down. The slightest movement can detach your retina. We are taking you to the operating room as soon as Doctor Stein helps you sleep. Here he is now. Nurse Forenzo will hold your hand."

He felt something like a cup being slipped over his mouth and nose. It didn't smell good. Almost made him sick.

"Now, Johnny, count to ten. Backward," said a different voice.

"One, two."

A new voice greeted him, not as gentle as the old doctor's, more authoritative, "Count slowly. Start with ten. Count backward."

"Ten, nine."

The nurse saw the boy's muscle tighten as the gas was administered.

"It's okay, Johnny. This is nurse Forenzo. You can call me Jenny. Sleep."

—

The softness of her hand, her voice, were his last remembrance before his mind darkened, joining the ink dark that smothered his eyes.

It was still dark, at least to Johnny, when he heard the words of the old doctor. "We took it out."

"I know. You took out both my eyes. I still can't see."

"No, no, God *no*! We took the metal sliver off your retina, removed the lead from your eye."

"My poor baby." It was the soothing voice of Jenny Forenzo. Her soothing fingers that softly rubbed his temples in small circles. She must be so beautiful . . . her voice . . . her hands . . . so soft . . . Jenny Forenzo . . . She's probably as beautiful as Bernadette Clarkson . . . but not known as many boys and Bernadette . . . My nurse . . . my very own nurse Jenny knows only me . . . not other boys . . . I'm a man . . . I can feel my beard sandpapering the pillow . . . No, Jenny is not like Nookie . . . I mean Bernadette . . . Jenny's like Yelena . . .

"Your eyes are bandaged." It was the old doctor's voice.

"You paralyzed me when you operated. You hit my brain with your knife. I can't move anything but my legs."

"We have straps on your forehead and chest and hips so you can't move and jar that retina loose."

"Can I get them off pretty soon? So I can go to the bathroom and eat my supper."

"Not for a while. A long while. All the white must come back into your eye. The nurses will help you to eat and wash and everything . . ."

"Not everything!"

"We'll have an orderly help you with that whenever we can. Now we're going to help you sleep awhile."

"When will I see."

"We'll see."

"Do you like carrots?" It was Nurse Jenny.

Do you mind if I call you Jenny? You can call me Johnny . . .

"They help you to see."

"Nurse. No practicing medicine without a license."

Her giggle was like the bells on the Belgium dray that pulled the sleigh on the farm, but it was a throaty, a Marlene Dietrich laugh.

"Carrots! Yuck! Yuck to the third power, squared to infinity."

"That's a lot of yucks, young man," she said.

"Don't you have something like ice cream or chocolate cake that helps you to see again?"

"Boy," she said, "aren't we the lively one. Yes, I'm sure we can find a doctor who will prescribe just that and as soon as you wake up."

—

"I'm not sleepy."

"Yes, you are. I believe that young man with the wonderful voice is Mr. Raschi. His brother pitches for the New York Yankees. I believe he got hit in the eye with a baseball or something."

"Me and the Red Sox hate the Yankees. I'm not going to sleep."

"Johnny, you're like me. You can't hate anyone."

"Yes, I—" She was rubbing those soft tender circles in his temples again. The last thing he felt before he fell asleep was her brushing back his hair. *I think I love you, Jenny . . . Is it okay if I call you Jenny? Can I have . . . you . . . smothered in . . . ice cream?*

The time strapped to the bed passed very slowly.

Sometimes his mother could catch a ride with friends or relatives to the Mass General to visit her son. Other times she had to take the trolley from Rockledge to North Station and then walk halfway across Boston to visit him. Other times, if she didn't have the trolley fare to spare, she would walk the twelve miles into Boston.

More than one vehicle pulled up beside her while she was walking. "How about a ride there, beautiful?"

"No, thanks."

"Aren't you cruising? I've got the cruller, so if you want your honey dipped."

"The only thing you're cruising for is a bruising."

"Tough, huh?"

"She stepped aggressively toward the car. She was not in the mood for mashers. His car left two giant broken back snake tracks as the result of burning rubber. "Nutty old broad!" he yelled once he was sure she couldn't catch his old Plymouth.

But now she was beside his bed. "Johnny, you have to get better. Your sister and brother need you. I have to work so much it's nearly impossible to keep an eye on them, and they need you. Romola might need a brazie— some support upstairs. And your brother, God will get him. I found some pages from the underwear section of the Sears catalog hidden in that section of his brass bed. Where the knob screws off. And he's only ten, ten going on twenty. He thinks he's so big. He isn't. I can't even tell him to check and make sure my underwear is clean if I get hit by a car."

She looked out the window. Students from BU, BC, and Harvard were rowing their sculls on the Charles. "What are those skinny boats with those guys in their underwear rowing? What's this world coming to?"

"They're okay. That's—"

"Don't you sass back to your ma, or the next time I come in here, I'll bring my broom."

—

"You'd hit a helpless kid."

"Just enough to leave straw whiskers on your face."

Johnny was enjoying teasing his mother. "Ma, don't hit me!"

"What are you talking about? Do I beat children." She didn't want an answer. "Especially blind children. Oh my god, I didn't mean to say that."

"Ma, can you ask Righty or someone to come in sometime. What's out the window there, Ma?"

"It's just some dirty river, the Charles, Smarles, whatever, with a bunch of boys in their long johns paddling these skinny boats."

"Sculls, Ma. Rowing sculls, Ma."

"Don't you go correcting me, young man, if you know what's good for you."

"Will you come back a lot, Ma?"

"Of course. But I can't miss work. I have to buy your sister a brazi—there, I almost said that word again. I have to purchase her an upper support. And I have to beat your brother for that dirty stuff he hid in the bed. And I have to be there when I buy Romola her first brazi—her first upper garment. Otherwise, she'll get one too big so she can stuff handkerchiefs in it."

"The pages from the Sears is not Jazz's, Ma."

"Don't you lie to me, young man. Or the next time I'll just bring a bar of soap and wash out your mouth. It's certainly not yours, Johnny. That I know. Sure as God made little green apples."

"I wish I had some little green apples. I can't take a—"

"Don't you dare talk that way. Say I need help going number two."

"What else is out the window, Ma?"

"Just those young men on that smelly river in undershirts, showing their bare arms, with some sort of H on the shirt."

"They're from Harvard. And that's the Charles."

"Some skinny little guy with a megaphone is in the back of the boat, just like Rudy Vallee. I love that man. The skinny little runt is calling out numbers."

"He's the coxswain, Ma."

"Don't you dare talk that way in front of your mother! Just who do you think you are? Your brother?"

"Oh, Ma. What else is there out there?"

"Across the river, there's some kind of big blue lighted-up sign. It says Carter's Ink or something. Guess what?"

"What?"

"When I was coming in on the trolley, I went by the Big Bear. When you get better, I'll take you there shopping. It's a new giant market with a big bear on the roof. You can see the big bear and maybe you can pick out some fruit."

"Let's go to Faneuil Hall instead. They have—"

"I'm not taking you to any place your grandfather Shiverick says is evil. He said that's where the colonialists started plans to steal this country from our English people who discovered this country. They just slurped clam chowder at the Oyster House and planned to take this country away from the king and their betters. Why don't they tear that old place down? And now all those Micks are all over Boston as a result. Pope, politicians, every one. Mean and small. God hates the pope. He can't even speak English. And he would even have Santa's helpers talking a foreign language. Those priests talk to their parishioners with their backs facing them. What kind of church is that? I ask you—what kind of church is that? I'll tell you. It ain't no church. I'd like to take my broom to everyone of them."

"Ma, I've got lots of friends that are Catholic. You too."

"That's different. They're good people. They forget they are Catholics around me, just as well."

"That ain't something you can change by making them your friends. If the pope found out you were trying that stuff, he'd kick ass."

"First, don't you ever use no swear words around your mother. Did you get brung up in the gutter or something? And 'ain't' ain't in the dictionary. There isn't nothing worse than Catholics. Except Jap and Nazi awful people."

"Ma, there are good people everywhere. All kinds of good people . . . and Bernadette is Catholic . . . She is so nice . . . her voice so soft . . . her eyes so blue . . . bluer than a Siamese cat's . . . I would marry her . . . if I wasn't going to marry Yelena . . ."

"If you ever married a Catholic I don't know what I'd do."

He could hear her start to cry. "You certainly wouldn't be allowed in the front door of Grandpa Shiverick's house. How would you like that for starters? It would kill us both if you did that, but you won't. You've always been a good boy. God loving. God fearing. And it don't hurt no one to be that way."

"Ma, Dad was a Catholic when you married him."

"Don't you ever talk to your mother that way ever again. And I mean it. Don't you ever, ever say in public that your father was a Catholic. Your father loves and fears God and—"

"Ma, you don't have to come back too often. It's such a long way in here."

"That's the appreciation I get for coming halfway across the world to visit you. I had to push all kind of Chinamen aside to get here. There's so many of them they must be digging holes from Hong Kong twenty-four hours a day to get here. How many do we need? We don't got that many shirts to be starched. I did all this traveling to see you when I should be looking for a brassiere—there! I've said it!—for your sister."

Just hearing the word "brassiere" was a thrill, although coming from his mother took something off it. *Brassiere . . . wow . . . When Dad brought home that new washing machine . . . and Ma danced around the kitchen using the old scrub board as her partner . . . that was really great . . . and Dad said, "No woman of mine has to scrub with her hands."* And his father looked knowingly at the warning near the rollers that squeezed the clothes dry. *It said, "keep hair and breasts free of the roller," and when I read it, "keep hair and breasts free." Free breasts . . . I couldn't get upstairs fast enough . . . to remove that brass ball from my bed . . . and get my Sears pages out . . . Lingerie . . . I'd like to linger in ladies' lingerie . . . I'll have to get a new set of pages from Sears now that Ma found my pages . . . what is it that when I looked at the girls in their . . . in their brassieres . . . Great balls of fire . . .*

"Ma, you don't have to come every week."

"I'd crawl to my son every day. Through alligators and lightning. Will you talk to your brother as soon as you get home? When you get home, remember you had all that medicine that makes you drowsy and dizzy, so remember the fourth and ninth stairs are missing."

"Don't worry, Ma, four and nine, how can I forget my favorite numbers?"

"Oh, my baby Johnny, I love you so. I wish God would let me give you my eyes. I love you more than life itself."

"Come on, Ma. Someone might hear you."

CHAPTER 22

IT WASN'T JENNY

"You can't count it as losing your cherry," Righty said, looking down at his friend, wondering what it must be like to be strapped to a bed day after day. "What if it was a queer orderly or somethin' and not a nurse?"

Johnny strained at his straps, only making them tighter, hurting his breathing as they tightened against his chest, making hot irons sear his brain as the strap across his forehead tightened until his eyes bulged, and he feared they would be forced out of his skull. *My eyes have gotta be bulging like a fat frog . . . when dink broke its leg to win . . . the frog-jumpin' contest . . . What a horse's patootie . . . Of course the perfect asshole . . . Sorry, Ma . . . was Dirk the dirty . . . selling doughnut holes like Righty said . . . Danny the Doughnut Man would kill him . . . selling the holes he gave away free . . . but Danny can't kill him . . . the Japs . . . or was it the Nazis . . . killed Danny . . . Maybe both did it . . . Danny was gentle . . . but tough . . . He would kill Dirk for selling free doughnut holes to kids . . . that were free to us kids . . .*

Dirk had shown up at Duck Pond one day that the kids picked as a vacation day off from school. He knew they'd be there. He'd heard Rhesus say, "If this scrounge is going to try and sell us doughnut holes, he can put them in his oven, where the sun don't shine. We'll head to Duck Pond and fry up some fish." And he led the charge out the bakery door.

They were all bare ass and fishing when Dirk showed up.

"You punks better not get a fishhook caught in your peckers, if you have whackers, that is," he had called down to them.

"Hey!" Rhesus yelled back. "You squat to piss, you pussy!"

"Hey, monkey face, you want your kisser washed with your asshole?" Dirk said, heading down to the group, Rhesus in particular.

He stopped short as Johnny and Righty stepped toward him, backed up by the rest of the group. Even old skin and bones Fat Burns stood up to be counted.

Dirk stopped short.

Rhesus pushed past his friends and glared up at Dirk. "Ya got the rag on?"

"Back off, monkey. Or I'll do this to you." He picked one of the frogs out of the live bait bucket, snapped off a pieced of straw from a nearby clump, stuck it up the frog's rear end, and started blowing.

The frog got bigger and bigger; its eyes started to bulge.

Thinking about Dirk blowing up the frog, Johnny could feel his eyes bulging under his bandages.

Righty's words still rang in his mind. *What if it was . . . a queer orderly . . . or something . . .*

Johnny's eyes bulged even more as he repeated Righty's words to himself, "What if it was a queer orderly?"

His eyes started acting strange beneath his bandages. He saw a chicken's rear end open, like he had seen hens do so often to lay an egg. Instead of an egg appearing, it was an eyeball. Then he felt his eyes turn to eggs, all white. Like a monster's. The doctor said the white had left his eyes and that the white held his retina in place. The eye that appeared in the chicken's escape hatch popped out. Johnny tried to catch it, but it slipped out of his hands. He wouldn't ever see again. *It's my eye . . .*

"Are you okay, Johnny?" Righty asked. "Everyone wants you to come back to school. If you get better. And see. And come back. I'll even join the marines with you."

Righty took Johnny's hand and squeezed it tight.

"You were gonna join with me anyhow."

"Are you okay?"

"Ya. I dreamed for a second that my eye popped out of its socket like an egg from a chicken's touch hole."

"Oh, wow, an eye with chicken shit on it. Wait till I tell the guys about the great and crazy dreams you're having. They'll want to come here to the hospital."

They both laughed. It was the first time in the month since Johnny showed up at the hospital that he had laughed.

He hadn't laughed since the day his gun blew up and his ma rushed him to the hospital. She didn't have transportation to get him into the Boston Eye and Ear Infirmary, so she had borrowed a car. Well, sort of

—

borrowed it. Someone had left the keys in it. No one ever stole a car in Rockledge.

His mother had packed him in the backseat wrapped in a shawl that Grandma Shiverick had crocheted.

She had no trouble starting the old Plymouth with the big silver clipper ship emblem on the hood. Although she had never driven a car, she had seen a hundred drivers start their cars. She finally figured it out. The whoom of the engine starting terrified her.

The real trouble started when she attempted to find the right gear. She understood there was a forward and a backward. The car did a jerky cha-cha-cha, bumping and grinding forward and backward.

She attempted to go forward in third gear and gave it the gas, but the high gear left the car bucking like a horse with its bit on its balls. Then stalled.

Second was more interesting. She got a little further before it stalled. Perhaps twenty feet.

Reverse proved worse. Really bad. The car bolted backward, knocking over two trash cans, which was bad enough, but there was a big tomcat in one. It gave a scream. Interestingly enough, its scream drew an interested female that had ignored the tom over the years.

Her only thought was that she had run over an old woman.

Charity finally found first, and her take off was almost smooth. But she didn't dare search for the other gears that had played her for dirt earlier as the grinding set off a group of kids playing nearby, chanting, "Hey, lady, grind me a pound."

So she drove all the way through Rockledge, Medford, Somerville and much of Boston in first gear. The last part of the drive was down the wrong and oncoming lane on Storrow Drive.

Johnny lay in the backseat, not knowing what was happening, except his ride was not unlike his first ride on the Cyclone, Revere Beach's highest and fastest roller coaster.

It was terrifying, but they did arrive at Mass General Eye and Ear, and he had laughed as he was carried from the car to the stretcher, and he heard his mother ask the attendant, "Could you please drive this car back to Rockledge, corner of Washington and Pomworth Streets? But please take the keys out of the ignition when you leave it there and hide them under the seat. And don't worry about me getting home. I'll take the trolley."

And now he laughed again. *An eyeball with chicken shit on it . . . Righty wouldn't say shit if he had a mouthfull . . . Well . . . perhaps . . .*

—

Righty brought him back to the present. "It probably was a nurse, not no orderly. And all the nurses are really pretty. I'm sure you lost your cherry like you said."

Righty continued, "Ya, it probably was a nurse, but that doesn't count. You're supposed to look the girl right in the eyes when she cops your cherry. But first you gotta look down below and decide whether 'it' is in front or down below. Near the old scat chute."

Righty thumbed rides into Boston to visit Johnny second most. Bernadette Clarkson visited him the most, but how she got there he didn't know. But it wasn't that he tried not to think.

She had actually hopped a ride on the yellow peril and climbed on top, terrified of the sparks that shot from the rod that ran along the electrical overhead. Then she walked and jogged the rest of the way to the hospital. A far cry on how she used to get rides, but she had changed since that first day when he defended her.

She didn't say anything. Just sat there beside his bed.

She wanted to hold his hand.

He wanted to hold her hand.

They didn't hold hands.

"Are you there?"

"Yes."

"I know. I can see the blue of your eyes, Bernadette."

Silence. He knew she was staring at the bandages. He still hadn't seen the slightest ray of light as the flashlight beams were shone into his eyes day after day by the doctors and nurses who checked for dilation.

"Are you there, Bernadette?"

"No one calls me Bernadette," the girl everyone called Nookie whispered so low Johnny wasn't sure he had even heard her words.

"I do."

Silence.

"Are you there?"

"No one ever said anything about the color of my eyes."

Johnny knew that his friends, all the boys and not out of meanness as much as putting a lot of importance in being part of the gang in the know, thought of her large breasts and rear end as round and juicy as a Thanksgiving turkey, both of which bounced slow and languid and as rhythmically as a basketball dribbled to a slow and sultry New Orleans Basin Street glide and bounce.

Hadn't the football team named a play after her, one they always called when they had the ball close to the goal line? "Nookie Clarkson," the quarterback called, "We need a big hole. On five. Break!"

—

That always pissed me off . . . like the fly on the toilet seat . . . Bernadette is a good person . . . I'm sure of this . . .

He would bolt out of the huddle to his guard position when they called her play. His anger helped him to push the defensive guard opposite him backward until the player he blocked took out the linebacker as well.

The play became more and more important because it worked nearly every time. Then some wise ass would holler out, "And we all scored on Nookie Clarkson!"

Until the Thanksgiving game, when the Reading linebacker had called out, "Look out for the Nookie Clarkson!"

Johnny jolted past the guard he was supposed to block and sunk his helmet so deep into the linebacker's stomach that he thought his head would come out the opponent's rear end.

Now she was beside his bed. He wanted to ask her to hold his hand and instead said, "Thank you for coming. Not too many come to visit anymore. I've been here so long. Except Ma and Righty. It's just too tough to get to this place. How do you get here?"

"Mostly walk." It was a good twelve miles walk.

"There is some rough territory before you can get here, my mother said. You shouldn't be walking in here alone."

"Sometimes I get a ride."

Johnny winced. "You shouldn't take no rides from no guys. You could get hurt."

Silence.

"Did you leave?"

"No."

"You can be so quiet sometimes."

"That was one of the nicest things anyone has ever said to me, not to hitch rides. Sometimes I'm quiet when someone is nice to me, but sometimes when someone is nice, I think about the bad times. Other times I think about what is good. It is sort of like a battle in my mind."

When she was young, up until the age of eleven, her aunts and mother and even strangers said how lovely and happy child she was, always smiling.

Then her mother died.

What had been the times she was bounced on her father's lap changed to kneeling before him, her face pushed downward, the words ringing in her ears. "You have to say you love your old daddy he lets you do this."

The first time she was forced to open her legs, it hurt so much, and she fought so much that he threatened to change his attention to her younger sister.

—

"Don't do that to her. Do me."

So anytime Mr. Clarkson wanted his "beautiful Bernadette" and she wouldn't respond, he merely went through the motions of forcing himself on her baby sister in front of Bernadette.

"See what you are making your father do? You're no good, no good doing this to your poor dad. You're no good. The police will lock you up forever and send your sister to Russia, if you ever tell anyone. And it will mean you don't love your sister and old daddy. Won't it? You love your daddy, don't you? Of course you do. Come here. Go down on your knees and show your daddy how much you love him. When you are on your knees, it's just like you are praying. Tell your daddy you love him."

"I love you, Daddy."

"Bernadette, are you there? You're so quiet," Johnny said. "Maybe, when I get out of here, we could take a walk down to Dolefull's Pond, and I could swim out and pick you one of the water lilies. They are so beautiful. I know how to dive deep and grab the stem at the roots. They last lots longer that way. One time I had a bunch of them wrapped around my neck as I swam, and there was a water snake in 'em, and I swam so fast that Rhesus and Reynard, who were picking the lilies, thought someone stuck an Evinrude Motor on my tail. I carried the flowers they picked, and then they sold them to the rich people in Melrose Highlands.

"You must have a lot of girl visitors, and you'll have to give lily flowers to a lot of girls."

"No, I don't. But it is really too far. You shouldn't be coming in."

"Oh . . ."

"But I want you to. My ma comes in a lot. Perhaps you could meet my ma and come with her."

"No one ever wanted me to meet their ma before. Perhaps I better not."

"Perhaps. My ma cries a lot when she's here. Real low she cries. And tells me she caught a cold. My aunts come sometimes, and they bake me so many brownies and gingersnaps and apple pies that it hurts where the strap that strangles my stomach is. Righty comes in. Sometimes the whole gang, Skinny, Dick Tracy, Tim Yanders, Rhesus and Boattail, Scoff Burns, Soupy Campbell, Bobby Butt Burner. They come sideways to visit when they play Southie in football. But they made so much noise the hospital invited them to stay away. And Reverend Newhall comes in. He told me God didn't do this to me, but God will make me see the light one way or the other."

"Does Reverend Newhall bring his daughter Mandy and her cousin Mabel? They frighten me."

"How come?"

"They can be mean."

"How?"

Silence.

"You don't have to answer. It's has to be getting late. Doesn't your father worry about you walking home in the dark?"

Johnny couldn't see the glistening of her eyes.

"He has to worry. Fathers worry about their daughters. I know I'd worry about mine if I had one. Someday," he added.

"I try to get home real late. After he is done worrying and falls asleep. So I just check to see if my little sister is all right."

"You're lucky. My dad got all shot up in World War II. I was too young. They wouldn't take me. Or Righty. Or Rhesus or anybody."

"Where's your dad now?"

"He just got out of the hospital. Two years he was there at the Fort Devens Army Hospital. He walks with two canes now. He bought a brand new Packard with the Dunlop Gold Cup white walls. He takes my brother Jazz and me fishing, but we can't have worm juice on our hands."

"Does Yelena ever come to the hospital?

"Sometimes."

"She is the only one in the college course that isn't mean to me, I mean of anyone. And she's the most beautiful, the smartest, and the nicest. I voted for you and her to be king and queen of the carnival ball."

"Her father is a church deacon, and my grandfather Shiverick painted our church for nothing."

"She likes you. I heard her whisper to the other girls one time that you're awful nice. And awfully cute. I heard her whisper that in the library. She didn't know I could hear her."

"She's so good for me. She's got nice clothes. Look, we'll take a walk when I get out. It won't mean anything though. I mean we can take a walk or something."

Johnny couldn't see her rest her chin on her chest, look down.

"Are you still there?"

He could sense another presence.

"Can you see any light?"

"I think so."

"How about now?"

"It's like seeing headlights through a windshield in a rainstorm."

"How about this eye?"

"Yes."

"You're going to see someday. Someday soon. How much, we'll have to wait and see."

—

423

"Thank you."

"How's your back? The nurses giving you plenty of back rubs. You don't have any bed sores. You had a close call. We could look in your pupil and see that silver shining on your retina. Calls don't come any closer than that."

Johnny said, "I've had some close calls. Once I was playing catcher in a pickup baseball game, and this guy came sliding in just as the ball hit my glove and I put the tag on him. And the umpire called him safe, yet when the dust cleared, there is the guy, flat on his back. His toe about four inches from home plate. Then the umpire called him out."

"And you won the game!"

"Nah. We lost sixteen to zip. But the guy looked funny, just a couple inches from the plate. That's a close call."

"Once when I was a kid, the old doctor treating me for poison ivy told me he started a slide into second base way too early and stalled about four feet from the base. And the second baseman had to come off the base and tag him. Which he did, after he was done laughing."

Johnny laughed telling the story.

"That's the first time I heard you laugh in the three months you've been here," Bernadette said.

"I laughed when my friend Righty was here. He told me about this egg with chicken sh—. He told me this real funny story about Humpty Dumpty."

A new doctor came in and checked his chart at the end of the bed and said, "I think your eye will come back a little each day until you've regained your eyesight. It certainly appears that way. But we can't say how much will come back. You most likely will need glasses."

"Will I be able to play ball?"

"I think so. Oh, when you're fielding a fly ball on a sunny day, you might see a half dozen baseballs in the form of dust devils. These little spots in your eyes will be where the tiny pieces of metal pierced your eyes. Actually, they will look like pieces of dust on a projector lens, but things could have been a lot worse."

"Will I really have to wear glasses?"

"We'll wait and see. At the start you'll have to wear glasses that are all blacked out on the sides and the front except for a little pinhole for you to look through. This will keep you from taxing your eyes and risking them. Once a week you can go to an optometrist who will make that hole a little bigger each time, and pretty soon you'll be able to catch football passes as well as passes made by pretty young girls."

"Doctor, I didn't realize what a romantic you are." It was Jenny's voice. He didn't even realize the nurse was there.

Bernadette looked at her feet.

"The first thing I want to see when I can see again is you," Johnny said to the nurse.

"Oh. Why, thank you. Aren't you the little romantic as well. I guess you are getting better."

He loved her throaty laugh. He wasn't sure if it was that laugh, her rubbing little circles in his temples with her fingers, the heat he felt from her hands as she reached under his back to rub it without removing the straps he wore, or was it the warmth of her breath, that sweet sourness, or the warmth of her, whatever that very soft, very warm part of her was that touched him as she changed the sheets of his hospital bed with him in it. Or was it all of the previously mentioned.

It wouldn't bother me one bit . . . If Jenny was the one . . . who copped my cherry . . . whoa up Buster Brown . . . Merry Palm was the first . . . Boattail said some girls have dozens of cherries . . . professional virgins . . . but what about Bernadette? The guys say she still has her cherry . . . but its pushed so far back . . . she uses it as a taillight . . . Shut up, you bastards . . . you shut up too, DaSilva . . . her eyes are so blue . . . as soft as her voice . . . she was the one that said . . . Yelena liked me . . . Why would she say that?

Johnny smiled.

"Well, aren't you the cunning cutie," the nurse said, "smiling at me when you can't see me. Never have seen me."

Bernadette wished she had been the nurse.

CHAPTER 23

GOING HOME, GOING HOME, I AM GOING HOME

Jenny wasn't working the day Johnny was checked out of the Mass Eye and Ear Infirmary wearing glasses whose light was blocked out except for a tiny hole through which he saw the world in tiny sections. The doctor had told him that each week the miniscule porthole would be made a tad larger.

He had never seen her face and wondered whether he would ever see her. Johnny had heard her voice, felt her hand rubbing his painful bed-ridden back, felt her fingertips' soft circles on his temples; this beautiful woman was of his imagination.

He was wheeled to the front entrance in a wheelchair and lifted gently out in the powerful arms of his uncles Matthew and Mark Shiverick, who were just home from the wars.

The Germans and Japanese had both surrendered during his months in the hospital.

They had given up before he and his gang could get a whack at them. *Too bad . . . I could really work a peep sight . . . with these glasses . . . or be a night fighter . . .*

"You be careful with him." It was his mother's voice.

"Yes, sir," Uncle Matt said, clicking his heels, wincing, having forgotten about the Japanese machine gun bullets he had taken in the left leg while on Tinian. "Your little boy is a man now. In fact, why don't we

—
426

take the boy to Scully Square? He looks like a blinded vet. We could get his ashes hauled for free by some patriotic lady of the night."

"I'm not sure what you are saying, brother Matt, but if they are what I think they are, you are not going to be walking because I'm going to put some dents in your good leg."

"Come on, Sis, you'd hit someone who can't defend himself?"

"Hit you and your dirty talk? I'll press your pants with you in them," she said. "Now have that boy duck getting into the car and put his foot on the running board first."

"Wait one moment," Johnny said.

"Do you need to rest?" his mother asked.

"Nah, I want to see if Uncle Matt still has a foxtail on the antenna."

"'Course I do. And my lucky rabbit's foot on the key chain. If I had been thinking I would have brought both of them with me on the Tin Can to Tinian. Although it doesn't seem it did much good for the rabbit or the fox."

"But the fox's wiles and the rabbit's speed are a tough combo to beat."

"No one outruns a bullet," his uncle said.

Johnny was in the backseat beside his mother, while his uncle gave the gas to his old Hudson.

She pressed hard on the floor with her right foot, doing her part as a backseat driver, an art she had down to perfection.

"Where would you have kept the foot and tail, Uncle Matt?"

"Footentail," Uncle Mark said. "Didn't think you knew Kraut. I learned the language in German from a träulein friend. A pure, despite being mature lady. Gutentight, untouched."

"Enough! You naughty nitwits. Drive. My son wants to get home so he can talk to his brother.

"Ah yes, the nine-year-old who can only talk about owning a brothel," Mark said.

"Oh, brother," Matt said, then turning to his sister asked, "a brothel? Is that where they make soup, Sis?"

"I say, ol' chap, a spot of tea and broth," Mark mimicked.

"Could you stop here for a second, Uncle Matt?"

The driver pulled to the breakdown lane.

The three adults wondered why the boy was staring across the Charles; there was only the giant ink company there.

Johnny tried to focus his eyes through the peephole in his glasses. At first, the distance was merely out of focus. Then slowly the blue blur of the giant Carter's Ink sign across the Charles River came into focus. Jenny had said it was there, describing the blues whose neon impulses changed

—

as the atmosphere changed. "Johnny, the colors look like the deep blue of the ocean. The light blue of the sky. But not near as blue as the eyes of that little girl that comes to visit you so often."

And there it was, for Johnny to finally see. *There it is . . . the blue of the sky . . . blue like the ocean . . . like Jenny said . . . and I'm going home . . . like Jenny said I would . . . Righty . . . and Pointer . . . and Dink . . . Bernadette . . . Yelena . . . Jenny . . . I must forget Jenny . . . not to ever see her again . . . never more . . .* "Quote the raven."

"Are you talking to yourself?" his mother asked.

"Got money in the bank?" his uncle asked. "You talk to yourself. You've got money in the bank." Turning to his brother, he said, "I was wondering where you would have carried that foxtail and rabbit foot, with your backpack already full of long underwear, a shelter half, and extra socks and mess gear and ammo and all that stuff. Plus the extra skivie shorts to change into every time one of those little Japs jumped out and said, "Sayonara, Yank," and you did some double doody in your fun-to-wear un-der-wear."

The brothers were working overtime, trying to keep their young nephew entertained, his mind off his peephole glasses.

"Try corny," his brother said. "You carried not a single extra thing in your combat pack. Even a mess kit spoon that weighed a ton in the field. The first thing I got rid of was my gas mask."

"If you had a farting foxhole buddy like I had, you would have got rid of all your gear except your gas mask. And you wouldn't throw away your M1. You'd need the gas mask to stay alive and the M1 to shoot the purveyor of the flatulence."

"Young ears," Faith said. "Could we limit the toilet talk?"

"It's funny some of the crap different guys carried. Especially when a spoon and a fork and even mess kit were tossed away as weighing too much, and all the eating from the helmet was done with your KA-BAR knife. I remember one guy pulled his trench knife during some infighting and looked at the ketchup and beans on it before he stuck the bad guy."

"Come on, brother, it's up to my knees."

"Some guys shat-canned the things that'd help feed them or could save their life. One guy carried the baseball cards he collected when he was a kid. He'd pull them cards out at the strangest times and look at them. He loved Pistol Pete Reiser of the Bums. This guy said he liked Pistol Pete because he was a member of a drinking and shooting club. 'Drink all night. Piss to dawn.'"

"Little ears," Faith cautioned.

"Another carried a little music box that played 'Home Sweet Home.' I'll tell you, he was the only guy in the outfit the GIs wanted to kill more than Japs. He liked Stan Musial of the Cards. Joltin' Joe of the Yanks. Guess he liked spaghetti. King Kong Keller. Maybe he liked monkeys."

"And how about Johnny's uncle Manny? While everyone had pictures of their girlfriends or kids in their wallet, he carried a photo of a big buck he shot up in Maine."

"Down Maine," Johnny said.

They all laughed.

"Another world heard from," his mother said, brushing his hair back from his forehead.

"Now you done it," Matt said to his sister, your slamming on the brakes in that backseat. There's a blinking blue behind us, and it isn't Queen of the Tassles Sally Rand batting her eyes at the boys. Should I pull over or do a U turn and see if the silly bastard will follow us up Storrow Drive against the traffic?"

Faith told her brother, "You never swore before you went into the service."

"Well, that's because they stopped giving me merit badges for being good," Matt said.

"How do we know when you are telling the truth or kidding?" Charity asked.

"Don't you worry one bit, Reach in the glove compartment and get those ribbons out," Matt replied.

"Holy cow, you never told me you got this stuff."

"Just pin it on my Ike jacket."

"The Silver Star, the Bronze Star. The Purple Heart with two other hits! I'm impressed. I thought you only caught the leg shots."

"Hey, real heroes hide. You're decorated. I also have the Tijuana Theater Ribbon with a case of Clap Battle Star."

The large red-faced officer signaled to Matt to roll down his window. "Now what do we have here, lad? A gentleman wanting to help the city of Boston pay its bills. Oh, my little woman, Mrs. Murphy will be so happy. She needs happiness. She can't find out who threw the overalls in Mrs. Murphy's chowder. Now isn't that a good laugh? Lots of people I stop think I should be tossing them out at the Old Howard or casino, and I can get even funnier. And what do we have here? A hero. Surely, a man such as yourself understands that others besides yourself were in the corps. Like your officer Murphy that stands before you on this very day."

—

"Third Marine Div, FMF, Officer Murphy, be it," Mark said in an Irish brogue no one in the family knew he had and one his father, Mr. Shiverick, would have cut his son's tongue out for. Pretending he was Irish. How low can you go, the old man would have asked."

"Irish be ya?"

"On me late mother's side. Ya name be Murphy?"

"Yes, 'tis. Be you wanting to make something of it!"

"No, no, lad. Just want to determine if we're related. My muuthuur was a Murphy. Be you from South Boston originally."

Charity's eyes rolled skyward when Matt said his grandmother, who was as straight Scotch as a bottle of J&B, MacGreggor with a burr, by maiden name, was a Murphy. *Oh my good god . . . he made our mother Irish . . . God will have nothing to kill after Dad gets him . . . with his terrible swift sword . . . Oh my good holy Lord in heaven . . . his mother was a Murphy . . .*

"No, I was from Charleston," the police officer said.

"I don't believe it," Matt said. "We're relatives! Our family was from Charleston."

"You might be Irish, Mr. Shiverick, you're so full of bullshit blarney. But me relatives are from the North End. But it was sure an begorra a nice try. Now why don't you shift your limey arse into gear and trot trot to Mac-Rockledge, like a good unticketed lad."

"Thank you, Officer Murphy," Matt said, slamming the Hudson into gear, burning rubber, tossing gravel into the officer. He floor boarded it and, within seconds, put a dozen honking cars between him the officer.

"I hope you're happy now" his sister said. "You've probably jarred Johnny's eyes back into his ear sockets."

"You okay, kid?"

"Yah. You sounded just like Pat O'Brien in *The Fighting 69th*. And tough like Jimmy Cagney. Who taught you to drive like Maurie Amsterdam?"

"Amsterdam himself between races."

"No wonder we won the war," Charity the sister said. "The Axis found out we were all crazy."

Johnny put his head against his mother's shoulder and whispered low to her, "We could of won it sooner if they had let me in."

"I know, my Johnny baby."

"Maybe the next one."

"There won't be a next one. This was the war to end all wars."

"It's the second war to end all wars," Matt said.

"If there is a third war to end all wars, I'm going."

—

"Sleep, my Johnny baby."

"Ma?"

"Yes?"

"Would you rub my temples soft in little circles?" *Like Jenny . . . did . . .*

The last words he heard were his mother's "Not being able to see too good for a while you're going to have to remember four and nine, the four and nine steps are still missing. You go through those stairs and catch your head on the stair risers. Well, you might never see again."

"Rub my temples some more."

She did.

He slept. Blue ink ocean and sky sleep.

CHAPTER 24

A LITTLE BAG OF FLEAS

His mother couldn't keep him down.

Despite knowing a good jolt could prevent his eyes from healing correctly, perhaps forever.

She would have guessed that wearing the pinhole glasses was like walking in a tunnel, a long tunnel at which the opening at the end was miniscule, wondering what was beside him, on top of him. Or below. Where he stepped.

If he cracked his head on something high or stepped in a hole, that could be it.

He understood this. At least in part, he never forgot it was the treads of stairs four and nine that were missing. That he had to drag his feet to get the feeling when he was at the edge of the curb. But being careful alone wasn't enough. Add the fact that he would do a fancy dancy step when he was feeling his full ration of oats, especially as the holes were made gradually larger as the days progressed. But you still had to be lucky.

Luckily, he had learned to drag his feet long before to keep the flapping soles on his shoes from folding under his heel and tripping him and, more important, holding him up to self-ridicule in front of his friends.

He could have used a cane. Tap . . . tap . . . tapping . . . quote the raven . . . nevermore . . . He'd take his chances without the cane in his you-can't-keep-a-good-man-down game of Blind man's bluff.

He wished as the pinhole size was increased, now the size of the tip of a fork's tines, that the doctors would remove the leather shields on the sides of the glasses that cut out the light. Nope. Too much light was risky, they said. For it's . . . whiskey, whiskey, whiskey . . . that makes it mighty . . . risky . . . Of course he didn't drink. He never wanted to. Besides, hadn't his mother told him that beer and whiskey have worms in them?

Each week, his goal of larger peek holes meant trekking to the optometrist at Massachusetts Eye and Ear Infirmary to have the pinholes slightly enlarged. Johnny laughed at the blinders in front of friends, whinnying, making believe he was an old plug horse, thinking, *Makes me sort of . . . like the old horse . . . that pulled the milk wagon . . . over the cobblestone . . . The horse's hooves tap tap tapping . . . like a cane . . . no cane . . . for this kid . . .*

He was warned not to jerk his head swiftly or to suddenly look down. It meant everything was to be done in slow motion.

Then after a million light-years, the glasses, with that final large peephole and the side blinders were needed no more.

Now he often sat, the warm sun on his face, with his eyes closed. He never knew whether he did this sunning for a minute or an hour.

When the glasses came off, he was cautioned that he was still healing. He could lose everything he gained, could self-destruct, if he wasn't careful. He gave the warnings much thought. *Be careful, Dopey Johnny . . . Johnny be good . . . Jenny used to call that white thing I wore in the hospital . . . that thing without a back that left your ass in the air . . . a Johnny . . . and* sang, "Oh, Johnny, be good . . . to me . . . but for now . . . self, be good to me . . . *Be careful . . . or it's Helen Keller . . . here I come . . .*

Johnny did a lot of thinking, kept it to himself, as he wandered around town, always careful to not to be too close to the action. Not wanting to get hit by a foul ball or have some little girl whizzing a hula hoop clipping him, taking him down. *That's a fifteen-yard penalty for you, hula hoop kid . . . a lifetime of seeing eye dogs for me . . . I wonder whatever happened to Wendel Wilkie . . . I liked him . . . but I liked Roosevelt for president more . . . It was when he was on the radio . . . He told us the Japs . . . had invaded . . . Pearl Harbor . . . and I wanted to get them . . . just to . . . get them . . . Poor Mr. Roosevelt . . . a president that had to spend his life . . . in a chair on wheels . . . A cow's tail is long and silky . . . Lift it up and you'll find Wilkie . . . Wonder if us kids running around chanting this helped President Roosevelt win . . . Maybe we did help win the war . . . We couldn't have won without Mr. Roosevelt . . . and how about Dewey? Did we help the president beat Dewey . . . A cows tail is long and gooey . . . Lift it up and there is Dewey . . . a cow's tail is long and gooey . . . Lift it up and you'll smell . . . pew ey . . . up with cows tails . . . down with Dewey . . .*

—

Johnny opened his eyes and left his sunny spot to enjoy a drowsy meander.

The screeching of car brakes froze him. A car had come to a stop just feet from him.

"Hey, kid, waddaya, blind or somethin'? Get a dog."

"Sorry." He could see the red-faced driver, his nose a sore red bulb laced with purple veins, like a radish just pulled from the earth. "I wouldn't be sorry if I wasn't afraid of losing my eyesight . . . fat ass . . . You'd make W. C. Fields look sober . . . Christmas bulb nose . . ."

"Ya, I bet. You'd really been sorry if I clipped you. And if I had and you dented my grill, I would have backed over your sorry ass. I just don't like your attitude. With that sorry shit."

"Sorry."

"Don't get wise with me. I've got a good mind to get out of this car and fix your sorry ass. Your father should have kicked your ass when you were younger. Where is he, delivering garbage?"

"Your mother wears—army boots!" Johnny said, hightailing it behind a hedge where his old mongrel Rags had limped onto the scene.

"What did you say? You punk! Coward!" the driver yelled after him.

The word "coward" stopped Johnny in his tracks, and he reversed his running, stopping just short of this winner of a W. C. Fields look-a-like contest. He could smell the whiskey on the driver's breath.

"I said take a crap in your hat and pull it over your ears."

The door of the car swung open so fast it hit Johnny full force, knocking him to the ground.

The driver jumped out and stood over the boy. All Johnny could see was a huge belly that disappeared as its owner lifted his foot over Johnny as if to stomp him.

Practically toothless old Rags grabbed the shoe in his combination of worn flat teeth and gums and held on.

"Hey, hey! What the hell. Get this little bag of fleas away from me!"

Johnny heard Rags growling through his grip.

He knew the sound of his dog, all thirty-five pounds of fur and fury. He had heard when the old dog was young, had warned other dogs and nere-do-wells that he suspected, away with his then-toothy, true-grit growl.

Even now the would-be boot deliverer saw the true grit in the toothless growl.

"The driver shook off the dog and kept his shod foot high, that is until Righty showed up on the scene, jumped on the driver's back, and yelled to

Rags, "Bite his balls, Fang!" Righty had changed the old dog's name to fit the situation.

The driver only saw the foam in the dog's mouth but didn't back off. Instead, he kept his foot high in the air to deliver it to Johnny or Rags, whichever made the first move.

"Bite his balls, Fang!"

"What the fuck!" the boot lashed out at the little dog, caught it in the ribs, driving it into the ground.

The dog didn't whine. In fact, the growl did sound like one that would be an order issued by a ninety-pound German Shepherd called Fang.

Johnny went to his knees, found his dog, and rested its head in his lap.

He heard the hurried footsteps of the boot that had put the little dog down, heard the car door slam and speed off.

Rags moaned as Johnny picked him up, cradled him in his arms. They walked the three miles to Wakefield and the SPCA there.

"Can I help you, son?"

The veterinarian there had a kindly face, what Johnny could see of it through the glasses.

"Rags, he's hurt. Bad. Can you help him?"

"Hmmmm. You're right. He's hurt bad. Sounds like fractured ribs punctured a lung. I don't think you can afford that kind of care. I can put him in with the other dogs that we're putting to sleep tomorrow morning."

Johnny remembered his uncle Manny DaSilva telling him about the time he tried to get this English setter the SPCA had, and it was all set until his uncle was asked, "This will be a family dog, won't it? It won't be used for hunting, will it?"

"Both. This dog will be treated in a way I wish I could be treated, and we'll be the best of hunting buddies."

Johnny had heard the story many times around the campfire, when his uncle visited him and Dink and Pointer on the hill behind the farm, where they camped when they were afraid Pie would do something real mean.

"This dog is spoken for."

The SPCA veterinarian turned and walked away, but his uncle had still heard his words, "the policy is no dogs are let out to do some more killing."

Two days later, he had his brother Francisco go to the pound and ask for a dog. He said he loved terriers, boxers, setters.

"Too bad, we had a lovely English setter, long soft ears, the gentlest eyes, a lovely, special animal. But no one wanted him, so we put him to sleep."

—

Francisco's brain nearly exploded. He had helped slaughter many farm animals—pigs, chickens, cattle—but this made him sick. It was the fact that suddenly he had to throw up that saved him from thirty days in jail, as he could barely see the veterinarian through the blood red fog that made him ill. He walked out.

And Johnny, on this day, walked in with the words, "Look, sir, I can do with you what I do with my dentist. I give him the money as I get it, and when I have enough, he fixes a tooth. Rags needs fixing."

"Interesting."

"And I could give you some money now and keep putting it into your envelope until I paid you all up. Just fix him now."

"Sounds good. Bring the dog back when the envelope is full."

Johnny spit in his face.

The vet took a step toward him, but the little dog still had a growl left in his body, and he took two steps backward.

It was tough carrying the little white mongrel the three miles back home. It was tough enough looking through the pinholes, but the salt stinging his eyes made it even rougher.

The little dog licked his hand. The tongue that hung long as he had followed Johnny as he'd run to fishing or to a pickup baseball game now had little strength. "I know you don't want me to feel sad, Rags . . . I can't help it . . . Oh, please don't smile . . . That grin hurts too much now . . ."

It was nearly dark. He realized he was walking in the street when a car came directly at him. It only had one light on. *Kadiddle . . . if I was with Bernadette . . . or Yelena . . . Nah, she wouldn't have me . . . I could claim a kadiddle kiss . . . I wonder if Bernadette saw the one light first . . . if she'd claim a kadiddle . . . Yah . . . the guys say she gives more than a kiss . . . I gotta get a girl to cop my cherry . . . Oh, Rags . . .*

"Please hold on."

"Where have you been? You've frightened me clear out of my mind."

It was his mother. She was on their front steps.

"I gotta get to bed, Ma."

"You okay?"

"Yah."

"What about supper."

"I ain't hungry. And ya, I know, 'ain't' ain't in the dictionary."

"You're not hungry? You're okay?"

"I ate at Grandma Shiverick's." He hated to lie to his mother, but sometimes a white lie is better for everyone concerned. Otherwise, in this case, his mother would have kept arguing that he had to eat. The only problem with fibber-a-dibbing was that you had to look around, make sure there were no darning needles in the air looking for kids that fibbed so they could sew up their lips.

"Okay. Go to bed, and don't forget to take your socks off and air them out."

He had to hang his socks out the window each night so they would be clean smelling the next morning. This turned Johnny into quite a weatherman. If it rained or snowed during the night, it meant he had to wear his Sunday go-to-church socks to school the next day.

In the spring, they smelled good, like new-mown hay. Sometimes in the summer, they would smell like the Concord grapes that hung in lush clumps from the Pinellie's vines or even a little bit like Mrs. Pinellie's apple pies that she baked once a week. Fall was the most fun. Sometimes the maple tree's winged seeds that whirly birded down in an effort to provide future trees caught in a sock. He would sometimes take one of the parachute pilgrimages of jumpmaster Mother Nature, split the seed apart at its base, and stick it on the end of his nose, making it appear as if a small, green butterfly had landed there to rest until such a time as Johnny's sneeze set it afloat.

The winter socks were tough. Especially if his feet had been sweaty and they froze in the cold. Trying to get a warm foot into a sock frozen thin as the hockey stick blade of Bruin's center Dit Clapper was no easy task.

The few times he tried to secret them under his pillow rather than hang them out the window led to his mother sniffing up a storm like a beagle on the bunny trail and pulling painfully upward on his sideburns with the words, "Whose feet do not smell sweet?" Charity didn't particularly want to hurt Johnny but didn't want him getting into a fight in school with one of the big kids who called him Chief Stink Foot.

He told Righty the cold winter socks made him shiver more than from fright when listening to *I Love a Mystery* on the radio or a visit to the House of the Seven Gables in Salem, where witches walked.

He told Righty, "That day we visited the witches' home, my dad, Jazz, and I also fished Salem Willows. We always rowed way out of Salem Willows harbor, past all the other rowboats, and caught the most and biggest fish of anyone."

Righty said his mother heated his bed with the flat iron she kept on the stove for such jobs as warming sheets, socks, and gloves.

Johnny continued, "We caught flounder and mackerel and an occasional sand shark. Sometimes we hooked into a dogfish, and the shark would drive its spike of a tail into the side of the boat Dad rented, and it had to be dug out with a knife while all the time keeping a weather eye out for its teeth."

Then they were at Johnny's house, where he was greeted by his mother, "Get in the house, missing person, and watch out for those two missing stairs! And give that Rag dog an extra hug. He's shivering in your arms. You don't look good. I'm gonna bring some supper up to your bed. For both of you. So don't go giving it all to the dog."

Boy and dog no sooner got into bed than Charity showed up with steaming corn chowder and thick tear offs of Grandma Shiverick's homemade bread. The day's leftovers mixed in warm gravy were especially for the dog.

Rags didn't eat. Johnny didn't either. They were shivering and warming up was more important than filling up at that moment.

"Jazz. You asleep?"

"Yah."

"Help me hug Rags. He won't stop shivering."

"Okay."

"Don't hug too tight."

"Okay. You feel like a piece of bread?"

"Nah. I'm not hungry. You eat it."

"You forgot our game. Do you feel like a piece of bread? I feel like a piece of bread. So Rags is a piece of baloney. We made him a sandwich between us."

"I can't play, Jazz. Rags doesn't feel all that good. So no funnies tonight, okay, huh?"

"I know, but you know how Rags is. Anytime we don't feel good, he tries to cheer us up, dancing on his back legs. Gives us that shit-eating grin."

"You don't want to swear, Jazz."

"I gotta learn to swear, Johnny, 'cause Ma thinks when I grow up I'm gonna run a whorehouse, and you gotta know how to swear to run one of those."

"How old are you, Jazz?"

"Ten."

"Going on thirty. Why does Ma think you're gonna run one of those places, anyway?"

"She found one of those books with girls in them that I had hidden in the bedposts. You know, the hiding places only you and I know about. You never looked in my bedpost, did you, Johnny? I never looked in yours."

"You know better than that. You never looked in mine I know."

"Nah. Well, maybe once, by mistake. Where in unholy Hanna did you get a book like that?"

"In the drugstore."

"They don't sell those to us kids," Jazz said, sort of sad.

"It sort of fell into my hands while I was looking for a Valentines card for Ma. Ya, that's it."

"You'd better look around for a darning needle bug on that one."

"Jazz. Go get Roma."

"Why?"

"I think Rags feels real bad."

Johnny heard his little brother get out of bed and walk softly down the hall, so their mother wouldn't hear him. Then he heard the two sets of footsteps returning.

"Johnny?" It was Roma. "I love Rags."

"I know."

"Me too, Johnny," their little brother said.

"Yah, I know, Jazz," Johnny said. "I'll rest him on my chest, and you two guys can hug him from each side."

"Johnny, I know you're not supposed to love people cuz it makes you a sissy," Jazz said, "but it's okay to love dogs, ain't it?"

"Ya. But shut up and hug."

"We gotta lift the irises out carefully," Johnny said as the three of them dug the hole, "so no one will know Rag's is in here."

"Except us," Roma said.

"Yah, just us and Rags," Jazz said.

They each had put a piece of their favorite clothing on the dog. Johnny, his Red Sox hat. Jazz, his Popeye the Sailor sailor shirt. Roma, her last two pair of bobby socks.

Jazz looked at his big brother. "He won't be cold now, will he, Johnny?"

"Nah, kid."

The three of them lifted the little dog wrapped in Johnny's jacket off the ground. He knew his mother would be angry that the winter coat she had bought him two sizes too big so he could get two seasons out of it was lost.

"Waste not, want not," she had said. "And until you grow into it, you can carry Rags under it."

The coat now carried the little dog as he was lowered into the iris bed.

Roma hesitated in lowering Rags.

"It's okay, Roma," Johnny said. "We'll be with him again someday."

"I know, but Ma will kill you when she finds out Rags was buried in your coat, and you'll get to have Rags all the time," Roma said.

—

"What about your two pair of bobby socks, Roma?"

"I won't tell on you guys," Jazz said.

"I'd guess not," his sister said, "with Rags wearing your best Popeye shirt."

Their mother, who watched and listened to her three children from behind an upstairs curtain, bowed her head and covered her eyes with her hands. *Your mother won't . . . kill you . . . little ones . . . but I sure can't wait to hear . . . your little fibs . . .*

Below, Johnny prepared to carefully place the first shovel full of dirt on the little Rag's grave. "You put your arm around your sister, Jazz."

"I ain't hugging no sister."

"Okay then, say a prayer for Rags then."

"Okay. Dear God, take care of our dog, Rags. Or else. I hope God didn't hear that."

"What?" Johnny asked.

Roma looked down at her little brother. And both started sobbing.

"Cut it out! We ain't no sissies." They both stopped crying. "Did you bring your Jew's harp, Jazz, or did the teacher take it from you again?"

"I got it. But I don't know how to play no taps."

"You heard it at the Fourth July parade when they played it at the cemetery and fired their guns."

"Why can't we fire guns in the air instead?" Jazz asked.

"We just can't," his sister said.

"It's because we don't got no guns," Jazz said quite disappointedly.

"That's a double negative," Romola said.

"Oh, Ms. Smarty Pants," Jazz said.

"Just play your Jew's harp, smarty pants yourself," his sister said.

"Nah. We ain't no Jews," Jazz said. "We're piss-in-the-pail agains."

"Episcopalian, dummy," his sister said.

Jazz played taps.

They all thought his effort sounded fantastic but an unbiased judge would have ventured that the spring metal musical instrument sounded more like two skeletons shagging on a tin roof.

Johnny shoveled while Romola put her arm around her little brother's shoulder while she crossed herself, not knowing what to do. She had seen Catholics do it when they were sad or frightened or didn't know what to do. *Us protestants got nothing . . . to make us feel good . . . when we feel bad . . . except God . . . that ain't so bad . . . I guess . . .*

She felt guilty about her thoughts. "Jazz, you play awful."

"Shut up," her little brother said.

"You shut up."

"You both shut up."

"We ain't got no Rags no more," Jazz said.

"Yes, he's in doggie heaven," his sister answered.

"Will we see him when we get there."

"You only get to doggie heaven if you're real good," Johnny said, "and don't swear or answer back or have that type of book fall out of hell into your hands."

"I think I hear Rags under the dirt," Jazz said, tears suddenly streaming down his face as his body racked with sobs.

Roma and Johnny hugged their brother.

It was much like the night before.

Except on this hugging there was no little dog between them.

CHAPTER 25

THE INVITATION

"You were the one who visited me most while I was in the hospital."

"Righty visited you most," Bernadette said, quickly glancing at Johnny, then lowering her eyes when he returned her gaze.

"He doesn't count. He's my best friend."

"Everyone in the class wanted to visit, but teacher said we had to be careful not to bother you too much. It was so far to go, and after the yellow peril lets you off, you have to walk miles through traffic and everything. Unless you take a taxi."

"You did it. Walked miles."

"That's different. Most of the kids have so much to do, sports and clubs and hanging out."

"Yes, I know. Today's the first day my glasses came off. Five weeks of wearing blinders. It seems longer than the months I was in the hospital, and I never would have seen you behind me just now if I still was wearing them."

"I was just, well, sort of just out walking."

"Want to take a walk to Duck Pond?"

"It will be dark by the time we get there."

"You don't have to afraid of the dark when you're with me. Besides, I learned to get around in the dark."

"I'm not afraid of the dark." She looked down at her feet. "Except when I'm in bed."

"You don't have to be afraid of anything when you're with me."

"I know, but you're not in bed," she looked down again. "Not with me when I get scared."

Not in bed . . . with me . . . It was Johnny's turn to check out his shoelaces.

They walked in silence, Johnny kicking a stone in front of him, taking the tinfoil off the paper that had protected the cigarettes inside their package, discarded carelessly, collecting the tinfoil that was growing to golf-ball size. Tossing the ball in the air and catching it with his left hand, his right, behind his back. He put the tinfoil in one pocket and reached in other front pocket and, with his right hand, pulled out a ball of string he had been collecting and tossed that in the air again and again so he wouldn't have to look at her.

She was glad he was tossing the string ball in the air and had to watch it so she could look at him rather than her having to walk watching her feet each time he glanced at her.

He took the tinfoil ball out of his pocket and tossed both in the air at the same time, catching both each time, until he glanced at her and both fell to the ground. "Once I had three balls I played with."

They both looked at the ground.

Johnny blushed for himself. Bernadette blushed for Johnny.

"Let's walk the railroad tracks to Duck," he said, cutting off Main Street at the Corporal John Williams Swimming Pool, named after Rockledge's World War II hero. Williams had won the Congressional Medal of Honor after he destroyed three German machine guns nests that had pinned downed his outfit.

"The pool is named after a guy I used to deliver the morning paper to. He wiped out three Nazi machine gun nests. The last one after a mortar shell landed near him. Damaged his leg so bad he had to cut it off before getting the last one. He spoke to our Boy Scout troop. He spoke so low we could hardly hear him. He didn't talk about the war, just told us to be good Scouts and not fight. Unless you were forced to. I liked him so much. He liked to hunt and fish and walk around all alone in the woods, sort of bashful-like. Then he died."

"Gee."

"Probably his heart was broke."

"Oh that poor, poor Corporal Williams. He should have been a general."

"That wouldn't have worked so well. 'Cause generals don't have to get out of foxholes and do that sort of stuff. I want to be a corporal someday."

"Promise me you won't get hurt and won't have to live in some kind of hole you dug."

—

"I promise. Hey, who wants to lose a leg and not be able to find it?"

"No one."

"Hardly anyone who swims here knows who he is. All they got to do is read the plaque. It's only been three years since the war ended. Everyone's forgot. Not everyone forgets. My father uses two canes to walk, wherever he is."

"You're lucky."

"What do you mean?"

"Your dad being away someplace," Bernadette said.

"What do you mean?"

She looked at the ground. "So your sister can sleep."

He shrugged his shoulder, trying to indicate he understood or he didn't understand. To end the confusing conversation, he said, "Let's see who can walk on the rail the longest without falling off."

"I don't have good balance," she said.

He searched in the woods, found a sapling, and cut it off with his jackknife and trimmed off the small branches.

"You walk on that track, and me on this, and we'll hold the branch so you can balance."

"It will be sort of like holding hands for balance," Bernadette said, looking down. "Not like when you and Yelena hold hands. 'Course not."

"'Course not. Yelena is my girlfriend. Sort of."

"You know what?"

"What?"

"It's sort of like playing electricity," she said.

"What's that?"

"Well, say if you were playing tag, and someone was trying to tag, and say 'you're it,' but someone else reached out and touched you and said 'electricity.' You would be safe from the person trying to tag you."

"I don't get it."

"Well," she looked down at the ties, nearly losing her balance on the rail, "if you're holding the stick and I'm holding the stick and one of us said 'electricity,' it would mean sort of like we were we were holding hands, but not really."

He looked down at the rails and said, "Electricity." Then looked up quickly, again catching the flash of her China-blue eyes just before her lashes veiled them.

And they both looked down.

The sun was setting quickly now, causing the trees to cast their dark shadow hands over them, around them.

—

Johnny fell off the track when the shadow of one branch, appearing like a small dark hand, fell on her breast. *I've never fallen off before . . . I've never fallen . . . before . . .*

"A penny for your thoughts."

"I was thinking, ah, I hope I make the football team next fall." *Liar, liar . . . pants on fire . . .*

"You were a starter last year. The best football player in the world, the whole world."

"Ya, but you can never be sure, completely sure, of anything."

"Well, maybe one thing."

She looked down.

"Ya," he said, "sometimes I get confused. Look! You can see the sun and the moon both."

"And you can see 'em both on the surface of the pond. It's the most beautiful sight I've ever seen," Bernadette added.

Johnny looked at her, and then down at his feet before she could see his glance. *You're the most beautiful sight . . . I've ever seen . . . 'cept for Yelena . . .* "Ya, maybe. The Duck at night, with the sun and moon on it, is really pretty. Thought one time I saw two butterflies kiss in midair. Remember in Bambi, the birds and the bees and the butterflies were twitterpated. Dizzy. Like some silly kids get."

"Ya. Twitterpated."

It was dark now. They could see the cars on the opposite side of the pond, their lights on.

Johnny spotted a car with only one headlight. "Kadiddle!" *You have to kiss me . . .*

"What's that mean? Tell me." *Tell me I have to kiss you . . . that's what kadiddle means . . . one light . . . one kiss . . .*

"Oh, nothing. It means nothing." *Oh, you sorry little coward . . . coward . . . coward . . . coward . . . but I already kissed . . . Yelena . . .*

"Yes, sir. It means something." *Oh, he's so different . . . the others want so much . . . more . . .*

"Ya. It does."

"What? Tell me."

"Well, the moon just came out."

"Yes?"

"Well, when you first see it, the first one who sees it says, 'Hi diddle kadiddle, the cat and the fiddle, the cow jumped over the moon." He stepped off the track, walked the rail, using the stick as a clicker behind him, like when he used a stick on a picket fence to make the rat a tat tat of a machine gun. Looking down all the while. "Ya, kadiddle means nothing.

Although my uncle Franchesko said once, "When you see a car with one headlight or the first moon on the water, you have to say 'kadiddle, the cat has to piddle.' Sorry 'bout the language."

"Oh." No one, ever, had apologized to her.

"Hey, there's Duck Pond Rock. When we skip school, we go there and fish and sun and swim. Sometimes we cook up a yellow perch. And share a bottle of Royal Crown. You get the most tonic in Royal Crown Cola."

"It sounds like fun."

"I'm in charge of making sure no one drinks more than their share. One time we filled an empty bottle with water and kept measuring what we poured out, and then measured each section of the bottle and put a tic mark on the back of the bottle. It's kind of important we share and share alike."

"Yes, it sounds important," she said.

"It is."

"Very important, I bet."

"I'd love, I mean I'd like to swim and fish with you sometime. Yelena doesn't like to swim or fish, although she said she loves to sun where her family goes to the islands. She said that we would go to the islands together later in life, when I become a lawyer or doctor. She said I can accomplish anything I set my mind to."

"I'd like it to fish or swim here."

"We can't. We don't wear no bathing suits when we dive in Duck. Your father would kill you."

Her voice became very sad, "No, he wouldn't. He wants to keep me alive."

As the moon lowered in the sky, its rays reflected along the surface to where they sat.

"Can we sit for a moment before we go back?" she asked.

"Sure. No, wait a sec."

She looked at him when he stood abruptly and disappeared into the nearby woods. "Don't leave me alone." She tried not to sound frightened. Don't leave me alone . . . Don't leave me alone . . . in my bed . . .

Then she saw him in the nearby woods take the jackknife out of his pocket and open it. The blade caught the moonlight, flashed steel for a moment, and then disappeared. A cloud covered the sky, and he disappeared.

She was looking into the dark where he appeared nearby.

"Here. Over here," she said, trying not to be worried about being in the dark.

He returned from the woods holding a handful of balsam and fir. "It will make a nice seat for us. Smells good, and they're not sticky like pine can be."

"Oh."

"Sometimes, my cousins and I made a lean-to out of pine. Then we make beds with balsam and fir and hemlock, and we sleep out all night."

"I'd be afraid."

"You'd never have to be. If you were one of the guys, I'd protect you."

"My father, Gord, said nobody can protect somebody all the time, 'cause you can't. Nobody can protect nobody else."

"He's wrong. I don't mean to disrespect your father, but he's wrong. There is always someone who can protect someone else. Always."

"You think so?" She tilted her head softly to the side as she looked into his eyes for a brief moment; even in the night sky, her eyes remained the color of the day's.

"I know so." *Bernadette . . . I would protec . . . You are so beautiful . . . I want to kiss your lips . . . No . . . No way . . . has she done . . . it . . . for as many guys as they claim . . . No . . . they lie . . . but I love Yelena . . . and she . . . me . . .*

"A penny for your thoughts."

"I was thinking, the moon is so beautiful."

"You're like a poet."

They both looked down, holding their glance low for several seconds, looking up at the exact same moment.

She looked into his eyes, closed hers halfway, moved closer to him, her lips parted.

She wants to kiss me . . . She wants me to kiss her . . .

He moved his face close to her, could smell her. *She smells like apple blossoms . . .*

Closer. Her lips were puckered. Reaching out for his.

He moved his mouth closer to her slowly. *Our noses . . . they're going to . . . collide . . .* Johnny was close to panic. *What do you do . . . not to have . . . the noses . . . collide?*

At the last moment, close to panic, he tilted his head, swerving like a car trying to avoid a collision.

Their lips met. His head swirled, dizzying him with mind and heart dust devils.

He pulled her close. Felt her breasts crushed against his chest. He kissed her harder, his mouth opening slightly. *Are we . . . going . . . to do . . . it?*

—

She pushed him away, flattening him against the evergreen bed he had made.

"Why?" He felt like crying. She had done "it" with dozens of guys, maybe hundreds.

Her answer was so soft he could hardly hear it. "You're a nice boy."

"No! No, I'm not." Please . . . please . . .

Bernadette sprung to the sitting-up position at the cry of a faraway loon. "What's that noise?"

"A loon."

"I'm frightened."

"Don't be, but we better go," he said.

"Can we stay just a little while longer until he's asleep?"

"Loon's stay up all night."

"I mean my fath—, Gord."

Bernadette looked at her hands, which she held in front of her, palm up. "Did you really mean you're not a nice boy? I don't believe you."

"Nah. I lie sometimes."

"No, you don't. You were just kidding."

"Bernadette?"

"Yes?"

There is a giant beechnut tree in the woods. The moonlight shines on it. Its bark is so smooth. "Come with me."

She looked at the dark of the trees, the shadows. "Why? I'm afraid of the dark."

"Don't be. Take my hand. Don't be a stranger in paradise. (He remembered the words from the song on the radio) Wait. He picked up a small stick, handed one end to her. "Electricity! Any goblins come out from under a toadstool, I'll clock them with double the power."

He led her through the dark of the thick pines stand and to the hardwood where the giant beech was.

She watched as he pulled out his jackknife and opened the blade. "I'm not afraid. Like you told me not to be."

She watched as he carved into the smooth bark. "J.D. & N.C."

"Who's N.C.?"

Oh my god . . . Bernadette Clarkson . . . not Nookie . . .

"Oh, ah, it stands for, ah, No Clue."

"No, it doesn't. You're like the rest of them! My name is Bernadette."

She ran through the dark woods, the limbs slapping her face like hateful witches, until she came to the trolley tracks, and then ran down the tracks blindly, still holding her hands over her eyes. Not so much as to continue to defend herself against the trees no longer there, but rather to block out his carving. "N.C."

Johnny stood frozen in the woods. His hands covering his face.

He walked all the way home with his hands spread across his eyes, wishing he was blind again, just catching an occasional glimpse of where he was going. Surprised to find himself on his own porch.

"Did someone try to strangle you and miss?" his mother asked as he walked through the door.

"What do you mean, Ma?"

"You've got a set of hand prints embedded in your cheeks and forehead."

"I was just thinking."

"Pretty deep thinking. It appears your fingernails are branded into your brain."

"Can't be. I'm a no brainer." How in a million years did I . . . ever do that . . . carve N.C. It's Bernadette . . . B . . . Clarkson . . . B . . . B . . . C . . .

"Are you thinking too much again, Johnny? You'll wear out that brain someday."

"No, Ma, I just thought yesterday."

"Don't you be fresh with me, young man, unless you want your tail tanned."

"Yes, Ma."

"Don't you yes me, young man."

"Yes, Ma."

"Go to bed, young man!"

"Yes, Ma." *I'm a naughty little kitten . . . who has lost . . . a mitten . . .*

He headed up the darkened stairs and counted to himself, "Three. Eleven," despite knowing it was steps four and nine that were missing.

His leg slipped through the missing step, and as his body, his legs in a split, descended cellarward, the stair tread came up to greet his groin like the uppercut of a giant fist.

His groan was that of a huge wounded beast leaving the earth.

His mother bounded out of the kitchen, up the stairs, not having to count out the missing steps. "Are you trying to commit suicide?" she screamed.

She fell to the steps beside him and enfolded him in her arms. "My baby Johnny. Oh, Johnny. Oh baby, please don't be dead."

He looked up at her and, through a painful grin, said, "I'm okay. I did what you always said. Fell on my head so I wouldn't get hurt."

"You darn little piece of poop. You can't even count anymore. You scared the living life out of me."

—

"Ma, you're messing up my hair."

"Mr. Wise-mouth again. You're all right. God takes care of little children and fools."

"Yes, Ma."

"You'll be the death of me."

"I know, Ma. I'm no piece of poop. I'm just a stinking bird turd."

"Don't you use that language around me. Go to bed. Leave my lightbulb alone, and don't put no books against the bottom of your door to keep me out. Only the Good Book could stop this woman."

He slowly pulled his leg out of the missing step, where it had dangled in the cellar like some stalactite with a foot covered by a white sock with a hole in its heel, jumped to his feet, and bolted up the stairs after first smacking her on the butt. "Gitty-up, old horse."

"You do that again, young man, and I'll sell you to the Gypsies, minus a head. Someone's feeling their oats."

"You can't sell me to the Gypsies, Ma. You forget you sold me last week to the chinky, chinky Chinaman."

"Don't you dare slur any ethnic group. Anyone, for that matter!"

"Not even the Catholics, Ma."

"That's different, and you better not ever marry one."

Johnny could hear his sister in her bed, singing to herself. Or one of the paper dolls he had drawn for her. He had also designed and drawn clothing for her paper dolls in exchange for her making him french fries and fudge and promising not to let the word out that he drew paper dolls and their clothing for her. He'd kill her first, slowly, with a barbwire garrote, and then any wise guy she had told.

He peeked in through the crack in the old door.

The crack was the result of his father's partially playful, partially peeved swing at it. He had planned to take Johnny fishing the next day, but radio warnings were for a severe storm. It was the rattling of the loose windowpanes in their cracked putty settings, informing him of the coming bad weather that initiated the swing. The door forgot to duck.

And now Johnny looked in through the crack at his little sister. She was growing. He smiled to himself. *Man . . . what would she say if she knew I smiled at her . . . probably bats in your belfry buddy . . .*

Their mother had tied her hair in rags so she'd have nice curls the next day. She apparently planned to join Romola in bed shortly, as her teeth soaked in a glass of water on the nightstand. He could see the salt she had poured in the glass so the water wouldn't freeze, making little bubbles rise.

Good . . . Must be payday . . . She bought salt . . .

—

"I'll get a good brushing tonight. The baking soda brushing gets tiring." *Makes me feel like a darn . . . biscuit preparing to be baked . . . while I'm brushing . . .*

Romola had a rag doll on the pillow beside her, usually with a bonnet on her head, a bonnet with a bright-red ribbon around it and bright yellow and green daisies. Rags had it on this night. She used him as her live baby doll.

She was singing softly, "Rags, my little baby. Don't run away and join the naby. And don't you ever go and die on me ever again." She shook her finger in the rag dog's face. "Never. No, no, no."

Johnny strained his ears to hear. *Probably a hymn . . . Ma shouldn't feed her so much religion . . . She believes everything . . . 'cept her big brother . . . who should be a gosh-darned god to her . . .*

"Florence, Florence Nightingale," she said to dog doll that was now dressed as a front line nurse, "let us hurry to the battlefield to tend the soldiers. Let us help win World War II, the war to end all wars." It was only later, in high school English, she learned that Florence Nightingale was in the Crimean War and that hero Lord Cardigan, an undiscovered cad, the man the famous wool sweaters were named after, had unsuccessfully tried to starve her to death.

Romola changed from her soft nurse's voice to her "soldiers heading to the front" voice, singing, "Roll me over, Yankee soldier, roll me over, lay me down, and do it again."

Johnny was going to throw open the door and spank her little behind but thought better of it, remembering her temper whenever her privacy was invaded. *She'd kill me in my sleep . . . with Lizzy Borden's . . . ax . . . after she dulled it . . . and got it rusty.* Johnny loved to keep adding denouements to his imagination.

"Johnny!" his mother's voice rolled up the stairs like thunder over Cape Cod Bay. "Reverend Newhall is here to talk with you."

"I didn't do nothin' wrong, Ma, honest." He would catch the broom, despite the fact he hadn't done a single thing wrong in a week, that is if you didn't count his discovery of an uncut cud of chewing tobacco. Which he proceed to chaw in the Big Woods until the juices had completely loaded up his weapon, his mouth and its deadly barrel, a pair of front teeth he could spit a powerful stream of spit or juice ten feet from. He had enjoyed his fine-honed natural skills while he sat under the Big Tree, spitting at any careless or innocent ant that happened nearby.

Johnny wondered how old Newhall the preacher discovered about his chaw. He couldn't wait to tell his mother, the old tattletale. *And I'll now get the old broom bayonet treatment . . .*

451

His mother's voice was less patient the second time. "Are you coming or not? And don't forget to reverse the order." She had taken to reminding him of both the missing stairs since his unscheduled fall through the stairs to a hanged man's sudden stop.

"Hello, Reverend."

Reverend Newhall looked into Johnny's eyes, then his mother's, benignly, like the gentle old man he really was. Always trying to send out a soft-eye message of love. He was often misunderstood by some who believed he was myopic, senile, or just checking his target's eyes for guilt.

"I knew it. The moment he came home with those hand marks on his face. A fight."

"No. No. He wasn't fighting," the good reverend said.

"Something worse then?" she asked, glaring at Johnny.

"No, no Ms. Shiverick, ah, Mrs. DaSilva. No, my dear. Your son has done nothing wrong, and you can now call me father. As you most likely know, the elders are considering the transition from the low to the high Episcopalian church, and my title would then become father. This would be good practice to get a jump on other parishioners. Wouldn't that turn heads if the daughter of *the* Mr. John Shiverick was the first in town to call me father?"

"Why, thank you, Mr. Newhall."

The good reverend bowed his head in modesty. "Why, thank you, Ms. Shiverick. Ah, Mrs. DaSilva."

"But no, thank you," she said. "I already have two fathers and will dispense with a third. You, of course, know of my father on Pond Street, Mr. John Shiverick. And you know of my father who art in heaven. Yes, I find two quite enough."

"Well, ah, thank you, ah, for the consideration. Perhaps we should move on."

She glared at Johnny, who had worked his way behind Reverend Newhall and had painted a grin on his face that was wider than his ample ears. Years before, Charity had Scotch taped his ears against his head, and they had pretty much held. Each time her son had his hair cut she would call him, "My own little Clark Gable."

Johnny could never figure that out. Clark Gable a coward who refused to fight in the Civil War. Johnny would put his life on the line for his country, like his father and uncles did.

Charity was taking no truck with her son's cat-that-ate-the-canary grin.

Her return glare told him this—"Wipe that smile off your face before I wipe it off for you."

Johnny slowly wiped his face from forehead to chin, and when he was done, the grin was replaced by a Cherubic half smile dropped from the dome of the Holy Chapel of Rome.

The reverend reclaimed their attention. "Actually, I came by to invite Johnny to join our family on our summer visit to Cape Cod. It would be a wonderful cure for his poor, ruined eyes."

"A vacation would be pretty exciting for him. The last time we were on a Cape beach, his father was nearly arrested. He took the top off his bathing suit, if you can imagine such a thing. To get more sun, he claimed. If he was a woman, he would have been painted and punished as a hussy. Of course things have changed now. There is no more modesty. He was let off with a strong warning and reprimand. There is no modesty in today's world."

"No, there doesn't appear to be any, but please do not tell me more than I need to know."

"Why, just yesterday I saw—"

"Ah. Yes. Well. He certainly didn't escape the wrath of the Lord for that topless escapade of his."

"Oh?" she questioned.

"Why, yes, you surely know how your husband was shot up in Europe."

"Why, yes, I surely know that, but I didn't realize it was because he wanted to get some tan on his upper body."

"Well, the Lord worketh in strange ways."

"Yes, but I didn't know our good Lord carried a German water-cooled machine gun."

"Of course not. That was just a figure of speech, but it is certainly most true. The good Lord works in strange ways. Who are we to second guess what form his terrible swift sword takes as he trampath out the village?"

She tilted her head sideways ever so slightly, smiled at him, and then with a method she had perfected over many decades but very rarely utilized, she released a silent but rather odoriferous piece of flatulence. She did this terrible thing while looking heavenward, appearing not unlike Ingrid Bergman in *Joan of Arc*.

"You'll have to excuse me for a brief moment," she said and left the room.

"An amazing woman, an amazing woman, quite different, quite gifted."

Johnny looked at Mr. Newhall and said, "Yes, quite." *But of course . . . you mean her ability . . . to fart like a billy . . . when she thinks . . . no one is around . . .* "Reverend? The Cape?"

"Yes. Ah, hello, John. Yes, my thoughts appeared to have fled for a moment."

While Reverend Newhall was checking the heavens one last time before continuing his thoughts, he noticed a small box hanging from the wall with numbers on it. The number used to alert the elders who counted the collection after service, just who gave what.

The top and bottom box lids were both open.

"A reminder to give, John?"

"Nope." John wadded up a piece of paper in his hands, pumped the hand holding the wad a couple times in the air, and shot the paper through the makeshift basketball hoop. "Two, for the Couz! Bob Cousy, Reverend."

"You didn't throw away the tithing envelopes did you?"

"Oh no. I keep them in the drawer over there with the playing cards."

"Your grandfather Shiverick would turn over in his grave. I'm aghast."

"Grandfather Shiverick can't turn over in his grave. He isn't dead. He's still painting your church and kids' shoes too. I was just kidding about the cards, Reverend, although I must admit there are cards there."

"God help me."

"They're just my baseball cards."

"You young sir are a funny maker. The good Lord loves that. I'm sure he must love us to make others laugh."

"Although I did use playing cards at one time."

"God save us."

"I used them as baseball cards."

"Pray tell how."

"Sure. Babe Ruth is the king of clubs. Ted Williams, the ace of diamonds. The joker was Rudy York. One time before a Red Sox game, York stuffed Johnny Pesky in a baby carriage and pushed him around the bases. Did you know that Johnny Pesky's real name was something like Peskovitch?"

"Ah, very interesting I'm sure. Concerning your duties on the Cape, if you should so chose to be our guest."

"Williams was the Kid, while Ruth was the Babe, York was the Chief because he was part Indian. Crazy names, the Sox had a Catfish Metkovich in right field. One time a seagull dropped a catfish, a sort of horned pout, on him when he was out there. That's how he got his name . . ."

"Yes, of course, very interesting. We will need you to bring your bike along."

"Interesting. Great. I didn't know you followed baseball. The Red Sox have three right fielders hitting over .300. Catfish, Leon Culbertson, and Tom McBride. Along with Williams and Dom 'the Little Professor' Dimagio, all hitting over .300 five, awesome!"

"Yes, yes, of course, but—"

"If Peskovitch and Metkovich were on base when Ted hit one through the box—can't you just imagine the announcer—'Look at Peskovtich and Metkovich run and that son of a vitch Williams's hit!'"

"Enough! Where did you learn that type of language?"

"Just from listening to games on the radio. 'It's a high can of corn! He ripped the cover off the old horsehide! It's high off the green monster! Birdy Tebbitts is up. In his last forty-seven trips to the plate, he has— eaten!' Not everyone on the Sox hits .300."

"If I may say so," Reverend Newhall said, "I do not believe I've ever seen the same enthusiasm from you during our Bible discussion as you display when discussing Codfish Demachio or whatever his name is or when you talk about the Splendid Sphincter or whatever his body part name is. Let's remember, before we forget, baseball doesn't save. The Lord saves!"

"Yes! But Rocket Richard scores!"

"You certainly can be enthusiastic."

"They say that when the Rocket skates in on Brimsek alias Frankie Zero, it's like two Greek gods coming down from the mountains to face each other. Brimsek had six shutouts in his first six games in the NHL. The Rocket had a season where he averaged a goal a game. Wow!"

"They said that when the Rocket gets close to the goal, his eyes turn red, just like the goal light when a player scores, and they say when a forward skates in on Brimsek, his eyes show zeros, sort of like little orphan Annie. But a lot of rink rats say Eddie Shore would have cut Richard down at the knees without giving a timber warning."

"That was quite a long speech. But very edifying, of course." Reverend Newhall closed his eyes and tightened his lips until they were thin lines in his face. "If I may progress, I came here to invite you to the Cape with my daughter Mandy and myself."

"Oh?" *Mandy Pandy . . . Puddin' and pie . . . kissed the boys . . . and made them cry . . .*

"And her cousin, Mabel Newhall."

"Yes, I know her cousin." *Maybelle, Maybelle . . . get off the table . . . The fifty cents is for the beer . . . talk about two prissys . . . and Goody Two-shoes . . .*

—

"Did you think something, ah, say something," Reverend Newhall asked, frowning deeply, puzzled. "Never mind. Would you like to go to the ocean with us? It would offer you a chance to become—how shall I say it?—whole again. The Lord's ocean will say, 'Let there be light,' and you will see again. So long strapped to that bed, blindfolded, like some sort of madman. You poor lad. Once we settle in Long Pond in Wellfleet, we'll walk to the ocean, and you can sit and relax and read the Bible and listen to the waves."

"That would be the greatest." *Reet reet dada, with a wha wha . . .* "When I went to the ocean with my father before the war, we were so busy catching flounder and mackerel that we didn't hear nothin'."

"Pronounce your g's. N-o-t-h-i-n-g. Ing."

"Ing."

"I always tell young people to pronounce their g's. Otherwise, we could raise generation of youths that couldn't say 'God.'"

"That would be odd."

"I hope you're not mimicking me, young man, or trying to be funny. It is one thing to be funny but another to try and be funny with God or his servants, such as me. It would not serve the Lord well to have a callous youth praying to 'God, who art in heaven.'"

Johnny bit his tongue. *Don't blow a trip to the ocean, nitwit . . . Just don't be . . . od . . .*

He bit his tongue a second time, tasted the slight bitterness of his blood's copper.

He bit his lip much the same way his mother was biting her lip while listening in on their conversation from her perch in the unlighted stairway, partway between missing steps four and nine.

Charity feared she would be discovered and quietly climbed the stairs on all fours. *I'll give that little wise guy a good sweeping in the morning . . . being so flip . . . and to his pastor . . . of all people . . . Sometimes things are so bad you wish you were a Catholic . . . so you could cross yourself . . . No . . . things could never be that bad . . . making fun of our pastor . . . then again . . . Father Newhall . . . that will be the day . . . over my dead body, Father . . . such a silly man . . . Maybe I'll let Johnny get away with it . . . this one time . . . but no . . . there is no excuse to be flip with your pastor . . . No way . . . he'll never get to heaven . . . on a pair of skates . . . Now cut that out . . . 'cause he'll skate right by . . . that golden gate . . . Please . . .*

Charity abandoned her thoughts as she reached the upstairs landing and stood up and started singing softly to herself, "No, Johnny will never get to heaven on a pair of skates 'cause he'll skate right by that golden gate. I ain't gonna cry my Lord, no more." *Now I know where the little scamp got it . . . from me . . . God help him . . . May the devil take him . . .* "You can't get to heaven in a limousine, 'cause you drive right by."

"Did you hear something, Johnny?"

"Sounds like somethin'."

"G's, Johnny, g's."

"Geeze, pastor."

"Just for one second Johnny, please be serious. You were named after John the Baptist. Where were we? Oh yes, on the seashore. You could listen most all day to the ocean, except of course when running errands on your bike or doing chores. Doctors say just being near the ocean is therapeutic. Of course too much can make you lazy and idle hands—well, you know."

"Yes. Grampa Shiverick told me about idle hands. He loves the ocean. He has a conch shell. Says the Jewish people used it to call out to their God."

"Yes, yes, of course, they did. Calling in all the glory on themselves."

"Grampa Shiverick thinks that shell is very special. Makes me hold it with two hands. I think it's special too, but for a different reason than just calling to God. When he looks away, I hold it to my ear, one hand, and I can hear the ocean every single time."

"I'm sure. Now are you interested? It would be so therapeutic, and you and I could sit by the ocean and move some of enthusiasm for baseball players that are named after candy bars to the true Savior. Who gave his only begotten son."

"I'd love to go."

"Well, that certainly took a long time," the good reverend said, poking his middle finger inside his collar to allow some cool air in. *This boy can make it . . . warmer than . . . it really is . . .* "We'll take the train to Boston. Catch the ferry to Provincetown. There you will see the Portuguese lads jump off the gunnels and the masts of our ship into the sea to retrieve passengers' coins."

"Sounds great." *Maybe I'll take a dive or two . . . matey . . . for a couple shekels . . .*

"Then we hop a bus from Provincetown to Wellfleet, where we get off. We then walk the three miles to Long Pond. We load up your bike. Everyone else, Mandy, Mabel, and myself carry our share. Then you make return trips until you get the rest of the gear. Nothing will be touched waiting there by the bus stop. Good English character has survived since the Mayflower. The good citizens of Wellfleet do not even know what the word 'steal' means. But you must be careful not to hit any bumps when you have the crock of night crawlers in your basket. The crock could bounce out and break. And our crawlers could escape. Lord forbid."

"Yes, I'll be careful." *But would the Lord really forbid . . . I forbid you crawlers to crawl away . . . escape . . . make a break for it . . . my slimy friends . . .*

"I see you're thinking about the results of losing our bait. "When you taste those giant yellow perch and those horned pout taken out of that crystal water, you'll know the safety of our bait is important. I just salivate thinking of them. That is the fish, of course."

Like one of Pavlov's pups . . . Father . . . forgive me . . . for I have . . . finned . . . oh, funny Johnny . . . you break me . . . up . . .

"Then after we're set, there are Cahoons Hollow and Coast Guard Beach. Our lunch and towels will travel in your bike basket. Sometimes the coastguardsmen coming from town to the station will pick us up and all our gear. Including your bike. A bonus. Their truck is like a fire truck. To help in rescues."

"What do the coastguardsmen do there?"

"They do something they call 'real good duty.' I overheard them say that one time. You still have that Western Flyer red and white bicycle, I assume, you rode to church one day. It had an oversize basket. That's one reason I asked you to come. It certainly will be helpful. And you can watch after my nieces, make sure no one is forward with them."

"Yes, my uncle Francisco made the basket for me. Big, so it could hold all my newspapers. And also hold Rags when he was alive. I could take turns warming one hand and then the other on him. Made some good tosses with the warmed hands—tossed 'em out at home! Yah, even in the summer I rode Rags around. I don't anymore."

"I certainly hope not."

"Nope, now he's pushing up daisies." *Rags . . . my little guy . . . I bet you look spiffy with those flowers growing out of your nose . . . and your angel wings . . . I'm gonna have Jazz and Romy . . . bury me there someday . . . under the irises . . .* He had dug up a batch of wild irises in the Big Woods and transplanted them in their yard.

"Do you still have a clip for your pant leg so you won't get it caught in the chain? Of course you do. You're a smart young man. That's why I picked you."

Oh . . . thank God . . . it was not because Granddad Shiverick paints your church . . .

"We couldn't have you taking a tumble, with all our precious gear and especially our most precious possession, crawlers."

"Crawlers, most precious?"

—

"Of course. After our Bibles, of course. There are no worms on the Cape, too sandy. So after a rain some night, I'll drop by your house and pick you up. We'll go to the White Horse Golf Course with flashlights and quietly approach the greens. Lights out, like during World War II, when I was CD, civil defense director, on our block. After a rain, the night crawlers come out for a drink—and we grab them!"

The pastor's hand shot into the air, causing Johnny to duck, surprising him that any movement from the little old man could be so swift, powerful appearing. He made a note of this and how long his reach was.

"You have to be quick, like quicksilver, and you must get a good grasp. Otherwise, you can't hold them. They are that strong. Sometimes you can get two at a time as they are enjoying tea for two."

"Ya, I've seen that tea for two thing." *They're shaggin' . . . Pronouce your g's . . . even when just thinkin' . . . thinking . . . they're a lot luckier than me . . . concerning cherry copping . . . outsexed by a worm . . . Oh dear . . . bread and beer . . . If I was dead I wouldn't be here . . .*

Reverend Newhall watched Johnny's mind working. "A penny for your thoughts."

"I was just wondering what was that white stuff between the worms where they were having their . . . tea for two."

His mother, now sitting in the dark near the top of the stairs but ears still working like a air raid radar early warning system, bit her tongue. Wondering how many more nips it could take to prevent her killing her son immediately rather than in the morning. *I'll kill that little . . . Baby Johnny . . .*

"I would guess," the pastor said, "they are salivating. After all, it's tea and crumpets." He chuckled to himself, thinking, *Quite a good joke, even if I do have to say so myself.* "Anyway, we'll be leaving in about a week. Pray for rain, but not so hard to carry over onto our time in Wellfleet. By the way, bring an old pair of shoes. We'll be picking oysters in the Wellfleet Harbor backwater. And they can be sharp!"

"That's all I have."

"Have what?"

"Old shoes."

"Yes. We'll leave July 19. You'll meet us at North Station. Look for us. No later than 9:00 a.m. Or we'll go without you. Time, tide, and Father Newhall wait for no man."

"July 19. 9:00 a.m. North Station. And ride my bike in."

"Right on." He likes to slip phrases like that in as sort of a reminder to himself, and others for that matter, that indeed while he was one of *the*

Newhalls on that first of the three boats that landed at Plymounth, that he at heart was one of the common people, just one of the boys."

The good man of God also believed, after having said these things for decades, that it was the Newhalls and the Shivericks who built those high-masted ships on stilts on the banks of Sesuit Creek. Yes, and when completed at proper high tide, with everyone for miles watching, the Newhalls and the Shivericks knocked out the supporting platform planks, settling the craft into the creek to launch another vessel to sea. "Yes, my returning to the Cape is as a captain returning to the sea," said the good Reverend.

"Aye, aye."

The reverend liked that. *A good boy.* he thought. *Could be a Shiverick, if he wasn't quite so dark and didn't have that foreign name. Why would anyone do that to a child, make him dark, give him a foreign name?* "Make sure you check the air in your bicycle tires, carry a grease gun for your chain and sprockets, extra spokes as you never know when some little dog chases you and runs into your wheels. And of course, a flashlight. It's a must, no flashlight, no Cape Cod."

"Yes, I have a flashlight." But no batteries . . . no bulbs . . . but he only asked . . . if I had a flashlight . . . Johnny had found the shell of a flashlight at the dump. Thought it would make a good ray gun when they played Flash Gordon. On that giant blowdown oak in the Big Woods behind Grandma Shiverick's they used as a spaceship. Johnny loved that tree. It was everything, not just a spaceship, not just a ship in a storm on the high seas, it could be anything the imagination desired. It could be a bucking bronco when the wind was high. One time, when no one was around, he had climbed up closed his eyes and gently got it rocking up and down. Moaning ever so softly, "Oh. Yelena." It started to grow down there in his trousers, a growth cycle cut short when a red ant, a traveling man, sneaked through the buttons on his fly and bit the good bite.

"Yes, I have a flashlight." He hated lying, only did so when it was absolutely necessary to save his tattered tail. He once again wished he was a Catholic, so he could cross himself after a fib and get it off his back. Catholics were lucky. *Crib . . . cross . . . clean . . . clear conscience . . . Maybe I'm telling the truth . . . in a roundabout way . . . it's practically the truth . . .*

"And don't forget your Bible, young man. To forget your Bible is to forget your conscience, your heart. And don't forget clean underwear. Cleanliness is next to godliness, and on those words, I must go. Let us say goodbye to your mother."

Johnny yelled out to the darkened hallway, "Ma! Reverend Newhall says goodbye. Careful of stair nine."

Charity, now safe in the darkened upstairs hallway, was less than happy with her son. *I'll kill him . . . first thing in the morning . . . if he brings the reverend to the bottom of the stairway . . . I'll kill him right now . . .*

She held her breath.

She heard the front door open and close. Reverend Newhall had left.

The door opened and closed again. Charity realized immediately that Johnny had read her mind and made good his escape into the night, where he would remain during her cooling off period.

"You'll have to come home someday, and you'll get it!"

Johnny was hiding just outside the door, behind the lilac bush.

Little brother's Jazz's voice came down to him in a whisper, "It's okay. Ma's in her bedroom. She's already soaked her teeth. Sleep under the bed tonight. Ma won't check there."

Johnny heard Jazz snicker and whispered upward, "I'd shut up if I was you and if I wanted to live."

"Ya, who's gonna make me?"

"You, bucktoothed twerp, shut up."

Jazz was quiet for nearly ten minutes. "Johnny?"

"Yah?"

"Why'd you call me bucktoothed? You beat up the big guys that call me that."

"That's different, Jazz, and I always pound the piddle out of anyone that picks on you."

"Ya, I know. I love you too, Johnny."

"Shut up, you faggot."

"Hey, I'm a big guy too, Johnny. I know when you like someone you have to be mean so you won't seem mushy. Sort of the way we call Romy 'Stick, stick, your legs are skinny, and your butt is thick,' and we'll kill anyone else says it to her."

"It's sorta that way."

"Did you have enough to eat today?"

"Ya, sort of."

As much as Johnny hated to dip into his secret savings for Jazz's teeth, he was going to be the big guy in the sky, the Big Dipper, and buy him a package of Devil Dogs. And a penny's worth of candy. Mint juleps, bull's-eyes, maybe Nigger Babies. Maybe Kits, the pink ones; you get several of those.

"Johnny, are you making droolin' noises down there?"

"Nah, just salivating, thinking how I'm gonna spank your butt."

"I know you're salivating. You're touching yourself."

"Don't be stupid."

"Better not let Ma catch you doing that. Ya know she told you that if you do that, you'll need glasses."

"Nah, that's an old wife's tale. The scientific truth is that if you touch yourself, you grow hair in the palm of your hand."

"Ugh."

"It's not that bad. Then you don't need to buy a baseball glove."

"Yah, but how do you throw a baseball when you have a palm full of hair."

"Only one palm grows the hair."

"Yah, but then you have to learn to throw lefty."

"Nah, you salivate yourself, lefty, your glove hand."

"I don't know which I'd rather have, hair in my palm or wear glasses."

"What grade you in, Jazz?"

"The sixth."

"Look, you don't have to worry for three more years. You don't start doing that until the ninth grade."

"I've been doing it since the fourth grade. Kenny Moson taught me. I guess I'm just precautious."

"Precocious."

"Can you just sort of do it once in a while? Say until your eyes grow a little weak but not until you need glasses?"

"Please. Please! Jazz. Go to sleep or I'll kill ya."

"Johnny?"

"Yah."

"Don't ever have no kids."

"Ma only had one. Me. Now shut or I'll really kill ya."

"Okay, but bring up a pillow from the couch. I put the other pillow beneath the blanket like you're sleeping under the covers. In case Ma comes up and whacks your pillow with her broom. You can sleep under the bed."

"I only need one favor from you."

"Anything."

"Shut up."

"Ask a different one."

Chapter 26

CAPE COD COMETH

July 19 and Cape Cod did not come very quickly for Johnny. It had been on his mind since he was invited by the Reverend Newhall to be his guest during his vacation on the Bay State's sandy arm that reached out and attempted to grab the Atlantic Ocean and hold on. Holding on only lasted for moments each day before the moon and tide won out time after time.

Johnny's vacation, included many trips into Welfleet Center from the Newhall's Long Pond cottage for anything needed. Whims were thrown in as many as a dozen times a day. But there was diving, fishing, and other fun in between pedaling the seven mile round trip.

Back on the farm, there was some work, earning money at catch as catch can work; and if the work was fun, well, what in heck was there to say.

There was spearing frogs for five cents a pair of fat legs and grabbing snapping turtles underwater for two cents a pound that turns a young man's fancy to making a dollar.

There was also blueberry picking, ten cents a quart, with a bonus—you got to stuff your face with the berries that looked like tiny blue-faced and bonneted little ladies.

There was wild grape picking where you got to climb the swamp trees where the wild grapes grow and take a break by swinging on the ten— and fifteen-foot vines that hung from the swamp trees that allowed you to swing like Tarzan or, even better, swing like the Ape Man's long-armed, long-tailed ape Cheetah, all the time chattering like a baboon, scratching your chest, then taking time out to search and destroy the imaginary bugs that inherited Cheetah's chest, chattering "ugh, ugh, ugh" in joy with each pretended find.

His cousins practically piddled their pants with each of Johnny's bug discoveries.

It was a swinging good time, one that made time fly fast.

Add Poe to the mix and who needed more, that is until July 27.

The baby crow that Johnny and his cousins, Pointer and Dink Gouveira, had found at the farm under the power line had had its tail sizzled off when it had landed on a live wire during its first flight. Its tail feathers had fried off; he had suffered a broken leg when it crashed to the ground.

Every time they tried to make a little splint for the leg, the angry and frightened little bird, now named Poe the Crow, would strike out with its sharp beak and give a nip that had the bite of a raw shot of wild turkey. That is until Johnny snapped an elastic band around the rapier beak. The splint, made of tongue depressors, was held on by adhesive tape, giving not only a chance for the leg to heal, but also allowing the bird to land.

Poe not only acted like the little pirate he was, stealing anything that glittered, despite the fact in his wisdom; he also realized that all that glitters is not gold. Once he swiped a magnet and was drawn beak first into a tough steel bar that protected a shed window.

Completing Poe's pirate picture was the fact that he limped like a one-legged Peg-Leg Pete complete with swagger, his bare bottom shining like a bald man's pate, except at the wrong end.

They had fabricated a little diaper to keep its little arse warm until he grew a new set of tail feathers.

The cousins taught the brilliant bird its first word, "Merdre!"

Poe kept kicking the diaper off while announcing the first of its new vocabulary, "Poe dirty bird, dirty bird. Haw, haw, haw." Later, he added, "Don't quote me," to his confession of Poe being a dirty bird.

Johnny convinced his cousins that Poe was so egotistical he would grow a peacock tail rather than a crow's tail and would be killed as an outcast by marauding ravens.

The three boys were certain the crow was a him. They agreed it had the intelligent look of a man in its eyes and was fearless and venturesome. And the bird's demeanor was in general horny, although they were not certain what made a bird appear horny.

Dink was first to admit, "It ain't easy to tell what a bird's slong looks like. A dog is easy. It's always hanging out in public like a trolley strap handle. And It's always licking itself. And you know it isn't licking the jelly off its fingers."

"And a dog's thing isn't hidden by feathers," Johnny said, "and you don't have to blow the feathers away and take a real quick look."

Pointer said, "Ya dogs are easy to tell which is which. The boy dogs all give that three-legged salute to fire hydrants."

"You can tell when a cat's horny," Dink said. "The girl cat just sort of struts around, licking her whiskers, slanting its eyes, making its tail move like one of those hula-hula dancers in slow motion. And the tom lets out a meow as loud as a cow."

"Yes, cats and dogs are easy to tell which is which," Johnny said knowingly, "but birds are like human women. They keep their private parts hidden, and you don't know whether they hid them in front or underneath, and you don't have the slightest idea what they want."

Pointer wanted the crow to be named Doctor Death, for hadn't it escaped the electric chair, the power line's full surge.

Dink wanted the little squawking black baby to be named Ass Bestest. He said his hero, the foot-shuffling, slow-talking Steppin' Fetchit, supposedly said on the radio, "Honest Injun," that his name was Asbestos, as he likes ass bestus.

Johnny asked Dink why he didn't want to name the crow Wee Willy in honor of his wanger.

"Don't you go poking fun at my sir Wonder," Dink said.

"Self knighted," Johnny said.

"Be honest now, most beloved of my cousins, who are you to comment on a man's paraphernalia? You are still a cherry, as low a royal title as one can attain at the age of sixteen."

Johnny knew that not every sixteen-year-old had got a little, but most of those that hadn't, for self-survival, proclaimed to the heavens in voices so loud that their earthling friends also overheard, "I'm getting tons of noo . . . kie! Can never get enough of that wonderful stuff," a declaration that often ended on one knee, ala Al Jolson, a ritual for all, with arms outstretched, hands facing heavenward, eyes rolling with such delight that any witnesses to the confession of having gone all the way, plus an extra yard or two, whatever that meant, just had to be believed. Especially when the lying devil crossed himself. The Al Jolson ritual performed by all who confessed to getting a little ended with, "Mammy, how I jammed ya, how I jammed ya, down by the levee."

It was during these Christian heart crossings that Johnny wished he was a Catholic. You could never call a Catholic a liar if he looked heavenward and crossed himself.

But Johnny asked himself, *What can a Protestant do to cover a lie or ask for some extra help when you come to bat in the ninth inning, needing only a scratch single to tie or even win the game, if Skinny Potts gets the lard out of ass and makes it all the way home form second? Nothing.*

Anyway, June and a large part of July went fast. *Nothin' . . . that's what . . .*

Poe was great. They taught the baby crow to smoke. This means the three practically nonsmoking cousins had to ask their smoking friends for butts, meaning they only had stubs to offer Poe. Although the crow learned to swipe a cigarette from a package being shown off in a shirt, front pocket, or if the package was twisted into a T-shirt sleeve.

Johnny got to name the bird Poe over Doctor Death and Ass Bestus because he told them about the Edgar Allan Poe tales, "The Pit and the Pendulum," "The Raven," and had not only the cousins, but also himself believing Poe was evil and could bring them all kinds of good evil fun.

It was Dink. "Ya, I can live with your choice, Johnny, cuz you scared the living piss out of me."

Dink even checked to see if Poe had fangs, no easy task, as when a crow doesn't want to open its beak, it really doesn't want to open its beak.

They had a plan to find out whether the crow had fangs or not. When Pointer offered the crow a cigarette and it opened its beak, Dink inserted a tongue depressor instead, and Johnny looked for werewolf fangs.

Seeing his cousins' disappointment at his announcement, "No fangs," he cheered them up with, "He probably only grows them at night."

Once having named the bird, Johnny became its falconer, a position of royalty in older days, which he pointed out.

Thus, Johnny ended up more bug free than his cousins but also suffering one bad earache, paying the price for being a wise guy.

He was bug free because Poe had no problems plucking the bug out of the air from his position on Johnny's shoulder as he picked blueberries in the swamp.

Johnny rewarded him with a deep-blue, plump, ripe, and juicy berry every time Poe scoffed a mosquito out of the air.

If the berry was purple rather than blue, the baby crow merely dropped it on the ground.

That tickled Johnny, and he wondered what would happen if he gave the greedy little piglet a green berry.

He found out. "*Ouch!*" he yelled as Poe stuffed the green one in his ear, and Johnny snapped his finger, flicking the crow's beak. "That's enough of that, my fine-feathered fiend."

It was the summer of '48. Fun filled. No more worries about wars. World War II was long over. War cards showing Jap Zeros strafing school children, holding babies up on bayonets, leading American nurses off into the jungle at gun point. Their white uniforms were dirty and soaked with the blood of wounded GIs they had treated. The blouses often missing several buttons, their skirts running high on their thighs as they were prodded on to their fate were long gone, replaced by Joe D, Stan the Man Musial, King Kong Keller baseball cards, the way it's supposed to be when you're a teenager and it's summer.

It was three years since Johnny had walked to Boston to try to sign up with the marine raiders, the Flying Tigers, navy frogmen, army rangers, coast guard minesweepers, merchant marine U-boat spotters, civil defense close-those-shades persons, and others in uniform.

His only real accomplishment was that he managed to get Righty drummed out of the Boy Scouts before he was in the Scouts.

He had taken Righty to join his troop that met in the basement of the Episcopal Church. Righty, after many years of friendship with Johnny, had learned the great joys of exploration. Exploration became a necessity after someone in authority such as Scoutmaster Bolson dictated at a preinduction session held on the church lawn the night before the big ceremony, "The upstairs of the church is off limits. A no-no. Thou can't. Thou shan't."

While the scoutmaster hadn't been in the service, he had served with the Civilian Conservation Corps planting seedlings in the Depression Days of the '30s and had maintained that military bearing and certain military language like "off limits." Add the fact that Bolson was also the chemistry teacher in the high school, an elder in the church. Well, the combination made him a man to absolutely be disobeyed.

And he demanded his proper title due at each posting—Scoutmaster Bolson, Elder Bolson, and Mr. Bolson in chemistry class.

Johnny decided that it would be best to introduce his friend to the inside of a Protestant church the night before his induction into the troop, and they waited while the Scoutmaster and the last of the Scouts went their ways.

Then they were in the basement window and in the dark. When Johnny lost sight of Righty and failed to hear a squeak from anywhere, he knew his friend was headed upstairs to no-no land and had to be rescued as he knew the Scoutmaster could and would find a way to have a recalcitrant punished. Or so he said. And no one particularly wanted to test him.

Johnny found Righty sipping wine from the chalice scheduled for a coming Communion service. "Not as good as us ginnys make."

"Come on, let's get downstairs and out of here. Oh no, here he comes."
"He" being the suspicious Scoutmaster who had returned.

Righty slid under the nearest pew. Out of sight. Quiet as a church mouse.

Johnny stood straight as the Scoutmaster approached him. "Who's here with you? Where's your Catholic friend?"

"What do you mean, Catholic—"

"Don't you pontificate with me, young man. Where is your friend?"

"It's just me." *That's not quite a lie . . . I am just me . . . If we were playing tag . . . I'm slow . . . I'm it . . . It's just me . . .*

"This is your last chance. Where is he?"

Johnny stood in silence, looking at his shoes.

The scoutmaster slowly reached down to his knee-high laced leather boots, felt for the knife case sewed into the boot, unsnapped the top, all the time staring at the boy who he had personally chosen to be the next den leader for the Cub Scout pack that would graduate its bears, lions, wolves, and finally Webelos into his troop. The Scout he handpicked because of his fine Christian stock, English stock, the grandson of Mr. John Shiverick, blue blood, despite the thinning by the brood DaSilva.

Johnny watched as Scoutmaster Bolson slipped the knife out of its case, brought it up slowly, pulling the blade that shined like the wheels of a steam engine from constant honing to an edge that could cut toilet tissue without tearing.

"Where is he?"

The knife passed close to his crotch. Then his stomach. Up to his shoulder. "I'm cutting that Life Scout badge right off your uniform."

He looked into his Scoutmaster's eyes as the much larger man grabbed his shirt and slipped the point of the knife into the Life Scout badge.

The tip cut around the perimeter of his Life Scout badge, slowly, until only four threads connected it to the shirt. The Scoutmaster bent, sliding the knife back into its case on the boot, never taking his eyes off Johnny's, then straightening up.

He glanced at the Life Scout badge on the boy's chest; there were three threads holding it to the shirt. The pounding of Johnny's heart had broken the fourth. "Where is he?"

Silence.

"Where is he? Or you lose your last threads that tie you to decency."

The large man reached out, grasped the Life badge that took ten merit badges to earn, making time to earn them between working a dozen different jobs, school, sports, and hanging out.

Johnny felt like his raw heart was in the grasp, being torn out as the Life Scout badge was stripped off his shirt. Much like an Inca high priest tearing the pounding Heart out of a virgin and crushing it into the small

—

hole in the block near the temple's top, doing this repeatedly until the base of the temple flowed with blood.

After this Johnny waited in the dark, behind a giant oak, across the street from the church until he heard the squeak, the telltale sign that a basement window was being opened. Then he saw Righty running low to the ground, keeping in the shadows, toward him.

Out of breath from the dash, Righty still found the ability to cough out, "You didn't tell."

"You wouldn't have either."

"I don't know. I don't know."

"I know. So let's cut the shit and take a swim in Spot Pond. I haven't pissed in a scoutmaster teacher's mouth in my life, and I just feel that it would just feel fine to do so."

They started the two-mile jog to the town's drinking water supply and the best fishing and swimming in town, Spot Pond, owned and operated by the MDC, Metropolitan District Commission, whose guards were not only slow runners but also wore patent leather shoes with leather soles.

"Jesus, when I saw him reach down and take that knife out of his boots just inches from your face, I thought Johnny will have to tell him where I am.

"I sure hope Bolson is really thirsty," Johnny said.

"Hope he's hungry too. I really did mess my pants."

"I'm not going in."

"Relax," Righty said, "I'll find some ferns."

"Ferns." Johnny closed his eyes as he jogged.

Fern Osterhouse was eighteen. A farm girl endowed like a thirty-six-quart Hereford. She always had that 'it's-nearly-milking-time' full look. Farm boys from miles around tripped over their tongues when she was about.

Back at the farm, Uncle Manny DaSilva was alerted into their youthful streams of thought when he spotted them in the high hay observing her sitting on the Osterhouse farm mule as it pulled a plowing sled.

Sneaking up behind them, he said, "Listen, guys, I've got some unbelievable news for you."

"You're pregnant, "Johnny said.

"This is what my brother Tony raised. Another W. C. Fields? If you don't want to hear—"

"Go ahead, Uncle Manny."

Dink said, "We'll kill him, and he'll be quiet."

"You know that Fern Osterhouse, Old Farmer Osterhouse's granddaughter?" He had to turn aside to keep from laughing as their eyes lit up to show a jackpot six lemons.

"Ja," they said, sounding like a battle-weary platoon of German soldiers being asked if they wanted to go on leave in Paris, "well, sort of."

"Well."

"Yah. Yah."

"She swims in the nude." *Oh . . . it's fun to lie . . . to these little liars . . .*

"I'll tell you where, but you tell me first where you've been catching all those giant bucketmouth bass."

"Swims in new what?" Pointer asked.

"Dummy," his brother said. "Nude. N-U-D-E, like she swims without any bathing suit on."

"Where?" Johnny asked, failing miserably in his attempt to appear not to give a good rat's ass.

"Ya, where?"

"Ya, where?"

"I'm not telling. I just don't trust you. You'd probably try to sneak up and grab a peek. Do you think that would be fair. Peeking at an innocent farm girl that was just trying to float her lilies?"

"You just don't love us," Dink said, trying to look hurt, "wanting us to tell you our hot spot."

"Yes, I do. I do. But I also love wild grapes and mushrooms. And frog's legs."

"What's that got to do with it?" Dink asked.

"Well, I'd like to see these things, much like you'd like to see, let's say other things."

"Okay, okay. We'll get the wild grapes and mushrooms," Dink said.

"What about where you catch those big largemouth bass? The real hole this time."

The cousins looked at each other.

"I guess we weren't too clear on our directions," Johnny said.

"Yes, I'd guess that," their uncle Manny said, turning aside, biting his tongue to keep from smiling. Their dilemma fueling his funny bone. *Do these little ant turds . . . think I'd tell them where pretty pumpkins was bathing bare ass . . . If I knew . . . I don't think so . . . A man can only love wild grape wine and frog's legs and big bass . . . to a certain cutoff point . . .*

"No sweat. No sweat," Dink said.

"Yah, no sweat," Pointer added.

"We give you our word," Johnny said.

"Like you gave me your word on where the bucketmouths were. Anti up, first. Then the spot."

Two days later, the skinned frog's legs, the grapes, and directions to the secret bass fishing hole were laid out to their uncle.

And he in turn told them of the secret cove of Fern Osterhouse, "But I can't tell you the exact time. I do know that she loves to swim in the nude,"—the cousins shivered when he said that word—"during heavy thunder and lightning storms."

They spent hours, days in the high grass near the spot, often in heavy rain and lightning.

"What if we get hit by lightning?" Pointer asked.

"Who cares? Some things are worth it."

They took turns on watch while the other two would gain some semblance of being out of the storm by taking shelter under a nearby pine with thick low-drooping limbs.

Other times they were very, very happy in their discussion. "What jubes (Jubes only being a piece of mint candy that had a lewd sound to teenagers, a very important element) I bet you a nickel her basketball boobs have 'A. J. Spalding' printed on them," Dink said.

"Do you think she'll wash them in front of us?" Pointer asked.

"With heavy hangers like hers, she must have nipples the size of lily pads. In this cold rain, they'll look like little neck clams gone insane."

Their uncle Manny, having recruited his brothers Tony and Franchesco, were insane with laughter as they sat fully outfitted in rain gear under a tarp, drinking a combo of Portagee Port and White Lightning, eating Mine's pickled pork chops.

They took great glee each time the lightning struck and the boys flinched.

"They quit soon," Franchesco said.

"They're DaSilvas all right," Manny said.

"Nah, they wouldn't ever have told you about that bucketmouth fishing hole," Tony said.

"The little craps lied again. That's what makes this most enjoyable. Let's break out the linguica and sour bread. Got that homemade horse radish. Pass the lightning. Let them dance. Lying to their uncle Manny again," Manny said.

The only thing that would be more fun than watching those horny little goats would be if Charity and Sis found out why they don't have enough sense to come in out of the rain."

"How would we explain it to Sis if they got hit by lightning?" Franchesco asked.

—

"Not to worry, they're lying on their lightning rods," Manny said

"Yes," Tony added, "they look like big-keeled sailboats in the sand, the way they're tilted."

"I bet this is more fun than that new invention they say will be on the market pretty soon. Television. They say it's like having your own movie house in your own home," Franchesco said.

"I believe it when I see it," Manny said.

"Hope it rains bad again next week," Franchesco said.

"Hey, look, they're all excited. What gives?" Manny asked.

"Over there! Coming around the corner! That wake!" Tony said.

"Couldn't be," Franchesco said.

"It ain't," Manny said, "it's only a beaver. A big one."

The three brothers looked at each other. Laughed. Watched as the three boys edged forward to see better through the high grass.

The three brothers grabbed their sides. "It hurts," Tony said.

"A beaver!" Manny said.

"My sides hurt," Franchesco said as he slid from his back against a tree to the ground.

Manny rolled in the rain.

"They're DaSilvas all right," Tony said, "don't know enough to come in out of the rain where titingers are concerned."

The sheets of rain prevented the boys from seeing that the wake they had viewed approaching was merely that of giant beaver and each allowed himself to dream.

And these were Johnny thoughts as he and Righty made their escape from the church.

Thus, Johnny was fully primed and ready for Cape Cod, where rumor had it that women without clothes on hid in the sand dunes off Provincetown and Truro, hoping to get what some of the guys whose dads surf fished off Race Point called an all together tan.

Johnny was ready for July 27. Really ready.

CHAPTER 27

WILD BEACH PLUMS

July 27 arrived.

Johnny was ready for Cape Cod.

Almost.

He had all his gear stuffed in a sweatshirt; he had tied the neck and sleeves closed. His bike was ready and raring to go, and you couldn't tell Johnny that a bike couldn't be raring to go.

The plan was simple. A quarter mile from the station starting point back home in Rockledge before the train could build up a head of steam, the two of them, boy and bike, would hide in the reeds to get to Boston.

As the caboose pulled near his hiding spot, he would commit himself, ride alongside of it until the rear railing was even with him. He'd grab the railing, clamping the bike between his legs, and pull himself up onto the platform.

His only worry was scratching the Western Flyer when he pulled it aboard or when climbing up onto the caboose roof.

But the best-laid plans of Mice and Men and Western Flyers can go astray, especially when a conductor who was never on the caboose as it left the station appears.

The engine, with the coal shoveled in with gusto, flexed its huge piston muscles that tried to burst out of their pipe sleeve confines and broke out of the blocks with a spurt.

The conductor was on the rear platform, letting a wicked whiz as the night before he'd traveled to Woburn (Rockledge was dry) to share a schnapps or two or three.

—

He was doing an outstanding job of covering up as peeing over a platform was not part of the uniformed person, public trust job description, not to mention that the platform railing was above his waist.

The conductor skillfully camouflaged his actions by utilizing his all-aboard megaphone.

He hadn't expected that the one extra brew would change nature's schedule nor that a hefty woman would have claimed the train's only toilet despite the warning on the water closet door, "Do not use until this train is fully under way."

Spotting the piddling conductor who was spoiling his schedule to meet Reverend Newhall and his family, Johnny angered and yelled out, "I'm calling the cops and telling them you're leaking off the caboose."

Nonplussed, the conductor looked up to spot his tormentor and ended up misaiming and mistakenly polishing off his leak into the wide mouth, megaphoning hefty stream out the narrower mouth section.

Johnny jumped on his bike and pedaled like a jackrabbit with a promise to Rockledge Square, where the yellow peril trolley was due to head to Sullivan Square. The train plan was out the window; trolley imperitive.

It was getting close. The electric trolley conductor had another dozen passengers to bring aboard, an action he would string out to keep himself center stage.

Johnny pumped until the spokes of the Western Flyer were a blur. It was a mile to the Fellsway, where he could hide in ambush, hopefully hop on the large taillight that would serve as a headlight on the return trip, and pull himself up, bike clamped between his legs.

He barely had flung himself into the alders when he heard the trolley coming at him.

Something was wrong. It wasn't slowing down like it usually did as it entered the Fellsway. He could see it in the distance. It would be too fast.

He took the sweater loaded with his gear and laid it by the tracks. Took off his shirt and arranged it like a pair of trousers beneath the sweater and quickly placed a large round stone near the sweater neck.

The yellow peril slowed down when the conductor spotted what appeared to be a body but then saw it was a dummy. "Shit! The little bastards!" he said as the trolley swayed like a bucking bronco.

All attention was drawn to the little old lady nearest the conductor on hearing his words. No one saw Johnny pick up the shirt, the sweater suitcase, hook them on his handlebars, hop on the bike, and ride like the wind along the bumpy trolley car railroad ties, sending cinders spraying from his tires like the wake of a speedboat until he could grab the large light.

He pulled himself upward, the bike clamped between his legs with the power of a rodeo cowboy on a bucking bronco, his bike bumping the tracks as sparks from the overhead arm that got its electric life from the live wire overhead showered down on him.

Johnny knew he had used too much strength in his high-powered bicycling, couldn't pull himself onto the lamp, stand on it, and then pull himself up onto the roof, where he could lay flat between the roof and the live wire (being very careful not to have a handlebar touch the line).

The yellow peril had picked up too much speed for him to drop off, rattled the tracks until they sounded like great clashing swords, terrible swift swords. He had promised his mother to never jump a ride on a train or trolley. *Grandfather Shiverick said the Lord seeth all . . . To lie is mortal sin . . . To lie to your mother is to lie directly in the eyes of God . . . The only time you can lie to your mother is to save your ass . . .*

Now he was up and on the giant lamp. He had to rest before trying to pull himself up to the roof. *Don't rest . . . the lamp might snap off . . . like it did when Marly Brown sat on it too long . . . and he got spattered on the tracks like shit hitting the fan . . .*

He pulled himself upward, digging his fingers and toes into the various protrusions and windowsills as the sparks wrapped around his head like a fireworks display gone awry.

It took seconds that seemed like hours to get his upper body on the roof. *Keep your head low . . . Handlebars . . . Don't let handlebars touch the wire . . .*

With his upper body on the roof and his lower torso hanging free, the bike clamped between his legs, he started bringing the Western Flyer upward. He couldn't release both hands from his hold on the roof, but he needed to grab the bike. The pain in his thighs and knees felt like a Great Dane had sunk his teeth into his lower body and was slowly feeding hot lead through its fangs into his body. *Gotta get one hand down there . . .*

He released one death grip, prying his fingers off the handhold with the mental strength needed to pry the fingers of a drowning man off its rescuers's neck.

The crossbar of the Western Flyer was in his grasp, but he couldn't pull it up. He tugged until he thought his shoulder would come out of its socket and both bike and shoulder would fall to the tracks that sped behind them. The dizziness made the inside of his head spin into faster and tighter circles, like his brain was attached to a rotating helicopter propeller and threatened to spill his brains out his ears. But all the tugging in the world would not bring the bike up.

That is until he released the death grip his thighs had on his bike.

—

With a great tug, he brought the bike up beside him, onto the roof, and watched in horror as the handlebar touched the live wire. *Oh shit . . . Oh shit . . .* He closed his eyes so tight they felt like grapes being squeezed to popping in a mighty palm. He could feel the deadly bolts surge through his body. Could visualize the electrical power that drove the great trolley turning him as black as an eight ball, then turning to soot and disappearing in the slipstream, never to be seen again.

But the electrocution didn't come.

He opened his eyes slowly. Only the rubber grips at the ends of the handlebars had touched the wire.

His body went limp as the fear oozed out of him. "Ooooh." *Ma . . . Ma . . . I'll never hop a ride again . . . Oh, Ma . . . do you hear your baby Johnny?*

He had little room for movement, but by slight movements of his head, he managed to check out the red and white Western Flyer. Not a scratch on it. He carefully reached out and plucked a cinder from the balloon tire tread. The whitewalls appeared undamaged. He brushed a piece of dust off the tire. It was then he noticed his missing fingernail on his right forefinger, the result of the trolley lamp.

The trolley barn maintenance man would scratch his head that night as he washed the dust covered lamps of his fleet. "What in sweet Jesus is a fingernail doing in the butt of my kaaar? The old girl was probably scratching her arse. Funny creatures, my little ones."

He lovingly patted the butt of his yellow peril. "Good girl, with your Hemingway butt two ax handles wide."

The maintenance man could picture his ten-ton girl sashaying down the tracks, the undulating sway of her buttocks topped off by the sparks that she showered down.

Johnny patted his Western Flyer and gave it one last check before looking at his finger. The nail had been ripped out by the roots.

As the trolley pulled into Sullivan Square, Johnny slid from the rood, bike clamped between his legs, and was on the platform.

Johnny spotted the platform safety officer checking him out closely, and as he walked toward Johnny, he hopped on his bike and attempted to pedal off slowly so as not to alert him.

The officer started running toward him, "Hey, you can't ride a bike in here."

The officer was gaining.

"Hi-Ho, Silver," Johnny sang out as he poured the coals to the pedals and widened the gap between the two, despite the fact the officer had run track at Boston Latin. Of course it was twenty years before.

—

Johnny tossed the salute usually given by the youth of the day when they were certain they had outstripped their pursuer. The devil's horns, fore and littler fingers still, while the middle fingers were folded into the palm. The salute meant whatever the passer or the receiver wanted to interpret. And Johnny gave him an ear-swallowing smile.

"Hi-Ho, Silverware, Hitler lost his underwear!" the guard yelled after him, then to himself, said, "Nice young kid. Not all today's yoots are bad apples. Reminds me of when I was a young whippersnapper."

Once on the streets Johnny gave his steed a little scratch behind the ear, the ear being the chrome light that was clamped on his handlebar.

His arms and legs ached with the effort of pumping toward the Boston Wharf where Reverend Newhall and family waited by the Provincetown ferry. "That boy better be here soon."

Johnny sped through one red light as taxis blared their horns at him, got up to the line of traffic that had gone before him, found one taxi, a Checker with the window open, put his left arm through the window and his leg on the running board, and hitched a free ride for several blocks. The hackie had never glanced over at Johnny, but as the boy ended his hitchhike, knowing that in the heavy traffic that had set up, that he could make better time on his bike, the driver called out, "That will be seventy-five cents, kid."

Without looking back, Johnny gave him a wave.

"Nice kid. They're not all rotten apples."

Johnny spotted Reverend Newhall standing with the two teenage girls and came to a brake squeaking stop, balancing on one leg.

"Any problems, Johnny?"

"No, sir."

"You only made it with fifteen minutes to spare. You know my daughter, Mandy. She's a senior, but of course she goes to private school, and her cousin, my niece, Maybelle."

"Hi."

The two girls pretended not to hear him. He was not only an underclassman, but also one with a foreign name to boot. They turned their attention to the ferry, giving Johnny the split second he needed to whip out his comb and run it through his hair, straight back, rather than fluffing it up into a pompadour like he did for the girls at Rockledge High. He figured the more worldly cousins would appreciate the Euro look. Nope . . .

They turned away again, this time checking their fingernails. Johnny didn't exist for them. He was less important than a fingernail.

One of which he was painfully missing. *Perhaps they'll like a pompadour . . . a high one . . . like a young Einstein . . . without the frizz . . .*

They were still looking away. Out came Johnny's comb with a Svengali slight of hand, and it was run through his hair again. This time, instead of leaving it flat, he applied pressure to the back of his hair with the comb and pushed forward, forcing the front of his hair skyward.

Rev. Newhall frowned at him, combing his hair in public, of all things.

He barely had his comb back in his pocket before the girls returned their attention to the elderly minister.

It was then that Maybelle glanced at him. "Cool, man."

"How did you ever do it? Fantastic, a racing stripe," Mandy said admiringly, moving closer in an attempt to figure out how he had dyed his hair into a racing strip, a green line with a white line on each side of it streaked through his hair.

"GROSS!" Mandy said, realizing that it was not some sort of quick-fix dye miracle but rather the residue of a passing pigeon dropping unbeknownst on Johnny, and he had combed the bird turd back into his hair, forming the nearly perfect racing stripe that wasn't missing much more than a car number. Number 2 would have been fitting.

He felt his head, saw the pigeon mess on his fingers, and bolted to the toilet, hearing Maybelle's "disgusting" burning into his back.

With the water turned on full force, Johnny soaked his head, washing with one hand, covering his eyes with the other. Oh no . . . why me, dear Lord . . .

A red-faced Boston cop approached him, twirling his baton with all the arrogance of the chief drum major leading the Rose Bowl parade. "*Hey*, kid, this ain't no Roman public bath. Get your arse into gear and outta here."

Johnny fled, but not until checking the tin mirror and grabbing a handful of paper towels for drying, taking a moment in his flight to hold his little finger up on his right hand while folding the others downward, a symbol meaning his tormentor deserved less than the best.

"Little shit head!"

The words hurt Johnny more than the officer could ever believe they could and had him checking his hair several times for pigeon droppings.

Johnny locked his eyes onto his shoes as he approached his pastor and the cousins.

"Come along, they're loading," Reverend Newhall said, loading Johnny's bike basket with two suitcases and hanging bags of clothes from the handlebars that already held Johnny's sweatshirt with his belonging.

He handed Johnny two more cloth-carrying bags for his left hand. The right was needed to push the bike aboard the ferry.

Reverend Newhall carried two bags in one hand, three in the other.

The cousins went aboard holding hands.

A crowd of friends and relatives and those who merely liked to see ferries leave the pier waved.

The girls waved to the crowd as if they were personally there just to see them off. As the ferry pulled away, it headed out through Boston Bay, headed to Stellwagen Bank. A line of herring gulls lifted off to follow, knowing the passengers would be feeding them the entire trip.

Johnny heard the girls chatter as he hung over the railing, hearing the wump-wump-wump throb of the mighty diesels.

"Maybelle, that's Quincy Bay. Named after John Quincy Adams. Mandy, that's the roller coaster at Revere."

Johnny could feel his stomach joining his head in a death dance with the movement of the boat. *Think of something else . . . the roller coaster . . . the hurricane . . . No . . . not a roller coaster . . .*

Although roller coasters ran in the family. His uncle Luke Shiverick's picture was posted at the entrance gate to every roller coaster in the northeast.

His hobby was taking the front seat of the coaster, and when it headed down the steepest section, he'd stand up, knees locked against the sides, staring down into hell as it dove down and off into heaven as it climbed.

When Grandfather Shiverick heard the family telling each other that Luke could die or suffer serious injury and they would have to make him stop, he said, "Leave him be. God takes care of little children and those adults less endowed with gray matter."

The girls were joining the good reverend, backing up the holy man's chant, "Thank yee for your bountiful gifts, oh Lord" with their singing "Oh, what a beautiful morning. Oh, what a beautiful day. I have a wonderful feeling, everything's going God's way."

The old man nearly passed out with the holy passion.

The roll of the boat started to get to Johnny, and he wanted to barf so bad his toenails ached. *Don't get sick . . . Don't get sick . . . Look at the horizon . . . Look at the horizon . . .*

"Isn't God great?" Maybelle asked.

"God is beautiful and great," Mandy said, knowing the answer.

"My angels on earth," the Reverend Newhouse said, patting their heads as they mewed upward to him.

Johnny wanted to pat the heads of the girls, thinking they looked like twin angels complete with tits, but the surge, the hot bile burned upward, ready to burst his safety valve.

He held it back. Checked his pastor, the girls, now waving and smiling up to the captain, certain that their safety and comfort was the only thing on his mind.

"Oh god, cookies," he moaned as he threw up over the side, the collection of food setting up a thin slipstream that in part caught a jolly appearing and austere gentleman in his seventies in the face. "Fucken seagulls!"

His three companions, hearing the hollow sounds and giddyup of Johnny's barf, turned their attention to him.

Please, dear Lord . . . please . . . No racing strip in my hair . . .

The gods smiled on him. His hair was barf free.

Passengers tossed bread to the gulls that glided effortless beside the steaming ship, drafting, their eyes small and mean, the whiteness of their feathers pure as a baby's drool.

A pod of right whales fluked and sounded beside the ship, soaking in the propeller vibrations they recognized as friendly. Several ventured closer, nearly touching the vessel.

One curious calf approached the boat but was nudged away by its mother.

Johnny hung way over the railings, hooking his feet so he wouldn't go overboard, to get a better look at the giant whale's blowhole.

He was just in time, the whale let fly, its breath catching him full bore. *Bad breath in whales . . . Hope mine doesn't smell that bad . . . Whew . . . Seaweed must not have had . . . any chlorophyll in it . . .*

"The tower! The tower!" Mandy cried out in delight.

Johnny could barely make out the tall needle of the Provincetown Tower in the distance. He hoped they would have a chance to climb it. He had hitchhiked to Salem to visit the House of the Seven Gables, where he managed to swipe a splinter from the clapboards despite the sharp-eyed guard.

He had also ridden his bike to Plymouth, where he chipped a small piece of Plymouth Rock and the guard had chased him down the beach, nearly catching him as he pedaled through the sand. It was a tough ride, but running in sand was tougher. Especially for guards that liked a six-pack while listening to the radio news after supper. Later, after leaving the panting guard behind, he sat in the sand, hoping not too many kids would take chips, worrying Plymouth rock could disappear. He sifted the sand through his fingers, dreaming of the Pilgrims setting foot right where he rested, and put some sand in his pocket his collection.

Soon he would add Provincetown sand to his collection. And he wouldn't be chased. He thought, *No stupid guard will . . . chase me for grabbing a sand . . . unless they think I'm trying to swipe dog turds . . . Why do people bring their animals to the beach? My Rags was different . . . He wasn't no pig like those other ass wipes . . . His little heinz fifty-seven different varieties loved the beach . . . Somehow he managed to dog paddle his little tail to the bottom . . . and scoff up a horseshoe crab in his mouth . . . and he'd swim to me . . . the saber tail of the prehistoric animal cutting a dangerous swath through the air . . . My Rags . . . proud as a fur-covered peacock . . . Oh, dear Lord . . . why don't dogs live as long as their masters? You should be smarter than that . . . Nah, nah . . . I didn't mean that . . . I promise you, Ma . . . Your baby Johnny will live longer than you . . . just long enough so you won't be sad . . . just long enough so I won't be sad . . . Grandfather Shiverick said we all meet together . . . in the great by-and-by . . .*

The whistle of the ferry jolted Johnny out of his reverie.

"Didn't you hear us calling your name?" It was his pastor. "We thought you were comatose. Does this happen often? Do you take medicine? We're here."

A crowd of people had gathered to watch the fishing and lobster boats unload. Wonder how these Portuguese fishermen could go to sea in those bucket of bolts, one even had a piece of plywood nailed over what had to be a hole high on the bow. Now they turned their attention to the ferry and the people on board. Waved. When you don't fish on Cape Cod, there isn't a lot more to do.

Mandy and Maybelle were thrilled that so many people had gathered to welcome them. The ferry was alongside the wharf. Lines were tossed and hitched. Sun-soaked curly hair kids, six to sixteen, piled aboard like pirates boarding a spice-laden clipper ship on the high seas.

"A coin, a coin!" they called out as they climbed the gunnels, the rigging, and then sailed after the Indian head pennies and buffalo nickels flipped high in the air, catching the sun, a Lorelei.

And the offspring of the Portuguese that had settled in Provincetown for no other reason than the fact you couldn't jut any further into the sea.

Johnny wanted to join them, not only for the coins that could bulk out his three years of saving for Jazz's teeth fixing, but also for the sheer joy that made the bronzed treasure hunters not just dive after their fortunes, but do beautiful swan dives and flips, gainers, and great frog leaps, legs and arms out to the side, forming the shapes of airborne green leapers.

—

Johnny couldn't contain himself. He was on the railing. This would be a greater dive than any off Duck Pond Rock.

His bomb burst with the foam of other geysers of other divers as he entered the water. They all swam downward, snapping up the coins like feeding goldfish, returning skyward as their lungs emptied.

Johnny continued downward, his eyes on a descending sideslipping quarter. He snatched it in his hand just before it reached the bottom. Something dark shot out at his hand. It was a large lobster, tossing its claws toward his hand. He thought of Joe Louis tossing punches.

Johnny had opened his hand when the lobster threatened and the shiny quarter fell out.

The lobster clamped it in his crusher claw.

"That's mine." He swam over the lobster, hoping to grab it from behind and avoid the threatening claws.

Oh, Johnny, you are so . . . smart . . .

The thought fled swiftly. The lobster had snapped its tail and also shot backward. Its ripping claw extended upward and pinched the end of his penis.

Johnny could feel the tears burst from his eyes. He looked upward for help. The divers on the surface looked like tiny toys.

He was out of breath.

He freed the ripper claw from his private part and freed the crusher claw containing the coin with a yank.

Then he pumped with all his power upward, lungs feeling like a balloon that water was being forced into and would soon burst. The sky was closer now. He could see the clouds through the ocean surface. Then he was free of the ocean's crushing maw and dragged in the air so deeply he felt it had filled him down to his toes.

The Portuguese kids who could stay underwater for three or four minutes at a time gathered around him, and one asked, "How did you stay down so long?"

"I wasn't down that long."

A small kid floated on the surface nearby. A larger boy pushed down on his head, sinking him below the surface, "Worthless brother, no coins."

When the small boy bobbed up, he gave Johnny a smile. "You're not a P-towner, but you can stay cuz God made the ocean for everyone."

Johnny looked at his hard-earned quarter and said to the kid, "Bet when you show this to your brother with the coin in the lobster claw, they won't duck you anymore."

"I can't take it from someone who isn't one of us. My brother would kill me."

—

482

"Then take it from the ocean," Johnny said, flipping the claw and coin in the air, watching it sink as the boy dived after it, his feet slipping beneath the surface like the tail of a sounding whale.

Moments later, the boy was on the surface holding the coin trapped in the lobster claw high over his head. "See! See!"

Johnny flipped over on his back, his mouth filled with salt water, and spouted it into the air like the right whale had spouted earlier, watching the stream disintegrate in the sun rays into a multitude of small silver coins of pure silver.

Then he saw the boil-sore red face of his pastor glaring down at him. "You will pay for this. You will pay for this brazen display, mister. Mr. DaSilva."

Johnny swam to a thin piling and shimmied up with a skill developed when shimmying up the black birch to reach the highest of the wild grapes that grew on the python-thick vines.

He was greeted, a wrong term, by the pastor and the cousins; he was covered with the tar and pitch from the pilings.

The looks he received from Mandy and Maybelle had an even more turned-up nose and curled lip than when they discovered that the magic racing strip in his hair back in Sullivan Square was pigeon scat. Barf.

"What could you have been thinking of? You could have gotten killed. Or drowned. What would I tell your grandfather, Mr. Shiverick?"

"You could practice by telling my mother first."

"I hope you aren't being flippant, young man. Your vacation could end before it starts."

"I'm sorry. And stupid."

"Why, yes," Reverend Newhall said," but young, and of some good English stock. Young Mr. John Shiverick, named after your grandfather."

"John DaSilva."

"That's quite enough, young man."

"Yes, sir."

"Now we must catch the train to Wellfleet."

"We'll run ahead, Father. The salt air just makes you want to hop, skip, and jump," Mandy said, grabbing Maybelle's hand and running along the pier laughing, holding her straw hat tight to her head as its wide brim filled with air. "I could just fly. Just fly."

Reverend Newhall rearranged the giant load in the basket of the bike, slipped the handles of the clothes bags over the handlebars, handed Johnny two sacks for each hand, loaded himself up, and said, "We're off."

The conductor helped the two girls aboard the train and went aboard himself, leaving the pastor and the boy to try to get their luggage aboard.

—

After several aborted attempts, including nearly losing the crock of night crawlers, Reverend Newhall climbed up the steel stairs to the small platform between railroad cars. Johnny handed up the bags and boxes they had brought. Then his bike. They were ready to steam to Wellfleet. Just in time.

The conductor's "All aboard" was in sync with the engine's spewing steam.

The conductor watched as Johnny attempted to bring his bike inside the railroad car.

When the Western Flyer was almost into the car, the conductor blocked Johnny. "You can't bring that aboard my car. What would you bring next year, an automobile? Then an airplane? Don't answer. I'm sure you would. Get it out to the back platform. You stand there with it until we get into Wellfleet."

Johnny bit into his lower lip to stop it from quivering.

"And don't you dare to give me any lip, young man, or am I using the term 'young man' loosely?"

Johnny was about to give the conductor a piece of his mind, the piece that worried him, that dark section that made him worry about himself, made him worry about his future as a Christian.

At Wellfleet, Johnny started to carefully work the bike off the platform down the narrow steps when the conductor attempted to grab the bike and speed it along.

"I wouldn't," Johnny said.

The conductor jumped back at hearing the barely audible words. Then collecting himself, pulling his jacket blouse down with a huff, said, "You wouldn't. You wouldn't. You little gutter snipe . . ."

"What's going on here?" The reverend had opened the car door and poked his head out.

"I think there is a need for your lessons in good manners here," the conductor said.

"John, you are not causing more trouble. Why do I ask?" He looked at Johnny's still-soaked clothing. "Don't bother to speak. I know the answer."

"Hurry, or else," the conductor said.

Johnny gauged the old man's ability to hear as he eased the bike down the steps to the platform and turned to the now-smiling conductor and whispered, entering his own smile onto the scene, "Take a flying fuck at a rolling doughnut."

"What?" the conductor screamed, his eyebrows pushing into his hairline, the red spreading upward from his too-tight collar to his ears.

"Just what did you say?" Reverend Newhall questioned. Johnny looked up as his pastor's face, which he thought had a look that is usually reserved for a person entrapped in the dual death of having both his boxer shorts riding up with toward his throat with a razor's vengeance and his shoes so tight it felt like an elephant had used his feet as a PLP, public leaning post.

He knew he was in trouble. "I'm sorry I spoke so low. I said," pointing skyward, then at a nearby fishing hut, "that flying duck is so low it will hit the roof of that low hut."

The conductor started down the steps.

Johnny placed himself between the conductor and his bike.

"Yes, yes, it could have," the reverend said, "it could very well have run into the hut."

The conductor looked up at the pastor with an are-you-for-real look.

Reverend Newhall helped Johnny rearrange all their gear on Johnny's bike and placed two more cloth bags in his free hand as he balanced the Western Flyer, hefted five bags himself, and they started off, the girls skipping ahead.

"Go slow, my dears. It is a long walk, two miles to our cottage."

The both slowed, patted their laced handkerchiefs to their foreheads.

The sun was setting as their turned off the narrow tar road onto the sandy one that led along the edge of Long Pond. "We're here. That's it," the old man said, "That one over there, John."

The cottage looked like the other two on the pond, never having seen a lick of paint in forty years, the cedar shingles fighting a war, weathered to turn the salt silver of a whitecap or the dark brown of the seaweed that slip slided away just beneath the surface.

A screened in porch traveled the entire length of the front and was entered up steps where rusty nail heads showed through as the boards had shrunk in the sun. Scrub pines stood guard around its perimeter, the tree limbs nearly hiding the wooden shingle roof that had lost the battle to the sun decades before but still managed to swell when it rained, blocking out the elements.

The cottage had a small kitchen, a smaller dining room, a bedroom that housed a single bed, and the screened porch, which had a double bed at one end and a cot at the other.

The reverend started lighting the oil lamps on the porch, living room, and kitchen, keeping the flame as low as it could go without turning off. "A penny saved is a penny earned. John, would thou please get a bucket of water so we can prime the pump."

Johnny took the bucket that was handed him and headed out the door. The porch was only fifteen feet from the water's edge.

—

He turned the pail over, sat on it as he watched the moon come over the treetops and set up a gold ribbon road the entire length of the pond.

A bullfrog started its throaty, sorrowful croaking nearby. "Kaaaaponk, kaaaaponk."

Johnny checked the pickerel weeds to the left side of the sandy beach that housed the croaker. "Don't be sad . . . We'll be friends . . . I won't sell your legs . . . Yes . . . they are lovely . . . I'll get you a set of heels . . ."

The assurance appeared to do little to allay the bullfrog's fears as its baritone voice reached octaves so low its sad song seemed to come from distant jungle drums.

Then the faraway call of a quail added its lonely voice, "Bob white, bob white, bob white." Its brothers and sisters joined the choir, and the choirmaster, maestro bullfrog, added his deep vibrations, taking over all the very air of Johnny's world, entering his head, causing his ears to join the drum section, then his chest and his very breathing.

He took one last at the moon road down the pond, closed his eyes, and breathed deeply, bringing the salt odors born of the Atlantic's waves beating off the great sand dunes of Cahoon's Hollow, the swamp blueberries from the end of the lake, wild beach plums, honeysuckle, and heather.

"It is beautiful." His pastor's voice was barely audible from the porch. "We can be certain of only one thing in life, that if this is a hint of heaven, it isn't that bad a goal to work toward. Please don't forget the water when you come in."

A short while later, he was holding the bucket high in the air, tipping it so the water could prime the pump as the old man smiled at him, working its handle with surprising vigor.

"I'll take the bedroom. The girls want the porch. Can't blame them. You will take the cot. You can hang the small tarp from the ceiling for privacy."

"Reverend, can I use the tarp to cover my Western Flyer instead. I'm afraid some pine pitch might fall on it. Or a seagull or something might strafe it."

"I certainly see no problem other than it will mean you will have to change from your clothing into your pajamas under the blankets and only after the lamp is turned off. And of course you will have to wash the tarp off before we leave."

"Yes, sir."

"Would you put the night crawler crock in the shade under the porch? We'll hope the raccoons don't get into them. And take the Sears catalog up to the backhouse. It's uphill to the left, tucked in behind the scrub pine. Don't stub your toe in the dark."

Johnny placed the crock under the porch, locating it directly beneath where he would sleep. That way he could hear if any raccoons wanted any night crawler spaghetti and chase it off. *Pretty good thinking, Johnny . . . unless the spaghetti draws a family of skunks . . . cheee . . . if a skunk gets me . . . its . . .* "Nobody likes me. Everybody hates me. I think I'll go eat worms, big fat ugly ones, little, skinny slimy ones. I eat worms three times a day," he sang.

"Got money in the bank," Mandy called down from the darkened porch, "talking to yourself, little boy?"

"Nah." *Little boy . . . I'm sixteen . . . You're only seventeen . . .*

"Don't go looking for anything special in the Sears. My daddy took care of that, little boy."

"Sure." *What in hell does she mean by that, don't go looking for anything special?*

She opened the screen door, placed the dog-eared catalog on the top step, closed the door, turned her back on him, and said, "And don't go trying to see anything when we're in the kitchen changing into our 'jamas."

"There ain't nothin' to see."

"Wanna bet?"

He picked up the Sears and headed to the outhouse in the dark. A bough in the eye and two toe stubs later, he located the two seater. He thought of his and Dink's and Pointer's efforts of a month of digging to get a mole's eye view of a woman's it only to have their grandfather nearly burn them to death, escaping suffocation from the smoke to nearly suffocate in the droppings of ten years of visitors to the farm fudge and corn and berry stand. No, Johnny wouldn't be trying to get any mole's eye view.

A bird's eye view might be a little different. Maybe some night he'd climb a nearby pine and try to look down through the half-moon cut over the privy door. Surely the girls were afraid of the dark and would bring an oil lantern with them.

He didn't know whether a minister's daughter would even have an "it." *Perhaps even a minister's niece might not have one . . . but they certainly have boobs . . . big ones . . . little ones . . . some the size of your head . . . unless they're stuffing socks in there . . . I'm going to be up front with you . . . but if Reverend Newhall ever caught me . . . I'd burn in hell . . . forever . . . but then again . . . how many forevers can you burn in hell? Ma already sentenced me to burn for eternity . . . if I ever dated a . . . Catholic . . .*

—

The door squeaked as he opened it and closed it behind him. He pulled down his pants and sat on the butt-smooth wood. He placed the Sears catalog beside him. There were only a few sheets of newspaper left from the last cottage renters. He felt the box beside the seat. Matches. Left there to strike to kill any odors after your business had been done. *Wonder if holy people like Mr. Newhall leave any odors . . . How about Mandy? Her bum has to be close to her . . . whatever you call that girl part . . . that part . . . wherever it is . . . under . . . or in the front . . . God, I feel . . . real dizzy . . .*

He reached between his legs, took himself in his hand, and applied a firm pressure, then told himself he was only directing his stream downward, if he had to go.

He struck a match. Opened the Sears, flipping toward the section where the women wore the bra and panties. What did Amanda mean? Mandy what did you . . . mean?

He wondered what Amanda meant by her "and don't go looking for nothing special in the Sears."

Then suddenly Johnny knew. His pastor had torn those special pages out of the catalog. He released his hand from his private. *Why would such a great and brave soldier . . . be called private? Why not general? You have a great general hanging there, Johnny boy . . . General Pecker . . . General Pecker, sir, your troops are waiting for you to review them . . . Is Amanda dropping her dress . . . her uniform . . . at this very moment . . . while trying to pull her nightgown down . . . over her body . . . with the same continuous motion . . . but if I was looking in the window . . . it wouldn't work . . . I'd see where it was . . . but would I . . . if there is hair there like on men? What would I see?*

He could feel himself grow as he pondered the question. Then shudder.

Johnny nearly jumped through the half-moon above the door when Mandy's voice greeted him, "Don't hog the palace."

Through the crack in the door, he could see the bouncing kerosene lamp the cousins held between them.

"Okay. Okay. Give me a break. I'm just leaving the paper here. Nothing else."

"Sure."

He made one last check to make sure the Sears wasn't left open to where the special section had been ripped out.

He was out the door and disappeared in the dark, cutting a big circle through the woods to reach the cottage, ground covered so swiftly and so fearlessly that he didn't even hear Mandy's mocking voice, "And don't you go trying to see something special. My father, who art on earth, will have you burn in hell."

Maybelle laughed as her cousin slapped her shoulder. "Now stop that. Be a good girl."

"Woman."

"Why, yes, we are. We shouldn't be making fun of little boys. Now should we."

"No, we shouldn't. Shouldn't we."

They both laughed at the Scarlet O'Hara accents.

"Oh, that rogue DaSilva boy," Mandy said, "he does give a damn, my dear. Would you sing outside the door while I draw my toilet, dear? I don't want that silly boy listening for my tinkle."

"Yes, my dear."

Their laughter drifted down to Johnny, who was now beneath the blankets, searching for the gallant steed whose mighty muscles had flexed only minutes before, but had turned into a simpering, flaccid minutia pony, gelded by the cousins' sneers.

The bullfrog and the covey of quail had ceased their songs. Their music that had made him hum love songs to himself was now replaced by the crazy laughter of a loon.

Or was it the cousins laughing at him?

CHAPTER 28

CHERRY PICKING

Each night it was a battle between the lovely, lonely song of the whip-poor-wills and the magpie chatter of Mandy and Maybelle at the far end of the porch that determined how swiftly or how slowly Johnny got to sleep.

The soothing song of the whip-poor-will repeated endlessly as they sought the punishment of the poor boy.

The punishers of 'poor will' won the first two nights on the Cape, and Johnny nodded off quickly.

Because of the jabberwocky of the cousins, Johnny was given to a variety of methods to try and put himself to sleep.

He needed his sleep as while the girls slept in the next morning, Johnny was up and at 'em rowing the good reverend around Long Pond as he trolled for pickerel with a spinner and worms.

After several hours of rowing and when Johnny was positive his arms were made of rubber and a good three feet longer than when he got out of bed in the early morning dark, the Reverend Newhall would dispense his mercy, and they anchored and settled down for some serious yellow perch fishing. Or perhaps quietly luring some of those late-feeding nocturnal horned pout that apparently had caroused all night and had to catch a snack before catching a nap.

He tried a number of methods to help himself go to sleep despite the girls chattering. He counted sheep; that didn't work. He tried to hold his head under his pillow. Nope.

Johnny next counted breasts, and he quickly discovered that didn't work. To the contrary. And slowly, the nipples turned from brown to pink to blue.

And he found himself staring into Bernadette's light blue eyes, clear as a baby's, and then into Yelena's now-cat-green eyes. At times, the pair of eyes he visualized had one blue and one green. And he'd doze off wondering which to change. *Should I get a second blue . . . and have a pair or a second green . . . discard the blue . . . Is it possible to have both . . . two separate pairs of mixed . . . Had a cat once . . . had two different eye colors . . . yellow and blue . . . or somethin' . . .*

The final solution to getting to sleep was thinking of one of his chemistry lectures. The problem here was it made him snore, and the guffaws from Mandy and Maybelle were intended to wake him up, at which time Mandy would say, "Little boy. Little snoring boy. How I hate people who snore. Especially little boys."

Each night Mandy called out, not loud, "Little boy?"

"Ya," he'd answer, trying not to show how angry it made him. That would mean she won. There was less than a year in age difference. And he was way taller than her.

"Nothing. Go to sleep."

The sixth night, he decided not to give her the satisfaction, and when she called out, "Little boy?" he didn't answer.

"Little boy, are you sleeping, like a good little boy should?"

He didn't answer.

"He's asleep," Mandy whispered to her cousin.

"It's about time," Maybelle said, a husky tone to her voice rather than a peeved one.

"Did you see little boy Johnny in that bathing suit at Cahoon's today?"

"So?" Maybelle said.

"Did you see the hair on his chest went right down his stomach to the top of his bathing suit, and you could tell that the hair from the you know what came up and met it."

"So?"

"Did you see the bulge where his you know what was?"

"No," Maybelle said, "but once I saw Jackie McBey's thing. Well, I didn't really see all of it. His fly was undone. I always wondered how he kissed."

Johnny cupped his ears, being careful not to move the blankets so they'd know he was listening and make fun of him.

"I could give you just a little kiss like I think he'd kiss you but . . ."

"But what?"

—

"Then you'd have to give me a little kiss like you think Johnny might kiss." Silence.

"That was good," Maybelle said. "Do you really think he'd stick his tongue in my mouth like that. I hope so."

"He would," Mandy said, then lowering her voice so Johnny could barely hear, "Your turn."

"For what."

"You know, how he'd kiss."

"Okay . . . Is that okay?"

"Oh yes, Johnny. Oh yes. Lick my tongue. Lick it when I stick it out."

"Oh wow. I don't know. Okay."

"Oh, Johnny. Oh. My nipples hurt. Do my nipples. Do my nipple."

"What about me? What about Jackie McBey? How would he touch mine? Ummm. Oh yes, Jackie."

"Oh, Johnny, oh. Touch me where I'm wet. The wet hair first. Where it came from."

Their moans were soft, low. There were fewer words. They were too low for Johnny to hear.

He lay awake long after he was certain they were asleep. He wanted to pump himself. What if they're not . . . asleep . . . and saw the blanket moving . . . Oh, God . . . help me . . . How do I do it without moving the blanket?

He squeezed his eyes tight, stiffened his hand and pressed it against his upper lip at the apex of the nose where you press to stop yourself from sneezing, a very painful action. He wasn't sure whether the tears came to his eyes because of the painful hand pressure or because he squeezed his eyes so tight he saw vertigo.

He tried to blank Mandy's dark-brown eyes from his mind, but the best he could do is conjure Bernadette's robin's-egg-blue eyes and Yelena's deep-silver sea-green ones. There's no rest for the weary . . .

It was the light snoring that put him to sleep. Johnny thought it was himself snoring. That he was asleep. It couldn't be Mandy or her cousin. Girls don't snore . . .

But actually, he was awake. The light snoring was Mandy's.

While Johnny was weary, she was exhausted.

He was awake enough to wonder what he could do. What in heck do you do in a case like this? Mandy was doing it with me . . . Why can't I do it with her?

From the furthest distance on the lake, a loon laughed.

Not sounding unlike Red Skeleton.

"My, my, aren't we the sleepyhead."

—

Johnny opened his eyes.

The figure that bent over him was blurred.

"The early bird gets the worm. The early fisherman gets the fish." It was Reverend Newhall. Johnny leaned out of the cot, scooped up his dungarees, and pulled them under the old woolen army blanket, glancing down the porch. The girls were asleep.

"I'll meet you in the boat," the old man said

Johnny pulled on his trousers, zipped them, being very careful not to catch his pubic hairs in the zipper, like he did that first morning under the adverse conditions of dressing under the covers. He was more careful the second morning. His hair escaped. But not so his foreskin, and the piranha-like zipper made him gasp.

After that, he was very careful about his zipper's travels past the pubic and the foreskin, but he should have been more careful with his travels past his testicles. Pain? All he could think about was that the grip by the zipper, whose teeth Johnny was positive were set in a combination smile and snarl at that moment.

He couldn't free himself.

He worried whether the two girls would see the action under his blanket and attribute the cause to self-flagellation. *How does a girl accuse you of . . . how do they accuse you of what the guys call . . . twanging your banjo . . . tooting your flute . . . tutoring your toy . . . Most likely a girl would say . . . batoning the Boston pops . . . little boy . . .*

His progress of freeing himself from the pit bull zipper was nil. The pain, on a scale of one to ten, was an eleven. He even considered asking for help. *God bless me . . .*

The "God bless me" must have worked. The zipper, as if it had a mind of its own and had quenched its thirst for a fun time, released its grip, and his tender sack fell free, accompanied by his sigh so singular in relief that it could never be confused for anything but a zipper release.

"You coming fishing?" The reverend's voice was an attempt to wake Johnny but not the girls.

It worked. The cousins were sound asleep as Johnny tiptoed to the screen door, opened it so slowly that the usual cry of pain from the hinge was silenced.

Reverend Newhall sat in the stern of the boat, two telescoping, steel rods at the ready, as Johnny, barefoot, pushed off, and then hopped over the gunnels and into the middle seat where the oars, already in the oarlocks, awaited him.

Once the wooden lapstrake was moving out, the reverend, like a Harvard scull crew coxswain on the Charles River, called out, "Stroke,

—

stroke, stoke," as he checked his watch to move the boat at a speed he knew would lure the chain pickerel out of the pickerel weeds to strike the spinner and worms that was trolled close to shore in two feet of water. Meanwhile, the second line dragged a red and white Daredevyl wobbled on the starboard side in waters that dropped off to six feet where perhaps one of the stray largemouths that was just offshore catching the first morning sun would strike out of anger.

Johnny hoped that neither the needle mouth pickerel nor the bucketmouth bass would hit. He wanted to get to where they would anchor, and he could fish for the perch and cats. Besides, the pickerel were bony, and the bass was tasteless.

"Steady as she goes, me laddie," the preacher said, putting his pocket watch away.

By the time they reached the deeper waters, the sun sparkled on the slight wake the boat had set up.

"Lower the anchor quietly. We don't want to frighten the fish off," the reverend said. "Mustn't frighten the fish off."

Johnny lowered the anchor, an old window sash weight tied on by clothesline until he felt it bump bottom. *Should of tossed it with a splash . . . make the fish curious . . . that's what Pa always said . . . Fish is curious like all dumb animals . . . and the most curious is the dumbest of all . . . man . . .*

Johnny reeled in one rod and his pastor the second. They took two drop lines and unwound a couple feet of line so as they could bait up.

The reverend unfolded the top of the heavy brown paper bag saved from a shopping foray to the Big Bear in Boston and took out the container of worms. The needed worms had been unceremoniously removed from the large clay crock stored beneath the piers that helped hold up the camp. They were transferred to a cardboard container that had once served the noble task of holding a large order of french fries from Parkers in Wakefield.

Johnny watched his pastor remove the worms. *Wish he wouldn't store the darn worms . . . in the same bag as the sandwiches . . .*

Reverend Newhall read Johnny's thoughts, "Don't worry none about the two being together. We all have to eat a peck of dirt before we die."

Johnny remembered both his grandmothers saying the same thing. In fact, at that time everyone's grandmother said, "We all have to eat a peck of dirt before we die."

The words of wisdom were probably first uttered in Hebrew to calm a daughter whose child's mouth looked like she had just eaten a ball of mud and faced certain death.

Most kids ate a little dirt on their hot dog. Hey, if you drop it on the ground, you pick it up, make sure there is no dog turd on it, plop it back in the bun, and yum.

"Yes, sir, my grandmothers said the same thing. 'Everyone has to eat a peck of dirt before they die.'" *But no one ever said we had to eat a peck of worms . . .*

Each drop line had two hooks. One on the bottom for the whiskered cats and one up several feet for the perch. Both baited with crawlers. The bottom one with a full worm hooked through the collar so the cat could slowly slurp it like a strand of spaghetti and the higher hook with only the tiny tip torn from a crawler. Otherwise, the green striped bandits would steal your worm supply blind.

The perch cooperated, with volunteers being towed into a pail of ice chips. The ice chips had miraculously survived for several months. They were originally large blocks of ice stored in hay.

Johnny had helped his uncle Matt Shiverick cut ice in local ponds and horse haul it to HP Hood in Boston and sell it. They always stopped at the Ford Plant in Somerville, where his uncle would stare at the Model T trucks and flivvers and dream of setting his old horse "horse" out to a well-earned pasture.

The sun warmed his face as it climbed higher and the perch went lower, bit less. He thought of his uncle. *Wonder what Uncle Matt will do . . . when he has to get into the truck and drive to each customer . . . rather than just walking to the next one . . . knowing horse would be there waiting . . . probably known the route better than Uncle Matt . . . He'll probably find out what Uncle Tony found out when sugaring . . . and changed over to the tractor . . . got rid of ol' Pete the big Belgium gelding . . . and had to get aboard and drive that tractor from bucket to bucket . . . maple to maple . . . couldn't just whistle . . . like he did for Old Pete . . . and Old Pete never got stuck in the snow or mud . . . Matt just had to whistle, and that ol' horse would pick up those snowshoe feet and clippety clop up to him . . .*

Johnny remembered cutting pine boughs with his dad, tying them to his feet, and using them as snowshoes so they could go jackrabbit hunting. He tried to imitate the whistle his uncle gave when he wanted the sapping horse to come to that next spigot.

The whistle was a failure. Perhaps because he didn't have that big gap in his front teeth that his uncle Matt had.

He heard his uncle Manny once tell his younger brother Franchesko, "Wish I had that Cumberland Pass gap between my front teeth that Matt Shiverick has. He only uses it for whistling for horses."

"What would you do with it?" Tony had asked.

"Well, first, it would be great for holding a piece of straw while you fished. But it could clamp down on a tiny but nice nipple just enough so it couldn't get away but wouldn't hurt it none." That's what Tony always said . . . a man could do a lot worse than having a piece of straw or a nipple in his teeth . . . That's what his uncle always said.

"What are you whistling, son?" the old man asked him. "Sounds a little bit like the Old Rugged Cross. Your grandfather, Mr. Shiverick, sure loves that song. Maybe as much as the words. 'He loosed the fateful lightning of his terrible swift sword, his truth is marching on.'"

The old gentleman swung from repeating the words to singing them, loud and proud, "Yes, his terrible swift sword! His truth is marching on. Glory, glory hallelujah. Glory, Glory hallelujah."

Lucky you ain't no priest pastor . . . your hormerlie . . . or whatever Catholics call it . . . would make people . . . wish they had a tin ear . . .

Johnny glanced as the song continued; his pastor was gloriously happy, a bucket full of fish and holy words. I bet he thinks it wasn't the crawlers that did it . . . but rather his breakin' bread on the waters . . . He sure is a great ol' scat . . . and his Mandy sure has a great set of waterwings . . .

"Bet I can read your thoughts."

Johnny nearly jumped out of the boat, dropped an oar in the water, and had to make three passes before he could hold on to it he was so nervous.

"Of course I'm not a betting man, but if I was, I'd bet you wish you could climb on the wings of a pure white dove and fly to your grandfather, Mr. Shiverick's side. Just sing your heart out with him."

"Yes, sir, you are exactly right," and to reinforce the fact that his thoughts were of dove wings not water wings, he sang his frightened heart out like a heldentenor, "Glory, glory hallelujah!"

They upped anchor, and Johnny started the return trip to Reverend Newhall's coxswain chant as he played out the trolling lines.

It didn't hurt his high spirits one little bit when a two-inch perch grabbed at the Daredevyl and managed to hook the corner of its jaw on one of the trebles and a two-foot pickerel parted the reeds like a baby Moses gone berserk and took the perch, Daredevyl, and a foot of line into its belly, making it angry enough to come out of the water four times before the old man had it alongside. And the teenage boy had it by the gills and hoisted it out of the water and high over head for its conqueror to see.

Johnny laughed out loud as the old man's grin appeared to swallow his too big ears and those white John L. Lewis super eyebrows lifted enough in joy to show eyes so happy that you knew this was some sort of holy vision.

"It's the biggest I've ever caught. And you brought it aboard. It isn't caught until it's in the boat. God is good!" He smiled up at God after he lowered his flapping wings brows to protect his eyes from the sun.

"Move over, son."

The boy slid to the side, and the old man took the seat beside him and grabbed one oar, singing out, "Pull, me bucky! Today old John Harvard owns the Charles."

The two pulled with amazing power and rhythm, especially considering there was more than fifty years difference in their age.

"Girls! Girls," the pastor sang out, "Mandy, Maybelle, come see!"

Mandy and Maybelle ran from the porch to the beach as the bow of the boat ground onto the shore.

"Look at this! We celebrate! Cahoon's Hollow and the surf this afternoon and ice creams in town this evening.

The walk to Cahoon's and the ocean was about three miles, but it was much shorter when an old fire truck full of young coastguardsman, which at first rolled past the four hikers, backed up on realizing that two of the walkers were girls.

One coastguardsman hopped into the back between two long ladders as Reverend Newhall climbed up beside the driver and Johnny and the cousins hopped into the back, Johnny without a helping hand. Maybelle, and especially Mandy, had several hands offered.

Mandy didn't sound unlike Scarlet O'Hara in her shy, lid-lowering thanks.

Johnny frowned. *She never looked at me that way . . . except in the dark . . . when Maybelle was me . . . and she got wet . . .*

His heart quickened. He looked around guiltily, hoping no one noticed his thoughts. But no one was looking at him.

It seemed the driver who turned repeatedly to smile at the girls drove slower than they had been walking, and why not, hadn't they been driving back and forth on the road between Wellfleet Center and the Hollow that housed the coast guard station and its wooded rescue boat that was powered by the strong arms that helped the girls aboard, hoping for just that, girls wanting a ride?

Of course a kid and an old man with his collar on backward, like a priest but not a priest, were a little tough to take.

The truck drove down between the dunes to the wooden station with the flagpole that towered up some fifty feet between it and the giant whitecaps that carved at the high dunes. This was much more effective than the Chinese water method of water wearing out a stone. It appeared that the dune had started its unrelenting capture of the flag, that a good five feet had already been buried.

The truck came to a sudden stop, rattling the ladders, as the guardsmen emptied the truck liked rats from a sinking ship, hoping to be able to help the girls from their lofty perch.

"No need," the old man said. "They are athletic lasses."

Their chins appeared to bounce off their knees as the old man waved them to follow.

The travel down the steep dune made all that took it realize that indeed they weren't in the camel class of sure-footed sand travel.

"We'll set up between those two groups of ladies. They look very nice." He wasn't about to travel down to the beach where sections of sand and dune could be claimed for privacy, and under the devil's temptation, certain type of individuals were known to remove their tops, even their bottoms. Hadn't he happened upon such a pair, sent them scurrying like a cat before a broom with his *"Damnation! Damnation and hell!"*

Reverend wasn't completely happy with himself as he viewed the fleeing buttocks of the girl and couldn't help but think it moved somewhat like that of Mrs. Morton, who, during her holiest moments in church, stood on her tiptoes, hands high in the air, shifting her weight from one foot to the other, flexing her buttocks' cheeks with a disturbing, less-than-holy, silent chant. He had called out to the heavens that day, "Get thee from my door, devil!"

And thus, the two girls and the boy found themselves between two set of older ladies with knees that hung like the jowls of a red tick hound and were just as lugubrious.

"Last one in is a rhesus!" Mandy yelled out, dashing for the surf.

Maybelle caught up to her with a bound, grabbed her hand, and they entered the surf together.

Johnny sauntered to the beach trying to flex his biceps, his pecks as he walked, as if it was their natural movement. No luck. He promised himself he'd spend more time in the weight room when football started that fall.

"Monkey, monkey," the girls chanted, pointedly staring at his hairy chest, then waded away from him to share their secrets.

Johnny dove beneath the surface, came up between several rocks that hid them from their sight but allowed him to spy on them. Are they touching each other out there? Is Maybelle me? Is Mandy squeezing her thighs together? Oh, God, help me . . .

The girls were having a water fight. When they glanced over at Johnny, he caught a wave and body surfed until it broke close to shore. He

—

landed on the hard sand with a painful grating that knocked the breath out of him and filled his bathing suit with sand.

He tried to get the sand out of the suit but only managed to shift it all to the crotch of his suit. He felt it packed there. He stopped trying to rid himself of the sand and instead reshaped it.

He waded out of the surf, faced the ocean, and closed his eyes, but not really, as he peered out between his heavy eye lashes toward the cousins.

"Wow," Maybelle whispered.

"Double wow," Mandy said. "I'm going to be exhausted tonight. Johnny."

Johnny saw them both looking at him, laughing. *They know it's sand . . . They know it's just a sand castle that'll be washed away . . . Prince Valiant gone . . . with the first wave . . . the magic wand . . . gone . . .*

Then he remembered his uncle Tony's words, "It's not what you got, it's how you use it."

But Johnny remembered his uncle Manny ruining it with his braggadocio. "Yah, little brother, but what if you've got it and can use it too?"

Johnny frowned as he walked into the surf and his sand phallic slowly washed away. What if I don't have it . . . and I don't know how to use it . . . Oh Lord . . . the pain . . .

He moaned out loud, a painful sound that came across more as one of delight, causing a large man whose jet black handlebar mustache and long heavy eyebrows hung down like shades during a World War II blackout to look at him strangely and then quickly put some distance between them with the muttered words, "P-Town faggot."

Johnny had no idea what he was talking about.

And returned to shore, spread out his towel, and lay face down in the sand, thinking of Mandy, hoping he would not leave some little sand nest where his thing was warmed to the point where it no longer needed the bulking out of sand. *If anyone notices, I'll . . . I'll tell them there was a plover nest there . . . yes . . . a plover nest . . .*

He didn't know how long he slept. He did know when he heard the old man's words. "Best we travel on to Avalon. Everyone going to be sore in the morning."

He reached into a small bag he had brought with him. Johnny figured it was his private stash of goodies, as he hadn't broken it out when they ate the tuna sandwiches packed in chips from the icehouse and drank the water drawn up by the old squeaking pump and kept cool in the last survivors of the ice age, chips crisscrossed with straw.

The old man pulled out several small green leafs. "Aloe leaves. Break them and spread the white on each other's backs."

"I'll do Mandy's," Maybelle said.

"And I'll do Maybelle's," her cousin said.

"And I'll do my own," Johnny said.

The old man didn't have to worry as he was fully dressed in a white linen suit and a huge brimmed straw hat. Even his neck was protected from the sun by the clergy collar that led many to believe Episcopal ministers were some sort of priests.

Johnny loved Rev. Newhall's straw hat. It reminded him of the time his father had taken him to a Red Sox game at Fenway. It was the day he had left Johnny for a short while, and Johnny had spotted him going into the Old Howard, the burlesque house in Scully Square; and when he came out, they had a hot dog at Joe and Nemo's. His father had said, "They're good, but wait until you have one of those Fenway dogs. They're the cat's meow."

They both had laughed.

His father had paid a buck and a half for his seat, seventy-five cents for Johnny, no small outlay.

The game was fantastic. Bobby Doerr and Rudy York put one over the Green Monster. Ted Williams sent a tower of power twenty rows over the visitor's bullpen.

Then Jim Tabor hit a long one, foul, and some old gent stuck out his straw hat to catch the ball. And it knocked the top out of the hat. The crowd exploded with laughter.

"Williams hit a second high can of corn!" the excited announcer cried out.

And his father said, "Now let those damned Yankees dig themselves out of that grave."

The Sox were up by eight.

But Joe D. and King Kong Keller and the Pride of the Yankees. Was it Gary Cooper . . . stupid . . . Lou Gehrig . . . got pissed . . . and sent out a few . . . Chinese fireworks of their own . . .

The Sox lost 9 to 8.

The Reverend Newhall's voice woke him out of his walking reverie. "The low bush are in here," the old man said, leading them off the road into the scrub pine that lined the edge and to a small mound, blue as a bluebird's back, with blueberry clusters that little ground birds sing about.

"Don't eat too many, save a handful to put on your ice cream. I'm going to remain at the cottage. Continue your walk into town and get the ice creams I promised. That giant pickerel is proving costly. Here's a nickel each. No, wait. Get a double scoop. Here's two more cents each."

Each took the change taken from a small cloth bag whose drawn string tightened with much more ease than it opened. "Don't eat too fast or take too big a bite, or you'll suffer temple freeze."

"Coming back, if you have time before dark, stop by the big hole in the road about a mile from here and fill your pockets with beach plums. We'll make beach plum jam."

The old man turned down the sandy road to the cottage. "And stay together."

The three moved quickly toward town fortified with blueberry energy as the thoughts of a double dip of homemade ice cream waltzed in their heads.

"Here's the pothole for when we come back," Johnny said. "The beach plum bush must be in there."

"So," Maybelle said.

Johnny looked at the large girl, his expression blank, as he didn't want anyone running to his pastor with any stories. Sew buttons on your fly . . .

"Don't go thinking any thoughts. Don't let no sugar plums dance in your head, little boy."

The ice cream stand was beside the Wellfleet theater, an old wooden structure that seated about twenty moviegoers. The size didn't really matter, as it was a rare day when more than a dozen persons attended. It was ten cents to go. And money didn't grow on bushes.

Maybelle got chocolate and vanilla.

Mandy ordered strawberry and chocolate.

Johnny got two coffee scoops. Maybe the caffeine will keep me awake . . . after they think I'm asleep . . .

Johnny watched as Mandy licked the ice cream, resting her tongue on a giant strawberry that protruded disturbingly from the dome of the cone.

He moaned. His cone appeared to be melting much faster than theirs. He hoped they didn't notice.

They ate as they walked as the evening slowly crowded in.

Maybelle, with her long legs stepped out, opening a distance between them.

"The pothole," Mandy whispered. "The wild plums are just in the woods a piece."

"Yes."

"You know you're not really a little boy." He could see her smile in the dark. *I'm gonna lose my cherry . . . I'm gonna lose my cherry . . . Oh . . . thank you, good God . . . I'm going to lose my cherry . . . oooh . . .*

—

Mandy walked into the dark woods.

Johnny followed.

"The beach plum tree," she whispered, plucking two plums from the bush, cupping them in her hand. He could see her smile in the dark. He closed his eyes. Held them closed. When he opened them, he was more used to the dark. He could see the stain, a thin line of sweat, just below where the bottom of her bra would be. *She made love . . . to me . . . last night . . . Of course it was . . . really Maybelle . . . . but Maybelle was . . . me . . .*

She looked into his eyes.

He moved his face toward her. *What do you do with your nose? They'll hit . . . They licked tongues last night . . . Tongues are longer than noses . . .*

Johnny rested his hands on Mandy's shoulders, lowered his face into hers, closed his eyes, feeling his lips heat, swell ever so slightly.

"You pig! You pig! I'm telling my grandfather you tried to . . . you tried to kiss me."

She ran from the woods, giving a small cry.

That night, the cousins didn't whisper in bed. Didn't ask if he was awake.

Johnny could hear Mandy's soft sobs at the other end of the porch.

While she didn't tell about the attempted kiss, Mandy did not look at Johnny the final week of their vacation, not while swimming in Long Pond nor on the sand at Cahoon's. Not on the walk back to Wellfleet Center all loaded down with their gear to catch their train to Provincetown nor on the train to Provincetown. Or the ferry back to Boston nor on the yellow peril return to Rockledge.

Johnny knew he was the rottenest son of a bitch that ever lived.

He wished he was a Catholic so he could tell this to someone, someone who just couldn't tell anyone else. He crossed himself. *Ma would kill me . . . if she found out I did that . . . It would kill Granddad Shiverick if he knew I did it . . . Oh, Lord . . . I want to ask your help . . . but you're not supposed to ask for stuff for yourself . . . in your prayers . . . I'm supposed to ask how I can help others . . . but right now all I can do is try and help myself . . . What if someone tells my ma . . . She's one tough lady with a broom . . . Please, dear Lord . . . help me not to want to get it so bad . . . Dear Lord, please help me get laid . . . Oh, God . . . why me?*

CHAPTER 29

SENIOR YEAR—1950

The Big Tree gang's last year of high school was a potpourri of pleasure and pain.

And much of summer of that followed was spent cruising and confusing, according to Johnny. Add Righty's classification of Johnny as a poet. "He is a poet and doesn't know it. His feet are Longfellows." Righty could deal out the corn with the best of them, with his oversized blurbs.

The sum and total was complete confusion; they did not know if they were coming or going.

Dink had a Model A Ford. When they pooled their change on a given day, they knew the seventy-five cents would buy them enough gas to hit Revere Beach in the morning. If it was so crowded there, they couldn't lay down their towels, they'd tool up to Canobie Lake, with all the cool stuff they learned at the reet pleet Revere, such as "What's cookin', good lookin'" at least got the girls to look at them that first time.

There rarely was a second glance as the gang only had an opening line, not near enough to "make the sweet tootsies of Canobie hot to trot."

Sometimes they traveled all the way to York Beach or Old Orchard, Maine, counting the white broken lines that made up the center strip of Route 1, as it made the counters very dizzy.

It wasn't easy as the counting was done through the section of floor they had removed to keep the car cool. The updraft through the floor was augmented by the fact that the bottom of the windshield could be tilted a foot above the dash. This could mean a passing bug or small piece of debris could invade the driver's eye. Meaning a copilot had to take the wheel, with the blinded driver never taking his foot off the gas pedal and the balance of the happy passenger posse hooting, "Yippie-i-yay-ki-yay."

Dink and Pointer had hitched up a radio for the car complete with two antennas. How cool can a car be.

One antenna would always have the high-flying foxtail flapping in the breeze, a sure way to get girls. Of course it was on the driver's side. The other antenna had up to nine bathing suits drying on it, just about the max of friends they could squeeze into the car.

They had made fantasy plans to attempt to meet with the Ringling Brothers to declare they could get double the number of humans into the Model A than the Ringling clowns could get into their tiny vehicle and without using a trapdoor beneath it to secret up rascal clowns.

Each soiree always had Righty as a regular, along with Johnny, the brothers Boattail and Rhesus, Scoff Burns, Soupy Campbell, Fats, and others rotating on the trips. Usually the one who had the most loose change for the gas got the nod.

For a while, they carried as many as thirteen passengers by putting two on each running board. Two things ended this practice.

One was the Model A had trouble making it up the steeper hills, and two, the police were always stopping them.

Oh ya, and three—one day Dick Tracy fell off the running board while trying to wave to a leggy blonde girl who was walking along the side of the road. And no one ever bounced as high as he was reported to.

Dick Tracy always had to one-up his buddies, so one day he hitched his belt to the speeding car's door handle and waved with both arms while Dink laid on the horn they had installed, one that gave those loud tugboat a-oooog-gaar's.

His belt held on the doorknob, but the knob pulled out of the door, and Dick Tracy became the flying young man on the flying trapeze without benefit of trapeze or safety net.

Luckily, he hit the grass on the side of the road. Boattail and Rhesus, who later visited the injured Dick Tracy, reported, "He broke his ass. Ya, he broke his ass in ten places."

Actually, the brothers were more interested in borrowing the injured boy's unicycle than inquiring about their friend's home recuperation. Mrs. Tracy, who understood their motives didn't lend them her son's bike despite Bird's eloquent plea, "Why not? can't sit on the seat with a broken butt."

When it came to going to the drive-in theater, Scoff Burns convinced his father, an antique car buff, to accept Dink's generous offer of letting him drive the Model A some night.

They would be willing to drive Mr. Burn's Packard to replace the Model T for the night.

The big Packard could fit six into the trunk, two more on the floor of the backseat covered with a blanket, one huddled beneath the dashboard, and six in the regular seating.

Dink would drive to the ticket box at the entrance to the drive-in and purchase six tickets for those in view of the ticket seller. The ticket taker was to hold a trunk search if the rear end of the car was suspiciously low, but no matter how many you packed into the trunk of the Packard, the rear suspension system never sagged. A true mechanical buddy.

Scoff Burns bragged about the family car. "The Packard was made for bootleggers but constructed mostly to get kids into the drive-in without having to pay financial homage to the capitalists."

Despite the fact it was Scoff's dad's car, Dink insisted on driving as fair is fair, and after all, it was his Ford flivver Mr. Burns was driving.

Johnny was the passenger as he had the most imagination, and if the ticket seller had any questions, he'd turn on the double speak and charm, a skill that Fat Burns said gave him the ability "to sell refrigerators to the Eskimos." A comment that drew the same retort each time, "corn".

Scoff ended up in the trunk on more recent ventures to the drive-in despite the fact he argued, "It's my car."

But he was regaled to the trunk by unanimous vote when Rhesus pointed out, "Your farts are without mercy and would gag a maggot." Of course his fellow trunk inhabitants did not have a vote, as often Johnny was granted the authority of a benevolent despot.

Boattail said, "If he won't get in the trunk, let's kill him and feed him to the skunks."

Rhesus said, "The skunks have standards. They'd reject him."

Luckily, the summer came to an end as their moviegoing careers came to a dead end when Rhesus and Boattail had taken to sneaking around the rear rows of cars in sneak-a-peek soirees and claiming great victories of seeing some real sex stuff.

Rhesus said, "We saw them doing it!"

His brother said, "In another car, we scared the hair off this old guy's balls. He had his tool out when Marlene Dietrich came on the screen in that gypsy dress. It was in a popcorn box and up through the bottom. Just like a pigeon in fuckin' Boston Commons. And he was beating the hell out of his bongo, right there in the popcorn. And Rhesus yelled, "Hey! Leave that midget alone or I'll call a cop!"

"Hey, I saved the dipshit, he was gonna come just as Marlene was going to disappear and Ray Malland appeared."

—

Soupy Campbell, who lived near the drive-in and night after night sat in the pines near the back row of cars, memorized all the lines and, when he went to the drive-in in the gang's car of the day, tripped around between cars. One moment he was Jimmy Cagney singing, "Yank your doodle it's a dandy" or "She's a grand old bag, she's a high-flying bag." The next moment he was Abbott and Costello. "No, who's on second? What's on first?" and then his favorite, a suave Clark Gable, "Personally, my dear, I don't give a damn." Although at times the Soup ad-libbed, "Personally, my dear, I don't give a good shit."

The fire and brimstone end to Soupy's in-house acting career came when he was playing the parts of both Pat O'Brien and Barry Fitzgerald between cars and was spotted by his parish priest who cried out, "My young Mr. Campbell, I'll see you at confession. You'll pay. You'll see!"

While a good man in a fight or a rough football game, he was one of twelve children and some of the good Catholic family fears were instilled deeply in him; and when he recognized Father Coffey, he went screaming into the dark, "I'll never do it again!"

No one believed him. But he never did it again as the only person other than a priest who can put the fear of the Lord in a good Irish lad is a nun.

When fall came, Dink and Pointer headed back to Chelmsford, while the rest of the gang, with the exception of Tim Yancy, who was in the college course, stayed together, either selecting the general course or being assigned there under heavy-handed recommendation from school superiors who felt they would disturb the studies of the serious students in college and business courses.

The principal had all senior students assembled on opening day of school when they were informed, "This is your final year in high school. It will dictate your future. Some of you will go on to become doctors, lawyers, maybe even presidents. Others who fail to take advantage of the education being offered will become, ah, will not realize their full potential.

"Good luck and give it your best shot." But while this sounded like a sign-off, the students knew this was the start of a long, boring, and deadly denouement.

It was at this point that Skinny cut one he apparently had been saving since midsummer. After the roar of laughter, there was a dash for safety due to the closeness of quarters.

Skinny was hero of the day.

Within a few weeks, he was Saturday's hero. Football season was under way.

—

Rockledge was a small town locked in between larger cities, Melrose, Malden, Medford, Winchester, Wakefield and had a much smaller student body to pick its players from.

One result was its heaviest lineman, Skinny, went 189 pounds.

Johnny played guard at 142 pounds. Righty was the other guard at 149 pounds, and Soupy Campbell was the center at 165.

Boattail and Rhesus were the ends, and the line often left the huddle, not having heard the called play as both kept insisting the ball be thrown to them.

Tim Yancy was the triple-threat quarterback; he ran, passed, and punted. He was captain.

Football was gigantic for them.

Wandering aimlessly after dark was a strong second.

Talking. They had nothing to talk about, but it was vital.

They talked about nothing.

Talked about something. Everything.

"What do we wanna be after we get out!" Soupy asked.

They made "getting out" sound like an escape from a prison life sentence at times, while other times it sounded like they were being pushed out of a heaven of laughter and adventures.

"Somehow we all gotta stay together. The Big Tree is the answer," Johnny said.

"Get real," Scoff Burns said.

"Yah. You're right. But we can still get together."

"Yah," they all agreed and walked in silence for some time.

"I'm going to run my own auto body shop," Righty said, "fix people's cars up good. They'll be happy and I'll be happy. I'll make enough money to own my own race car on the Hudson oval, Riverside, Topsfield, and someday Daytona."

"A regular Morey Amsterdam," Johnny kidded.

"I'm going to be a banker," Boattail said. "They'll call me Reynard the Fox. I'll get to keep other people's money. Seriously. It's legal."

"I'm going to rob Reynard's bank," his brother Rhesus said. "He wouldn't shoot his brother."

"Dick Tracy will drill you. His uncle's a cop and is saving his badge for him," Skinny Potts said.

"Hey, remember the movie where one brother was a cop and the other a bad guy and the good brother drills him in the end . . ."

"You mean he shoots him in the ass," Scoff said.

"Nah, he means the good brother drills him in the end, the butt," Fat Burns said. "He's a fudge packer."

"Get serious," Righty said. "We gotta work when we get out of here. What're you going to do, Johnny?"

"I'm not sure. My grandfather Shiverick wants me to become a minister."

"You're kidding."

"Nah. Since I was a little kid he wanted me to be one. You could do worse. My minister took me pickerel and perch fishing. He's a good guy, one that takes care of people. He visited my aunt when my uncle died and everything."

"What does your grandfather DaSilva want you to be?" Righty asked.

"Some sort of sex fiend, I think. He never really said."

"Forget that. You're the only one in the gang that hasn't been laid," Rhesus said.

"Sure, I am. If you believe all that other stuff, but I think all you guys all dated Merry Palm."

"Oy, corn," Righty kidded, making a sour stomach face.

"Timmy, how about you?" Johnny asked. "You ain't going to have to shovel camel shit like the rest of us."

"I've gotta wait and see which schools will take me."

"Maybe you won't talk to us when you make the big time," Rhesus said, hitching his thumbs in pretend suspenders, like a big shot.

"Maybe I will, and maybe I won't," Tim answered, hitching his thumbs in pretend suspenders, shooting his chest out.

"Laaa dee dar," Rhesus said, trying to rough up his hair, "Hey, it's like an SOS pad! What gives?"

"Get with the game, you sound like a ferken cracker," Tim said.

The gang stopped in its tracks. They had never heard Tim swear or even come close or utter a word in anger. He turned and headed away. "I have to get home. Got some studying to do."

"What's with him?" Rhesus asked.

"Smarten up," Johnny said.

"Why me? He's got the bug up his butt."

"We got a game tomorrow for openers. Let's all have a bug up our butt," Johnny said. "Concord can be tough. They have all those farm boys, and they lift weights all year round. The *Boston Morning Record* reported they've won a thousand straight games and should win a thousand more."

"You sound a little scared," Rhesus said.

"Sure. For them."

The Concord game was the first of the season. Rockledge was famous for its small guards who had turns leading the running plays around end, and on one play, both guards pulled out and led the end around.

—

In the Concord game the 142-pound right guard Johnny, after taking a knee to the head from a 200-pound fullback busting the center of the line a play earlier, pulled in the wrong direction and met the left guard Righty.

They met head-on and both went down.

A little old lady screamed. She was always behind the Rockledge bench, and no one knew who she was. Or why she was there. Her only son was a star football player in the midforties who left school to end up with the Screaming Eagle paratroopers. He never got to show the Nazis what he could do as while he drifted down in his parachute, machine gun bursts from the waiting Nazi storm troopers honeycombed him.

She attended all Rockledge athletic contests and was the town's leading cheerleader.

On seeing the two guards run into each other, the tiny lady with the voice like a calliope chanted, "Wrong way, wrong way—yet we love you most this singular day."

Both Righty and Johnny got up, and both ran the wrong way, and quarterback Tim Yanders found himself running a naked reverse without a single blocker in front of him.

Concord was so confused by the two guards running left and a lone Rockledge back heading right that Tim ran untouched for a touchdown, leaving the little old lady rooter yelling, "Genius! The coach is a genius!"

Tim stood in the end zone, wondering what fantastic faux pas he had made as he heard the crowd chant, "Wrong way, wrong way! Wrong way wonders."

"Right way, right way, atta way, Timmy!"

Concord was a heavy favorite, but that one play caused it to come unglued.

All the expert sportswriters could not figure out the cause of the upset 7-0, but Rhesus simplified it with, "We met ass and kicked same!"

Tim was the first Saturday night hero, but Johnny was also the toast of the town. Sort of burned toast.

That evening, he asked Bernadette if she wanted to take a walk. He was broke and couldn't ask Yelena out. Besides, he was too ashamed of his wrong way caper that day.

Sharing his paper route and pin setting earnings with his mother to help buy food and leaving the balance with the dentist until there was enough to get Jazz's teeth fixed left money more scarce than hen's teeth.

Johnny and Bernadette walked in silence along the dark trolley tracks and through the woods of the Fellsway.

They both walked looking down.

—

"Can you believe it? I pulled out in the wrong direction."

"Things happen. You have to keep saying to yourself that you can learn from it," she said, "and you made dozens of tackles."

"No one will remember that."

"I will."

He wanted to hold her hand. *"You're a nice boy . . ." Yes . . . that's what she said . . . "You're a nice boy . . ." and I said . . . "No, I'm not . . ." I said, "No, I'm not . . . Oh my god . . .*

Her hands were held close to her side, except the one closest to Johnny turned ever so slightly toward his hand. He did not see this in the dark.

And his hand, its palm slightly open and facing hers, did not know.

Rockledge was blown out of the water the next three games. After beating a team everyone considered the best high school team in the state. Ipswich, Lexington, and Punchard played the tattoo on them. The only bright lights were Tim Yanders, who had several Ivy League schools looking at him, an athlete with smarts, and the two pocket guards who were not going to college. One sportswriter for the *Boston Globe* wrote, "The blue and white's two pocket guards, Minichelli and DaSilva, with a combined weight of one good lineman, are mighty midgets that do not realize how small they are and thus hit like runaway freight trains. The rest of the team, while hanging tough, are also Lilliputians, tied down by their small size, and while they will get the butts kicked all season, it will never be enough to send them off with their tails between their legs."

So when Rockledge was on Winchester's menu, they figured to be chewed up. Winchester had a line that appeared to be made up of Budweiser brute Belgium horses. They had a fullback that should have had a bulldozer blade mounted on his knees and a halfback called Swivel Hips Switzer, who one writer said, "If some fishing lure manufacturer could copy Switrzer's hip action, there wouldn't be a striped bass left in Cape Cod Bay."

On the kickoff, Rhesus tried to boot the ball to the left side of the field away from Switzer. The Rockledge team lined up heavy on that side.

The kick sailed high to the right and into Switzer's open arms.

Spotting that Rockledge overloaded on the left, Switzer headed straight down the right side lines.

The announcer's voice rang out over the loudspeaker. "Switzer's off and running. Only DaSilva, our mighty midget, has a shot at him!"

Johnny saw Switzer coming right at him. *Watch his fly . . . Watch his fly . . . Where the fly goes . . . he goes . . .*

He knew he had the fancy stepper dead to rights. Johnny had nailed the likes of such football giddy gods many times. *This is the guy I want . . . Stay on your feet . . . death to your fly, hero . . .*

Johnny lunged at the runner.

But Swivel Hips apparently took a sharp left turn while giving a right-hand signal, and Johnny fiercely clutched air, pulled it to him. And Switzer sidestepped to a touchdown.

Johnny got to his feet, looked around, certain the halfback was on the ground somewhere.

He heard the crowd roar. Looked behind him. Saw the Switzer doing what later dance crowds would call the dance of the live wire in the end zone.

And was involved in what many football fans felt was a first. A *Boston Morning Record* sportswriter thought so and said so for posterity, "Perhaps one of the best pound-for-pound linemen in the state, but the greatness limited by so few pounds of body, Rockledge's DaSilva, after missing an open field tackle on Winchester's Swivel Hips Switzler, well, the pocket guard got to his feet and gave himself an uppercut to the jaw that sent him backward, tea kettle over tail feathers. Yes, folks, teakettle over tail feathers! And where have you seen that lately?"

What the writer didn't write about was the love chant that followed Johnny's uppercut. The crowd, following a single chant from a little old woman who always sat behind the Rockledge bench, "Rocky, Rocky, Rocky Marciano," picked up the cry and added it own variation, "Rocky, Rocky, Rocky DaSilva!"

Righty blocked the try for the point after shooting through the center of the line after Johnny grabbed the Winchester center by the collar and yanked him into the end zone, leaving a hole you could drive a Mack truck through.

But no one paid much attention, as many had already written the score onto their cards, Winchester 55-Rockledge 0.

The problem was that Righty and Johnny played the rest of the game like feeding frenzy piranhas, and when Rockledge ended up winning seven to six, ending their opponents' undefeated streak, the captain of the Winchester team said off the record, "They ought to give those two little piss cutters a saliva test. They're as crazy as a bedbug."

What the sportswriter and the Winchester captain didn't know was that Johnny was insane with shame and Righty insane with his friend's pain.

A small blue-eyed girl on the sidelines also felt his pain.

That night after the game, Bernadette waited hidden in the dark of the Big Woods until Johnny climbed out of the Big Tree and back to earth.

And she silently walked up to him and then beside him. Bernadette and Johnny didn't speak as they meandered in the cool October night, the moon as soft and desirable as a homemade apple pie with vanilla ice cream.

She could still feel Johnny's hurt cut into her heart.

Her hand nearest Johnny turned outward toward him.

But again, his hand didn't know.

Rockledge lost the next three games, and only the Woburn and Thanksgiving games against undefeated Reading remained.

The season had a number of off-field highlights. Singing on the bus on the way to the games was an Indian chant, repeated from the moment the bus pulled out of the school and until it arrived at the opponents' field. "Boola, boola, boola, boola, that's the war cry of Rockledge High School. We will down them, we will crown them, until they holler—boola boo! Rah-Rah-rah!"

They also sang it all the way back after the game.

The coach was a benign old-fashioned gentleman who believed the most important things in playing sports were doing your level best and enjoying yourself. Winning was a weak third on his scale, a scale that eventually ended his coaching career.

Being of this character, the coach allowed them to sing on the way to the game to drum up the fever attributed to the Indian war dance. And he allowed the singing on the return trip, even after a good pasting, as it showed that the spirit hadn't been whipped out of them, that they weren't ashamed of their efforts. Certain sportswriters over Rockledge's season attempted to make the coach, the team, and the town ashamed of them. But the coach and the town saw what they saw. And weren't ashamed, as to the contrary, their little guys had made their enemies pay, and pay dearly.

Although Johnny went into a mental closet because of his Wrong Way Corrigan pulling out of the line in the wrong direction to lead the play and his Rocky Marciano belt to his own chin—both happenings the entire town and much of the state was informed of—it was the third little known incident that led his list of humiliating happenstances, bar none, despite the fact it was only known by the center and right tackles who played beside Johnny. And even they weren't sure of the full extent of the incident that happened in the game against Woburn.

There were only minutes left in the half, and Woburn had the ball on their own ten-yard line, and a punt was called for.

Johnny had entered the game with a queasy stomach, a situation that got worse as the game went on and was now at the point he feared he'd crap his pants.

But if they could rush the punter and make him get off a quick kick, they could find themselves in the position of maybe kicking a field goal before halftime.

So Johnny stayed in.

Righty whispered to Johnny that he'd crash the center. When the ball was snapped, he banged into the Woburn center, and the surprise move left a hole in the offensive line. Johnny cut behind Righty, rushed the kicker, and fully extended arms in the air, hoping to get a hand on the ball when the startled punter hesitated for a split second, and the kicked football caught Johnny full bore in the stomach, triggering a jump start peristalsis that led to an unplanned problem in Johnny's football pants.

Rockledge recovered on the Woburn five, and when they lined up for the first play, Johnny's line mates suspected something, perhaps a pea soup fart at worst. They all knew he never had enough to eat, but Johnny felt the entire world knew what happened.

Rockledge pushed it over for the touchdown that started them on a roll, as they won twenty-one to zip, leading Rhesus to say, "We really kicked the shit out of them, and they kicked it out of us," leading Johnny to utilize one of his best efforts to come up with a smile, a weak one but a smile.

That night after the knockout-punch game against Winchester, walking toward Spot Pond in silence, Bernadette did more than turn her palm toward Johnny's hand. She brushed her fingertips against his.

He was thinking of the Thanksgiving football game against Reading.

Rockledge had the ball on the Reading four-yard line with time running out and with Reading up six to three.

Everyone would be looking for Tim Yanders to get the ball and scoot around end, but the ball was going to the fullback Ted Nitzke, who was built like a Sherman tank. Nitzke, also the place kicker, had made the game 6-5 with a field goal. The plan called for a fullback plunge through the middle of the line. If it worked, it would be Rockledge's first win over Reading in a decade.

Beating Reading was everything. Especially to Johnny, whose love for football was second to none. He found himself digging his cleats into the ground like an enraged bull as the play was called by Yanders, "32 fullback smash."

But before the quarterback could slap his hands together and yell break, Nitzke said, "Let's open a Nookie Clarkson."

—

"What in hell's that?" Righty asked.

"The biggest hole in town!" The fullback grinned.

The fullback had spent the night before tossing and turning in bed, trying to think of something he could do or say that would set him apart and above Tim Yander's sensational season in a losing cause and above the two pocket guards that the men townsfolk proudly declared, "Little as babes but with the balls of a bear," and spur his team onto victory. So repeating his knocking of the girl he called Nookie when looking for a dirty laugh, Nitzke called his play and yelled break before Yanders could stop the momentum. The Nookie Clarkson play called for the interior linemen to create an opening for him to run in the winning touchdown! "Through the biggest hole in town!" he mocked. He had called for the play one too many times.

All the adrenaline Johnny had built up for this one play was transferred to his right hand, which he threw into the fullback's face with such power the snap of his neck, pop of his eyes, and the cracking of two front teeth appeared instantaneous.

The fullback went down like he was poleaxed. He was carried from the field to the gate when the town ambulance was always at the ready in case of a football injury.

Both Reading and Rockledge coaches were furious with some fans and the Reading coach calling for his arrest. Instead, Johnny was escorted by cruiser back to the school and dressing room.

It was going to be Tim Yanders; everyone knew he'd be running around end.

He never got started as the Reading defensive guard head faked Johnny's substitute out of his jock and dropped the quarterback before his fingers even tightened on the ball.

The Rockledge Thanksgiving Day loss, always a Greek tragedy, was placed squarely on Johnny's shoulders.

Righty found Johnny late that night high up the Big Tree in the Big Woods.

He called up, "That was some breakfast cereal punch, snap, pop, and crackle," in a failed attempt to cheer up his friend.

Why Righty just knew Johnny would be there, he did not know. They had not visited the Big Woods since they made the transfer from cowboys and Indians to football.

He had checked the Rockledge town square first looking for his friend. It was there he found Bernadette wandering the dark alleys looking for Johnny.

Bernadette had tears streaming down her face. They shined in the moonlight like a brook cutting through snow and ice.

"What happened?" Righty asked her.

"He never swears." She looked at the ground.

"Hardly ever."

"He told me go get the "f" away when I asked if he was okay, and he said he never the "f" wanted to see me ever again. What did I do?"

"It's not you, Bernadette." Johnny and Righty were the only boys in town that called her by her God-given name.

"It's Johnny. He blames himself for losing to Reading. He can't help it. He knows right from wrong more than anyone else in the world. But that doesn't stop him from being wrong."

Now Righty tried to cheer his friend up and climbed the Big Tree, shimmied out on the thick limb, and sat in silence with him.

They sat, feet dangling in the air, alternating between staring into the moon and peering down into the darkness, alternating, with periods of sitting with eyes closed, balanced wholly on the skill of their buttocks. Righty tried to touch Johnny's fingertips with his, and Johnny said, "Why don't you get the fuck out of here and stay away?"

And Righty did.

Johnny met with the principal and football coach the following Monday.

The principal said, "To strike a teammate on a field of play where the birth and cultivation of good sportsmanship are the ultimate goal of school leadership is a reprehensible action that cannot be atoned for."

"I'm sure there must be some logical explanation. Johnny just isn't the type to—"

"Coach, you will have your time to speak. When your hearing is held. Meanwhile, please consider your coaching on hold until this is all sorted out. And now, young man, what do you have to say for yourself, in your self-defense?"

Johnny looked up at the principal and back down at his feet.

"Where I come from, young man, silence is an admission of guilt. Did Mr. Nitzke incite you? I take your silence for a no."

Johnny looked up again.

"So the cat's got your tongue. Maybe I'll encourage some speech from you. If you do not want a permanent suspension from school. No, you say. Well, let us also declare that further silence is a further admission of guilt worthy of suspension of right to play ice hockey and baseball. Now let me say that if you admit Mr. Nitzke was guiltless in this debacle and you

—

alone are to blame or if you can tell me that Mr. Nitzke predicated this disgraceful act, then we can settle on a two-week suspension. You know among other things we could have won our first Thanksgiving football game in more than a decade if it wasn't for—"

"I know."

"Do I take this as an indication that the cat has returned your tongue, and you are willing to proceed with this dialogue?"

The coach got to his feet and rested his hand on Johnny's shoulder. "Mr. Principal, I know this boy and—"

"You may leave, Mr. DaSilva. Coach, you will stay."

Johnny slowly got out of his chair and headed from the room.

"By the way, your suspension is immediate, and your schoolwork will be made up each day when you return to these hallowed halls at just about the time I'm sure you planned to be going to hockey practice. Good day."

The halls were empty, except for Righty, who had sneaked out of the front of his math class when on cue Fat Burns let out a sorrowful moan. The teacher was shocked when she saw Fat's thin face looked the color of a boiled lobster.

It was obvious he was being eaten alive by fever. And why shouldn't he look that way? He had been shuffling his feet in the same area for fifteen minutes, a proven practice as far as not only looking like you had a fever but actually giving you one as well.

Johnny joined his friend who had made his classroom escape in the hallway, and both were out the door and in moments heading for the Big Tree and a long silent sitting.

Some routines could not afford to be broken. He delivered the morning papers starting at 5:00 a.m. and arrived home just in time to go to school. But his mother had to head to work first. She always gave her son a once-over to make sure he was as passable as possible.

Johnny's jockey shorts were old and frayed and tickled where tickling enjoyment is optional—enjoyable or aggravating.

"Why're you wiggling like you want to dance with worms in your pants, son?" she asked.

"I don't want any worms anywhere. Unless they are those little red wigglers that the pumkinseeds and crappie want."

"You watch your language, young man."

"Crappie are fish, Ma."

"And you're full of crappie, young man, if you think I buy that song and dance 'Crappie are fish.' That's a hot one. You have to avoid the temptation of lying."

She also continuously cautioned him against the great variety of temptations the world would offer him, warnings made in a voice that would make the deadly swing of Edgar Allan Poe's "The Pit and the Pendulum," sound more like a church bell in a belfry calling worshippers to service. "And while on the subject of worms, young man, remember that beer has worms in it."

Another day it would be, "Remember, you reap what you sow."

And his answer, "Yes, Mum, you sew what I rip."

"Reap. So what did I do, give birth to a comedian?"

She'd also make a squinch face at him.

He made a face at her, putting his thumbs to his ears and wiggling his fingers. Sometimes he would thumb his nose. Sometimes it would be a double thumb. This was followed up by his rolling his eyes and then crossing them while managing to drool spittle down his lips.

She laughed. "Your face is going to freeze like that someday, young man."

Working with his mother at the box factory during his suspension was more togetherness than Johnny could imagine. During past summers, when he worked in the box factory, he felt like he could crawl between two sheets of cardboard and hide when she cautioned her fellow female workers, especially the older ones, "Just stay clear of my little boy."

At first he pretended he wasn't suspended. He would just have to pretend he was going to school and then keep out of her sight.

He had practice in avoiding her.

As whenever Johnny spotted his mother outside the home and she was easy to spot as she walked at a pace that many believed would lead to the breaking of the four-minute mile, he would walk a mile out of his way, two miles when with friends, just not to have to nod to her. She was different than other mothers. Old man Minichelli had said, "She had the cajones of a kicking mule."

This honorary title was cemented when a knife wielder had tried to hold up a passerby in front of their home. She almost beat him to death with a broom with the words, "Shame on you. You should be working for a living like the rest of us."

When the police arrived, he begged them to keep her away from him, wanted her arrested for assault. Officer O'Toole kicked the would-be hold up man in his tail, and they hauled him off.

Many towns folks wondered how she could look anyone and everyone in the eye when it was disclosed her husband was a bigamist, had two wives. How could she ignore the fact that the other wife had three

—

kids and that those kids and their babysitter died when their gas stove malfunctioned.

Other towns folks pretended it didn't happen; that sort of thing just did not happen in their town.

But it was Charity's kids whose pictures were published on the front pages of the *Boston Post* rather than those of the three that lost their lives. A reporter had stolen Johnny's, Romola's, and Jazz's photos off the wall, and they were run in the paper as if they were the three that died.

The three dead children had names the same as Charity's children.

There is poor, and then there is poorer than poor, where the Rockledge family found itself.

The townspeople asked each other how she could kick the Thanksgiving basket down the steps that the Elks had left off. And then chased their car up the street, came back, and sat her kids down and told them, "We are not poor, and don't you let anyone tell you that you are."

Some good citizens asked how beggars could be choosers. How could she turn her back on food while her kids obviously needed a good square meal. Only an unfit mother would do that.

Of course none of this was said so she could hear it; who knows what a crazy woman might do if you upset her.

Johnny didn't walk big circles around her because others thought she was crazy, nor did he walk big circles because her clothes were poorer than his, so his could be better than hers. He walked circles around her just because she was his mother.

He didn't know why he didn't want anyone to know she was his mother when he was in public. He was very ashamed of the fact, and he wondered whether he was ashamed of her.

Despite the fact he was her Johnny baby.

The mail came at ten each morning. He had to sneak home under full view from the tower of power, the box factory, where his mother often looked down to check their home.

At exactly 10:05, he traveled through three backyards over four fences to his own backyard, out of sight of the box factory crow's nest. He would creep and crawl, butt working like he was humping woodchuck holes.

The creeping and crawling to the mailbox was followed by the moment of truth, that horrible moment he had to get up and grab the mail in full sight of the box factory window, and each time he feared he would be greeted by his mother's yell, "I will skin you alive, boil your butt in oil, and feed it to the dogs!"

On the third day, there was the letter. The corner of the envelope read: from the office of Otto P. D. Graffdinger, Principal, Rockledge High School.

It informed his mother of his suspension from school and all participation in varsity sports until further notice.

There was a self-addressed envelope for her to return and a required answer to the effect that she received the notice and comprehended the seriousness of Johnny's misdemeanor and his punishment.

Principal Graffdinger was pleased to read his mother's return. The letter was on his desk beside a copy of Johnny's handwriting in the form of a written book report he did for English.

"Dear Principal Graffdinger. My son John is mostly a good boy. But pretty often is not. I punished him till his butt nearly fell off . . ."

It was Boattail Eurasian's first attempt to forge a letter to a principal. Although he was a forger par excellence who had altered numerous report cards, changing Ds to large economy-size Bs for a mere ten cents per B, two bits for As.

"You can imagine our shock at receiving your parlance concerning John DaSilva's attitude and actions. You can rest assured his punishment will be most severe." That every moment, out of school will mean double time to his studying.

Boattail's forged letter to the principal continued, "While I cannot describe some aspects of his punishment, rest assured they will not be pleasant and will be repeated until its gets into his thick skull. With the utmost respect, Charity Shiverick DaSilva.

"PS. Believe you when I say that the doubling of his hours of studying, plus what I assume will be your makeup requirements of him, will only serve to make sure that his first semester at Princeton this coming fall will be little more than a review of the works of our fine school system, especially our high school under your leadership."

"Didn't your spread the good happy horseshit a little thick?" Johnny asked, "Princeton?"

"You wanted the works, the fifty-cent contract. It comes complete with song and dance."

Johnny looked at his friend, well, his friend most of the time. *How much did you make on those water lilies? Did you cheat me and Rhesus?*

Boattail said, "For two bits more, I'll tell you who likes you."

"Hey, that's a simple one, no one."

"Nope."

"Okay. The devil."

"Close but no cigar," Boattail said, puffing on a pretend cigar. "Nope."

—

"When you punch your own teammate in the huddle, you're not on anyone's all-American team. Especially in a Bible belt like Rockledge."

"Maybe that was a Bible belt you threw to Nitzke's chin," Boattail said.

"Look, I know there are some people who think Nitzke's a donkey's rear end, an ass's ass, but everyone thinks I'm the perfect, undiluted epitome of an asshole, bar none, squared to infinity."

"There might be some out there, on learning that lesser asshole Nitzke got what was coming to him when you, white knight, came to the defense of a lady, Nookie, ah, Bernadette Clarkson, in that huddle. Believe me, Brother John, there are some out there who believe in shining armor."

"Were these people in the huddle?"

"Get with it, dink drop. Do you think you can pull a caper like that and not have the entire town know what took place? Now there are those who think Nitzke's naming of the fullback plunge Nookie Clarkson was funny, fitting the lady in question. There are a few who grabbed hold of the hope that perhaps chivalry isn't dead. Perhaps one of them is a special lady. And I know who it is. And I know she is class, and she isn't about to say, 'Sir Johnny, you're my hero,' and she isn't about to say, 'Come and get it,' like a fullback plunge girl we—'" Boattail's hands were up in front of his face in defense. "Back off. I'm only trying to earn two bits here by letting you know the that wonders never cease. That a thoroughbred is interested in a half-breed like you. Look, unflex. Get cool. I'm just trying to earn my way through college."

"You're going to the same school I'm heading to, the school of hard knocks, where all you get is the third degree."

"Look, do you want to know who the princess is? I'm handing you the glass shoe."

"Sure, I'd like to know, just out of curiosity, but I'm not paying any bribes."

"Oh, Mr. Ivory Soap, 99 and 44/100 percent pure! Of course the other 66/100s involves things like paying to have a letter forged to the principal, and how about that time you broke into the bakery?"

"I was just trying to get everyone a honey-dipped doughnut."

"You forget you were the one that was hungry. I can still see you climbing up that drainpipe, up on the rooftop, ho ho ho, and down the skylight."

"Ghosts of Christmas past."

"Ghosts. You hit it. We shit our pants when the cops showed up. We hid behind the library and waited when the baker unlocked the front door and one cop went in with him and the other stood by the back door. And

—

found nothing. Nothing. They looked and looked. Someone had called the cops. They saw you go in. They could have gunned you down."

"Not in America. This country doesn't want anyone to go hungry."

Boattail started humming "God Bless America."

"And I would have paid them back when I got rich."

Boattail's next selection was "Holy, holy, holy," complete with heavenly eye rolling.

"No, I'm serious. When I got a job after graduation, I would put the money, with interest, in an envelope and send it in."

"And the farmer took another load away," Boattail sang as he shoveled imaginary bullshit. "I remember the cops searching and searching. The baker even looked in his oven. An hour later, they came out and left, and we waited and waited and wondered whether the Wizard had whipped you up to Oz. Then the back door opened, and a ghost appeared. We all started stuttering and all that other stuff you do when you're frightened. This pure white figure floated toward us. It was some sort of ghost. Had the cops found you and beat you to death? Did the baker make you eat doughnuts until your body burst? Was this your ghost? Nah. You son of a gun, you had hidden in the flour barrel, in the fucken flour barrel. We hugged you and kissed you and ended up covered with enough flour to make a dozen doughnuts each. We would have elected you president that day. You were our hero, plain ass as that, our hero. And now, again, you're a white knight, this time to a beautiful woman, a lady, and only I know who she is."

"Hey, I'll buy you a Harley when I strike it rich. Who is she?"

"Ha! A bribe! That 99 and 44/100 percent pure ratio is evaporating."

"Nah. It would not be a bribe but rather a thank-you because you're a sweet guy."

"No one's ever said that to me before," Boattail said, lowering his head, flickering his eyelids. "I'll tell you what."

"What?"

I'll give you a clue, just one little clue. Her initials are—Yelena Smoltz."

"You are full of what makes the grass grow green!"

"I shit thee not, white knight.

I was hiding in the janitor's closet where I had drilled a tiny hole through the wall to the girl's showers . . ."

"You never told me that," Johnny said.

"Well, you wouldn't have paid the two bits I charge per peek, Gentleman Jim Corbitt," Boattail answered.

"You bet your ass I wouldn't have taken a peek. You would have taken a poke. But I know you're kidding about this."

"Ya, okay, I'm kidding about the peeking," Boattail crossed his fingers behind his back, not particularly afraid of God, but he didn't like to lie to a friend.

"But while I was peeking, Yelena was fully dressed, honest Injun, and you've never heard of an Injun talking with forked tongue. I did overhear her tell her girlfriends about you. That she would swoon if anyone did such a gallant act for her. Who would have ever expected that the queen of Sheeba, her majesty, Yelena Smoltz, would ever say that she would swoon over anyone, let alone you, a lowly piece of crapola."

"Swoon?"

"I shit thee not. Couldn't anyway. You're too big a turd—Swoon, big S. You know, the way a swan flies—swooning. Well, that little bird said she was gonna swoon, fly to you."

"No."

"Yes. The best-looking, best-built, smartest, richest, nicest, and with-her-cherry-still-intact girl in ten towns around has tapped you to hoist her onto your horse."

"Where did all this poetry come from?"

"Yah, I know, I'm a poet and don't know it, but my feet are Longfellows. Look, you wouldn't pay a bribe. You've got standards, but you do pay forgers to sign your mother's name. How about two bits if I write Yelena a love letter for you?" asked Boattail.

"I don't think so. Look, I've got to beat it. I'm meeting with the dentist. I've finally saved enough money to get Jazz's teeth pulled back inside his mouth."

"You mean pulled out."

"No one's pulling his teeth out. I'm just going to get them unbucked. The Doc told me $90, and Jazz wouldn't have buckteeth anymore. I've been saving in an envelope the dentist has been holding for me for six years, and I've got it. The whole amount."

"Hey, good luck." As Johnny walked away, Boattail whispered under his breath, "Poor silly don dilly."

"See ya."

"Ya."

"And thanks."

"For what?"

"The initials. Yelena Smoltz."

"Look," Boattail called after him, "it's our secret. If the guys knew I do stuff for nothin', I'd be out of business."

—

"No sweat," Johnny said.

"Okay, buddy, keep your finger on it."

"You too."

The mile run to the dentist's office flew as he saw Yelena's face in the bursting colors of the autumn maples, saw her high overhead in the giant V of Canada geese that cut the sky like the prow of a great-winged vessel leaving the white of cumulous clouds in their wake.

He ran through the fields, eyes closed, seeing Jazz smiling, his teeth as even and as white as piano keys, biting the noses off all those who snorted, "Ya can eat corn through a picket fence." His mind's eye told him he was coming to the end of the field, to Franklin Street, leading into the square. He avoided a large crack in the hot top. *Step on a crack . . . break your mother's back . . .*

He skipped over a caravan of ants. *Step on an ant . . . make an uncle sad . . . Where did all this kid stuff come from?*

But he knew it was his joy for his brother and the news that Yelena, Yelena the beautiful, thought he was a white knight. That made him feel that he could fly. *I can fly . . . I can fly . . .*

Rockledge Square was a blur to him as he neared it. Something seemed to be in his eyes, something like a tear. *Nah . . . big boys . . . don't cry . . .*

Yet he could make out that white tooth that hung over the door to the dentist. Beside it was a pawnshop where three white balls announced its venue.

He didn't see the giant pool cue with its blue-chalked tip and often had made him wonder whether the cue stick decided to leave the mock up of a rack of fifteen pool balls to take a shot at one of the big boys, a white one that made up the pawnshop display.

He multiplied that giant tooth to a perfect thirty-two, Jazz's future display to the little teeny bopper girls that either snickered or felt sorry for him. What little girl wouldn't have some desire for a young stud that the Tooth Fairy obviously had a crush on to be so generous.

Johnny ran up the stairs that led to the dentist's office, skipping over the fourth and ninth steps, as was his habit at home, and into the waiting room.

"Well, well, well, who do we have here? No matter that question, what dated Indian heads do you bring me?"

"Better than that. I've been collecting newspapers to sell to the ragman. I've taken a couple weeks off from school just to be able to pay you." *Liar, liar pants on fire . . . what a windy . . . breeze . . .* "And I've earned eleven dollars and fifty-three cents at two cents a pound of paper.

—

You add it to what you've got in my envelope, and it comes to $99, just what you said it would cost to get Jazz's teeth uncrooked."

"Whoa up. Slow down. That was years ago when you started. Have you ever heard of inflation? Of course you haven't. You're too young to worry about money, but some of us do. Today you're talking $200 plus a promise to pay me all future Indian head pennies you receive. And that's doing you a favor. I admire your tenacity to help your brother's teeth. Because of your dedication to your brother, yes, I could go as low as $200."

Despite his efforts, tears welled in Johnny's eyes.

"Now tears will get you nowhere, only hard work and honesty will. Now give me that money, and I'll put it in your envelope, and it will all work out. Why so few Indian heads?"

He extended his hand for the eleven dollars and fifty-three cents, representing pounds of paper collected and sold to the ragman. The ragman had deducted a percentage for what he assumed would be the undetectable wetting of some of the paper tied deep within the bundles to make them heavier.

And now the dentist standing before him sounded like the ragman. Johnny did not know where the pick came from, the one the dentist used to check for cavities, but one moment it was in the dentist's hand, and the next moment it was sticking in the back of his hand.

Even before the dentist's scream ended, he was yelling, "You'll be going to jail for this, you gangster!"

Johnny looked down at his right hand where the pick had been moments before. Now he grasped the envelope he had been saving in for years, stared at it, heavy with pounds of change. And threw it in the dentist's face.

"You'll get the electric chair for this, you little piece of shit. You're no good, just like your father. It's in the blood."

Johnny was surprised at his dentist's swearing. He was always such a friendly man, especially when he counted the Indian heads Johnny brought to him. But Johnny had to address the situation at hand. He had stabbed the doctor.

An apology might help, maybe begging for forgiveness, but what came out was "Doc, you were whelped from a skunk's asshole."

That didn't help at all. He felt this immediately and was certain the headlines in the Rockledge weekly would be "Dentist Stabbed by Teenage Patient."

But the dentist was not without a sense of survival, visualizing a newspaper report pointing out what went before the stabbing.

—

The majority of the towns folks in 1949, after Johnny's punch thrown in the Thanksgiving game wondered, "What is wrong with today's youth? Can the world survive?" and agreed "The world is going to hell in a hand basket."

A tight circle of friends and family gathered tightly around Johnny. Although Righty remained in the background, unsure whether Johnny wanted him near. Righty had not forgotten Johnny's words in the Big Tree. "Why don't you get the fuck out of here. And stay away."

"I'm telling you, Johnny, you've got it made in the shade," Boattail said, appearing on the heels of the *Gazette* article about his punching Nitzke. "Yelena wanted you after you pulled that crap in the football game, your white knight bit belting Nitzke the nerd. But your saving for one hundred years to get your brother's bucktee . . . ah, to get Jazz's smile among the perky and fighting the greedy has got this lady primed, ready, willing, and able. Doctor Dentist DaSilva, you have Lady Yelena ready, willing and able to have two pulled and one filled despite the fact her teeth are perfect."

"You're full of what makes the grass grow green. And I wouldn't talk about Yelena."

"Yes, I can make the grass grow green, but in this case, I'll even be the nurse and lead her to your dental chair."

"Now you're a pimp as well as a forger. You won't even have to study to become a lawyer. You're there," said Johnny.

"Sticks and stones will break my bones, and names are good advertising. Think of me as a matchmaker. I'm just trying to make a dishonest living. You've got it. Anyone who can throw five years of saving in someone's face has surely got four bits tucked under his mattress."

"Forget it."

"Hey, stay cool. You're not fooling with some dipshit here. Mickey Spillane wrote about me in 'My Gun Is Quick.' Remember Mike Hammer's words. I've had hot nuts since I read them. Every time I think of his writing, 'my blonde had a brunette base,' I can't help myself. It's diddle diddle dumpling with my horn, John."

"Boattail. Come on. Call it quitso. No flimflam. A girl like Yelena thinks in terms of fraternity presidents, captains of the Harvard football team, doctors, lawyers, Indian chiefs. Not some skinny guy whose inside cheeks touch each other as he looks for a couple Hires Root Beer bottles to cash in to buy his next meal, a package of Drakes Cakes."

"Look, and this is free," Boattail said, "there are those who need Don Quixotes. Need them to soothe the wounds of you stupid bastards who get hacked to pieces by windmill blades smarter and faster than you. Keep the four bits, you cheap sucker. This introduction's on me."

"Nope."

"Listen."

"No speaka da hinglish," answered Johnny.

"No wonder your ears are growing long, and you've started braying. You're so stupid you don't even realize you've broken Righty's heart. And he's so stupid he would pay me two bits to patch it up. You both get bit by the same idiot of something catchy or something?"

"Righty," Johnny whispered to himself. *No wonder there are fewer horse's heads around with horse's asses people like me running free . . . Oh, John . . . you stupid . . . mean . . . horse's ass . . . to the tenth power . . . squared . . . to infinity.*

The town was pretty much divided in two. One group that either glared, sneered, or looked through him, and the second that said "attaboy" with words or look.

Both were greeted the same way by Johnny. He looked at the ground and kept on walking. In fact, there was a case to be made that he was walking, looking at the ground, and saw neither.

That's the way it was when he was walking along Spring Street in that patch of road free of homes.

He didn't see Bernadette standing in the shadow, watching him with tears on her cheek, trying to work up the courage to just say a simple hello or just quietly catch up to him, walk beside him in silence like they had those times he needed someone there, not doing anything, not saying anything. The palm of the hand closest to him would be turned, just ever so slightly, toward him, just in case he wanted to touch fingertips or even hold her hand. They wouldn't have to say anything.

She didn't know what it was all about. She perhaps was only one of a handful of people who didn't know why he had hit a teammate in the huddle. She had no one to tell her like others had someone to tell them. She had no one to share with other than Johnny, who for that brief moment would catch up to her as she walked alone those few nights, and even then they just walked, side by side, silent.

Bernadette had nothing in common with other girls in the town, and although she had been with many boys, she had nothing in common with them.

The only girls who might have had something in common, those whose lives had been also ruined by fathers so sick that rabid animals appeared well in comparison, were well hidden.

—

These girls would never admit what had taken place as they most often felt it was their fault, as did some of the town folks.

In Bernadette's case, it had been brought to public notice. Very few believed that it was her fault, yet everyone knew of it. That's why no other girl took her hand.

Yelena had reached out but not far enough.

And Bernadette walked alone.

This day she watched Johnny's shape in the distance, could see his face as he got closer when he'd look up at the clouds. Sometimes he would only roll his eyes upward to check the high-flying cirrus clouds drawing Indian war bonnets some forty thousand feet up.

Bernadette looked upward whenever Johnny did, wondering what he saw there. The wisps were beautiful, and she wondered whether someday they would use them as feather beds and be carried along, side by side, each reaching out to hold the other's hand. She thought of that first time, when he had asked her to take a walk in the dark and tried to do it to her, like so many others had tried and succeeded.

She said, "No, you're a nice boy," and he had cried out, almost in agony, "No, I'm not." And he never tried again. And she never let another boy do it again.

"But you are, Johnny. You are a nice boy. The boy I want to walk with forever, with my hand always open to you. And tell you I want you now, like I wanted you then. But I couldn't let you become one of them—the faceless."

He was so close now that she feared he could hear the words she whispered to herself, could hear her thoughts, feel her closeness.

Did she have the courage to step out so he could see her? Now her words to herself were voiceless. "What if he said the same thing he said the day after that football game. What if he knew what all the boys did to me. He must know. If he ever knew about my father. He knows. She drew some strength from the fact that she had had the courage to walk and thumb despite being followed on foot, mauled by some of those who picked her up so she could visit Johnny at the Boston Eye and Ear Hospital after the gun had exploded in his face. "Please, someone give me that courage now."

She could feel the strength slowly seeping into her. What would she say? Her first words would be so important. Maybe she'd just walk toward him. Her hands by her side, but one palm turned open slightly toward him.

"Well, well, look who doesn't care whether they break their mother's back, with all the cracks in the sidewalk and all."

Who jumped the highest, Johnny or Bernadette, when Yelena's voice greeted him, would be a toss-up. Neither had seen the tall blonde girl with the cool eyes as light and gray as the last of the night on the morning horizon.

Bernadette drew deeper into the shadows as Yelena walked toward Johnny, her arm extended, her hand high, as if it was being presented for him to kiss the back.

Johnny could think of nothing to say, felt foolish with an insipid. "How do you know I'm afraid on stepping on cracks?"

"I've seen you walking several times, many times. You also do not step on ants. I like those who protect the weak, the small, at all costs. We, the gentle, are all too few in number."

We . . . the gentle . . . are way too few in number . . . Geez . . . I've kicked the bejesus out of half the town . . .

"Cat got your tongue?" she asked, coyly looking up at him, her eyes gray ice with flames burning in their centers. "Cat got your tongue?"

A bolt of lighting fired through his skull, his heart, his groin, sizzling and searing where it struck, and he feared he would tumble, with a timber coming from out of nowhere.

He looked at the girl the town thought its most beautiful, whose peers chose as captain of the cheerleaders, president of the senior class, and chairman of the 1950 yearbook selection committee.

"Too very much." It was written in the yearbook under class statistics. "To be the most beautiful and most likely too succeed. Even the heavens are too low for the goals of our Yelena."

He was stunned! This was the girl in front of him.

Bernadette watched in heartbreak as the beautiful girl walked directly at Johnny, took his hand in hers, and held it, until he looked into her eyes. Eyes that held his, not allowing him to lower his, try as he may. "Johnny, you will never walk alone. And we will never be afraid of anything as long as we walk together."

My god . . . is she quoting Shakespeare? Is she talking to me? Why would a girl like Yelena want to talk to a nothing . . . like me?

Bernadette turned away toward the old house that blocked her escape, her hideaway tree now cloaking her back from view, and rested her head against the old, long-ago creosote-stained clapboards. A spider came from beneath one of the warps in the sun-ravaged siding. She felt the daddy longlegs walk across her temple to the corner of her eye, change directions down her cheek when a leg was flicked by her eyelash, and stop, unsure what course to follow when it reached that first tear. Then it retreated, its fear leaving an acid-etched trail on her cheek.

"You make me so happy!" Yelena said to Johnny, looking over at him, squeezing his hand until he returned her glance. "There are so few true heroes today. With everyone, it is 'What can you do for me today?' 'I've got mine. How you doing?' Forget the sick, the old, those down on their luck. Give it all to the lame and the lazy and the bully. No one steps forward today to be counted, that is until at that football game when you said 'to hell with the world' and let Mr. Nitzke know what it is like for a bully to pick on the very lowest—Bernadette. You are what I've been waiting for without knowing it. Without knowing what I was waiting for."

Johnny was weak. *What's happening here? Am I crazy . . . dreaming . . .*

How long they walked, neither knew. They did not realize that they held each other's hand so tight that their knuckles hurt. That she never stopped talking. He never hearing the words she spoke, was simply dizzy with the fact that the most beautiful girl in the world, for some crazy, crazy reason, wanted to hold his hand.

She smiled. "Let's walk together, think about what we can give each other."

The most beautiful girl in the world . . . wants to hold my hand . . . and more . . . a kiss . . . not possible . . . no way . . .

"When the police led you from the field that day and everyone was stunned into silence, it was me, Yelena, who cheered, 'Yea for Don Quixote,' without knowing what others called dastardly was a deed rarely done probably not since the old antebellum south was killed by our northern rabble. That this wonderful act that held you up to scorn to all, all but one, was done for a poor woman, used and abused by all until she was but one of Dante's shades, whipped back and forth in space, by the shifting winds of eternity."

Johnny heard only her tones, felt her euphoric mood, and just as well, as her words were those of a student enthralled with her college course advanced readings.

Johnny listened, wondering what it would be like in the college course, brain aching with new thoughts from another world, and believed his general course required reading was little more than the-dog-chased-the-cat-the-cat-chased-the-mouse-the-mouse-chased-the-cheese primer.

No matter that they floated on clouds, she on a fine-lined cirrus, a lace white on a blue blood background, and he on a cumbersome cumulous, stained with storm warnings. They were in the same sky.

Yelena and Johnny drifted on friendly breezes like hawks in the heavens as one, unlike the skies he visited with Bernadette, where they were Dante's shades flapping like torn and injured clothesline sheets in a storm.

As their senior year went on, Johnny underwent many changes. Yelena got him interested in visiting nursing homes, talking with old people, writing poetry, helping her with the speech she would give at graduation.

This also kept him out of trouble's eye; although the one time he fell off the good-boy bandwagon, the only piece of slippage during their senior year, Johnny was innocent, well, almost.

It seems the chemistry teacher, Mr. Van deClyde, looked on the world and those who peopled it as elements, matter, which can neither be created or destroyed. He placed most general course students in the H2S category, hydrogen sulfide, which smells like rotten eggs or, more poignantly, according to Skinny Potts, smelled like the flatulence of a dead flounder given off after a four-day sojourn on an July beach in Quincy Bay.

A few of the general course members who had taken umbrage to what they considered as offhanded, often underhanded, 'looking down the nose treatment' by Mr. Van deClyde, had taken to collecting eggs. Old eggs, stinkers, perfect for tossing as specific targets.

This plot was not selected as was the usual hullabaloo of wolf whistles, farts made by cupping your palm under your armpit and bringing your elbow down sharply to your ribs, thus trapping the air which escaped with an explosion worthy of diarrhea in an elephant, not to mention cat calls and a muffled word, "prack," a substitute for the word "prick."

Prack was the perpetrators' way of calling out prick without offending some of the girls in the class who were downright nice and didn't deserve the profanity. This nicety was the unofficial ruling of the loosely knit prack practitioners who were bored well beyond tears with the chem class and the teacher's class distinction.

The reason Mr. Van deClyde escaped much of the prack and cupped underarm farts was his practice of allowing the disinterested to sleep during class as long as they didn't snore or keep sleeping during a surprise visit from the principal.

Thus, those who wanted to sleep, either out of boredom or because they needed sleep badly like Johnny, who worked one or two part-time jobs, policed their peers.

Van deClyde had made this out of character snooze arrangement in an attempt to have a chance to get through to the few students who actually wanted to learn something. Scoff Burns, who planned to run an auto body and welding shop when he got out of school, wanted to know all about mixing the gases for the needed torches and the reaction of various auto paints.

Righty and Johnny and the rest wanted Scoff to get into a profession that would keep him on the straight and narrow, as they were certain he needed to keep busy and away from the free time he could spend indulging his kleptomania. In their young imaginations, they could visualize Scoff graduating from stealing anything from a Rolls Royce to a piece of penny candy and graduating into bank robbery and his eventual dying in a hail of bullets or a four-by-four cell.

But it was the appearance of their friend Skinny Potts, who was not only a college course egghead but was also invited by Van deClyde to drop into his lab at any time and take on advanced work that upset their fine understanding of domain. Skinny's first visit to general course chem was announced when the door opened, and his belly arrived well before the rest of his body. This college course visitor, friendship aside, was an invader. No outsider was allowed to witness just how little members of the general course would allow itself not to be taught.

And of course, Skinny made the mistake of not only truly knowing what he was doing concerning chemistry, but also flaunting it before his friends.

Almost immediately, his friends started poking their fingers in his belly, an action that would have gotten an outsider a good poke in the nose.

Skinny was also asked by his friends, "How many months pregnant?" "Don't name it after me," "So you're the sunnamumbitch that stole the medicine ball and swallowed it," "Must be jelly cuz jam don't shake like that," "You can't be having a baby elephant because your trunk is too small."

But every dog has his day. And this was Skinny's. He mixed and matched the chemicals, not looking unlike a benign Einstein and fearsome Frankenstein offshoot, with a confidence that shook what little his friends had out of their chemistry trees. The breaking point was Van deClyde's continuous beatific glances at his prima donna Potts.

After a behind-the-hands tete-a-tete, the friends decided to change their plans concerning their stinky egg stash that they had planned to be used against teachers they thought treated them unfairly or looked down their noses at them.

Van deClyde wasn't one of those earmarked for a stink bombing because of their uneasy and unspoken sleeping peace agreement. But this was a lot more than a little much.

And the eggs they had collected and treated with the little chemical knowledge all year and then hidden in a long-forgotten closet corner and covered with a collection of cobwebs and dust balls discovered in the darkest corners were for the first time returned to the light of day.

Johnny, with the help of his cousins, Dink and Pointer Gouveira, had secretly relieved the farm's chickens of a dozen eggs and informed their grandfather Pie, who barely understood English but didn't want anyone to know it, that the laying hens were suffering from lazy ass.

The three, with an ice pick to drill a tiny hole and straws of wheat had sucked in on them, had the shells free of their yolks and whites.

Johnny carefully transported the shells from Chelmsford to Rockledge wrapped in goose down and protected from breakage by being cuddled in his crotch.

He thumbed homeward, catching five rides without drawing much attention except from an old lady, perhaps thirty-five or so, who superstitiously glanced several times at his bulked out crotch cargo.

When she stopped for a red light in Reading square, she slid her hand to his crotch, crushing one egg shell before Johnny could bolt from the car.

The woman, angered at her spur-of-the-moment fit of desire as well as being thwarted during a moment of desire, unthinkingly called, "Police!" but quickly burned rubber from the scene.

She questioned herself as to why she ceased getting her jollies off via visits of kleptomania to local clothing stores rather than having this new fixation on the denim-clad crotches of young hitchhikers.

Rather than risk another such threat to his eggshells, Johnny walked the remaining three miles home, no easy task as he easy stepped along with thighs wide apart, fearing his hidden load would suffer some sort of Humpty Dumpty demise.

Getting the shells into the chemistry class, unbeknownst to all except those involved, was not the most difficult task Johnny and his partners in crime faced.

Filling them with H2S and then capping the contents with bubble gum was.

The stink gas eggshells were then secreted, perhaps to be used later against teachers who had offended the honor of friends.

To their surprise, it wasn't a teacher that lit the fuse but rather a friend who had invaded their domain and was the recipient of beatific smiles from their teacher.

Dick Tracy, whose uncle was a cop, was considered tops at subterfuge. He was selected to retrieve a couple of the hidden eggs and, unbeknownst to their chemistry teacher and Skinny, tape them on the bottom of the lab table.

Dick remembered the day he had secreted the eggs in the closet and at first covered them with spiderwebs fabricated by Scoff with his mother's crochet hooks. But then they collected the real dust and webs. His uncle once told him during one of his story telling braggadocios that if he was a crook, he would cover his hidden stash with spiderwebs as "all cops are afraid of spiders."

Now the eggs were out of hiding.

It was agreed long before this zero hour, when the friends drew their battle plans as they sat around in the dark in the Big Tree, that come the day the smell was to hit the fan, that Soupy Campbell would be called into action.

Soupy had gained the reputation of being the one person who could handle any smell invented, a reputation well earned after he had dropped the flat rock on that sleeping skunk.

He would pluck the bubble gum seal from the eggs with a Boy Scout Life pin purloined by Scoff.

And that he did. While Skinny was sojourning in the chemistry closet after reading a note slipped to him by Bobby Burnham that "Nookie Clarkson will show you her tits in the chem closet if you promise to do her chem term paper. She's in there now, knockers to her knees!"

No matter that Bernadette was in General Two, a Gorky's "Lower Depths," beyond the General One. Here she dreamed up Johnny's, a dream often interrupted when Yelena appeared. Then Johnny and the town's most admired and beautiful girl rode off into the sunset. Bernadette, even in her hurt at the theft of her dream, believed they were the most beautiful couple she had ever seen, even more beautiful than Nelson Eddie and Jeanette MacDonald. And in her eyes, Johnny's dungarees turned into the gaudy colors of the Jamaican doctor bird colors of Nelson Eddy's Northwest Mounted Police uniform. Bernadette viewed Yelena in an outfit of splashed colors too beautiful for words, riding sidesaddle beside the giant white steed Johnny rode.

Yelena was wearing a white angora sweater, pleated plaid skirt, and angora bobby socks that capped the brown and white saddle shoes, whose leather was curried into perfect presentation by the family maid, Mrs. Yanders, Tim's mother.

Yelena's father, the good Dr. Smoltz, praised Mrs. Yanders, who worked several jobs to help Tim's future attendance at medical school. "All families should be graced with a maid like my Mrs. Yanders," he said but was quite content that his small section of town was the only one graced with the ability to hire a maid. And in the back of his mind, which he rarely visited, lurked the question, "Who would ever want to receive medical treatment by a person of color?"

She watched as Yelena took a red rose, like the one she had secreted behind her back to give to Johnny, and placed it in her mouth, quickly following up with several staccato flamenco steps and a handing of the rose to Johnny as she slowly lowered her eyes and then glanced up at him.

Bernadette looked at the two mint juleps in their light-green candy wrappers she had purchased for Johnny, hoping to hand them to him this very evening and be asked to share with him. Or perhaps just leave them on his steps, hoping he would know whom they were from.

She dropped the candies as if they were molten ingots. They struck her penny loafers, which that very morning had been relieved of the two shiny pennies she had been so proud of to purchase the candy.

Bernadette was in the lowest class, although school administrators avowed there were no class distinctions at Rockledge High.

And now the chem teacher unintentionally reminded the general division members that they did not avoid distinction, and they in turn were about to remind him that they did not appreciate this by raising their own what they termed "dis-stink-shun."

The plan was set into action, and Skinny inched his soft-shoe way toward the chemicals closet.

Dick Tracy secured the eggs they had hidden in a hollowed-out chemistry one book he had borrowed from a college course nerd and inched his way toward Skinny, where the exchange was made. Skinny placed the eggs in a vacant lab desk where he removed the bubble gum stoppers from the eggs with a pair of hair tweezers he had borrowed from a girl who was combing her hair using a mirror in her hallway locker and had left her tweezers unattended and open to a slight of hand tweezers-napper.

The word got around the class that perhaps it wouldn't be all that bad an idea to have some sort of handkerchief or rag handy a little later. The word wasn't passed to everyone as there were a couple classmates suspected of being two-tongued tattletales.

When Bobby Burnham told Johnny that the caper was ready to roll, Johnny said, "Perhaps we can do this a little differently. Why not let me tell the teacher we're pissed?"

"Yelena got you wearing skirts now?" Bobby immediately knew he had made a mistake and that retaliation would be immediate. *Any guy that could feel a thug like Nitzke in a huddle . . . in front of hundreds of fans . . . would have no trouble decking someone . . . someone like me . . .*

He wished his survival common sense was as quick as his mouth.

Bobby wondered whether he would get it on the nose or in the pit of his stomach and was completely shocked when Johnny turned and walked away. Bobby immediately puffed up and ventured, hopefully low enough so Johnny wouldn't hear it and that only a few near admirers would say, "Next she'll have you wearing panties. You better not squeal on us."

Johnny heard but kept on walking. *Yelena would be . . . proud of me . . .*

Not everyone was proud of his walking away. In fact, no one was.

"Wattaya, suddenly a major highway," Nancy Nadeau, a corpulent girl with a face like a disgruntled grasshopper and suspected of being a tale carrier said, "a major highway with a yellow line down the middle."

"Hey, grun-doon," Skinny said to the girl, "Johnny doesn't give no shit, take no shit, so you couldn't do better than grunting and squatting around his teepee. That goes for Burnham and his mother, and it goes for you."

Johnny turned his back on the girl.

"Cat got ya tongue, can't speak for yourself," she repeated to Johnny. "You suddenly a major highway. With a yellow line painted down your back."

Bobby laughed as Johnny went to his chemistry table and appeared to study the formulas in front of him but not seeing them, and Johnny's antagonist was glad he hadn't buttoned his lip. Feeling perhaps it was time for a new big man. He smiled as he thought to himself, *A new rooster . . . with some real spurs . . . for ruffling feathers . . . then kicking ass . . . a real cock . . . one who knew how to crow . . . Sure, Johnny's part of the gang . . . but you gotta grow . . . or you gotta go . . .*

But Johnny's participation was a mute point as the H2S crept through the room like some insidious green fume, appearing to rot the skin and intestines of those who had not been forewarned and didn't have a handkerchief or rag or kerchief to hold over their nose.

The chemistry teacher could not see the stink itself, but he saw the white of the handkerchiefs appear as the odor surged toward him like a great tidal wave.

He was frozen in place, like a person suddenly finding himself at gunpoint. When the threat arrived at his domain, his desk, he reacted like any great monarch. The class door was closed, "Everyone stays!"

And armed with a Paul deGaullian nose that had lived in concubinage with a variety of less-than-desirable odors, he followed said proboscis toward the apex of the offending odor.

Van deClyde arrived at the lab desk only moments before Skinny appeared there, discovered the source emanated from his station, and closed the drawer just as the teacher who, along with Skinny, was entitled by student knighthood grantors, the Trainer and his Pet.

Pet would have stuck as a nickname, but those who tore wings off butterflies loved calling the roly-poly fat boy Skinny because it hurt. A lot.

His friends who called him Skinny did so out of affection. And when the name was used by the party of the first part in front of the party of the second part, the fur flew. The gang was hard on each other, but lo and behold, outsiders beware.

"Well, Mr. Potts, I see you have a little something brewing here," the Trainer said. "I take it you enjoy such odoriferous presentations."

"No, sir," Skinny moaned, "not in the least, sir." Skinny looked like he was going to break out crying.

"Well, I believe that you are being quite modest."

Johnny took a step toward the teacher.

He felt Righty's hand on his shoulder.

"In fact, Mr. Potts, I believe you relish in it. And are just being modest in front your peers, in the general division I might add."

"No, sir, I'm not modest about enjoying H2S."

"Oh, sir, you admit you enjoy it."

"No, sir."

"Yes, sir, you do enjoy it," the chemistry teacher said, completely losing it and opening the drawer with one hand while grasping the young man by the neck and forcing his head down into the source. Quickly he grabbed a nearby fire blanket and tossed it over Skinny's head and the top of the drawer.

Johnny brushed off Righty's hand and moved toward the situation.

This time, Righty had two hands on him and whispered in his ear, "I have a way."

Spotting Johnny, the chemistry teacher said, "Come on, Mr. DaSilva, please don't be detained by Mr. Minchelli, your right-handed friend with a left-handed brain. Please proceed. It will make it easier to arrange for your criminal character to serve some sorely needed time in reform school, or perhaps in your case, jail. After that you will repeat your senior year, perhaps for several years, and I can again have the privilege of tutoring you on right from wrong and on how foolish you are to believe that you can just get away with anything."

"I have a way," Righty whispered again as they walked from the lab with their stink-soaked friend between them.

Righty lifted his shirt and displayed a Phillips head screwdriver he had taken from his shop class and tucked in his belt, "The way."

The "way" would take place a week later, when Mr. Van deClyde would have their general course class in lecture along with his advance honors College One students who would serve as one-on-one aids.

The week passed, and it was time. Both skipped their homeroom attendance check and sneaked to the basement. They locked themselves in a toilet stall, and both stood on the seat until the potty check was made by the custodian, Charlie McCarthy.

Charlie was a tiny man, thus named because of the two deep lines leading down from the corners of his mouth and missed upper teeth that made him appear to be controlled by a hidden Edgar Bergen ventriloquist whenever he talked.

The little old man they all loved, as he never told on anyone but threatened all perpetrators that he would kick their ass if they didn't "straighten out and fly right." Most of the students towered over him and told each other not to breathe too heavy on him as a stiff wind would blow him away.

But he had their respect. They loved his looks, his face like a shrinking rotten apple complete with eyes and mouth while lacking a nose. Best of all, they loved the fact that the little man who couldn't fight his way out of a paper bag was so feisty and actually believed he could kick ass.

The kids would never retreat after the janitor's kick-ass threat without first putting up their fists in mock battle and challenging him to "put up your dukes."

They threw a few funny punches into the air and retreated. The tiny custodian commenced to kick the living shit out of the air between them.

The girls loved him too. They were asked politely to move. The boys' kick-in-the-ass threat was replaced by a sweeping bow that would do Robin Hood's greeting to Lady Marion proud.

For them it was his "Now, ladies, be you moving your pretty little tail feathers to class" that got to them, and a number of the more daring or humor-prone girls had a variety of sashaying walkaways that added to the collected glee of bored-to-tears kids.

One little lady, Mary Kulas, who had an unusually long neck, would stroll off moving her head and neck far forward of her body and back, imitating an emu in strut.

A second girl, Jeanne Pool, whose physical endowments meant at least two other girls had to go without, exited in such a seductive 1949 Old Howard "Stripper of the Year" Sally Rand movement you could almost hear the throaty mood drum beat of the Scully Square strip joint when young teen boys stood outside listening, imagining, getting their jollies off.

Charlie McCarthy's remark to her exit made the rounds of the Rockledge Spa that day and became part of the school's history, a tale that got better each year.

One day in the main hallway, Charlie asked Ms. Pool to move on, complete with his sweeping bow.

And she did. And Ms. Pool's jugs, as the story later went, swung in a circular unison like the ticking hands of London's Big Ben, and her hips swayed like a mare in moisture.

Little Charlie, seeing the exaggerated exit, called after her sweetly, "You go chipping any of the corners off our hallways, you'll have to pay for their repair."

"That little janitor," Johnny told the guys that night, sitting on Big Rock in Big Woods, rotating conversations with baleful howls at the full moon. "Everyone could learn from Charlie McCarthy."

"How so?"

"Hey, if everyone in the world knew his humor was without meanness, it could help solve a lot of problems. It would be a better place. Sort of a 'make laughs, not war.'"

"Oh wow," Scoff had kidded, "aren't we the great philosopher, Socko Platohelmentes."

"You make him sound more like a boxer and a many-headed amoeba," Skinny had said. "They were Socrates and Plato."

"Thanks, I needed that."

Mr. McCarthy's all right," Johnny said, ending the discussion. Johnny put the little man right up there on a pedestal with the English teacher, Mr. Leaders. The two had always treated him with respect, understood that anyone could make a mistake or two or three, but the intent was more to be judged than the mistake. Johnny always performed high for those in this category and performed down for those who had little respect for people. And this case, he was going to realize a low point and was going to pay dearly for it.

Charlie took his job seriously. And he would use any method possible to ensure it was not only done, but also done well. Hadn't he lived with the potato famine in Ireland and escaped it only to wait in the dole line during the U.S. of A depression.

No one was to be in the school basement when the bell rang announcing the first class. Johnny and Righty were set up to make an exception to this regulation.

Charlie looked under the door for feet and looked over it to see if anyone was standing on the seat. Spotting either, he would encourage the lollygaggers to hurry along.

Righty and Johnny were both balanced on the same toilet seat, bent over so their heads would not show above the door. They hadn't talked since they rendezvoused that morning. Righty basically was staying the fuck away, as Johnny had commanded that day after the Nitzke incident. And Johnny wasn't much into apologizing. In fact, he had never apologized to anyone. Unless you consider being extra good, caring, and kind to someone you wronged as an apology.

They passed the custodian's inspection, but barely.

As the little custodian farted and said sweetly, "A little kiss for the principal who has a habit of looking down his nose at people."

The boys bit into their lips, their eyes opening wide with suppressed laughter until the tears ran down their cheeks. Only by painfully squeezing their testicles did the suppressed laughter lose its battle.

But they finally heard the door close behind him.

They didn't leave their hiding place as they knew Mr. McCarthy had developed a certain cunningness having dealt with a great many generations and varieties of students over the decades.

"*Aha!*" the door was thrown open, and the custodian glared back into the room of toilet stalls, feeling that despite he was certain the basement was empty, an "*aha!*" might take a nervous student to commit himself.

Johnny had just been ready to step down form his perch but swiftly drew his leg back.

The tiny old man farted again. "And a kiss for the principal's bride as well."

He left again, and this time, he stayed away.

"What a cute little bugger," Johnny said.

"Come on, over here. We've got to hurry. The lecture starts pretty fast. As soon as our class starts fist flexing the college boys into line," Righty said. Taking the Phillips head screwdriver out of his belt, he headed to the huge vents of the school's antiquated combined heating and cooling unit.

He fit its bite into the large commercial Phillips head screws that held the four-by-four vent on.

"Hope they don't have the heat turned up," Johnny said.

Righty removed the last screw and removed the grate that had covered the duct.

Johnny crawled into the giant hot air duct, and Righty put the grate back in place, replaced the screws and tightened them.

Righty looked at his watch. "10:15, just after third period starts."

Johnny's voice came back muffled as he had already started to slowly climb upward in the giant ventilation system, wiping off cobwebs and dust balls, always trying to keep the three-point contact rock climbing rule as the higher he got, the longer the fall.

His toe and handgrips, which jutted out an inch and a half, were four feet apart on the seams where the sections were bolted together.

It got darker as he climbed. The only light available was from the smaller tunnels that led into each room and provided the heat through vents located in the wall close to the ceiling.

General Custer . . . What am I doing here?

He took a brief detour at the first-floor level and looked through the vent there.

Dog shit on a bulky roll . . .

He found himself looking down at the principal who was staring into the vent.

But the principal didn't see him; all he saw was a dark silhouette of what looked like John DaSilva's face that he believed was some sort of an open-eye nightmare caused by eating at the school cafeteria in a gassy effort to show the kids once and for all that he was one of them. And that the food was fit for a human being, him being the only human he knew.

He shook his head and vowed it would be a month of Sundays before he ate there again.

It wasn't only the food, but rather the opened-eyed fear he instilled in some of those eating. One ninth grader held a fork full of spaghetti in front of his mouth watching the principal for a full five minutes. It would probably still be there if one of his buddies hadn't yelled boo, causing him to wear it on his fly.

At first, no one knew where it landed. It was a frail young girl with long strands of curly hair painfully set in rags for four hours the night before who spotted the spaghetti on the boy's trouser crotch and, for some unbeknownst reason, let out a howl that set the cafeteria in a turmoil.

The principal jumped to his feet. "Everyone stay cool! Don't panic. I'll go for help."

When he got back to his office, he realized he didn't know what type of help you send for when the emergency involved spaghetti on a young boy's lap. He questioned himself as to why in a million years what inspired him to tell the rapt students that he would go for help.

He found himself sitting in his office, staring at the ceiling where a daddy longlegs spider with great effort was slowly skating along upside down. The principal was overwhelmed with the feeling he wanted to send it all the way back to where it had started? For forgetting to say "May I."

But he had lost all confidence in his authority and was overwhelmed with the desire to climb into the dark overhead vent and hide.

It was then as he peered into the dark of the duct that he fantasized that he saw the face of his hated nemesis, Mephistopheles DaSilva. *I have to . . . graduate him . . . my retirement . . . I must survive the next . . . two years . . . three months . . . thirteen days . . . and . . .*

—

He checked his watch and said aloud, "Twenty-two minutes!"

Johnny's backing away from the principal's vent was probably the quietest thing he had ever done in his life.

When he backtracked though the duct to the giant Y that sent one set of vents heading upward and the other to the end of the school, he went in the wrong direction and suddenly was lost.

There was another vent. *Directions . . . I need directions . . .*

In a silent Elmer Fudd voice, similar to the one the cartoon character asked no one in particular about the direction Bugs Bunny went, he asked himself, "Which way do I go? Which way do I go?"

He heard girls' voices at the end of the vent. Then he saw the shower sprays, the tops of girls' heads being shampooed. A few more feet, and he would see what he'd never seen before. Tits . . . and down below . . . where guys have hair . . . and perhaps he could finally decide once and for all whether a girl's . . . it . . . was in front . . . or sort of underneath . . .

He had felt more and more stupid, the older he got, not having seen a single it. *I'm probably the only stupid . . . son of a gun . . . in the world . . . who has never seen one . . .*

The girls were singing and screaming, seemingly having as good a time as the guys have in the shower. He wondered whether any of the girls pulled some of the stuff the guys pulled.

Like the time Boattail asked Soupy, when they were showering after baseball practice, whether he felt that the water was getting warmer, and Soupy said, "I don't think so."

Boattail had smiled at his friend and then looked down.

It took Soupy some time to realize that mingled in the clear water of the shower was a yellow stream, quite warm now that he felt it on his hip, emanating from Reynard's fountain of youth.

Boattail disappeared out of the shower faster than the wink of a cat to avoid the Soup's wrath. *Nah . . . girls can't do that . . . They don't have . . . spigots . . . but what do they have for an . . . it?*

He wondered whether they wet the ends of their towels, snapping them at each other's asses, leaving marks similar to those administered to punished pirates.

Even if the girls snapped towels, they didn't have to put up with what the guys had to put up with. A stray snap that missed the buttocks and zipped between the legs could catch a foreskin, or even worse, a testicle.

That meant war.

He stayed there some time, thinking the girls were like the boys yet were so different.

—
541

That was all. He couldn't figure it out as he backed into the main tunnel that led to the vent leading upward.

He looked down the shaft once. It was a long, long fall into that black hole.

Johnny climbed until another artery of vents went off to the side. *Third floor . . . women's sweaters . . . lingerie . . .*

He had seen bras and panties hanging from hooks on the distant side of the girls' showers.

He enjoyed looking at them but remembered the embarrassment the time he was hanging around the women's underwear section at Sears. The floor manager had told him, "Move along, Sonny," which would have been a palatable order, but when he added, "We can't have you lads lingering in ladies' lingerie," and laughed at his witticism as he had done many times in the past, Johnny had picked up a pair of bright-red bikini panties and thrown them at the man.

He had sort of wished he'd kept them; the feel of the slippery material left the hair on the back of his neck standing up. He told himself he only wanted them for informational purposes, that perhaps he could, once and for all, by their structure, determine whether "it" was up or downstairs.

He knew he lied to himself.

The vent was getting darker and dustier as he continued to climb. Then there was a small square of light, the vent, to Mr. Van de Clyde's room

The chemistry teacher's voice filtered through, "I noticed Mr. DaSilva and Mr. Minichelli aren't in class today."

Johnny inched forward until his face was against the grate. The entire class had got the word he would be there for a vent flyby at 8:45. The entire class knew the Skinny Potts Revenge Plan and what they had to do.

"I believe John DaSilva is in class, sir," Mary Kulas volunteered, stretching her long neck high in the air like an ostrich vacating its head hole in the ground.

Michelle LeMoine, who was described by the boys that took auto body repair as having a body designed in a custom auto body shop with spectacularly large headlights, squirmed.

"Yes," Mary Kulas said, "he is here in my holy vision." She closed her eyes and crossed herself.

"Okay, then, Mr. DaSilva is here for Mary's holy vision but absent from my attendance sheet, which will be turned into the principal's office."

Johnny had backed into the dark of the vent where he checked his two containers. The covers were on tight, the chemicals Skinny Potts had secured with the help of the brothers Rhesus and Boattail. The concoction was blended the night before, mixed with the gang's voodoo chants. Johnny and Righty stood by, listening to their instructions from Doctor Skinny as to what the chemicals' properties were and their dangers.

"You get N_2O, Nitrous Oxide in your eyes, and you can end up like the nearsighted Mr. McGoo. And you get the el stinko on you, and you'll be dead meat when they start questioning everyone."

Zero hour in the vent neared, but Johnny still jumped when the class-ending bell rang, and the class filed from the room.

The General One course was leaving the room as the College One course was coming into its chem lab.

Yelena wouldn't be there. She was in Newton, participating against other top students in the Debate Decathlon where the state's most outstanding debater would be chosen. She successfully defended her statement that "attainment of high goals in wealth and power were directly related to the educational and economic status of their parents.

All the classes back at Rockledge High got to hear her winning debate played through the school.

"Only a rare talent, a dedication rarely ever seen, can lead to an escape from the American nightmare, a caste system that allows only a few to succeed. Anyone can escape the drudgeries of life if he has the talent, the desire and the right girl to lead him out.

The principal had sat in his office smiling as the tape played out to the classes and could barely wait for the student body as one to chant her name, "Yelena, Yelena, Yelena!"

But the silent chant was "Johnny, Johnny, Johnny" seeing a boy unscrewing the cap on the large vial that contained a double-duty dosage of H 2S along with N2O. The fumes were moved through the vent and into the classroom by a small battery activated fan Johnny switched on.

Within moments, the college division students joined the general course rushing out of the room and down the hall.

The chemistry teacher started an immediate search of the lab heading first to the back of the class where he had uncovered Skinny's unpalatable action just a week before. When he lifted Skinny's desktop, he was greeted by the scent of an entire container of splashed Old Spice and a note, "Nope. It twernt me."

Johnny sneaked one last peek, feeling a hint sorry for the chemistry teacher but only a hint. *He should never have . . . held Skinny's head under the fire blanket . . .*

The hallways outside the chem lab cleared.

—

Johnny backed out of the small vent into the main duct as the results of the drop took over Mr. Van DeHyde, and he gagged and laughed, very difficult things to coordinate.

It was at this point that Johnny made his first big mistake. He rubbed his left eye with his right hand that was covered with $HNO2$, an unstable acid and salt mixture.

The burning was immediate.

Concentrating on returning down the vent was difficult, he felt like his eyes had been sprayed with kerosene and a match struck.

Going down backward was much more difficult than the difficult climb upward. Finding the toe holds was difficult enough, but releasing the grip of one of the hands holding the narrow lip and searching for the lower lip was near impossible. It called eventually for the release of the second hand and the immediate finding of the lower lip the toehold was on.

The principal arrived at the third floor chem lab to find the chemistry teacher looking through the glass at him, tears streaming down his face, gagging and roaring with laughter, and to an audience of students that had gathered.

The principal gave his teacher a read-my-lips glare as Van deClyde continued to laugh. "You'll get a king-size laugh out of my plans for your future."

Van de Clyde's last stand was just about at the same point in time when Yelena Smoltz was announced winner of the state debating championship. And as Johnny missed his grab for a lip with his right hand as he also released his grip with his left above.

He plunged the final twenty feet to the concrete floor of the shaft, hitting with a sickening thud, breaking off his two front teeth approximately halfway up. A nice even break that gave him somewhat the appearance of a young boy waiting for his second teeth to grow out fully.

He lay there moaning. His mouth in broken bone pain, a pain only relieved as the searing in his eye increased.

It's okay, Jazz . . . we're fixing your teeth . . . Until we do . . . no one will remain standing . . . if they call you buckteeth . . . Ma, did you call your Johnny baby? Ma . . . did you call me baby? Ma . . . just call me baby . . . one last time . . .

Righty backed off the Phillips head screws of the vent with hands that hadn't shaken like that since he read that telegram from the government when he was a young kid, that his brother, Big Lefty, had been killed by enemy fire in a place called Monte Casino. *That's where Ma and Pa were from . . . Don't moan, Johnny . . .*

The moans continued, and Righty's thoughts escaped him as he pulled the grate from its receptacle. "I feel like crying."

Johnny half crawled and was half pulled from the vent by Righty.

Righty propped his friend against the wall and washed the blood off his face and scooped the blood and broken teeth pieces out of his mouth.

"Eyes."

He cupped his hands full of cold water and threw it into Johnny's eyes time and time again.

Finally exhausted, Righty sat on the floor beside his injured friend.

How long they sat, neither knew.

"We better screw the vent back on," Johnny said, holding his left eye closed.

They left by a no-exit basement door. They hadn't been in school that day, at least according to the attendance sheets, and there was no good reason to make themselves known at this particular point in time.

Not one of the five hundred plus students made them known either, although some considered them lowlifes, criminals, and dangerous but kept that to themselves for a variety of reasons.

In a few cases, it was sheer fear. There were boys and girls who could give a warning glare similar to the one Michelle LeMoine had given Mary Kulas when she thought the latter was going to point to Johnny in the vent.

"What happened to your eye?" Righty asked as they headed to the Big Woods, waiting until school was over in two hours before thinking of checking in at home.

"I got that acid stuff in my eye."

"You okay?"

"Yah. It's just that everything is blurred in that eye, like someone pulled some sort of laced curtain over a window."

"You'll be all right."

"Yah. I know."

"Well, I'll head out."

"Righty."

Yah?"

"Don't ever get the fuck out of here."

The two hugged.

"You know I wouldn't ever do no such thing."

The good news after such a school and town shaking incident is that things would be very quiet for a long time. The teachers and administrators knew this, and the investigation within was held, thus no real pressure was put on, as even an uneasy peace can be a good thing.

—

Many of the teachers whose hue and cry would have eventually led to the breaking of the tight-mouthed will of some student was not forthcoming. Many felt it was probably better to keep this class moving onto graduation. So as not to have to face them an added year.

And it was quiet for some time. In fact, the rest of the school year.

Johnny never got to play hockey or baseball due to his suspension extension.

He did get to work more hours, enough to convince a Tufts University Dental School Lab made up of advanced students to fix Jazz's teeth and to glue his two chipped teeth together.

Jazz, on viewing his new picture book, smiled, mocked, and scolded Johnny, "I won't be able to eat corn through a picket fence. You ruined me."

He would be able to give the money he had saved to fix his brother's teeth to his mother to help her partially pay Massachusetts General Hospital Eye and Ear Infirmary for the operation he had had on his eye when his rifle exploded in the sandpit at the farm.

She was paying off thousands of dollars in bills at a dollar a week.

Undaunted, she sent a dollar a week to the hospital administration, despite the fact they first asked, then pleaded that she cease because it cost more and was more effort to service her payment than the dollar was worth.

No matter their problems, she had her own. The dollar out of her pay, plus paying for the money order and the stamp and envelope, was more than could be afforded.

She only had a year to save for dresses for Roma's senior year. And she squeezed every penny until Honest Abe wet his pants and every nickel until the buffalo fell before her apron like a bull falling before a matador's cape to fatten her daughter on malted milk, Ovalteen, and real milk rather than a concoction you added to water to make it into a pretend milk. *I better not hear no one calling my daughter . . . no scarecrow . . . or they better have six backsides . . . cuz I'm gonna flay off five of them . . .*

When Johnny wasn't working and Yelena wasn't leading the cheerleading squad or debating or fighting for a cause, she was with Johnny.

She had let him know early on that she was saving herself for their marriage.

Her main cause was Johnny. She saw something in him that had won her the state debating championship.

She was driven closer to him when she overheard her father tell her mother in the maid's kitchen, "Yelena's new cause is trash, but I guess every young girl has to go through a dump-picking period."

She had pushed open the swinging door between the dining room and kitchen and accosted her father with. "You are an evil-viewing man. This boy has all the makings of success. And I am his maker."

And that she nearly became, despite her I'm-saving-myself pledge.

It was after her president's speech at graduation.

She was brought to tears by her own words, "The world can only be saved if we save one individual at a time.

"It is a puzzle that only we individuals can fit together. Each must give the other a chance, a chance to succeed." She looked directly at her father, who was so proud of the fact that his daughter addressed hundreds of people that he missed the meaning of the words directed at him.

"I'm ready to do my share. To help one single person first." She turned her glance to the row of graduates sitting behind her, gazing down the line, stopping at Johnny, a tear in her eye.

Embarrassed, he looked away. To his right he saw Bernadette standing beside him. Looking at him. *What's she doing here . . . beside me?*

Then he remembered the alphabetical order of diplomas, receiving C, as in Clarkson, was just before D, as in DaSilva. *And what's she doing crying?*

The applause brought him back to the graduation.

He watched as his friends received their diplomas and wondered whether he would see some of them ever again. They had been in nearly every day of his life up to this point.

"Clarkson."

Bernadette stepped forward, took a fleeting glance at Johnny, her doe-shaped eyes, bluer than that of a bluebird, sadder than the call of a mourning dove, and then terrified, she lowered her eyes quickly.

Her words in his head, as soft as her look, her voice. "I can't . . . you're a nice boy . . ." How they had almost touched fingertips on one of their walks.

He heard the snide and disguised "new key, Nukie, Nookie" remarks and wanted to rip into the line of male faces and erase each smirk with a swing until something told him it would ruin this graduation for her and the entire class.

He was more overwhelmed with the desire to take her at arms length and slowly pull her to his shoulders.

"DaSilva."

They looked each other in the eyes as they passed, her eyes wide, like a frightened fawn in the bright beam of a jacker's light.

He closed his eyes as they passed.

"Hey, good looking."

The voice wasn't that of the principal who clutched Johnny's diploma with a death grip, not wanting to give it up. Johnny hadn't come to him and begged to be allowed to play hockey, baseball, but especially to play in the Thanksgiving football game.

Johnny held his open palm out for the certificate, looking past the school head and at the president of the class. Yelena's smile was as white and warm as desert sand. Her gray eyes as cool as the mist on the early morning Scotch gloaming penetrated his soul and wondered how far she could take him. His potential.

She picked him up at his home that evening. She had borrowed her father's Jaguar. The Mercedes he had promised her for graduation had not come through in the color he expected and was reordered.

Johnny had insisted that he be allowed to walk to her house, and they would set out for their graduation dinner at the Hotel Statler in Boston from there.

She had insisted on picking him up.

They had known each other for several months. She had never been to the Statler.

He met her as she came up the steps. "I love your house, Johnny. It's not all that glitz and cold marble and modern Danish that I have to put up with. I love wooden shingles. Our country was built on wood. By fighters, fighters with honor. I'd like to meet your mother."

"She's gone out. To the, ah, to a benefit she's giving for the poor."

Charity, his mother, hunkered low, out of sight, and drew further up the darkened hallway stairs. *Oh, Johnny baby . . .* Holding her arms tightly around herself, not paying attention to stairs four and nine, her leg slid through the missing step, her crotch hitting the riser and leaving her with pain similar to getting hit there with an ax.

She cried out in pain. She didn't want to.

"*Ma!*"

His shoulder hit the door, tearing it off its rusting hinges. Yelena followed him in.

He pulled his mother upward as Yelena helped remove her bleeding leg from the step. They led her to the couch, placed her head on a small throw pillow that was covered with an embroidered pillowcase that showed a tower with the words "New York World's Fair, 1939" stitched in.

Johnny held her hand and smiled down at her. He could not remember ever smiling at her.

"Whatever happened to your front teeth," she said, looking up.

"Oh ya. You're right. Something happened."

Before she could ask what she was right about, Yelena was cooling her forehead with a piece of an old towel she discovered hanging near the sink.

Charity looked at her son, but her vision of him was blurred, and what she saw spun in circles, counterclockwise. She was losing consciousness and tried to ask Johnny what had happened to his chipped teeth again. He answered, "We having chipped beef for supper?"

Her mouth was dry, and her forehead broke out in a cold sweat. A huge native with a bone through his nose pounded on a tom-tom in her head. Darkness was closing in.

"There, there," she heard Yelena's low voice, then a whisper to be heard only by Charity, not by her son, "It's no fun to be poor."

Charity's eyes grew huge at the words. She used the last of her energy to sit up and tell the lovely young girl with gray eyes as cool as distant smoke that they were not poor. But she fell back onto the pillow, her eyes inches from the New York World's Fair embroidery. They had gone there. Somehow they had gone there. The entire family. *Johnny . . . James . . . Roma . . . me . . . Tony . . . We were one . . . then . . . Tony was there then . . . My husband . . . the handsomest of all . . .*

The beautiful girl was now patting the back of her hand. "Sleep. Sleep," she sang low, "lullaby, and good night. To your mother's delight."

Johnny had tried to keep from crying when his Grandmother Shiverick had died last month.

He had looked at her for two days, waked in her own bed, in her own home.

The undertaker, Mr. Beaudette, had made her look like she was only sleeping.

But she wasn't—no fancy lip and cheek colors like the dead women at other wakes. There was no place for that sort of thing with the Shivericks.

Never a tear that young boy shed. And immediately after the burial, Johnny disappeared.

It was his grandfather Shiverick that spotted Johnny in the dark of the Big Woods, high up the Big Tree, silhouetted against the ink-stained sky.

The old man thought he heard a sob but then again thought it could have been the wind, for hadn't he not sobbed for those two days.

Johnny had sat with this old man and his old dog, Pal.

The old dog sat there, looking at both, first one then the other, licking first one's hand then the other's hand.

—

Neither the man nor the boy cried, stoic as the photo of the king of England that hung in the Shiverick dining room.

Mr. Shiverick first met Yelena when Dr. and Mrs. Smoltz attended Grandmother Shiverick's wake.

The old man looked at Yelena's features. *Like some holy Catholic statute . . . Please, dear Lord, don't let this lovely girl be a Catholic . . . Let her find one of her own if she is . . . Smoltz . . . Yelena Smoltz . . . Jewish maybe . . . God's chosen people . . . God loves everyone . . . and we must love each other . . . but surely he meant we should marry our own . . . not out of the faith . . .*

Now it was Johnny's Mother.

"She's sleeping," Yelena whispered to Johnny. "She's way above now."

"You know, Yelena, we're not poor."

"I know you're not, Johnny."

No, you don't . . .

Yelena held his mother's cold hand and felt the fine down on her forearm.

Johnny looked down at his mother, the constant frown she wore in life was etched on her forehead like acid on stone. The results of worrying and working for her kids.

Each time Yelena leaned forward to wipe Charity's brow, the young girl's breasts struggled to get out of the top of her gown like two rambunctious babies attempting to get out of their blankets in the nursery.

Johnny wanted to look away. He couldn't. *How low . . . can I . . . crawl?*

One time in the past, at a party, Johnny believed he saw her nipples, like pink nonpareils out of their silver wrappers. They were very often just a call away.

He closed his eyes, knowing it was unfair to take advantage of someone unsuspecting, someone caring for his own dead mother. *I am . . . sick . . . scum dog . . .*

But dealing with the present and the past at the same moment in time, left him spiraling in free fall like an autumn leaf. Where am I? What am I?

He didn't close his eyes all the way. For some reason, try as he may, they would not close tight so that his mother was all he viewed.

Yelena blocked out his mother. There was the most beautiful sight he had ever seen. Rosebuds . . .

He groaned in grief, in ecstasy.

And now she was leading him off his front porch, her hand in his, down the rickety front steps to the elegant lines of the Jaguar—hers.

"Not a bad graduation gift, huh? Daddy loves his little girl."

She held the passenger side door open for him.

"Thank you, James." He laughed, and then he immediately felt ashamed

She ran around the car, her head thrown back in joyous laughter, jumped into the front seat and hoisted her gown just high enough to be able to work the pedals.

"Hold on," she said. "It's me, Flash Gordon, and his rocket to the moon. The night is ours!"

He watched her as she drove, the world's most beautiful girl, in her elegant car.

She knew he was watching her, causing her breast, already heaving from the excitement of the mad dash to the car, to build up the momentum of the ocean, its waves exciting themselves to the point where they threatened to inundate the very seawall meant to harness them.

Johnny was dizzy. He forced his chin against his chest in an attempt to keep his head from falling off.

What followed was a blur. He was at the head table where the class president was seated when Yelena whispered, "A penny for your thoughts."

"I was thinking of the pounding surf lapping against the sand and writing your name in the sand, only to have the waves smooth it out. I wrote it time and time again, and each time the ocean erased it. And I fought the ocean."

"And you won. You were punished for it, punished again and again, but your heart, so strong, so valiant, fought on. I heard about what you did months ago for Winston Potts."

Who in hell is Winston Potts? Oh ya . . . Skinny . . . Skinny Potts . . .

"And I know why you hit that boy in the huddle because he had talked about that Bernadette."

Cheee . . . I sound like Jack Spratt . . . would eat only a rat . . . and not the accepted fat . . .

"And I know why you knocked yourself out that time against Winchester after that boy scored a touchdown. You are the last crusader."

I'm the last windmill dueler . . . whose ass was sliced to salami . . . and hot mustard and searing horse radish was smeared in the wounds . . . Oh, the cheeks of my burning ass . . . I'm nothing . . . minus one hundred . . .

She leaned over and kissed his cheek.

The banquet was a blur to him.

As they had entered the country club, the entire class stood and applauded Yelena.

But Johnny saw nothing, except the vision of moments before.

Just before they entered through the giant double doors, he was certain that he saw Bernadette's face lit up for a brief moment by the lights of a passing car, in the dark of the giant rhododendrons. She had a gown on. Her large blue eyes were moist, aflame with the panic terror that he had seen her. Dress in a gown for a prom she would not get to attend.

In that split second, when the door was opened by the clubhouse boy, he wanted to run to her, hide in the bushes with her. *Touch her hand . . . like we never did . . . hold each other close . . . like we never did . . . tell her . . . yes . . . I'm a nice boy . . .*

But he didn't.

And now he was on the inside.

Bernadette on the outside.

The boy from Woburn, who had asked her to the banquet, had told her, "We'll fuck first."

"I don't do that anymore."

"Since when?"

Bernadette had walked the two miles to the country club, much of the time carrying her high heels under her arm, then in shame, hid in the rhododendrons before someone spotted her. There was Johnny. With Yelena. In that car. She was in her silk stockings, now worn through in the heel. Hiding. And he had seen her. And she had wanted to call out to him. And didn't.

Now they were outside, the dinner dance over. Bernadette still stood in the dark of the thick bushes where she had remained the entire time and heard Yelena say, "Quite a shindig. How about Crane's Beach?" And they drove off.

There were no other cars at Crane. Even the surf fishermen who hunted the lunker striped bass that entered the shallow waters in the dark had left.

Johnny started walking toward the soft slurring of the easy-rider waves, the full moon lighting a path from the horizon to the shore, catching the caps. *Is that Bernadette's face . . . there . . . right there . . . in that wave . . .*

But the waves washed her face out of the moonlight like they had washed away Yelena's name each time he wrote it in the sand.

He watched a hermit crab caught in a small backwater left behind by the outgoing tide. Its trail through the sand was an arduous one, but it had an even more difficult choice at hand. An empty shell confronted it. It was the next size needed as it changed neighborhoods upward. Yet the present shell still was comfortable. But for how long?

"Hey, Dopey, come help Snow White."

Yelena stood on the dune behind him, aglow in the moonlight.

He ran to her side. "Now I'm happy."

He took the blankets from her. She took his hand. "Say something, Johnny, don't be Grumpy."

"Ca-choooo!"

"My poor Sneezy. Here." She took the blankets from him, spread the larger one on the ground, folded the end several times, making a pillow, which she patted. "Here, sweet prince."

I feel more like a rhesus than a prince . . . in this monkey suit . . . and Jazz's teeth work is delayed . . . I can't pretend . . . I'm a rich boy . . .

"Take it off if you're uncomfortable," she said, undoing his white bow tie, unsnapping his cummerbund.

She put the cummerbund over her head in such a manner it pushed her ears forward, snapped it under her chin, and crossed her eyes and stuttered, "I don't do . . . do this for every . . . for every buddy."

He wasn't sure whether he was supposed to laugh. This was a new Yelena. The one he saw in class was a serious student; on the cheering field she was prima ballerina Maria Tallchief. When they met after school or the early evening before she went home to study, she was Emily Dickinson.

She placed his bow tie at the top of her gown, hiding her cleavage, an action that drew his eyes there.

"No, No, Nanette," she said, shaking her finger at him, shaking her head from side to side, "Tisk, tisk."

I wasn't looking at . . . at them . . . not this time . . .

He looked down at the sand. The moonlight bounced off the flat water of the trapped retreating tide. The hermit crab was half out of its old shell.

She took the cummerbund off her head, shook her mane like a wolfhound coming out of the water and flicked it over one eye. "Veronica."

Veronica Lake . . . I sure as heck don't feel like Alan Ladd . . .

Then she was up, danced around him, doing adagios, playing the part of both the man and the woman, taking the tempo slower and slower, then exploding, throwing her head back. She slipped down tempo until it appeared she was involved in a ballet, ending with a pirouette high on her toes that spun her hair in a moonlit golden blur.

She collapsed to the sand, holding her arms open and beckoning him, palms outspread, "Come."

Rather than going into her open arms inviting him on top of her, he settled down beside her, propped himself on his elbow, and looked at her. *What in . . . unholy fuck . . . am I doin'?*

—

"The prince not only duels to defend the honor of fair maidens; he also respects what he duels for," she said, smiling at him. "So rare a man."

He returned her smile, but it was the uneasy smile of the foot testing the first pond ice of winter.

She took his hand and held it tight in hers as they stared into the moon.

He was startled by her voice, how long had they lain there in shared silence.

"My breast. Pure as a dove's."

She guided his hand beneath the top of her dress until it cupped her. She squeezed his hand on her, repeating the action, ever so slowly, bringing his hand higher each time, then moving her hand from the back of his to his fingers, which she directed to a nipple as erect as the tip of a thumb hitching a ride, to where.

He could feel his cock force its way past the bottom of his jockey shorts, like a boxer shouldering past his opponent to an infighting position.

The wetness on his thigh was like the broad strokes of a painter's brush, warm, sticky. *My god . . . my god . . . my good holy god . . .*

It no longer seeped like a small leak in a dam but now spurted like it had breached all shackles. He felt spent yet felt his tankard being refilled, as if his Musketeer companions had poured endlessly into his cup, keeping it continuously frothing until the foam streaked down its side.

He felt her other hand drawing his downward. She used her hand to direct his under her dress, upward. Until she said, "There," and it rested against the warm wetness of her panties.

Her legs parted, slowly, tenuously, her voice ever slower, more tenuous. "I had been saving. I had been saving. For marriage. But my prince appeared early. I'm yours, sweet prince, to duel for me. And protect. And you will grow under my hand to be a king. Under my hand you will grow. Oooh. Give me heaven on earth. Now!"

"It" wasn't in front. Nor underneath. "It" was—just there.

Her perfume, the smell of her body, mixed with the salt air and stirred by the moon left them both dizzy, like when they were kids, blindfolded, spun in circles by their friends, and then released to meander like ludicrous drunks.

Reaching out for support.

His on her breast. Her's now on his cock, both of which throbbed with the intensity of a kettle drum being beaten with passion by an invisible drummer signaling the end of a Beethoven symphony.

—

"No." His voice was so soft he could barely hear it despite the fact it thundered through his head, echoing endlessly.

Her "What?" was the plaintive wail of a banshee.

His voice so subdued that he listened closely, wondering where it was coming from, what it was saying. "We'll save it. We'll save together. By us. For us!" *A treasure to be saved . . . forever . . . by us . . . for us . . . Where did this good happy horseshit come from? I want to get it . . . with my private . . . no, my general . . . and I want to taste it . . .*

"Yes, yes. My poet. My poet. You've already grown from my crusader knight to poet laureate."

He was stunned, thunderstruck, didn't know what to say. He had waited a lifetime, and at the moment of truth, some asshole that sounded like him had said, "Let's save it."

"Yes, my poet laureate," she said with an even deeper passion.

Johnny was afraid he was going stutter,. "Ah, rah, and daaa," but instead offered, "I'm a poet and don't know it. My feet are Longfellows." *Insipid . . . What the hell did I say? Am I a pure . . . undiluted idiot.*

"Give me your sweet hand."

He removed his fingers from her curly fire down below, tufts they had been entwined in, like a wild grapevine on its host swamp maple. Sipping that one sweet finger before placing his hand in hers. He grew dizzy. *Oh . . . so sweet . . . What kind of asshole am I?*

"You are so special. You are a prince. So very special, my love."

They sat holding hands into the early morning. "I've got a little chill," she said. "Perhaps we better head back."

"No. We'll gather driftwood."

The fire was in a scooped-out hollow in the sand. The wood burned softly, its salt-soaked body giving off embers that drifted skyward.

"See how our embers join the fireflies in dance."

He nodded silently.

"It's your turn," she said.

"For what?"

"Poetry," she said. "The embers joined hands with the fireflies, doing a Virginia reel, spiraling upward to join the stars in an endless forever."

They sat, warming their hands at the fire, then stood, turning their backs to the flames, lowering their rear ends close to the flame for warmth.

"Hot, cross buns," she chanted.

"Toasted tushie."

"Johnny? What do you want to be? Who do you want to be?"

"An ordinary person."

"There is nothing ordinary about someone who will stand and defend what is right."

"Start me with ten, who are stout-hearted men, and I'll soon give you ten thousand . . ."

"You're not being serious. What would you like to do? Be a surgeon who saves little children. Travel to Africa. Feed the starving. And then write poems about it, encouraging others to help."

"I sort of thought about being a state police officer."

"Stop joking."

"Well, you are surely joking when you say I should be a surgeon. A poet."

"I surely am not."

"Yelena?"

"Yes?"

"I just graduated from the general course. We learned that 'ain't' ain't in the dictionary. We learned that two and two are four. We learned that most of us only graduated because the teachers wanted to be certain they wouldn't have to have us one extra day, let alone another year. They felt the devil they know is not as much a threat as the devil they don't know."

"There is nothing that can't be overcome. Prep school. Andover. Choate. Then Harvard, for your medical degree. And before Africa and the children, Amherst College. Your degree. Then Babson, so you can spiral our riches upward."

"Medical school? I foul up trying to put a Band-Aid on my finger. Amherst College too? All this on a part-time paper route?"

"My father, once he understands how I feel, who you are, what your potential is. Your brain. Your courage, will move the world for me. You."

"Yelena, my school is the school of hard knocks. Where I got the third degree."

"Hold my hand. It will all work out. I will work it out for both of us. Remember my speech at graduation—'The world is us. We cannot make it flat again. We are the new centurions. Ours is the new age. There is television where pictures are projected over the airwaves and look out at us, urging us onward in our very homes. There is the jet plane, and now we can travel faster than sound. Our thoughts, dreams, and hopes must keep up. We are the ones with hands of fearless steel that reach into the fire and pulls out the chestnuts for all. The world is at peace. This peace is what we carry as our mantle. Our potential is only as limited as our imagination, our desire to go forward. Ours is the country of promise. We must fulfill our promise to the world.' I love you, my Johnny DaSilva."

Johnny looked at her as she glanced skyward, her eyes moist. *I just don't know . . . I just don't know what she wants . . . what she's talking about . . .* "I can't take help from your dad. It's a hang up. I've had it since I can remember. I can't help myself. Not taking. But I will help myself. For us. I can do it."

"Yes. Our love is pure. Forever."

Dawn sifted in a silence broken only by the low woosh of tern and gull wings over waves.

Johnny looked down on the hermit crab. It had made no progress. The tiny tidal pool had dried up. Its tracks through the sand ended at the shell it had attempted to make its new home. It appeared too exhausted from its efforts escaping from its too-tight home to its planned abode. The hermit crab, naked in the new sunlight that crept over the ocean's horizon and the sand, appeared to grow to giant proportions through his eyes. Then suddenly shrink.

They walked hand in hand back to the Jaguar.

He glanced back once, in time to see the hermit crab plucked from its path between shells into the beak of a laughing gull, which held it there, appearing to smile at its final futile efforts to live. It disappeared down the gullet as the bird tilted its head skyward and racked the air with a wild life-is-good scream.

For some, that is.